TODD HERZMAN

ACCIDENTAL CHAMPION

BOOK ONE

aethonbooks.com

ACCIDENTAL CHAMPION
©2024 TODD HERZMAN

Aethon Books
www.aethonbooks.com

Print and eBook design and formatting by Josh Hayes.

Published by Aethon Books LLC.

Aethon Books is not responsible for websites (or their content) that are not owned by the publisher.

Also by Todd Herzman

Accidental Champion

Accidental Champion 2

Check out the entire series here! (Tap or scan)

Chapter 1
I Choose Champion

THE SKY TURNED A VIVID, BLOOD RED.

Xavier Collins stared at it, a frown lining his face. *That's odd. Some sort of blood sunrise, like a blood moon?* He shook his head, shoved his ear buds back in and put his hands in the pockets of his plain black hoodie.

He walked over the wide bridge that separated the two halves of his city, ignoring the red sky. No one else seemed to have noticed it, after all. Traffic crawled across the bridge so slow he could walk faster than it moved. Sleepy drivers sipped coffee, rubbed eyes, and shook fists at the people in front of them.

It was a long trek to campus. He couldn't afford the inflated price of the university dorms—even if he did have the money, he'd always been more of a loner and knew the noise would drive him crazy—and housing "across the lake" was far cheaper. He could have caught the bus, but the walk was the only exercise he got, and he enjoyed his ritual of listening to audiobooks on the way.

The soothing voice of the narrator drifted into his ears. He was listening to his favourite fantasy author's newest release. He took a deep breath, the smell of water on the air. In his mind, he was on a four-masted ship a part of a fleet of thousands, mages throwing flames over the waves.

1

He couldn't help but enjoy the escape. It wasn't that he disliked his life. It wasn't *bad*. It was just that the ones in books always felt so much... more.

If I could move things with my mind, wield a magic sword, or fly upon a dragon...

He supposed he was like most young people inching into adulthood, slowly stumbling into the "real world" and wondering "Is this it? Is this all there is?"

He just wanted there to be *more*.

Xavier struggled to focus on his morning classes. He had three lectures in a row and sat at the back of each one, right at the top of the stairs. He had a million tabs open on his laptop and kept switching between them and a story he was writing.

If Xavier wasn't reading or actually studying, he tried to spend his time writing. He was an English major, hoping to get into an MFA in Creative Writing—what his mother had called an "infinitely unemployable career path." But he wasn't here just so he could get a job after he left; he wanted to *learn*.

Xavier *loved* learning. If he had any superpowers, it would be that. Problem was, the things he enjoyed learning didn't tend to have easy ways to earn money.

In high school, he spent an entire year learning how to do parkour. He vaulted over benches, climbed walls and jumped from one gap to another. Learnt how to fall from height and roll smoothly out of it to reduce the impact on his knees.

But what exactly was he going to do with that? Become a stuntman? A thief? He'd briefly considered that—the former, not the latter—but stuntmen tended to get hurt in their jobs.

He'd rather not make getting hurt his profession.

A couple of years later he'd stumbled on someone twirling two balls of fire at the ends of long chains. Poi, they were called. The balls were made of Kevlar—like in bulletproof vests and motorcycle gear—and soaked in kerosene before they were lit aflame.

He'd taken to it fast. Earned a few hundred dollars busking downtown.

Until he'd wrapped one of those chains around an arm and got, well, *burned*. Because, play with fire and... you know the rest.

His earlier desire—not getting hurt in his profession—made him shy away from continuing. Besides, there didn't seem to be much career growth in that kind of performance art.

When he'd found writing he'd figured that was the way to go. He was always trying to escape into books. Writing was simply the next logical progression. If *he* couldn't move things with his mind or fight a dozen orcs with only his trusty sword and shield, he could at least write about it.

Seemed like a good idea to him. Not to his mother, but he... well, he stopped taking her advice when he realised she couldn't handle her own life, let alone his.

In his third lecture, Professor Manning, a man in a suit one size too big and old-fashioned half-moon glasses, droned on about the Hero's Journey and Joseph Campbell in a rasping monotone, things Xavier had learnt plenty about before he'd even gotten to this class. Two girls sat in front of him, whispering back and forth about some TV show. A guy three rows down openly played World of Warcraft, not even looking up from the screen. Xavier frowned, turned his head and looked out the window. The sky was still blood red. Dark clouds had gathered.

The whispering stopped. The guy playing on his laptop removed his earbuds.

A storm's coming.

That definitely felt ominous. He was about to check his weather app when hail the size of golf balls plummeted from the sky and lightning flashed. The lightning forked off in six different directions. They were on the fourth floor here, and Xavier got a good view down to where one of the forks struck.

He blinked, inching sideways on his seat. The lightning pooled into the courtyard, congealing into one yellow-glowing mass. It sparked, electricity shooting off it and setting a trashcan on fire.

"What the hell?" Xavier muttered.

He stood and walked straight to the window. He wasn't the

only one. As the *boom* of thunder was released, the lecturer stopped his droning, finally noticing what was off.

The congealing lightning rose, forming an arc as tall as a tunnel on the freeway. It buzzed and spat sparks until it appeared to stabilise.

Then something stepped out of it. Xavier blinked. Rubbed his eyes. Squinted. *Am I hallucinating?* Others were pointing, panicking. The lecturer was saying something, his voice a discordant mix of acute stress and strained calm.

Maybe I'm dreaming.

What he saw couldn't be right. It was green. About three feet tall. Wore rough spun clothes one might find at a renaissance fair or the set of *Game of Thrones*. It had sharp features. A long, curved nose. Needle-sharp, yellow teeth. Pointed ears. And it carried a sword.

It was a goblin.

The sky had been painted blood red. Lightning had created a portal. And a bloody goblin had stepped out of it and straight into one of the university's courtyards.

Xavier took a stumbling step back from the window just as the world went grey and everything froze.

Including him.

Text appeared, transposed over his vision.

Interlopers have discovered your world. Your Solar System has now been marked for integration into the Greater Universe.
System integration begins in:
5...
4...
3...
2...
1...
System integration commencing.

A blinding flash of light erupted in Xavier's vision. The world shifted until he appeared in a completely black room. He blinked, trying to see some shapes in the darkness, but there was nothing there.

He reached out, but there was nothing to touch.

"Where... where am I?" His mouth was dry. So dry. His voice cracked and shaky.

Then more text appeared.

Subject identified as XAVIER COLLINS.

Subject? Xavier thought. *Where is this text even coming from? Why can I read it in the dark?*

Subject's physical skills deemed as: Minimal.

Minimal! Xavier rubbed the back of his head. He looked down —though he couldn't see anything in the darkness of this place— and supposed he *had* gotten out of shape since he stopped parkour... four years ago.

Subject's intellectual skills deemed as: Middling.

Xavier pursed his lips. He didn't much like being judged, though he had to admit he couldn't fault whatever the hell was judging him, even if he wanted to cuss it out. "Minimal, middling," he muttered into the darkness.

Subject's spirit skills deemed as: High.

Xavier tilted his head to the side with a frown. *What are spirit skills? And... why are mine* high?

"Hello?" he said, his voice sounding no more confident than

before. "Is anyone out there?" He wasn't sure if a response would help.

Please choose a Moral Faction.
Do you wish to:

1. **Fight for your world.**
2. **Fight for yourself.**
3. **Fight for chaos.**

Xavier shifted his weight from one foot to the other. What kind of choices were those? He chose what he considered to be the obvious one: Fight for your world.

"One," he said aloud. "I choose one."

You have chosen Moral Faction 1.
Do you wish to become one of your world's
Champions, Soldiers, or Support?
Speak or think one of the options to learn
more.

Xavier's frown deepened. He still wasn't sure if this was a dream, but as someone who'd consumed vast amounts of fantasy and science fiction novels, television and movies, he figured his best approach was to *assume* it was real until proven otherwise.

If it ended up being real, assuming it was a dream would likely get him killed.

Besides, since when were his dreams this... elaborate?

Xavier licked his lips. "Champion."

Champions are a world's best fighters, and so
they are given the best opportunities. Once a
Potential Champion has been tested against
other Potentials and found to meet the require-

ments, they will be sent to a pocket world to experience their tutorial, where they will be pitted against other World Champions to fight for rewards, upgrades, and powerups...

Xavier's eyes widened as he read the text. There was more, but he couldn't help but zero-in on what the second line said.

Champions would be sent to *another world*? He still had no idea what was happening. It was beginning to feel like some weird video game. *Champion, Soldier or Support?* He could guess what Support would be, and he couldn't imagine Soldier would be near as interesting as becoming a Champion.

And he had to guess that only Champions would get to be sent to another world. Isn't this what he'd always wanted? Something... more?

If this wasn't just some dream or weird hallucination, he would forever be kicking himself for not getting the opportunity to be sent to a whole *different world*. His imagination went wild, and he spoke before checking the other options or even reading the rest of the text.

"I choose Champion."

You have selected Champion.
Subject's full integration will not commence until after the first test.
Prepare yourself for battle.
Fight to the death.

"Battle? What do you mean, *battle*?"

Before Xavier got an answer, another blinding flash assailed his vision. He blinked it away. This time, he didn't end up in total darkness. Instead, he stood in a grassy plain that seemed to stretch on forever. The air was still. The sky was a clear blue, no sun, though it was bright as day. Not a speck of cloud.

This doesn't feel real.

Your opponent, another Potential Champion, will be arriving in:
5...
4...
3...
2...
1...
Your opponent has arrived.

Another Potential Champion? Opponent? He supposed this is what the text meant when it said he would be tested. *Perhaps I should have read to the end.*

Xavier swallowed as he looked over at his opponent. The man appeared to be in his late thirties and was built like a bear. He wore a military uniform. A tactical vest, helmet, and goggles. There were several patches on his shoulder, one was of an eagle carrying a trident.

Crap, is that a bloody Navy SEAL?

He didn't only come with the uniform, either.

Xavier didn't know much about guns, but he'd played a fair amount of Counter Strike in his day... which he knew meant absolutely nothing. Still, even he could identify the man's weapon.

It was an assault rifle. An M4A1 carbine, if he was right. Not that the distinction mattered. Xavier checked his pockets. His keys and phone had been in his backpack, which currently sat under his desk in the lecture hall, and all he had on him was... a pen.

A writer should always have a pen...

To test the preparedness level of your world's pre-integration elite, Potential Champions will not be supplied with weapons and armour, and will have to fight with what they came with

**before they can be fully integrated into the
Greater Universe and receive their new
abilities.**

Fight to the death.

Xavier took a stumbling step back. He pulled the pen out of his
pocket. He felt like a kitten pitted against a lion in a cage fight.

The soldier took a few steps forward. He had his hands on his
rifle, but his finger wasn't on the trigger. His uniform looked dirty
and roughed up, like he'd been on deployment when this had all
happened, which explained why he was decked out in full gear.
He looked left and right. He'd been in a ready position when he
arrived, but seeing only Xavier there, he relaxed.

"What the hell is this?" The man's voice was deep and gruff
and carried far. Standing across from him, Xavier couldn't help but
feel... not-very-manly. The soldier looked up at the sky and
gestured toward Xavier. "I'm not going to fight an unarmed, non-
combatant! This isn't protecting my world!" The man swore something fierce. He sighed, pulled the strap of his rifle over his head,
then made to place it on the ground.

**Surrender recognised.
XAVIER COLLINS is the victor.
JULIAN MYERS forfeits his chance at
becoming a World Champion.
One cannot walk backward on the path.
Extermination imminent.**

The soldier—Julian—scrunched up his face. "Extermination?"
he muttered before his eyes widened.

A bolt of lightning struck him, jolting his entire body until he
fell, unmoving on the ground.

Congratulations XAVIER COLLINS. You have passed the first test!
You have gained 100 Mastery Points.
You have gained 100 Spirit Energy.
You will be returned to the waiting room in 0 seconds.

Chapter 2
Full Integration

XAVIER BREATHED. FAST AND SHALLOW.

Someone had just died in front of him. *Julian. Julian Myers.*

The man hadn't wanted to fight. He'd put his rifle on the ground. He could have killed Xavier in a second. Could have won the challenge. But he'd surrendered.

And paid for it with his life.

And that's the only reason I'm still alive.

Xavier had been yanked back into the "waiting room." The black expanse of nothingness. He put his hand to his chest, heart beating so damn hard it hurt.

He'd expected to feel the fabric of his hoodie. Instead, he felt his bare chest. He looked down but couldn't see himself in the darkness. He touched his jeans—

They were gone.

I'm naked. Why the hell am I naked!? It wasn't the weirdest thing that had happened that day, and it didn't overshadow that Navy SEAL's death, but it still made him feel ever more vulnerable.

He shut his eyes. When he did, he saw lightning shoot down from the sky. Saw it strike the soldier. Julian.

He snapped his eyes back open. A notification appeared,

superimposed over his vision. He stared at it, blinking, still in shock.

Congratulations XAVIER COLLINS. You have passed the first test!
Prepare yourself for Full Integration.

"Full integration?" Xavier frowned. "How do I prepare myself if I don't know what that is? And why in the world do I have to be *naked*? That doesn't make any—"

Pain spread over Xavier's entire body. Pain like he'd never felt before. He'd broken a wrist once while trying to learn how to ride a skateboard. He'd burned himself. He'd been punched in the face. He'd pulled something in his back and been laid out for two weeks.

But this? This made everything he'd ever been through *combined* pale in comparison.

He shook violently. His mouth was open, and he was sure he was screaming, but he couldn't hear himself over the pain.

As suddenly as it came, it went.

A bright flash of light illuminated the room. It turned from a black expanse to a white one. There was still nothing to be seen, but now his own body was visible.

Xavier gasped in a breath and looked down at himself.

Nothing had changed, as far as he could tell. And he was still very much naked. "Wonderful." He hoped he wouldn't be sent into another fight to the death in this condition. If what he'd been through could even be called that—he hadn't *done* any fighting.

Someone died in front of me. Because they refused to kill.

He swallowed, waiting for something to happen, hoping he wouldn't be stuck here to linger in his own thoughts.

You, XAVIER COLLINS, have now been integrated into the Greater Universe! The honour is yours.
The System welcomes you.

"Thanks?" Xavier muttered, wondering what exactly the "System" was.

Based on your pre-integration abilities, your attributes have been distributed as follows:

XAVIER COLLINS
Level 1
Strength: 5
Speed: 5
Toughness: 5
Intelligence: 7
Willpower: 7
Spirit: 10
Mastery Points for this level: 100/1,000
Available Spirit Energy: 100/1,100

Xavier took a moment to absorb the information.

This looked like some sort of character sheet. *Definitely like a video game.*

This was why the System had judged his physical, mental and spiritual abilities. So it could quantify them? *This is insane. All of this is absolutely insane.*

It also made a thrill run through him. *Spirit.* That had to do with... magic, right? The sky had gone blood red. Weird lightning had created a portal. A goblin had stepped out.

Now this.

If everything else had been real, why couldn't *magic* be?

Choose your preferred basic fighting class:
Warrior
Mage
One cannot walk backward on the path.

Xavier blinked. That was it? Two choices? For some reason,

he'd expected more variation. Though he supposed the classes were only *basic*. There might be opportunities to specialise as one got stronger. But he was thinking too far ahead. *One step at a time.* He had already rushed one decision today, choosing the path of Champion without fully reading what the consequences of that choice would be.

That choice had almost gotten him killed. It *should* have gotten him killed. *Thank you, Julian, for sacrificing yourself.* Xavier wondered if the man would have put his gun down, had he known it would mean his death...

He pushed that out of his mind. It had already happened. It couldn't be changed. And... he didn't want it to be.

I'm still alive. I'm still alive, and I need to focus.

He eyed the two choices. Warrior. Mage. Both paths felt incredibly exciting to him. He imagined himself wearing full-plate armour, riding on a horse, slamming his sword into—

People?

Did he really want that? To kill *people*?

Maybe I'll be fighting goblins...

He shoved his worries into the back of his mind. This choice was an important one, as the System said: One cannot walk backward on the path. He'd seen that firsthand when he'd watched that Navy SEAL surrender and die for it.

Stop thinking about that! He shook his head.

His attributes indicated that he would be a better mage than warrior. *If I choose mage, will I be able to move things with my mind? Throw fire from my hands? Call lightning from the heavens?* Warrior sounded cool, but magic? Magic sounded *awesome*. You could wield a sword in "real life." You couldn't wield *magic*.

At least, not in any life he'd known before this.

But before he decided, he cleared his throat and spoke into the white room. "Can I have more information?" His voice didn't echo. It fell flat, barely travelling past where he stood.

Warrior Class:

A warrior is a physical fighter. They can be an expert in hand-to-hand combat, melee weapon combat, or long-range combat. A warrior's path is as varied as any other.

Mage Class:
A mage is a magical fighter. Like a warrior, they can fight at close range or at long range. They can wield the elements, commune with spirits, summon magical creatures, or a thousand other possibilities. A mage's path is as varied as any other.

There are infinite paths to walk, with infinite choices to make. Each choice you make will form who you are, and can never be undone.

That's ominous.

Xavier sighed at the descriptions. They didn't exactly tell him a great deal. Though he was interested to see the different things a mage might be able to do. He wondered how a mage could be a close-combat fighter...

Xavier could have stood there, umming and uhhing about what choice to make for hours, but doing so would just be lying to himself. He'd made the choice the moment he'd seen the option.

"I choose mage."

There was no pain this time. Something he was infinitely glad for. A flash of blue light consumed his vision, then slowly faded. When he looked down at himself, he was pleased to find he was no longer naked. Instead, he wore bland grey robes. *Mage robes.* On his feet were thin leather boots, and a satchel had appeared over one shoulder. In his hand, he held a seven-foot staff with a small, white crystal at its end.

"Huh," was all he could say.

Congratulations, you have chosen the basic fighting class of Mage!

You have gained the spell Cast Element.

You have gained the spell Spiritual Guidance.

You have gained the spell Summon.

You have gained the spell Telekinesis.

Xavier's eyes widened. Four spells? He'd just gained *four* spells? He rubbed his hands together. He had no idea how any of them worked. His brain hadn't been infused with the information like Neo in *The Matrix*. But he was very eager to learn.

Is this where I get sent to a new world for my tutorial?

Xavier cleared his throat and asked the question aloud.

The System responded, text flowing across his vision instantly.

You have not yet met the requirements to enter the pocket world. First, you must protect a settlement from destruction.
Only then will you be sent to the Eternal Tower.

Requirements? Eternal Tower?

Xavier's vision went white. When it cleared, he stood back inside his lecture hall, where he'd been when this had all started. For a moment he wondered if this had all been a dream. If he'd fallen asleep. And... sleepwalked to the window?

He shook his head. No one else was here. No lecturer. No students. Not a single person. He wondered how much time had passed since he'd last been standing in this room. It couldn't have been long.

Xavier looked around. He still clutched the seven-foot staff in his hand.

Protect a settlement. Those had been the words. Though he would hardly call the university campus a settlement, he supposed that's what the message had meant.

He stepped over to the window, clutching the thick staff in both hands.

The portal in the courtyard was still active, though the goblin—or whatever it was—was nowhere to be seen.

Something clattered to his left. He spun about. The lectern on the stage had been knocked over. A small green man ran up the middle aisle of the lecture hall.

Xavier stared at it. Took a step back. It was one of the goblins. As he stared, he wished he had more information. *If I'm Level 1, what level is that goblin? Does it have a level?* Xavier was quickly losing his grip on how the world worked.

He got an answer to his question in the form of a notification popping up in his vision. It looked like the text he'd seen before, but this was instead a small box that hovered over the head of his enemy.

{Lesser Goblin – Level 2}

The Lesser Goblin made a beeline toward Xavier. Xavier hefted his staff, wondering how in the hell he was supposed to cast one of his spells. He thought of the one he wanted, then said it aloud, hoping that would help.

"Cast Element!"

Nothing happened. Well, his voice cracked. Nothing *useful* happened.

"Fire!" he said, hoping that would make some sort of difference. That flames would shoot from his staff and hit the little beast.

Again, nothing happened.

Oh, no.

Chapter 3
Stealing a Purse From a Goblin's Corpse

The Lesser Goblin cackled. It leapt into the air, kicked off the back of one of the seats, then fell straight at him, its short sword swinging down.

Xavier swore. He managed to block the strike with his staff, hoping the sword wouldn't be sharp enough to cut through the wood. The strike hit with a solid *thunk*.

The Lesser Goblin landed on the ground in front of Xavier. It slashed out at his leg. There was a stab of pain as the sword bit into his flesh.

Xavier wanted to run, but he stood his ground. *If I don't figure this out, I'm not going to survive.* He struck out at the goblin, swinging the long, heavy staff like a baseball bat.

When Xavier had learnt how to fire-twirl with poi—two chains with balls of fire at the ends—he'd also learnt how to use a fire staff, as a few friends he'd busked with used them.

Those movements hadn't been for fighting, they'd been for performing, but the old patterns—the muscle memory, long embedded into him—kicked in. He twirled his staff around his body in a way that made him look like some formidable expert.

The goblin's eyes widened, its posture hesitant. Xavier grinned. He struck out again. The goblin tried to block with its short sword, but as the Lesser Goblin was half his size, it simply wasn't strong enough to stop the weight behind Xavier's strike. And Xavier had a huge amount of reach on the little beast.

He actually managed to push it back down a few of the steps.

Another strike and the goblin tumbled to the ground.

Maybe I should have chosen warrior...

Xavier went in for a killing blow.

He didn't think about it. He just *moved*. He'd seen what happened when people hesitated in this new reality. Seen what it meant *not* to fight.

The head of his staff bashed into the goblin's skull. Xavier winced as green blood and something that looked suspiciously like brain matter spurted out and onto his new leather boots.

"Eugh." Xavier stepped back. He wiped the goop off on one of the chairs. Should he feel bad about what he'd just done? He examined his feelings.

That goblin would have killed me. I had no choice.

You have defeated a Level 2 Lesser Goblin!
You have gained 200 Mastery Points.
You have gained 200 Spirit Energy.

Instead of feeling the guilt he'd expected, Xavier felt a burst of pride. He still wasn't sure what Spirit Energy did—was it some type of mana?—but he'd figured out that Mastery Points were basically like gaining experience points in a game. It was what would bring him to Level 2.

What happens at Level 2?

He shrugged off the question. If this were like a video game, or like a fantasy novel, he knew what his next move needed to be.

Xavier walked over to the Lesser Goblin corpse. Pain shot up his left leg. An adrenaline spike during the fight had made him forget about being wounded. Now the fight was over, that pain hit him in full.

I don't suppose there are health potions in this new world...

He grunted and struggled into a kneeling position. The Lesser Goblin had a purse tied to its belt. Xavier, leaning heavily on his staff in one hand, grabbed the short sword that had fallen to the ground and sawed through the string. He tucked the purse into the satchel he'd received when he'd gotten his staff.

This is really weird. I'm stealing a purse from a goblin's corpse.

Unfortunately, the satchel was empty. When he'd opened it, he'd hoped to find some potions inside. Something to heal his wounded leg. He slowly lowered himself until he was sitting on one of the steps, then he leant his staff against a chair and cut a length of fabric off the goblin's threadbare clothes.

He was about to wrap his leg when he paused. *What the hell am I doing? I'm not in a bloody fantasy novel.* There was a first-aid kit on one side of the lecture hall. He passed it every time he came into this room. Not that he'd ever had any need for it. *Until now.*

Xavier tried to shove the short sword into his satchel, but even though it was rather small—being a sword for a goblin—it jutted out awkwardly. Instead, he managed to stick it through the cord that tied his robes shut.

Not finding anything else of worth on the Lesser Goblin, Xavier climbed back up to standing. Using his staff like a cane, he made his way down the steps to the first aid kit.

He'd been hoping to find the wound half-closed already. This "System" had brought magic to the world, after all. But that wasn't the case. It looked normal.

Yes, because a sword slash in my leg is normal.

He did the best he could. He dressed the wound and wrapped it with the bandages. He'd never taken a first aid class, so he had no idea if he was doing it right, but he figured it was better than nothing.

At least it won't get infected. Can wounds still get infected, now the System has integrated us into the Greater Universe? He had no idea.

His mind had kept turning as he cleaned his wound, trying to understand this new reality he'd found himself in. He climbed to his feet and limped to the room's door. He shut it, turned the lock.

There would be more goblins out there. He was sure of it. The System's message had told him to protect a settlement. If he'd succeeded in doing that by killing the Lesser Goblin, he would have been transported out of here, or received some sort of success-notification.

He went through his reasoning again. Nodded to himself. *Sounds logical enough.*

Once the door was locked, he leant heavily against the wall. He looked at the corpse of the Lesser Goblin. Killing one of those things had left him limping. He may have been able to defeat it, but what happened if he had to fight two, four, *six* at once?

He needed to play to his strengths. Whatever those were. Saying "Cast Element" clearly hadn't been enough to use his spell, so it must work in a different way. He couldn't go into his next fight unprepared.

He'd be dead if that Navy SEAL hadn't surrendered.

I can't rely on luck to survive.

He focused. Before, when he'd needed to choose from options the System had provided, he'd either said them out loud or *thought* them with purpose. He had an idea. A simple one.

When he'd thought he wanted more information about the goblin, it had appeared.

Xavier frowned, and thought, *Spells*.

Spells List:
Cast Element – Rank 1
Spiritual Guidance – Rank 1
Summon – Rank 1
Telekinesis – Rank 1

"Huh," Xavier said. "Is it really that easy?" He wondered what the different ranks were, and if he could see any descriptions of the spells. So, he thought what he wished: *Description for Cast Element.*

Cast Element – Rank 1
Cast Element is a basic mage spell learnt by all starting human mages. It gives the caster the chance to call upon each of the elements of fire, air, water, and earth. As a mage advances, they may choose to specialise in one of these elements, generalise in several, or abandon the path altogether.
One cannot walk backward on the path.

Xavier smiled as he read the text. Though the description was quite general and didn't tell him anything about *how* to use the spell, he was glad his hunch had paid off.

He took note of the references to "the path." In video games, one never tended to "lose" a spell once it had been learnt, but this seemed to indicate that might change. The path of casting elements could be abandoned completely, perhaps in favour of one of the paths his other spells provided.

I wish I had some sort of manual that explained all of this. The thought struck him. *Manual!* He frowned. No text appeared.

It was worth a shot.

He thought about himself and the information he'd seen—his attributes. At the simple thought of "attributes," nothing happened. But he realised he wasn't thinking it *with purpose.*

Xavier tilted his chin up. *Attributes and personal information.* He threw in that last bit to see if it would change anything.

XAVIER COLLINS
Age: 20
Race: Human
Grade: F
Moral Faction: World Defender (Planet Earth)
Class: Mage

Level: 1
Strength: 5
Speed: 5
Toughness: 5
Intelligence: 7
Willpower: 7
Spirit: 10
Mastery Points for this level: 300/1,000
Available Spirit Energy: 300/1,100

Xavier frowned. Why hadn't it shown him this information before? The fact that it mentioned his race as human made him wonder what other races were out there. *Goblins, of course. But what else? Elves? Orcs?*

Weird grey aliens?

He shook his head, moving to the next thing.

Grade: F

He tilted his head to the side. Grade F? What did that mean? It didn't sound good. Was he being graded on how well he'd done so far? *I'm still alive, aren't I? Shouldn't that at least be a pass?*

Maybe it meant something else...

Moral Faction: World Defender (Planet Earth)

Xavier had already figured there must be *other* worlds, what with there being goblins coming through portals and all. But this only further confirmed it.

He looked down at the text at the end. Seven hundred more Mastery Points and he would reach Level 2, which made him excited even though he didn't know what gaining a level would do.

Spirit Energy, he still had no clue about.

He licked his lips and thought—with as much purpose as he could muster—*What is Spirit Energy?*

Nothing happened. He deflated.

Well, that wasn't helpful.

A clatter sounded, somewhere out in the hall. Xavier mentally pushed the notification away—at least *that* worked—and limped over to the door, wincing when he put weight on his injured leg. He placed his ear against the door.

There was a massive *thud* as wood splintered.

The point of a blade thrust straight through the wood, coming out an inch away from his face. He stumbled backward, heart racing. Almost fell. The sword was pulled back. An eye pushed up against the hole it made.

Another goblin. The eye flicked toward Xavier. The goblin cackled. Another one cackled out in the hall. Then another.

There were at least three.

Xavier glanced about, considered hiding for a moment, then thought better of it.

Time to fight more of these little beasts.

Chapter 4
I Can't Live Up to Being a Champion If I Die

I DON'T DESERVE TO BE HERE, XAVIER THOUGHT AS THE goblins outside the lecture theatre's door kept slamming their swords into the wood. Wouldn't be long until they broke through. *I'm not a Champion. Not a defender of this world. I'm just a college kid who likes to read and write fantasy and chose the wrong damned option.*

He released a breath. His hands shook, the staff gripped in both of them.

If Julian Myers hadn't put his gun down and surrendered, I would be dead. Very, very dead.

But he *wasn't.* He was here. Alive. He'd chosen "Champion" because he wanted to protect people. Because he wanted to be strong. It embarrassed him to think it, but he'd chosen Champion because he wanted to be a hero.

Heroes don't hesitate. They don't cower in fear. They don't run away from fights. They don't hide from them.

The goblins kept slamming their swords into the door. Any second, the wood would fail. Any second, it would give in.

Any second, he would die.

Maybe I don't deserve to be here, but I am here. Xavier steeled himself. Clutched the staff tighter. *I'm going to* earn *the title of Champion.*

The little green beasts broke through the door. Xavier didn't wait. Didn't hesitate. Didn't back away or back down. He slammed the head of the staff straight into the first goblin that stepped through, not even bothering to scan it.

The clear crystal at the end of his staff smashed into the beast's head, caving in part of its skull. Blood spurted from the wound.

But the goblin was still moving. His attack hadn't done enough.

Xavier followed it up with another strike as the Lesser Goblin stumbled into the room.

A notification popped up in his vision. He dismissed it instinctively, hoping he could read it later.

The goblin wasn't alone. It had come with four of its ugly, green-skinned little friends.

Xavier gritted his teeth as the second goblin entered the lecture theatre. It leapt over the first, eyes wide, nose flared, lips pulled back.

He yanked his staff up in a block, surprised he was fast enough. Again, he wondered if he should've chosen warrior. The System's words entered his mind, however. *One cannot walk backward on the path.*

Second-guessing his decisions wouldn't help.

The goblin didn't carry a short sword like the previous two. Instead, it wielded an axe. The head of the axe bit into the shaft of Xavier's staff, and he was surprised the wood didn't snap.

The other goblins streamed into the room and surrounded him. One flanked him on either side, another cackling behind him.

I can't live up to being a Champion if I die!

In that instant, it occurred to him that most every fantasy caster he'd read about manifested their powers in a time of great need.

He focused, and thought—with heavy intent—*Telekinesis!*

He didn't know how the damned spell worked. Didn't know what he was supposed to do. He just clenched his jaw and *willed* what he wanted into being, hoping it would work.

The goblin in front of him flew backward. It crashed through the lecture theatre's door and slammed into the wall in the hall.

Xavier didn't have time to admire what he'd done. He whirled his staff around him in a wild swing. Though he'd heard a loud crack when the goblin had slammed into the wall, he knew it was still alive as he hadn't received a notification congratulating him for killing it.

I cast my first spell! A smile slipped onto his face. He'd moved the goblin with his mind. Shoved it ten feet without touching it.

Three goblins still standing.

He wondered how long it would take for the one in the hall to get back up.

Xavier swung his staff at the closest little beast, but it slipped backward and one of its buddies pounced and cut a line into his ankle.

He almost collapsed. Both legs now struggled to hold his weight. *Crap, crap, crap!*

Cast Element!

It was like something took over him, then. Power built up inside him. Then entered the staff. The clear crystal turned blood red. The energy flowed into the staff until it could no longer contain it. Flames burst forth, straight out of the crystal. Fire streamed toward one of the goblins and consumed it in flame.

It wasn't a simple fireball that crashed into the enemy. This was more like a conflagration of flame. Every inch of the goblin was covered, its skin melting off.

The other two goblins exchanged a glance, eyes wide.

The flaming goblin flailed but soon fell. It writhed for a moment, then died.

Xavier stood tall. Tall as he could with both his legs injured. Gripped the staff tight. The two goblins backed away from him. *Aren't cackling anymore, are you?* The one in the hall was standing up, stretching its back.

They looked like they were about to run.

Xavier wasn't about to let them. He'd been tasked with

protecting this "settlement," which he'd figured must be referring to the university. Only then would he be yanked back out of this place and sent to the pocket world.

Whatever that is.

Besides, there was an addictive quality to defeating his opponents. To gaining more Mastery Points. If this was what he could do at Level 1, what could he do at Level 2? 10? 50?

He used Cast Element again.

Cast Element has a cooldown of 30 seconds. It cannot be used for another 25 seconds.

He blinked. *So much for throwing fire around.*

The goblins, seeing he hadn't blasted another of them into ash, were no longer backing off. In fact, they looked as though they were emboldened.

Telekinesis! Xavier thrust his staff forward.

Telekinesis has a cooldown of 30 seconds. It cannot be used for another 15 seconds.

Again, nothing happened.

Xavier swallowed. He snapped out with his staff, one of his legs giving in as he did so.

The goblins began their insane cackling once more. Wicked grins alighted on their faces. The one he'd thrown into the wall was back, and Xavier was surrounded on three sides.

Xavier only kept on his feet out of sheer force of will. He narrowly avoided a sword-strike from the goblin on his left. But as he did, he moved into range of the one on his right. An axe bit into his knee. He slammed into the ground and yelled out in pain.

This no longer felt like a video game. Video games weren't this painful!

I can't die like this. I refuse to die like this!

He was outnumbered and gaining injuries by the second. He

had no idea what to do. He scrambled, trying to remember what the other two spells he'd learnt were.

If he'd been smart, he would have parked himself at the back of the lecture hall and sent spells down at his enemies from afar in hopes of taking them down before they could reach him, but he hadn't even known if he *could* use his spells.

He recalled his other two spells—Summon and Spiritual Guidance. He hadn't read their descriptions. He hadn't had time, after he'd been injured by the first Lesser Goblin. He used Spiritual Guidance, worried Summon might have some ritualistic component that would make it longer to cast.

He thought the command as forcefully as he could.

Spiritual Guidance!

Xavier didn't know where the spells came from—he didn't know if he had mana like in a video game, or if he did, how much—so he hoped he had enough energy left to cast another spell.

Something came over him, then. Much like it had when he'd used Cast Element and thrown fire at one of the goblins. Except this felt quite different to that. It was... taking over his body.

A silver glow spread over him, and he felt himself gaining insight. His head snapped up, and it was as though he knew what he needed to do. It was strange, but he didn't question it—he didn't have *time* to question it.

He'd been gripping his staff with his right hand. He tossed it quickly into his left. The goblins were walking around him. They still looked cautious, and Xavier realised something about them—the little beasts were cowards.

They had the numbers. He was injured. And yet now they saw him as a threat, they were *still* hesitating.

Whatever force was guiding him through the spell helped him use that to his advantage. He drew the short sword he'd shoved through the belt tying up his grey robes—the one he'd taken from the first goblin he'd killed. The staff now in his left hand, he leant heavily upon it and pushed himself to his feet.

He lunged toward the closest goblin. His arms being longer, he still had the reach. He swiped straight for its neck. Still felt strange. He didn't know if he would have gone for a strike like that without the Spiritual Guidance spell influencing his actions.

Xavier took the goblin's head clean off.

The silver sheen disappeared. All the pain he'd been feeling from his injuries flooded back. In that moment when he'd stood and lunged, decapitating the goblin, he hadn't even realised the pain was gone.

The Spiritual Guidance spell had worn off. It had been like a surge of adrenaline. But now that it was gone, he felt an emptiness he never had before. A wave of exhaustion slammed into him. Like he hadn't slept in days. And the pain? It wasn't just back. The pain felt three times as bad. He didn't even know how he was still standing.

The two last goblins looked more wary than ever. As though about to bolt. Part of Xavier wished they would. But he imagined that would be a mistake. Mostly because he didn't know how many of the little beasts there were.

What if they left only to gather reinforcements?

Whatever pain and exhaustion he endured, he couldn't let the goblins see it. If they saw his pain. Saw how tired he was. And worse, if they glimpsed his fear, they would pounce. He gritted his teeth. An image of the Navy SEAL, Julian, getting struck by lightning assailed his mind.

That's what refusing to fight will get me. Dead.

He wouldn't let that happen.

Xavier stood as tall as he could manage. God, the pain felt unbearable. He gritted his teeth ever harder. Remembered a quote by Marcus Aurelius, the Roman emperor and stoic philosopher.

If its endurable, then endure it, he thought to himself, the words like a mantra. *If it's unendurable, then stop complaining. Your destruction will mean its end as well.*

It wasn't the first time he'd thought of that quote. It felt absurd, however, contemplating the last time he'd used those words as a mantra—he'd been struggling to stay awake during a particularly boring lecture about poetry.

Why Creative Writing teachers insisted on making everything about poetry, he would never understand...

He repeated the mantra once more, standing tall. A swell of confidence ballooned in him, then. He swung his blade out wildly at the nearest goblin. In his mind, he felt something *shift*. He wasn't sure what it was for a moment, until he realised—it was Telekinesis.

It had reached the end of its cooldown.

Xavier did the last thing he expected considering the dire circumstances he'd found himself in: he grinned.

Chapter 5
At Least I Know I Can Handle Myself

Xavier cast Telekinesis on one of the goblins. The little beast slammed into the wall behind it. Something cracked in the creature, just as it had the first time Xavier had used the spell on an enemy.

Only this time, the wall he flung the goblin at wasn't as far away. It was right behind it. Xavier took an aching step forward, the pain in both his legs stabbing at him. His ankle—the one a line had been sliced into—threatened to give out.

It faltered, but not enough to stop him from doing what he needed. He lashed out with the little sword. The Lesser Goblin hadn't made it back to its feet yet, so striking the little beast was easy enough.

You have defeated a Level 2 Lesser Goblin!
You have gained 200 Mastery Points.
You have gained 200 Spirit Energy.

Congratulations, you have reached Level 2!
Your health has been regenerated by 50%!
Your Spirit Energy limit has increased by 100!

You have received +1 Intelligence, +1 Willpower, and +1 Spirit!
You have received +5 free stat points!
All your spells have refreshed and are no longer on cooldown!

An odd sensation ran through Xavier's body. It was similar to when he'd cast Spiritual Guidance, but even more invigorating. He felt like he could do *anything*. He was caught by a thrill of excitement, and he couldn't help but smile.

Which he knew would look strange to anyone witnessing the scene. A young man in odd, grey robes killing green goblins, covered in their blood and *smiling*.

That didn't put a stop to his feeling of elation, however.

The pain in his legs faded, and he could stand without difficulty. The remaining goblin looked afraid. *You should be afraid,* Xavier thought. He threw the short sword down, took his staff in both hands, then used Cast Element.

Energy ran from him and into the staff. The crystal at its top turned red, then fire flowed out of it. Flames streamed toward the goblin, which had turned and tried to run, but it wasn't fast enough to outrun the spell.

The flames caught the Lesser Goblin, consuming it in seconds.

You have defeated a Level 2 Lesser Goblin!
You have gained 200 Mastery Points.
You have gained 200 Spirit Energy.

Xavier breathed hard. Still grinning. He looked around at the dead Lesser Goblins in the room. His grin faltered. Suddenly, he felt... embarrassed? As though he shouldn't be smiling about what he'd just done.

He straightened and shook his head. The door to the lecture theatre was still broken, which meant more Lesser Goblins could find him at any moment.

At least I know I can handle myself now.

He took stock of the situation. First, he looked at his legs. His robes had slashes through them. They were covered in blood—his red and goblin green. He gripped his staff in his left hand and hiked the robes.

Xavier had only bandaged the first wound he'd taken, not others. He looked at the line in his ankle. All he saw was blood. When he narrowed his eyes and looked more closely, he found the wound almost healed.

When I gained that level, it said my health had regenerated by 50 percent. That made him wonder what his health *was*. Did he have health points, like in a video game?

Health points! he thought.

Nothing appeared. He did, however, get a vague sensation, something that told him he was on the right track, almost as though he was beginning to get a feel for how the system worked.

Health status.

Your health is at 90%.

Had he really lost so much health in that fight? He'd taken perhaps three strikes, all to his legs—thank God those little beasts had been short. Looking down, he supposed he *had* lost a lot of blood. *Perhaps I lost more health as I bled?*

He wondered if that percentage would go up as time passed, and if so, how quickly.

Xavier paused. He hadn't been taken away from this place yet, which meant there were still goblins out there. At least, he hoped it would only be goblins...

Okay, what's my next move? So far, he'd been blundering through on not much more than blind luck and sheer force of will. If he were to get out of whatever the hell this was alive, he needed more than that.

He had received five stat points when he'd gained that level, along with one point into Intelligence, Willpower, and Spirit. He didn't know which did what, only that he was deemed to have a strong spirit by the System.

Whatever that means.

He looked at his attributes and personal information once more.

XAVIER COLLINS
Level: 2
Strength: 5
Speed: 5
Toughness: 5
Intelligence: 8
Willpower: 8
Spirit: 11
Mastery Points for this level: 300/3,000
Available Spirit Energy: 800/1,300
Free stat points remaining: 5

All right. My Mastery points are 300 of 3,000, which means it takes three times as many Mastery Points to reach Level 3 as it did to reach Level 2. He supposed that made sense. In any video game he'd ever played, gaining levels became harder as one went along.

Why would this System be any different?

When he came to his Spirit Energy, he frowned, tilting his head to the side. He only had 800. How could that be possible? He thought back to all the fights he'd been in, and the notifications he'd received at the end of them.

Whenever he'd defeated an opponent, he'd received the same amount of Spirit Energy as Mastery Points. Shouldn't his Spirit Energy be maxed out at 1,300, if that were the case?

Also, shouldn't his maximum Spirit Energy only be 1,200?

One thing at a time.

He stood there for a moment, frowning. He *should* have 1,300 points of Spirit Energy, yet he only had 800. That was 500 less than he'd gained after killing six goblins and "winning" the fight with the Navy SEAL.

Xavier stopped himself from tapping his foot as he thought it all through. The last thing he wanted was to alert any goblins in the area of his presence—though he imagined the fight's noise must have travelled far.

He strained his ears but heard nothing. He was alone. For now.

Spirit Energy... Where could that 500 have gone?

It clicked. He raised his chin. How many spells had he cast? He'd used Telekinesis twice, Cast Element twice, and Spirit Guidance once—he had yet to use Summon.

I used five spells. Each time he'd used one of the spells, he'd felt energy leaving him. That must have been Spirit Energy! And each of the spells had cost 100 Spirit Energy each!

Xavier couldn't help but smile. It was like figuring out a little puzzle. *Spirit Energy is mana.* Except, since when did one gain mana from killing?

He shook his head. Just because this *felt* like a video game didn't mean everything would line up. How could it? This was real life, now. *Unless I've had a stroke or been in a coma. Or, worse, some terribly vivid hallucinations and the goblins are actually classmates I've murdered.*

Except somehow, those eventualities felt more ludicrous to him than what was *actually* happening.

He halted that line of thought immediately.

Okay, now I know where the Spirit Energy went. Why do I have a maximum limit of 1,300? His limit had been 1,100 and, when he'd gained a level, he'd gotten 100 added to his limit.

He looked at his stats again—his Spirit attribute was at 11, as he'd gained 1 point from the level-up. That clicked then, too. At least, the math added up.

Each point in Spirit gives me 100 to my Spirit Energy limit. Each level gives me 100 as well. I was Level 1 with 10 Spirit, so I had 1,100. Now, I am Level 2 with 11 Spirit, so I have 1,300.

He figured there was an easy way to test this theory.

Xavier willed what he wanted to happen next.

You have added 1 point to Spirit!
Spirit increased from 11 → 12!
You have 4 free stat points remaining.

Xavier then thought to bring up his available Spirit Energy, seeing if he could have *only* that appear, instead of his entire stat sheet.

Available Spirit Energy: 800/1,400

He pumped his fist in the air, even though he knew he would look ridiculous doing so. He felt a bit proud for having figured that out. Though he was a long way from getting a handle on the System and whatever had happened to the world, this felt like a step in the right direction.

Before applying his other free stat points, Xavier moved around the room. Each of the Lesser Goblins he'd killed had a purse just like the first one. Coins jingling inside. Using one of the short swords, he cut the purses from their belts and shoved them into his satchel.

I wish I had some sort of bag of holding. Do those exist? He would find out. Assuming he lived long enough. He clenched his jaw, resolve settling into him. *I'll see this all through. Whatever it is.*

He'd *chosen* Champion, after all. Now, it was time to live up to that.

Chapter 6
Is This What I've Been Looking For?

Xavier stalked the halls of his university, ears pricked for any goblins on the loose.

He stifled a laugh at the absurdity of what he was doing. He'd walked these halls a hundred times. Going from one class to another. Carrying his bag and laptop.

Today, he wore grey, slashed-up robes covered in red and green blood. He carried a seven-foot-long staff with a clear crystal at its end that helped him channel his magic.

The belt tied about his waist had a short sword shoved through one side and an axe shoved through the other. A satchel hung from his shoulders, six purses of jingling coins inside. He hadn't looked inside the purses yet. There were more important things to do than count his spoils of war.

That morning, as he'd been walking over the bridge on his way to class, he'd been wishing he could move things with his mind. Wishing he could live in a fantasy world. Now, it seemed as though a fantasy world had come to him.

His smile fell away. He'd already seen one life lost because of the System integrating Earth into the Greater Universe.

Xavier still didn't know what the wider ramifications of that were. He wondered how many others had chosen Champion. How many other fights to the death had there been?

How many people had actually fought? Killing each other because of words that appeared superimposed over their vision? And how many others had been transported to a place like he had, forced to fight goblins, or who knew what else?

Xavier swallowed. The integration wasn't exactly a dream come true, but there was no use complaining about it. A guilty part of him didn't *want* to complain about it.

I always wanted more. Now I can wield magic. Throw fire. Fling goblins across a room with my mind... Is this what I've been looking for? The very thought alone made him feel like he was doing something wrong by *enjoying* this.

That Navy SEAL had died for him. Then he'd killed six goblins. Creatures that appeared just as sapient as he was.

But the guilt fell away surprisingly quickly. If this were to be the new order of the world, why shouldn't he embrace it? Why shouldn't he enjoy it? Wouldn't that be better than suffering through it?

This was surely just the beginning. Xavier didn't know what trials he would need to endure, but he did know that what he was doing right now was nothing more than a *test*.

Though he worried about his mother, there was nothing he could do for her right now except hope she'd been taken some-where safe. *She would not have chosen Champion.* He imagined her choosing something like Support. The thought of her choosing Soldier was laughable.

His mother wasn't even *in* this city. It would take him hours to get to her, assuming the roads weren't clogged and he could get a car to work.

So, like many other things, he had to put his mother out of his mind and focus on the task at hand.

Once he'd taken the purses from the goblins, he'd remembered his bag, laptop and phone had been at the top of the stairs. His wasn't the only laptop still sitting on one of the little desks in the room.

He'd ran up the stairs and grabbed his phone. Tried to use it. It had been on, but there had been no signal.

He supposed he shouldn't have been surprised.

His laptop hadn't connected to the internet, either. The university's Wi-Fi was down.

Xavier had shoved the laptop, his phone, and earbuds into his satchel, along with his water bottle, but he'd left his backpack there. It would feel strange to carry it around, considering what was going on. There wasn't anything useful in it, anyway.

There was still so much he needed to learn. But he wouldn't go into his next encounter unprepared.

He thought of the different spells he had available, thinking to bring up the list again, and was surprised to find new information.

Spells List:
Cast Element – Rank 1 – Upgrade Quest Unlocked!
Spiritual Guidance – Rank 1 – Upgrade Quest Unlocked!
Summon – Rank 1
Telekinesis – Rank 1 – Upgrade Quest Unlocked!

Upgrade quest? Xavier frowned. He focused on the first one.

Cast Element – Rank 1
Upgrade Quest:
As you have now used this spell, you have taken your first step on the path to upgrading it to Rank 2.
Available paths:

1. **Cast Fire. To upgrade, use Fire to help kill 10 enemies. Progress: 2/10**

2. **Cast Water. To upgrade, use Water to help kill 10 enemies. Progress: 0/10**
3. **Cast Earth. To upgrade, use Earth to help kill 10 enemies. Progress: 0/10**
4. **Cast Air. To upgrade, use Air to help kill 10 enemies. Progress: 0/10**
5. **Cast Elements. To upgrade, use all four elements to help kill 5 enemies each.**

Choosing one path may eliminate some or all other paths. This will both limit your ability and strengthen it.
Upgrading a spell from Rank 1 to Rank 2 will make you immediately forget another Rank 1 spell of your choosing. Once a spell is forgotten, it is almost impossible to be learnt again.
One cannot walk backward on the path.

Xavier stopped walking as he read Cast Element's different paths. He wasn't as prepared for his next fight as he'd hoped.

He slipped into a small classroom on his left, ensuring it was deserted before he shut the door. He almost took a seat before thinking better of it. There was only one exit—the door he'd walked through.

The blinds were closed. He flicked on the lights. He wasn't surprised they worked, as a projector screen was still running, pointed toward the room's front wall. He looked at the heavy desk near the door where a teacher should have been sitting. An abandoned cup of tea rested atop it.

Xavier walked around the desk and shoved it in front of the door. It took longer than he'd hoped and made him sweat more than it should have. Now the door was blocked, he took a seat facing it.

I still have 4 free stat points, maybe I should put one into Strength...

He hadn't invested them in anything yet, as he wasn't sure which attributes would best help him as a mage. He assumed Intelligence and Spirit were the more important ones but couldn't be sure.

Xavier sighed and plopped himself onto one of the seats. He looked at the information again.

> **Upgrading a spell from Rank 1 to Rank 2 will make you immediately forget another Rank 1 spell of your choosing. Once a spell is forgotten, it is almost impossible to be learnt again.**

If he used Cast Element on enough enemy goblins with the fire element, he could upgrade its rank. But that would mean losing the chance of using the other elements.

Unless he diversified the spell's usage, using the spell twenty times instead of ten. It would take longer for him to rank up the spell, and something told him focusing on all four elements would mean none of them were as strong as if he were only focusing on one or two.

Assuming it lets me focus on two...

And if he *did* rank up the spell, he would lose one of his other ones. He bit his lip. That meant he could only keep two out of the four spells. And out of the three he'd used, he liked them all.

Xavier put his head in his hands. He hadn't even *used* the Summon spell yet. He supposed he could do that now. It probably used 100 Spirit Energy like the other spells had, and he still had 800 Spirit Energy left.

What does Summon even do?

The information came up as he raised his head.

Summon – Rank 1
Summon is a basic mage spell learnt by all starting human mages. Summon has several different paths, and is a difficult spell to master. It can be used to

42

> *summon an ally to your position, summon a trained*
> *familiar, summon the help of a lesser deity, or even*
> *summon the dead. As a mage advances, they may*
> *choose to specialise in one of these areas, generalise in*
> *several, or abandon the path altogether.*
> *One cannot walk backward on the path.*

Xavier swallowed. *Or even summon the dead.* A shiver ran up his spine at the thought of necromancers creating zombie hordes. Was this really a spell *all* starting human mages got?

At least it says it's difficult to master.

Xavier wondered what he could even *do* with this spell. He definitely wouldn't use it to summon the dead. That... wasn't his style. He didn't fancy having walking corpses around him, reminding him of all the people or creatures he'd slain.

Though having his own army didn't sound *too* bad, except for the fact that he was a loner who would far rather spend his time alone.

The part about summoning a trained familiar did sound interesting. He wondered if he could train multiple familiars. Starting with a wolf, making his way toward a dragon... He closed his eyes, imagined himself riding on the back of one.

But how could he train a familiar *here*? Maybe if he'd appeared in a forest. All he'd encountered at the university were goblins, and something told him those didn't qualify. Even if they did, he didn't want a goblin as a pet—that seemed more like slavery.

He tilted his head. *Summon the help of a lesser deity.* What would that look like, exactly? Perhaps it should have surprised him that deities—*gods and goddesses*—existed in the first place. Xavier had been an atheist since the age of ten, when he couldn't get a good answer from his mother about why she believed in God. But... well, after the day he'd had, it would take a lot more than that to surprise him.

Besides, his lack of belief had always hinged on there being a lack of *proof*. If he could actually summon the help of a deity, that seemed like proof enough of their existence.

Would summoning their help give him some sort of boon? Or would a god appear in front of him and kill his foes? He doubted it would be the latter.

There's gotta be some strings attached to summoning a god's help. He didn't like that idea on principle.

He didn't *know* anything about the Greater Universe. The last thing he wanted to do was get mixed up with gods and goddesses. What if he ended up worshipping a malevolent one by accident?

Though he still liked the idea of riding a dragon, he couldn't make this decision based on something he didn't know was possible. If he had to fight for his world, he needed to become as strong as he could be *now*.

That meant choosing a path and sticking to it.

He looked at the next spell.

Telekinesis – Rank 1
Telekinesis is a basic mage spell learnt by most starting human mages. Telekinesis has several different paths, and is a difficult spell to master. It can be used as a blunt force instrument, or an instrument of precision. As a mage advances, they may choose to specialise in one area, generalise in both, or abandon the path altogether.
One cannot walk backward on the path.

Xavier frowned. It was only learnt by *most* starting human mages, and not all? He wondered why that was. The two different paths made sense to him. He supposed it was the difference between flinging something at an enemy, or flinging the enemy, like he'd done with those two goblins.

He brought up the upgrade information.

Telekinesis – Rank 1

Upgrade Quest:
As you have now used this spell, you have taken your first step on the path to upgrading it to Rank 2. Available paths:

1. **Heavy Telekinesis – This path allows you to move heavier items or opponents but lacks accuracy. To upgrade, move ten heavy objects. Progress: 2/10**
2. **Precision Telekinesis – This path allows you to move light items with high accuracy. To upgrade, move twenty light objects with great precision. Progress: 2/20**
3. **General Telekinesis – This path combines the best and worst of both worlds. To upgrade, move ten light objects with great precision, and move five heavy objects.**

Choosing one path may eliminate some or all other paths. This will both limit your ability and strengthen it.
Upgrading a spell from Rank 1 to Rank 2 will make you immediately forget another Rank 1 spell of your choosing. Once a spell is forgotten, it is almost impossible to be learnt again.
One cannot walk backward on the path.

Xavier blinked, then smiled. He didn't need to kill any enemies to upgrade Telekinesis to Rank 2! He just had to move heavy or light things—assuming he ended up *choosing* this spell.

He sighed, once more wishing he didn't *have* to choose.

Then he looked at the information for the final spell.

Chapter 7
Quest Log Activated

HIDING IN THE SMALL CLASSROOM OF HIS GOBLIN-INFESTED university, a heavy desk in front of the door, Xavier read the spell description for Spiritual Guidance.

Spiritual Guidance – Rank 1
Spiritual Guidance is a basic mage spell that is rarely learnt by human mages and is only available to those with a naturally strong Spirit. Spiritual Guidance has several different paths, and is an incredibly difficult spell to master. It can enhance one's body, mind, and magic, and subtly guide one's actions while in combat. As a mage advances, they may choose to specialise in one area, generalise in all, or abandon the path altogether.

Unlike other spells, generalising in Spiritual Guidance does not hinder the power of each of this spell's abilities, as achieving Rank 2 and upgrading the spell to Spiritual Trifecta is only achievable by rare individuals.

One cannot walk backward on the path.

Xavier's eyes widened. The spell was rarely learnt? Required a naturally strong Spirit?

The System deemed my Spirit skills high. Is that why my Cast Element spell was able to take out the goblins in one hit despite only being Rank 1? Because I had a high Spirit attribute?

He narrowed his eyes and brought up the Upgrade Quest right away, wanting to learn more.

Spiritual Guidance – Rank 1
Upgrade Quest:
As you have now used this spell, you have taken your first step on the path to upgrading it to Rank 2. Available paths:

1. *Spiritual Strength - Enhance one's physical and mental strength while in combat. To upgrade, fight an enemy while this path is active. Progress: 1/10*
2. *Spiritual Defence - Enhance one's physical and mental defence while in combat. To upgrade, fight an enemy while this path is active. Progress: 0/10*
3. *Spiritual Magic - Enhance one's magical power while in combat. To upgrade, fight an enemy while this path is active. Progress: 0/10*
4. *Spiritual Trifecta - Enhance one's physical and mental strength and defence, as well as one's magical power, while in combat. To upgrade, fight an enemy while this path is active. Progress: 0/5*

Choosing one path may eliminate some or all other paths. This will both limit your ability and strengthen it.
Upgrading a spell from Rank 1 to Rank 2 will make you immediately forget another Rank 1 spell of your

choosing. Once a spell is forgotten, it is almost impossible to be learnt again.
One cannot walk backward on the path.

Xavier's interest piqued even further. He stared at the fourth path, Spiritual Trifecta, and reread part of the spell's information:

Unlike other spells, generalising in Spiritual Guidance does not hinder the power of each of this spell's abilities.

He grinned. *That's the path I'm going to take.* It seemed like the obvious choice. It made him wonder why there were multiple paths to begin with. Wouldn't everyone choose Spiritual Trifecta? It even had fewer requirements to upgrade, only using the spell to fight against five enemies instead of ten!

It didn't even specify *killing* the enemies.

Then again, it did say it was only achievable by rare individuals. *I'll have to become one of those rare individuals, then.*

He realised he'd been a fool earlier, when he'd left the lecture theatre, for not having looked at his spells first. There'd been far more for him to do before facing his next enemy.

I hope there are enough enemies for me to face to upgrade these spells.

He bit his lip. He needed to make a difficult decision. He was *definitely* going to pursue upgrading Spiritual Guidance to Rank 2. As he could only choose two out of his four spells, and he'd already put aside Summon, he needed to decide between Cast Element and Telekinesis.

Why does this feel like such a difficult choice? He sighed. *I can't spend all my time on this decision. There are goblins to kill.* He chuckled to himself. *Goblins to kill. Yeah, that's a completely normal thought to have.*

Xavier stood. As though standing alone would help him feel more assertive.

Cast Element helped me kill my enemies faster. Throwing fire was the quintessential mage spell. But moving things with his mind? The way he had flung those goblins against the wall?

He thought about which spell would help him better in the long run, and which he would prefer to use. Though he didn't have knowledge of the System and how it would let him develop those spells, he'd read plenty of books...

Fire is too volatile. What if I can't control it? What if I set fire to an enemy army and the fire can't be contained? As powerful as fire was, it was chaotic, too. It might have helped him kill his enemies faster, but there was something about Telekinesis that he liked even more.

Perhaps it wasn't the most logical choice, but he'd always wanted to fling things with his mind. It was an insane dream he'd had since he was a kid.

Now that he could actually make it happen? How could he refuse?

Seeing as he *had* to choose, he decided to go with Telekinesis—Heavy Telekinesis, to be precise.

He imagined using it to move a mountain, or fling an entire army to the ground, and couldn't help but grin. It gave him a better image than simply setting everything on fire. Besides, he couldn't say he liked the smell of burning flesh.

For a moment, he considered using Telekinesis in here. He could move the desk out of the way of the door with his mind, but he only had so much Spirit Energy. Eight hundred points, to be exact. Even if he could gain the next rank, he'd be without Spirit Energy for his next fight.

I need to figure out a way to gain more Spirit Energy without killing enemies.

It was the same thing that stopped him from using Spiritual Guidance, even though he needed to practise with the spell.

He looked at his legs. His tattered robes. He'd taken a lot of damage when those goblins had attacked him, and he still didn't know how to regain health without levelling up.

He checked in on his health.

Your health is at 91%.

He blinked. Grinned. It had gone up! Though it hadn't gone up *much*, not a whole lot of time had passed since last he checked. Perhaps ten or fifteen minutes. *Maybe sleeping makes it regenerate even faster. Or, like, meditation?*

Xavier shook his head. There was so much to figure out, but he couldn't spend all his time trapped in this room. He'd spent too much time here already.

If he was careful enough, he wouldn't have to worry about losing health.

Just to be safe, he put one of his free stat points into Toughness.

You have added 1 point to Toughness!
Toughness increased from 5 → 6!
You have 3 free stat points remaining.

Hopefully that will help.

He also decided to use the rest of the stat points. He didn't know how much difference they made, but there was no point hoarding them if it meant the difference between survival and death.

He threw one point each into Intelligence, Willpower, and Spirit. Those three attributes appeared to be the most important for a mage. He might have killed a lot of those goblins by whacking them over the head with his staff or using one of their short swords, but such tactics would only be effective for so long.

He paused before moving the desk as the attributes were distributed. Tilted his head to one side. Narrowed his eyes, furrowed his brow.

Did he *feel* smarter? *How am I supposed to tell?*

Xavier sighed and shoved the desk along the ground again. The heavy legs scraped against the floor louder than before. Once he'd moved it aside, he readied himself, then opened the door quietly.

The hallway was clear. Not a person—or goblin—in sight. He worried about heading out to the courtyard. Worried about being in the open. Since he'd seen his spells had quests to upgrade them, he'd wished he had some sort of quest screen for defending this outpost.

Quest Log Activated
Current Quest: Protect a human settlement
from invaders taking root on your world.
Defeat all of the enemy invaders.
Progress: 6/50
Rewards:

1. **You will be sent to a pocket world.**
2. **Unknown item.**

Huh. Xavier ran a hand through his hair. "Would have been nice if that had shown up from the start," he muttered. He stared at the last reward. *Unknown item.* Could that be a better staff? Maybe new, untattered robes?

Forty-four more goblins to kill. He hoped they were all Level 2.

Xavier gripped his staff in both hands and stalked down the hall as quietly as he could. Seeing that quest log gave him a renewed sense of urgency. Honestly, he hadn't expected there to be so many. A part of him was terrified, as he should be. This was life and death, and all that.

But another part? Another part was excited. That was a lot of Mastery Points. He could rank up his spells. Gain more levels. More stat points.

He felt giddy. Like he hadn't in a long time. Not since he was a kid. A sense of adventure swelled inside him.

Cackling sounded around a corner. *More goblins.* He grinned.

Slowed his stalking walk to a creep and popped his head around the corner.

Two goblins, standing alone. He scanned them.

{Lesser Goblin – Level 2}
{Lesser Goblin – Level 2}

Good. He could take two Level 2 goblins. He needed to gain a lot of Spirit Energy. Enough to practise Spiritual Guidance.

And he wasn't going to miss an opportunity to use Telekinesis.

The goblins both faced away from him. They were speaking to each other, though Xavier didn't understand what they were saying. The language was harsh and guttural, their voices high-pitched. Honestly, it sounded like they were mumbling to each other.

What do goblins have to talk about, anyway?

Xavier stepped into the hall, unseen, and cast Telekinesis. The goblins had been standing quite close together, and both of them were struck by his spell.

They flew farther than he'd expected. The vicious *crack* when they slammed into the ground made him wince, but no notifications appeared.

Still not strong enough to take them out in one. Perhaps if he'd flung them at a wall. *Or off a roof...*

Xavier sprinted at the closest goblin, which struggled back to its feet. He needed to use Spiritual Guidance. And not in the same way as before—he needed to draw on all three of its qualities.

Spiritual Strength. Spiritual Defence. Spiritual Magic.

He repeated those three things in his mind as he cast the spell, trying to imagine what they might feel like.

The power seized him, as it had before. *Exactly* as before. Fear alighted in the Lesser Goblin's eyes. *I'm not using all three.* He didn't know *how* he knew; he simply did. It was instinctual.

But he couldn't hesitate.

He slammed the staff's head into the goblin's skull.

**You have defeated a Level 2 Lesser Goblin!
You have gained 200 Mastery Points.
You have gained 200 Spirit Energy.**

The skull caved in easily. Xavier felt how much stronger he'd hit. Far stronger than the last time he'd used Spiritual Guidance.

The silver sheen of the spell remained on him. It nudged him to bash in the other goblin's skull. One smooth hit and it would be done for. But if he did that, he'd be one more step *away* from upgrading to Spiritual Trifecta.

He recalled the upgrade's requirement:

Enhance one's physical and mental strength and defence, as well as one's magical power, while in combat.

It didn't say *use them all at once.*

Xavier faced the last goblin. The goblin slashed out. Xavier, silver sheen still enveloping him, caught the sword on his staff, diverting it. The silver sheen wore off. Exhaustion struck him, but less severe than last time. Perhaps because his leg wasn't injured, or because he'd expected it. Maybe even because he had more points in Spirit or Willpower than before. He didn't know, but he took it as a win.

He tried to use the spell again, focusing on its defensive aspect.

Spiritual Guidance has a cooldown of 10 seconds. It cannot be used for another 7 seconds.

Of course, the cooldown! Xavier hadn't known what the cooldown was before this fight. It was the first time he'd tried to use it twice in one fight.

Xavier backed away down the hall. Was this a stupid plan? Should he just attack the goblin? Kill it while he had the chance?

Only if I have to. He wanted the Spiritual Trifecta upgrade. He needed to do something exceptional if he were to become powerful enough to be a Champion. *Let's send it on a merry chase for a few seconds.*

He pretended to look afraid—which, admittedly, wasn't the hardest thing in the world to do, considering the circumstances—and ran down the hall, toward the classroom he'd hidden in while figuring out his spells.

Every few seconds, he checked the cooldown. It wasn't until he made it around the corner that it finally reached zero. He heard the goblin's pursuit, its mad cackle echoing off the walls.

I wonder if that will attract more of the little beasts...

The second the cooldown ended, Xavier whirled. He didn't know how powerful the Spiritual Defence would be, but he hoped it would be strong enough to take one of the goblin's hits.

Because when the Lesser Goblin leapt into the air, short sword cocked in a backswing ready to strike, he hadn't raised his staff to block the attack.

Xavier cast Spiritual Guidance. As the sword came down, a silver sheen enveloped him once more.

Chapter 8
This New Reality

I THINK I'M AN IDIOT.

The Lesser Goblin's short sword came down to strike Xavier's head, and he wasn't moving out of the way. But the moment the silver sheen of Spiritual Guidance had enveloped him, it infused him with confidence.

It felt different to last time, however. It didn't guide his attacks, it simply made him feel as though he could take anything the enemy could dish out. Without the spell, Xavier would have winced and tried to dodge the goblin's strike. With the spell, he stood tall, raised his chin, and waited for it to hit him.

Pain split his skull as the strike came down. He stumbled back a few steps. Touched a hand to his head. To his surprise, there was no blood. The strike had hurt, but it hadn't split his skull.

Hell, it hadn't even split his skin!

The Lesser Goblin looked as surprised as Xavier. Maybe more. Xavier had already figured out the little beasts were cowards. The goblin backed away, glanced behind him, ready to run.

The silver sheen had dissipated the second the short sword had hit him, so Xavier knew the cooldown's timer would have already begun. *I can't let the goblin run. I can't let it get away. But I can't kill it until the cooldown reaches the end, or I won't be able to use*

Spiritual Guidance to strengthen my magic during this fight. Should he run again? The goblin might be afraid, but it was still a predator. If Xavier wanted to make it think he was prey, he had to act like prey.

So he backed away, checked his cooldown.

Seven seconds.

He widened his eyes, made his movements jerky.

Five seconds.

The goblin hesitated. Stopped backing away. Tightened its grip on the short sword's hilt, steeling its gaze and smiling wickedly.

Three seconds.

Xavier shook his head. Raised his hands—his left still holding his staff—as though in surrender.

The goblin approached. Looked about to run straight at him.

One second.

It sprinted forward. Leapt up into the air again. Cackled louder than before.

Something *clicked* in Xavier's mind as the cooldown ended. He cast Spiritual Guidance, focusing it on his magic.

The goblin cocked its sword back.

A silver sheen enveloped Xavier.

The goblin's sword came down.

Xavier thrust his staff forward and cast Telekinesis. A massive amount of energy infused him. The power moved through his body. Before the goblin's strike reached Xavier, it was yanked backward, thrown across the hall. Must have flown forty feet until it crashed into the far wall. It dented the wall, bones breaking, and slid to the floor in a heap.

You have defeated a Level 2 Lesser Goblin!
You have gained 200 Mastery Points.
You have gained 200 Spirit Energy.

"Yes!" Xavier pumped a fist into the air. The silver sheen wore off. Mental, physical, and perhaps even *spiritual* exhaustion slammed into him. His body ached to fall to its knees. His legs faltered, worse than when he'd been injured.

He inhaled deeply. Let it out slow. And kept standing. The exhaustion soon left him. When it did, he felt a deep emptiness where the power once sat. That, too, soon left him.

He brought up his Upgrade Quest for Spiritual Guidance, looking only at the one for Spiritual Trifecta.

> *Spiritual Trifecta - Enhance one's physical and mental strength and defence, as well as one's magical power, while in combat. To upgrade, fight an enemy while this path is active. Progress: 1/5*

Xavier smiled. Couldn't help it. He'd been right. He didn't need to use all three of the spell's abilities simultaneously—perhaps that wasn't even possible while it was still at Rank 1. He just needed to use all three of them during the same fight.

Though he instantly saw the problem with this approach when he looked at his Spirit Energy.

Available Spirit Energy: 700/1,500

While his capacity to hold Spirit Energy had gone up to 1,500, that hadn't added any to his pool. He'd defeated two Lesser Goblins, gaining him 400 Spirit Energy, but it had taken five spells to manage it.

I need to be careful of that. He held up his staff. Green blood coated the crystal. The description said that mages could be close-combat fighters. Now he was starting to realise how. *Spiritual Guidance. It can make me physically and mentally stronger.* There must be other, similar spells. Should he add a point to Strength and Speed each on his next level-up? Was he going about this all wrong?

The Lesser Goblin lay crumpled at the far wall. Forty feet, he'd flung that thing. Its corpse was mangled, the neck turned the wrong way from the force of hitting the wall.

How much farther could I have thrown it if the wall wasn't there?

Xavier frowned. Was that a twisted, morbid thought, or a practical one?

He shrugged it off and cut the goblins' purses. *I need to manage this four more times.* Stalking down the halls, searching for more goblins, he wondered how other people were faring in this new reality.

Alistair Reed had planned everything *perfectly*.

His target was alone. He'd studied the building from every side. Knew how he would get in and out without being seen. Knew how to make the kill a quiet one.

The last thing he needed was to become a target himself, especially when this was going to be his first kill. *First of many.*

He'd gotten to the target's door. Picked the lock as silently as an expert thief. His weapon was sheathed at his hip, beneath his coat. The lock clicked and he almost laughed. Adrenaline surged through him. Hadn't felt this excited in a long time. Not since he was a kid, playing with the neighbour's dog.

Watching it squirm and listening to it whine as he poked holes through its flesh with a freshly sharpened hunting knife.

That's when he'd heard a noise outside. Thunder booming. It had been rather dark and gloomy. The sky had an odd colour to it. Reminded him of blood. Then again, most things did.

Then time had frozen.

Interlopers have discovered your world. Your Solar System has now been marked for integration into the Greater Universe.
System integration begins in:

5...
4...
3...
2...
1...
System integration commencing.

He'd been terrified, at first. Then confused. Then enraged.

Something had pulled him away from the most important moment in his life. He was finally going to achieve his childhood dream. Something he'd been working up to, something he'd been fantasising about for *years*.

The murder of another human being.

Now he'd been yanked out of his reality and thrown into darkness.

Text kept appearing over his vision. It knew his name. It judged him in three categories: physical skills, intellectual skills, and spirit skills. He'd achieved "High" in all but the last, which had only been "*Minimal*."

Then it had asked him to choose a moral faction. He didn't know what was happening, but he was nothing but delighted when he saw that "fight for chaos" was an option.

Much of his rage had dissipated by then. Instead, he was caught in the clutches of curiosity.

This was *new*. This was *different*. Like the murder he was about to commit, this was something he'd never experienced before. Perhaps someone else might have thought they were going mad, with all this happening.

Alistair Reed had long ago realised going "mad" was a matter of perspective. From where he stood, everyone else looked like the mad ones.

When he'd chosen to fight for chaos, he'd been forced to make another choice. A choice between two classes—that of a Warrior and that of a Mage.

Alistair had never been much for playing video games. His

mother had thought that was a good thing. Always droning on about how violent they were. Alistair had simply never found them to be as violent as his dreams. As violent as his fantasies.

They'd never lived up to his imagination.

This, however, might be different. Very different. As he was someone who liked to use his hands—he touched the hunting knife strapped to his belt, beneath his oversized coat—he couldn't pass up choosing warrior.

The System then sent him into the middle of a city he didn't recognise, where something called a "tutorial" was going on. He was given a quest. One he quite liked the sound of.

Quest Log Activated
Current Quest: Destabilise the tutorial.
Progress: Incomplete
Reward:

1. **Unknown item.**
2. **Bonus Mastery Points.**

Alistair grinned. He'd been given three weapons when he arrived back in the world: a sword, a dagger, and a bow. His coat was gone, replaced with thin leather armour, cheaply made.

He tucked a strand of shoulder-length blond hair behind an ear, then strode into the middle of a mess of people.

The quest wasn't specific. There was no time limit. But that made it seem all the more fun—he had the freedom to do... whatever he wished.

What looked like a hologram flickered into life in the middle of a large city square. The hologram was of a wizened-looking, bearded man in shining golden armour. He had a hand resting on the pommel of his sword and a serious look about him.

And he stood fifty feet tall.

The hologram spoke. "Citizens of Planet Earth, I am here on behalf of the System to welcome you to the Greater Universe."

Alistair slipped into the crowd. One among hundreds of confused-looking people wearing an odd assortment of robes—grey and white—medieval-looking trousers, tunics, and dresses, and leather armour identical to his own.

Something told him this "Greater Universe"—this new reality the world had fallen into—was going to be fun.

Melissa Donovan sat alone in her one-bedroom, studio apartment, eating cold baked beans straight from the can. She could hear her neighbour screaming at her kids through the thin walls. But that was nothing new. *Mother of the year, that one.*

Reminded her far too much of her own mother. Her own mother being the reason she was here.

Her place was a dump. The only damned thing she could afford. But it was *her* dump, and she was proud of it. She worked evenings and weekends just to afford the place, trying to get through her last year of high school. She was at that age of life where she was legally old enough not to be forced to live at home, but also nowhere near being able to properly support herself.

That will change. She had a scholarship to the local university. A full ride. Accommodation. Food. Tuition.

She'd worked herself to the bone to get the opportunities she had. All she needed to do was get through the next six months.

And I don't need anyone's damned help.

When she was finished with her poor excuse for breakfast, she rinsed out the can and threw it in the recycling.

It froze in mid-air. *Every*thing froze.

What the...?

Text appeared across her vision. Something about interlopers and being integrated into the Greater Universe. *Am I dreaming?* She was yanked from her room. Judged by emotionless text. It deemed her physical skills to be middling, her intellectual skills high, and her spirit skills middling.

She had no idea what any of it meant.

Then, she was given a choice. Three moral factions. Though she didn't understand what was going on, not making a choice didn't seem to be an option, so she chose the only one that made sense. *It's what I've been doing for my entire life.* Maybe this was some sort of dream. She didn't know.

But she would always choose to fight for herself. She was given stats, then made to choose a class.

Choose your preferred basic fighting class:
Warrior
Ranger
Mage
One cannot walk backward on the path.

This was all beginning to feel very strange. *Like some sort of video game.* She'd never had the time for those. There simply wasn't room in her life for leisure activities.

Not knowing any better, she chose Ranger.

The moment after she'd chosen her class, she was pulled from the weird room of nothingness and taken to a forest. Her clothes had been changed—she now wore sleek leather armour, a green cloak adorning her shoulders. In her right hand was a bow, at one hip a quiver, at the other a dagger.

Quest Log Activated
Current Quest: Survive in the wilderness.
Progress: Incomplete
Reward:

1. **Unknown item.**
2. **Bonus Mastery Points.**

Melissa frowned. She still had no idea what was going on. Perhaps she should have been afraid. All alone in the middle of a forest. She had never used a bow before. Never hunted. Never needed to gather food in the wilderness in all her life.

But why should she be afraid, when she had the only person she would ever need with her?

Me.

There was a *crack* nearby, like the snapping of a stick. Clumsily, she pulled an arrow from her quiver and fumbled, trying to get the nock on the string. Something bounded along the forest floor. Heading toward her. She whirled. Spotted it through the trees.

She frowned. *What is that?*

{Rabbit – Level 3}

It looked nothing like any rabbit she'd ever seen. Its teeth were sharpened to a point, and it was the size of her mother's annoying beagle.

And it looked like it was out for blood.

Whatever happened to the world, it changed everything. Even the animals.

Melissa drew back the string of her bow and took aim.

And loosed.

She didn't understand this new reality, but she *would* survive it.

Chapter 9
Who Knew Fighting Monsters Would Involve So Much Math

Xavier slammed his staff into the head of the first goblin in the cafeteria.

A massive *crack* sounded as the green beast's skull caved in. Blood and brain matter sprayed into the face, but he'd learnt to keep his mouth shut when fighting in close quarters.

The little beast died in a single strike. Xavier dismissed the notification out of habit.

The other three goblins noticed him, then. He'd snuck into the cafeteria when his stomach had started rumbling, only to find a pack of goblins hovering around the little soft-serve ice cream machine. One of them had been shoving what looked to be chocolate-flavoured ice cream into its mouth, its eyes wide with wonder.

As none of the goblins had a ranged attack, now Xavier had gained their aggression, he turned and ran, waiting for Spiritual Guidance to reach the end of its cooldown. Since he'd reached Level 3, he'd put two of his free points into Toughness, two into Speed, and one into Spirit.

Though he knew he should add points to Intelligence, as he was sure that helped his magical strength in some way, he figured Toughness and Speed were more likely to keep him alive when facing goblins. He was more of a reader than a gamer, but he'd played his fair share. He knew about the concept of min-maxing, but doing so when his life was on the line probably wasn't the smartest choice.

Besides, each level he gained brought more Intelligence, Willpower, and Spirit as it was.

Spiritual Guidance lasted longer now he had a total of 15 points in Spirit, but fortunately the cooldown timer started the moment he cast the spell, not when its effects wore off. The silver sheen was on him for at least three seconds before it disappeared, giving him a boost of speed after he'd killed that first goblin.

He was getting used to the sensation of it falling away, so when the silver sheen disappeared and the exhaustion hit him, the boost to his strength—both mental and physical—gone, he was more than ready for it.

The second the cooldown ended, he whirled around and cast the spell once more, this time for defence.

He didn't flinch when his enemy's sword came down.

When it came time to run again, he did it with a grin. His plan was working perfectly. And this would be the last time he would need to do it.

Spiritual Guidance didn't only last longer, its cooldown had also been reduced. What had taken ten seconds before now only took nine. Though it didn't seem like much, one second could be the difference between life and death.

Finally, when the cooldown timer on the spell reached its end again, Xavier whirled around, staff gripped tightly in both hands. He'd led the three goblins out of the cafeteria into a hall he'd already ensured was clear. They were bunched up in a line, close enough together for what he planned to do.

He cast Heavy Telekinesis—the spell already having gained Rank 2. After gaining the second rank on the spell, he'd quickly realised it now required 200 Spirit Energy to cast. The cooldown had also been reduced significantly, making the spell even more effective. It had been taken all the way down to 20 seconds. Though some of that reduction could have been from his gain of

Spirit or Intelligence when he'd levelled up—he hadn't realised how much the cooldown had reduced until after he'd gained those stats.

The spell flung the goblins backward so hard that it made their heads whip violently. He aimed the spell to the side, straight at the wall instead of down the hall. A symphony of cracking bones sounded as they slammed into the bricks.

You have defeated a Level 2 Lesser Goblin!
You have gained 200 Mastery Points.
You have gained 200 Spirit Energy.

The kill notification repeated another two times. Xavier dismissed all three, his grin widening as another notification popped into his vision. This was the one he'd been waiting for.

Spiritual Guidance has taken a step forward on the path, upgrading to the spell: Spiritual Trifecta.
Spiritual Trifecta is a Rank 2 spell.
As you only possess a single Rank 1 spell, you may not choose which spell to forget.
Cast Element – Rank 1 has been forgotten.
One cannot walk backward on the path.

Xavier quickly read the notification, nodding as he did so. Now that he'd brought both Telekinesis and Spiritual Guidance to their second ranks, he'd forgotten Summon and Cast Element. Out of the four spells he'd gained when choosing the basic Mage class, only two remained.

When he'd ranked up Telekinesis to Heavy Telekinesis, he'd been given the choice of what spell to forget. Now, it simply forgot his other spell automatically.

He considered the consequences of that. *I'll need to keep an eye on all my spells and their upgrades in the future, to make sure I don't forget a spell accidentally.* Fortunately, now that the spells were Rank 2, the information he gleaned from the System implied he wouldn't need to forget any other spells to get them to Rank 3.

I wonder what would happen if I learnt another Rank 1 spell, and it was the only one I needed to upgrade? Would I not need to forget anything? He hoped he would get a chance to experiment in the future.

Xavier knelt by the closest goblin, slumped down from the wall, and cut its purse off its belt. He didn't bother collecting its weapons or its clothes. He knew that in a video game, he would be looting everything he could from the enemies' corpses, but he didn't have enough space to store it all.

He wasn't going to leave the purses, though. That would just be foolish.

He did the same for the other four goblins he'd slain, placing the purses in his bag. The satchel dug into his shoulders from the weight.

When he'd finished, he checked the Quest Log.

Quest Log
Current Quest: Protect a human settlement
from invaders taking root on your world.
Defeat all of the enemy invaders.
Progress: 32/50
Rewards:

1. **You will be sent to a pocket world.**
2. **Unknown Item**

Only eighteen goblins left.

Xavier was getting the hang of this. He'd have thought the hardest thing would've been killing the goblins, but so far, the hardest thing had been keeping his Spirit Energy in check. That's why he'd needed to herd those three goblins into the hallway. Casting Spiritual Guidance three times during a fight took 300

Spirit Energy, while using Heavy Telekinesis used 200. If he'd had to use Heavy Telekinesis twice more, he would have used more Spirit Energy than he gained.

Who knew fighting monsters would involve so much math. He shook his head, chuckling to himself. Not for the first time, he thought there must be a better way to gain Spirit Energy than simply killing enemies.

He took a quick look at his stats.

XAVIER COLLINS
Level: 3
Strength: 5
Speed: 7
Toughness: 8
Intelligence: 10
Willpower: 10
Spirit: 15
Mastery Points for this level: 2,500/6,000
Available Spirit Energy: 1,000/1,800
Free stat points remaining: 0

Xavier was glad to see he had 1,000 Spirit Energy. It was the most he'd managed to gather so far. He always worried what he would do if he ran out. He hadn't added any points to his Strength, so he could only hit harder when he had Spiritual Guidance—now Trifecta—active.

As his stats rose, he'd started to notice some differences. It hadn't been obvious when he'd added points to Toughness—not until he'd been struck by an enemy.

He'd still been injured, but he *knew* it would have been worse had he not added any to the attribute at all. The slash had caused another leg wound. Fortunately, the wound hadn't lasted long as he'd gotten it shortly before reaching Level 3, and his health got regenerated again.

When he'd upped his Speed, he'd noticed it the first time he'd ran. He wasn't just faster, running was *easier*. It took less breath, less energy. He could only imagine what it would be like as his stats grew even higher.

When it came to Intelligence and Willpower, he still struggled to discern what difference they made. But, then again, Xavier hadn't always been the best when it came to numbers. Now, it was coming much, much easier to him. He barely had to think about the calculations for Spirit Energy and Mastery Points.

He was also able to think faster on his feet and take in information faster.

Once he'd reached Level 3 and started to notice things had been changing, he hid himself in a classroom and took out his phone. Though it didn't get any reception anymore, it still had more than 60 percent charge. He'd brought up an ebook on his Kindle app and timed himself reading through the pages.

Since gaining 3 more points in Intelligence, he was able to read *at least* 50 percent faster than he had before.

I wonder what else is happening to me.

He hadn't noticed Willpower's effects. But, then again, killing his enemies, finding the courage to move through the university's campus... it had become easier and easier. He wasn't sure if that had anything to do with his Willpower attribute, or if he was simply getting used to this new reality.

The only difference he'd noticed with Spirit was how it affected his use of the Spiritual Guidance spell. It didn't only make it last longer, it made it *stronger*. He was quite sure Spirit had also made his Heavy Telekinesis spell stronger as well.

He dismissed his stats and brought up the description of his newly upgraded spell.

Spiritual Trifecta – Rank 2
Spiritual Trifecta combines all three paths of Spiritual Guidance. When cast, it improves one's physical and mental strength, physical and mental defence, and magical strength.

This power comes at a cost, however. Spiritual Trifecta costs twice as much as the average Rank 2 spell to cast. One cannot walk backward on the path.

Reading the spell's description gave Xavier mixed feelings. On the one hand, he was thrilled that casting the spell would give him *all three* qualities at the same time. He hadn't been sure that's what the spell would let him do.

On the other hand, he was pretty sure the Spirit Energy cost would now be 400 instead of the 100 it had been at Rank 1.

I really need to find a way to regain Spirit Energy without killing.

Xavier sighed. He dismissed the description, adjusted the heavy shoulder strap, then walked down the hallway into the cafeteria.

He hadn't just come here to kill a few goblins. He'd come here for *food*.

Chapter 10
A Really Great Excuse to Eat a Lot of Food

XAVIER'S STOMACH GRUMBLED AS HE TOOK A PLATE AND PILED food onto it. He tried not to look at the corpse of the goblin he'd killed, dead by the soft-serve ice cream machine.

He couldn't remember the last time he'd felt this hungry, and he didn't think it was because he'd skipped lunch. Another thing he'd noticed when putting points into his Speed attribute was that he'd... well, lost weight. The bit of pudge he'd carried around his waist for the last few years had disappeared.

He'd pulled up his tattered, bloody robes and been surprised to find his abs visible. They weren't chiselled. He wasn't super-ripped. But it was a definite improvement.

Though the fact he hadn't added any points into Strength showed, as he looked fairly skinny.

When he'd piled enough food onto his plate, he took a seat in the corner of the cafeteria. The plate had mashed potatoes, scrambled eggs, and strips of bacon all atop one another in a mess. Where he sat, he could see every exit to the place.

Perhaps he should have gone somewhere safer to eat, but this way he wouldn't have to go far to get seconds. And he would *definitely* be getting seconds.

He grabbed his fork and shovelled the mashed potatoes into his mouth first. He was probably eating too quickly, but he didn't care. His eyes darted from one exit to another, ears perked. Though other things had improved, one thing that *hadn't* was his senses. *Shouldn't there be some kind of Perception attribute?*

When the plate was clean, he went back for more. God, it felt good to *eat*. After three plates—far more than he usually consumed in one sitting—he felt full. He placed the fork on his plate and leant back in the chair, sighing in relief.

Had his metabolism improved dramatically with only 2 more points into Speed? Had his other stat points affected it? *The brain burns a lot of calories, and my Intelligence is now three points higher than it was...*

He frowned. He felt fuller not just in his stomach, but... in a different way. A way he couldn't quite define.

A hunch made him check his Spirit Energy.

Available Spirit Energy: 1,300/1,800

Xavier's eyes widened. He shook his head. Let out a chuckle. His Spirit Energy had only been at 1,000 before he'd eaten all of that food. Now, it had gone up by 300!

Eating increases Spirit Energy.

He facepalmed, feeling foolish. Now he knew, it seemed obvious. Food *was* energy. Though he'd imagined he would need to do something else to gain Spirit Energy other than simply eat.

I guess I was wrong.

That made him wonder if eating would increase his health as well. Right now, it was completely full, so he wasn't able to check. He looked down at the short sword at his hip, then rolled up his left sleeve.

Worth a try...

Despite being full, Xavier grabbed another plate of food then returned to his seat. He drew the short sword from his robe's belt and cut a small line across the top of his forearm—he wasn't foolish enough to cut a line in his palm. If he couldn't heal easily, it would only give him trouble holding his staff. And what if he sliced an important tendon? That always bothered him when characters did that in books and on TV.

He stared at the small wound for a moment, then brought up his health.

Your health is at 99%.

His health would regenerate naturally if he let it. The wound would heal faster than before the System, and not only because he'd added three points to his Toughness.

But it would take roughly ten minutes for him to gain 1 percent of health. *Though it might be faster, now I have more Toughness. Do I also have more health?* As it wasn't shown in points, he didn't know.

He ate the food quickly, shoving mashed potatoes into his mouth and chewing as fast as he could. Then he checked his Spirit Energy and health again.

Available Spirit Energy: 1,350/1,800
Your health is at 100%.

Xavier grinned. He was learning. Learning fast. He noticed his Spirit Energy had only gone up by 50 points that time. Was that because the food went to his health as well as his Spirit Energy? Or did eating more bring diminishing returns?

Part of him wanted to gorge himself until his Spirit Energy reached its current limit of 1,800, but now he felt uncomfortably full to the point where he had to loosen his belt, so that didn't seem wise when he was about to fight more goblins.

Still, he'd gained almost enough Spirit Energy for his most powerful spell. *And I found a really great excuse to eat a lot of food.*

He chuckled and stood, reminding himself that he still had a job to do. *Eighteen more goblins to kill, then I can get out of this place.*

He was eager—*very* eager—to see what this pocket world would be like.

Xavier strode out of the cafeteria, past the dead goblin, and out into the courtyard. When he thought about how many goblins he still needed to kill, he noticed it was just the right number for him to reach Level 4.

Is that somehow by System design? He supposed he might never know.

The second he made it outside into the late afternoon light, he ducked behind an archway near the cafeteria's exit. He poked his head out. He thought it would take him a while to find the last eighteen goblins...

But they were all out here. Clustered near the open portal. When he'd looked through his classroom's window after being returned here, the portal had still been active, but the courtyard had been empty of goblins.

He counted them, just to be sure. *Yep. That's all of them.* He bit his lip. How in the world could he kill them while they were together? He'd never fought this many at once before.

Maybe I can lure a few of them away somehow...

A notification appeared.

Quest Log Update
Kill the remaining enemies within 10 minutes to gain a bonus reward.

Xavier's forehead creased. It almost seemed like the System had heard what he'd been thinking, and this was its response.

He sighed. He didn't know how to lure the goblins away. Perhaps taking them on all at once was his only option. He scanned them, glad to find none above Level 2. Xavier had assumed he'd start to find stronger goblins but wasn't about to question his good luck.

All right. I have the element of surprise. All I need to do is use
it. The enemies are all clustered together. He could use that to his
advantage. His Heavy Telekinesis might be able to hit them all at
once. He *had* killed those three goblins all at the same time, after
all... though he doubted the spell would be strong enough for
that.

I can run faster than them, he reassured himself. He didn't
much care if running away looked cowardly. It was practical.
Gaining an enemy's aggression—or "aggroing"—and then kiting
them was a staple of video games he was happy to steal and use,
and he had a lot of space in the courtyard for such a strategy.
Though he supposed it would be harder to cluster his enemies
together out here than when running through hallways.

He poked his head out again. So far, the goblins hadn't noticed
him. He looked at their weapons, then smiled. *Still no bows. Still
no staves.* Not a single one of the goblins was an archer, and none
appeared to be mages. In fact, he hadn't seen *any* goblin use a
spell yet.

So far, it felt as though the System had given him an easy challenge. Then he remembered that Navy SEAL. Julian Myers. *That*
hadn't been easy. That had been luck.

Eighteen enemies. If he wasn't careful, if he didn't play this
right, his luck would run out. *And there's no margin for error. Not
with this many enemies.* If he got a leg wound that slowed him
down, it would mean the end of the fight—and the end of his life.

Xavier leant back against the archway. He gripped his staff
tightly. *I only have ten minutes. No time to second guess myself.*
None of the goblins were facing his direction. They were all
looking toward the portal. Almost as if they were waiting for
someone to arrive. *Or something.* Though there was nothing in his
quest log about more enemies appearing, who knew if he could
trust that? It's not like the System wasn't happy to throw him into
life-threatening situations. *Or kill someone with a lightning bolt for
refusing to fight.*

He didn't think that would happen now, though he couldn't

help but wonder what *might* happen if he tried to leave the university campus instead of protecting it.

He took a breath, let it out, and steeled himself. Then he stepped out of the archway.

I hope these little beasts are still cowards.

Chapter 11

Who Knew Choosing a Mage Class Would Have Me Bashing In so Many Skulls

XAVIER SPRINTED INTO HIS UNIVERSITY'S COURTYARD, straight at eighteen goblins, all of whom wanted him dead. They were too far away to be in range of Heavy Telekinesis. He couldn't simply stand behind cover and attack them from afar. Besides, knowing how cowardly these little beasts were, they'd likely run if he started picking them off. Then he'd be sent on a merry chase through the university, tracking them down.

He had to get in closer, especially if he wanted to take advantage of his melee abilities with Spiritual Trifecta.

The sun slowly dropped below the horizon. The sky was no longer the blood red it had been that morning. The lamps in the courtyard all came on, but it was the portal behind the goblins that was giving off the most light.

He ran as fast as his legs could carry him, which was far faster than it had been that morning. He didn't cast Spiritual Trifecta. Not right away. He hadn't used the spell before, but he had to assume it only lasted for three seconds and that the cooldown on the spell remained at nine seconds.

Xavier wasn't made for stealth. He had the element of surprise, but he wouldn't be able to sneak up on these things. They would have spotted him if he'd tried, so his best bet was hitting them as hard and fast as possible, then getting the hell out of there until he could use his spells again.

One of the goblins turned at the sound of his swift strides. It released a startled yell, which notified its kin of his imminent arrival.

The goblins scattered backward a bit, no longer neatly clustered as they had been before. But a second later they rallied, all eighteen running to intercept him.

Good. He'd rather them not run away—rather not have to hunt them down. That didn't stop a shudder of fear from running up his spine. He swallowed as he was only a few feet away. *Bravery isn't the absence of fear, it's acting* despite *fear.*

When he was one step away, Xavier cast Spiritual Trifecta for the first time. He felt the energy drain from him, then infuse his body and mind. Maybe even his soul, assuming those existed.

He felt stronger and faster than ever. His mind moved more swiftly. And his magic. It was crackling. Ready. *Eager* to burst forth.

All three qualities of the Spiritual Trifecta spell enveloped him, powering him beyond his imagination.

Xavier didn't hesitate. He cast Heavy Telekinesis. The eighteen goblins had spread out around him, so he wasn't able to hit them all at once even if the spell *was* capable of that. But he still managed to throw four of them straight up into the air. He didn't know how far they flew—it wasn't as though he could stop and watch.

As they flew up off the ground, Xavier swung his staff into the head of the nearest goblin and watched it practically explode in green blood. The goblins were surrounding him now, striking him with their swords, but they weren't causing him any damage. They *couldn't* cause him any damage.

Not while Spiritual Trifecta was active.

He managed to slam his staff into another goblin's head, then he high-tailed it out of there.

As he ran, he heard the goblins he'd thrown into the air slam into the ground. The kill notification for the two goblins he'd struck with his staff, along with four more he'd used Heavy Telekinesis on, popped up. He rapidly dismissed the notification, glad that throwing those four goblins had been enough to take them down.

There was also a seventh notification, but he didn't have the time to read it. It said something about reaching his Spirit Energy limit.

I just killed six goblins in three seconds. He couldn't help but be surprised by how well that had turned out. Though the second he started running away, the silver sheen of Spiritual Trifecta dissipated, and with it, all of the power it had infused within him.

He was ready for the exhaustion. He'd been through this before. Many times, now. He knew how to push through it. Knew how to run while feeling like this.

What he hadn't anticipated, however, was that using all three of the spell's qualities at once exhausted him *three times as much* as when he'd only been able to use one.

That certainly hadn't been in the spell description.

He gritted his teeth and pushed on. His body felt heavy. Weary. Weak. But he knew that exhaustion was just an illusion of the spell.

With a nine-second cooldown, and it lasting three seconds, I just need to run for six more seconds before I can use it again.

Now that the spell gave him physical strength *and* defence, he wouldn't need to wait for Heavy Telekinesis to be ready again. He could just pummel a few more of the little green beasts with the head of his staff.

Who knew choosing a mage class would have me bashing in so many skulls...

Xavier had been counting down in his head, waiting for Spiritual Trifecta to reach the end of its cooldown. When it didn't, he attempted to cast it, a little confused.

Spiritual Trifecta has a cooldown of 24

seconds. It cannot be used for another 14 seconds.

Xavier's eyes widened in shock as he read the notification. The cooldown for Spiritual Trifecta had changed! It took more than twice as long as Spiritual Guidance had! Was that because it was a generalised spell and did three times as much as the Rank 1 spell had?

No time to think about why.

He set his jaw. It was fifteen seconds longer than he'd expected, which meant this whole fight would play out differently than he'd thought. He threw a glance over his shoulder. His legs being longer than the goblins', he'd actually made some space between them in his little sprint.

Now he knew he was faster than them, he slowed his sprint to a run and waited. *Don't panic. Just adjust. This can still work.*

He let them close the distance behind him as the spell crawled toward the end of its cooldown. When it was ready, he whirled around then twirled his staff around him in an extravagant move and slammed it into one of the goblin's skulls, casting Spiritual Trifecta mid-swing to give him the most time with the spell active.

He cast Heavy Telekinesis—the spell now having a shorter cooldown than Spiritual Trifecta—but the goblins weren't as clumped together as before, and he only managed to throw two of them. He whirled back around, ready to run.

Only he couldn't. The little green beasts—the little green *bastards*—had surrounded him, closing off his path of escape. They must have seen through his plan and come up with one of their own.

Xavier panicked. It wasn't the first time he'd been surrounded by goblins, but these ones weren't hesitating like the first lot he'd killed back in the lecture theatre had, and there were still nine of them left.

More than enough to do him in.

Xavier slammed his staff into another of the goblin's heads, but the silver sheen about him fell away before he'd hit. The exhaustion slammed into him once more. It felt worse than before. The goblin was still struck, but the strike hadn't killed it. It stumbled back two steps before regaining its footing, a wicked gash in its forehead.

He swung his staff around him wildly, just like he had back in the lecture theatre. He'd already killed half of the group—surely they would be afraid of him *now*.

But if they were afraid, they didn't look it. And they certainly didn't *act* like it. One of the goblins leapt up and grabbed his staff, weighing it down. Though the little beast was small, it must have weighed at least sixty pounds.

Sixty pounds at the end of a staff, and he hadn't put a single point into his middling Strength attribute.

Another goblin pounced on his staff, and before he knew it the damned thing was already out of his grasp, pulled straight out of his hand. He hadn't been strong enough to keep a hold of it. *Not good.*

Xavier didn't hesitate. No matter how tired he was—no matter how afraid he was—he wouldn't let these goblins win.

Them or me.

He pulled the short sword he still kept at his belt and slashed straight at a goblin leaping up at him. Took the goblin in the eye. It yelled but still tumbled on top of him, taking him to the ground.

No, no, no, no. The ground was the last place he wanted to be! None of this was going to plan! *Maybe I would have been better off picking Cast Element, flinging spells at them from a rooftop.* He cursed not having tested Spiritual Trifecta—he hadn't wanted to waste Spirit Energy.

But it was too late for doubts.

One couldn't walk backward on the path.

Xavier tried to throw the little beast off him with his left arm even as sharp teeth bit into him. *The little bastard is biting me!*

Then something stabbed into his legs. Then another. Blood was pouring out of him.

He tried to cast Heavy Telekinesis.

Heavy Telekinesis has a cooldown of 20 seconds. It cannot be used for another 10 seconds.

Ten seconds. Can I survive for ten seconds? He bloody well *hoped* he could.

He jammed his short sword into the goblin on top of him. Felt the blade slide into its flesh and further soak his robes in warm, green blood. Saw the kill notification come up. The goblin went slack on top of him.

Finally, he pushed the goblin off. Its teeth were still clamped onto his forearm, and doing so ripped a chunk from his flesh. When he shoved the goblin off, it revealed the remaining goblins standing over him, thrusting down with their swords.

Xavier didn't know how many times they'd stabbed him in the legs, and now he'd pushed the goblin off him, he'd exposed his torso and face to their strikes. He thought he'd felt pain before. Back in the lecture theatre. The first time he'd been injured by these invading monsters. But this... this was so much worse.

I'm probably only still alive because I put 3 points into Toughness. But I won't be able to last much longer.

He was lying on his back, feeling more defenceless than he ever had.

I'm going to die here, aren't I?

Every decision he'd made that day flashed through his mind. He should have chosen warrior. Maybe that class would have given him armour. He should have put points into Strength, then he wouldn't have let go of his staff. He should have never chosen Spiritual Trifecta in the first place. Or maybe he should have kept running away from these goblins until he'd led them into a narrow hallway, where he could have hit more of them at once with Heavy Telekinesis.

He saw a dozen ways this could have gone differently. A dozen ways this would have ended up with him surviving, instead of lying on the cement riddled with holes and gashes by short swords and vicious little axes. Not to mention a damned bite in his arm.

At least he'd gotten to go on an adventure, though he wished it would have lasted far, far longer.

Xavier gritted his teeth and waited for the strikes to fall.

Chapter 12
I Can't Fight for This World If I'm Dead

Xavier lay on his back in the university courtyard, ready to greet his death, eight goblins striking down at him with swords and axes, blood gushing from who knew how many wounds in his legs, his satchel—filled with purses, his laptop, and phone—digging into his back beneath him.

When one of the swords was an inch from his face, he felt a surge of adrenaline. Or maybe some hidden reserve of self-preservation. He *pulled* the corpse of the goblin he'd just killed back on top of him so it could soak up the fatal blow.

Thunk.

The sword dug into the goblin corpse's skull instead of his own. *Still alive.*

The attacks stopped briefly as the goblins yanked the corpse off him. They gave him evil grins, cocking their swords and axes in overhead strikes.

Heavy Telekinesis reached the end of its cooldown. The feel of it being ready took him by surprise. He felt it *click* in his mind. In the same instant, he thrust his hands into the air—he didn't have his staff, though the short sword was still clutched in his right fist.

He didn't know if not having the staff would make his spell less powerful. He supposed it didn't matter.

The spell was cast. He pushed it all around him. In his mind, he could feel how the spell worked. Could feel it stretching to push every one of the enemies away in a wave emanating outward, instead of in one direction. Could feel how that diluted the spell and made it less powerful.

But it didn't need to kill any of the goblins—as much as he would have liked the spell to kill *all* of them—it just needed to get them the hell out of the way.

He saw the goblins thrown off their feet. They didn't fly forty strides away. More like twenty. But it was enough. *Not having my staff, and diluting the spell, plus not having Spiritual Trifecta active, made it much weaker.*

Xavier wanted to stand, but his legs were in so much pain. He looked down and found them covered in gashes and soaked in blood. Far more blood than before. He felt weaker than ever.

Your health is at 15%.

Honestly, he was surprised his health wasn't even lower. He forced himself to sit up and spotted his staff a few feet away. The goblins were already making their way back to their feet. Eight still living, though a few of them looked beaten up from being thrown. Their movements looked sluggish and painful.

Not as painful as mine.

He crawled toward his staff, his wounds scraping against the cement, gasping in pain until he was close enough to reach out and grab it. He wrapped his fingers around the staff and checked the cooldown for Spiritual Trifecta.

Spiritual Trifecta has a cooldown of 24 seconds. It cannot be used for another 4 seconds.

Maybe I can get out of this.

Xavier wished he had some sort of health potion, or was closer to his next level-up. He wanted to wait until Spiritual Trifecta was ready. Wanted to use it to help him get back to his feet—assuming he could stand in this condition. But that wasn't an option.

Even if he *could* use the spell, it would be a waste. The spell would likely run out before the goblins got to him. He'd fall straight to the ground from pain and exhaustion and be in the same damned position as before he'd cast Heavy Telekinesis.

Xavier let go of the short sword and gripped the staff in both hands. He moved it until he had the butt of the staff on the concrete, then pushed with all his might, all the way up to his knees, letting out a yell as his legs scraped along the ground again.

I can do this. I have to do this. He heard the goblins. Their little feet reminded him of the pitter-patter of children running. But it wasn't children running toward him.

It was monsters from another world. Monsters that wanted him dead.

I chose Champion because I wanted to defend Earth. I wanted to fight.

He pulled himself up the staff, one hand over the other, using every ounce of willpower he had. Every ounce of energy.

I can't fight for this world if I'm dead!

His legs shook. Blood poured from a half-dozen or more wounds. But somehow, his legs held. Somehow, he was on his feet.

I can do this!

He couldn't run. Probably couldn't even walk. Soon, he wouldn't be able to rest his weight on his staff, not when his enemies reached him.

He would have to trust Spiritual Trifecta would strengthen his legs enough.

Just the effort of standing threatened to drain him of every-thing he had. He leant heavily on his staff. He was only standing through sheer force of will. That wouldn't last long.

Heavy Telekinesis has a cooldown of 20

seconds. It cannot be used for another 11 seconds.

Xavier gritted his teeth, struggling to believe such a short time had passed since he'd cast Heavy Telekinesis. It felt like an eternity.

Then, finally, Spiritual Trifecta reached the end of his cooldown. He wanted to cast it. It would bring him the strength he needed to keep standing. Maybe even take away some of this pain.

But he waited. Until the last possible moment, like he had the last time. Then he cast Spiritual Trifecta. A silver light enveloped his body. Infused his muscles. Infused his mind. Energy poured into him. His grip around his staff tightened. His legs had been shaking keeping him up, now they felt *strong*. Stable. Immovable. Despite the wounds. Despite the blood still pouring from them.

He yelled. In anger or pain, he wasn't sure. Maybe both. His staff slammed into the skull of a goblin running right at him. The kill notification came instantly.

Another sprinted at him. Went down, blood splattering onto his already soaked robes.

He swung his staff. Clocked two more. For perhaps the third time that fight, he saw a notification telling him he'd reached the limit of his Spirit Energy. He'd killed four of the little bastard beasts when the spell wore off. *That didn't feel like three seconds!*

The weakness was the first thing to hit him. His legs felt like they didn't have any bones. Like they were made of jelly and nothing was holding them up. The pain came next, as though he were being stabbed all over again. He had to flick his gaze down to his legs just to make sure.

The wave of exhaustion was the worst he'd ever felt. Like he hadn't slept in a week. Like he'd been on a forced march for three days straight.

His legs wobbled. Threatened to make him fall. Threatened to take him back to the ground.

Your health is at 11%.

I'm losing blood. Losing health.

He couldn't fall. If he did, he would get stabbed. And die. There were still four goblins left. Four goblins to *kill*. He might regenerate health naturally, but even if the goblins—by some miracle—decided to run away, he doubted he would be able to bind his wounds in time.

Which meant they would keep bleeding, and he would keep losing health. And die.

He needed to kill these last four goblins. Not only to complete the quest, but to get to the next level and regenerate his health.

For the first time during the fight, Xavier saw fear in the goblins' eyes. The trepidation in their posture. He'd killed ten of their friends before he'd hit the concrete, then he'd taken out four more when he shouldn't even be able to stand.

I can't stand. Not for much longer. Now he was no longer swinging it, he leant heavily on his staff to keep his balance, glad his arms hadn't taken any damage.

The goblins stared at him, then glanced back at the portal. *Are they waiting for someone?* The thought had occurred to him earlier. But something else occurred to him now. *What if they want to run?* Xavier didn't know if that would mean he would complete this quest. Technically, he would have protected the settlement...

It doesn't matter if them escaping lets me complete this quest if it ends in my death.

These little beasts were cowards, and now they'd seen what he was capable of, and their superior numbers continued to dwindle, that cowardice was coming to the fore.

I need to appear weak. He laughed out loud at the thought. Even his laugh startled the goblins. One of them looked like they were about to make a run for it. He coughed as he laughed, almost expecting blood to stream from his mouth, and was glad when it didn't. *Okay, I need to appear even weaker.*

Right now, his enemies' hesitation was a good thing. He

needed to stall them long enough for Heavy Telekinesis to reach the end of its cooldown again. He would just have to hope it would be enough to kill them without Spiritual Trifecta active.

Appear weak... appear weak...

He wondered if these little green bastards would understand him. "Please, leave me alone!" He motioned toward the portal, as though encouraging them to leave. "Just... just go home!" It was a gamble, but he was pretty sure he could tell two things from their hesitation.

One, they were afraid of attacking him—which, of course, was the most obvious. And two, they were afraid of returning home defeated. Xavier could imagine some sort of goblin lord awaiting them on their home world. He didn't think their boss would be impressed that they let a single human kill so many of them then scare off those left standing.

He tried to think about this as though it were a story he was writing. *How would I make the character look as vulnerable as possible?* He *wanted* them to come to him. He just didn't want them to come too *quickly*.

One of his legs trembled, the muscles spasming in pain.

He checked on Heavy Telekinesis.

Heavy Telekinesis has a cooldown of 20 seconds. It cannot be used for another 4 seconds.

How can it still not be ready? I need them to attack me. Which meant he needed to fall. *At least that won't be hard.* Xavier took a sharp breath in, tightened his grip on his staff so he wouldn't lose it, then let his legs buckle.

He fell to the left. Saw the pavement come up to greet him. With his hands gripping the staff, he couldn't slow his fall or halt it in any way. His shoulder slammed into the ground, made his head snap to the side. The pain in his legs doubled.

Xavier was jolted, disorientated—he hadn't anticipated how

much this would throw him off. For a moment, he couldn't focus. Didn't know what was happening at all.

Heavy Telekinesis has a cooldown of 20 seconds. It cannot be used for another 2 seconds.

Almost there. He blinked. Tried to get a read on what was going on. Something tugged at his gut. He felt... cold, as though it were the middle of winter and he'd walked outside only wearing shorts and a T-shirt. Something was draining from him.

Your health is at 6%.

The fall... it hurt me more than I thought!
He heard the pitter-patter of little feet running. Sprinting. *Away or toward me? Toward me!* Just like he'd planned. He gritted his teeth. Heavy Telekinesis hadn't snapped out of its cooldown yet, but it would be there in less than a second.

He gazed up and saw all four remaining goblins sprinting straight for him.

Your health is at 5%.

As they got close, he waited. Then grinned. The spell was ready! Xavier cast Heavy Telekinesis. He didn't know if it would work. Didn't know if it would be enough to kill them. All he could do was hope it wasn't his last action on this world.

But if he *was* going to die, he would take as many of these little green bastards with him as he could.

The last thing he saw before he lost consciousness was four goblins being thrown off their feet and high into the air.

Chapter 13
If This Were a Video Game... I Would Definitely Be Overpowered

Xavier's eyes snapped wide open, and his vision was assailed by a stream of notifications.

The first four were kill notifications.

The goblins. I killed them. I won!

He dismissed those and read on.

Congratulations, you have reached Level 4!
Your health has been regenerated by 50%!
Your Spirit Energy limit has increased by 100!
You have received +1 Intelligence, +1
Willpower, and +1 Spirit!
You have received +5 free stat points!
All your spells have refreshed and are no longer
on cooldown!

Xavier sat up. The first thing he noticed was that his legs were still very much in pain, though they were no longer bleeding.

Quest Complete!
You have completed the quest: Protect a human

settlement from invaders taking root on your world.
All titles earned during a quest are withheld until the quest is completed. Now that you have completed your quest, you have received your titles.

Title unlocked!
Bloodied Hands: You are not afraid to get your hands dirty. You have become the first fully integrated person on your world to kill within the Greater Universe.
You have received +5 Strength and +5 Willpower!

Title Unlocked!
Born on a Battlefield: You know your way around a fight. You are the first on your world to defeat ten or more enemies in lone combat.
You have received +5 Toughness, +5 Willpower, and +2 Spirit!

Title Unlocked!
Settlement Defender: You are the first on your world to defend a settlement, however small, from enemy invaders.
You have received +5 Toughness and +5 Intelligence!

Title Unlocked!
Quester: You are the first person on your world to complete a quest.
You have received +2 to all stats!

Xavier rubbed his eyes. He had gained titles? Four of them?

His eyes widened as he read each one, thinking of all the stats that he'd just gained. His body surged with sudden strength. He felt the subtle shifts in his mind.

All this because I was the first?

And there was more.

Congratulations on completing your quest! Here are your rewards:

1. **In 5 minutes, you will be teleported to a pocket world where you will experience your tutorial as a World Champion.**
2. **You have received the item: Storage Ring!**
3. **For killing the remaining enemies within 10 minutes, you have gained a bonus reward: +1 Skill Point.**

Xavier couldn't hold back his smile. He did it! He defeated all fifty goblins, and—most of all—he didn't die! He moved to leverage himself to his feet with his staff, but... he didn't need to.

He felt stronger than he ever had in his entire life. He looked at his body. Though much of him was covered by the grey robes and all the goblin blood—not to mention more than enough of his *own* blood—he could already see the difference.

His shoulders had become broader. The muscles in his legs, arms, and torso thicker. He let go of his staff with his right hand and touched his left bicep, flexing it. It felt... huge.

Xavier shook his head and stood with ease. The timer was visible within his vision. Forty seconds had already passed, and there were still more notifications to read.

Title Unlocked!
100 Stats: This is a common title that everyone receives when they have reached a total of 100 combined stat points.

You have received +1 to all stats!

Title Unlocked!
First to 100 Stats: You are the first person from your world to reach 100 total combined stat points.
You have received +5 to all stats!

Xavier's eyes widened. Doing some quick math, he realised that just that morning, he'd only had a total of 39 stat points, now he had *over a hundred?*

Not only did I get a common title for achieving 100 stats, I got another one for being the first! On top of that, it was his biggest title yet. He felt another shift in himself. He looked down. His muscles weren't larger, but they *must* be denser, right? He remembered when he'd put points into Speed, he'd gotten slimmer. *Maybe those two stats level each other out. Speed doesn't make me too bulky to move fast.*

If this were a video game... I would definitely be overpowered. He wondered what other things he might gain for being the first in his world to do it, but he also wondered *how* he was the first. He had to imagine there were other people out there who'd chosen Champion who were more suitable than him. *Maybe... maybe they've just taken longer to complete the first quest.*

For a moment, the Bloodied Hands title had confused him. How could he have been the first from his world to kill in the Greater Universe, when other Champions would have been pitted against each other? *He* hadn't killed Julian Myers, after all.

Then he realised it specified first *fully integrated* person. *I wasn't integrated until after that match with the Navy SEAL.*

Either way, he couldn't complain, could he? He was gaining *massive* advantages, advantages that no one else on Earth would ever be able to get. He frowned, that fact making a weight of responsibility fall upon his shoulders.

That Navy SEAL died for me without even meaning to, and

now I've gained titles no one else will be able to get. If I die, it won't just be Julian Myers's sacrifice that goes to waste, all these titles will be lost with me. He clenched a fist around his staff. *I need to keep gaining more advantages. Stay the strongest, so I can defend Earth and earn the right to be one of its Champions.* He looked around at all the dead goblins. *Or have I already gained that right?*

Xavier glanced at the countdown timer again. There were only two minutes left now. He'd spent too long looking at all the titles, checking out his new physique and getting lost in thought. Though he really wanted to check his status, he should get moving.

He frowned, thinking about one of the rewards he'd gained. *A Storage Ring.* He looked at his right hand. It was already on his ring finger. *Storage Ring... Is that like a bag of holding?*

Xavier focused on the ring. As he did, a space was revealed to him within his mind. A dark space with four walls, roughly the size of his bedroom. He tilted his head to the side. "Whoa! That's huge!" His eyes widened, looking at the space. "How do I get things *inside* it?"

That's when he remembered—he had eighteen goblins to loot purses from. He grinned and got to work, plucking a short sword from the ground and cutting one purse after the next, except his satchel was getting too full.

He paused, a goblin's purse in his hands. He looked from it, to the Storage Ring. *Everything else works by thought...* He *willed* the purse into the ring. It disappeared from his hand. When he looked into the Storage Ring's internal space, the purse sat on the black room's floor.

Xavier smiled broadly. He only had a minute and a half left before he would be teleported out, and he used it wisely. He put his satchel into the Storage Ring and looted every purse and weapon from the eighteen Lesser Goblins he'd slain in the courtyard.

Then he activated Spiritual Trifecta and sprinted into the cafeteria, throwing as much food into the space as he could. If it worked like in books he'd read or games he'd played, the Storage

Ring would keep the food fresh. He went to one of the vending machines, smashed the glass with the head of his staff, and touched each of the beverages, focusing first on the water, putting them into the Storage Ring one by one.

Then he realised how foolish he was being.

He touched the vending machine itself, putting the entire thing into the ring. *Much faster.* He moved to the next vending machine—this one held snacks. Bags of chips. Bars of chocolate. Not the healthiest things, but he would need whatever he could get to help restore his Spirit Energy. Not to mention his health.

It was then that he realised he was missing the most important thing of all: coffee.

He had no idea how long he would be trapped in this "pocket world." And he had no idea what kind of beverages they would have.

Xavier couldn't remember the last time he'd gone a day without coffee. He knew it wasn't *actually* the most important thing for him to have—he *could* go without—but if he were to be fighting for Earth against goblins and who-knew-what type of other monsters, he would *definitely* want some coffee.

He went to the café area, where full pots of coffee still sat there hot. Part of him was tempted to take the espresso machine and grinder, but he doubted he would have electricity wherever he was going.

You will be transported to a pocket world in 5...

Better keep moving.

4...

Xavier placed a hand on the coffee pots, rushing from one to the next.

3...

He let out a breath. Before the timer reached the end, he'd put all ten coffee pots into his storage. He stood there, gaping at the cafeteria, empty of vending machines and every food tray in each of the self-serve windows.

Did I really just do that, acting as though it was a life-threatening situation?

2..

Maybe I'm going a little crazy, after all I've been through...

1...

Though, admittedly, who wants to go without coffee?

Commencing transfer of XAVIER COLLINS.

Chapter 14
First Defender of Planet Earth

One moment Xavier Collins was standing in the cafeteria of his university's campus, scrambling to get as much food, drinks, and *coffee* into his Storage Ring as possible after being pulled from his class earlier in the day and forced to "fight" a Navy SEAL, then thrown back to his campus to fight fifty little green goblins from another world.

The next moment, *he* was the one being sent to another world. A pocket world.

Whatever that is.

It wasn't the same as being pulled into that room filled with nothingness where he'd first been judged by the System. It was faster. Instantaneous.

Xavier stood in a small room that looked somewhat medieval. Stone floors. Brick walls. A bed was pushed up to the bricks on one side of the room, with fresh grey robes folded at the head. A solid wooden chest sat at the end of the bed. It had an open padlock and a key sitting atop it. The chest was empty.

On the other side of the room was a small writing desk, with a shelf large enough to fit perhaps five books in it. There was a wooden stool in front of it, but no writing implements to be seen. A lit candle burned atop the writing desk, providing the only light in the entire room.

What... is this place?

He'd imagined many rooms like this. When reading fantasy novels or trying to write his own. *It looks like... like the room of an apprentice?* Was this supposed to be *his* room? He looked at himself and blinked. His robes were still in tatters. Covered in red and green blood. Plus other things he'd rather not list. But while his clothes were ruined and dirty, his body was entirely clean.

Did the teleportation do that? Thinking of all the sci-fi novels and shows he'd consumed, he had an awful thought and wondered if every atom in his body had been split apart and put back together during the transfer. *Am I even me anymore?*

For a few seconds he stared off into space having a full-on existential crisis. Then he shook his head and changed into the fresh set of robes.

A notification popped into his vision.

XAVIER COLLINS, World Defender of Planet Earth, as you are the first of your world to reach the Tower of Champions Pocket World, you have unlocked a unique title.

What? Xavier thought. *Another one!?*

Title Unlocked!
First Defender of Planet Earth: You are the first Potential Champion of your world to reach the Tower of Champions Pocket World. You have received +5 to all stats!

Xavier felt a little shaken as more power coursed through his body. After having changed into the new robes, throwing the old ones into the corner of the room, he plopped himself on the bed and took a deep breath, letting it out slowly.

So much had happened, and only a single day had passed. He was getting all of these advantages that no one else had access to. *The first this, the first that...* He wasn't complaining, he was just... a little overwhelmed.

Before I leave this room, I need to look at my stats. I need to see where I'm at, and apply the five free stat points I got from reaching Level 4. He had no idea what would be outside that door. No idea what the "Tower of Champions" even was.

He brought up his status and personal information for the first time since he'd finished his first quest and gained all of those titles.

XAVIER COLLINS
Age: 20
Race: Human
Grade: F
Moral Faction: World Defender (Planet Earth)
Class: Mage
Level: 4
Strength: 23
Speed: 20
Toughness: 31
Intelligence: 29
Willpower: 34
Spirit: 31
Mastery Points for this level: 100/12,000
Available Spirit Energy: 2,000/3,500
Available Skill Points: 1
Free stat points remaining: 5
Titles: Bloodied Hands, Born on a Battlefield, Settlement Defender, Quester, 100 Stats, First to 100 Stats, First Defender of Planet Earth
Spells List:
Spiritual Trifecta – Rank 2
Heavy Telekinesis – Rank 2

Xavier's heart pumped hard against his chest as he saw how high his stats had become in such a short time. He knew that whatever this was, it was only the beginning. *I'm only Level 4... but with all the titles I've gained...*

He bit his lip and did some math. The answer came quickly. He gained a total of eight stat points every level—three of which were automatically assigned, and five of which he could assign freely. With all the titles, he'd gained 110 *extra* stat points.

That's 13 levels worth of attributes—13.75, to be precise! Which would make his effective level for someone who *hadn't* received all these titles... *Level 17!*

All right. Let's not get ahead of myself. I still don't know what awaits me outside. He looked at his attributes another moment before throwing all five of his free points into Spirit, bringing it up to 36 and making his Spirit Energy limit 4,000. Though he still wasn't sure *exactly* what each attribute did for him, he knew Spirit helped his most powerful spell: Spiritual Trifecta.

Without that spell, he wouldn't have survived, and he certainly wouldn't have killed those goblins so quickly. *It's a rare spell, and I chose to generalise in it, which is even rarer... and I seem to have an affinity for Spirit, starting at 10 stat points. Is that why I was able to complete my quest faster than everyone else?*

He also wasn't worried about min-maxing his stats anymore, not after he'd received all those titles. He likely had as much Strength, Toughness, and Speed as any warrior at his level and far more than any other mage.

One thing he didn't know what to do about was the skill point he'd received. He looked at the door of the room. *Maybe there will be people out there who can help me. This is supposed to be where my tutorial is, right?* He remembered what the information had said about being a Champion:

Once a Potential Champion has been tested against other Potentials and found to meet the requirements, they will be sent to a pocket

world to experience their tutorial, where they will be pitted against other World Champions to fight for rewards, upgrades, and power-ups...

He hadn't read more than that, and right now, he really wished he had.

Why am I still waiting in here? I've already proved I should be here. In fact, I'll be the first from my world to arrive! He smiled. *A tutorial is just the thing I need to figure out what the hell is going on.*

Xavier stood, looked down at his robes, then nodded to himself and muttered, "Time to see what this new world has to offer." He made sure the Storage Ring was on tight—it seemed to magically adjust to the size of his finger—held his staff in his left hand, then opened the door. As he did, he realised there was a key sitting in the lock. He took it, stepped out of the door, and locked it behind him, then placed the key into his Storage Ring.

He frowned, placing his palm on the door and tilting his head to the side. There was no number on the door—nothing to show it was *his* room. But something was odd about it, like... he could *feel* it was his. *Add it to the list of strange things.*

The hallway was long. *Really* long. Looking off to the left, he saw hundreds—maybe thousands—of different doors. The same was true for the right. The architecture was like the room he'd been in. Stone and brick. Sconces along the walls held lit torches, illuminating the space with flickering, flaming light. It reminded him of a castle, which only made him more excited.

Every twenty doors or so was an archway. He headed to the closest and found a circular stairwell leading up and down. There hadn't been any windows in his room, so he had no idea what might be outside.

I guess I'll head down. Maybe I'll find out.

He wished he had more information about what this place was. He had thought he might be greeted by someone when he arrived, but so far it looked like he was the only one here. *I suppose I am the first one here...* Though when he'd read that he would be pitted against other World Champions, then that he was the first from "Planet Earth" to arrive, he had to wonder if there were *other* races from *other* worlds here.

Maybe I'll meet some races who are more friendly than the goblins...

He sighed and headed down the stairs. As he walked, he checked in on his health.

Your health is at 65%.

He blinked when he saw it. His health should have been around 50 percent. Maybe 55 percent. Though it felt like a lot had happened since he'd reached Level 4, less than ten minutes had passed. How had he regenerated 15 percent of his health in that time?

I guess that's thanks to all my Toughness? He supposed the Toughness attribute was a mix between the Vitality and Endurance attributes found in video games. *And Speed is Dexterity and Agility. But I'm still wondering why I don't have a Perception stat. Surely my senses are important?*

As he walked down the stairs, he took a few chocolate bars out of his Storage Ring, eating them with the excuse that they would help his health regenerate and gain him more Spirit Energy.

He'd chomped down ten chocolate bars by the time he'd made it to the bottom of the steps. Disappointingly, that had only added 50 points to his Spirit Energy and healed his health by about 5 percent. *Still worth it.* He stashed the wrappers in his Storage Ring, not wanting to litter. *I should make sure to keep it clean in there...*

At the bottom of the stairs was another hallway, far wider than the last. Though it lacked all the doors the floor he had just left had, it did have the same archways. To the left was a dead end. To the right, a single door.

He headed down the quiet hallway, his steps echoing ominously in the empty space. There hadn't been any enemies here—not yet—but he couldn't help but feel wary. *I haven't spoken to anyone since all of this began. I'm a loner... but I could really use some company right now.*

When he opened the door at the end of the hall, he had been expecting to find an exit. A way outside. Instead, he'd entered...

"A tavern?"

Chapter 15

Kvothe? Gandalf? Dumbledore? You Know, Something... Fantastical?

THE TAVERN WAS QUITE LARGE. THERE WERE ENOUGH TABLES and chairs to seat at least five hundred people. Several fireplaces burned bright, wood stacked beside them, making the room warm and toasty. A lit candle sat on each of the heavy wooden tables— tables that looked to be bolted to the ground. *In case of a bar fight?*

Xavier's gaze trailed around the place. When he'd opened the door, this had been the last thing he'd expected. There was a long bar on one side of the room, with a single barkeep standing behind it, idly wiping down the wood.

This is straight out of a fantasy novel. Xavier didn't know whether to be excited or confused.

The barkeep looked up at him, eyes widening when he saw Xavier. Then he smiled. "Welcome!" He motioned toward all the empty chairs. "Looks like you're the first one here!"

Xavier's brow furrowed. *He doesn't seem like a threat.* He tried to scan the man, like he would one of the goblins.

???

A sharp pain stabbed his head. *It's blocking me?* He put a hand to his forehead, but the pain passed quickly. Besides, after all he'd just been through, it was barely a blip. Perhaps that had something to do with his higher Willpower.

The barkeep chuckled. "Sorry about that. I'm sure you won't be the only one." He tapped a finger on his forehead. "Can't scan someone of my level. At least, you can't." He beckoned him over with a sigh. "Something tells me you haven't been through orientation."

The tavern wasn't the only thing that looked like it was from a fantasy novel. The guy behind the bar had a heavy beard and burly arms. His clothes were of good quality, but clearly medieval chic. *Like I can talk, wearing this grey robe.*

Xavier walked over, hiding the hesitation in his steps. "Orientation?" he said, thinking, *like at a university?*

The barkeep sighed again and shook his head. He took a mug and turned, pulled ale into it from a barrel stacked against the wall. "Ah, Champions from baby worlds... The System really doesn't do much to prepare you, does it? Just..." He waved a hand. "Throws you straight to the wolves." He placed the mug in front of Xavier and nodded at one of the stools in front of the bar. "Take a seat. Maybe I can give you some answers."

Baby worlds? Xavier got the sense he was being talked down to, but the man's manner was easy and casual as he did it, so he didn't feel offended. Besides, none of what the man said was wrong. The System *hadn't* prepared him. It wasn't as if he had a clue what was actually going on yet.

But the way he talked... Xavier took a seat. Grabbed the handle. He looked into the cup. *Probably not poison, right? One way to find out.* He took a sip. He'd never drunk ale before. He frowned. While he didn't think it was poisoned, it also wasn't very strong, and it had kind of a bready taste. *Weird.*

Xavier looked at the barkeep. "You're not from Earth... are you?"

The barkeep chuckled, tapped his nose. "You're a quick one, then. No. I'm not from Earth. I'm from..." He frowned. "Well, that doesn't much matter. Would probably just confuse you at this point." He put a hand to his chest. "I'm human, though, same as you. That's why I'm here, actually. To make you feel at home."

Xavier looked around the tavern and thought about his small apartment across the river from his school. "This is nothing like my home."

The barkeep opened his hands. "But it's *cozy*, right?" He rapped a knuckle on the bar. "Classic architecture. It's a part of your history, and mine. Many places in the Greater Universe still look like this." The man was smiling. Beaming, actually. He seemed happy to talk. Xavier wondered how long he'd been waiting behind that bar.

Xavier, on the other hand, wasn't the biggest talker. *I'm a writer, not a talker,* was something he often thought. He looked at the ale, realising he hadn't paid. "I'm sorry, I don't have anything —" He paused. Looked down at his Storage Ring. He focused on it and searched the space within until he found one of the goblin purses and summoned it into his hand.

"A Storage Ring, huh? Must have been a reward for your first quest." The barkeep raised a brow and peered at the purse. "Don't worry, first drink's on the house."

Xavier nodded. "Thanks. But... I was wondering if you had anything stronger?" He still held his staff in his left hand, but it no longer felt appropriate. He eyed the man for a moment before leaning it on the bar. He could have placed it in his Storage Ring, but thought he would be faster at grabbing it than summoning it.

Though, to be honest, he didn't feel like this man was a threat. And even if he was... *If I can't scan him because he's too high-level, would I even have a chance at defeating him? What level could he be...* 20... 50... 100? He didn't know if there was a level cap in this... He almost thought "game," but this *wasn't* a game.

Thinking that way might get him killed.

The barkeep raised a finger. "I've got just the thing." He pulled a bottle from one of the shelves. Took a glass from under the bar, a tumbler—which didn't really fit the theme of the place. He poured a mostly clear, brownish liquid into the glass, filling it with about two shots.

Xavier tilted his head at the bottle. "Jack Daniel's?" Out of everything that happened that day, somehow this was the most perplexing. "How do you have... Jack Daniel's?"

"As I said, I'm here to make you feel comfortable." The barkeep slid the glass to him. "Making food and drink from your world is a part of that."

Does that mean they have real coffee? Xavier shrugged that thought away and upended the contents of the goblin's purse with a clatter of coins. The coins were round and thick, larger than any he'd used before. They were silver. *And are they... glowing?* He picked one up, inspecting it. The coin had an odd weight to it, and there was something about it that felt strangely familiar. "How many of these do I need to use?"

He counted what he had in small stacks of five. The goblin's purse had twenty-five of the strange silver coins.

"Five Lesser Spirit Coins should be plenty."

Xavier held one up. "And that's what these are?"

The barkeep smiled. "Indeed. That's what those are. Spirit Coins are the main currency of the Greater Universe. Suppose you haven't got the Identify skill yet, then?"

For a moment, Xavier wondered how much he should reveal to this stranger. But he saw no reason to lie. He wanted to learn from him, and keeping things from him didn't seem like the smartest way to go about that. "I haven't learnt any skills at all, though I do have one skill point. I gained it from the quest I just completed to get here."

Xavier pushed a stack of five Lesser Spirit Coins toward the man. *He could tell me any price and I'd just have to believe him, not knowing what these are worth.* Though if each goblin purse held roughly the same amount of Lesser Spirit Coins—and they'd all weighed about the same—he would have over a thousand of them now. And if he could sell the eighteen weapons he'd looted from the last goblins, he'd be able to gather more.

The barkeep tapped a finger on the stack and it disappeared. Then he offered a hand. "Sam."

"Sam?"

The barkeep chuckled. "My name."

Xavier raised an eyebrow. Took the hand and shook it. "I was just surprised your name was so... normal."

"What were you expecting?"

"Kvothe? Gandalf? Dumbledore? You know, something... *fantastical*."

"Well, Sam *is* a nickname for Samericalian, but most people just call me Sam."

Xavier frowned. "I don't know if you're pulling my leg."

The barkeep blinked. "Thought I was shaking your hand."

Xavier released the man's hand and sighed. "I'm Xavier. It's good to meet you. I think. I still don't really know what's going on." He started putting the coins back into the purse, though he paused when Sam frowned. "What is it?"

"Your Storage Ring can contain your coins separately. You don't need to keep them in purses."

Xavier stopped. "Oh." He tapped a stack of coins with his finger.

You have added 5 Lesser Spirit Coins to your Storage Ring.

Xavier looked inside his Storage Ring, as he did, a notification popped up along with his view of the room.

Coins
Lesser Spirit Coins: 5

He focused on the coins and willed two into his hand. The stack appeared atop his palm. "Huh."

"If you and the person you are dealing with both have Storage Rings"—Sam raised a finger, pointed at his own Storage Ring—

"then you can make the currency exchange with a shake of the hand." He held out his hand, nodding down at it.

Xavier took it again.

Samericalian would like to give you 5 Lesser Spirit Coins. Do you accept?

Xavier thought, *No*, and the notification was dismissed. He withdrew his hand and bowed his head. "Thanks." He grabbed the tumbler and took a sip. This wasn't the first time he'd drank Jack straight. He remembered it having more bite. *Is that because I have more Toughness?* Still, it was far better than the ale. "So... what exactly is the Greater Universe?"

Sam stood back, folded his arms over his chest, and stared off into the distance. "It's..." He waved a hand. "*Everything*. At least, it will be. One day." He furrowed his brow. "The universe is larger than any normal human can ever fathom. I believe that's something your world already figured out, pre-integration. What you haven't figured out is shortly after the universe was born, the System was too. As to knowing what the System truly is... That's well above my pay grade."

Xavier's eyes widened. "The System is over thirteen *billion* years old?"

Sam smiled. "Something like that, yeah. Though 'years' are relative depending on where you live." He put a hand to his head. "It all gets a little confusing sometimes. Anyway, what everyone *can* agree on is that the System expands slower than the universe does." He pulled the mug of ale Xavier decided not to drink toward him and tapped the middle of the liquid with a finger. "The System ripples outward from its origin, crawling over everything like a wave until it encompasses all it touches."

Xavier's eyebrows scrunched together as he recalled the first System notification he'd received. "When the integration happened, it said... 'Interlopers have discovered your world. Your

Solar System has now been marked for integration into the Greater Universe.' What you're talking about sounds different."

The barkeep's eyes widened. "Ah! That's how your world was integrated? Well, that... that changes things."

"It does?"

The barkeep bit his lip. "Yes. Unfortunately. You see, usually when a new world is integrated, for the first five years, the only thing they have to contend with is the flora and fauna having been changed and evolved."

Changed and evolved? Is he saying that plants and animals are going to turn into what... monsters? Xavier kept the question to himself, not wanting to interrupt the man.

"But now... now you'll have to deal with something far worse. I did wonder where you got those coins from."

"What do you mean... far worse?"

The barkeep sighed. He pulled that bottle of Jack Daniel's back off the shelf, took another glass from under the counter, and poured himself a drink. He sipped it, then looked Xavier in the eye. "Usually a world is integrated because of the wave I mentioned. The System rippling outward from its centre, assimilating everything into the Greater Universe. But sometimes... sometimes a world can be discovered by *other* means. Sometimes a Denizen of the System can reach *beyond* the Greater Universe and travel to a world not yet under its dominion."

"What does that mean?"

"It means..." Sam looked down into his drink, no longer holding Xavier's eye. "It means your people are unlikely to survive."

Chapter 16
Failure Here Means Death

"*WHAT?*" XAVIER BLURTED. HE STRAIGHTENED ON HIS STOOL, staring at the barkeep of this strange tavern on the bottom floor of the Tower of Champions, the pocket world he'd been sent to. "What do you mean my world won't survive?"

"Oh, your *world* will survive. It's a new resource, one that will be coveted by the more predatory kingdoms, empires, and collectives among the Greater Universe. It's your *people*"—he waved at Xavier—"who probably won't last." He tilted his head to the side. "Though you might..." His expression soured. "You might be made into slaves."

Xavier's shoulders slumped. He stared down at his glass of Jack. Downed the whole thing, then slapped the glass back onto the counter with a loud *crack*. For a second, he thought he'd broken the glass, but it was still intact. "Pour me another." He pushed five Lesser Spirit Coins over to the man. He still had a few piles sitting on the bar. He tapped them, placing each of them into his Storage Ring.

The barkeep grabbed the bottle and gave a generous pour. Xavier snapped up the glass and downed every last drop, placed it back on the counter, then wiped his mouth.

Okay. I need to process this information and find out more. I already knew I would be fighting for my world, that's why I chose Champion... This doesn't really change anything. I mean, does it? He eyed Sam. "You said newly integrated worlds usually only have to deal with fighting evolved fauna and flora, so... why does my world have to deal with outside threats?" He thought of the goblins. He'd taken those invaders down and lived to talk about it.

"As I said, usually a newly integrated world is locked out of the Greater Universe until they have had a few years to... find their footing. But because interlopers discovered your world *before* it was integrated, that door has been opened, so to speak, and there is no way to close it again. Word will spread that your world isn't locked down, and those looking to claim it... will send through their armies."

"How many... how many worlds like mine survive being integrated this way?"

The barkeep rubbed the back of his neck. "Well, I think it's roughly... one in a thousand."

"One in a thousand," Xavier muttered. "That's... I mean, better odds than winning the lottery, I suppose, and people win that all the time..." Though a 0.1 percent chance of survival wasn't exactly something to bet on.

"That, however, doesn't take into account the race of those in the world. Humans are versatile! We *thrive* in the System. But..." Sam sagged. "We don't tend to start off strong. So your chances are probably more like... one in *ten* thousand."

The hits just kept on coming. Xavier produced another five Lesser Spirit Coins from his Storage Ring. Placed them on the counter. "Another drink. Please."

He sat there and talked with the barkeep for a good long while as the man explained to him what was likely to happen to his planet. When Xavier mentioned the quest he'd done, that he'd been fighting goblins, the man perked up and no longer looked quite as dour.

"Goblins!" Sam smiled, slapped a hand on the bar. He'd had a few drinks himself by this point. "That's good. That's good! They are one of the weakest—and, between you and me, *dumbest*—races in the Greater Universe. They're intelligent, sapient beings, but far weaker on average than humans."

Xavier nodded along. "I guess that explains why I was able to defeat them."

"Let me guess, they were all Level 2?" The barkeep raised an eyebrow.

Xavier blinked. "They were. How did you know?"

Sam leant his elbows on the bar. "Well, see, the System doesn't leave worlds like yours *completely* defenceless. There are *some* restrictions in place. The main restriction is in the level of the Denizens the System allows onto a new world."

Xavier frowned, remembering when the first goblin had stepped out of that portal.

But that was before our world was integrated. "How can the System restrict the level of a... Denizen in a world that isn't integrated?"

Sam smiled. "Good question. Well, you see, the System isn't going to let *any* Denizen that is more than one level higher than the highest-level person on your world travel to it. And that's specific to *people*, or Denizens. It refers to the sapient races, not the animals and plants that will have been changed by the integration."

Xavier stared at the bar, trying to figure things out. "So, a wolf in the woods could be Level 20, but if the highest human is Level 10, a Denizen from outside of our world can only travel to Earth if they're Level 11?"

"Precisely!"

"And what happens if they're a higher level?"

Sam shrugged. "They'll die. Instantly."

Xavier nodded. "Good." He sighed. That was a damned relief. It was good to know that some Level 200 beast couldn't suddenly appear on Earth and destroy everything in an instant. "So that's why they sent a Level 2 goblin through the portal. Because the second they did, my world would become integrated."

Sam nodded. "And Denizens above Level 2 would have been destroyed."

"Is that why there are titles for being the first to achieve something?" Xavier asked. Again, he wasn't sure how much he wanted to tell the barkeep, but he wanted to figure these things out.

Sam chuckled. "You *do* catch on fast. That's another thing the System rewards to newly integrated worlds. They give what are called Progenitors—the first, second, third... all the way to tenth in a world to achieve things—advantages that no one else can ever gain. Gives them a fighting chance, and that's not just worlds like yours. That's *all* newly integrated worlds."

That makes sense. I'm only Level 4, but as per my math earlier, my stats are that of someone at Level 17. Or, at least, a human at Level 17. Those goblins must have had weaker stats than humans. And there is no way they would be able to send a Progenitor from another world, someone with stats well beyond their level. Any Progenitor with titles like mine would be at a far, far higher level. That will be a real advantage if they can only send in enemies one level higher than me.

Though... he supposed that last part wasn't true. He didn't know if he was the highest-level person on Earth. "I need to get training." He looked the barkeep. "If all that you're saying is true." He stood. "I... I can't just sit here." He grabbed his staff, which had been resting against the counter. "I need to get stronger as fast as I possibly can!"

The barkeep smiled again. "You've got a good attitude. A man hears their people have a one in ten thousand chance of being annihilated or turned into slaves, usually they might crumple into a little ball and lose themselves to anguish." He pointed at Xavier. "Not you. You're raring and ready to go!"

Xavier tilted his head to the side. "My world's at risk, what else *is* there to do?"

"Crumple into a ball, remember?" Sam shook his head. "There isn't much you're going to be able to do right now." His eyes flicked up, as though looking at something, though they were a little unfocused. *Is he reading a notification?* The barkeep nodded. "It will still be another three days until orientation. Usually it takes a while for Champions from newly integrated worlds to complete their first quest."

Xavier frowned, realising something. "You're saying there will be Champions from worlds that *aren't* newly integrated?"

"Of course. Once a Denizen gains access to the System at age sixteen, they're given the chance of becoming a Champion, just like you were given the chance. Though, as you know, choosing Champion has its risks. The first test is a fight to the death. Slightly more than 50 percent of people don't make it past that. Most Denizens of integrated worlds make it past their second test—a quest of varying difficulty—as they know what they're getting into and have access to knowledge and items someone such as yourself does not, but not all make it. People from worlds like yours... perhaps." He tilted his head to one side. "Ten percent of those who choose Champion make it to a tower."

Xavier balked. "You mean... only one in five survive the quest? And what do you mean *a* tower? Are there more places like this one?"

The barkeep raised his palm and tilted it left to right. "Roughly that many survive. It varies. And of course, there are thousands of instances of the Tower of Champions." He scratched his head. "Probably millions, actually." He waved at the tavern. "Just like there are countless versions of this room." He pointed at the door. "This section of the Tower of Champions is reserved only for those from your planet, though not everyone who walks through that door will enter my tavern. There are countless other establishments like my own within the Tower of Champions, but you're locked to *this* one, along with five hundred others from your world. They'll be considered your cohort."

"Cohort?"

"Kind of like a class."

"The Tower of Champions is an academy?"

"In a sense, though failure here means death. Unfortunately."

Xavier slumped back down onto his stool and ran a hand through his hair. "I think I liked it better when I was in the dark," he muttered, though that wasn't strictly true. He *needed* to know what was going on, and considering the titles he'd received, he was likely the first person on Earth to learn *any* of this stuff. Though perhaps that wasn't the case. Perhaps he was simply the first who'd chosen Champion to learn of it. Others on Earth would be going through their tutorials even as he spoke. "My tutorial will start after orientation?"

"That's right. The rest of your cohort will be here by then. Though the orientation will be a rehash of much that I've just said, there will be other things it will teach you." Sam wrapped a knuckle on the bar. "Like how to get more of those coins."

Xavier gripped the shaft of his staff tightly. "Can I... return to Earth? Before the tutorial starts?" He couldn't help but wonder how many other places those goblins were turning up. Or what if there were other, more dangerous races who'd found his world?

Sam sighed. "I'm afraid that's impossible. You're stuck here, in the tower, until the end of your first challenge. There... isn't really much more I can tell you than that. There is a lot to learn about the System, but I'm only *allowed* to tell you so much."

"But... these Champions from other worlds... they'll... they'll have been training for this all their life, won't they? They'll know everything about the System? How to take advantage of it?" He remembered the stats he'd been given when he was first integrated. If he'd been stronger, or perhaps studied harder, or *something*, he would have started off with higher stats. He didn't know *how* high, but it would have made a difference, wouldn't it?

"Aye. That they will." Sam's gaze dropped to the bar. "I'm sorry for the lot you and your world have been given."

"It's not your fault. You've been kind to me. Taught me things I didn't know when all of this..." Xavier flapped a hand. "Is just insane." He sighed. "If I can't get home yet, what can I do? I don't want to just sit here and drink until orientation starts." Though he had to admit, a small part of him wondered if he had anything better to do. But he knew if he let himself wallow, that wallowing might never end.

Sam bit his lip. He glanced at the tavern's door, then leant forward on the counter, inching closer to Xavier over the bar. He spoke in a hush, "There's only so much I can say. But there are ways for you to train outside of gaining levels."

Xavier waited for Sam to say more, but apparently that was it. He opened his mouth to ask another question, but the barkeep raised a hand.

"I can't say more than I already have. I'm sorry, you'll have to just wait until the orientation begins, and figure things out on your own until then."

Chapter 17
You Currently Have No Skills

Xavier didn't let himself have another drink. He said his goodbyes to Sam the barkeep then headed out of the tavern. At first, when he'd been learning more about what being integrated into the Greater Universe meant, it had invigorated him with more energy and motivation than ever.

Now, he wasn't sure what to think. What to *feel*. Sam had told him there were ways to train without gaining levels, but what exactly *were* those ways? Did it have anything to do with the skill point he'd gotten as a bonus reward from his first quest? He still didn't know how to use that.

He wondered what types of titles he might be missing out on by getting locked in this place. Part of him felt like those stuck on Earth who hadn't chosen Champion had a better chance of becoming stronger than him, though he supposed he had no idea what they might be going through. *At least they aren't stuck in a pocket world with only one person to talk to.*

He trudged back up the stairs. As he did, he retrieved a pack of chips from his Storage Ring and munched on them. His health had already made its way back to full just from the time he'd been sitting at the bar. It felt good seeing it at 100 percent, but it wasn't like he was in any danger right now.

Should I just go up and sleep? He didn't feel tired. He didn't know whether that was because of his stats, or all of the excitement from the day he was having. *Has it really only been one day?*

That in itself was difficult to believe. He supposed it made sense then—him being the first to arrive in this place.

As he walked up the stairs, he noticed his legs weren't finding it difficult. He wouldn't have climbed this many stairs before the integration without breathing hard and breaking a sweat. *With all the titles I gained, my Strength is at 23.* He wondered how much Strength the strongest person on Earth would have started with. *Is 10 the limit? Or would they have been more like 12?*

He clenched his fist, felt the strength in his arm. *How do I... make this more without gaining levels?*

When he made it back to his room, he threw the empty chip packet back into his Storage Ring and slumped onto the bed, deep in thought. He contemplated the skill point he had, then tried a few things, attempting to see if he could use it.

Finally, after trying about ten different things, he thought, *Skill list,* and a notification popped up.

Skills
You currently have no skills. Do you wish to purchase a skill with your Skill Point?

He didn't like the way the System said he had "no skills." *I have plenty of skills, thank you very much.* Still, he thought, *Yes,* as this was what he'd been looking for.

He blinked as a massive list appeared with a vast number of options. His eyes widened, looking at all of them. They were in different sections and disciplines: Cooking, Baking, Blacksmithing, Tailoring, Fishing, Hunting, Performing.

There were even sections for Engineering, Alchemy, and Medicine. When he saw a section for Writing, he had to restrain himself from selecting it to see what skills he might gain in that field, wondering if it would be in sections for prose, dialogue, descriptions, scene setting, and worldbuilding.

He shook his head. *There are more important things to do right now...*

There were also sections for general skills, things ranging from jumping or running to climbing. *Can't I already do those things? What does gaining the skill "running" do, exactly?*

Xavier put his staff on the bed and rested his chin in his hands. The barkeep mentioned something about an "Identify" skill, which he ended up finding in one of the lists of general skills, but he didn't feel as though choosing that would give him a large enough advantage at this point.

I gained the skill point as a bonus reward, which means I'll likely be one of few Champions who already has a skill point. I need to pick something that will give me the greatest advantage.

That's when he came upon Martial skills.

His eyes widened as he looked at things like Unarmed Combat, Staff Mastery, Sword Mastery, and Dagger Mastery. There were even things for Physical Resistance and Magical Resistance, and a skill for Magical Potency, which he assumed would improve the strength of one's spells. Unfortunately, there didn't seem to be a way to learn more about a skill. All he got were their names, though usually they were fairly self-explanatory.

What if I can improve a skill without needing to gain Mastery Points to do so? That would be one way to train without gaining levels. He wasn't sure that was how it worked, but he was eager to find out.

He needed to decide *which* skill to choose. As much as he wanted to ask Sam, he doubted the man could answer that question.

Considering how many goblins he'd killed by hitting them with the butt of his staff, Xavier was *very* tempted to choose Staff Mastery. But he wanted to check what other skills were available first.

To his surprise, he came upon the skill Meditation in the list of

Martial skills, which made him frown. How was that a "Martial" skill? *If the Meditation skill is anything like in video games or novels I've read, it will help regenerate my health, maybe even Spirit Energy.*

In fact, now he thought about it, Meditation giving him Spirit Energy was incredibly likely, and there were probably other advantages. Like, maybe getting it to a high enough level would let him meditate while walking, or eventually while fighting...

But that didn't seem like something that would help him over the next few days. He imagined he would gain a lot more skill points in the future. *I'm only Level 4, after all.* He already felt envious of Champions coming here from worlds that had been integrated for decades, centuries, even millennia. *They would know exactly what to do with this skill point.*

He stared at his staff on the bed, then looked at the Staff Mastery skill. He *could* choose Magical Potency, but he figured his magic strength was already quite high.

It was his physical combat ability that was lacking. *If there are other Champions like that Navy SEAL, they will be miles ahead of me in combat skills, even if they're pre-System combat skills. Then there's all those from other, already integrated worlds... My stats may be high, but stats alone won't be enough to get me far, will they?*

Xavier chose Staff Mastery.

You have learnt the skill Staff Mastery!
Staff Mastery – Rank 1
You are a student of the staff. Your weapon is one of range and versatility. Of defence and offence.
+5% physical damage with staff weapons.
+5% Speed when wielding staff weapons.

Xavier raised an eyebrow, looking at the bonuses the skill gave him. These were the first bonuses that used percentages. Initially, he was disappointed—5 percent didn't seem like much. Then he supposed it was only Rank 1.

He also realised... even if right now it was worth less than five attribute points, down the track, if his Speed stat were in the hundreds? It would be worth *far* more. *Perhaps I'm thinking too far ahead.*

He tried to will some sort of upgrade quest to appear, like they had for his spells, but nothing came up. *Maybe I need to use the staff first.* He grabbed his staff, then looked around the small room that he supposed was his for the foreseeable future. There wasn't much space to move.

He stepped into the hall. It was wide, with plenty of room. Gripping his staff in both hands, he felt rather foolish about what he was about to do. Like a kid in the backyard playing with a stick. But he'd done fire twirling in front of crowds before, and here he was alone. At least for the moment.

There's nothing foolish about training. He stepped forward and swung the staff. That's when he realised something. He swung the staff *differently* to how he had before. He had one hand all the way down near the butt of the staff, and the other up about a third of the way. The strike felt far more powerful.

He hadn't noticed he'd been holding the staff that way. He stood back up from his lunge and frowned.

Did choosing that skill download information into my brain? He probed his mind but couldn't for the life of him find anything he didn't already know.

He swung the staff again. This time in a series of strikes. Overhead, underhand, side to side, taking a step with each strike as though he were putting an opponent on the back foot.

The way he moved felt so much different to before. His steps more... calculated, smooth, even graceful, if to a small degree. After the sixth strike, he stopped again, looked down at himself. *Something has definitely changed. Like... like there's muscle memory that wasn't there before.*

Xavier couldn't help but smile. He recalled how he'd fought

against the goblins. The way he'd hit them with the staff. It had been so clumsy compared to this. *And I'm only at Rank 1!* He wondered how he would be able to improve this skill.

Xavier didn't have much concept of time in that hallway, but he figured he'd spent at least two hours swinging that staff almost nonstop. Though his muscles were somewhat strained and his breathing had quickened a little, he'd never gotten close to pushing himself hard. He wondered if that was his Strength, Toughness, or Speed helping him out there. Perhaps all three.

As for his Speed, though it was currently his weakest stat, he was sure he was swinging his staff faster than Bruce Lee, Jet Li, or Jackie Chan could in their primes.

This is insane! I'm faster than a Shaolin monk!

By the end of his session when he finally stopped, he wasn't feeling anything improving anymore, though he supposed that didn't mean the training was for nothing. Just because he wasn't seeing his "stats go up" didn't mean he wasn't improving. *I'm stronger and faster, tougher and even smarter, but the only reason I'm moving differently is because of the Staff Mastery skill.*

He put the staff in his Storage Ring and looked down the long hallway. There were other things he should train, or test. For one, he didn't really know how fast or strong he was now. He needed to make sure he could properly judge his speed and strength while in the middle of a fight, lest he try and do something he couldn't, or misjudged how fast he could block.

Or what if he accidentally jumped over an enemy instead of at them? *That would be embarrassing. And potentially lethal, for me.*

So that's what Xavier did. He ran. He jumped. He performed push-ups, then handstand push-ups against a wall, then finally freestanding handstand push-ups in the middle of the hallway. He sprinted down the spiralling stairs, to the door of the tavern, then back up to the door of his room.

It was when he was doing those sprints that something finally changed.

You have gained +1 Speed!

When the notification had popped up, it had taken him by surprise so much that he'd slipped on a step and fallen straight into the wall of the stairway, slamming one knee and his head against the stone. Even so, he laughed and pumped his fist in the air—once he'd regained his footing.

He'd gained an attribute point, and he hadn't needed to get a level or a title to do it!

Now he'd done it once, he would surely mange to do it again.

Chapter 18
Looks Like They've Already Destabilised Themselves

Alistair Reed wiped his dagger on the dead man's cloak. He stood, tilted his head, admiring his handiwork.

You have defeated a Level 3 Human!
You have gained 300 Mastery Points.
You have gained 300 Spirit Energy.

The man had had the basic Warrior class. His cheap, thin leather armour hadn't been enough to stop Alistair's dagger, especially since he'd struck the back of the man's neck.

The man hadn't even seen him coming. He'd been one of the fools who'd chosen to fight for this world, chosen to be a Soldier. Once the fifty-foot-tall wizened, bearded hologram man had finished explaining what the Greater Universe and the System was —in fairly broad terms—this man, *Daniel*, had taken charge.

Those gathered in the square had a myriad of different reactions. Some had screamed, searching for their children or younger siblings—apparently anyone under the age of sixteen had been transported to "Safe Zone" cities where they would come to no harm and be looked after by those who'd chosen Support roles.

Others had broken down, squatting or sitting where they'd stood, shoving heads in hands and going quiet or weeping miserably.

Alistair didn't understand what their problem was. Why were they all so distraught? He thought this new world order was rather fascinating. Looking at those people, he'd wondered why he even *needed* a quest to destabilise the tutorial.

Looks like they've already destabilised themselves.

That had made him want to chuckle, though he'd suppressed the emotion. He was used to suppressing his true feelings around others, so it wasn't difficult.

Then men and women like *Daniel*, who might be described as stoic and strong-willed, had taken charge. Not everyone in the crowd had broken down, either. Many had no more than frowns on their faces, or slightly wide eyes. Almost everyone seemed at least a little shocked. Though there were some among them who had smiles on their faces, similar to the smile Alistair wasn't letting slip onto his own face.

He wondered if those were kindred spirits. People who revelled in chaos like he did. Or perhaps they were simply video game addicts and enthusiasts who thought their wildest dreams were coming true.

Alistair looked at his Quest Log again.

Quest Log
Current Quest: Destabilise the tutorial.
Progress: Incomplete
Reward:

1. **Unknown item.**
2. **Bonus Mastery Points.**

Alistair frowned. *No change.*

Footsteps sounded near the mouth of the alleyway he stood in. *People coming.* He sheathed his dagger, wiped clean of the dead man's blood, and nimbly climbed a fire escape. *Putting points into Speed and Strength was a good idea.*

It was the third day since the System had come and the chaos had begun. He still hadn't appeared to make any progress on his quest, despite this being the third "leader" he'd killed. Perhaps he was thinking too small.

So far, the tutorial had been incredibly basic. Monsters—things that were once animals, but had been twisted and changed with the arrival of the System—spawned in small enclosures in the middle of the square, and one by one, the people gathered received notifications that it was their turn to kill them.

Mostly, the "monsters" were Level 1 mice and rabbits no more dangerous than an angry dog.

Alistair pulled himself to the top of the building. He couldn't believe how easy the System had given it to these people. When the fifty-foot-tall hologram had spoken, it had told them of a universe with vast kingdoms, empires, and planetary collectives that vied for domination of the stars. Of entities that possessed the raw power to destroy entire worlds and solar systems. Of monsters large enough to eat *suns*.

And yet the tutorial had consisted of them fighting... bunnies?

It was utterly ridiculous. Made further ridiculous by the fact some had said, before they requested to step into the enclosures by the System, that they refused to kill the rabbits and mice that spawned.

The people quickly realised refusing a System's command was a very, very bad idea. The only person to actually do it hadn't been warned of any consequences. They'd simply shaken their head and said something about being a vegan.

Then they'd lost their left hand. It had been sliced clean off.

Alistair had found it difficult to keep a giggle inside. He'd had to stifle it so hard it almost looked like he was crying. Considering some people in the crowd *had* been crying didn't make him feel any better for his pitiful appearance.

The woman—crying about her missing hand—had stepped into

the enclosure, pale and shaking with fear, and killed the bunny with some sort of fire spell after it had bitten her arm.

No one had refused the System since.

From atop the building, Alistair let his smile roam free, watching as a woman noticed the corpse in the middle of the alleyway.

The woman screamed, loud and high-pitched. She fled, running back to find help. Alistair chuckled. It reminded him of the crime shows he'd watched. When someone had stumbled upon a body. The women had such terribly dramatic screams. He'd always thought they came off as fake.

Perhaps if the murderer were standing over the body and looked ready to kill them too. But screaming simply because they've seen a corpse? It had never rung true to Alistair.

Now, he supposed he'd been wrong about that.

Over the last few days, Alistair had been very careful with his kills. Cornering people when they were alone. Never taking on more than one person. He didn't want to be found out.

But now, after having killed three people already without his quest having changed, he wondered if "careful" was the right approach.

I'm still thinking like this is pre-integration. Like I'm worried about getting caught by the authorities. He tilted his chin up, thoughts occurring to him. *The world is nothing like it was.* He thought of the vast kingdoms and empires that the hologram had mentioned, and his ambitions grew beyond simple murder.

In this new reality, killing brings strength. Power. The more I kill, the more Mastery Points I gain. The more Mastery Points I gain, the more levels I accrue. He smiled sinisterly. *Levels make stats go up.*

Why should he worry about getting caught? What did getting caught matter if he became the most powerful human on the planet?

The hologram had spoken of other things, too. Of the fact that their world wasn't "locked" like other, newly integrated worlds apparently were, which meant that portals had been opened up around the planet—and more would follow—with enemies from other planets coming through. Though Alistair hadn't encountered any of those portals yet, which he was glad for. He didn't feel ready.

If Alistair destabilised this tutorial, it would mean fewer people to help with the defence of Earth. That was information he'd not had when he'd chosen his moral faction.

Alistair didn't care what happened to the people of Earth, of course, but now, with the prospect of becoming powerful enough to perhaps one day rule it... he didn't want his playground falling into enemy hands.

Plans formed within his mind. One after the other. He concluded that these people—the thousand he shared his tutorial with—were not important to the defence of the planet.

If there were entities in the Greater Universe that could destroy entire worlds, what did a thousand weak individuals *matter*? They couldn't compare to a *single* strong individual, could they?

And their deaths will make me strong.

Alistair Reed now knew what he had to do to destabilise his tutorial and complete his first quest.

He had to kill everyone in it.

Quest Log Update
Kill every member of your tutorial before the tutorial ends to gain a bonus reward.

Alistair laughed again. *It appears the System agrees with me. And that it's listening to my thoughts.*

Melissa Donavon drew back the string of her bow, an arrow

nocked. She breathed slowly and deeply, sighting her enemy through the trees.

{Wolf – Level 6}

It was the strongest enemy she'd seen yet, but she didn't doubt she would be able to take it down.

She activated her spell, Precision Power Shot. Day three of being stuck in the woods, and she'd managed to upgrade the spell to Rank 2, from Power Shot to Precision Power Shot. She'd had to practise her bow skills on a tree for hours on end that first day, without ever sleeping, before a notification popped up.

Melissa had been fairly hopeless at aiming the bow at the beginning, but after she'd added more points into her Strength attribute, it was becoming easier to pull the heavy string back and hold it steady.

Then, for her, it had simply been about patience and perseverance. Two things she had in spades.

The notification which had appeared when she'd first begun training had said she needed to land one hundred accurate shots upon enemies to learn a skill called Bow Mastery.

If all went well, this would be her hundredth shot.

The point of her arrow glowed as she loosed the string. The arrow shot through the air, whistling past the trees. The wolf had its head raised, sniffing the air, when the arrow slammed into its skull.

It didn't have time to yelp.

You have defeated a Level 6 Wolf!
You have gained 600 Mastery Points.
You have gained 600 Spirit Energy.

Congratulations, you have reached Level 7!
Your health has been regenerated by 50%!
Your Spirit Energy limit has increased by 100!

You have received +1 Strength and +2 Speed!
You have received +5 free stat points!
All your spells have refreshed and are no longer on cooldown!

You have completed 100/100 accurate shots on enemies with a bow. You have learnt the skill Bow Mastery!
Bow Mastery – Rank 1
You are a student of the bow. Your weapon is one of range, power, and precision. May your enemies never see your arrows coming.
+5% physical damage with bow weapons.
+5% piercing damage with bow weapons.
+5% Speed when wielding bow weapons.

Melissa didn't smile when she reached the next level. She simply released the breath she'd been holding, slung her bow about her shoulders, and drew the dagger from her belt.

She stalked over to the wolf's corpse. Melissa had only gone hunting once in her life. One of her mother's ex-boyfriends had taken her bow-hunting. She'd been thirteen years old, and he had this weird, creepy smile whenever he looked at her.

The last thing she'd wanted was to go hunting with the man, but he was paying for their rent, and her mother hadn't given her a choice.

He'd carried a crossbow with a scope. Something he never let her touch. He went hunting with three of his buddies, and the only reason he'd wanted to bring her along was for someone to cook the meals and fetch the beers.

Though she'd hated playing little fetch girl, she was now glad she'd had that experience. When she'd given the deer he'd killed a sour expression, he'd frowned at her and made her gut and dress it.

At least I know something of this.

As she knelt, assigning her free stat points—one to Strength, two to Speed, one to Toughness and one to Willpower—she rolled the wolf onto its back and sliced into it. A thought entered her mind she'd never imagined having before: *I wonder what wolf meat tastes like.*

It was the third day of being "integrated into the Greater Universe" and Melissa still didn't know what was going on. It was like she'd been thrown into some sort of video game. All doubt of it being a hallucination, dream, or psychosis had left her once the rabbit that had attacked her had sunk its abnormally large teeth into her shoulder.

Perhaps she should have been afraid, all alone in the middle of the woods with animals transformed into monsters, but she felt a sudden sort of peace the first time she'd killed something and gained those Mastery Points. Seen that she could gain levels. A peace that only intensified when she'd gained her first stat points and allocated them.

Now, out here, she didn't need anyone else. She didn't need to go to university. Earn a degree. Find some job she didn't truly want. All she needed was to hunt and become stronger.

She would never run out of food again. And out here, she would never have to rely on someone *else*.

Melissa Donovan hadn't had a single worry but for her basic needs since entering this forest. That was, at least, until lightning struck the ground half a mile away and something that looked an awful lot like a portal opened up.

It happened once she'd finished dressing the wolf. She'd stalked through the forest as quietly as she could, approaching it, and watched as something—some*one*—had stepped through.

It looked and walked like a man, except it had ears that tapered to a point. Long, silver hair tied up in a ponytail. It wore some sort of medieval armour. Ringmail, she supposed it was called. In one hand it carried a long, slender sword. In the other, a round shield with a protruding bump in the middle.

Hidden behind a tree, Melissa scanned the strange-looking alien.

{Elf – Level 8}

Elves are real? She'd seen *Lord of the Rings*, and supposed that's what this man looked like. After all that had already happened, why *wouldn't* elves be real?

Quest Log Update
Remain within the forest and survive the
arrival of the enemy invaders for five days to
gain a bonus reward.

Melissa quickly read the notification, silently nocked an arrow, and sighted her new enemy. She was about to activate Precision Power Shot when another two elves stepped out of the portal.

Gently, she held the string as she put it back into a neutral position, then, arrow still nocked, gaze still looking toward the newly-arrived elves, she slipped back through the trees and disappeared into the woods.

Looks like I need a plan.

She wasn't about to let her sanctuary be stolen from her.

Chapter 19

If That Happened to a Normal Person, It Probably Would Have Broken Their Back

EVEN WHEN OTHER CHAMPIONS APPEARED, XAVIER HAD NOT ceased his punishing training regime.

Since the first day that he'd arrived in the Tower of Champions, he hadn't slept more than four hours a night. He wasn't sure if it was healthy or not, but he felt more energetic than he ever had in his life.

One thing he'd discovered when he slept was that sleeping *did* increase his Spirit Energy. It seemed to increase at a rate of 500 points per hour of sleep, as after his first night of sleep it had topped out at 4,000.

That solves that mystery. He was pretty sure that meditation would solve that problem as well—a skill he'd yet to gain, as he'd chosen Staff Mastery first. Though with eating food, killing monsters, and sleeping all able to gain him more Spirit Energy, he wasn't sure if he needed a fourth way or not.

But he certainly *wanted* one.

That first day, he'd trained for hours. Mostly sprinting up and down the stairs and doing as many handstand push-ups as he could manage. After a little while, he realised the handstand push-ups simply weren't cutting it, and he'd done something he'd at first thought would be foolish.

He'd taken one of the vending machines out of his Storage Ring and picked it up. There was some information on the side, warning of how heavy it was.

It weighed 990 pounds, or 450 kilograms. He'd looked at it a little dumbfounded, lying on the ground. Xavier hadn't been to the gym in... a long time, but he was pretty sure the record for the heaviest deadlift wasn't much higher than that vending machine's weight.

He'd looked at his Storage Ring, glad he didn't have to carry the weight of everything that was inside of it around with him. *It must put everything in some sort of pocket dimension. I mean, there are pocket worlds, so why wouldn't there be interdimensional storage spaces? How else would the ring work?*

At that point, he hadn't managed to gain any points in Strength despite all of his attempts. The only attribute he'd gained through physical training was Speed.

He'd looked at his Strength attribute—at twenty-three points—and wondered how strong that made him in "normal" terms. He could do handstand push-ups absurdly easily. He'd be able to do them on one hand if he had the balance for it—which he didn't. Yet.

But picking up something that was almost a thousand pounds? That seemed... even more absurd.

He'd stared at the vending machine a moment, then shrugged his now-large shoulders and figured it was worth a shot.

Xavier had leant down, picked it up, and had it over his head in seconds. He'd stumbled backward, felt a massive strain on his joints, but he'd managed to keep it steady and push it all the way up, his arms extended.

He'd laughed out loud into the empty hallway until someone stepped out of one of the other rooms, peeking at him with wide eyes. The surprise of someone being in what he considered his hallway made him falter, stumble back, and fall onto his ass.

The vending machine had slammed into the stone floor. The

glass broke, and snacks had fallen out everywhere. *If that happened to a normal person, it probably would have broken their back.* His backside felt a little bruised, but otherwise he was fine.

A notification had popped up in his vision before he regained his footing.

You have gained 1 Strength!

The man who'd seen him had stepped out with a frown, arms crossed, looking at him as though he were a little crazy. Xavier snapped back to his feet, placed a hand on the vending machine, and deposited it back into his Storage Ring.

Five more people had opened doors after that. Though he *had* been the first to complete his quest, others had only been perhaps ten hours behind.

Xavier, being a bit of a loner, had run a hand through his hair and sent them down to the bar to talk to Sam. They'd looked a little perplexed to discover there was a tavern downstairs in this place, but considering what they'd all been through, they took it in stride.

While it was good to see others here, he didn't feel as though he had time to socialise, not when he was finally making some progress.

The second they'd all stepped through the archway—four warriors and one mage, by the looks of them—he'd taken out that vending machine and started again.

The first point he'd gained must have been a fluke, because after three whole days of training, he'd only managed to gain one more point in Strength, one more point in Speed, and a single point in Toughness.

Toughness, he had trained in his small bedroom. He remembered watching a documentary about Shaolin monks. The monks, when they trained, performed conditioning on their bodies to strengthen themselves. First punching water, then sand, then stone. They'd taken shots to the gut, too. Punch after punch after punch. He'd also seen Muay Thai fighters condition their shins by kicking banana trees.

So he figured... in a world like this... hitting himself with his staff might be the best way to train Toughness when he couldn't add to the stat.

It had taken him six straight hours of slamming the wooden staff across his legs, arms, stomach, head and back until finally he'd received a notification. He only wondered what people would think he was doing in there if they could hear him through the door.

He hadn't learnt how to increase his Intelligence. When he'd tried reading books on his phone, opening his satchel which he'd been keeping in his Storage Ring, he'd found his phone was long out of battery with nowhere to recharge it.

And his laptop had been smashed. It must have broken in that last fight he'd had with the eighteen goblins before he'd been whisked away to this place—he remembered falling onto it. The screen was cracked in about four different places, and it couldn't turn on.

He'd sunk onto his bed, then, lost in dismay, his laptop cradled in his arms, wondering about all the writing he'd done over the last few years. All the short stories. Assignments. The outlining. Ideas he'd jotted down. The unfinished novels...

Had they all been... lost?

He'd always backed up everything he wrote onto the cloud, but after the System had come, he hadn't been able to gain any signal.

Xavier wasn't sure how long he'd sat there, staring off into nothing, thinking about all the work he'd lost. After a while, he realised that while it was important to him, right now... it wasn't important *enough* for him to lose time. His world was in turmoil. Under threat. His people had only been given a one-out-of-ten-thousand chance of survival.

Half of all people who had chosen Champion—like he did— would have died. Then more would have died failing their quests. And that was just those who'd chosen Champion.

Xavier had no idea what other people were going through. Whether the invaders had attacked them. He hoped they would be safe in their tutorials, but with Sam telling him this world wasn't "locked," he sincerely doubted it.

And he was worried about a few lost written words?

I can write things again. Who knows, maybe I'll be a much better writer now I've gained so much Intelligence. And with my Willpower stat, I might actually finally finish something...

On the day he knew orientation would finally come, Xavier sat on the stone floor of his room, closed his eyes, and breathed steadily. He wanted to test something out. So many of those skills that he'd seen when looking to use his skill point were things people already *knew*, so he'd wanted to find out how good the System was at picking that up.

What if he were to demonstrate his proficiency in a skill? What if he *showed* the System that he could already do something? When he'd been using his staff to smash in goblin skulls, he hadn't been doing it with any particular skill.

Would it have been different if he'd *shown* skill when fighting with the staff, as though he already had some mastery at it?

He wanted to see if he could unlock a skill through the simple use of it. And, being rather stubborn, he'd sat there meditating for a good five hours before a notification had finally appeared.

Skill Quest Unlocked: Meditation
To unlock meditation, successfully meditate
for 100 hours.
Progress: 5/100

Xavier smiled. *It worked.* One hundred hours felt like a long time, and he imagined it might be easier simply *learning* the skill with a skill point, but he was glad that he'd discovered this option. *I wonder what other skills I could unlock Skill Quests for.*

He soured, wondering why he hadn't unlocked a Skill Quest for running, considering all the damned running he'd been doing since he'd gotten to this place. *Maybe I don't have good running technique, so it isn't registering properly?* He'd been relying heavily on his newfound Speed and Strength stats as he ran, not thinking about technique at all. Running wasn't something he'd really done since his parkour days, and those days had been short-lived.

Even though other Champions of Earth had arrived, he hadn't had a real conversation with anyone except for the barkeep. Late in the first day, only a few people had arrived. The ones he'd sent down to Sam in the bar. On the second day, however, *hundreds* more came. Way more than Sam said would be in his cohort.

Now, there were thousands of people out there, heading back and forth from their rooms down to the tavern. Somehow, the hallway never seemed too crowded. Neither were the stairwells, as there were so many of them every few rooms, on both sides of the hall.

But it did mean he couldn't run up and down the stairs anymore without getting in people's way. It didn't stop him from running down the hallway, though. Even if he got a lot of weird looks.

On the second day, he'd done a little exploring. Well, exploring was a bit much. He simply went up the stairs instead of down them. What he'd found at the top was a locked door. He'd tried to scan it, like he might with an enemy such as the goblins, but it didn't let him. He wondered if that was because it was just a door or if it was because he didn't yet have the Identify skill. He figured it was the latter.

When Xavier wasn't training in the hallway, he spent his time in his room, where he had more than enough food taken from the cafeteria in his Storage Ring. He'd sorted out all the goblins' coin purses he'd looted, and found he had 1,231 Lesser Spirit Coins. Not that he knew what to use them for other than buying alcohol down in the tavern—not that he'd *been* down to the tavern since that first day.

He should have gone out and talked to people, but... he'd

always been a bit of a loner. Though the demographics of the people outside varied considerably, and people didn't exactly seem excited about what was going on, it felt like he was stuck in a university dorm, surrounded by a bunch of strangers he didn't want to talk to.

I've faced goblins from another world, and I'm afraid of making new friends?

It seemed incredibly foolish, especially since he was pretty sure he was the strongest one among them. *Hell, I might very well be the strongest person on Earth right now...* Though he wasn't happy he couldn't gain any more levels over the last few days, he doubted he'd fallen too far behind.

The Tower of Champions is an opportunity for me to get strong, gain rewards... I still don't really know what the tower really is, but I'm sure it will accelerate my progress beyond anything anyone on Earth can manage.

Xavier was in the middle of a strength training session, holding the vending machine aloft in his tiny room. *Good thing it has high ceilings.* He pushed it upward. Managed to press it twenty times before another notification popped up.

You have gained +1 Strength!

Xavier practically dropped the vending machine onto the floor, his arms were trembling so much. But as he'd gotten used to this, instead of dropping the 900-pound weight, he put it straight into his Storage Ring.

Suddenly, he felt as light as a feather. *Another point in Strength! That's 26 now.* He was getting really close to two hundred stats. *I wonder if there's another achievement or if there won't be one until I've reached five hundred combined stats...*

A second notification appeared in his vision soon after the first.

Orientation begins in 5 minutes. Please head

**upstairs to the next floor where you will meet
the rest of your assigned party.**

Xavier blinked. *I guess I finally need to talk to some people
around here.* He wasn't sure why that made him more nervous than
the prospect of fighting monsters.

Chapter 20
Meet the Party

Xavier felt oddly giddy and nervous as he walked up the steps. He wasn't the only one heading up there. About twenty people walked up the same set of stairs. None of them talked to each other, but they all had a mix of eagerness and dread on their faces.

As he looked at them, Xavier couldn't help but remember how many people Sam had told him would likely even *get* to the Tower of Champions. *Only 10 percent of people who chose Champion made it*. Not only that, he knew that people died while *at* the Tower of Champions, especially as they would be pitted against *other* World Champions. Xavier got the feeling that meant they might have to go up against World Champions from other, established worlds. People—whether humans or those of another sapient race—that had been Denizens of the Greater Universe since the moment of their birth.

Unlike Xavier and those around him.

How many of these people will survive? He wasn't worried about himself. Perhaps he should have been—maybe it was arrogant not to be—but the fact he had more stat points than anyone else lent him that confidence. *I can do this. I will do this. Maybe I can help keep some of the others alive, too...*

He was the first to reach the top of the stairs, which wasn't too much of a surprise given he was the fastest. He reached the locked door he'd come upon the day before when he'd been exploring.

He put a hand on the handle and was about to turn it when a notification appeared.

Would you like to enter this instance?

Xavier frowned. This hadn't happened the day before. He'd just tried to turn the handle and hadn't been able to. *Another instance, like the tavern?* The tavern hadn't had this notification, though he supposed the door hadn't been locked, either. *Maybe it only lets certain people in at certain times.*

As he didn't want to hold up the line forming, he thought, *Yes*, as quickly as he could. Instead of stepping through the door like he had to the tavern, he was teleported straight into a large room with four chairs facing a stage. The room had torches burning along dark stone walls and looked a little like a theatre. *Maybe it* is *a theatre.*

If anything, it reminded him of one of his classes. Except, fewer chairs. He sat at the chair on the far right, shifting in it, feeling oddly uncomfortable. He checked to ensure his Storage Ring was still on his finger. It was there, as it always was. It had never disappeared or fallen off—checking had simply become a habit.

His staff was inside his ring. He didn't expect to have to do any fighting during the orientation, but he also didn't know *what* to expect. Another thing he'd been practicing while locking himself in his room was summoning his staff to his hand quickly.

When doing so, he'd felt almost like a child drawing a fake gun while staring into a mirror. Like *he* thought he was cool, but anyone looking might think he was just being silly.

I'm sure the skill will come in handy.

It wasn't long before another person arrived. Oddly, it wasn't one of the people he'd seen on the stairs. *I suppose if they were teleported here, they could have come from anywhere in the hallway.*

The man looked to be in his mid-to-late forties. He'd chosen the basic class of Warrior and was wearing the typical thin, light leather armour that Xavier had seen the other warriors wearing. A sword and dagger were sheathed at his belt. Though there was no sign of a bow, he may have had one stashed in his Storage Ring.

The man had dark brown hair and a close-cropped beard with grey streaked through it. He had a stocky build, but Xavier had no idea if that was from stats or from pre-integration. He gazed about the room with a critical eye before nodding sharply at Xavier then taking a seat beside him.

He offered a hand to Xavier. "Howard."

Xavier took it. "Xavier."

Howard leant back in his chair, crossed his arms over his beefy chest, eyes narrowing as he looked at the stage. "You have any idea what this orientation is all about? We've been chatting about it in the tavern. No one has a clue. That barkeep's tight lipped." The man grunted. "Least he's been keeping the drinks flowing. Lord knows we need 'em."

"I... I'm not sure. I guess we'll be finding out what our mission will be."

Another person appeared. A woman in grey robes much like his. She carried an almost identical staff to Xavier, though a bit shorter, and had a wide-eyed look about her. When she saw Xavier and Howard, she smiled, giving a small wave. Xavier struggled to pick her age. Mid-twenties, perhaps. She had red hair, sharp green eyes, and a spot of freckles on her cheek.

Though she didn't look like as much of a fighter as Howard did, Xavier wasn't about to underestimate her. Anyone who'd made it here had been through... well. A lot.

That was another thing he'd tried not to think about. The real reason he hadn't talked to any of these people. Xavier had killed. *Goblins.* Fifty of the little green bastards. But these people? Unless they'd had opponents like Julian, well... then they'd killed another human being to get here. They'd been thrown into a one-on-one deathmatch and not only decided to fight for their lives against another human, they'd come out on top.

Right now, if he were thrown into that situation, knowing what he did—that he would be struck down if he refused to fight—he would have done it. He would have fought. For himself. For the world. He shouldn't judge those around him if he would do the exact same thing, but it still gave him an odd feeling in his stomach when he thought about it.

I'm surrounded by murderers.

The woman sat next to Howard. She gave them both a smile. "I'm Siobhan. I guess the two of you are my party?" She had a slight accent. Was that Irish? He supposed it must be, with a name like Siobhan, that red hair, and those freckles. Though the accent sounded a bit diluted, like she didn't live there anymore.

"Howard," Howard said. "This here's Xavier." The man frowned. "A party is like a team, right?" He scratched his beard. "I've never played one of them video games, though people keep telling me that's what everything has turned into." He shook his head in obvious dismay.

Siobhan's smile didn't slip away. "Yeah, a party's a team. Looks like we have two mages and a warrior." She looked back at the door. "I wonder who'll step in next."

Howard raised an eyebrow. "You're taking all this well, aren't you?"

Siobhan shrugged. "I figured I should either embrace it or I'd go a bit insane." She smiled, a bit too brightly.

"Suppose that's... healthy." Howard's raised eyebrow didn't drop until the next person arrived.

It was another basic warrior. To Xavier's surprise, the man looked younger than him. Couldn't have been more than sixteen. He was the youngest person Xavier had seen so far. Sam had said that Denizens gained access to the System at sixteen.

Everyone from long-integrated worlds will be his age, won't they? Which means, what, we'll be pitted against teenagers? It was a strange thought, not that he was all that much older. Though four years felt like a large gap when it was the difference between a teenager and an adult.

The kid had dark hair long in need of a haircut and a whisp of stubble on his chin that looked like a weak attempt at a beard. He gave a small wave. "Hello." He had his bow slung over his shoulder and a hand on the hilt of his sword. He dropped the hand. "I'm Justin."

"Hey, Justin!" Siobhan beamed. Xavier wasn't sure how she was so calm, let alone happy. "Come on over, meet the party!" She patted the last chair in the line, then introduced herself and the others. "We've only exchanged a couple of words. I don't think I've chatted to any of you down in the tavern yet." She looked up at the stage. "I think we still have a few minutes before orientation starts. Maybe we could go around, say something about ourselves?"

Xavier shut his eyes and suppressed a sigh. This reminded him of sitting in a new class at the start of the term and going around a circle one by one. He'd never really known what to say then, and he didn't know what to say now.

"I guess I'll start, then. Like I said, my name's Siobhan. I am— well, I suppose I *was*—an Assistant Marketing Manager... which sounds more important than it is. It was for a small, indie game company. That's actually why I know a bit about them. I... play a lot of video games in my spare time." She rubbed the back of her head. "I'm also a 2nd dan black belt in Taekwondo. I used to fight competitively. In my teens..." She looked at Justin. "What about you?"

Justin blinked. "Uh. I'm still in high school. I don't really play much video games." He looked at the sword at his hip. "I'm actually an Olympic fencer, so when I'm not studying, I'm training for that."

Xavier frowned. Looked at Justin. *An Olympic fencer, really?* He hadn't expected that from the kid. Then again, he hadn't expected Siobhan to be a 2nd dan black belt. Though he supposed he *should* have expected something like this. There had to be a reason these people survived their deathmatches, after all. *Did*

Justin have his rapier, foil, or whatever it's called, on him when the system integration started? He didn't think they'd be effective in a fight, but what did he know? *And did Siobhan... kick her opponent to death?* He bit on the inside of his lip. *I don't think I should think about this,* he told himself. *If we're going to be a team, I need to learn how to trust them, not imagine how they might have killed people.*

"Guess it's my turn." Howard had a gruff, somewhat clipped manner. "I'm a cop. Was a cop. Before all this." He sniffed, arms crossed at his chest again. "Got a wife and two kids back home." His voice cracked, ever so slightly. "Worried sick about 'em."

Siobhan nodded, her smile slipping. She ran a hand through her hair. "I suppose... that's something we should mention... I've got a little sister out there, somewhere. Only fourteen. My parents... I just hope they're with her."

Justin looked away from them. "Just me and my mum." He sniffed. "Hope she's all right."

After a moment, their eyes fell on Xavier. He hadn't said a word yet. Not since he'd spoken with Howard before the other two arrived. Honestly, he'd been hoping the orientation would start before he had to speak. *A cop, a martial artist, an Olympic fencer, and I'm a... writer. Yeah, they're not going to think much of me, are they? At least, not until they see me fight...*

"I am—was—a student at university." Xavier didn't mention where. None of the others had. "I wanted to be a writer, but... that doesn't seem like it'll be an option. Really." He scratched the back of his head. "My mum's out there, somewhere..." He probably should have sounded more concerned. He was a little concerned, to be honest, after he'd heard what might be happening to the rest of the world, with Earth not being locked and people able to invade. But mostly, he knew he needed to focus on what was in front of him. He wouldn't be able to help her, or anyone else, if he got too stuck in his own head about it.

Besides, they'd grown distant over the past few years. Ever since he'd admitted what he wanted to do with his life, really. The others waited, staring at him, as though they were expecting more. Maybe they wanted to know if he was secretly trained as an assassin or something. Surely they were wondering how he'd made it here.

After a few moments of awkward silence, a notification appeared.

Orientation begins now.

On the stage, a man wearing glowing, golden full-plate armour appeared. He was ten-feet tall, though he looked human, and... Xavier frowned, narrowing his eyes. Was he *transparent*?

Chapter 21
Greetings, Champions of Earth!

"HOLOGRAM," SIOBHAN MUTTERED. "GOTTA BE A hologram."

Howard grunted. "The world's gone to hell, it has..."

"I think we should be quiet," Justin whispered.

Xavier straightened in his chair, looking at the bearded hologram.

For a few seconds, it just stood there, then it began to speak. "Greetings, Champions of Earth! And welcome to the Greater Universe!" The hologram had a deep and commanding voice. Xavier could easily imagine him as the general of some intergalactic space army of knights.

What, like the Jedi? I suppose I can move things with my mind, though I don't have a laser sword... Maybe he has a laser sword.

"Are you the one who's finally gonna tell us what the hell's going on here?" Howard asked.

"You are each World Defenders of the Planet Earth. The few who selflessly not only chose to walk the path that would let you fight for your world, but the path to becoming a *Champion*!" the hologram replied.

"I don't think it can hear us." Siobhan stood up. She stepped over to the stage, went on her tiptoes, and waved a hand in front of the tall hologram's face. Well, a fair bit below it as she couldn't reach.

Justin's eyes widened. He looked like he wanted to pull her back down.

The hologram continued, "Look to the people beside you! They are your party. You have each suffered through gruelling tests of character and might to get where you are now. Of those on Earth, approximately eight million of you chose to become Champions." The Hologram didn't so much as glance down at Siobhan.

Howard grunted. "Well, that's bloody useful."

Xavier frowned, taking in the hologram's words. With his Intelligence at 29, the math was easy enough. With a population of eight billion in the world, only 0.1 percent of people had chosen Champion. *One in one thousand.* He supposed that wasn't an indicator of how many had chosen to fight for their world, instead of the other two moral factions he'd remembered seeing, as Champion hadn't been the only option.

Billions of people might have chosen Support or Soldier roles. Though he'd honestly expected more people to have gone down this route than they had. He bit his lip. Then again... *Maybe they actually read the entire description, unlike me.*

Still, eight million people... was a lot. There must be other hallways like the one with his room in it. There were thousands of rooms in that hallway, but not *millions.* There must have been other instances of it, just like there were no doubt countless instances of this room.

The hologram kept talking. "Of those eight million, half made it to the second test. Their proving quest."

Xavier's heart sank, and it felt like he'd been punched in the gut. He saw the others all drop their heads, as though coming to the same realisation as he did at the same time. *Four million dead...*

"Of the four million who began their proving quest, roughly one million of you made it *here.*" The hologram smiled. "To the Tower of Champions!" He raised his hands, voice booming around the space.

Xavier shut his eyes. Taking it all in. Things he'd known already. Things Sam had told him. But now he had a number to put to the dead.

Seven million... The chances of me making it here, out of everyone on earth... One in about ten thousand.

Xavier leant back in his chair. He frowned. *The exact same odds Sam gave the people of Earth for surviving, are the same odds of me getting into this chair. Of all the Champions of Earth being here, right now.* When he thought about it in those terms, it was oddly comforting. *If I can make it here, then maybe the people of Earth can make it through this. At least... those of us who are left. And those of us who survive.*

The orientation went on like that for a little while. Much of what the hologram told them were things Xavier had learnt by trial and error—how spells worked, how to select from a skills list, how to gain upgrade quests for spells and unlock skills, without any further information than the basics—and about the wider universe, which Sam had told him about.

The hologram didn't mention titles, however, which Xavier found interesting.

Then the hologram had mentioned those under the age of sixteen who were yet to gain access to the System were in "Safe Zones," taken care of by people who'd selected the Support role. Howard and Siobhan had both visibly relaxed at this. Howard no doubt thinking of his two children, and Siobhan, her little sister. Xavier hadn't realised how tense Siobhan's shoulders had been until they'd loosened. *Maybe she isn't taking this all as well as it seems.* She still stood by the stage, examining the hologram with interest.

The hologram didn't mention anything about their world not being locked down, which Xavier found strange. He wanted to ask questions about that, but they'd already confirmed the hologram couldn't hear them. That it was just a recording. Likely every other orientation of Champions from Earth—and there would be roughly

250 thousand of them—would be experiencing the exact same words.

Finally, the hologram pointed at each of them—at least, it pointed at each of their *chairs*. Siobhan, still standing, smirked with a quick shake of her head when the hologram pointed straight past her and at the chair she no longer occupied.

"In a moment, the four of you will take your first step inside the Tower of Champions!"

"I thought we were already in the Tower of Champions," Howard muttered.

Xavier was thinking the same thing.

The hologram stepped aside. Behind it, a door appeared. "In the future, the room you sit in right now will be your staging area. Here, you will gain rudimentary access to the System Shop and be able to purchase a variety of items appropriate for your levels. The room will also expand, turning into one where you may perform physical and mental training to naturally increase your attributes to gain an advantage against your peers, as well as spar with your fellow party members."

The hologram waved a hand downward. Four small books appeared. "This book is your Tower of Champions manual, and it is specifically tailored to an audience of people from a newly integrated world. It will explain much of what I already have, as well as how F Grade Denizens can create Lesser Spirit Coins."

F Grade Denizens. I suppose that wasn't how the System was grading me, then... And we can create Lesser Spirit Coins?

Siobhan snatched up one of the books, flipping through the pages. Xavier stood and grabbed his. It was a thin, leatherbound book with English script on the cover that read: "Tower of Champions Manual: New Denizens Edition." He frowned, depositing it into his Storage Ring with a thought.

The hologram motioned to the door. "Your first mission in the Tower of Champions is to reach and clear floors one to ten. Each floor is filled with monsters and enemies of increasing levels, and each floor has a Champion of its own that you must defeat before gaining access to the next floor. When you have cleared the tenth floor, you will be allowed to return to Earth for a short period of time between missions.

"In your manuals, you will find more information about the typical completion time for each floor, and the mission as a whole, depending upon the experience of the Denizens undertaking said mission. Clearing each floor will garner your party rewards such as items, skill points, and bonus Mastery Points. There are also rewards for being the first to clear a floor, and the first to clear the entire mission.

"However, you are being ranked not only against your peers on Planet Earth, but against other Denizens from four other planets, all of whom have spent at least ten generations within the Greater Universe. Therefore, it will be very unlikely for anyone from your world to gain a reward for being the first to clear a floor, and even less likely for you to finish the mission in a good time." The holo-gram clapped its hands together. "Speaking of time, the clock is ticking! The mission begins now."

The hologram disappeared.

"I was expecting..." Howard waved a hand in a circle. "*More.*" The man stood, stepped over to his manual, and bent over to grab it. "Should we read through this first?"

Xavier's gaze turned toward the door, locking onto it. *There are rewards for being the fastest to clear each floor...*

"What was that about being pitted against other planets?" Justin asked. "Planets that have been around this System for *gener-ations*? That... that doesn't seem fair, does it?"

"Life isn't fair, kid," Howard said. "Never has been. There's always going to be those who start off better than others just because of where they were born, and who they were born to. On Earth, the rich got richer and the poor stayed poor. Looks like the same is true of this Greater Universe. The powerful get more powerful, hand that power to their offspring, and the weak... get crushed under their boots."

"That's..." Justin swallowed. "An inspiring speech."

"That's assuming their lifespans haven't been improved," Siobhan said musingly. "With enough levels, people might live longer. Hundreds, maybe thousands of years. Think of the power they would gain... They wouldn't just hand that out."

Xavier was still staring at the door. Why hadn't they stepped toward it yet? "That just means we'll need to scrape and claw for every inch we can." He stepped toward the door. Grabbed the handle.

Tower of Champions.
The Tower of Champions is where World
Defenders prove themselves, fighting for
rewards, upgrades, and powerups.
Open Levels:
Level 1 of 1,000.
Would you like to enter?

One thousand levels. The first mission was only for *ten.* Would they eventually have to clear every single one of them? *That's a lot.* Xavier tilted his head to the side. *It doesn't say I have to enter with my party... That's good to know. Not that I'm going to leave them behind.*

"Shouldn't we talk about our classes? You know, come up with some sort of battle strategy?" Siobhan was still staring at her manual, which she'd opened. She pointed at something on the page. "It says it will take about a week for a party from a newly integrated team to clear the first floor." Her eyes widened. "It might take up to *three months* for us to get through all ten! That's... assuming we survive."

"Does it say anything about what we'll face?" Howard asked.

Siobhan shook her head. "It says the monsters and enemies that spawn on each level will vary depending on the party that steps through and that... if we exit the instance before clearing the level, the monsters will respawn."

"Respawn?" Howard asked. "That mean they'll be back, even if we killed 'em?"

Siobhan nodded. "Guess we shouldn't step back out, then. Unless we want to take advantage of farming them."

"Farming?" Howard asked.

Xavier cut them off. "If it doesn't say what they are, then we need to move. We haven't got time to stand here and talk. The parties from the other four worlds will already be in their instances, killing monsters!"

"Calm down, kid. You can't expect us to clear it faster than them, can you?" Howard frowned.

Xavier tilted his chin up. He summoned his staff from inside his Storage Ring. "Not if we stay standing around here. And please, don't call me *kid*," he said, thinking, *even though I am less than half your age...*

He bit his lip. Should he tell them about his titles? That he had higher stats than a normal Level 4? That made him realise he hadn't even *scanned* the others. That should have been the first thing he'd done when they entered the room. He supposed he'd been feeling a bit awkward about chatting with strangers and knew what level they would be anyway.

He did so now.

{Human – Level 4}
{Human – Level 4}
{Human – Level 4}

I should have expected that. So far, everyone he'd scanned had been Level 4. *Unless they have titles like mine... which they literally can't... I'm effectively at least thirteen levels stronger than them.*

Xavier took his hand off the door and sighed. The notification asking if he wanted to enter the first floor of the Tower of Champions disappeared. He looked Howard, Siobhan, and Justin in the eye. "I think I need to tell the three of you something."

Chapter 22
I'm Not That Kind of Mage

STANDING BEFORE THE DOOR THAT WOULD HAVE THEM ENTER the first floor of the Tower of Champions, Xavier explained to his party members what different titles he possessed, and what that meant for his stats.

For the most part, they'd looked at him with scepticism, but as he had no reason to lie, they seemed to take him at his word.

"Your stats are *really* that high?" Siobhan said for the third time. "That's such an interesting gaming mechanic! Having the *first* to achieve something gain a reward like that!"

"Sounds unfair to me," Justin muttered. "If you get a strong start, no one will be able to catch up."

That's exactly my plan.

Howard clapped the kid on the shoulder. "Remember what I said? That's life. Learn to live with it or don't."

"Whatever it is," Xavier said. "I..." He swallowed. He wasn't good at talking to strangers, and what he was about to say would sound incredibly absurd and arrogant. "I think if any party from Earth has a chance of clearing these floors faster than those from established worlds, it's ours."

"Because of you?" Howard raised an eyebrow.

Xavier nodded. "Yes. Because of me." He locked eyes with

Howard. "You know about the invaders, don't you? That our world isn't locked from others being able to travel toward it?"

Howard grunted. "Word got around. 'Bout the only thing they talked about down in the tavern."

"Then you know how seriously we need an advantage. You want to get back to your kids? Your wife?" He looked at Siobhan. "You want to get back to your sister?" At Justin. "And your mum? The faster we clear these floors, this mission, the faster we get to Earth and help protect our people." He gripped his staff tightly. "That book says it will take us three months, but if we don't return for that long, it might be too late. Who knows what state the world will be in."

It felt like an awful thing to do to a world. Remove those who wished to protect it the most, when it was most in need of protection.

Howard raised his chin. "Right, then." He looked at the other two. "Xavier's right. Whether we can clear these floors faster than those rich bastards from old worlds remains to be seen, but I want to get back to my family."

Siobhan nodded. "I want to make sure my sister's okay. And... I want to see if we can do this."

Justin drew his sword. Looked down at it. "I've been practising fencing most of my life. Since I was seven." He gave a small grin. "I'm used to winning tournaments. Maybe this will be no different."

Howard smirked, giving a rare chuckle. "That's the spirit, kid. All right, then. We've dallied enough." He motioned to Xavier. "Lead the way."

Siobhan raised a finger, stalling them. She still had the book open in one hand, her gaze locked on it. "Remember what the hologram said about the System Shop during the orientation? And about this room? Apparently, the second we step out and step back in, that's when this place will change." She looked up from her book at Xavier. "Are you sure we shouldn't check out the shop first?"

Xavier frowned. He had over a thousand Lesser Spirit Coins, and he supposed the others might have some coins on them as well. He looked down at his grey robes. At his staff with the clear crystal at its head. He supposed new gear *would* be a good thing, but he didn't want to delay. He could imagine the four of them looking at the shop's contents for ages, trying to figure out what the best things to buy were. That would only slow them down.

He supposed that was another thing those parties from established worlds would have over them. He had to imagine that they would all have much, much better starting gear.

Siobhan, Howard, and Justin were looking to him, as though he were the leader. *I guess I am the strongest.* He knew what he would do if he were alone, so that's what he said. "I'm sure we'd find something useful in the shop, but it would slow us down. If we want a chance at being the first to clear this floor, we need to start moving *now*." He touched the doorhandle. Text appeared in his vision, asking what floor he wished to enter.

Floor one.

Xavier was transported out of the orientation room and found himself standing in the middle of what appeared to be a cabin. It wasn't particularly big. There was a bit of clear space on the ground. There wasn't much in the room. Just a round, wooden table with four chairs. There were two doors: one behind him, and one ahead of him.

You are currently in a Safe Zone. You party has a combined 24 hours they are allowed to spend within this Safe Zone, starting in 5 minutes.

The others didn't take too long to arrive.

"A Safe Zone?" Justin muttered.

"If it's anything like in a video game, it means we shouldn't be attacked by enemies while we're here," Siobhan said.

"Awfully convenient," Howard grunted. He walked up to what Xavier thought of as the front door and opened it. It was dark outside the cabin, almost pitch black, though Xavier could make out some trees.

Justin stepped up behind Howard, peering through the door. "That looks... ominous."

"We don't appear to be in the tower anymore." Howard closed the door. Four minutes remained before the countdown on the Safe Zone would begin.

"This door leads back to the room we just left," Siobhan said.

"We're still in the tower," Xavier said. "It's just not what we expected it to be." Considering all he'd seen so far, a "floor" of the tower containing a cabin and a dark forest wasn't about to take him by surprise. This System was powerful enough to change their entire world and, eventually, the entire universe—according to Sam the barkeep.

He was sure it had the power to create anything.

Xavier walked over to the open door. "Now come on. Let's get moving."

The others gave each other wary looks, but they didn't complain. Xavier gripped his staff tightly and checked his stats before stepping out, wondering how they might change by the time he was out of here.

XAVIER COLLINS
Age: 20
Race: Human
Grade: F
Moral Faction: World Defender (Planet Earth)
Class: Mage
Level 4
Strength: 26
Speed: 22
Toughness: 32
Intelligence: 29
Willpower: 34
Spirit: 36

Mastery Points for this level: 100/12,000
Available Spirit Energy: 4000/4000
Available Skill Points: 0
Free stat points remaining: 0
Titles: Bloodied Hands, Born on a Battlefield,
Settlement Defender, Quester, 100 Stats, First
to 100 Stats, First Defender of Planet Earth
Spells List:
Spiritual Trifecta – Rank 2
Heavy Telekinesis – Rank 2
Skills List:
Staff Mastery – Rank 1
Lesser Spirit Coins: 1,231

Xavier nodded minutely as he looked at his stats. Since he'd sorted his Lesser Spirit Coins out of their purses and put them back into his Storage Ring, he'd been able to see them whenever he looked at all of his information. He still had no concept of how much the coins were valued, but he supposed they couldn't be worth a great deal if they were called "Lesser" Spirit Coins.

The hologram said something about being able to create our own coins. That the information will be in the manuals we received. He just didn't feel like he had the time to actually look.

We need to move forward.

It wasn't just that Xavier wanted to be the first to clear this floor and gain a reward for it, though that was high up in his mind as a priority, taking up almost all of his mental space.

He also felt... a thrill of excitement. He *wanted* to do this. *Wanted* to fight. Xavier couldn't wait to see how much stronger he had become after gaining all of those titles. Couldn't wait to see what difference it would make to his spells.

Xavier hadn't wanted to practise with Heavy Telekinesis while in his room or out in the hall. It wasn't a very precise spell, and he would just end up breaking furniture, though he wasn't sure how the cooldown had been changed by his jump in stats.

Spiritual Trifecta, however, was something he'd used a few times, trying to see what the new cooldown was like, as his Spirit attribute had increased by 20, all the way to 36, making it his strongest attribute.

When he'd tested the spell, his cooldown had gone down from 24 all the way to 15. It didn't regenerate as fast as it had when it had been Spiritual Guidance, but it was a huge step up. And it still made him feel exhausted when it wore off, but the fact that Willpower was his second strongest stat made that weakness far easier to handle.

The ground was soft underfoot as he stepped out of the cavern. His eyes adjusted to the darkness of the forest, and he gazed about, straining his ears, wondering what monsters they might face.

Part of him had expected a notification to appear. Something that told them how many enemies they would need to kill, but nothing showed up.

He heard the others behind him, footsteps in damp earth. Howard stood to one side of him. Justin at the other. Both with their swords in hand, steel bare, glinting in the faint moonlight that filtered into the clearing where the cabin sat.

Siobhan came to stand behind him. Like Xavier, she was a mage. He would have assumed someone with a background in Taekwondo would rather choose warrior, but she had foregone that. *She plays a lot of video games. Maybe she's always wanted to wield magic.*

Howard looked Xavier up and down. "Perhaps I should go first. You're some sort of magical ranged fighter, aren't you? Isn't that what basic mages are? And I can't imagine those robes would soak up too much damage."

Though Howard had said he didn't know anything about video games, he'd likely spent a lot of time talking about everything with people down in the tavern.

Xavier smiled. "I'm not that kind of mage." He glanced behind him at Siobhan. "Does the book say anything about the first floor?"

"Unfortunately, no. There isn't any information but the timeframe."

"A week for a party from a newly integrated world," Xavier said, remembering what the woman had told them. "What about for a party from an established world?"

Siobhan was quiet. She bit her lip before speaking. "It says... they would take one to three days."

Xavier nodded. "Then we need to be faster than that."

He took a step forward when he heard a rustling to his left. A big, dark shape bounded out of the trees and leapt straight at him. Xavier saw a flash of bared teeth and outstretched claws.

The beast looked like some sort of black puma.

Chapter 23
You Want to Do This All by Yourself?

THE MONSTER WAS ON HIM BEFORE HE HAD A CHANCE TO scan it, but Xavier was still faster. He cast Spiritual Trifecta as he heard a roar permeate the air and watched as the big, black cat soared toward him.

Perhaps it thinks I'm the weakest because I'm not wearing armour.

A silver sheen enveloped Xavier. Power flooded through him. It infused every single one of his muscles. It infused his mind, making it work ever faster. It infused his magic, making it *stronger*. With his Willpower at 34 and his Spirit at 36, the Spiritual Trifecta spell made him feel stronger than *ever*.

Grasping his staff with both hands, Xavier swung it straight at the head of the enemy monster before it could reach him. His staff crashed through the big cat's head. Blood splattered his robes.

The roar that had been unleashed from the beast's throat died the instant Xavier's staff made contact.

You have defeated a Level 10 Black Puma!
You have gained 1,000 Mastery Points.
You have gained 1,000 Spirit Energy.

That thing was Level 10?

Xavier stared at the enemy he'd just killed. The enemy he'd taken down in a single strike. He shook his head, eyes wide. The speed at which he'd struck the beast, the damage he'd done... he knew part of that was from having Staff Mastery adding 5 percent to his Speed and 5 percent to his damage when wielding a staff, but the rest?

My higher stats and Spiritual Trifecta. He couldn't help but feel a little... invincible. Especially since the others were gaping at him, mouths wide.

"That... that beast was Level 10!" It was Siobhan who spoke. She must have had a chance to scan it before it had been killed.

"You killed a Level 10 monster in one hit?" Justin stepped over to the beast. "I barely even saw the thing coming and it's already dead." He raised his sword, gaze darting about the trees. "Do you think there will be more?"

Howard frowned, his eyebrows pinching together, eyes narrowing as he searched the trees. "Was lying in wait. Knew we'd come out of there." He shook his head. "If this is what other parties will have to deal with..." He ran his left hand through his hair. "Don't know how many will survive."

Xavier knelt by the Black Puma. It was huge. Far larger than any big cat he'd ever seen. Though the only ones he'd seen in the flesh were at zoos. Still, it must have been twice the size of a lion. He touched it. The monster disappeared into his Storage Ring.

"You're... keeping it?" Justin asked.

"We might need the food later," Xavier said, standing back up.

"Or we might be able to sell it at the System Shop," Siobhan mused. "And buy better, cooked food. Can't imagine puma meat will be all that tasty."

"We need to keep moving." Xavier didn't wait for the others. He walked straight into the trees. Perhaps he should have been wary, especially as Spiritual Trifecta had just worn off, a wave of exhaustion slamming into him—a wave that had become easier to ignore—but he didn't want to waste any time.

It took a moment for him to hear their footsteps catch up. "Did you guys gain any Mastery Points from that kill?" Siobhan asked.

"N-No," Justin said. "I didn't."

"Neither did I," Howard added.

Siobhan made a "hmm" noise. "Suppose that's because neither of us attacked it. That means Mastery Points aren't shared just because we're in the same party. We'll have to participate in kills if we want to gain levels."

Xavier's gaze tracked through the trees. He wished the others would stop talking. He doubted that was the only Black Puma around. If they were silent, maybe they'd be able to hear the next one coming. He wondered what might have happened if the beast had launched itself at one of the others. Would they have died? Would the System really have done that? Put a monster so powerful right outside the Safe Zone?

If this were a normal team, it could have seriously injured or killed one of them until the others got organised. If it did kill one of them, they'd only have three people in their party now. That made him wonder what might happen if someone lost their entire party. Would they be able to join another, or would they have to clear the floor on their own?

I'm not going to let any of them die. If another Black Puma leapt out of those trees, he would be fast enough, even without Spiritual Trifecta. *Heavy Telekinesis could throw it backward, negating its sneak attack before it reached us.*

As he searched for their next opponent, in the back of his mind he worried about how this was all going to go. He hadn't thought about how Mastery Points would be split. If he took out all the enemies, then his party wouldn't get a chance to gain any levels. He would be taking every single kill, leaving nothing for them.

That wouldn't only stop them from gaining Mastery Points, it would stop them from gaining combat experience. He frowned, thinking about the predicament. He figured he had two options.

He could try and solo this floor—in which case they would be better off staying back in the Safe Zone—or he could try and help them level up at the same rate as him.

Xavier turned the problem over in his mind. *If it takes other parties from established worlds one to three days to complete the first floor, then we need to do it faster than that. I can't hang around waiting for each of them to strike an enemy before I kill it.*

He halted, stopping midstride. He heard the others stop behind him a moment later.

"What is it?" Howard whispered.

Xavier turned to face all three of them. He wasn't used to taking a leadership role. Wasn't used to any of this, to be honest. He didn't know if this was the right choice, but all he could do was go with his gut. "I think... I think the three of you should return to the Safe Zone."

"What?" Howard stepped toward him. With that sword in his hand, he looked rather threatening. Xavier felt a thrill run through him at the prospect of violence but doubted the man would attack him. "You want to do this all by yourself?"

"If you do that, we'll stagnate," Justin said. "We won't gain a single level."

Siobhan narrowed her eyes. "He knows that."

Xavier sighed. "I don't want to deprive you of Mastery Points, and I certainly don't want you three to stagnate." He pursed his lips. "I'll need the three of you. On the higher floors. I'm sure of it." He wasn't sure of it, but he wanted them to *feel* needed. They had to know they would be useful later; otherwise, they would fight him on this.

"The faster I clear this floor, the better. If... if I'm able to do it faster than parties from the other worlds, then we'll know I've done the right thing. We'll be able to gain a lead on them. I'll gain more levels alone than with the three of you with me, and that would give me enough strength to do the *next* floor faster, and the next."

Siobhan put a hand on her hip, the other holding her staff. "You want to clear *more* floors without us?"

Xavier nodded. "If I can clear this first floor faster than any other party, that will *prove* that this plan will work. Then I'll clear the next four floors on my own. Once I've reached the sixth floor, I'll bring the three of you back in and level you up. The monsters will no doubt be much stronger by then, and it won't take the three of you long to gain levels faster with my help." He looked at Siobhan. "You said the floor will respawn if we step out, then back in?"

Siobhan bowed her head. "Only until we clear it. Which means if you clear this floor, we won't be able to re-enter it."

"That's all right. If we gain a big enough lead, we can farm the sixth floor. Fight monsters without fully clearing it, then have them respawn. If I'm right, it will gain all of you a *lot* of levels."

Howard frowned. The man was good at that. Had the right face for a frown to look sceptical, disappointed, and slightly angry at the same time. "What happens if you can't clear this floor faster? What if you reach the end and don't get a reward?"

Xavier noticed the man didn't ask "What if you can't succeed?" They'd seen what he could do when the Level 10 Black Puma had come at them. They knew he could handle this. "Then there will be no point trying to clear the second floor on my own. I'll already be too late. Whatever party did the first floor faster would gain a reward, making them even stronger. Which means I can bring you three in on the second floor."

"The rich get richer..." Justin muttered.

Siobhan nodded at Xavier. "It makes sense." The manual appeared in her hand, summoned straight from her own Storage Ring. She nodded again, staring down at it. "I'll read this, back to front, while you clear the level. I'm sure it's got a lot of information inside we can use. And if I read it, I can just give you the information you need without you having to slow down." She tilted her head to the side. "I don't want to try stepping back through the door to the Staging Room in the cabin, in case it changes things in here, but once you've cleared this floor, the rest of us can train in our Staging Room and look at the System Shop while you clear the *next* floor."

Xavier sighed in relief, glad the woman approved of his plan.

As she spoke, it got the other two nodding. Justin, who'd looked disappointed a moment ago, now looked determined. Howard's face was fairly clear of emotion, but at least his frown was gone.

"I guess that makes us your support team, then," Justin said.

Howard grunted. He stared Xavier in the eye. "Don't die out there. And if this plan is to work, you've gotta move. I'll get the others back to the cabin. We'll hole up there. Been standing around talking long enough. If you're gonna do this, you've gotta do it now." With his sword, he pointed through the trees. "*Go!*"

Chapter 24
Sharp Claws and Dagger-Like Fangs

As much as Xavier appreciated Howard pushing him on, he wasn't sure how long the other three would be holed up in that cabin. He hoped it would only be a few hours, but if it was longer, they would definitely need something to eat.

So he withdrew a few things from his Storage Ring that he'd pilfered from the cafeteria, plopping enough food and drink onto the ground to get them through the day without having to go hungry.

Siobhan smiled with a shake of her head. Justin's eyebrows shot up. And Howard, a cop, pointedly looked *away* from the tray of donuts.

Once he left the three of them with something to eat while hiding in the Safe Zone, Xavier left, thoughts turning through his mind. They'd barely been walking for a few minutes from the cabin, but he hadn't seen a sign of any other monsters.

Is another one of those Black Pumas stalking me? he wondered. *And will all the enemies be Level 10? Will they be lower, higher?* He sighed. *One way to find out.*

He figured the best way to find the enemy was to make as much noise as possible. Though, of course, the party had already managed that with all the talking they'd done.

Xavier started with a jog. Then, moments later, he was sprinting through the trees. As he ran, he focused on his steps. On his technique. He had been running a lot for the past few days, yet he hadn't gained any Skill Quests, yet he'd seen that Running, like Staff Mastery, was a skill.

I wonder if Justin has gained a Sword Mastery skill, as he was an Olympic fencer before all this. And could Siobhan gain an Unarmed Combat skill?

Xavier, however, didn't get much time to practise his running technique before he was attacked again. He heard movement in the dark trees to his right. Now he'd been out of the cabin for a while, his night vision had adjusted quite well, and the moonlight filtering through the canopy above was more than enough for him to see by.

Another Black Puma. Xavier grinned. He'd already reached the end of his cooldown for Spiritual Trifecta, and he'd gained more than enough Spirit Energy from the last kill to refill what he used.

Crack.

You have defeated a Level 10 Black Puma!
You have gained 1,000 Mastery Points.
You have gained 1,000 Spirit Energy.

The Black Puma went down instantly, just as the first had. This time, Xavier had seen its vertically slitted eyes widen as his staff had come down to crack its skull. He almost felt bad for the beast, which was clearly outmatched, but he couldn't let feelings of sentimentality into this process, not if he were to clear this floor fast enough.

Three members of your party have entered the
Safe Zone. The Safe Zone timer begins now.
Once the Safe Zone timer reaches its end, you
and your party will either be ejected from the
Safe Zone and never permitted to return,

making you and your party unable to exit this floor until it is cleared, or you and your party will need to exit to the Staging Room.

A timer counting down from twenty-four hours appeared in Xavier's vision. He dismissed it but sensed he could recall it if necessary. *That will give me an idea of how long this is taking,* he thought.

He wondered about the text that had shown up. If clearing this floor took more than a day, the others would have to leave the Safe Zone, or they would *all* have to leave the first floor. At least, that was his understanding of it.

If all the Safe Zones on other floors have the same time limit and restrictions, it will be very difficult to carry them through other floors. He got the feeling they could only gain a reward for the floor if they were in it when it was cleared. *Good thing they'll be staying in the Staging Room, like Siobhan said.*

He quickly deposited the Black Puma into his Storage Ring before standing tall and straining his ears. *Doesn't sound like there are any more around here. Then again, it's not like I heard the first two before they came for me. Who says I'll hear the next one?*

Xavier sighed and started running again. He didn't focus on running silently. Quite the opposite. In fact, he started stomping down ever more heavily across the forest underbrush, crushing twigs, sticks, and branches underfoot. Crumpling leaves and kicking stones, scuffing his cheap leather shoes across the ground, hoping they would last him. *This definitely won't earn me a Skill Quest.*

As he ran, he summoned the countdown timer, wanting to try something out. He knew that some video games let you alter the HUD, or heads-up-display, moving information across a screen wherever one wanted. This new reality *wasn't* a video game, but it had sure worked a lot like one so far.

After a moment, he managed to will the countdown timer to appear in the corner of his vision. It was out of the way, and he was sure it wouldn't bother him during a fight. But it was also easily in view if he ever wished to look at it.

Two minutes passed when he heard footsteps padding across the forest floor to his left. He glanced over. Saw another Black Puma running toward him. Looking at how fast it was running, the puma seemed slightly slower than him.

I could kill it in a second. Or... He thought about how many more Mastery Points he needed and that he needed to clear this level as fast as possible. *If it takes an established party a day, or three, to clear this floor, that could be because the Black Pumas are spread out far and wide through the forest.* That was assuming there weren't *other* monsters around this place—and he knew there would still be a boss for him to find.

He thought all this through as the Black Puma trailed behind him. Xavier kept glancing over his shoulder and listening intently to the beast bounding through the underbrush, hoping it wouldn't lose interest in him when it realised it couldn't catch up.

It takes a normal party from a world like mine at least a week. That's probably not just because there's a lot of ground to cover, but because they would need a lot of rest and recovery between each fight. A Level 10 monster would no doubt be able to grievously wound someone only at Level 4. If they survived, they would need time to heal, especially if they lacked access to food. And they wouldn't have as much Toughness as me.

Xavier smiled, the idea coming to him as the Black Puma showed no sign of ceasing its chase. *If I keep running through the forest, gain more and more of these Black Pumas' aggression and have them chase me, then take them all down at once as fast as I can, it will be far faster than me stopping each time. And I probably run faster than almost anyone at my level, and everyone else doing this will be Level 4.*

The only way someone would have *more* Speed than Xavier at his level would be if they'd started with a good amount, then added all their free stat points at each level into it. That, or they'd been able to gain a *lot* more than him by training naturally, like he'd done in the hallway. Though he got the feeling there must be a limit on how many attribute points someone could gain from that kind of training.

At least, I hope there is. Because if I'm wrong, there could be people way stronger than me at the same level who don't possess any titles at all.

It wasn't a thought he liked having, so he pushed it away, sure it couldn't be true.

After roughly two and a half more minutes, Xavier heard another Black Puma chasing him. When he looked over his shoulder, he now saw *two* of the monsters on his tail. He couldn't help but smile and laugh. His running hadn't faltered since he'd started. He wasn't sweating, breathing heavily, or feeling tired at all. Of course, it had only been a few minutes, but he wondered how long he might be able to run like this...

Just as he'd guessed, another two and a half minutes later, and a *third* Black Puma was chasing him.

They appear evenly spaced out through the forest, though I wonder how many directions they're in. So far, he'd been following a rough path through the woods. According to Little Red Riding Hood, he should have been safe as long as he *didn't* stray from this path. But so far, that didn't seem to be the case.

Are all the enemies across this path? That seems... a little easy. Did he just have to keep running, then he would eventually have every Black Puma following him? Did it take a week for a normal team to fight each one of them because they were so weak and slow, having to regain health between every fight, and not running from one monster to another? *That's probably why more established parties can manage it in a day, by speeding from one encounter to the next.*

If he was right about how the floor worked—with all the Black Pumas spread across the same path, with some sort of Boss Puma at the end—then all he would need to do was keep running until he'd gathered them all. Or, at least, until he'd gathered as many as he figured he could deal with at once.

I imagine the other floors will be much, much harder than this one. Then again, fighting a bunch of Level 10s—even if only one at a time—would be very tough for a normal group of Level 4s. *They'd become a really solid team by the end of it.*

Maybe that was part of what this floor was about—teaching the party to work as a team against foes stronger than them. If that was the case, then he was doing it ass backward by soloing it. Not that he minded.

When Xavier had ten Level 10 Black Pumas following behind him, enough to gain him another level, he figured it was time to stop and fight. He might feel invincible from how he'd handle the first two, but he didn't really know how many he could handle all at once, and he didn't want to get into as much trouble as he did when fighting those eighteen Lesser Goblins.

He might not be so lucky if he did something like that a second time.

Xavier steeled himself. He was confident he could take all the Black Pumas down—he just didn't know how difficult it would be. He whirled around and saw ten massive black cats all bounding at him at once, all coming at him from the same direction.

Their booming roars sounded as loud as thunder cracking the sky. It echoed off the ground, off the trees, through the forest. Xavier wondered if the rest of his party could hear them all the way back at the cabin.

Seeing all that powerful muscle, those sharp claws, and dagger-like fangs, Xavier swallowed. Maybe this plan wasn't as smart as he'd first thought.

Chapter 25
Lesser Butcher

Xavier stood in the middle of the dark forest on the first floor of the Tower of Champions, staring down ten massive Level 10 Black Pumas, each twice the size of a lion. Their eyes glowed an eerie yellow, and their fangs and claws looked sharper than ever.

The grey mage robes Xavier wore felt thinner than ever, too, and he worried his Toughness, even at 32, wouldn't be high enough for him to survive an onslaught from so many foes.

But if he did everything right, he wouldn't have to worry about that.

Xavier cast Spiritual Trifecta. The silver glow engulfed him, and any ounce of doubt he'd felt disappeared in a flash as power thrummed through every vein and muscle in his body.

He stepped forward, casting Heavy Telekinesis a split-second before the first of the ten Black Pumas reached him.

As all ten of the Black Pumas were clustered together, Xavier managed to capture every single one into his spell. They were flung up off the ground. Yelps released from their terrifying maws, making them seem far less threatening than a moment before.

It was the first time Xavier had cast Heavy Telekinesis since gaining his titles. Not only that, but Spiritual Trifecta also further strengthened the spell, infusing its power into his magic.

The Black Pumas soared backward through the air. A part of Xavier was simply astounded that his spell was strong enough to pick them up at all. *How much do these things weigh?* He recalled hearing something about male lions weighing over 400 pounds, and these beasts were *twice* that size.

And with one spell, he'd flung ten of them!

Can my spell, infused with Spiritual Trifecta, really move more than 8,000 pounds at once?

The first of the Black Pumas soaring through the air slammed into a tree. The tree snapped in half, breaking at the trunk. And it wasn't the only thing that snapped. There was a symphony of cracks, as though every bone in the monster's body broke at once.

You have defeated a Level 10 Black Puma!
You have gained 1,000 Mastery Points.
You have gained 1,000 Spirit Energy.

Xavier's eyes widened. *With one spell?*

Another Black Puma hit a tree, and he received a second kill notification. The rest followed quickly after, until all ten Black Pumas had been defeated.

Congratulations, you have reached Level 5!
Your health has been regenerated by 50%!
Your Spirit Energy limit has increased by 100!
You have received +1 Intelligence, +1
Willpower, and +1 Spirit!
You have received +5 free stat points!
All your spells have refreshed and are no longer
on cooldown!

Xavier shook his head, a little surprised by how easy that had been. He wasn't surprised by gaining the next level. That was the *reason* he'd wanted to gather ten of them together.

Then another notification popped up.

Heavy Telekinesis has taken a step forward on the path!
Heavy Telekinesis is now a Rank 3 spell.
One cannot walk backward on the path.

Spiritual Trifecta has taken a step forward on the path!
Spiritual Trifecta is now a Rank 3 spell.
One cannot walk backward on the path.

What? How did that happen? Xavier hadn't unlocked any Upgrade Quests for the two remaining spells he possessed, like he had when they were Rank 1. He'd thought he hadn't done what he needed to unlock them yet. *Maybe Upgrade Quests are only from Rank 1 to Rank 2?*

He was tempted to take out his Tower of Champions manual and riffle through it to see what it said on the subject but stopped himself. *That's what Siobhan will be doing. I need to keep moving.*

Xavier stepped over to the first of the Black Puma corpses when yet another notification appeared.

Title Unlocked!
Lesser Butcher: This is a common title. You have slain 10 enemies in a single strike. Whether you have slain small field mice or fearsome dragons, this feat's reward is the same.
You have received +1 to all stats!

Xavier laughed. He couldn't help himself. He certainly hadn't expected to gain a title for *that*! And the fact that the title was called *Lesser Butcher* made him wonder. How many more enemies would he need to slay at once to gain the next title? Would slaying twenty or fifty at once gain him Minor Butcher? What would he need for *Greater* Butcher? Was there a Legendary Butcher title?

I think I'm getting ahead of myself.

He turned his attention back on task. Though glad for the level he'd gained, the ranks he'd gained for his two spells, and the Lesser Butcher title, he couldn't let it slow him down.

As he put all the enemy corpses into his Storage Ring, which he noticed was filling up fast, he applied the free stats he'd received. At first, he thought he should put a point into Speed, but then he realised he could already run faster than the Black Pumas. If he started to run a *lot* faster than them, they wouldn't be able to keep up, and his plan would no longer work.

More Speed will surely help me on the higher levels, but I have to focus on what's in front of me. Besides, I just gained a point in Speed—and every other attribute—from the Lesser Butcher title.

Instead, he put two points into Intelligence, two into Spirit and one into Toughness—because one can never be *too* resistant to enemy attacks.

The Intelligence would further strengthen his Heavy Telekinesis spell, the Spirit his Spiritual Trifecta spell along with his Spirit Energy limit—he was sure that the spells would require even more Spirit Energy now they'd gained another rank, though he hoped they hadn't gone up by too much. And the Toughness would, well, help keep him from dying.

Because as it had been incredibly easy to take down ten of the Black Pumas at once, he wanted to see if he could *double* that.

I've been in here for over half an hour now, he thought as he started running again. *I wonder how many enemies the teams from established worlds have taken down. And how many enemies there are in this place to begin with...*

As he ran, he looked at how many Mastery Points he needed to gain for the next level.

Mastery Points for this level: 100/24,000

Double what I needed last time.

As he ran, capturing more and more Black Pumas' aggression, having them trail behind him one by one, he thought about the first floor of the Tower of Champions, a theory forming in his mind.

Every single other person I've seen, both in the hallway, in the tavern, and in my party, is at Level 4. I already think that every other Denizen in the Tower of Champions came here at Level 4. If they, like me, only had a few Mastery Points, they would need to gain roughly 12,000 to get to Level 5.

Xavier couldn't imagine a team going through the first floor *without* gaining a level, and if the whole party were participating in the fight, they would gain about 250 Mastery points per kill, which meant there would need to be... forty-eight Black Pumas here for each party member to gain a single level.

Would killing forty-eight pumas really take some parties an entire *week*? *I've already killed twelve.* Then there would be any Mastery Points gained from the boss. The System seemed to have some sort of odd logic to it. His first quest had fifty enemies.

What if this floor had fifty enemies in it too?

It's a working theory...

If it did, he might only gain one more level from this place, unless the boss gave a *lot* more than the average Black Puma.

I'm making a lot of assumptions. He found that with the added Intelligence, his mind worked more efficiently. He also found it worked *faster*, and *never wanted to stop*. Something was always running through his mind, no matter what he was doing.

Except when he was fighting. Then it just seemed to be him against the world. His mind, for the most part, would clear, and all he had to do was survive. Maybe that, and being so damn powerful for his level, was why he felt so excited to keep fighting. To keep gaining levels.

He knew *why* he was doing this. He wanted to gain these titles so he could give the people of his world a fighting chance against the invaders on Earth. But he had to admit there was a selfish part of him that really loved thinking of himself as the hero. Not only that, he really, *really*, enjoyed being powerful.

That's not such a bad thing, is it?

Maybe that was why, as he ran, he didn't stop when he reached twenty Black Pumas trailing behind him. Nor did he stop when there were twenty-four—enough to gain another level from.

He ran until he'd gathered thirty-five of them. Glancing behind him every few minutes, he'd made sure they were all of the same level. Not a single one had been over Level 10.

This is... ambitious.

He wanted to gather more. If he'd been right about how many enemies were on this floor, that would be two more Level 10 Black Pumas, then the boss of the level. But he didn't want to risk encountering that boss with this many other enemies around him.

It had taken him an hour and a half to gather these enemies. His legs *still* hadn't become tired and heavy, though a thin sheen of sweat covered his forehead, and he breathed a little heavier than usual.

Here goes nothing. I really, really hope I don't die.

He was pretty sure he wouldn't.

Chapter 26
Don't Get Yourself Killed

Xavier whipped around and faced all thirty-five Level 10 Black Pumas. Fear welled up inside him. Instincts, ancient and primal, begged him to run. But other instincts were forming inside Xavier. Ones that told him to fight. To stand his ground. These were the very same instincts that had gotten him through the quest with the goblins.

If he had run, if he had hidden, it never would have put him in this position. He never would have gained those titles. He wouldn't be anywhere near this strong.

All right, Xavier. You did this to yourself. Now let's make sure it pays off and you don't get yourself killed.

The closest of the Black Pumas leapt high into the air. Twice as high as Xavier was tall. It bore down on him like an eagle swooping at a field mouse. Xavier gritted his teeth, his Willpower attribute doing the heavy lifting in that moment.

Hold.

The other Black Puma's surrounded him. They didn't all come from one direction like the first batch he'd fought. There were simply too many for them to be able to cluster in that close, especially considering how damned big they were.

It also means they won't all be able to attack me at once.

He felt a prickle at his back. Heard their paws padding through the underbrush. The low rumble of their roars.

Hold.

As Xavier had been running, he'd flung a Heavy Telekinesis spell off to the side, felling several trees in the process, so he could check how long its current cooldown was, as the last time he'd used it he'd gained a level—refreshing all his spells—and hadn't had a chance. The cooldown had gotten all the way down to three seconds, something he hadn't thought would be possible for a long, long time.

He had no idea how the spell had been reduced so much. Had all those titles really made such a huge difference? He hadn't figured out the calculation of stats—it must have been affected by multiple attributes.

Either way, he wasn't going to look a gift horse in the mouth.

The Black Puma soaring through the air roared, claws outstretched and ready to rip him apart. It was inches away.

Now!

Spiritual Trifecta engulfed Xavier in a silver light that bloomed outward, alighting the small patch of dark forest he stood in, casting shadows of all the monsters he was fighting over the nearby trees.

Xavier loosened his grip on his staff, not wanting to hold it too tightly, and smashed its head into the skull of the Black Puma. It went down like a sack of potatoes, the kill notification popping up instantly, though Xavier was becoming adept at ignoring those in the middle of battle.

As he'd run, capturing the aggression of more and more of these big cat beasts, Xavier had thought through his strategy. Spiritual Trifecta was his biggest chance at winning this battle, and he didn't want to squander a single second of it. Though he hadn't been struck by one of these Black Pumas yet, he was sure enough to risk his life that the spell would be strong enough to protect him from their claws and fangs.

It was after the spell had worn off—a spell that last time he'd used it, lasted only five seconds—that he was *less* sure of. *I've already gained four points in Spirit since then. Maybe it will last longer.*

The first Level 10 Black Puma down, Xavier whipped his staff around and slammed it straight into the head of another leaping for his back. The beasts were fast, but he was faster even without the spell active. With it? They didn't stand a chance.

Two down. Only thirty-three to go.

It almost felt like Xavier's body was taking over. Gaining the skill of Staff Mastery and all those hours of solitary practise in the days leading up to this made every movement seem natural. *If this is what it's like with the skill at Rank 1, I can't imagine what it will be like later.*

He kept a fraction of his attention on the countdown timer in the corner of his vision, working from the assumption that Spiritual Trifecta would only last five seconds. In *two* seconds, he'd already taken down three of the Black Pumas.

Xavier grinned as they clustered in close around him. He cast Heavy Telekinesis on his left flank, flinging about a dozen of the cats. Before the beasts could hit the nearby trees or slam into the ground, he was already cracking the skull of another.

Though now he'd revealed his power, the Black Pumas—like the Lesser Goblins before them—showed hints of hesitation. Xavier gritted his teeth, waiting for Heavy Telekinesis to refresh its cooldown. He didn't know how skittish these beasts would become, and in all the time he'd been formulating this plan he hadn't considered what he might do if the monsters actually ran away from him.

They could scatter around the forest and hide from me. They probably have excellent hearing, and they're as black as the night which might very well permanently blanket this place. He'd have to go hunting for his prey, and that could take a long time if he wasn't lucky about it—especially since he knew absolutely nothing about tracking wild animals.

So he couldn't let any of them get away.

Three more Black Pumas went down while he waited for his spell to refresh, and he could hardly believe he'd almost taken down *half* of them before the Spiritual Trifecta spell ran out.

The instant Heavy Telekinesis was ready again—the silver sheen of his other spell still enveloping him—Xavier cast it on his right flank, picking up maybe four more of the big cat beasts. The roars that had filled the air were replaced with yelps as they were yanked off their feet. He wished he could have used the spell on more of them, like the first time he'd cast it during this battle, but the Black Pumas were far more spread out than they had been even seconds ago.

Xavier had lost count of the number of beasts he'd slain during this encounter, and he didn't exactly have the time to count his notifications, but as far as he could tell, maybe thirteen of the Black Pumas remained.

He swept his staff around, trying to strike the nearest of the beasts, but it leapt out of the way before his staff could make contact.

As he missed the strike, that was the moment Spiritual Trifecta ran out. A sudden weakness overtook every limb and every inch of Xavier. His legs, which had been extended in a lunge, threatened to falter.

Before he could steel himself, one of his legs *did* falter. The atmosphere around him shifted. The dozen or so Black Pumas that surrounded him no longer showed any hint of hesitation in their posture. They were predators, and they could tell when their prey was vulnerable.

Xavier felt sluggish and slow without the spell active. Felt half as strong as before, even though he knew that wasn't quite true. He didn't hear a roar behind him. The pounce was soft. Quiet as a feather touching down. It was the *thud* when the Black Puma slammed into his back that was loud.

Xavier tumbled to the dirt. He might have been able to press the weight of the massive beast over his head like he could with the vending machine, but that didn't mean he could take the weight slamming into his back and keep standing—especially when he wasn't braced for it.

Something in his back *cracked* and a pain like nothing he'd ever felt stabbed at him. He had a sneaking suspicion that something in his spine had given way. He had quite a lot of Toughness for his level, but that didn't mean it could withstand the onslaught from several Level 10 Black Pumas tearing into him.

In fact, he was quite sure it *couldn't* withstand such a thing, especially since he wasn't wearing a lick of armour.

Nothing about his plan included him being taken to the ground.

Burning lines of pain alighted over his back as something slashed deep into him. *Not something. The beast's dagger-sized claws.*

Your health is at 75%.

He stifled a scream at the intense pain. His staff was still clutched tight in his right hand. His face had been slammed straight into the dirt and he heard the roars from the other approaching beasts, ready and eager to feast on him, to pay him back for the slaughter of their brethren.

Another slash. Another bite of burning pain. His health was falling fast. He tried to push himself off the ground, knowing he should be strong enough to, but another weight slammed into his back.

Your health is at 50%.

No no no. I am not *going to die here!* He tried to cast Spiritual Trifecta, though a part of him knew he wouldn't be able to.

Spiritual Trifecta has a cooldown of 15 seconds. It cannot be used for another 8 seconds.

Xavier finally let the pain he felt out, releasing a yell louder than the roars of the Black Pumas. They tore into him again and again, and he wasn't exactly sure *how* he was still alive.

Your health is at 25%.

No. No. No. I'm not going to give up!

The attacks kept coming. Xavier still couldn't move. He could take a hit from these beasts, but not from so many at once. Not from such a sustained barrage.

So many times since the System had come, he'd thought he would meet his death. When he stood across from a Navy SEAL holding an M4A1 carbine assault rifle. When he'd first been injured by the Lesser Goblin that had leapt at him with a bloody sword. When he'd been fighting those eighteen goblins and they'd gotten him to the ground—just like these damned pumas had gotten him to the ground.

And right now. When his health was the lowest it had ever been.

I got myself into this mess. I'm going to get myself out of it!

Your health is at 1%.

Chapter 27
I Won't Let This Be the End

Your health is at 1%.

THE NOTIFICATION STARED AT HIM. GOADED HIM. IT WAS THE only bloody thing he could see.

I won't let this be the end.

Heavy Telekinesis—bless the short cooldown of that spell—was ready to be used again. The feeling in his mind was like being let free. Though he wasn't free. He had at least two Black Pumas on his back tearing into him with claws as large and sharp as daggers, and if he was hit even one more time, he would be dead.

I might even die from my wounds, though my Toughness should be strong enough now to regenerate my health faster than the bleeding effect takes it.

Focusing all his might and concentration toward a single point, Xavier did the only thing he could in the position he was in—face down in the dirt, unable to see and barely able to move his arms, let alone the staff he held.

He focused the spell *downward*, straight into the earth, hoping it would do what he wanted. Though he'd managed to make his Heavy Telekinesis spell spread outward around him like a wave in the past, he'd needed his staff and hands to *direct* it. He wished more than anything that he could send the two beasts on his back flying away from him, but it simply wasn't an option.

In a movie or TV show, this next move might have launched him straight backward, up into the air. But Xavier knew that wasn't how it would work. If Heavy Telekinesis anchored him against the weight he pushed against, he would have been flung backward when he'd tried to fling those ten Black Pumas that added up to over 8,000 pounds.

His Heavy Telekinesis spell slammed into the ground with all the force he could muster. It wasn't as strong as it would have been had he had Spiritual Trifecta active, but it was still damned strong, and more than able to dig a ditch—or, more accurately, a crater—that must have been twelve feet deep and thirty feet wide, which wasn't all that big considering those two Black Pumas were each at least twenty feet long with all four paws on the ground.

He'd sunk down into the crater. Knowing it was about to form, he was ready for it. The Black Pumas ripping into his back? They were not.

Xavier felt like the luckiest guy in the Greater Universe when he found his feet down in that ditch, though he knew he was still in an incredibly volatile situation. His health wouldn't magically regenerate faster than he could take the hits from these beasts, and now he was stuck in a large hole with two of them.

But those two beasts had been disorientated by the fall. The confusion they felt wouldn't last long. He capitalised on it instantly, slamming his staff into one of their skulls.

Unfortunately, without Spiritual Trifecta active, one hit wasn't enough. The first Black Puma fell backward in the pit—the pit that was barely large enough to hold him and the two massive beasts—just as the second Black Puma gained its feet.

Xavier's body was weak. Blood leaked from his back, and he could barely stand for the pain. Whatever had cracked in his spine made his back arch at an odd angle, and sending out that last strike against the first puma had made all the wounds stretch and tear—

fortunately not enough to dash away that final percent of health. He was surprised he could even stand.

But he had to push through the pain if he were to survive.

He didn't have time to check, but he knew he was close to a level-up. A level-up would grant him 50 percent more health. Refresh his spells. It would get him *through* this.

Xavier unleashed a roar of his own. The pain in his back doubled as he smashed his staff into the puma that had just gotten to its feet and was swiping its massive claw toward his face. Xavier slammed the paw away with a parry—a little surprised that he was even able to—then thrust the staff straight into its eye. He kept pushing the staff, half-wishing it was a spear. The eyes being a weak point, Xavier managed to puncture straight through them and into its brain.

You have defeated a Level 10 Black Puma!
You have gained 1,000 Mastery Points.
You have gained 1,000 Spirit Energy.

Xavier almost fell back to the dirt when he didn't gain a level from the kill. But there was no time. The Black Pumas circled above the crater, roaring down at him. Any moment they would leap into the fray.

He pounced at the remaining puma in the ditch and once again struck it in the head. He didn't know if it was his higher Strength stat or his Willpower that was keeping him on his feet, but he was surprised his legs didn't falter. Surprised they were strong enough to hold him up.

You have defeated a Level 10 Black Puma!
You have gained 1,000 Mastery Points.
You have gained 1,000 Spirit Energy.

Congratulations, you have reached Level 6!
Your health has been regenerated by 50%!

**Your Spirit Energy limit has increased by 100!
You have received +1 Intelligence, +1
Willpower, and +1 Spirit!
You have received +5 free stat points!
All your spells have refreshed and are no longer
on cooldown!**

Yes! Yes! Yes!

Xavier's wounds stitched back together, causing a terrible itch. But he would take the itch over the pain. Whatever had broken in his back cracked back into place. *Mostly* back into place. He'd only gained back 50 percent of his health, after all. And he was sure some of his wounds would still be open.

At least one more hit won't kill me.

His spells active again, Xavier didn't hesitate. He cast Spiritual Trifecta then leapt straight out of that twelve-foot-deep crater he'd created. When he landed on solid ground near the edge of the hole, one of the Black Pumas leapt at him. But Xavier wasn't having any of it. He'd lost his patience for this fight after the pumas had gotten him down to 1 percent health. He wasn't going to let anything like that ever happen again.

I shouldn't have taken on so many.

Xavier struck the Black Puma down then cast Heavy Telekinesis on the largest cluster he could find, flinging them into the air.

The beasts crashed into the trees around him, cracking bones and snapping trunks as more roars sounded and more kill notifications popped up. He could see four more massive Black Pumas left around him. Four more targets for him to eliminate.

He went in for the kill, smashing his staff into one after the other until the final Black Puma turned and bolted. It ran on near-silent feet. If Xavier let it get out of sight, he'd lose it to the forest.

He needed to clear every monster from this floor. He wasn't about to let one get away.

Xavier sprinted after it. He'd already discovered he could run faster than the Level 10 Black Pumas without Spiritual Trifecta active. With it? He outpaced them easily. After about ten strides Xavier leapt into the air and cast Heavy Telekinesis down at his enemy.

As the force went downward, the beast was crushed.

You have defeated a Level 10 Black Puma!
You have gained 1,000 Mastery Points.
You have gained 1,000 Spirit Energy.

Title Unlocked!
Survivor: This is an uncommon title. You have been taken to the brink of death and came out of it alive. You have shown great fortitude and sheer force of will. Most who have been in your situation have given up and died, but not you. You have received +6 to Toughness!

Xavier released a small gasp of pain as whatever had cracked in his spine snapped fully into place. He fought the impulse to scratch his back, either with his nails or his staff, itchy from his healing wounds.

Another title! That's two from this mission. He was glad to find he wouldn't have to wait until the end of the floor for the titles he gained to come into effect, like he had when he'd done his first quest. But he was worried he'd received this title at all. He should never have let his health get that low in the first place. *I need to learn from this. I need to be better.*

Xavier couldn't take any more of the Black Puma corpses with him. They were simply too big, and there was no longer enough room in his Storage Ring for them. Instead, he stretched out his still-sore back and looked through all the notifications he'd received, hoping he hadn't missed one of the Black Pumas.

At the start of the battle, he'd had thirty-five trailing him. He counted the notifications, dismissing the ones that told him he'd reached his Spirit Energy limit—that was easy enough when killing beasts that offered 1,000 Spirit Energy.

Thirty-two... thirty-three... thirty-four...

Thirty-five!

Xavier couldn't help but do a little victory dance, one he was glad no one was around to see. *All right. That's... forty-seven monsters I've killed on this floor. If my theory about there being fifty monsters on this floor is correct, then there should only be two more and the boss left.*

He twirled his staff about him and couldn't help but grin. Though when he looked down at himself, covered completely in beast blood, wearing robes torn and tattered—mostly at the back— he wished he had some way to clean himself. That, and sturdier robes.

Why do I even need mage robes anyway? While his spells were stronger when wielding the staff, he wasn't sure the robes offered him anything. They certainly didn't offer him protection. Maybe they were simply too low-level to do so.

Xavier shook his head. *A problem for another time.* He was hurt, but he couldn't give himself too long to heal. He was glad he'd gained six Toughness from that title, but considering what he'd just been through, he put the five free stat points he'd received for gaining Level 6 into Toughness as well, bringing the attribute up to 45.

It's now higher than my Spirit attribute. What kind of mage am I? He chuckled at that last thought. He didn't know why he found that funny. Maybe it was just the release of tension after almost dying.

He checked his health and was astounded to see it was already at 61 percent. He was sure he must have pushed the limit higher by gaining eleven points in Toughness over the last minute, and yet it had already healed by 10 percent—plus the 50 percent from gaining that level—since he'd been down in the pit.

That's way, way better than it's ever been. He felt hesitant throwing himself into another encounter while not at full health, especially after what he'd just been through, but he couldn't imagine whatever he faced next would put up as much of a fight as the thirty-five level 10 Black Pumas he'd just defeated. Besides, if he were to have a chance at being the first to clear this floor, he had to keep moving.

Xavier pressed onward through the dark forest, toward what he hoped were the final few monsters of the first floor of the Tower of Champions.

Chapter 28
A Planet of the Apes Scenario

THIS LOOKS PROMISING.

Xavier raised his staff, gripped in both hands, over his head as he stretched out his sore back. He'd been running for the past ten minutes, through the forest's underbrush, and was yet to encounter another monster.

The number of monsters had been spread out so equally across the path he'd been able to predict when he would encounter another one up to the *second*. What had changed? He certainly hadn't cleared the first floor of the Tower of Champions yet. He would have received a notification if that were the case. And he hadn't fought anything he would consider a boss, just the same Black Pumas again and again.

But now, Xavier had come to the end of the path. It terminated at a large stone temple. It looked as ancient as the Egyptian pyramids, but was more like something the Mayans might have built.

The step-pyramid had a central staircase at its front that led to a small structure at the top with a single, doorless entryway.

If I know anything about final bosses, I'm guessing this is where the one for this floor will be. He checked his health and was pleasantly surprised to find it at 85 percent. His running slowed its regeneration, something he would keep in mind, but it hadn't halted it completely. Though he didn't know whether that was because of his high Toughness attribute or because that was simply the case for everyone. *Another reason why other parties will go even slower than me. If they're injured after every encounter and don't have something like a healer or health potions—if those even exist—then they'll need to rest a lot more, and apparently they won't be able to walk during that resting time.*

Not even three hours had passed since he'd entered this floor. *I have to be the fastest. There's no way I'm not.* He steeled himself before heading up the stairs, checking his stats.

XAVIER COLLINS
Level: 6
Strength: 27
Speed: 23
Toughness: 45
Intelligence: 34
Willpower: 37
Spirit: 41
Mastery Points for this level: 11,100/59,000
Available Spirit Energy: 4,700/4,700
Available Skill Points: 0
Free stat points remaining: 0

Okay. I'm definitely strong enough to face whatever's up there. And the longer I spend down here the more I ruin my chances of being the first to clear this floor.

Xavier gripped his staff and sprinted up the steps. Over the last few days, he'd gotten plenty used to running up stairs. There must have been at least three hundred steps, but it didn't take him long to reach the top.

He paused at the entrance. It was pitch-black inside the temple. He put a hand to the stone doorway and leant in, straining his ears. The stone was cold, as though never touched by the sun.

Looking back at the dark forest, Xavier wondered if that might be the case.

Though Xavier heard nothing, he was sure he was in the right place. He swallowed, feeling a hint of fear. Just because he'd become powerful, didn't mean he didn't feel fear every now and then. He'd be a fool not to, especially after what he'd just survived.

He stepped over the temple's threshold. The instant he did, torches along the walls began to alight one by one. *That's cool. And more than a little ominous.* He shook his head with a smile at the sight.

With all that had been going on. Everything that was on the line—like the entirety of planet Earth and every person on it—sometimes Xavier forgot to stop and think about what was actually happening around him.

In a way, his wildest dreams had come true. Though instead of being flung into a fantasy world, it was more like a fantasy world had been flung at his world. And here he was, not only experiencing it, but *thriving* in it.

Xavier was becoming more powerful than he ever imagined possible in reality. He'd wanted to be a writer because magic wasn't real, and neither were fantasy worlds.

But he'd been proven wrong.

As torches on each side of the wall lit one-by-one every few feet, the flickering flames illuminated the large temple's hall. Xavier shivered. The space was as cold as the stone he'd touched at the entryway—the torches' flames didn't seem to impact that at all. He crinkled his nose at the musty smell. *It even smells old.*

When the final torches at the end of the hall were lit, they illuminated a throne on a raised dais. For a moment, Xavier thought he saw a man sitting on that throne... But what he saw was no man.

It was a beast.

The thing *was* humanoid. Two legs. Two arms. It even wore some semblance of armour, though it wore no shoes. The dagger-like claws that extended from its paws were eerily familiar, and made a twitch run up Xavier's back. With good reason.

The beast's head resembled that of the Black Pumas.

An anthropomorphic sapient being, Xavier thought, tilting his head to the side. It wore crude armour, rusted ringmail that looked salvaged from several people smaller than it, poorly stitched together around its huge frame.

A spear was balanced across its legs. No, more like a halberd. The axe blade at the end of the shaft was huge. Xavier imagined it would weigh a *lot*. The halberd itself must have been twenty feet long—which was about as tall as this beast probably stood.

Is this what the Black Pumas might become if they gain more levels? Might they... evolve?

If that were the case, he couldn't help but wonder if that might happen to other animals back on Earth. Xavier could imagine pushing back the threat of otherworldly invaders, only to end up fending off a *Planet of the Apes* scenario. The thought almost made him chuckle at its absurdity, if not for the possibility of it actually being real.

Xavier's gaze trailed from the anthropomorphic beast to the two beasts flanking it, which he hadn't noticed at first, as his attention had been solely on the one sitting on the throne.

I was right. Three more enemies. That's fifty enemies on this floor. He felt a swell of pride at that. He supposed everyone liked being right.

He scanned each of the enemies before him. None had yet to make a move.

{Black Puma – Level 11}
{Black Puma – Level 11}
{Puma Prime – Level 15}

Puma Prime, huh? And only Level 15? The other two Black Pumas were the highest he'd faced so far, but that didn't worry him. He put this scenario in the context of a normal party.

Assuming the normal party had not farmed the first-floor instance—something a small part of Xavier wished he could do—

then they would have likely each gained a single level from all the fighting, or be close to doing so. Which meant they'd be no stronger at this point than at the beginning, which he thought was rather unfair.

And if facing one Black Puma at a time had been a challenge... facing two at once would be far harder.

And then there was the Puma Prime.

The anthropomorphic beast smiled, revealing two massive, jutting, sharp fangs. The beast peered down at Xavier as though he were an insect in front of a king. *He is sitting on a throne. Perhaps that's the way he sees himself...*

The Puma Prime made a show of looking behind Xavier and to the left and right. The beast opened its mouth, revealing more sharp teeth. "All. Alone?" The voice came out like a guttural growl, loud enough to echo off the walls and make it all the way to him. "Your party. Died?" The beast seemed to have trouble forming words, its forehead creasing.

Xavier's eyes widened. He wasn't sure if he was more surprised that the beast could speak, or that he could understand it. Was the System translating for him? *If it's translating for me, why couldn't I understand the goblins?* He pushed that question aside. The fact the beast could talk didn't change Xavier's plan. He needed to fight it. Besides, every single one of the Black Pumas that he'd fought had pursued him first.

Do I really have to justify this? Just because it's sapient doesn't mean I shouldn't kill it. The goblins were sapient. The System has thrown us into the Greater Universe. A universe where countless worlds and races fight for dominance. If I worry about killing other sapient beings... I won't be able to protect the ones on my own planet.

He knew what happened when "good guys" refused to kill. Like when Batman kept putting the Joker into Arkham Asylum. That bastard would always escape. *And that's how Robin dies.* Xavier didn't *want* to be a killer, but he didn't want to be weak, either. This new reality demanded more of him than he ever knew

Todd Herzman

he would have to give, and he wasn't about to back down because of morals he'd held before that no longer applied.

Besides, he *needed* to kill the Puma Prime to clear this floor.

Xavier raised his chin. He didn't want to stop and talk. He strode forward, staff gripped in both hands, and headed for the throne at the end of the long hall.

The Puma Prime smiled as he watched his prey enter his domain. It was rare that prey came to him. He knew that it was his fate to fight anyone who came through those doors, but he'd been expecting more opponents than this.

The human looked weak. Thin, tattered robes hung off the man's body. Robes drenched in the blood of his kin. Robes that were nothing compared to the great armour adorning the Puma Prime's own shoulders. Perhaps a rage should have boiled within him at all that blood, but he was glad his kin had been slaughtered. Less competition for him. Fewer mouths to feed, and more opportunities.

This foul creature dare believes he can defeat me? His thoughts flowed so much easier than his spoken words, though that would change as he became more powerful. He had been granted intelligence above his previous station, and he was not going to squander it.

A low, rumbling laugh built up inside the Puma Prime's chest as he watched the small human stride across the stone floor of his temple toward his throne.

The Puma Prime looked to his two guards, then flung a hand in the human's direction with a sigh that sounded more like a growl. "Kill. It."

His two guards did not hesitate to respond to his command. They were at a level where they could understand him but could not respond with any semblance of *real* language.

The Black Pumas had already assumed offensive postures,

their hind legs bent, poised and ready to pounce, fangs bared, roars aching to be unleashed. At his command, they bounded across the stone floor directly for the human foolish enough to enter his hall *alone* and *weak*.

The human stopped walking and waited for the two Black Pumas to come to him. The Puma Prime frowned, leant forward in his chair, staring at the man. When the man had entered the hall, the Puma Prime had smelled a hint of fear. That fear should have grown when the Puma Prime and his guards had been revealed, yet now...

The Puma Prime smelled no fear at all. The man stood tall—as tall as a human could stand, at least—and looked... *confident*. He did not shiver nor quail as two beasts bounded toward him, even though his level was identifiable as almost *half* that of the beasts ready to kill him. He stood firm.

Why? Why is he not afraid?

The human raised his staff. A flimsy looking weapon that did not even have a blade attached. It was nothing like the weapon the Puma Prime possessed.

A weapon fit for the king of the forest!

The man slid one foot backward, a defensive stance, and waited for the pumas to reach him. Then a great energy emanated from him, and the two Black Pumas were flung into the air. They crashed into the stone ceiling with a startling *crack* that echoed off every wall of the temple.

Then they fell to the floor, dead, and once more, the Puma Prime could smell fear.

But now that fear came from him.

Chapter 29
First-Floor Climber

Xavier watched the two Black Pumas slam into the stone floor of the temple.

You have defeated a Level 11 Black Puma!
You have gained 1,100 Mastery Points.
You have gained 1,100 Spirit Energy.

You have defeated a Level 11 Black Puma!
You have gained 1,100 Mastery Points.
You have gained 1,100 Spirit Energy.

Huh. He'd been right. The Heavy Telekinesis spell could take out the two beasts without needing a boost from Spiritual Trifecta. Something he was glad for. He didn't want to waste the Spiritual Trifecta spell facing the two weak guards, only to have it wear off before he faced the main boss.

Xavier looked over at the Puma Prime. He didn't like the look of the halberd it wielded. That thing looked *dangerous*. Its reach was massive compared to Xavier's own staff. Honestly, it seemed ludicrous to have to face an enemy that much taller than himself.

I wonder if some parties farm the first Black Puma outside of the cabin, over and over, so they can gain a few levels before going after the rest and the boss at the end. He nodded to himself, thinking that would be a smart approach. It was probably the advantage that established parties gained that most others didn't.

That, and they likely had far better weapons and armour.

All right. Stop dallying. It's time I finish this, clear this floor, and get out of here.

The Puma Prime stood from its throne. Its eyes were wide, and was it... afraid? The beast opened its mouth. "You." It waved a shaking hand at the dead Black Pumas. "How?" Its other hand gripped the long halberd.

Xavier glanced at the tall ceiling. *I suppose that's why it's so tall.* He glanced left and right. *And why this hall is so wide. The Puma Prime wouldn't be able to fight in here otherwise.*

Again, he didn't want to stop and talk. Xavier sprinted toward the scared looking cat with a smirk on his face, whispering under his breath, "Here, kitty kitty." He figured if he had to live and fight in this new reality, he might as well enjoy it.

His Spirit Energy was completely full. Killing those two Black Pumas had restored the paltry 300 points he'd needed to use Heavy Telekinesis. And by the time he reached the end of the long hall, the spell's cooldown ended.

I'll make this quick.

The Puma Prime took his halberd in both hands and pointed it toward Xavier. Anger contorted its face. It opened its massive maw wide, showing off those large, sharp fangs once more, and released a roar louder than anything Xavier had heard in the forest.

An observer might think he was running straight at the enemy's weapon, the Puma Prime standing there awaiting him like a pikeman awaited a cavalry charge. Shaking in fear but determined to hold. But Xavier was just closing the gap. He wasn't going to puncture himself on that thing.

When he deemed himself close enough to the Puma Prime, he activated Spiritual Trifecta, infusing his body, mind, and magic with power, and engulfing him in that familiar silver sheen.

The brightness of the spell further illuminated the temple, and he was sure he looked like a beacon in the middle of it. An easy target. Something he might have to consider in the future. *Not a good spell if I'm going for stealth.*

The Puma Prime, still roaring, didn't look as though it could bear holding anymore. It bounded forward on two massive legs, its strides longer than Xavier was tall, its halberd pointed down at him. Xavier had the absurd thought that right now the beast looked like a pole-vaulter.

The moment Xavier had seen the massive beast stand he'd played the fight out in his head. At least, played out how he *wanted* it to go. He didn't know if it would work, but he damn sure hoped it would.

They were but a few strides away from each other when Xavier leapt into the air, as high as his legs could take him. Which only brought him up to chest height with the beast.

That's when Xavier cast Heavy Telekinesis. He angled the spell downward as best he could, wanting to push his enemy toward the stone. The spell hit, though it didn't hit as hard as on other enemies he'd used it on.

Does the Puma Prime have some sort of resistance to magic? It wasn't something he'd considered, as he hadn't come up against it yet, but he supposed it must be possible. He'd seen such skills available when he'd been looking to spend his skill point.

But just because the Puma Prime could resist his spell, didn't mean it had no effect. The beast was flung downward. It stumbled back two steps before it overbalanced and fell onto its ass on the temple's cold stone floor.

Xavier had been hoping—*expecting*—his spell to deal far more damage. He'd thought to crush the beast's bones and leave it crippled and barely able to move, if not completely dead, considering he'd been able to take out the two Level 11 Black Pumas so easily.

But this didn't change what he did next. Xavier landed atop his downed enemy, right on the beast's chest, and slammed his staff—his muscles infused with extra strength—straight into its cat head.

He cracked the beast in the left temple. Its head snapped to the right. The strike boomed outward like stone crashing against stone.

Crack.

He slammed his staff into the beast again.

Crack. **Crack**. **Crack!** **CRACK**!

He used every second of Spiritual Trifecta, smashing his staff into the beast's skull over and over. Blood spurted from the wound and every strike snapped its head one way then back the other.

God, how much health does this thing have? Any one of these strikes would have killed the normal Black Pumas, but it was like the Puma Prime had extra resistance to not just magical attacks, but physical ones as well. *I have enough points to be a higher level than this thing, shouldn't it be easy for me to kill it?*

When Spiritual Trifecta ended, he'd cracked his staff into the beast's head six times. It still breathed but wasn't moving. When the exhaustion hit Xavier, he'd been worried the beast might notice and attack back, but it hadn't tried to move out of the position it was in at all.

Heavy Telekinesis was ready to be used again. Xavier, standing on the anthropomorphic beast's chest, stared at its drooping eyes. The beast locked gazes with him, blood covering its face that was caved in on two sides. The Puma Prime raised its head from the stone. Made the struggle look like it was lifting a heavy weight. Like it was using every ounce of strength it had. "Finish. It," it rasped out.

Xavier felt a twinge of guilt at the state he'd left the beast in. At the pain it must be suffering. *Not for much longer.* Heavy Telekinesis might not work as well on this beast as on others, but it still worked.

He angled the spell over the Puma Prime's head, then cast Heavy Telekinesis facing downward, focusing it as narrowly as he could. As the spell wasn't built for precision, it wasn't perfect, but it worked.

Most of the spell's force hit the top of the Puma Prime's head and snapped it back to smash into the temple's stone floor. The Puma Prime had breathed its last breath.

You have defeated a Level 15 Puma Prime!
You have gained 3,000 Mastery Points.
You have gained 3,000 Spirit Energy.

Xavier frowned. 3,000 Mastery Points and 3,000 Spirit Energy? That was *twice* as much as he'd been expecting for a Level 15 enemy!

More notifications appeared.

Congratulations! You have cleared the First
Floor of the Tower of Champions.
Party Member Contribution:
Xavier: 50/50 Kills.
Howard: 0/50 Kills.
Justin: 0/50 Kills.
Siobhan: 0/50 Kills.
No shared attributions apply on this floor.

Party member contribution? I didn't know the System tracked that.

Title Unlocked!
First-Floor Climber: This title has the opportu-
nity to be upgraded. You have cleared the First
Floor of the Tower of Champions, and shall be
rewarded.
You have received +2 to all stats!

Plus two points to all stats. That's not too bad, I guess. Though I expected more than that. The way the System had mentioned the rewards gained from the Tower of Champions, this really didn't feel like much.

The notifications didn't end there, of course.

Title Unlocked!
Solo Tower Climber 1: This title has the opportunity to be upgraded. You have cleared a floor of the Tower of Champions by yourself. You are either very brave or very stupid for attempting such a feat. Know that whether this feat was achieved through sheer skill or unbridled luck, you shall be rewarded.
You have received +8 to all stats!

Xavier couldn't help but smile. *Now that's more like it!*

He hadn't expected to gain such a title, as the other members of his party were still technically on this floor—even if they were in a Safe Zone. But as the System tracked contributions to kills, he supposed it was inevitable.

I'm glad I didn't let one of the others attack that first Black Puma.

He shook his head. Eight attribute points to all stats. It was the best title he had—even better than his First Defender of Planet Earth title. *Is clearing a floor solo really that much of a big deal?*

Xavier's eyes widened as he spotted the next title.

Title Unlocked!
1ˢᵗ First-Floor Climber: Out of Champions from five competing worlds, your party is the first to clear the First Floor of the Tower of Champions within your instance.
You have received +5 to all stats!

Xavier was about to celebrate when another notification took him by surprise.

Title Unlocked!

First Floor Ranked 42 (Completion Time – 2 hrs 47 mins): Out of all the Champions from all the worlds in the Greater Universe who have completed the First Floor of the Tower of Champions in every possible instance, you have edged into the Top 100 fastest times at No. 42.
This title is a Temporary Title. If your record is edged out of the Top 100, your title will be lost.
You have received +10 to all stats!

Xavier's jaw dropped. He struggled to believe what he was reading.

Out of all the Champions from all the worlds in the Greater Universe...

How many Champions would that *be*? There were one million people here from *his world alone*, not to mention the four other worlds. For a moment, he contemplated how large the universe was and how many thousands, millions, billions, perhaps even *trillions* of worlds must have been integrated into the Greater Universe by the system since the Big Bang... Then there was the fact that it wasn't only new worlds who came to the Tower of Champions. Everyone who gained access to the System at age sixteen and chose Champion... They were the ones who came here.

Which means there are probably countless new Tower of Champions instance created every day...

Even with his high Intelligence attribute, he couldn't fathom how many would have tried to do what he'd just done. *And I'm ranked 42. In all the universe.* Despite the sheer number of Denizens who'd likely done this before, Xavier couldn't help being a *little* disappointed he wasn't the first, but that was sheer arrogance.

He also liked the number 42.

And +10 to all stats? That was *insane*! With the four titles he'd just received, he'd gained... +25 to all stats, totalling 150 stat points! Doing the math, he was now equivalent to someone at Level 40! Though he imagined his stats were more balanced than the average Level 40.

And here I am, still only Level 6. It made him wonder about the powerhouses out there in the Greater Universes. How long they lived. How powerful they'd become over the years. How many titles they'd received.

What about the first person who ever received any titles at all? Are they still out there, somewhere, billions of years old? He shook his head. Another notification popped up.

In 30 seconds, you and your party will be returned to the Staging Room.

Chapter 30
Loot Boxes

Xavier made sure he didn't pass up the opportunity to loot the dead Puma Prime. In fact, as he only had thirty seconds, he decided to make some room in his Storage Ring for the big beast and its halberd.

He looked around the temple. The part of him used to playing video games expected a treasure chest to be hidden around here, but even looking behind the throne itself made him come up with nothing.

The throne was unadorned as well. No jewels encrusted its arms. No crystal adorned its head. And there was no crown of gold—or crown at all—anywhere to be found. He sighed, thinking of a normal Champion climbing this tower. Would all they have gained from this floor be two points to their stats?

Xavier, of course, couldn't complain about what he'd received, and he supposed the title everyone got would be the equivalent of almost two levels. *I think I've just been spoiled by all the titles I've been getting. And this is only the first floor. Maybe the rewards for other floors are better.*

When the timer reached zero, Xavier was satisfied nothing of value remained on this floor for him to find.

There was a flash of white light, then he was standing in the Staging Room, surrounded by his party.

Howard, Siobhan, and Justin stood around him, blinking and shaking their heads at the disorientation of being teleported. Xavier noticed he'd adjusted to it much faster. *They're all still Level 4...*

Siobhan's eyes were wide. "You did it! And really fast too!" She looked down, her shoe scuffing the floor. "We were getting a little worried. Thought... thought we'd made a bad decision and that you would die out there."

Howard gripped Xavier's shoulder. "You did it. You cleared the floor." He nodded at the other two. "And we got the two titles even in the Safe Zone."

Two titles? Xavier had received four. His forehead creased. Of course. The 1st First-Floor Climber title had said "your party," not just him. He smiled. "That's great!"

"We each received seven points to all our stat points! That's... that's *huge*!" Justin smiled, ear to ear. Xavier hadn't seen the kid smile like that.

Before Xavier could respond, Siobhan pointed excitedly at something in the middle of the room. That was the first time Xavier really *looked* around the room. The Staging Room looked completely different.

It was far larger, for one. About the size of an indoor basketball court. There weren't practise weapons or anything like that, but on one side of the room were a series of large stone balls. Each stone was larger than the last, until the largest one, which was as tall as Xavier. *Are those for strength training? Like what strongmen use?*

A circle was marked out in the centre of the room, about twenty strides across. Xavier got the feeling it was a sparring circle. On the far side, near the exit, a pedestal stood with a large blue crystal atop it. The crystal gave off a slight glow. Xavier wondered if that was some sort of System Shop terminal.

Finally, his gaze fell on what Siobhan had been pointing at. In the middle of the room, near the sparring circle, were four wooden chests. Xavier grinned, scanning them.

{First Floor Loot Box – Xavier}
{First Floor Loot Box – Howard}
{First Floor Loot Box – Justin}
{First Floor Loot Box – Siobhan}

Loot boxes! And they were actually *called* loot boxes? Xavier chuckled, glad to find that the titles weren't the only reward for clearing the first floor. In fact, he couldn't help but remember the hologram talking about items, skill points, and bonus Mastery Points for clearing floors.

He was glad the others were provided with things too. Though, even before opening his loot box, he itched to get to the next floor. He was sure he'd be the first to clear the second floor, as he'd been the first to clear the first, but he wanted to solidify his lead.

I got the forty-second best record in the Greater Universe. I'm sure my lead is solidified. He hadn't told the others about that. He wasn't sure if he should or not. He didn't know how they'd feel if he told them exactly how much stronger than them he was.

He started to realise how large the divide between himself and others would become. Other Champions from his world would likely take a week to finish the first floor. When they did, they would only get roughly one more level and two points to each of their stats.

What floor would he be on by then?

The party headed toward the four loot boxes in the middle of the room, each kneeling before their own. Xavier put his staff down. It was only then he realised his previously tattered robes had been repaired and cleaned. In fact, there wasn't a drop of blood on him.

The System... repaired my clothes and washed me clean? He didn't know whether he should be thankful or a little creeped out. That's when he had a suspicion.

Your health is at 100%.

He frowned. The last time he'd looked at his health, which was when he walked up the step-pyramid to the temple at the top, it had been 85 percent. Only a few minutes had passed since then. He couldn't tell if his Toughness was simply so high now that his health had healed by itself, or if the System had healed him when he'd been brought back to this room.

He suspected the System had healed him.

Maybe Siobhan would know something about that. He didn't doubt that she'd been reading the Tower of Champions manual while he was clearing the floor.

Xavier pushed those thoughts aside and opened his loot box. There was no key, only a latch, but the fact the box had his name on it made him wonder if he was the only one who could open it. *It makes sense.*

He raised the lid.

You have gained +2 Skill Points.
You have gained 24,000 Mastery Points.
You have gained 10,000 Lesser Spirit Coins
Please choose your preferred item:

1. **Armour**
2. **Enchantment**
3. **Weapon**

Xavier raised an eyebrow and smirked. Twenty-four thousand Mastery Points happened to be the exact amount one would need to go from Level 5 to 6. Assuming the others received the same amount, it would easily take them from Level 4 to 5.

And they cleared the floor faster than anyone else from our world could have. Maybe by soloing, I'm not keeping them as far behind as I'd assumed. They will already be stronger than other Champions from Earth besides me, especially with the extra five stat points they gained along with the normal plus two.

He cocked his head, wondering which item he should choose.

213

He *definitely* wanted some sort of armour, but now he had so much Toughness, did he *need* it?

What would be the better choice for him?

I need to deal a lot of damage fast. A new weapon could help me achieve that. Xavier frowned, remembering when he was lying face down in the dirt, Black Pumas tearing and biting into his back, getting all the way down to 1 percent health...

He shook his head. *No. I don't want to get that close to death again. Maybe armour is the right choice...* He paused, wondering what the Enchantment might be. *Would that be some sort of jewellery with a modifier for stats? That could help me as well...*

Xavier sighed. This wouldn't be the only loot box he would get to open while clearing the floors. This was just the *first*.

He bit his lip, thinking—not for the first time—*I can't fight for this world if I'm dead.* And so, he chose the armour, wondering what he might receive. Besides, maybe there could be a weapon in the System Shop he would be able to buy. He had over ten thousand Lesser Spirit Coins now, after all.

The loot box, when he'd opened it, had been empty. Now, a set of silver robes sat within it.

Xavier took the robes out. *These don't look very sturdy.* He sighed. *Definitely not what I had in mind. They don't look like armour at all.* He tried to scan them but wasn't able to—just like he'd never been able to scan his own robes. *Maybe because I don't have the Identify skill. But I do have two skill points to use now.*

He looked around. There wasn't anywhere for him to change. Then a notification popped up.

Would you like to fast-equip Robes of Intelligence?

Xavier blinked. *Robes of Intelligence? Is that what these were?* He thought *yes.* The grey robes he'd been wearing were replaced with the new silver robes, and the old robes were now clutched in his hands. *Huh. Convenient.* Would that be possible during combat?

He smiled, looking at the others. Though he'd been disappointed by the item he'd received, he wanted to see what his party members had gotten.

Howard held a massive tower shield, one almost as tall as himself. Justin held a new sword, longer and more slender than the sword he'd started with. The new sword had a shining red crystal at the pommel. And Siobhan held a new staff, running her hand up the shaft. The staff wasn't wooden like Xavier's. This one was metal, and at the end it had a purple crystal instead of a clear one.

Beautiful, Xavier thought. Of the staff, not of Siobhan. Although, her red hair, freckles, and that smile which just now found its way to being turned toward him...

Xavier cleared his throat, turning his attention back on task. "I'm eager to get to the next floor, and unlike our initial plan, I think the three of you should come along. If you're able to get titles even in a Safe Zone, it might be worth waiting around in there for me to clear a floor. But before we move on, we should look at the System Shop. I... can almost guarantee no one will clear the second floor before us."

The leatherbound Tower of Champions manual materialised in Siobhan's hand, replacing the staff she'd held. She flipped the book open. "I was just about to talk about that. The System Shop. And other things. There are actually a *few* things I've learnt that you should know before we push on!" Siobhan looked up from the book, beaming.

Xavier nodded. He felt his cheeks reddening a little, though he was interested in far more than her smile. More than once, he'd been tempted to look in his own manual, but he was glad he hadn't —he wouldn't have gained the forty-second spot if he had.

"All right," he said. "What have you got to tell me?"

Chapter 31
The Whole Damned Game Is Rigged

THE OTHERS GATHERED AROUND SIOBHAN AS SHE BEGAN TO talk, though Xavier got the sneaking suspicion Howard and Justin would already know everything she was about to say, considering they'd all been holed up in the same cabin for the past few hours.

Siobhan raised a finger. "First, I can't believe how fast you managed to clear this floor!" She shook her head. "It's absolutely insane. The book says that passing the floor in twelve hours is considered to be an elite-level time. Only a few parties in every instance of the Tower of Champions are able to manage that."

Xavier raised an eyebrow. *Twelve hours is an elite time? Well, if most parties from established worlds complete the first floor in one to three days, that does make sense. And it definitely means we're well ahead of them.* Though that didn't mean he wanted to spend *too* much time chatting between floors. He might have a gain on other competitors, but he didn't want anything to jeopardise that.

"And that's because they have expensive armour and weapons and have managed to find a good team!" Siobhan shook her head once more. She had an excited, giddiness about her. "Did you know Champions can *choose* their party down in the shared space? The tavern, I mean. They can invite people to their party before orientation begins. That's how elite teams are formed. Cohorts—

the others who can enter the tavern—tend to be location-based, and you can only party-up with those in your cohort.

"You can even change parties, but if you've cleared more floors than one of your party members, you have to start from their most recent floor. Also, apparently only a few people are willing to take the risk of clearing the floor on their first way through. That's actually why so many people from worlds like ours die on the first floor. They don't think to grind out a few levels before moving on through the floor. They don't read the book, and they don't realise how difficult the final boss will be to face."

Xavier nodded along at what she was saying. "I had wondered about that. It's good that it has that information in there."

Howard closed his loot box and sat atop the chest. He leant forward, elbows resting on his knees. "I just hope that others are as smart as our Siobhan here and actually *read* the manual before rushing in."

Justin frowned. "Maybe we can let others know? At least those in our cohort. We could head down to the tavern..."

Xavier raised a hand and shook his head. "I don't think we have time for that. Not right now. And besides, I'm sure everyone will be on their floors."

"Not necessarily," Howard said, but didn't argue the point.

"The fact the three of you gained titles when I soloed the floor means I think you should stay in the Safe Zones while I fight. That way, you can each progress even without killing beasts."

Siobhan bit her lip.

"Is something wrong with that plan?" Xavier asked.

"It's just, according to the book, not every floor has a Safe Zone." Siobhan flipped to another page in the manual, ran a finger down it. "Floors 3, 6, and 9 don't."

Xavier leant forward. He was sitting cross-legged on the ground, the others in a semi-circle around him. "What else does it say about the floors?"

"Unfortunately, it isn't particularly detailed," Howard said. "I hoped it would give us a rundown of the floors. Apparently, the floors in the tower haven't changed in the past..." He looked at Siobhan.

"Fifty thousand years."

Howard nodded. "The composition of each floor has been identical for a long time, but the System restricts specific information about the floors from being distributed."

Siobhan flipped to another page, then turned the book around and pointed a finger at a footnote at the bottom. "It restricts distribution of floor knowledge via the written word and other recorded communications; however, it doesn't prevent people from talking about it."

"Which means those from established worlds who have experienced the tower before pass on valuable information on how to effectively clear levels to their children. Or the highest bidder," Howard grumbled.

"There's something about a ranking list. Apparently only those from the top families in the entire Greater Universe are the ones who are able to break into the Top 100 for a floor, though every thousand years or so there's an outlier."

Justin sighed. "Just like Howard said. Nothing is fair. The rich get richer. And the whole damned game is rigged."

"Most parties only manage to gain a ranking after farming a level over and over, leaving everything but the final boss alive," Siobhan said, speaking fast from excitement, like she had so much information bottled up within her and it was all exploding out. "It's a risk, because they might never get fast enough to get to the Top 100, and they don't know what the records are until they get there unless they personally know someone in the Top 100.

"And, of course, they can only do the floor *once*. So, if they finish the floor in 6 hours, but they needed 5 hours and 59 minutes, they'll never know if they could've edged in. It's easier for those elites to gain the title of being the first in their tower to clear the floor, like the title you gained for us."

"You're gonna have to tell us how you managed that," Howard

said. "I think I'm only just starting to realise how damned strong you are."

Xavier, who'd been nodding to Siobhan's words as she spoke, was starting to realise the exact same thing. He didn't anticipate that they would know about the ranking list. He definitely needed to tell them about the solo title to ensure they didn't try and take down any monsters, and now... well, he didn't know why he was keeping it to himself.

These people had chosen Champion because they wanted to fight for Planet Earth. And how exactly would they use this information against him, anyway? What was the harm in them knowing how strong he was?

What Siobhan had been telling him about elite parties having to grind out levels just for a chance at reaching the Top 100, and here Xavier was doing it on his first try without farming a single extra level from the floor, made him realise just how much of an anomaly he must be...

I guess I'm one of those outliers.

"So, ah, I think I have something to tell you guys." Xavier mentioned the Solo Tower Climber 1 title he'd received first and that it could be upgraded. Then he pursed his lips. "There's more. You know that list you were talking about?" He looked at Siobhan. "I... ranked forty-second."

Siobhan blinked. Justin's mouth fell open. Howard, who'd been drinking one of the Cokes Xavier had given them when he'd left them in the Safe Zone, almost choked on it.

"You... what?" Justin blurted.

Siobhan clutched the manual close. "According to the book... that... that should be basically impossible."

"You did say an elite team could clear it in twelve hours," Howard muttered. He stared at Xavier, a little wide-eyed. "He's got no reason to lie."

"Just how strong are you?" Siobhan whispered.

Xavier wasn't sure how to answer that. He didn't really know. Even after he'd accomplished what he had, he didn't *feel* as strong as he could be. He still only had two spells. While they'd reached Rank 3, they hadn't gotten any stronger than that.

And he only had a single skill. He'd wondered if he would gain any more skills while clearing the floor, but it had never happened.

"I... don't know. But I think what you've told me is giving me a good idea." He paused, not sure what else to say on the matter. "Now... I got two skill points from that loot box, along with ten thousand Lesser Spirit Coins. Does it say much about the System Shop?"

Siobhan nodded numbly. "We should be able to get decent gear through it, though higher-grade gear is stat-locked."

The word "grade" sparked a thought. "F Grade..." Xavier muttered. "Does it say anything about that? And did you find out how to make more Lesser Spirit Coins, like the hologram said we could?"

"We did," Howard said after Siobhan was quiet for a moment. It seemed she was still processing things. "It's a process that involves using Spirit Energy. Apparently, you can spend Spirit Energy to *make* coins. Five hundred Spirit Energy lets you make a single Lesser Spirit Coin."

Huh. Xavier had had his suspicions about that, what with the word "Spirit" being in there. "So we can... *make* money?"

"It takes a bit of skill." Justin raised his right hand, palm facing up. A silver coin appeared atop it. "I've managed to make about two." He smiled weakly. "But I don't have the Meditation skill, which also helps with health, so the only way I've been able to recoup my Spirit Energy is through eating. Though the book says sleeping works for that too."

Xavier smiled. *I knew Meditation would help with that!* He told them about his discovery on how to unlock the Meditation skill without spending a skill point, then wondered if that was the skill he'd purchase next, as he didn't have the hours to learn the skill without spending a point for it, but thinking about it, he'd never had an issue gaining more Spirit Energy, and with his Toughness where it was... He sighed inwardly. *There's too much to consider.*

"All right." Xavier faced Siobhan. "I know you have a lot to tell me from that book, and, well, I want to know *everything*, but right now I need to get outfitted for the next floor. Has it mentioned anything about what the best skills to get are?"

Siobhan seemed to snap back to herself. She nodded. "It mentions Identify and Meditation. Apparently Identify is a good skill because it helps parties prioritise what to loot, and as the skill levels it will give more accurate information about an enemy—like what their weaknesses are. Though that works better on beasts than it does on Denizens."

Xavier nodded. "I'm not sure those skills will be the best for me to choose right now, not when I'm specialising in clearing floors at speed."

Siobhan smiled. "No, speedrunning might require something else." She raised a finger, then flipped through the pages with her other hand. When she found the spot she wanted, she tapped a specific point on the page. "From the little you've said, I think your best options are the Physical Resistance and Magical Potency skills.

"They're passive skills that level up naturally while taking damage and dealing damage with spells, but they can only be learnt through purchasing them. You'll be gaining more skill points as you clear more floors, so perhaps that will be a good time to get skills like Running to make your movement speed more efficient. Right now, surviving and dealing damage seem like your best bet."

Xavier frowned, considering the two skills she'd mentioned. Without looking through the entire skills list again, he supposed she was right. *Physical Resistance will help me, well, not die. And Magical Potency... it should make almost everything I do better. It will make Spiritual Trifecta and Heavy Telekinesis passively stronger.*

"And these skills will gain more ranks as I fight?" He still hadn't managed to get Staff Mastery to Rank 2 and wasn't even sure *how* to yet.

Siobhan nodded. "Yep!"

"And are there... ways that I can learn more spells?"

"Not until Level 10," Howard chimed in. "Apparently that's when we can upgrade our class."

"The class upgrade will be based on our actions," Justin said. "Unlike the basic Mage and Warrior classes, it will take into account how you have fought and what other things you've done between Levels 1 and 10, and also what spells you've ranked up, and what ranks they've gained. There are even rarity ratings for different classes and class paths."

"Though you *can* buy spell books for certain spells, those are prohibitively expensive in the System Shop," Siobhan said. "According to the book. But we can outfit you with a new weapon from the store."

"And potions!" Justin said.

"Level 10 is what a lot of the elite teams try to reach before clearing the first floor within twelve hours." Siobhan was nodding as she spoke. "Because they want to gain their class."

Xavier stood up. "All right, then. Let's get me outfitted and ready. Then, I'm going to tackle the second floor."

Chapter 32
Welcome to the System Shop!

Xavier took Siobhan's advice, acquiring the two skills she'd recommended he learn: Physical Resistance and Magical Potency.

> **You have learnt the skill Physical Resistance!**
> **Physical Resistance – Rank 1**
> **You're used to taking a beating, and now you've got the skill to prove it.**
> **+5% damage reduction from physical attacks.**
> **+5% Toughness.**

> **You have learnt the skill Magical Potency!**
> **Magical Potency – Rank 1**
> **You are a student of magic. Your magic is infused with a potent energy that improves every spell you cast.**
> **+5% damage to all spells.**
> **+5% Intelligence.**

Xavier raised an eyebrow as he read the text for the two new skills. That was... actually far better than he'd expected. *And this is only on Rank 1.*

Right now 5 percent might not make a huge difference, but that difference would only improve the higher his stats became. Not for the first time, he wondered if titles would eventually have percentage modifiers for stats.

When it came time to look through the System Shop to find him a new weapon, the others glanced at each other, then Howard stepped forward. "We were talking in the cabin. When we weren't worrying about you having died out there." The man rubbed the back of his neck. "Well, we're hoping now that you've figured that you can change parties that you aren't going to... leave us."

"You can," Siobhan said. "I mean, if you want to."

Xavier paused, about to rest his hand atop the crystal on the pedestal—the System Shop's terminal. "Uh, do you want to..." He swallowed. Talking to them about the tower, about titles and clearing floors... that had all been easy enough. Just like talking about writing with others had always been easy because it was something he was interested in and knew a fair bit about. But this was an entirely different thing. "I guess if you guys want to leave the party, I'd understand why. You're not getting a lot of combat experience right now, saddled with me."

"Are you kidding?" Justin's eyes widened. "We don't want to leave! We were just worried because... you don't really need our help."

Howard rested a hand on the kid's shoulder. "Justin is right. We don't want to leave you. We know we might not be much help, but we've been thinking of ways we can be, like with Siobhan reading the Tower Manual and trying to come up with the best skills for you to use." He nodded at the System Shop terminal. "For instance, assuming you want to remain partied with us even though you're doing all the work... we thought we might offer you all of our Lesser Spirit Coins, so you had a better chance of getting what you need from the shop."

Siobhan nodded. "It's not like we would have been able to gain that title without you."

Xavier blinked. That... he hadn't been expecting. If he were in their shoes, the last thing he'd want was to be stuck in the Safe Zone, letting someone else do all the fighting. But it was what he wanted *them* to do; otherwise, he wouldn't be able to gain the Solo Climber title.

"You guys would really do that?"

Howard shrugged. "It's only fair. You're the one who would benefit the most from these resources."

Xavier lowered his head in thought. "I think... I think I've got another idea for the rest of the floors. What I said before, about levelling the three of you up when we got past the fifth floor, I'd still like to do that. But I don't want to clear the floor with the three of you. I think by then, we should have solidified enough of a lead over the other parties."

Siobhan smiled. "That's perfect. We don't need to clear the whole floor to gain levels! After we farm them, we can have all the monsters respawn before re-entering so you can gain the solo title. And besides, by the time you get to the sixth floor, most from our world probably won't have reached the second. We'll be miles ahead with the titles alone."

"Which will make us all the stronger when we get back to Earth," Howard said. "Then I can find my wife and kids."

"And I can find my mother," Justin chimed in.

"And me, my sister." Siobhan beamed. "And we'll be the first party to return to Earth. We'll really be able to help with the invaders." She came over and took Xavier's hand in both of hers. "Because of you."

"Oh." Xavier looked down at where she held his hand, surprised at her having taken it. Then a notification popped up.

Siobhan would like to give you 10,501 Lesser Spirit Coins. Do you accept?

Xavier felt a flush enter his cheeks. Why else would she have taken his hand but for this? He mentally accepted the prompt. Then the others came up, taking his hand. Howard was first, his handshake strong and solid.

Howard would like to give you 11,007 Lesser Spirit Coins. Do you accept?

Justin was next, shaking Xavier's hand with a nod.

Justin would like to give you 12,351 Lesser Spirit Coins. Do you accept?

Xavier wondered how Justin had gained so many more than the others. More even than Xavier had started with after fighting all of those goblins. But he figured that wasn't important right now.

"You should be able to sell off anything you looted while on the floor," Siobhan said. "The System Shop apparently takes entire corpses, though you would earn more money from them if they were dismantled, that isn't really something that classes like ours tend to specialise in. Better to kill more monsters and loot them than spend time learning how to dismantle them and craft from what's left over."

Dismantling? Crafting? Xavier hadn't even considered those things, and he supposed Siobhan was right. It was better for him, and in time the others, to focus on their offensive and defensive capabilities.

Xavier put his hand on the crystal.

Welcome to the System Shop! Would you like to buy or sell?

Sell, Xavier thought.

A blank box appeared over his vision with nothing in it. It took

Xavier a moment to think of what to do next. Then he willed one of the Black Puma corpses into the box.

He only had ten Black Puma corpses out of all the ones that he killed, as his Storage Ring simply wasn't big enough to hold them all *and* the massive Puma Prime, plus all of the food and other things he'd taken from his university's cafeteria.

Maybe I should clear this out, put most of the food into the Staging Room...

Willing the Black Puma corpse from the Storage Ring into the blank box had the feeling of dragging and dropping a document from one folder to another on a computer.

When the corpse had been put into the box, another prompt appeared.

Would you like to sell {Black Puma – Level 10 (Corpse)} to the System Shop for 50 Lesser Spirit Coins?

Xavier's eyes widened. Fifty Lesser Spirit Coins for a corpse. He still didn't really know how much things were worth in this new reality, and he had even less idea of how the economy worked —especially when one could *create* coins themselves with Spirit Energy, though only one coin per five hundred points.

I can kill an enemy with that much Spirit Energy and make far more by selling its corpse. What an odd universe this has become...

He shook his head and thought *yes*, placing the other nine in there as well. Then he placed the Puma Prime's corpse inside the System Shop's blank box and was disappointed to find it was only worth 75 Lesser Spirit Coins. *It's only giving me 5 coins per level of the corpse. That doesn't seem fair, considering how much stronger the Puma Prime was.* Perhaps that's what Siobhan had meant. Maybe he would have gotten a lot more had he "dismantled" it.

Maybe if I were in a town or city, I'd be able to sell it straight to someone who specialised in that kind of thing for a higher price than the System Shop takes. He pushed away that thought for now. He didn't know how things would work when he wasn't in the tower. He needed to focus on the task in front of him.

Once he'd sold the corpses, he moved onto the Puma Prime's halberd and armour.

Those appeared as "unidentified" when he placed them in the box, but he wondered if that was because *he* hadn't identified them, not because the store didn't know what they were.

The store priced them much, much higher than it had priced the corpses.

The halberd was 500 Lesser Spirit Coins, while armour was 250 Lesser Spirit Coins. *Even though it's all rusted and oddly cobbled together?* He supposed he shouldn't complain.

He was a little disappointed when he found he had nothing left to sell. *Am I able to use more than one Storage Ring at once? Maybe the others will let me borrow theirs so I can carry more loot.*

He frowned, thinking about beast corpses as "loot" seemed... disrespectful? Then again, he wasn't the one making the rules in the Greater Universe. He just had to live with them.

Xavier looked at his spirit coins in his Storage Ring.

Coins
Lesser Spirit Coins: 46,415

Whoa. I wonder what the conversion to dollars is... If it's near one to one, I've definitely never had this much money before.

It was time for him to look at his options. He wondered if there was any new armour he should buy, considering the robes he'd gotten from his loot box didn't seem to be the most durable of defensive wear.

He took his hand off the crystal, then placed it there again. This time, he thought, *Buy,* and a massive list appeared in front of him, with everything ranging from food, to potion ingredients, crafting ingredients and materials, blacksmithing equipment, building materials...

It was overwhelming.

Xavier bit his lip and willed the shop to narrow its focus, hoping that would help. That's when he found the options for armour and weapons. He picked the sub-menu for the Mage class, then staves.

His eyes widened. The first staff he saw was worth 1,000,000,000 Grand Spirit Coins. Xavier didn't even know what a *Grand* Spirit Coin was, let alone how much it was *worth*! And this staff required a *billion* of them? It was highlighted in red, which apparently meant he didn't have the stats to use it—which was no surprise, considering its absurd price—and it was called *Stave of the Otherworldly Void Reaper*.

He blinked.

What an incredibly ominous name.

Xavier took a breath, then let out a sigh. The equipment was listed from highest to lowest price. For a moment, he'd felt rich with his 46,000 Lesser Spirit Coins—even if most of them weren't technically his. Now, he felt dirt poor. But that was a feeling he was fairly familiar with.

All right. I can contemplate how absurd amounts of money like that are possible later. Right now, all I need to do is find a staff, maybe some armour or enchantments...

He shut his eyes and tried to will what he wanted to the System Shop. When he opened his eyes, the list had become much, much smaller.

And there were only three items that matched his criteria exactly, though there appeared to be vast quantities of each item. He selected the information for the cheapest of the three.

Staff of the Apprentice Mage
This staff requires 30 Intelligence and 20 Spirit to wield.
+5 Intelligence
+2 Spirit
+5% magical damage dealt
+5% Spirit Energy recovery
This item costs 15,000 Lesser Spirit Coins

Xavier was intrigued that the staff provided Spirit Energy recovery, but he had to say he was underwhelmed by the stats it provided. As to the 5 percent it added to magical damage, though he hadn't been able to analyse the staff he already wielded, he had a sneaking suspicion it was no better than that.

I've definitely been spoiled by the titles I've received. Does this really cost 15,000 Lesser Spirit Coins?

He shook his head and looked at the next item above on the list. Right now, the list was only showing him items he could afford, as he'd requested, and items that would fit into his style. This one really only seemed to fit the first criteria.

Stave of the Fighting Mage
This staff requires 25 Intelligence, 20 Spirit, and 15 Strength to wield.
+5 Intelligence
+5 Spirit
+2 Speed
+2 Strength
+5% Spirit Energy recovery
+5% magical damage dealt
+5% physical damage dealt
This item costs 30,000 Lesser Spirit Coins

Xavier was more impressed by the second item, but he didn't like the price tag. It was *twice* as much as the last, but he supposed it did offer twice as many boosts. Besides, he was glad to see there were staves that would add to his melee fighting ability and not just his magic, considering it was a strong aspect of his fighting style.

He found it strange that it required less Intelligence and Spirit to wield, but he supposed that could have been because it was for a different type of mage than the first staff. Or maybe that was one of the reasons it was more expensive—it didn't require very high stats to use.

If I bought that... it doesn't really leave much room for me to buy anything else I had in mind.

Xavier couldn't make his decision without checking on the last item.

Spirit Staff of Might
This staff requires 50 Intelligence, 60 Spirit, and 40 Strength to wield.
+5 Intelligence
+10 Spirit
+5 Speed
+10 Strength
+10% Spirit Energy recovery
+15% magical damage dealt
+15% physical damage dealt
This item costs 45,000 Lesser Spirit Coins

Xavier's eyes widened at the stats the staff offered. *That's more than many of the titles I've earned!* Though the stat requirements were quite high, he could clearly use it; otherwise, he wouldn't have been able to see the staff in the store per his search filters. He also couldn't help but like that it added 15 percent not just to magical damage, but *physical* as well.

It costs almost as much as I have. I definitely won't be able to afford anything else if I get this...

That wasn't going to stop him from getting it, however. Xavier smiled, and purchased his first item from the System Shop.

Chapter 33
Like Swinging a Heavy Barbell

XAVIER COLLINS TOOK UP THE SPIRIT STAFF OF MIGHT. THE staff looked rather different to the wooden staff he'd first received when he'd chosen the basic Mage class.

The moment he'd accepted the purchase of the staff, it had appeared in his hand. And... it felt *right*. He'd felt the boosts it offered him the moment he'd wrapped his fingers around it.

The staff was still made from wood, but the wood felt inherently different. It had a weight to it that didn't make sense to Xavier in anything but metal. Like the wood was denser than it should have been.

Is that a property of the wood that it was made from? Some kind of magically heavy tree in an enchanted forest in a galaxy... a fair distance from here? Or was that heaviness infused into the staff during the crafting process?

Had a normal, unenhanced human picked up this staff, they would have struggled to wield it. It would be more like swinging a heavy barbell around than a fighting staff. He supposed that's why it required 40 Strength to wield. As Xavier had 62 Strength, he found wielding the weapon to be a breeze, and looked forward to what kind of damage that heft could do to an enemy.

He wondered how Siobhan would fare with it. Wondered if

232

she would even be able to pick it up, given she wouldn't have the requisite stats to do so. *How did the System restrict someone from using a weapon they weren't ready for?* He could simply hand it to her to test, but he didn't want to let it out of his grasp.

Like a musician with their instrument, it felt wrong to hand it to someone else, even for a moment.

The wood was a dark brown that was almost black. He felt the grooves in the shaft, unique as a fingerprint. At the staff's head was a crystal like his previous staff, but where that one had been clear—unless he'd been casting a spell—this one was silver. It glowed slightly, reminding him of the silver sheen that enveloped his body when he cast Spiritual Trifecta on himself.

The crystal was roughly diamond-shaped—like two triangles attached together—and looked rather sharp at the point. *Could this be used to cut the enemy? Even penetrate armour?* It wasn't a spear, but something told him it could be wielded like one if he wished. He wondered if his Staff Mastery skill accounted for that.

The staff was longer than his last one. Perhaps eight feet tall. It was almost ridiculous, but he knew he would grow to appreciate its reach.

Now he'd purchased the staff, he couldn't see the stats and other boosts it offered him. *I really need to purchase the Identify skill.* But he could see the changes it made to his stats.

Xavier brought up his stats, seeing if he could fiddle with the settings of how they appeared. Ever since he'd gained Staff Mastery, he should be getting a 5 percent boost to his Speed when wielding the staff, but he'd never seen that reflected in his stats before.

Now, he realised if he willed it, he could make that information appear in several different ways. He cocked his head, deciding to put any stats modified by a percentage into brackets beside the stat. He also found that the percentage-modified stats were boosted by equipment. He'd wondered if it might make a distinction. Which meant the extra Intelligence he'd gained from his equipment—five from his Robes of Intelligence and five from his Spirit Staff of

Might—got boosted by the 5 percent boost to Intelligence received from his Magical Potency skill.

That must be another way rich Denizens gain such a huge advantage. I only filtered for weapons I could afford. I imagine there are very pricey weapons that need even less stats than this one to wield but offer more advantages and boosts to the wielder.

He made his equipment stats appear exactly where his normal stats would, simply adding to the total number like his titles did. Happy with how he'd set it out, he looked at all his information—attributes, titles, spells, skills, and all.

XAVIER COLLINS
Age: 20
Race: Human
Grade: F
Moral Faction: World Defender (Planet Earth)
Class: Mage
Level: 6
Strength: 62
Speed: 53 (56)
Toughness: 70 (74)
Intelligence: 69 (72)
Willpower: 62
Spirit: 76
Mastery Points for this level: 40,200/59,000
Available Spirit Energy: 7,000/8,200
Available Skill Points: 0
Free stat points remaining: 0
Titles: Bloodied Hands, Born on a Battlefield, Settlement Defender, Quester, 100 Stats, First to 100 Stats, First Defender of Planet Earth, Lesser Butcher, Survivor, First-Floor Climber, Solo Tower Climber 1, 1st First-Floor Climber, First Floor Ranked 42
Spells List:

Spiritual Trifecta – Rank 3
Heavy Telekinesis – Rank 3
Skills List:
Staff Mastery – Rank 1
Physical Resistance – Rank 1
Magical Potency – Rank 1
Lesser Spirit Coins: 1,415

It was the first time Xavier had taken a proper look at his stats since he'd received all the titles from finishing the first floor, and he had to say... he was impressed. With all those titles, his new robes and staff, not to mention the two skills he'd just gotten, he felt more ready than ever.

If this is how strong I am now, how strong will I be once I clear the tenth floor? That's when they would complete the first mission and be able to return to Earth. At least for a short time.

For a moment, his mind wondered. *When I entered the first floor, it said it was one of a thousand. Will we have to clear all one thousand floors before we can fully return to Earth? And if we do have to do that... how much stronger will I be by then?*

He gazed at the door, then at the ceiling. *One thousand floors...* And if he earned a title for each of them? *I would become unstoppable.*

Xavier gripped the new staff tightly. He already felt like he'd spent far too much time in the Staging Room, even though he knew they were well ahead of any other team. He was itching to enter the next floor. His heart beat faster as he anticipated it.

How many levels will I gain this time?

Without hesitation, Xavier stepped up to the door. He looked at Howard, Siobhan, and Justin. He had an idea. "I don't know what this floor will look like, but if we can..." He bit his lip. "I won't have time to loot everything I kill." He touched his Storage Ring. "Nor will I have the space to store everything. But the three of you..."

Siobhan smiled, excitement clear in her eyes. "You want us to trail behind you?"

Xavier nodded. "Only after I've slain the monsters. And, well, you might not be able to keep up."

Howard hefted his new tower shield, his forehead creased. "I suppose we'll have to get used to being outside a Safe Zone, as there'll be floors without 'em soon. But what if we get into some danger? If we so much as hit an enemy, you'll lose your solo bonus."

Justin glanced between Howard and Xavier. He leant forward, cleared his throat. "And, you know, we don't want to *die*. Don't forget that part."

Howard gave Xavier an intense look. "He's not going to let us die." The man tilted his chin up. "Are you?"

Xavier looked at the floor. He didn't want to put them in danger, but he couldn't think of a better, more efficient way to loot the floor than having them trailing behind him, doing it for him. It would save him a lot of time, which he would need if he was going to get into the Top 100 again. But if one of them were in danger, and he had to move backward to save them... it would mean a loss of time.

He raised his head. "I'm not going to let any harm come to any of you. Only move forward if it's safe. I'll kill everything in my path. Head back to the Safe Zone if you have to."

Siobhan nodded. "It's the least we can do for you."

Xavier smiled. Glad she was onboard. Though he still felt a little guilty, risking their lives by asking this of them. But if he put things into perspective... *Everyone's lives back on Earth are at risk. I've gained these titles, and it would be selfish not to do the best I can with them.*

The second floor looked entirely different to the first. The party had been teleported to the middle of a small, cozy cavern. The walls were rough, jagged rock, and dirt fell to the ground when they brushed against it.

The ceiling was covered by some odd-looking glowing moss

that was enough to illuminate the place in an eerie, green light. Xavier wondered what would appear if he had the Identify skill.

The cavern was their Safe Zone. Xavier preferred the last one. But it wasn't as though he would hang around. He walked to the archway leading out of it. At his back was the door to the Staging Room.

The wooden door looked strange in the cave. A part of him wondered if he should get a lay of the land before attempting this floor, as it would give him a better chance of clearing the floor fast enough to gain a record, but that shouldn't be necessary.

If I did that, it would slow our time getting to the next floor, which would mean it would take us longer to get back to Earth. That's what he was doing this all for, after all.

Xavier didn't wave goodbye to the others. He didn't want to waste a single second.

He held his new, heavy staff in both hands. There was a thin film of wavy air at the archway, almost like some sort of protective barrier. It obscured whatever was ahead. He stepped through it, sure that no matter what was on the other side, it wouldn't be able to do him any real damage.

The instant he stepped through, a series of screeching roars filled the musty air and two beasts barrelled toward him.

Chapter 34
I'm Just Going to Need to Kill Them as Fast as I Can

XAVIER STOOD BY THE SMALL ARCHWAY OUTSIDE OF THE Tower of Champions' second-floor Safe Zone, facing down two ugly beasts that bounded toward him.

They were coming at him fast, but with his Speed being what it was, he had plenty of time to scan them.

{Giant Mole Rat – Level 11}
{Giant Mole Rat – Level 11}

Xavier smiled. The beasts were barely higher level than the ones on the last floor, though he imagined they would pose quite the challenge to a *normal* party of Level 6s.

Will every floor increase in difficulty this slowly? Will the next floor be Level 12 monsters, then 13, and so on and so forth?

Though he supposed that would be rather difficult when it came to reaching the one-thousandth floor...

No point thinking too hard on it right now. I'll find out eventually.

The slavering beasts opened giant maws as they ran toward him, their screeches so loud they stung his eardrums.

Something was odd about their screeches. The air shifted,

reverberating forward from their disgusting mouths. Like their screeches were some sort of sonic attack. *If my Toughness was lower, would this incapacitate me?*

The Giant Mole Rats had no fur, were deathly skinny with no meat on their bones at all. He could almost see their entire skeletons through their pale flesh. Their white, taut skin contrasted beady, glowing-red eyes, and their teeth looked sharper and longer than any rat's had a right to be.

The sonic attack was interesting. None of the Black Pumas had used any spells. *I suppose this is a different floor, with different difficulties.* He'd keep that in mind. His enemies might have unexpected tricks up their sleeves.

But if the Giant Mole Rats were capable of anything beyond this, he wasn't going to wait and find out.

Xavier activated Spiritual Trifecta then slammed a Heavy Telekinesis into the two mole rats. He didn't want to waste more time than necessary. The mole rats flew into the rock walls with a loud *crunch.*

I'm getting far too used to the sounds of bones breaking...

He didn't know how much longer Spiritual Trifecta would last now he'd gained all those titles and was wielding the Spirit Staff of Might, but he was eager to find out.

It almost didn't feel worth keeping track, as his stats changed so damned quickly, but knowing how long his spells and their cooldowns lasted would make everything run a hell of a lot more smoothly.

He glanced around the cavern he found himself in after the Giant Mole Rats had been dealt with. More glowing moss on the ceiling. The same rock walls. Only one exit—that last part he was glad for. The first floor had been a straight line. Maybe, if he were lucky, this one would be a straight line too.

But something told him that wouldn't be the case. Something told him this would be a maze.

If this is a maze and I clear every cavern before moving through to the next tunnel in the underground world, then I'll need to make sure the others know which way I go if the tunnels go forking off in different directions.

If Howard, Siobhan, and Justin took a turn he hadn't through the tunnels, they'd likely be forced to fight. And that, he couldn't afford.

He sprinted toward the cavern's exit, glancing at the Safe Zone countdown timer at the side of his vision. *That timer won't be there when the others leave the Safe Zone, which means I won't be able to track how long this floor takes. I suppose that won't change how long I do it for.*

Only a few seconds passed before Xavier encountered the next set of Giant Mole Rats. Should he take the same approach as he had with the Black Pumas, making them run after him? Getting all of their aggression and taking them down at the same time?

There had been risks in that. He'd almost died, for one. But if he *hadn't* done it, he might not have finished the first floor of the tower as quickly as he had.

Except the Giant Mole Rats were too damned big for that to be a viable option, and the cavern and tunnels too narrow. The second cavern was far smaller than the first, and he couldn't see how he'd get past these beasts and run to the next cavern if they weren't dead first.

I'm just going to need to kill them as fast as I can.

The next cavern was a narrow one, and it had two Giant Mole Rats just as the first had. They bounded toward him with their slavering maws opening wide, and their screeching screams stinging his ears. Their bones shifting, pulling their skin this way and that as they ran. The silver sheen from Spiritual Trifecta had yet to dissipate—five seconds had passed since he'd cast it.

Xavier slammed his new staff into the first Giant Mole Rat's skull as it leapt toward him. The beast died instantly, but that didn't stop its momentum from moving toward him. The weight of the beast slammed Xavier into the rocky ground.

Something bit his ankle, puncturing his flesh. The other Giant Mole Rat.

Spiritual Trifecta chose that moment to run out. The exhaustion slammed into him, and the pain came with it. But the mole rat's teeth weren't able to penetrate more than Xavier's flesh—they were stopped at the bone, as though trying to gnaw through metal.

And the pain... wasn't as intense as it could have been. In fact, once he solidified his resolve, it felt more like something was pinching the flesh of his ankle rather than biting it.

A harsh pinch—like with pliers or something—but he could deal with that.

Xavier could have pushed the Giant Mole Rat's corpse off him, with raw strength or Heavy Telekinesis, but he went for the wiser, more efficient option. He willed the corpse directly into his Storage Ring.

A weight lifted off him. Or rather, disappeared completely. But the other beast still gnawed at his ankle like a starving dog on a bone with a bit of meat still on it. As Xavier hadn't let go of his staff, and its reach was incredible, he slammed it down at the Giant Mole Rat's head.

His ears stopped ringing the moment the rat beast died. He hadn't even noticed that screeching, roaring spell had still been coming from its mouth.

Xavier snapped back to his feet, stumbled one step, then kept running through the cave tunnels.

The pain in his ankle doubled, but it still held his weight. Felt like he'd rolled it a little on a jog rather than had it ripped into by massive teeth. *I guess this is what it's like, having effectively 74 Toughness.*

He didn't *quite* feel like a tank, but that might have been because of his lack of armour.

Looking through his notifications as he ran to the next chamber, one of them made his eyes widen.

Physical Resistance has reached Rank 2!

It was the first time any of his skills had actually ranked up.

Todd Herzman

Xavier couldn't help but be surprised. *All it took was being tackled to the ground by a corpse and having my ankle gnawed at by a giant rat monster.* All in all, he couldn't complain, though it seemed like a dangerous skill to train.

He would bring it up later and see what changes gaining a rank in the skill had brought.

Xavier sprinted down the tunnel, already disappointed in how he'd handled that last fight. Yes, he'd turned it into a win, and it hadn't taken him that long, but getting taken to the ground while fighting only two opponents made him realise how fragile he still was. If he was determined to solo every floor of this tower, he'd be the only one who could get himself out of danger.

If I make a single mistake, it could cost me my life. And if I die, the chances of the people of Earth surviving plummet. He knew how arrogant that thought sounded, but it was simply the truth. No one else would be able to get the titles he'd gotten. He might not be a force to be reckoned with yet, but that would change as he rose through the levels and gained more spells.

And my next class. He was still four levels away from that. He wondered what the class might be. What new spells it would offer. While he loved Heavy Telekinesis and Spiritual Trifecta, there was something missing from the way he fought. He could benefit from more variety.

He was disappointed to find Spiritual Trifecta still only lasted six seconds despite having 76 points in Spirit. The cooldown for the spell had only reduced by two seconds, as well, putting it at twelve seconds. *Maybe I've hit the limit for how long it lasts, and the cooldown as well. I wonder when that spell will gain another rank, and what that might do for it. Will it simply make it stronger?*

Heavy Telekinesis had an absurdly short cooldown time. It hadn't been taken down more than three seconds, which was frustrating, but the spell definitely felt stronger than before.

Now he knew the type of floor this was—tunnels and caverns filled with Giant Mole Rats with sonic, ear-piercing screams—he knew exactly what to do to clear it fast.

242

As long as no surprises come my way, I might be able to complete this floor faster than the last one. Especially as I won't need to worry about looting the corpses. The Safe Zone's countdown timer had stopped a few seconds ago, which meant the others had stepped out of it. They'd be coming upon the first two corpses now.

He made it to the next chamber and grinned. It was larger, and there were even more Giant Mole Rats to fight.

Shouldn't be long until I gain my next level.

Chapter 35
A Bloody Maze

Xavier felt like a whirlwind of death.

A whirlwind of death. That sounds awesome.

He didn't know slaughtering monsters could be so... *fun*. A small pang of guilt still lived within him because he was *enjoying* killing. But if he was to become strong enough to defend Earth, he had to feed this feeling.

Had to embrace it.

Xavier used Spiritual Trifecta to increase the speed at which he ran through the tunnels. He barely slowed down if he could help it. With Heavy Telekinesis having such a short cooldown, he rarely used his staff for physical combat.

The sound of screeching rats filled the cave tunnels until they were choked off by the death he brought them. The Heavy Telekinesis spell's casting net had widened dramatically now his Intelligence was over 70, and he knew that Spirit must be doing *something* to make it stronger.

Magical Potency had ranked up three times since he'd entered this floor. It was now at Rank 4. Every time it went up a rank, he *felt* his magic get stronger. The rats flew harder into the walls, making large holes in the rock and dirt.

At one point, he realised he had to temper the spell. If he kept going like this, he might bring the entire damned cave system down. *That's the last thing I need.*

After killing ten more of the giant rat beasties, Xavier had reached Level 7. He'd been tempted to throw all five of his free stats into Intelligence, but that would be a mistake. He didn't need his magic to be stronger. Not down in these tunnels. Not when he could already one-hit every one of these things. Apparently none of them possessed the same sort of magical resistance as the Puma Prime he'd faced at the end of the first floor.

Besides, his Intelligence would have gone up when he'd gained Level 7, and with his Magical Potency skill being Rank 4, his magic was getting stronger without him having to put any extra stats into it.

No, the one attribute that lagged the most out of *everything* he had was Speed. And right now, trying to clear this floor as fast as possible, Speed seemed like the most important of *all* his stats. The faster he could run from one cavern to the next through the tunnels, the faster he'd be able to take down the Giant Mole Rats.

And Speed didn't only help the pace of his movement, it also helped how fast he could react. His reflexes had grown *immensely* as his Speed attribute increased.

I've gotten it fairly high with titles alone, but now it's time to kick it into overdrive.

He threw those five free stat points straight into Speed, bringing it up to an effective 61. It was still his weakest stat, but considering how *high* his stats were, it was quite strong.

After that, he became even faster. Taking down the rats in groups of twos and fours as he sprinted from one cavern to the next. He'd been wrong about the cave system. It wasn't a maze. So far, he hadn't arrived at a single fork in the road. He was glad for that. A maze would be much more difficult to navigate, especially at speed.

And if this were a maze, it would benefit those who'd cleared much of the floor before heading back to the Staging Room and respawning everything to try again far more than it would benefit my raw speed of killing through it. I wouldn't have a chance at making the Top 100.

He had a feeling there would be far more than fifty beasts on this floor, as opposed to the last floor, but he wasn't about to do the math and the guesswork. Despite how quickly his mind now processed information and did calculations, he wanted to focus purely on the task at hand.

After he'd killed perhaps sixty of the beasts, his suspicions had been confirmed, and he was already halfway to Level 8.

This is feeling too easy. He supposed that was a good thing, but he'd thought that clearing floors as fast as he could would be a challenge. Right now he was just running and flinging Giant Mole Rats into one wall after another. It didn't take much skill or finesse. Only raw power.

Then he came upon something strange. Every cavern he'd entered had two exits. The tunnel he'd entered through, and the tunnel he would leave through. Those exits weren't always straight ahead. Sometimes they were off to the left, sometimes to the right. They narrowed and widened. They climbed and fell. One such exit was a sheer drop straight down a hole. When he'd dropped down, he'd wondered how anyone was supposed to get back up.

What if we wanted to get out of here and head back to the Safe Zone? It wasn't as though he'd brought any rope. He'd looked up. The walls were solid rock, but he reckoned a blade or spike of some sort could be lodged into them. *I'm sure it could be climbed back through.*

So even though the cave system was nothing like the dark forest he'd been in on the first floor, he'd figured it was a direct path, just like that had been.

Then he walked straight into a room with dead Giant Mole Rats lying on the ground, right by the wall, their bones crushed.

What the hell? Xavier stopped sprinting, which was a strange sensation after having been running for so long. His brow furrowed as he examined the dead Giant Mole Rats. He tilted his head to the side.

I was definitely the one who killed these two. He looked at the exit to the chamber and frowned. *How is this possible? How can I be back somewhere I've been?* As far as he was concerned, it *wasn't* possible. Shouldn't have been. There hadn't been a single fork in any of the caverns. He'd gone in a "straight" line.

There was no way that line could come back on itself like this. *Unless...*

Xavier swore under his breath.

Unless the walls are moving.

A deep rumbling sounded. The cavern he stood in shifted, ever so slightly. Vibrations ran up his legs. Into his chest. Dust and dirt fell from the rocky ceiling.

This had happened before, but only when he'd thrown a Giant Mole Rat—or four—into the rock wall of the cave. It was why he'd tempered how much power he used in his Heavy Telekinesis spell, something that was difficult to control.

The rumbling came again. More dust and dirt fell, bits getting into his hair and eyes. He brushed it off his face. *That definitely wasn't me.*

Footsteps crunched over the dirt. Xavier peered through the tunnel on the opposite side of the cavern. *Was that the way I came through earlier?* It was all beginning to look the same.

He gripped his staff tightly, but those footsteps didn't sound like Giant Mole Rats.

Howard stepped through the tunnel. The glowing moss on the ceiling illuminated him in a green glow, making his frowning features look somewhat sinister. "Xavier?" He glanced around. "What are you doing here?"

Xavier ran a hand through his hair as Siobhan and Justin came into the chamber. "I've been wondering the same thing." He explained what had happened. How he'd headed through the tunnels and ended up back here. The rumbling in the walls.

Siobhan caught on right away. "The walls are moving! The exits and entrances are shifting..." She stepped to the wall and leant an ear against it. Her forehead creased, eyebrows pulling together. After a moment, she nodded. "Something's tunnelling through the earth."

Justin stepped over to the two dead Giant Mole Rats. He placed a hand on each. They disappeared into his pack. "That doesn't sound good. How are you supposed to find the final boss if things change?"

"It's like a bloody maze." Howard peered at the ceiling, worry in his eyes. His sword was drawn, despite the fact that he shouldn't have to face anything in this place. "I hoped it wouldn't be a bloody maze."

The former cop had an odd look about him, shoulders tense. He looked more afraid than the others. *That's not what I would have expected.*

The deep rumbling came again. Louder this time. Xavier narrowed his gaze at the ceiling. "I think that *is* the final boss. Which means..."

"It might show up anywhere," Siobhan whispered. "So... we aren't safe out here in the tunnels."

Xavier considered that. *She's right.* "Should the three of you head back to the Safe Zone?"

"That's probably best." Howard nodded curtly, then turned around. He stopped abruptly as the rumbling became even louder and the tunnel they'd just walked through... *closed.*

A wall formed where there hadn't been one before, rock growing from the tunnel walls until it met in the middle, melded, and looked as though it had always been there.

Then another tunnel opened to Xavier's left.

Howard's shoulders drooped. "I don't think heading back to the Safe Zone is a viable option anymore."

Xavier shook his head. *This wasn't part of the plan. I need to keep moving.* But... where would he move to? And how would he be able to move fast if he had to keep an eye on these three?

"This... isn't good, is it?" Justin said.

"No." Xavier sighed. "It really isn't."

Chapter 36
I'd Like to Have a Chat with Whoever Came up with This Whole Thing in the First Place

Xavier thought about it and... he couldn't leave the others behind. Dragging them along would no doubt mean losing *any* chance at getting a spot in the Top 100, but chances were they would still clear this floor before anyone else in their tower, especially since he was already so far ahead.

And he could still get the solo title, as long as he didn't let any of the others contribute to the fight.

He wasn't going to let the others get hurt or killed because of his pursuit of power. Besides, if they did end up face-to-face with the final boss of this place, they would likely try and fight it. Even if they did end up dead, their contribution would be on record, and he'd lose out on that solo title.

Xavier blinked, a little worried about where his thoughts had gone. *Am I really thinking that cold and practically?* He shrugged the thought away. It wasn't worth delving into right now.

"We need to keep moving." Xavier turned to the new tunnel that had opened. "I don't know how we're going to get out of here, but nothing will get done standing still." His next words made him feel like a jerk, but he saw no way around them—they were in a rush, after all. "Just try to keep up. Shout if you're in trouble."

He jogged through the tunnel. Heard the others follow. He

didn't look back—didn't want to see what expressions they wore. *Should I have left them in the Staging Room?*

That rumbling sounded again, this time off to the left. The tunnel opened into a cavern he hadn't been in before. It was devoid of enemies. Not a single Giant Mole Rat. But as he passed through, he noticed blood on the wall.

I must have passed through here already, and the others stored the bodies in their Storage Rings, that's why it's empty.

Howard was right. This place was a bloody maze. Worse, it was a maze that changed itself as they went through it, making it impossible to navigate. *Wonderful.*

Xavier had to slow his jog considerably as the others trailed farther and farther behind. It took them another ten minutes before they encountered more Giant Mole Rats.

Xavier had them dead in less than a second, their bodies smashing into the rock wall, the *crunch* and *crack* of their bones making the others flinch. He hadn't tempered his power that time. The walls didn't shift. No dirt fell from the ceiling. *It was never me causing this. It was always... whatever is tunnelling through these walls. I couldn't cause this place to collapse if I tried.*

He still struggled to imagine the tunnels were made by a beast. They lacked any sort of uniformity. He imagined some giant rock worm slithering through, making tunnels... but they wouldn't look like this. The size was too varied, wasn't it?

It wouldn't be a worm, anyway. It's probably a really big Giant Mole Rat. Like, some Rat Prime or Rat King thing.

The very thought made him shudder, though he doubted it would be all that formidable. He'd taken down the Puma Prime easily enough, and that was *before* the titles he'd gained for clearing the floor.

He took down about thirty more Giant Mole Rats. Now that he was running even slower, to the point where it barely felt like running at all, this series of tunnels and beasts felt far too monotonous.

And the fact the tunnels kept shifting on them wasn't making things easier.

Xavier paused in one of the caverns, checking how long he had until he would reach the next level.

Mastery Points for this level: 84,200/100,000

He blinked, a little surprised. *Only fifteen more kills.* But it wasn't reaching the next level he was worried about. Having slowed a moment gave the others a chance to catch up. Howard was bent over, hands on knees, breathing deeply. "You don't know how to slow down, do you?"

Justin had fared better, though was still a bit out of breath. He glanced around the cavern. "Why are we stopping? Are we getting close to the boss?"

Siobhan's cheeks were flushed, making them redder than usual, even under the moss-green glowing light. She put a hand to the wall. It took a moment for Xavier to realise it wasn't for support. "I can still feel the vibrations. But I think it's farther away than before."

Xavier frowned. "I don't think it's going to appear until I've killed enough of the normal Giant Mole Rats. The tunnels shifting... it's probably just to make it harder for us to escape this place." He ran a hand through his hair. "Though why they'd want to make this place hard to escape, I don't understand."

"So people can't farm as easily?" Siobhan asked.

"Maybe," Xavier muttered.

"That doesn't seem very..." Justin trailed off. They all knew the next word out of his mouth was going to be *fair*.

And they all knew the System that had integrated them into the Greater Universe wasn't fair from the moment they'd been pulled from their lives and forced to fight someone else who'd chosen Champion.

"So what do we do?" Howard asked. "Keep running and killing

until we come upon the enemy we're after? I've noticed the enemies are thinning. Getting harder to find."

Siobhan leant her staff against the wall and crossed her arms, resting her chin on a hand. "It is strange the System would make it more difficult to farm here, especially when it's clearly designed the option of farming into the tower. Otherwise, why let us leave the floor in the first place?" She cocked an eyebrow. "It doesn't make a lot of sense."

Howard rested with his back against the wall. "Since when does any of this make any *sense*, eh? The System. The Greater Universe. Pulling us from our lives. Throwing us into this *madness*. Tearing us from our families." His knuckles turned white as he clutched the hilt of his sword. "I'd like to have a chat with whoever came up with this whole thing in the first place."

Xavier considered the man's words—the man's anger. *Should I feel angry about what's happened?* He feared for what might happen to the people of Earth. He worried for all those who'd already died. He felt guilt for what had happened to the Navy SEAL he'd faced, the one who'd died at the hand of the System. The one who'd died in his place.

But... fighting monsters? Gaining *power*? Being thrown into a magical fantasy universe where the fate of his world rested on his shoulders? *It's everything I ever wanted from all those books I read, all those books I tried to write.*

He wasn't angry about it. He was... *excited.*

Xavier didn't respond to Howard's words. He didn't know how to. "All right, we've stood still long enough. Let's keep moving." He pushed on, through the next tunnel. To the next cavern. Hoping his theory was correct—that all he needed to do was kill a few more of these rat beasties, then the final boss would show itself.

I've killed maybe ninety of these things. Definitely more enemies than the first level.

Contemplating the boss, he wondered if it would have guards —giant, rat-cronies—like the first-floor boss he'd faced. *I'd bet on that being the case.*

Though Xavier was excited to face the final boss and finally clear this stupid maze of a floor, he did worry about the others. The boss—and its guards—could come out from any side of a cavern. Up through the ground, sideways through a wall, down from the ceiling.

The odds of it attacking *him* first were only one out of four. And that's just the boss. If it had two or more guards... it would be difficult—very difficult—to keep the others out of danger. He would have to gain all the enemies' aggression right away, and he couldn't very well use Heavy Telekinesis on a Giant Mole Rat that was right next to one of them.

He'd send one of his party members flying into a wall. Probably kill them in one hit.

Xavier glanced back at Howard. *Hopefully that tower shield of his stops any attacks getting to him without him having to strike back.* The man had been a cop. Xavier had to trust Howard would protect the others when it counted.

They ran for a good ten minutes without encountering a single enemy. Xavier heard the others struggling behind him. Howard's breathing was the heaviest. The man must be specialising in Toughness and Strength, not Speed.

The rumbling in the walls grew louder and louder as they ran. The ground shook, more and more, until it felt like an earthquake. He kept glancing at the ceiling, hoping the rocks wouldn't fall down on them.

That would be a great way to go. Dying in a bloody mine collapse. Or is it a tunnel collapse, because this isn't a mine? Though he suspected he wouldn't die from being crushed. Not with his Toughness as high as it was.

The others he wasn't so sure about.

When the rumbling became louder than ever, and they *still* hadn't come upon any more beasts, Xavier made them stop. Howard once again bent at the waist, resting on his knees as he sucked in air. Siobhan breathed heavily, her face more flushed. Justin still looked mostly okay, considering.

"Why... did... we... stop?" Howard said between gasping breaths. "Not... that... complaining..."

Xavier came to stand in the middle of the cavern. The largest one that they'd found. "Because I think we're not the ones hunting anymore."

A rock fell from the ceiling, missing Siobhan's head by a hair-breadth and slamming into her shoulder. A massive, mole rat head stuck out from a gap where the rock had been.

Its giant maw opened in a screeching scream that had Howard, Siobhan, and Justin all falling to their knees.

Chapter 37
Time to Exterminate This Rat

THE SCREECHING SCREAM LAUNCHING OUT OF THE MOLE rat's throat was louder than any other Xavier had encountered.

He leapt toward the other members of his party, facing up at the beast and quickly scanning it as he raised his Spirit Staff of Might.

{Giant Mole Rat – Level 15}

It was the highest-level beast Xavier had seen in this place. The same level the Puma Prime had been. But he was sure this wasn't the floor boss.

This was just one of its rat-beasty cronies.

Xavier cast Heavy Telekinesis on the Giant Mole Rat.

You have defeated a Level 15 Giant Mole Rat!
You have gained 1,500 Mastery Points.
You have gained 1,500 Spirit Energy.

Well, that was easy.

The Giant Mole Rat looked like it had been crushed up into

the hole it had tunnelled through. Then the rock around it crumbled, and it fell down.

Straight at them.

"Move!" Xavier shouted, but there was blood running out of his party members' ears, and the screeching hadn't stopped. Nor had the rumbling. It was coming *through* the walls on every side of them.

Oh, crap, the bastard things are everywhere.

Holes formed at every side. Xavier lost count. They came so fast he couldn't wait for Heavy Telekinesis to come off cooldown. He activated Spiritual Trifecta, the rush of energy pumping through every inch of him.

Xavier wasn't afraid for his own life. He was sure he could take whatever came. But he'd brought these people in here and hadn't let them progress. He didn't want them dying, especially since he knew they would restrain themselves from attacking. For him.

They're my responsibility.

As Xavier sprinted past them at the nearest Giant Mole Rat, he saw Howard pull himself to standing, leaning on his great big tower shield. A glow emanated from the man, forming a transparent shield in front of him.

He waved for the others to huddle around him. The transparent shield spread outward, encompassing all three. *Some sort of tanky protective spell?* Xavier wondered.

If he was going to save these people, he couldn't focus on them. He had to put his entire focus into the fight.

His body glowing in silver, Xavier had six seconds where his physical and magical power would be boosted. He slammed the head of his new staff into a Giant Mole Rat rising from the ground by Justin's feet. Then he whirled, slamming it into the skull of another.

His strikes felt perfect, the knowledge he'd gained from acquiring the Staff Mastery skill guiding him through each movement. He knew exactly where to step. Exactly where to hold the staff.

And the staff... Its power reverberated in his hands. When his strikes contacted the enemy, he felt the extra power in them. The extra damage he caused. *Five percent from Staff Mastery. Fifteen percent from the staff itself.*

He grinned as blood spattered his face, revelling in the thrill of the fight like never before. *Is this Spiritual Trifecta, doing its work? Or is this enjoyment... all from me?*

Another Giant Mole Rat came down from the ceiling, ready to pounce straight onto Howard's head, teeth no doubt sharp enough to puncture the man's skull. Xavier slammed it into the wall with his Heavy Telekinesis, then swung around and slammed his staff into the ribs of a Giant Mole Rat that reared back on its hind legs.

The Giant Mole Rats came, one after the other. From above. From below. From the walls on either side. Until finally, they all lay dead before him. *Nine. This thing had nine Level 15 cronies. That makes ninety-nine enemies killed on this floor.*

With all those enemies dead, there was still no sight of the big boss. Howard and the others looked a bit battered—one of the Giant Mole Rats had gotten through Howard's shield before Xavier could stop it. There was a great big slash across the man's tower shield. He'd been knocked onto his ass, barrelling into the other two and taking them down with him.

Xavier helped Siobhan to her feet, then Howard and Justin next.

Siobhan clutched one of her ears, the other gripped tight around her staff. Her gaze shifted left and right. "Is it over?" she said quite loudly.

Has she gone deaf? Have they all?

Xavier shook his head. "Almost." He raised a single finger. "One more." He enunciated the words clearly, in case they needed to read his lips to understand what he was saying.

At least, I think it'll only be one more.

The rumbling became louder than ever. He turned to the direction it came from, standing in front of the others.

The wall exploded outward. Rocks pelted toward him.

Slammed into his legs. His gut. His head. He'd had time enough to cover his face and turn off to the side, the worst of it hitting him in the back.

How is a normal team supposed to survive this level?

The rocks kept plummeting toward him. Howard had his shield raised. The others behind him. But that tower shield didn't look like it would hold for long. Every rock left a massive dent and pushed him back two feet.

The idea came, Xavier hoped not too late. He turned, faced the rocks, one hand flung over his eyes, the other flung forward, staff in hand. He cast his spell.

Heavy Telekinesis!

Xavier dropped his arm, opened his eyes.

The rocks weren't flung backward like he'd hoped. Instead, they stopped dead in the air. No, not dead. They hovered there, vibrating on the spot and slowly rotating, being pushed forward and back minutely, as though it were being acted upon by two opposing forces similar in power. He peered through them and saw a large, ugly, rat-like face with a weird, wicked smile contorting it, two long, sharp teeth jutting down over its bottom lip.

Like the Puma Prime had been humanoid, so was this rat-thing. It stepped forward. The rocks fell to the ground, splattering it like heavy rain.

Xavier scanned the beast.

{Rat King – Level 20}

Level 20? He knew the System wasn't fair, but he'd thought the tower might be different.

How could a normal party, from a world like his, expect to survive against this thing? *Maybe they would be able to escape. But then, how could they get back to the Safe Zone?*

The Rat King held a staff. Unlike Xavier's, it was twisted and gnarled. It looked more like a massive branch than an actual magic staff, but it glowed with power all the same.

The beast had a long, thick, prehensile tail that whipped back and forth behind it, tearing rivets into the wall. The Rat King had more bulging muscles on it than a steroid-infused bodybuilder on comp day. It stood nine-feet tall and had an odd beard that made it look like some sort of homeless wiseman or Viking god, the way it was clutching at its staff.

At least, it would have looked like one if it weren't a damned rat.

Unlike the Puma Prime, it didn't wear armour. But fortunately for Xavier's eyes, it *did* wear clothes. Red robes the colour of blood. They were sleeveless and open at the front, but at least they covered its lower body.

"You have come far to meet your deaths, humans," the Rat King said. Its voice was absurd. Raspy and high-pitched at the same time, though still menacing.

Xavier stepped forward, hoping to put the damned thing's attention onto him. He raised his chin. Heavy Telekinesis had already reached the end of its cooldown, but Spiritual Trifecta had worn off and needed a few more seconds. *Maybe I can stall this big rat beasty for a moment.*

"We didn't come here to meet our deaths." Xavier clutched his staff, puffed up his chest. Honestly, he felt more than a little ridiculous, and the raised eyebrow of the Rat King told him it wasn't intimidated in the slightest. "We came here to mete out yours."

The Rat King threw its head back and laughter filled the cavern, echoing off the rock walls. Its laugh was so loud it made dust and dirt fall from the ceiling, but at least it didn't make his ears burn. *They've stopped ringing. That damned screeching has finally ceased. Maybe the others will be able to hear again soon.*

He didn't know how fast their healing was. *I should have looked for health potions at the System Shop. I might have still had a few Lesser Spirit Coins to afford them.* Honestly, he simply hadn't thought he would need them. He still didn't think he would. But he hadn't expected to have the others along with him. That hadn't been a part of the plan. *If I tell them to run, will it just shift the Rat King's attention onto them?*

Xavier grinned as Spiritual Trifecta's cooldown ended. He took his staff in both hands. *Time to exterminate this rat.* He sighed inwardly. *Did I really just think that? Damn, that's cheesy. At least I didn't say it out loud...*

The Rat King stopped laughing. It wiped a tear off its cheek. "You may have killed my children, but they were weak. They were nothing compared to me." It raised its staff. "I am the Rat King! I rule over the underearth with an iron—"

Xavier didn't have time for a villainous monologue, especially one from a rat. Not when he was trying to clear this floor fast. He cast Spiritual Trifecta then Heavy Telekinesis a second later, already leaping into the air toward his enemy.

The Rat King wasn't flung back far, however. It only stumbled a few steps, shock widening its eyes.

Just like the Puma Prime, it appeared resistant to magic. And that resistance must have been quite high, considering how much stronger Xavier had gotten between floors.

He gritted his teeth. *Maybe I just need to get some more versatile spells.*

Xavier, midleap, struck out for the Rat King's head. That's when he noticed the almost imperceptible glow about the king. *Some sort of protective spell? Is that why it was able to resist my telekinesis?*

Well, whatever it was, Xavier would break through it.

The Rat King's tail whipped out. Though Xavier was plenty fast enough to avoid it, the ten-foot tail wasn't aiming for *him*.

It was aiming for the others.

Xavier gritted his teeth, following through on his strike. The Rat King's head snapped to the side. Blood flew from its mouth and splattered the cave wall.

A loud *thud* sounded behind him. Flesh hitting metal. Xavier couldn't glance back. There wasn't time. All he could do was hope the others would be okay.

Xavier managed two more strikes before he kicked off the beast's chest. He flipped backward in the air.

Back when he'd done parkour, he'd learnt a few tricks. Flips, strictly speaking, *weren't* parkour—he remembered the vast number of arguments and memes about it. But they did look cool. So he'd learnt how to do a wall flip. Though, nine times out of ten, he hadn't managed it.

Hopefully this is the one time I do.

With his newfound strength and speed, he'd kicked off the beast way too hard. He almost slammed into the ceiling but managed to catch it on his feet and kick off that too.

I wonder if I can learn some sort of acrobatics skill...

He rotated in the air and ended up landing on his feet. As he'd been in the air, he'd seen the others. Howard picked himself off the ground on the far-left wall—that tail-whip must have thrown him into it, even though he'd gotten his shield up in time to block.

Rocks flew at his party members.

Xavier landed in a crouch facing the Rat King and cast Heavy Telekinesis again, once more blessing its short cooldown. He cast it on the rocks and stopped them from reaching his party just in time.

He wished he could fling those damned rocks straight at the Rat King, but that didn't seem possible.

The Rat King had a wicked smile on its face as Xavier ran toward it. It slammed its staff into the ground. The ground shook, opened up beneath Xavier—

And swallowed him whole.

Chapter 38
Rat Bastard, King of the Pests

ONE MOMENT XAVIER RAN ACROSS THE ROCKY GROUND toward the Rat King—the Tower of Champions' second-floor boss—the next he fell into a hole that had formed straight beneath him.

He hadn't been fast enough to avoid it. Hadn't even known what was happening until it was too late. He didn't get a chance to climb out before the earth shrank, the walls closing in until he was trapped on all sides, his arms and staff clamped to his body and only his head exposed above the earth.

Xavier's eyes widened. How had he found himself in this mess? How could this damned pest be powerful enough to be a match for him? *Did I get too cocky? The damned thing has earth magic. I've never faced anything like it before.*

Being stuck in that hole made him long for the Cast Element spell. Maybe he'd be able to get out of this mess if he had it.

"Form behind me!" Howard shouted as the Rat King turned its attention toward the other members of his party.

Xavier, stuck in the earth, wasn't in a position where he could move. He couldn't turn his head and look at them. He was stuck facing forward, straight at the smug-looking King of the Rodents. He wanted to shout. Yell. *Scream.*

None of this was part of the plan! He'd had to bring them along to *protect* them, yet now it looked like they would come to harm.

Spiritual Trifecta ran out, the silver sheen that had enveloped his body dissipating to nothing. With the spell's deactivation, Xavier felt even more trapped than ever. He couldn't move a muscle, no matter how much he strained.

He felt weak. As weak as he'd been before the System had come. And *so damned exhausted.*

How could that be possible? It was simply dirt and rock that surrounded him. He should be able to break out of it. Shouldn't he? Or was it simply that he felt weak, and so he *became* weak?

Xavier finally let that shout rasp from his throat as he opened his mouth wide. His face contorted in rage, staring at the laughing Rat King that approached Howard, Siobhan, and Justin.

I can't let them get hurt.

Heavy Telekinesis was ready again. He used it. Slammed it into the rock and dirt directly in front of him. Though he could barely aim it, unable to move his arms, all he needed was to push it forward. Make some room.

Once the spell had been cast, he could finally move an arm. He struggled, dragging it up his body as he heard one of the others shout.

"Don't strike it! He can still get the title!" It was Howard's voice, booming in a shout.

That fool. They should forget about that. Hell, they should run out of here.

"You distract it, we'll get him out." Siobhan. Her voice somehow panicked and calm at once.

Xavier heard footsteps. Two sets. He struggled, but still wasn't able to budge out of the damned earth. Then hands grasped his shoulders, digging through the ground.

He heard heavy breathing. *Siobhan?*

The earth shifted. Moving of its own volition, as though a spell had been cast. No, not *as though.* A spell *had* been cast. The hole around him widened just enough for it to no longer keep him stuck.

He was able to turn. Siobhan had a look of intense concentration on her face. *Of course. She's a mage. She must have Cast Element.* Justin stood above him. He grabbed the warrior's hand. The boy might be nowhere near as strong as Xavier, but he still had supernatural strength compared to a normal human, and pulling Xavier free was easy enough.

"Watch out!" Howard yelled.

The Rat King's tail swished straight for Siobhan's head. The woman gasped. Xavier ran toward her. He could get struck by that thing and survive. But Siobhan? She would likely die in one hit.

I won't let that happen!

But he was too slow. Fast as he was, as many points as he'd put into Speed, he was too slow, and he could *see* it. All this had happened in less than two seconds, and his Heavy Telekinesis spell wasn't ready yet. How could it not be ready yet? How could so much happen in such a short period of time?

Siobhan raised her staff as though to block, her other hand coming up over her head. The crystal on her staff glowed brightly. *Another spell. But what could she do to stop that thing?*

White light engulfed Howard. The man disappeared, reappearing directly in front of Siobhan, his shield up and ready to block the Pest King's whipping tail.

I know that spell. It's the Summon spell. She has both of the spells I lost.

The massive tail struck Howard's tall tower shield. He went flying to the side, knocking over Siobhan with him, but that didn't matter.

They're alive. They're both alive.

Xavier faced the Rat Bastard, King of the Pests, filled with a rage he'd never felt before. There had never been a time in his life when he'd been in a position to protect others. Never been a time when he was needed so much. Never been a time when people had *trusted* him like his party had.

And he wasn't about to let them down. He wanted to be deserving of that trust, just as he wanted to deserve the title he'd earned—*First Defender of Planet Earth.*

He raised his staff. The Rat King's face had blood plastered on it from the first time Xavier had struck it. *It must be injured. I won't fall for its damned tricks again.*

The spell ready now, Xavier shot a Heavy Telekinesis at the Rat King. That glow was visible about it once more. That protective barrier around it that seemed to work somewhat like armour.

Xavier didn't care. He ran forward. When the Rat King slammed its staff on the ground to create another hole, he leapt straight over it. In midair, Xavier cast Spiritual Trifecta then slammed the head of his staff into the rodent's face.

The rodent's head snapped to the left.

Bam.

To the right.

Bam.

To the left again.

Xavier was falling now. Just as he had the first time. But he didn't kick off the rat's chest and do another flip. Instead, while it was still disorientated, he hooked his staff around the rat bastard's neck, making him swing about its shoulders until he clung to its back, hands wrapped around his staff.

And he pulled. Choking the rat out with all his strength. With everything Spiritual Trifecta offered him. He pulled. And pulled. When Heavy Telekinesis was ready again, he slammed it into the back of the Rat King's head with all the power he could muster.

The glow about the rat was gone. Whatever protection it had before, it didn't have any more. The full might of Xavier's spell slammed into it.

The head exploded forward. As hard as Xavier was pulling his staff against its neck... the Rat King's head flew clean off.

Holy crap.

The Rat King's body went limp.

You have defeated a Level 20 Rat King!
You have gained 4,000 Mastery Points.
You have gained 4,000 Spirit Energy.

Xavier blinked. Just like when he'd killed the Puma Prime, this floor boss offered twice as much experience as he'd expected. Enough to push him over the line.

Congratulations, you have reached Level 8!
Your health has been regenerated by 50%!
Your Spirit Energy limit has increased by 100!
You have received +1 Intelligence, +1 Willpower, and +1 Spirit!
You have received +5 free stat points!
All your spells have refreshed and are no longer on cooldown!

Xavier leapt backward off the Rat King as it slammed into the ground with a loud *thud*. More notifications followed the first, and he breathed a sigh of relief now the party was out of danger.

Congratulations! You have cleared the Second Floor of the Tower of Champions.
Party Member Contribution:
Xavier: 100/100 Kills.
Howard: 0/100 Kills.
Justin: 0/100 Kills.
Siobhan: 0/100 Kills.
No shared attributions apply on this floor.

Somehow, Xavier was glad and annoyed at the same time. The others had *definitely* contributed. Howard had kept them out of danger, tanking the boss's attacks for the others. Siobhan had opened the earth for him, and Justin had helped get him out of being stuck in that hole.

He was sure he would have gotten out of it eventually... but the way things had been going, he might not have survived the fight had they not been there to distract the floor boss.

Title Unlocked!
Second-Floor Climber: This title has been upgraded. You have cleared the Second Floor of the Tower of Champions, and shall be rewarded.
You have received +4 to all stats!
Note: The title "First-Floor Climber" has been stricken from your soul.

The last title has been stricken from my soul? That... sounds strange. Also souls are real?

Though he was glad the second title combined with the first. He imagined what it would be like if he cleared a thousand floors. Reading through his status information would be quite the task.

Title Unlocked!
Solo Tower Climber 2: This title has been upgraded. You have cleared a floor of the Tower of Champions by yourself. You are either very brave or very stupid for attempting such a feat. Know that whether this feat was achieved through sheer skill or unbridled luck, you shall be rewarded.
You have received +16 to all stats!
Note: The title "Solo Tower Climber 1" has been stricken from your soul.

Xavier frowned. Honestly, he wasn't sure if he *deserved* this title, this time around. He hadn't done the floor *by himself*. Not strictly. Though he'd been the only one to deal any damage to the enemy beasts.

That's quite a loophole. A party could come in and tank for one member, letting them clear the whole floor... Though, he honestly doubted the likelihood of that. Maybe if that party member were paying a great deal.

Though he supposed he'd found himself in that exact situation...

Title Unlocked!
1st Second-Floor Climber: Out of Champions from five competing worlds, your party is the *first* to clear the Second Floor of the Tower of Champions within your instance.
You have received +10 to all stats!
Note: As you have a similar title, "1st First-Floor Climber" has been combined with this title and shares its stats.

Xavier smiled. He was glad they'd received that last title. He was sure they'd still be the first to clear this floor, even with the trouble they'd had when the tunnels and walls began to shift. *They'll be shifting for everyone, so it's not as if we'll be the only ones dealing with it.*

In 30 seconds, you and your party will be returned to the Staging Room.

The others snapped into action. Justin knelt down and snatched the Rat King's staff. Howard grabbed the head, transporting it to his Storage Ring with a disgusted look. Siobhan did the same for the body of the Rat King itself.

Xavier looked at his robes. Once again drenched in blood and dirt. But he couldn't seem to care about it.

He did frown, however, as he noticed the lack of another notification he'd hoped for. *I didn't get into the Top 100 for this floor...* He shouldn't have been surprised. It had taken much longer than before. Though he felt a tinge of disappointment, titles weren't the only thing he was aiming for.

It was in that moment that *another* notification did appear. His eyes widened. *Maybe I was wrong.* But no, this was something else —something he'd been hoping to receive but hadn't realised he was quite this close to getting.

He looked at the notification. *Two* notifications, he was happy to see.

Chapter 39
First to 500 Stats

XAVIER SMILED AS HE READ THE TWO NOTIFICATIONS, standing in the blood-drenched cavern where he and the others had faced the final boss of the second floor.

Title Unlocked!
500 Stats: This is a common title that everyone receives when they have reached a total of 500 combined stat points.
You have received +3 to all stats!
Note: As you have a similar title, "100 Stats" has been combined with this title and shares its stats.

Title Unlocked!
First to 500 Stats: You are the first person from your world to reach a total of 500 combined stat points.
You have received +12 to all stats!
Note: As you have a similar title, "First to 100 Stats" has been combined with this title and shares its stats.

Xavier's eyebrows shot up his forehead. He'd gained so much in such a short period of time. He wasn't sure how long this floor had taken them. It was much harder to judge without the count-down timer for the Safe Zone running in the corner of his eye.

He wasn't surprised his party had been the first to clear this floor, and he most certainly wasn't surprised he'd been the first from his world to reach five hundred combined stat points.

He must be the equivalent of Level 60 right now, which made him wonder why a Level 20 floor boss had given him so much trouble, to the point where it made him shudder thinking about how many others might lose their lives fighting it. Especially Champions from his world. Though he also knew they wouldn't be facing it for at least a week.

Maybe we can stop by the tavern, like Justin suggested. If there are parties there, we could give them tips, tell them what they might expect. As none of the other parties would have completed the first floor yet, they would still have a chance to farm the level.

The thirty-second timer ran out. Xavier and his party were returned to the Staging Room once more. Once again, four loot boxes sat in the centre of the room. They looked like the exact ones that had been there before, but Xavier was sure the rewards inside had been reset.

He looked down at his robes. A moment ago, they'd been covered in rat blood. Mostly from the Rat King. Now, they were as pristine as the moment he'd first put them on. His health and Spirit Energy were at their fullest, and he still had five free stat points to spend.

The others looked a little shaken. Howard had a frown digging deep ruts in his forehead that made him look older than he was. Or perhaps it just made him look his age. Justin clutched the hilt of his sword even though he'd not swung it while they'd cleared the floor. Siobhan had returned her staff to her Storage Ring and was rotating the ring around her finger, turning it around over and over like some nervous tic.

They'd been through more than he'd bargained for them, and

they'd still had the self-control not to strike a single enemy during that last encounter, which had no doubt been quite frightening.

Howard looked at his shield. Where it had been marred and dented by the Rat King's vicious tail, now it was clean of even a single scratch. The man's frown deepened. "Almost as though it didn't happen," he muttered.

"It happened." Siobhan stared at her Storage Ring. She let out a sigh, a smile returning to her face. A little more forced than usual. The redheaded mage looked at Xavier. "You fought well."

Xavier dipped his head. "Thank you. All three of you. You rallied together, got me out of that hole. And didn't strike the enemy once."

Howard rolled his shoulder, seemingly surprised it wasn't hurt. "You get the solo title?"

"I did. But not the record. Seems we didn't get through that one fast enough."

"At least we got through first," Justin said.

Howard grunted. "Siobhan's right. You fought well." His frown deepened, something Xavier hadn't thought possible. Even more lines crowded his forehead.

"Why am I sensing a but?" Xavier asked. He might not have known the former cop long, but he sensed he had more to say.

"But you should have been able to handle that Rat King on your own."

Xavier lowered his head. The words hit harder because of the truth in them. "I was thinking the same thing." He'd been sure he would have won even if the others hadn't been there to get him out of that hole.

Mostly sure.

But he shouldn't have *struggled*. He shouldn't have fallen for its tricks. And it shouldn't have taken him so *long*. In the end, it had been easy enough for him to kill. But that damned protective spell around it had thrown him off...

"You're strong. I'm not doubting that, not for a second. You're a scrapper, too. That's for sure. And you move with that staff quite well." Howard deposited his tower shield into his Storage Ring and sheathed his still drawn sword. "But you lack clear tactics. You lack *experience.*"

Siobhan leant against the wall. Her eyes downcast, still on the ring around her finger. "To be fair, we all lack experience in something like this. I think he's done incredibly well, considering."

Howard grunted. "Not saying he hasn't. Just saying he needs to do *better*. Considering his power, we shouldn't have been in danger in there." He raised his hands. "That's not me blaming you, Xavier. That's me wanting to help."

Xavier didn't feel blamed. Howard was only saying what had been niggling at his own mind.

Justin cleared his throat. "The other Champions, from other worlds... they'll have been practising for this. Even if they didn't come from wealth, they'll know what to expect. Know how to move in a battle, how to anticipate an enemy's movements." He cocked his head to the side. "Howard's right. You're strong. Powerful. You have a boundless amount of talent, but you need to temper that talent into skill. Forge it through experience." He turned his sword hilt around in his palm. "At least, that's what my fencing coach would have said."

"You're right." Xavier looked at his staff, thought about the two spells in his possession. Spiritual Trifecta. Heavy Telekinesis. Thought about his fighting style. Even with Staff Mastery, his fighting style was basically hit the enemy hard and fast and try not to let them hit him. There wasn't any finesse because he hadn't *needed* that.

All he'd needed was to throw those pests into a wall and break their bones on the rocks with one spell, then move onto the next. What kind of experience was that giving him?

That was just showing him that he was going through this tower on easy mode. So the moment it got hard—truly hard—he might make a mistake with real consequences. *Their deaths. Maybe even mine.*

And if he died? How would Earth fare against the forces of the

Greater Universe making its way to their world? No one could take the titles he'd hoarded. No one could use them but him.

He shut his eyes. "What do I do, then? We still have a lead. That means... we have time to train." He couldn't help fighting the words as he said them. He didn't *want* to stop and train. He wanted to keep pushing forward, faster and faster. Get through all ten floors as quickly as possible.

The sooner they did, the sooner they'd be allowed to return to Earth.

"We need to get you to Level 10," Siobhan said. "Get you to your next class before you clear the third floor."

Howard grunted his agreement. "True enough. But we need more than that. You need better spatial awareness. You're quick. Smart. But that's not doing *enough* for you. You move that staff well. Your Heavy Telekinesis is strong. But you need to be better."

"He should get more spells when he reaches Level 10." Siobhan was still turning her ring around and around. "But we didn't fully check the System Shop. We moved too fast last time because we were all filled with the thrill of getting those titles. We need to see just how expensive those spell books are. The manual said they're 'prohibitively expensive,' though, so perhaps that won't be an option. And we should see if there are health and... Spirit Energy potions."

The woman stopped turning the ring. She put her right palm facing up, then summoned the Tower of Champions manual. "Maybe there's something in here that can help." She flipped through the pages, clearly taking solace from doing so.

Justin walked over to the loot boxes. A smile kicked up the sides of his lips. "And we should see what's inside these."

Xavier looked at the three members of his party, beginning to realise how lucky he'd gotten to find them.

They're like my own personal support staff. Though his plan was to solo every level of the tower to gain as many titles as he could, part of him wished they could join in on the fight. That they could enter battles as a team.

But they were all too far behind him for that to be practical. Still, perhaps he should stop seeing himself as a loner. Maybe, even, he should stop thinking of them as just his party members. He wasn't sure how long he'd be connected to these people, but there were a thousand levels in the Tower of Champions.

Something told him they would all be connected to the tower itself until they cleared every one of those levels. And why not do that together?

Maybe, along the way, these people will become my friends...

Chapter 40
Like Some Cartoon Villain

XAVIER WALKED TO THE MIDDLE OF THE STAGING ROOM. He knelt by the loot box with his name on it. He'd put his Spirit Staff of Might into his Storage Ring, and he had the odd urge to rub his hands together greedily like some cartoon villain, or steeple his fingers and say, *Excellent.*

He smirked, pushed away those foolish thoughts, and opened the chest to see what rewards he'd gained this time.

You have gained +2 Skill Points.
You have gained 50,000 Mastery Points.
You have gained 20,000 Lesser Spirit Coins
Please choose your preferred item:

1. **Spell Book**
2. **Attribute Token**

Xavier felt the rush of receiving so many Mastery Points at once, and he smiled, having gained more skill points. The two skills he'd chosen last time—Physical Resistance and Magical Potency—had already gone up a few ranks from the previous floor. Staff

Mastery remained at Rank 1, but he would gain more soon enough, once he figured out how to improve the skill.

He tilted his head to the side, seeing his choices of items. His eyes widened. The choices seemed better than last time, at least to his untrained eye. *A Spell Book, or an Attribute Token...* He thought about asking the others, but he wanted to think about his decision first. While equipment was important, each of these would make permanent changes to him.

The manual does say Spell Books are very expensive from the System Shop. As to Attribute Tokens, I guess they up someone's attributes? He could imagine them being incredibly helpful for someone who didn't have so many titles like Xavier did.

His forehead creased heavily. Attributes seemed to be the most important thing in terms of raw power. The more attributes he gained, the better off he would be. Though he didn't know how many attributes the token would give him, or if he would be able to choose what they were, he knew it would make a difference to his level of power.

The Spell Book, however, would make him a more versatile fighter. And what Howard had been telling him was right. Xavier couldn't simply rely on brute force in battle. True, it *had* gotten them this far, but he would be even more powerful if he trained up his fighting ability and versatility.

He bit his lip, not sure what the right choice was. *Time to consult the others. Maybe they have the same choices. If one of them chooses the Attribute Token, it should give me an idea of how many attributes I'll gain if I use one, and if I get to choose which attribute it is. If one of them chooses the Spell Book, then I'll know if the spell given is random, and whether or not I can gain more than one spell.*

What if he gained a spell that wasn't even relevant to the way he fought? Like, levitation or something? Sure, it would be cool to hover off the ground, but it wouldn't be his first choice by far.

The others each had almost identical expressions on their faces to how he imagined he looked right now. Deep in thought, unsure what to choose.

They conversed for a short time about their options. Siobhan, as a mage like Xavier, decided to choose the Spell Book to help give Xavier an idea of what it would be. She also liked the idea of gaining another spell, so he didn't feel guilty about her losing out on attribute points.

Besides, she wouldn't be able to gain the title of being a part of the first party to clear a floor if she wasn't helping me out. She might not have as many titles as I do, but she'll have far more than most people by the time we're done with these ten floors.

The book appeared in her hand. She smiled and shook her head. "I'm still getting used to the fact that magic is real."

That brought a smile to Xavier's lips, too. With the people of Earth at risk, all the goals he wished to achieve, the power he needed—and very much *wanted*—to gain, he sometimes forgot to stop and appreciate how amazing this all was.

Even if it was more than a little bit terrifying, too.

Justin smiled as well, though his smile was smaller than Siobhan's. Howard was the only one who didn't smile. Seeing his face brought Xavier back to reality. Back to what each of them was trying to return to. Trying to protect.

Siobhan opened the book. A book that appeared to have a single place in which to open it. Her eyes darted back and forth as she read the script. "The spell has been chosen for me. There wasn't any option for me to choose it."

"What is the spell?" Xavier asked.

The woman frowned, tucking an errant strand of red hair behind her ear. "Well, first, it says this Spell Book is nontransferable. It will only work for me. And, second, it's a healing spell." She looked over at Xavier. "That's strange, isn't it? I thought we wouldn't get healing spells unless we chose a Support role? I didn't think there would be support roles once we chose Champion."

Xavier, standing by his loot box, put a hand to his chin. It had gotten stubbly in the last few days, and he idly ran his hand across the spikey hairs. "The information you guys told me about gaining our next classes at Level 10, you said the classes were based on our actions?"

Siobhan nodded. "Yes. The classes we're able to choose from will take into account how we've fought and what we've done between levels 1 and 10, what spells we've chosen and ranked up, as well as what skills we've learnt and trained."

Xavier nodded. He pointed at the Spell Book open in her hand. It felt strange to have a whole book for one spell, but if he questioned everything that was strange about the Greater Universe, he'd never get anything done.

"Perhaps that's what's happened here. You received this Spell Book because of your actions." Xavier motioned toward the door to the tower floors. "Any way we look at it, you *were* in a support role in that last fight. You helped me get out of that hole and you never struck the enemy. You've been gaining levels by trailing behind me and opening loot boxes, not by fighting."

Siobhan lowered her head and frowned. "That means my options might be limited, unless we farm some monsters to make things different."

"Are you disappointed by gaining a healing spell?" Xavier asked.

Siobhan shook her head and smiled. "Actually, no. I think it will be a very good thing to have." She pursed her lips. "But I don't want to lessen my fighting capabilities too much. Maybe the class I get to choose will be a mix—a mage-cleric hybrid of some sort. I can certainly see how my Summon and Heal spells could work well together." She glanced at Howard, perhaps remembering how she'd summoned him to her, and he'd tanked an enemy's attacks.

Cleric was typically a healer class in RPGs. It made Xavier wonder if there would be classes with names like that later on. And the woman was right—summoning a party member to her and healing them *did* sound powerful. "We'll make sure you get some more fighting in before you get to Level 10, to help influence your class choice."

"We should also see if her healing you while you kill a monster gains her Mastery Points," Justin said. "I haven't played all that many video games, but isn't that typically how a healer class gains experience?"

Xavier tilted his head to the side. "You're right. That could stop me from getting the solo title."

Siobhan sighed. "If that's true, it will basically make the spell useless."

Xavier had the impulse to put his hand on her shoulder and reassure her somehow, but thinking that only made him realise how short a time he'd known these people. Were they familiar enough for him to do that? "I'm sure it will come in handy." He looked to the others.

Both of the warriors had chosen the Attribute Tokens. Howard looked at his, the coin resting atop his palm. Justin flicked his into the air. The token appeared to be made from wood, of all things.

"What about the Attribute Tokens?" Xavier asked. "What do they provide?" He wondered if the tokens were nontransferable, like the Spell Book. Though he wasn't about to ask them for their tokens, the thought *did* occur to him. *That's more than a little greedy, Xavier,* he chided himself.

Howard cleared his throat. "Like the Spell Book, the attribute was random. I got Toughness."

Justin raised an eyebrow, glancing over at the former cop. "I got Speed."

"Interesting. Though, that does make sense. Xavier pointed at Howard. "You were defending people, using your tower shield and that protective spell of yours."

"Bulwark."

"Bulwark." Xavier nodded. "Good name." He looked to Justin. "And you, I imagine an Olympic fencer has to be fast?"

Justin smirked. "Yeah. We definitely do."

"And how many attributes do they offer?" Siobhan asked. The woman sat on the floor by her loot box, the Spell Book resting open on her lap. She hadn't used it yet.

"Ten," Howard said.

"Ten?" Xavier looked at the Attribute Token in his notification. "More than I'd thought." He still had five free stat points to allocate.

"I think you should choose a spell," Siobhan said. "Attribute points will always help, but you're not exactly low on those."

The others nodded, clearly thinking the same.

While Xavier did agree, he couldn't help but *always* want more attribute points. *Having a hell of a lot of them is how I've gotten us this far, after all.*

But he was also far too excited to find out what new spell he might gain. The desire to rub his hands together came again as he told the others he agreed.

It's time to finally gain a new spell.

He couldn't help but wonder what it would be.

Chapter 41
Do You Wish to Learn This Spell?

Xavier held his breath as he selected "Spell Book" from the loot box's notification.

A moment later, a Spell Book appeared in his hand. It was the same size as the one Siobhan had on her lap. It was a leather-bound book that looked like it had five hundred pages.

He ran a hand over the cover, feeling the indentations worked into the dark leather. Some arcane symbol had been carved into it. An eight-pointed star. *Does this symbol have some sort of significance?* He didn't think Siobhan's had been the same, though her book sat open, so it was hard for him to know.

Xavier sat, his back against his loot box, and opened the book. Most of the pages were stuck together. He could only open it to a single spot near the middle. *I wonder what will happen when I learn the spell. Will this book disappear?*

He read the page on the left.

This Spell Book is nontransferable. Only XAVIER COLLINS is permitted to learn spells from this book. If the book is stolen or lost, it will return to him within 24 hours.

Xavier raised an eyebrow. Siobhan hadn't mentioned the bit about it returning to him. The others were watching him. They clearly wanted to peer at the page, but they were patiently waiting for him to tell them what the spell would be.

He looked at the page on the right. Part of him dreaded seeing what was there. *If it's some healing spell like Siobhan got, I'll be sorely disappointed.* But if the System worked like he was beginning to think it did, the chances of that were basically nothing.

Spirit Break – Rank 1
Spirit Break is a rare mage spell that is rarely learnt by human mages and is only available to those with a naturally strong Spirit. Spirit Break has several different paths, and is an incredibly difficult spell to master.
Spirit Break is an offensive spell that uses the Spirit Energy within an enemy against them. It can break an enemy's body, mind, and magic. As a mage advances, they may choose to specialise in one area, generalise in all, or abandon the path altogether.
Unlike other spells, generalising in Spirit Break does not hinder the power of each of this spell's abilities, as achieving Rank 2 in Spirit Break is only achievable by rare individuals.
One cannot walk backward on the path.

Do you wish to learn this spell?

Xavier blinked. He tilted his head to the side. *Another spirit-based spell?* The wording sounded similar to that of Spiritual Guidance when he'd first learnt it. Though this was different.

Instead of enhancing himself, it... *weakened* others?

That could have a lot of potential. He imagined what it could have done to the Rat King. Might he have been able to cripple its magic? Destroy its mind? Break its body?

Though Xavier had yet to lose a fight, he'd never had a spell like this. Something that could seriously hinder a strong opponent like the floor bosses he would continuously face.

He smiled, looking forward to testing this spell. Though he wasn't sure how he felt about *breaking* an enemy's mind, he would have to use every tool at his disposal.

It's not like I don't break a lot of bones. What's adding minds on top of that...

"Well?" Siobhan asked excitedly. Her hands were folded in her lap, and it seemed like she was forcing them to stay there. "What spell is it?"

Xavier saw Justin looked just as eager as Siobhan. Even Howard leant forward a bit, though his expression was carefully blank. Xavier didn't make them wait. He explained to them what the spell was called and what it did.

Then, not wanting to waste any time, Xavier ran a hand over the text at the bottom of the page, beneath the spell's description.

Do you wish to learn this spell?

Yes, he thought, pushing his will.

You have gained the spell Spirit Break.

The Spell Book snapped closed with so much strength it hurt Xavier's hand. He pulled his hand out, flapping it with a wince, and the book snapped the rest of the way shut.

Xavier frowned. The pain vanished in a second or so. He looked at the Spell Book. Part of him had been expecting it to disappear once he learnt that spell, so he was a little surprised it was still there. He tried to open the book again, but it wouldn't budge, even when he put *all* his strength into it. And he'd gotten mighty strong in the last few days.

Still, it wouldn't budge. He frowned. "That's odd." He didn't think it was worth using Spiritual Trifecta to boost his strength and try again. Something told him that book wouldn't open until he had another spell to learn.

It must be connected to the System somehow. Maybe. I don't know how this all bloody works...

He grinned at the others. "I'll test the spell out when we enter the third floor. Maybe I'll be able to rank it up before I reach Level 10 and gain my next class." Something told him that would be an important thing to do, if he wanted to influence what classes he could choose from.

Now he'd learnt his third spell, he was curious to see if there were any costs to ranking it up to the second rank like there had been for his other spells.

Xavier looked at the door. He was eager to head to the next floor, but there were still a few things they needed to do.

Siobhan learnt her healing spell, which was called Heal Other. Howard and Justin consumed their Attribute Tokens. *Literally* consumed. Apparently they had to swallow the large, wooden coins. Xavier winced, touching his neck as their throats bobbed, imagining the coins leaving splinters.

When the tokens had been consumed, Howard looked a little broader and Justin a little sharper and more slender, though the difference might not be all that perceptible if one wasn't looking for it.

Xavier glanced at his robes and wondered what his body looked like underneath them now. *How ripped and strong have I become with all these attribute points?* It was a vain thought that he discarded, pushing on to the next task.

He allocated his five free stat points. Seeing that he had 97 points in Spirit, and now having just gained a second spirit-based spell, he put three points into the attribute to bring it up to 100. He put the other two points into Intelligence, bringing it to 92 without the percentage boost from his Magical Potency skill. As much as he enjoyed fighting up close, he wanted to strengthen his spells.

Next, he looked into what new skills he should learn.

After a brief discussion with the others, they agreed the most important thing for Xavier was still *staying alive.*

So he chose Magical Resistance as the first of his two skills, considering how well Physical Resistance had worked for him so far.

You have learnt the skill Magical Resistance!
Magical Resistance – Rank 1
You are a student of magic, and all those who wield magic must learn to defend against its power.
+5% damage reduction from magical attacks.
+5% Willpower.

Willpower? Xavier hadn't realised Willpower had something to do with defence against magic, but he supposed that made complete sense. He hadn't been attacked by very many magical spells.

Being trapped in the earth, and having rocks thrown at him, those hadn't been purely magical attacks against his person like throwing magical fire, or using telekinesis on him would have been.

Maybe I already have fairly strong Magical Defence. He supposed more could never hurt.

The next skill choice was a difficult one. He struggled to decide between Physical Damage and Running. The first time Xavier had seen the Running skill, he'd figured learning it would be a waste of time or a waste of a skill point. He'd figured at some point he would gain a Skill Quest for it, like he had for Meditation.

But despite how much he'd been running, none had come.

That's likely another advantage Champions from other worlds have... they would have trained skills before gaining the System, and would know how to get Skill Quests for them...

Now, Running seemed like a *very* important skill. No matter how quickly he'd managed to clear that previous floor, it hadn't been fast *enough*. He may have done it before anyone else in their instance of the Tower of Champions, but he hadn't gotten a Top 100 record for it.

Did I just happen to fall into the best strategy for that first floor? he wondered. *Am I going to replicate something like that again?*

He stared at the skill selection menu, looking at Running. Looking at Physical Damage. He knew which one he *wanted* to choose. Physical Damage was the obvious choice for him. He was all about raw power, and he was sure this would help with that.

But Running would make him faster...

He contemplated the floor he'd just cleared. *Had Speed been my downfall there? Or had it been a lack of strategy? A lack of preparation and awareness in battle?*

For all he knew, he could have been seconds away from getting into the Top 100. If he'd taken down that Rat King more efficiently...

I'm procrastinating too much. Doubting myself too much. I can always get Running later. He couldn't afford to waste time being indecisive. There was a difference between taking time to consider a decision and obsessing over it.

Sometimes you just had to *do it.*

You have learnt the skill Physical Damage!
Physical Damage – Rank 1
You are a student of hitting things really hard.
Your physical attacks are infused with a
strength that improves every strike you land.
+5% damage to all physical strikes.
+5% Strength.

Xavier felt the Strength boost instantly. His muscles tensed as the attribute points were boosted. When they came in titles, the rush was too much for him to perceive each difference. But the more it happened, the more he could feel it, and Strength was always the easiest to notice changing.

He was glad the Physical Damage skill had a percentage boost to Strength. He hadn't known if it would.

Xavier looked down at his hands, clenched his fists, and smiled. *And this is just what I gain when I'm not fighting.* The rewards between floors were beginning to feel more and more important, especially now he'd gained a new spell.

He looked at the others. It was time to check the System Shop. He wondered if they would offer him the Lesser Spirit Coins they'd gained once more...

Chapter 42
F Grade, E Grade... I Don't Understand Any of It Right Now

Once again, when they sold all of the corpses and items they'd looted from clearing a floor, they didn't get a *great* deal of coin for them. It added up to a little more than seven thousand Lesser Spirit Coins.

Not for the first time, it made Xavier wonder how much more they could have earned had they sold off those items directly to crafters and dismantlers. He was quite sure the System Shop was cutting them out of a great deal of money, but he didn't think on it too long. It wasn't as though there were crafters in the tower he could sell to.

Even though they didn't get much from selling off what they'd looted, after the others handed over the coins they'd gotten from their loot box just like they had the last time—and this time without any comment, as though it had already become a habit—Xavier ended up with 88,640 Lesser Spirit Coins.

To him, that number felt absolutely insane. But he supposed he'd spent 45,000 Lesser Spirit Coins on his Spirit Staff of Might, so gaining roughly double the number of coins as last time shouldn't have been too surprising.

Will that number keep doubling, as we go up and up all of the floors?

He imagined having millions of Lesser Spirit Coins, or perhaps one day having Grand Spirit Coins. *Maybe I already have enough to convert to Grand Spirit Coins, whatever they are...*

Xavier recalled the first staff he'd seen when he'd looked at them in the System Shop. *Stave of the Otherworldly Void Reaper.* That thing had cost a *billion* Grand Spirit Coins.

The thought made him once more feel rather poor, but he knew he was just getting started.

The pang of guilt he felt at taking his party's coins for himself was less than it had been before. It was beginning to feel more natural. They were all chipping in, helping him push through these floors.

But it did make him wonder if there was something he could do for them. They'd all risked their lives in that final fight against the Rat King. Part of him thought it would be better not to take them into the next floor when he cleared it, especially since they already knew it didn't have a Safe Zone, but he wasn't going to go with that instinct.

They were going to come along. And they were going to learn to fight as a team in a way that let Xavier still get all the kill contributions and "solo" the level. He had a few ideas he wanted to test when they farmed the next floor for Mastery Points—ideas that would work much better if the others gained their classes as well.

Though he did worry about how long that might take.

We've cleared two floors in about eight hours. We should definitely have a strong lead by now. He hoped.

But right now, he focused on the task at hand, opening the System Shop's menu. The first thing he searched for were Spell Books. Though Spell Books were something he was still a little confused about. The Spell Book he'd used to learn Spirit Break, the one he'd gained from the loot box, hadn't disappeared after he'd learnt the spell.

He still had it, it just... wouldn't open. He'd deposited it into his Storage Ring, but he didn't really know what to do with it. Now that he had a Spell Book, would gaining another one simply... place that new Spell Book into the one he already owned?

When he found the list for Spell Books, he frowned.

There were various different options, and all of them were incredibly expensive.

Spell Book Primer – Gravity Mage
This item costs 20 Grand Spirit Coins

Spell Book Primer – Elemental Mage
This item costs 10 Grand Spirit Coins

Spell Book Primer – Void Mage
This item costs 20 Grand Spirit Coins

Spell Book Primer – Necromancer
This item costs 15 Grand Spirit Coins

Spell Book Primer – Windwalker Mage
This item costs 10 Grand Spirit Coins

Xavier ran a hand through his hair. First, he didn't understand what it meant by "Spell Book Primer." The loot box had referred to the book he'd gained from it as simply a "Spell Book."

Would this add spells to his own book?

Second, there was no information as to what the spell books contained, other than what they were called.

Gravity Mage, that sounds pretty cool.

One of his favourite books had a magic system where some characters could change how gravity worked for themselves or others, shifting up to down and vice versa, or untethering themselves from gravity altogether.

It was... confusing, sometimes, especially during fight scenes, but was also incredibly awesome.

Void Mage sounded interesting, too, though he really didn't

know what it would entail. The Necromancer spell book made him crinkle his nose and shudder slightly. As cool as necromancers were in fiction, he didn't really want an army of decomposing, smelly corpses following him around.

And there were probably moral implications to creating undead creatures... right? What if the souls of the deceased were trapped in the zombie-body, eternally forced to watch actions out of its own control? That wasn't something he wanted to dabble in, was it?

Still, necromancy is real? That's awesome and terrifying at the same time. His mind was expanding, seeing all the new possibilities this Greater Universe could offer.

Third... he still didn't know what a Grand Spirit Coin *was*, and how much it was worth. *Twenty Grand Spirit Coins doesn't sound like a lot. Maybe I can afford one of these Spell Book Primers... The Gravity Mage one could be cool... or the Void Mage, but mostly because I like the sound of it.*

As he had that third thought, the System Shop shifted, showing a coin conversion menu he hadn't seen before.

1 Grand Spirit Coin = 10 Major Spirit Coins
1 Major Spirit Coin = 10 Greater Spirit Coins
1 Greater Spirit Coin = 10 Spirit Coins
1 Spirit Coin = 10 Minor Spirit Coins
1 Minor Spirit Coin = 10 Lesser Spirit Coins

You do not have enough Lesser Spirit Coins to convert to a single Grand Spirit Coin.

Xavier's eyes widened as he looked at the conversion. At first glance, it didn't look like much. One equalled ten, again and again... but his mind worked quickly.

I would need one hundred thousand Lesser Spirit Coins to make a single Grand Spirit Coin. Which means I would need two million Lesser Spirit Coins to buy the Gravity Mage Spell Book Primer.

He shook his head. Were there really *six* different types of Spirit Coins, and they only had access to the *worst* of them? *We can make them, as F Grade Denizens, but we wouldn't be able to make them faster than we can gain them from killing beasts and clearing levels.*

As he realised the conversion, the exact cost of the Stave of the Otherworldly Void Reaper began to sink in.

One billion Grand Spirit Coins would be... one hundred trillion Lesser Spirit Coins!

That number made him stumble back and realise just how bloody massive this Greater Universe must be, and just how powerful those at the top were. Just from looking at... money.

I'm pretty sure that's a higher wealth divide than someone in a third-world country versus the richest billionaire from before the System came.

Xavier shook his head, thinking about the different spirit coins. His mind was working, turning the currency over and over, as though on the cusp of figuring something out.

There are six different "levels" or "ranks" of coins. F Grade Denizens can create the lowest rank of coin, the Lesser Spirit Coin. If I were to logically play that out, then E Grade Denizens could create Minor Spirit Coins, D Grade normal Spirit Coins, and so on, until A Grade Denizens could make Grand Spirit Coins.

He chewed on the idea for a moment.

Six ranks of coins, six ranks of Denizens... It made sense.

He floated the idea to the others, explaining to them the currency conversion and the different types of coins.

Siobhan flicked through her Tower of Champions manual, shaking her head. "There isn't any mention of any grade other than F." She frowned, tilted her head to the side. "But this manual only appears to cover the first ten floors."

"Do you think clearing the tenth floor will get us to the next grade? To E Grade?" Justin asked. "Or do we need to reach a certain level?"

Howard ran a hand across his close-cropped beard. "What exactly would getting to E Grade mean?"

. "Maybe, when we get a chance, we can head down to the tavern," Xavier said.

Howard grunted. "I could definitely use a drink. A few shots of scotch would go down well."

"I think he means to ask the barkeep what he knows about this." Siobhan smirked.

Xavier nodded. That was what he'd meant. Though he supposed there wouldn't be any harm in having a drink. Maybe two. They could use the break.

Just... not yet.

"We'll clear a few more floors first. Move forward. Gain an even more solid lead before we risk it by taking a break," Xavier said.

Howard nodded. "Speaking of moving forward. You find any health potions in there?"

Xavier went back to looking. While he was there, he used the search term "manuals" and found an abundance of training manuals, skill manuals, even class manuals.

And, just like the Spell Book Primers, all of them were prohibitively expensive. In fact, they were *more* expensive than the primers. The cheapest of them cost 100 Grand Spirit Coins.

Ten million Lesser Spirit Coins, or over a hundred times more than we have right now. Champions from established worlds have access to even more than I'd thought...

He sighed. Bought the health potions—there were, unfortunately, no Spirit Energy potions that he could find, but as he had quite a large Spirit Energy reserve and had been fighting beasts a higher level than himself, killing them with ease, he'd never had an issue running out of it while clearing the floors.

The health potions were called—big surprise—*Lesser* Health Potions. The System Shop had Minor Health Potions, which he could have technically afforded, but they said that they didn't work on F Grade Denizens, only those at E Grade.

F Grade, E Grade... I don't understand any of it right now, but something tells me this will be very important later.

The Lesser Health Potions were somewhat affordable—as far as he could tell—at 500 Lesser Spirit Coins each, so he bought ten for each of them. He figured they'd only use them when it was life or death, or to get through a floor faster, so there was no need to be stingy with them.

As he had plenty of Lesser Spirit Coins left and didn't really know what to spend them on, he thought about outfitting the others with better gear.

For my plan to work, Howard will need far better than his basic armour. Justin got a sword from his first loot box, but that won't help for what we need to do, so I'm not sure what to get for him. I suppose they would all benefit from armour.

He thought about getting armour of his own, but apparently basic mages couldn't wear warrior armour. The restrictions weren't based upon stats, but rather *class*, which Xavier thought was utterly ridiculous.

Am I going to be stuck wearing thin, barely protective robes for the rest of my life? Though when it came to equipment, he'd only been using search parameters that let him see items he could actually use and afford, so maybe there would be other things available to him if he had more coin or a different mage class at Level 10.

He looked over at the others. *Before I outfit them, let's get some training in and see if my plan can actually work; otherwise, spending too much coin on them could end up being a total waste.*

Xavier looked over at the door.

It was time to head to the third floor of the Tower of Champions.

Chapter 43
Whose Call Will You Answer?

In the Staging Room of the Tower of Champions, Xavier walked up to the door that would take him and his party to the third floor.

Before moving forward, he looked at his stats and other information.

XAVIER COLLINS
Age: 20
Race: Human
Grade: F
Moral Faction: World Defender (Planet Earth)
Class: Mage
Level: 8
Strength: 81 (85)
Speed: 77 (81)
Toughness: 89 (94)
Intelligence: 92 (99)
Willpower: 83 (87)
Spirit: 100
Mastery Points for this level: 51,700/200,000
Available Spirit Energy: 10,800/10,800

Available Skill Points: 0
Free stat points remaining: 0
Titles: Bloodied Hands, Born on a Battlefield,
Settlement Defender, Quester, First Defender
of Planet Earth, Lesser Butcher, Survivor, First
Floor Ranked 42, Second-Floor Climber, Solo
Tower Climber 2, 1ˢᵗ Second-Floor Climber, 500
Stats, First to 500 Stats
Spells List:
Spiritual Trifecta – Rank 3
Heavy Telekinesis – Rank 3
Spirit Break – Rank 1
Skills List:
Staff Mastery – Rank 1
Physical Resistance – Rank 2
Magical Potency – Rank 4
Magical Resistance – Rank 1
Physical Damage – Rank 1
Lesser Spirit Coins: 68,640

Xavier couldn't help but smile at how much his stats had gone up. *I'm becoming a force to be reckoned with.* He clutched his Spirit Staff of Might tightly. Then frowned, remembering the difference between a Lesser Spirit Coin and that of a Grand Spirit Coin.

I wonder what the difference between an F Grade Denizen and an A Grade Denizen is... He'd only guessed it went from F, to E, D, C, B, A. For all he knew they could be ranked differently, but it made sense to him.

He sighed. Perhaps he was only a force to be reckoned with compared with others at his own level.

We'll farm this floor until I reach Level 10. If it doesn't take too long, maybe I'll get the others to Level 10 as well—or maybe on the next floor. He supposed that would all depend on how easy this floor was to farm.

There will be no Safe Zone. Hopefully it isn't some sort of maze of shifting tunnels like the last floor. Maybe it won't be dark this time. It had been a few days since he'd seen the sun.

He turned to Howard, Siobhan, and Justin. Howard held his tower shield in one hand, his sword in the other. Justin had his long, slender sword that he'd gotten from his first loot box. Siobhan her metal staff with the purple crystal at the end.

Xavier looked at the dark-brown wood of his own staff. It had lost much of its heft, as he'd already gained a fair amount of Strength since he'd bought it. *Maybe I need to invest in another staff soon...*

"Are we all ready?" he said to the others.

They each nodded. There was more eagerness on their faces than usual. Probably because they would actually get to fight on this floor. At least for a little while, before Xavier was ready to clear it.

"All right." Xavier put his hand on the doorhandle. "Let's do this."

The notification popped up the instant Xavier's hand touched the handle.

Tower of Champions.
The Tower of Champions is where World Defenders prove themselves, fighting for rewards, upgrades and powerups.
Open Levels:
3 of 1,000.
Which level would you like to enter?

Three, he thought, then was teleported straight out of the Staging Room.

Xavier blinked, shielded his eyes with his left hand. Wherever he stood, it was impossibly bright. Though it didn't take his eyes long to adjust. He furrowed his brow, narrowing his eyes at the sky as the others appeared on either side of him.

"Huh." Xavier looked from one end of the sky to the other.

"Two suns." The massive, glowing, orange orbs of fire seemed to hang closer to this planet than the sun back on Earth did. Either that, or both these suns were significantly larger.

This planet...

"We're on another world?" Howard asked.

"I don't think it's... *real*," Siobhan said. "Like the other floors, the system creates it for the Tower.

Howard scratched at his chin with the top of his tower shield. "How does that make it not real?" He raised an eyebrow at her.

Siobhan opened her mouth. Frowned. Then closed her mouth again and shook her head.

Xavier smiled. He didn't much mind whether this place had been created or not. It *felt* real. Just like the dark forest on the first floor had felt real. And the underground tunnels on the second.

The breeze was cool and calm, wafting in from the left—who knew whether that was north, south, east, or west. They stood in a large field, and the breeze played with the long grass that was all around them.

He picked a long blade of grass and looked at it. It was... *purple*. He chuckled and shook his head, letting the blade of grass go. It drifted in the air for a bit before falling to the ground.

"So, what now?" Justin asked, his gaze panning in front of them. "I don't see any beasts."

"And where's the door back to the Staging Room?" Siobhan asked.

Right. I should be looking for that.

Howard kicked something metallic with his heavy boots. "I think this is the door. Trapdoor, at least."

Xavier looked at his feet. There was a large trapdoor on the ground, making a smooth surface for them all to stand upon in the middle of the grassland, and he got the sense Howard was right. *Odd place for it.*

That's when they heard a persistent *thud, thud, thud*, coming from their right, almost like the beating of a heart. Though it'd have to be a bloody big heart to beat that loudly. Xavier gripped his staff, readying himself for a fight. He hadn't imagined the field would remain peaceful for long.

His eyes widened when he saw what was heading toward them. It looked like... like an *army*. At that moment, it was a fair distance away, almost as far as his eye could see across the field. But it was definitely an army. Rows of men—and women, no doubt—marching forward at a steady clip.

Toward *them*.

"Oh." Justin turned his hilt around in his hand. "Is that..."

"An army?" Siobhan finished.

Howard grunted. "Sure looks like one. And that thudding? War drums."

A thrill ran through Xavier at the sight of it. He couldn't quite tell how many soldiers there were. Maybe five hundred? "Are we supposed to fight the army?" So far, all they'd been expected to do was fight *beasts*. Not... humans. Or, other sapient races *like* humans.

Some of those beasts had been sapient, he thought. *The Puma Prime, the Rat King. They could talk... not that I much liked what they had to say. And the goblins. They might not have spoken to me, not in a language I could understand, but they were definitely sapient.*

Xavier considered their situation. Even if the soldiers ended up being human, if they had to kill them to clear this floor... he would do it. He couldn't just return to the Staging Room and give up his clearing of the tower floors.

He didn't *want* to kill people, but he would do whatever he had to do to save his world.

Still, fighting five hundred soldiers seemed like an impossible task, even for someone like him. The soldiers, at this distance, were too far away for him to scan, so he couldn't even tell what level they were at.

Then more thuds sounded. This time, the thuds came from the other direction.

Xavier whirled around.

On the other side of them, there was *another* army. This one looked about the same size as the first. Five hundred soldiers. Marching unrelentingly toward the very spot where Xavier and his party stood.

"They're marching toward each other," Siobhan said.

Xavier narrowed his gaze. "And we're stuck right in the middle."

Justin tapped his foot on the door back to the Staging Room. "They're equal distances apart. That means when the fighting starts... it'll be right over our exit out of here."

"So." Howard sighed. "We're in the middle of two opposing armies. What, *exactly*, are we supposed to do?"

Xavier, staring toward the army on their left, could make out the soldiers marching a little better now—though he still wasn't able to scan them. *Maybe if I had the Identify skill, I'd be able to use it at range...*

"Do they look like elves to you?" Xavier asked. From what he could make out of the people walking toward them, many of them seemed rather pale considering this world had two suns, and their hair was white-blonde. He could even make out pointed ears.

"Yeah," Siobhan said. "Those are elves all right."

"These ones look human," Justin said. "I think."

The teenager was facing the other direction.

"Is that who we fight with?" Howard asked. "Or is that... racist?" He scratched at his chin with his tower shield again.

Siobhan tucked an errant strand of hair behind her ear. "What's the odds that both armies just attack *us*? What if we can't pick a side at all?"

Howard grunted. "That... that'd be bad."

"Bad sounds like an understatement," Justin muttered.

Xavier, sick of standing around waiting for both of the armies to reach them, willed the question toward the System, hoping something would come of it. He was more than a little surprised when a notification popped up in his vision.

Welcome to the Third Floor of the Tower of Champions.

The Third Floor of the Tower of Champions is a test of your leadership capabilities and your might in battle. An army of Elves and an army of Humans are to clash on this world. You must choose which army to fight with, and which to fight against.

Each army is 500 soldiers strong, and they have each summoned a Champion to lead them. Whose call will you answer?

Chapter 44
Those Bloody Knife-Ears

XAVIER STOOD IN THE MIDDLE OF A LARGE FIELD OF LONG, purple grass. Two suns blared down at him and his party from above. And, on either side of them, two opposing armies marched.

One, an army of elves, five hundred strong.

The other, an army of humans, equal in number.

Xavier stared at the last line of the notification that had popped up in his vision.

Whose call will you answer?

He had to choose which army to fight with.

"Are you guys seeing this?" Xavier asked.

He looked at the others. Their eyes were slightly glazed over. A familiar expression he was beginning to recognise—when they were reading text he couldn't see. His eyes had probably looked the same a moment ago.

Siobhan nodded. She looked at Xavier. "Which side should we choose?"

Howard and Justin looked at him expectantly.

Xavier rubbed the back of his neck. "I... don't know. I suppose it doesn't really matter?"

Justin looked over at the human army. "Do you suppose these people are... real? If the System creates these instances for the Tower of Champions, and each floor is identical to what countless other people experience, and we'll be able to restart this whole floor if we leave through the trapdoor and return..."

"I'm sure they're as real as the beasts we faced on other floors," Howard said. "Don't think we need to question it more than that."

Xavier nodded. The man was right. They could get all existential about how *real* everything they were experiencing was, but that wouldn't actually help them. "I think we should fight with the human side this time, then the elven side next time. Rotate between them as we farm this level. Learn as much as we can about both of them." He looked at Howard. "I'm... not really sure how fighting in an army is going to help me train those qualities you were talking about, but I'll do my best."

Howard shrugged. "I know you will. I've seen that."

When they'd decided Xavier needed to train his fighting capabilities, rather than just brute-forcing everything, he'd been hoping they would be taken somewhere he could fight beasts in a more controlled way.

This floor? It wasn't that.

We work with what we have.

"How are we going to get back through the trapdoor when the fighting is underway?" Siobhan asked.

Xavier ran a hand through his hair, looking from one army to the other. "We'll just have to figure something out." It wasn't a great answer, but it was all he had at the moment. "We could leave one enemy alive at the end." Though he couldn't see a floor boss, he was sure one would appear at some point.

His forehead creased as he willed the choice.

Whose call will you answer?

The humans.

A bright, glowing white light came out of nowhere, enveloping the four of them. It was a light Xavier recognised. One he'd seen before, when Siobhan had summoned Howard to her while they were up against the Rat King, and he'd blocked a strike that would have killed her.

Xavier and his party were teleported straight to the head of the human army. For a moment, Xavier panicked, worried the army would attack them. How would they know they were on their side?

Xavier might be confident in his abilities, but he didn't know how to fight five hundred opponents all at once.

Not yet, at least. I wonder if that will be in my future...

Seeing the army up close, he could get a better look at them. The armour they were wearing was a step above the thin leather armour that Howard and Justin wore, but it wasn't as good as plate armour.

It looked to be ringmail armour, no doubt with gambeson—padded jackets—worn underneath. At least, if his research on medieval armour for his writing proved to be true.

Most of the soldiers at the front line were carrying spears, which he supposed made better sense than swords for a battle. It actually made him wonder why a basic Warrior class wasn't outfitted with a spear when they started.

Not the time to think about all of this...

He scanned the nearest soldier.

{Human – Level 12}

One level higher than the last enemies we faced on the previous floor.

Xavier was beginning to see a pattern. Though this floor was certainly *very* different to the last. He quickly scanned a few more of them while they were still a few feet away and found them all to be of the same level.

Five hundred Level 12 soldiers... They better not decide I'm an enemy.

One soldier, a grizzled looking man who appeared to be in his forties, raised his spear high. "Halt march!" he called in a booming voice that couldn't be natural.

Does he have some sort of skill that makes his voice louder? Xavier wondered. He supposed that would come in handy when leading an army.

Xavier stepped in front of the others, still holding his Spirit Staff of Might tightly in his grip. The grizzled soldier, spear in one hand, shield in the other, didn't look *actively* threatening, but Xavier wasn't going to take any chances.

"Bless the Expanse! Our calls were heard!" The grizzled soldier smiled broadly as he approached, stopping a few feet away from Xavier and his party. The man frowned, looking between them. "You are the Champions we called for, are you not?"

Bless the Expanse? What's the Expanse? Does he mean the System?

Xavier tilted his chin up. "We are." Honestly, he wasn't really sure what else to say beyond that.

The soldier raised his spear. He turned back to face the army behind him and used that loud, bellowing voice that sounded like it carried far enough to be heard by all five hundred soldiers. "The Champions have come! They heeded our call!" He faced Xavier and the others, lowering his head. "We will follow your orders to the word, O Great Champions, to our deaths if we have to."

Howard stepped forward. He had that blank but serious look about him. "What's the situation, uh?" He motioned toward the man.

The soldier blinked. "Sergeant Bradley, Sir."

"What's the situation, Sergeant Bradley?"

Sergeant Bradley looked a little confused. He pointed at the other army. "We're at war." He motioned to his own army at his back. "Battle's about to start."

Xavier had to keep himself from laughing. *Straightforward, I'll give him that. Suppose there isn't much more to it. Though shouldn't some lord be leading the army? With a cool-sounding last name like Stark or Aragorn?*

Howard sighed. "What do we know about the enemy?"

Xavier took a moment to look at the rest of the soldiers. They weren't all warriors. Behind the line of warriors there were soldiers holding bows—both flat and long—and robed soldiers that must have been mages. *Or clerics, if that's what healers are called.*

"The enemy, well, those bastard scoundrels have been waging war with us for centuries." Sergeant Bradley spat on the purple grass. "Excuse my language, sirs and madam—"

"*Madam?* How old does he think I am?" Siobhan muttered under her breath, sounding a little offended.

"—but those bloody knife-ears have been burning villages right up the coast for years." The sergeant rubbed the back of his head. "Course, we been doing the same to them, but I am sure it was *they* who started the conflict!"

"You... don't remember?" Justin asked.

Sergeant Bradley shook his head, his face lined and angry. Then he smiled again. Looked at the four of them. "But with you lot here, *Champions*, on our side, we'll finally be able to tip the scales in our favour! Our armies were evenly matched. Without you, we probably would have wiped each other out to a man. Or, er, to a woman." He nodded at Siobhan. "To both!" The sergeant frowned at that, as though just now realising how foolish that would have been. Two armies killing each other until no one was left standing.

The System definitely came up with this scenario. And it doesn't seem to have even fleshed out this world all that much. They can't even remember why they were fighting?

It sounded more than a little ludicrous, but, then again, he was sure wars had been fought back on Earth over even less.

As to whether these people were real... they certainly *looked* real, and he was sure their weapons would feel real if one of them hit him. Was sure they breathed real air and bled real blood.

Could the System have created these people from nothing, just for the purposes of the Tower of Champions?

It seemed, well, rather insane.

His memory flashed back to watching the Navy SEAL get struck by lightning for refusing to fight him. *Yeah, insane is right. I've already seen proof of that.*

"Enough talk," Xavier said. He'd been a little tongue-tied before. It wasn't every day he spoke in front of a bloody *army*. But these people, real or not, were nothing more than tools of the System, and he was more powerful than all of them.

Why should he be afraid to *talk*?

Xavier turned and faced the other army. Even from here, he could see the circular patch devoid of purple grass in the middle of the field. "You see that area in the middle?" He glanced over at the sergeant.

Sergeant Bradley stepped forward, looking over at the circular patch where the trapdoor to the Staging Area was. The man narrowed his gaze, bushy brows pinching together. "Aye, sir. I see it."

"Get your best soldiers to secure that area, and another twenty as honour guard to protect us with their lives." Xavier gestured toward Howard, Siobhan, and Justin. "Understood?"

The sergeant, though looking slightly confused, nodded. "Aye, sir. Understood."

Xavier looked at Howard. "You're going to be keeping Siobhan and Justin alive through this, all right? We all have some training to do here. If you want to be a stronger tank to better defend attacks for us, you'll need to train that quality. You've got the Physical Resistance skill?"

Howard nodded.

"Good. The more you're a tank in fighting and battles, the more likely you'll get a class suited toward that at Level 10." Though Xavier said the words with confidence, none of them were totally sure that was exactly how it worked.

We just have to assume it will be. Besides, he should be able to rank up that skill of his if he's taking hits. I've managed to do the same, after all.

Xavier looked at Siobhan next. "You're going to get some crowd control practise with that Cast Element spell of yours." He bobbed his head toward Howard. "And you can keep this one alive with that Heal Other spell."

"What about me?" Justin said, shifting from foot to foot.

Xavier's forehead creased. *What about him?* He hadn't really thought about what Justin could do. If his party were to help him clear floors of the Tower of Champions while he still gained the solo titles, they couldn't actually *attack* the enemies.

Which was a shame, considering he reckoned Justin would be quite good with that sword, having been an Olympic fencer and all. *He'd likely gain skill ranks* really *fast with that thing, too.*

Xavier considered what role the man could play. Howard would obviously be a tank, made even better if he was able to get some sort of Taunt spell along with his Bulwark spell.

Siobhan would be able to heal and also Summon people toward her, which could get them out of danger and out of the woods health-wise. Her spells lent themselves *perfectly* to support. They hadn't yet discovered if healing another would gain her experience if that person killed an enemy during the encounter, but even if it did, she'd be able to heal Howard and Justin.

Xavier, feeling more confident than usual, placed a hand on the teenager's shoulder. "I'm not sure what role you'll play yet, Justin, but I know it will be an important one. You're fast, and I'm sure damned good with that sword. Right now, maybe focus on your combat and gathering and looting corpses into your Storage Ring. We all need to gain levels while farming this floor."

Xavier paused, facing all three of them. "Remember, no unnecessary risks. We are here to *train*." He glanced over at Bradley, then ushered the others a little bit away, huddling together so the sergeant and the soldiers at his back couldn't hear him. "As heartless as it sounds, those soldiers are expendable."

The words came to him easier than they should have. It was a coin flip which side they ended up fighting on, and they'd be switching sides their next run through this floor... They couldn't be sentimental about these soldiers, whether they were truly real or not.

We're here to train. To get as much out of this floor, out of this tower, as we can.

Siobhan frowned. Justin looked at the ground. Howard's face was still mostly blank but for a crease lining his brow.

"Let them protect you. Fall behind them. Do anything you can to *survive*." Xavier pointed toward the elves. "We don't know how strong those soldiers are. And we don't know what to expect from that army. Which means we need to let the soldiers go first."

"Cannon fodder," Howard muttered, shaking his head. "Makes a terrible sort of sense, I suppose." He scratched his close-cropped beard with the top of the tower shield, then nodded curtly. "Xavier's right. Feels different, this time, cause they're human. But we can't think that way if we want to thrive in this place." He glanced over his shoulder at the army. Then over at the elves. "This is as controlled a situation as we're ever going to get in battle. We need to use it to our advantage. Learn to prioritise."

Xavier looked at Justin. The teenager swallowed. Nodded. "It's what has to be done."

Siobhan looked from one army to the other, as Howard had. "It's so much easier in video games. But..." She shut her eyes, let out a shuddering breath. "We came here to get stronger, to protect each other. To protect *Xavier*. That is the main goal."

She opened her eyes, bit her lip. "And, as much as it pains me to admit, this might be good practise for us..." She eyed Xavier. "For you. If you, with all your titles, all the power you'll gain from this tower... if you really are Earth's best hope, we can't let anything happen to you." Her gaze fell to the ground. "There may be times like this, where it's the lives of people from Earth. Maybe even the lives of people you know. They may have to sacrifice themselves for you, and you might have to let them."

Xavier had been holding his breath, waiting for her reaction. He hadn't expected her to say that. The words hit him hard. He hadn't known her, Howard, and Justin long, and all he could imagine was one of them—namely Siobhan—getting killed trying to protect him, and him... having to *let* her, lest he die himself?

That didn't sound like something a hero would do.

I want to become so powerful that it doesn't happen. That it can't happen. He turned and looked at the elven army. *I want to become powerful enough that I can face that army alone and not have to rely on* anyone *else, or risk anyone else.*

But before that time came, he would have to do whatever he could to *get* there.

Xavier turned and faced the elven army, which was still marching toward them. They had to move if they wanted to get the door to the Staging Room secured.

He'd never seen so many enemies so close together before. It made him wonder how fast he could take them out—how fast he could get to Level 10.

He looked at Siobhan. "If you see me in danger, summon me to you, yeah?"

Siobhan nodded. "Call my name. I'll hear you."

I hope you're right.

He raised his staff, and called for the army he suddenly controlled to charge ahead.

Chapter 45
There Are Only So Many Risks I Can Take

XAVIER, GRIPPING HIS SPIRIT STAFF OF MIGHT TIGHTLY IN both hands, ran toward the enemy army of five hundred elves.

Knife-ears, Sergeant Bradley had called them. It was a slur Xavier had recognised. Strange, hearing it from a real person talking about real elves.

Real elves. Elves actually exist, and I'm about to fight them. He supposed that shouldn't come as too much of a surprise, considering he'd already fought against goblins, massive Black Pumas, and Giant Mole Rats.

As he ran, he looked over at the enemy soldiers. *How many archers and mages do they have? And how long will it be until we're in range? Would they think to target me?*

He'd already called for "his" army to charge. The sound of five hundred soldiers—all of them superhuman compared to a *normal* army back on Earth pre-integration—was close to deafening.

Howard was to Xavier's left, Justin to his right, and Siobhan behind him. Surrounding them were twenty soldiers handpicked by Sergeant Bradley to stick to them like glue and protect them. They had their shields up as they ran. Twelve soldiers ahead, four flanking on each side of them.

Xavier wondered what would happen if projectiles came down

from above. Those shields they carried were massive, rivalling Howard's in size. Were these soldiers all tank classes? Did they have some sort of protective barrier spell, like Howard's Bulwark spell?

Xavier's first instinct had been to run ahead of the army. To slam a Spiritual Trifecta–reinforced Heavy Telekinesis strike straight at a cluster of enemy soldiers and see how many he could take down at once.

They would slam into each other, maybe even behind into their allies' spearpoints.

Rushing ahead of the army would be the wrong decision. He needed to learn from his mistakes. Despite the fact that nothing he'd done had caused his death, he knew it was only a matter of time if he kept acting the same way.

Howard had been right. He should have been able to take that Rat King on his own... but it wasn't only that.

I've almost died too many times. Everything I've done has paid off, but there are only so many risks I can take until they stop helping me. I can't keep doing everything so rashly.

He needed to train his instincts, lest they get them killed.

Howard was right, but he went too easy on me.

Bright spells, fireballs and fire arrows, bolts of lightning, and large shards of ice that reflected the sky's twin suns began to flare above them, coming from the human army—the army Xavier and his party were leading.

He looked ahead. The elves were charging forward, unleashing a volley of arrows and spells of their own. The ground began to shudder. *Earth mages?*

Xavier's eyes widened in wonder. This battle wouldn't be like anything from Earth. Wouldn't be like the medieval battles he'd read about when doing research, nor would it be anything like modern warfare.

This would be something altogether different. Something that none of them had any experience with.

The enemy arrows and spells began to fall upon the human

army. A bellowing shout rang out from ahead of them—Sergeant Bradley, shield raised above his head—"DEFENSIVE MEASURES!"

Howard had his own shield raised above his head. He activated Bulwark, and a transparent shield enveloped the four of them.

Xavier had to wonder how large that shield would become in the future, and how long it would last. Could the man control how large it became?

He worried about his three party members.

Howard and the others have strong titles, even if they aren't as strong as mine. They should be able to hold their own out here. Besides, this army will protect us with their lives.

Xavier didn't know how many different types of arrows fell upon them. They glowed different colours as they bounced off the Bulwark spell. There were the fire arrows—arrows he doubted would work without magic (he'd seen a YouTube video in his writing research detailing all the reasons why fire arrows are only a thing in movies and not history). Then there were green-glowing arrows. He wondered if those were poisoned.

A purple-glowing arrow penetrated Bulwark's protective barrier without trouble. It whizzed past Xavier's ear and lodged itself into the ground. Had he been just a little to the left, it would have lodged itself into his skull instead. It must have been some sort of penetrative, anti-magic defence arrow.

I have 89 Toughness. I'm sure that would have been enough to withstand that arrow... right?

It wasn't exactly something he wished to test.

The soldiers around them had better weapons and armour than a basic Warrior class, not to mention they would all have their next class, but he couldn't imagine their stats would be very high.

They might not have any titles at all.

Still, Xavier needed to be careful—this would be nothing like fighting beasts. The beasts that he'd fought rarely had any type of spell, for one. And he wasn't used to dealing with ranged attacks.

Maybe I need some sort of protective spell myself...

But that was what Howard would be for. Of course, he might not always be able to rely on others.

They were nearing the enemy army now. Xavier felt a little frustrated that he didn't have any long-range spells he could use in this situation. Packed in, with the honour guard of twenty soldiers ahead of him, and even more ahead of them, his Heavy Telekinesis spell would only hurt friend not foe.

He thought about the differences between this battle and a "normal" human battle. *They don't have any cavalry. I'm glad for that.* Especially since he imagined the soldiers might be astride bestial mounts, rather than normal horses. *Perhaps we just got lucky.*

Xavier got a glimpse of the trapdoor to the Staging Room— their exit out of this place. The elves had reached it first.

Denizens, unlike normal, unenhanced soldiers, could run and fire their spells and loose their arrows all at the same time without slowing or losing any accuracy. And they could run *faster*. All that talking he'd done after they'd met Sergeant Bradley had slowed his army down enough that the trapdoor was now beneath enemy feet.

We'll need to push them back. Secure that area.

The armies were near to clashing, though Xavier could barely see it with so many ahead of them. He wished he could have an aerial view of what was happening on the battlefield.

BOOM!

The sound was so loud Xavier was surprised it didn't sting his ears. And it didn't stop. Two charging, superhuman armies crashed into each other. The clang of metal on metal. The roar of flames. The boom of thunder. All of it came at once, mingling with shouts, screams and cries of men and women fighting and dying.

The battle began to feel more real than ever. A thrill of fear and excitement ran through him. He could see the enemy. Through the lines of soldiers ahead of him. They were close. *Very* close.

The barrage of spells and arrows had stopped falling upon

them. They must be launching those attacks farther back, lest they hit their allies.

Howard disabled his Bulwark spell. Either that, or he simply ran out of it. It had the same impact: the protective barrier was gone.

Xavier ran ahead, easily able to overtake those around him as his speed was far superior. Now that he wouldn't be a target ahead of the army, it shouldn't be too dangerous getting close.

Throwing myself into the fray isn't a risk. Not as strong as I am. At least, he hoped it wasn't, but he'd never experienced anything like this before. *Why am I worried? With all the titles I've gained, I have almost fifty levels more worth of stats than these guys.*

Even if the enemy soldiers received more stats when they gained their new class, they were only Level 12. They wouldn't have had long to take advantage of that.

It was easy enough to tell elf from human, something he was glad for. He yelled to the honour guard in front to make a hole for him. They responded instantly. *At least they're well-trained. More than could be said for me.*

The line of human soldiers that had been in front of the honour guard was already falling. It appeared as though an equal number of the elves had fallen too, but there was too much chaos for him to be able to tell.

He scanned a few of the elves now that he was better able to see them.

{**Elf – Level 12**}
{**Elf – Level 12**}
{**Elf – Level 12**}

Just as I thought.

He quickly did the math. Assuming he received 1,200 Mastery Points per kill, he would need to defeat 124 enemies without sharing any of the points with others to reach Level 9. And maybe twice that number to reach Level 10.

Wiping out the entire army myself might be enough. Not that I'm going to try.

Xavier made it to the front. All that lay ahead of him now were the enemy soldiers. He smiled. He couldn't help himself. The thrill of the battle was taking over, pumping excitement through his veins.

Time to do some damage.

Xavier cast Spiritual Trifecta and was engulfed in a brilliant silver light. The power he felt from it was like nothing he'd ever had before.

I have 100 points in Spirit. Did that break some sort of barrier?

He didn't know, but it sure *felt* like he had.

If it did, I'm close to doing the same for Intelligence...

Facing the line of elves, their expressions contorted with anger as they rushed toward him, wielding spears and shields, Xavier cast Heavy Telekinesis. A purple light flashed on the enemy soldiers—some sort of protection from magic?—but it didn't seem to help.

His spell broke straight through it.

Countless soldiers were thrust backward. Xavier heard a symphony of elven bones cracking as they crashed into their allies behind them, then behind them, and so forth, and so on.

How much damage did I just inflict?

Over thirty kill notifications came all at once. He quickly read the first.

Magical Potency has reached Rank 5!

Just from one spell? Xavier didn't look a gift horse in the mouth.

You have defeated a Level 12 Elf!
You have gained 1,800 Mastery Points.
You have gained 1,800 Spirit Energy.

1,800? Shouldn't I have gotten 1,200? That's 50 percent more Mastery Points and Spirit Energy than I expected! Xavier wondered why that might be. *Maybe they give more because they've gained their first class?*

He pushed the question away. He didn't need to know *why*—he would just take it as a win.

Xavier felt his Heavy Telekinesis spell refresh its cooldown. *Was that in two seconds, not three? It's gotten even faster!* He launched another spell, still benefitting from Spiritual Trifecta.

More and more enemies fell.

Magical Potency has reached Rank 6!

What, again!?

Heavy Telekinesis has taken a step forward on the path!
Heavy Telekinesis is now a Rank 4 spell.
One cannot walk backward on the path.

Spiritual Trifecta has taken a step forward on the path!
Spiritual Trifecta is now a Rank 4 spell.
One cannot walk backward on the path.

Reaching Level 10 might not take very long at all!

There was a giant *thud, thud, thud.* At first, Xavier had thought it was from war drums. Then he heard a familiar voice call out.

"The enemy's Champion has arrived!" Sergeant Bradley bellowed.

A shadow loomed over the battle, like a mountain in motion, and Xavier got his first glimpse of the floor boss.

He swore, loudly and colourfully.

Chapter 46
Wearing Glass-Cannon Mage Robes

Xavier, standing between two armies, glanced up at the floor boss for the third floor of the Tower of Champions.

He had no idea what the hell it was, but it *looked* terrifying. Far more menacing than the Puma Prime or the Rat King had been. This looked like a true beast. It stood on four thick, trunk-like legs. It looked like some sort of weird cross between a rhinoceros and a three-headed hellhound, though this thing would give Cerberus a run for its money.

All three heads were wreathed in flames. Each had a long horn jutting from the top of the head that looked more like sharpened metal spikes than they did bone.

The horns glowed, and Xavier couldn't help but wonder if they had some sort of magical properties.

If I kill the floor boss before the enemy soldiers, does that end the level? He was 99.99 percent sure that it wouldn't, which made him all the more tempted to try, as terrifying as the damned beast looked.

Xavier scanned it.

{Cerotri Infernum – Level 40}

Cerotri Infernum? What the hell is that? Didn't infernum *mean* hell?

That thought made him shudder, wondering what the System's version of hell would be like. The more he looked at the Cerotri Infernum, the more he realised the differences between it and a rhinoceros.

Like someone already bad at drawing had done a drunk sketch of one.

This beast wasn't like any of the others that he'd encountered since the integration. The Black Pumas and the Giant Mole Rats appeared to be animals from Earth that had been transformed—or from somewhere incredibly similar to Earth. Which he supposed could be possible, as apparently there were *humans* on other worlds.

Not apparently. There are *humans on other worlds.*

But this beast? This beast was totally alien. Its skin didn't look like skin. It looked like molten lava. Like it was constantly flowing and shifting and changing. The red glow of its flesh washed over the enemy's side of the battlefield, as though painting it in blood.

The beast roared—from all three heads. The roar was as alien as the Ceres Infernum itself. It sounded like explosions set off. Like bubbles bursting. Deep rumbling and high-pitched hissing mixed with the roaring of a jet engine.

That sound *did* sting Xavier's ears.

The level of the beast took him by surprise, too.

The last floor boss was Level 20. This is twice that level. Not to mention the bloody beast stands thirty-five feet tall!

He supposed he wouldn't have to face it alone. He had an army behind him. It would be more like facing a raid boss with a guild than facing a single boss solo.

And I could probably take that thing on my own if I had to.

He was eager to finally test out Spirit Break on the beast. It didn't seem like something that would be helpful against multiple opponents, especially when he could kill them all so easily. But against *that*? It might be a different story.

Xavier flicked his attention back in front of him. He must have taken out seventy enemies casting Heavy Telekinesis twice. Spiritual Trifecta was still well and truly active—and both of the spells had just ranked up, not to mention Magical Potency was at Rank 6, giving him an effective Intelligence of 101.

He would have been at 100 when it had hit Rank 5, which meant he'd broken 100 before casting the second spell.

That last spell... It hit harder than the first without me even realising. I think I killed ten more enemies than the first. He had *definitely* passed some sort of barrier when he'd gotten 100 points in Spirit, then again in Intelligence. *The next closest would be Toughness.*

Tearing his focus away from the Level 40 Cerotri Infernum, Xavier cast Heavy Telekinesis against the line of enemy soldiers. The elven warriors had been climbing over the corpses of their kin to get toward him. Half of them looked like they were already injured—they must have been hit by the soldiers he'd already thrown.

Crack!

Dozens of kill notifications assailed his vision. He willed only the things he wished to see to the surface.

Congratulations, you have reached Level 9!
Your health has been regenerated by 50%!
Your Spirit Energy limit has increased by 100!
You have received +1 Intelligence, +1 Willpower, and +1 Spirit!
You have received +5 free stat points!
All your spells have refreshed and are no longer on cooldown!

Magical Potency has reached Rank 7!

A level-up, already? And another rank in Magical Potency? The skill was adding 11 percent magical damage to every one of his spells now, and boosting his Intelligence by 11 percent as well.

Xavier could barely believe how much damage he was inflicting. Spiritual Trifecta was still active. *How long does that last now?* He stepped forward, over the corpses of his enemies. He remembered what Howard had said—that he needed to learn how to fight without simply using brute force.

But right now, that didn't seem quite as relevant, especially when he had no shortage of Spirit Energy and his Heavy Telekinesis spell kept refreshing every two seconds.

Xavier threw one point into Toughness—he was now five away from one hundred—and the other four into Intelligence, going for as much mass damage as he could muster.

This is a bloodbath. A massacre.

He cast the spell again. More enemies fell. He had to remember that he *didn't* want to clear this floor. Not yet.

He'd killed less on that last spell. The enemies were running away from him now, no doubt clearing a path for their long-ranged fighters to get a bead on him.

An arrow *thunked* into his shoulder.

Crap. He was out in the open again, mostly because he'd killed all the soldiers that had been standing in front of him, and the ones he hadn't had run away. *So much for not taking risks.*

Heavy footsteps thudded behind him. Within seconds, the honour guard were in front of him with their shields up.

Howard was at their front. "We'll push you forward, then break and let you through when you near their lines again!"

"Good plan!" Xavier shouted back. He looked down at the arrow in his shoulder, realising that... it hadn't really hurt all that much. It had glowed purple—*penetration arrow?*—on its way toward him, but now it was dim.

The conventional wisdom was *not* to pull something that had punctured through your skin back out, as it was plugging up the blood. Blades tended to do more damage coming out than going in. But Xavier figured this situation was different.

He yanked the arrow out of his shoulder, knowing he could pull a Lesser Health Potion—or even munch on some food—from his Storage Ring if he needed it, but looking at his health... *That arrow only took it down by 1 percent? And it's heading back up?* He'd need to get hit by a hundred of those things—at the same time —to get taken out.

And that's wearing glass-cannon mage robes. I wonder how much more resilient I'll be at 100 Toughness...

Once again, Xavier was realising just how great the divide between him and anyone else *was*. It lit a fire within him. A desire to push forward even faster.

That army is nothing compared to me.

The Cerotri Infernum roared once more. The enemy soldiers had made a path for it. When it had arrived, it had been at the very back of the elven army's lines.

Now, it was nearing the front.

It will be on us soon. Very soon.

Xavier stepped on something metallic between enemy corpses. Looking down, he realised he was standing atop the door to the Staging Room. He'd already pushed the enemy army back far enough to reach it. "Sergeant Bradley! Help clear the trapdoor! We need it ready to be opened!"

Sergeant Bradley, who'd been not far behind him, bellowed orders to the soldiers he'd gathered for this very duty, even if he didn't know what the door was.

Howard and the honour guard reached the line of enemy soldiers. Howard barked that it was time for Xavier to step in, and they made a hole for him to step through.

Xavier felt like the battering ram of a siege tower. Protected by the soldiers around him until he reached his destination.

And it was time to punch a hole through the elven army. A hole that would lead him straight to the third-floor boss.

Xavier cast Spiritual Trifecta upon himself once more, then inflicted as much death upon the enemy as he could muster.

He flung thirty or so soldiers one way, took three slow steps as he counted down from two to zero, then flung another thirty or so soldiers the other.

I must already be halfway to Level 10 by now!

He wasn't sure how many enemies he'd killed. Maybe two hundred. But with his efforts coupled with the efforts of the human army, it looked like only a hundred of them remained. If he didn't ease up, they'd all be dead before he took out the floor boss. And the last thing he wanted right now was to accidentally clear the floor.

This has definitely been the easiest floor so far. It felt different, having so many people there to protect him while he fought.

The Cerotri Infernum was close. Damned close. It loomed over him, casting its fiery shadow. There was no longer a single enemy soldier between him and the floor boss.

Time to face the hell beast.

Chapter 47
The System Doesn't Stand for Cowards

THE THUNDEROUS, EXPLOSIVE ROAR OF THE CEROTRI Infernum rang out once more, stabbing at Xavier's ears. The weird bubbling, popping, rumbling, jet-engine noise hit him threefold.

Xavier stared up at the hell beast. Behind him, his honour guard and party stood, along with the rest of the human army. Some of them were engaged with the enemy elves, which were scattered about the battlefield.

"Sergeant Bradley!" Xavier shouted. "Ensure you leave one or two of the enemy alive!" He paused briefly, coming up with an excuse. "I wish to question them thoroughly."

Questions and torture were by no means a part of his plan, but he figured saying it in that way would appeal to the man considering how much he seemed to hate the "knife-ears."

"Yes, Champion, sir!" Sergeant Bradley replied.

The man's voice was far louder than Xavier's. *Definitely using a skill or spell of some sort.* He was glad the man had been able to hear him at all. He'd worried the beast's roar had deafened him.

The Cerotri Infernum reared up on its hind legs, threw back every one of its three heads, and released that roar for one final time before it attacked.

Xavier wasn't going to stand there and wait for it to strike.

As terrifying as this thing looked, he had to remind himself that even though it was Level 40, it was still far weaker than *him*. As long as he played this fight right—unlike the last boss fight—it should be easy enough.

Kill it before it kills you, and figure out if it has any weaknesses or tricks up its sleeve. That way, he could take it down even faster when he fully cleared this floor.

Xavier, enveloped in the silver sheen of Spiritual Trifecta, sprinted to the right of the beast, getting on its flank.

The first spell he *wanted* to use was Spirit Break, but he hadn't cast that spell before. It had seemed like a useless spell to use upon the elven soldiers, considering he could take them all out so damned easily, and now he was regretting that decision a little bit.

Ah well, I can use this massive beast as a punching bag.

He flung Heavy Telekinesis at the beast, wanting to throw it off balance. It was still rearing back on its hind legs. A part of Xavier had expected the beast to be completely resistant to his magic. The other two floor bosses that he'd faced before this one had some magical resistance, after all.

So it didn't come as a surprise when a purple sheen flashed all about its body. But the purple sheen wasn't enough. Xavier's Intelligence was an effective 108 now, and his Magical Potency boosted his damage by a considerable amount.

Xavier grinned as the Cerotri Infernum was knocked off to the side. The damned hell beast was far heavier than anything else Xavier had used the spell on, which just made him all the more glad for the type of telekinesis he'd chosen to specialise in.

It flew about thirty feet off to the left, tried to catch itself and regain its balance when its feet hit the ground. Instead, its sharp hooves dug deep troughs through the grassy field. The beast overbalanced and fell straight down.

Xavier frowned. He was glad he'd been able to throw the beast, but he hadn't heard a single *crack* of breaking bone. *It's too big, and those muscles... They're insulating the bones.*

A cheer rang out behind him, a chorus of *whoops* from the army, as though what he'd done would spell their victory.

It's not dead yet. Far from it.

As the beast struggled back to its feet, it was finally time for Xavier to test out his new spell. The spell was only Rank 1. And like Spiritual Trifecta when it was Rank 1, there were three different ways for him to use it.

He could *will* the spell to break his enemy's body, his enemy's mind, or his enemy's magic. Like Spiritual Trifecta, his instinct was to generalise so the spell would let him do all three of those things at once.

He could only imagine how powerful the spell could be against single, strong opponents.

Soon, I won't have to imagine.

Xavier thrust his staff forward. The beast still hadn't made it back to its feet. Xavier thought *Spirit Break*, and the Cerotri Infernum broke.

He'd willed the spell to break his enemy's body, and the spell did just that.

Spirit and Intelligence were Xavier's strongest attributes, and that was clear as a symphony of loud *cracks* came from the hell beast. Having gotten back to its feet, it slipped straight back down to the ground.

Each of its four legs was twisted the wrong way, jutting out at absurd angles, jagged bones piercing through its flesh. All three of its heads were *yanked* one way, then the other. The sound of it—the sight of it—made Xavier flinch, unexpected as it was.

Those three heads opened their massive maws once more. But this time, it wasn't a weird, explosive roar that was released. It was an agonised, tortured moan. The sound tugged at Xavier's heart strings.

I caused this beast pain.

He wasn't trying to torture it, but he needed to practise this spell. Xavier pursed his lips, and stepped toward the enemy.

He checked the cooldown on the spell.

Spirit Break has a cooldown of 15 seconds. It cannot be used for another 12 seconds.

"Do you wish for us to close in and finish the hell beast, my lord?" Sergeant Bradley said. The man had come out of nowhere, standing beside Xavier.

Xavier blinked at the use of "my lord." The sergeant had been deferential toward them, but that was the first time he'd used such an honorific. Xavier wasn't sure how he felt about it. "No, Sergeant. Tell your men to stand back. You have some of the enemies in custody?"

"Aye, my lord. Knocked out three of them. Got them tied up good. They should wake up soon."

"None of them surrendered?" Xavier asked. The hell beast was still struggling on the ground. Xavier's forehead creased as he looked at it.

Sergeant Bradley's eyes widened. He stared openly at Xavier. "Surrendered? Elves might be right bastards, but they aren't cowards. The System doesn't stand for *cowards*." He shook his head. "Surrendered," he muttered.

Xavier raised an eyebrow at the sergeant. Perhaps he should have expected that. He'd already learnt that from the System, after all. In fact, it was one of the first things he'd learnt from it.

The System is ruthless. It wants us to fight. It killed that Navy SEAL because he wouldn't. He supposed that made surrender a dirty word in the Greater Universe.

Xavier checked his cooldown again. It was nearing its end. The hell beast looked miserable. Defeated. Though it was still trying to gain its feet, it simply couldn't anymore. Xavier hadn't even seen what spells it could cast, though he was sure it would have had something, being Level 40 and all.

Figuring he had time, he checked his spells. And, sure enough, he found that Spirit Break now had an Upgrade Quest available.

Spirit Break – Rank 1
Upgrade Quest:

As you have now used this spell, you have taken your first step on the path to upgrading it to Rank 2. Available paths:

1. *Spirit Break (Body) - Break an enemy's body, crippling their ability to fight. To upgrade, fight an enemy while this path is active. Progress: 1/10*
2. *Spirit Break (Mind) - Break an enemy's mind, hindering their ability to think. To upgrade, fight an enemy while this path is active. Progress: 0/10*
3. *Spirit Break (Soul) - Break an enemy's spirit, blocking their ability to use magic. To upgrade, fight an enemy while this path is active. Progress: 0/10*
4. *Spirit Break (All) - Break an enemy's body, mind, and spirit, crippling their ability to fight, hindering their ability to think, and blocking their ability to use magic. To upgrade, fight an enemy while this path is active. Progress: 0/5*

Choosing one path may eliminate some or all other paths. This will both limit your ability and strengthen it.
Upgrading a spell from Rank 1 to Rank 2 will make you immediately forget another Rank 1 spell of your choosing. Once a spell is forgotten, it is almost impossible to be learnt again.
As you have no other Rank 1 spells, this does not currently apply.
One cannot walk backward on the path.

Xavier tilted his head to the side as he sped through the description, glad he could read so much faster now.

Just like with Spiritual Trifecta, there don't seem to be any drawbacks to generalising with this spell. He was also glad to find that bringing it to the next rank wouldn't make him forget any other spells. *I guess it's best to learn one spell at a time, rather than several. I wonder if I'll have a choice when I gain my next class.*

He looked over at the still struggling Cerotri Infernum, which he had basically taken down with two spells, not even having to touch it or take a single hit from it.

And this spell is damned powerful. Or maybe the spell is powerful because I am?

He glanced back at the battlefield. He'd been able to take out dozens of the elves at once. And with Spiritual Trifecta active—boosting his physical defence, as well as enhancing his physical strength and magical potency—he would barely take any damage.

Maybe I could take the whole army by myself. Especially if I gained a few more levels. Not that he thought it would be a smart thing to try.

When Spirit Break reached the end of its cooldown, he stared over at the Cerotri Infernum, his forehead creasing. He muttered, "Sorry, little beast," under his breath, then he cast the spell, willing it to break the enemy's mind.

More agonised moans were released from the enemy's three mouths. He shut his eyes, not wanting to see the pain this thing was in. The pain *he* was causing it.

I'm torturing this beast to gain power. But... how is that any worse than all the death I've caused?

He recalled Sergeant Bradley's words: *The System doesn't stand for cowards.*

Xavier steeled himself, opened his eyes, resolve settling within him. He'd chosen this spell because he knew it would make him strong. He couldn't shy away from what it was able to do.

If he was going to remain the most powerful Champion of Earth, if he was going to lead humanity to victory against those who wished to destroy them or enslave them, then he would need to embrace every bit of power he could get his hands on.

Xavier took another step toward the hell beast and waited for Spirit Break to reach the end of its cooldown.

Then, he would cast it again.

Chapter 48
Thank You for Your Sacrifice

XAVIER STOOD OVER THE MANGLED, DESTROYED BODY OF THE Cerotri Infernum.

The hell beast with three heads must have had a massive amount of health. It had managed to survive five uses of Spirit Break to its body, mind, and soul each.

Fifteen uses of the spell. Seven and a half minutes of agony.

It still breathed, but it did not moan any longer. It *couldn't* moan anymore. No cheers came from the soldiers behind him. A silence had fallen upon the battlefield as he'd cast Spirit Break, waited for the cooldown to end, then cast it again. And again.

And again.

Unrelentingly. With no mercy.

He didn't need to worry about his Spirit Energy. Being a Rank 1 spell, Spirit Break currently only used 100 Spirit Energy, so Xavier had *plenty* to spare.

A part of Xavier hated what he was doing, but he'd shut that part of him down. This had been necessary. This was part of his training. It was the best way he could think to push the spell forward.

He read the notification.

**Spirit Break has taken a step forward on the
path, upgrading to the spell: Spirit Break (All).
Spirit Break (All) is a Rank 2 spell.
One cannot walk backward on the path.**

Though Xavier felt a sense of achievement at having gained
the second rank for the spell, he also felt a bit of disgust at how he'd
done it. Now he'd gotten all the use he could from the hell beast, he
walked over to one of its heads.

Its eyes turned up, widened, staring at him. Its breath struggled
in and out, a rasping whine in its throat.

"Thank you for your sacrifice," Xavier whispered.

Then he cast Heavy Telekinesis straight *down* into its head.
The hell beast's skull was crushed into the ground. And though
only one of its brains was destroyed, that seemed to be enough to
tip its health all the way down to nothing.

**You have defeated a Level 40 Cerotri Infernum!
You have gained 8,000 Mastery Points.
You have gained 8,000 Spirit Energy.**

Magical Potency has reached Rank 8!

Xavier held his breath, waiting to see if another notification
came. A small part of him still worried that killing the floor boss
would mean the end of the floor, but he'd been sure enough that
hadn't been the case.

Now, after a moment passed, his suspicion was confirmed—
they definitely had to kill *every* enemy, and with some of the elves
captured, that meant the floor wasn't fully cleared.

He let out the breath and placed a hand on the Cerotri Infernum's mangled corpse, placing it into his Storage Ring. It barely fit,
taking up the entirety of the space, but he wouldn't have it in there
for long.

Xavier turned. His party, and every soldier that remained of the human army—which appeared to be almost all of them, as barely any had fallen once Xavier got into the battle—stood, staring at him in awe.

The first face he saw was Siobhan's. Her forehead was creased. Her gaze flicked away from his, toward where the corpse of the hell beast had been. At the massive pool of blood it had left behind.

He didn't know why he worried about how she might feel about what he'd just done.

I needed to do that. To gain power. Siobhan and the others will understand. Though... that doesn't mean they will like it.

"That was..." Howard let out a breath. "Vicious." He stared Xavier in the eye. "Please tell me you did that to gain the next rank in a spell, and not because you enjoyed it or something?"

Straight to the point, I see. Xavier nodded. "I got Rank 2 in Spirit Break."

"Looks like..." Justin swallowed. "Looks like the spell is effective."

Siobhan loosened her grip around her staff. Her knuckles had gone white, though that wasn't hard with her pale skin. "You really are something, Xavier." She shook her head. "You're even stronger than I imagined." The words felt somewhat devoid of emotion compared with how she usually spoke, and her smile was gone from her lips.

Xavier supposed he couldn't blame her. He hadn't exactly enjoyed what he'd done, but... he didn't regret it. He was glad for what it had given him. It seemed like the easiest way for him to test out and rank up his new spell.

"This floor doesn't pose much of a challenge for you." Howard gestured about the battlefield. "Clearly. How close are you to Level 10?"

"If we farm this floor one more time, I'll reach it easily. Then, on our third time in here, I'll clear the whole thing solo." Or, at least, with only the help of the army. He had to assume the soldiers wouldn't take away from him solo-clearing this level and gaining the title for it.

Although... he could be wrong.

Maybe I'll have to think about that...

Howard nodded. The man looked a little tired. "Good. Then, I think it's about time we got some sleep. It's been... a very long day."

Sleep? Xavier hadn't even thought about *sleep*, but he supposed the man was right. Though he didn't feel tired, they would need a break at *some* point.

And they were on the third floor on the *first* day of entering the floors of the Tower of Champions.

If I've gained this much in one day... how much will I gain in a week? A month?

A year?

The party headed back to the trapdoor that led to the Staging Room. It was still being guarded by a few soldiers, and they'd opened it up. None of the soldiers—not even Sergeant Bradley—spoke with them. It seemed as though they were too stunned by what had just happened to speak.

The soldiers hadn't even cheered when the Cerotri Infernum had died.

They might have been expecting Champions to come to their aid, but clearly they hadn't expected them to be as strong as *him*.

When his party returned to the Staging Room, the sombre mood seemed to clear away, though the others did seem a little quieter around him.

Maybe I'm just imagining that. Surely they don't think of me as a monster, right?

They sold off the loot they'd gotten. Unfortunately, they didn't have enough space in all their Storage Rings for everything, so some things had been left on the field. Still, they gained 8,450 Lesser Spirit Coins from what they'd just done—a battle that hadn't even taken an hour.

If we really wanted to, we could farm that floor over and over rather quickly...

The thought was an appealing one, but the last thing he wanted to do was slow his ascent through the tower floors.

We'll clear it one more time. I'll gain Level 10, and let the others do more fighting if I can.

Though farming the floor *sounded* like a good idea, and Xavier still needed to train to be better in combat, stopping to gain as much from a single floor seemed like a trap more than anything.

We might gain levels and Spirit Coins that way, skill rank-ups and even spell rank-ups, but we won't get any titles. Titles are how I'll get as strong as I possibly can. I'm not going to let us slow down.

Xavier checked how close he was to reaching Level 10.

Mastery Points for this level: 224,700/400,000

More than halfway. Just as I'd thought. His mind moved through the math easily. *I'll need to kill 98 more of those Level 12 soldiers. That's like, three uses of Heavy Telekinesis.*

Maybe even less, as the spell had already gotten stronger.

After the others briefly discussed their gains—they had each reached Level 7 during the fighting—and the fact that Siobhan healing someone who defeated an enemy *did* gain her Mastery Points, they quickly entered the third floor of the Tower of Champions. The party wasn't very talkative. They knew they shouldn't stop and chat for long. At least not until they'd gotten Xavier to Level 10.

Though Xavier couldn't help but feel like they were quiet for another reason.

He remembered that he'd been planning on getting the others to Level 10 on this floor, to get them closer to gaining their classes, but he didn't want to wait that long. They would take far longer than him to get where they needed.

They'll get to Level 10 soon enough. They're already Level 7, after all.

Xavier was finding it difficult to make plans, floor-to-floor, as they never really knew what they would find on the next one. Perhaps he would need to play things a little more loosely. He would still turn his party into a formidable support team, but the third floor, with its two opposing armies, simply didn't feel like the right place to practise that.

They appeared in the field again. It looked identical to the last time they'd been here. The same long, purple grass. The same twin suns, sitting in the same spot in the sky as they had last time.

Xavier shielded his eyes, gazing up at that alien sky. He couldn't help but smile, taking it all in once more, feeling the cool breeze play with the sleeves of his Robes of Intelligence.

He could hear the *thud, thud, thud*, of war drums, coming from his left, coming from his right. He took a deep breath of that clean, crisp air, then looked over at the elves, willing the prompt to come once more.

Welcome to the Third Floor of the Tower of Champions.
The Third Floor of the Tower of Champions is a test of your leadership capabilities and your might in battle. An army of Elves and an army of Humans are to clash upon this world. You must choose which army to fight with, and which to fight against.
Each army is 500 soldiers strong, and they have each summoned a Champion to lead them.
Whose call will you answer?

This time, Xavier chose the elves.
How fast can I reach Level 10?

Chapter 49
Stop Trying to Hit Me and Hit Me!

Xavier, Howard, Siobhan, and Justin were engulfed in a white light and transported to the head of the elven army.

Xavier wasn't sure how this would go. He'd just slaughtered this army and their summoned Champion, the Cerotri Infernum, basically torturing the poor hell beast as he ranked up his Spirit Break spell.

Now, he was going to be fighting on their side? It seemed almost perverse. But... here the army was, all of them alive again. To his eyes, it looked like the same army. *Which means the human army will be exactly the same, and I'll be killing Sergeant Bradley along with other human soldiers who had just been protecting me.*

It was a strange thing to think about. He wondered how the floors *worked*. Did the System create them each time? Or were they time-looped chambers that restarted whenever someone entered them? Like a never-ending stream of alternate universes?

He shook his head. *Not the time to figure out how the System and the Greater Universe function, assuming such a thing is even possible at all.*

One of the elves ran forward, then stopped about six feet away from them. The woman looked exceptionally regal. She was tall and slender—perhaps an inch or two taller than Justin—and the picture of an elven beauty.

She wore ringmail armour that clung to her figure as best it could. Like the human soldiers at the front line of the opposing army, she carried a long spear and large shield, though somehow she managed to do it with far more grace. Her flaxen hair was braided into a fancy bun at the top of her head.

Flaxen hair? Xavier thought, chiding himself. *Really? Can't I just call it blonde?*

He shook his head, tearing his gaze away from her gorgeous blue eyes, reminding himself why they were here—and about the fact that he would have killed this very same elven woman in the last instance of the floor.

This is weird.

Xavier was glad they weren't going to farm this floor more than one more time. He couldn't imagine what it might feel like, slaughtering these same soldiers over and over. It might be an effective way to gain Mastery Points and Lesser Spirit Coins, but it still... didn't *feel* right.

"Hail, Champions!" The woman's voice carried far, just like Sergeant Bradley's had, but her face was blank. *Serene.* She nodded to each of them. "We are honoured that you have accepted our call, though—" She faltered, cleared her throat. "We weren't expecting *humans* to come to our aid." She gestured toward her army. "However, you should not fear, for we elves are a noble race, and we will follow your orders to the *word*." She bowed her head. "Great Champions."

Xavier didn't let Howard step in this time. He spoke first, giving nearly the same orders as he had the last time, getting them to secure the trapdoor to the Staging Room—not that it would be difficult to reach, when he was done with the other army. He added in the order of keeping several humans alive for "questioning," figuring it was better to get that in early.

He asked for an honour guard, just as he had the last time. This time, however, he wanted to test something. With the honour guard in place—twenty tall, proud elven soldiers wielding long spears and massive shields—Xavier spoke to Siobhan.

When they'd briefly spoken of the progress each of them had made, she'd told him that her Heal Other spell had reached its second rank, while her Summon spell had reached its third.

Though Xavier wanted to clear this floor fast, he didn't want to pass up an opportunity. When he'd taken an arrow in the shoulder, it had done 1 percent of damage to him, so he knew he could take a good beating from the enemy soldiers as long as he had an escape route, especially if Spiritual Trifecta was active.

Xavier was proud of getting his Magical Potency skill all the way to Rank 8, but his other skills were lagging behind. If he wanted a class that blended physical combat with magical combat, he knew he needed to up those skills while he could.

Staff Mastery, Physical Resistance, Magical Resistance, and Physical Damage. There's one surefire way I can help boost all four of them.

He explained his plan to Siobhan.

"You want to fight the enemies with *just your staff?*" Siobhan asked, her eyes widening.

Xavier rubbed the back of his head and gave a sheepish nod. "Yeah, basically. I think it will really help me rank up my other skills. But if my health gets down to a quarter, I want you to Summon me to you and heal me."

"How will I know when that happens?"

"I'll use Heavy Telekinesis on the enemy. That'll be the sign."

Howard, on Xavier's left, leant in. "Do you need me by your side?"

Xavier shook his head. "No. I'll be right in the thick of things this time around. I don't want you in too much danger. Stick with the others. Fight as a team."

Siobhan nodded. "All right. I... I think your plan will work. I'll make sure to summon you back." She winced. "You know this is going to hurt, right?"

Xavier had considered that, but it didn't really bother him. His Willpower was at an effective 88, and if he'd learnt anything by this point it was that he could withstand physical pain. "I know. But I have to do this."

He didn't *want* to get hurt, but this seemed like the best way. Besides, considering all the pain he'd caused, he could take a little in return. It only seemed fair, after all.

This time, unlike the last, he didn't stay behind the honour guard. Didn't remain behind their shield wall or beneath Howard's Bulwark. Xavier made a hole through the honour guard and stepped right into the open, feeling like an utter fool.

This is exactly the type of risk I'm not supposed to take.

Except this time, it wasn't a *risk*. He knew that. He had support behind him. Siobhan could summon him out of danger. He wouldn't take one hundred hits all at once. He could probably run faster than they could hit him with their arrows and spells, anyway.

Especially with Spiritual Trifecta active.

He kept that spell inactive for now, let out a breath, and sprinted straight for the five hundred soldiers that comprised the human army, gripping his staff tightly in hand.

Time to wreak some havoc.

Xavier's actions seemed to take the enemy army by surprise. He hardly thought they would have expected a single person to be sprinting across the great expanse of purple grassland.

The *whish, whish, whish* of the grass sounded on every stride as his legs ate up the distance between the two armies faster than ever. This was the first time he'd sprinted since he'd gained the titles from the second floor.

God, he was *fast*.

The arrows and spells began to come his way. He could take a good few of them if he needed to, but he was running too fast for them, and almost all of the projectiles fell short as the long-range fighters had to launch their attacks over the line of melee fighters at the front of their army, so they weren't loosing their arrows or firing their spells at him straight-on.

An arrow struck him in the leg, and he thought he'd be stopped completely. The pain hit him hard... but not *that* hard, and it didn't slow his run at all. Checking his health, he noticed he had taken 2 percent damage, but he wasn't worried.

That's just because I haven't activated Spiritual Trifecta yet.

A fireball struck him full on in the chest. Again, it barely hurt him. He would need more than that if he was going to rank up his skills.

"Come on!" he shouted at the enemy. "Stop trying to hit me and hit me!" He blinked. *Did I just quote Morpheus in* The Matrix?

His voice boomed, carrying across the field. Another voice sounded out, responding to him in turn, and he recognised who it was.

"Kill the bastard traitor! A human fighting with knife-ears? *Honestly*! Give him everything we've got!" Sergeant Bradley bellowed back.

A barrage of arrows and spells came straight for him. More than the first time, and Xavier wondered if this had been such a great idea...

Figuring he was seconds away from reaching the first line of soldiers running as fast as he was, Xavier activated Spiritual Trifecta, held his breath, and braced himself.

Siobhan can get me out of here if need be.

With the speed of his eyes and the speed of his thoughts, he counted roughly forty attacks that would *actually* hit him if he stopped running.

That won't be enough to kill me.

Xavier stopped running. Gripping his staff in his right hand, he opened up his arms. He looked like a man welcoming death, when that was the last thing he would ever do.

The arrows and spells fell. Arrows with flaming tips. Arrows glowing purple and green and blue. Fireballs, lightning, and ice shards too.

The constant barrage slammed into him, making him take one, two, three steps back. The pain was... the pain was...

Bearable.

He'd endured worse, and so he knew he could endure this.

Magical Resistance has reached Rank 2!
Physical Resistance has reached Rank 3!
Magical Resistance has reached Rank 3!
Physical Resistance has reached Rank 4!

Xavier did perhaps the last thing anyone observing might have expected him to.

He laughed. He threw his head back and *laughed*. He was... *enjoying* this. How could he be enjoying this?

Don't question it.

Having paused for a couple of seconds to take all those hits, he began sprinting again, checking his health.

Your health is at 56%.

I just took that many hits, and it brought me down by less than half?

Even though that's what he'd been expecting—that's what the math had told him would happen—it was still a surprise. Part of him thought he would need to be summoned straight back to Siobhan after taking those hits, even if that didn't logically make sense when adding up the attacks coming his way.

Still, it surprised him how *strong* he had become.

He did something he hadn't done before. He willed the health notification to remain in his vision, just as he had with the timer back on the first floor. It remained up in the top-right corner of his vision, so he could glance at it whenever he needed to.

Why didn't I ever think to do this before?

Finally, Xavier reached the army, his Spirit Staff of Might gripped tightly in both hands, the silver sheen of Spiritual Trifecta glowing about his body, strengthening both his physical damage and his physical defence.

It strengthened his magic, too, of course. But right now, that wasn't relevant.

It's time to bash in some heads.

Chapter 50
Like Some Berserker Warrior from Myth

Xavier kept a close eye on his health as he fought, but once he'd gotten into the thick of things, right up at the foot soldiers with their spears and shields, he wasn't taking near as much damage as he had been when he'd been out back in the open.

And now, his health was actually steadily regenerating.

Xavier heard Sergeant Bradley holler for his soldiers to create a shield wall to receive him, clearly expecting him to be strong after he'd taken all of their attacks and kept running.

Would be good if I can stop and take these arrows out, though.

He looked like nothing more than a human pincushion. Half of those attacks had been arrow-strikes, and so he had about twenty arrows protruding from all manner of places. His arms. His legs. His chest. His shoulders. His stomach.

Fortunately, none had entered his most delicate of areas, something he hadn't considered as he'd been standing there ready to receive the enemy attacks.

I really need to get some actual *armour.*

He couldn't help but wonder if his skin would be healing *around* the arrowheads. He may have to create new wounds when he pulled them out, worse than what the arrowheads themselves would create with their triangular, jagged edges.

When he'd reached the enemy, for a moment he'd worried his strikes wouldn't be enough to get past their defences. The soldiers had their shields up, and many of them had Bulwark—or a spell similar to it—active.

But he should not have worried.

You have defeated a Level 12 Human!
You have gained 1,800 Mastery Points.
You have gained 1,800 Spirit Energy.

His barbell-heavy staff slammed into the enemy shields, breaking through their protective spells with ease. The shields were metal and wood. Dents formed and splinters flew, and all the while his Spirit Staff of Might remained in perfect condition.

I'm glad I spent so much on this staff.

His robes, on the other hand, were a tattered mess to the point where it barely looked as though he was wearing many clothes at all.

While his staff didn't have much penetrative power except right where the crystal was, it had plenty of *blunt* force.

It was akin to a heavy foot soldier swinging a war hammer, except his staff was far faster and more agile. He struck about him with fierce accuracy, denting helmets and breaking skulls. When he struck a soldier in their shield, they went flying as though he'd hit them with Heavy Telekinesis.

Though they didn't have far to fly, so they would slam into the soldier behind them—sometimes straight onto their spear.

Each of his strikes was a one-hit-kill, at least while Spiritual Trifecta was active.

Physical Damage has reached Rank 2!
Physical Resistance has reached Rank 5!

That didn't take very long.

He got into a rhythm. He felt... absolutely unstoppable,

fighting in the middle of hundreds of soldiers. Blocking, redirecting, or simply *taking* their strikes because he knew he could. Bashing in skulls, knocking one soldier into another, hearing the metal *clang*, the wooden *thwack,* and the sharp *crack* of bones.

Xavier only blocked and redirected enemy strikes when he needed to—when he was trying to let his health regenerate—but it seemed to have an advantage he hadn't expected. When he'd struck down thirty soldiers, something miraculous happened.

Staff Mastery has reached Rank 2!

Yes! Finally!

Xavier would have pumped his fist into the air if he wasn't in the middle of an enemy army. He'd been waiting for Staff Mastery to reach the next rank for *ages*. Clearly, he hadn't been fighting with his staff in the way the System had expected him to.

Do I only gain more ranks with the staff when I'm fighting against armed enemies? It sounded a bit ludicrous, but as far as he could tell, that might very well be the case. *I wonder if I can gain Staff Mastery ranks simply through sparring.*

Xavier revelled in the fight, taking down one soldier after another. He knew he could have taken them down far faster with a single Heavy Telekinesis spell, but with each swing of the staff, and with all the strikes he was taking, he was getting stronger and stronger. Tougher and tougher.

As though to prove that to him, a notification popped up in his vision.

You have gained +1 Toughness!

The notification took him by surprise at first. He hadn't gained any attributes through training since he'd been running through the halls, hefting the vending machine over his head, and hitting himself with his staff.

Xavier smiled. He probably looked more than a little insane

right now. His face and robes speckled and damp with blood. His clothes tattered to ruins. The dead piling up around him. His staff battering a path through his enemies. Like some berserker warrior from myth.

But this was what he was training for.

The invaders will have armies. And I will defeat them.

What was he doing here? Fighting in the middle of five hundred soldiers and *winning*? That was simply proof of concept. What he was doing was *working*. It made him desire, all the more, to get back to Earth and see how his world was faring.

This floor, then seven more, and we'll be able to return. At least for a little while.

Spiritual Trifecta had worn off sometime during the fight. He'd been surprised at how long it had lasted—at least ten seconds, and he'd managed to do a lot of damage in that time.

He'd worried it was the only thing that had been giving him enough edge to go toe-to-toe in the middle of all these Level 12 human soldiers, but—keeping a close eye on his health—he tested what he could do without the spell active.

He was able to kill another thirty soldiers, and his health never dipped below 35 percent.

Xavier was getting closer and closer to his next level.

Spiritual Trifecta lasts for 10 seconds now, and its cooldown is 12. Which... effectively makes its cooldown 2 seconds, as the countdown starts the moment I activate it.

That meant that, soon enough, he might be able to keep Spiritual Trifecta active *indefinitely*. Assuming he had enough Spirit Energy to do so—but running out of Spirit Energy around this many enemies wasn't exactly an issue for him.

Two more notifications popped up in his vision.

Physical Damage has reached Rank 3!
Physical Resistance has reached Rank 6!

Rank 6 already? He supposed the extra damage he was taking without Spiritual Trifecta active was making his Physical Resistance skill rank-up even faster.

As the notification came, something crawled all across his skin. Then it... *burned* and *itched* like nothing he'd ever felt before.

What the hell is happening to me?

He glanced around him, worried he'd been hit by some sort of spell, but none of the enemy mages were yet in sight, and his health wasn't going down.

It was going *up*.

Xavier gritted his teeth, blocking strikes left and right as the sensation further intensified. He looked down at the skin of his arm, and his eyes widened.

His skin *was* crawling. Literally. Like there were thousands of tiny insects beneath it, skittering up and down across his bones.

He stumbled backward from the enemies in front of him and activated Spiritual Trifecta to bolster his physical defence against whatever the hell this was.

Snap!

One of the arrows in his arm snapped at the top of its shaft, up near where the arrowhead was embedded into his skin. His skin had healed over it, and had... eaten through the wood?

A chorus of *snaps* followed the last as all the other arrows around his body began to break, their shafts falling uselessly to the purple grass.

But the metal arrowheads were still inside him. They'd been healed over and were now trapped beneath his skin.

What. The. Hell!?

It was like his skin had grown twice as hard. He was taking hits even as he looked down at himself, the enemy melee soldiers parting to let the archers and mages get in hits.

The new arrows that came for him... were *bouncing* off him. They weren't damaging him at all!

The itchy, burning sensation continued, and he began to

realise what was happening. With Physical Resistance gaining so many rank-ups, he'd reached 100 Toughness, breaking through whatever barrier was at that milestone.

He looked at his health.

Your health is at 51%.

It was going up? Even as arrows and spells hit him, it was going *up*.

Unlike the arrows, the spells still did damage to him. Willpower was what gave resistance to magic, not Toughness alone, but his health had gone up high enough after breaking 100 points in Toughness that now the spells were only doing *half* a percent damage.

Magical Resistance has reached Rank 4!

Well I'll be damned.

Willpower was at an effective 91 now. Maybe he needed to push that all the way to 100...

Another notification popped up, one that made him raise his eyebrows.

Metal impurities detected during Toughness upgrade.
Attempting to purge metal impurities...

Metal impurities? The arrowheads!

A shock of pain ran through every inch of Xavier's body, to the point where it took him to his knees despite his strong tolerance. The crawling sensation beneath his skin intensified until it felt like nails were being dragged across the surface of his bones.

Error.

Unable to purge impurities in an F Grade Denizen.
Attempting to assimilate metal impurities into muscular structure...

Chapter 51
Attempting to Assimilate Metal Impurities

XAVIER KNELT IN THE LONG, PURPLE GRASS OF AN ALIEN world. Two large suns hung high in the sky, their heat bearing down on him. The breeze blew in, flapping the tattered remnants of his robes.

And all Xavier felt was the pain. A pain that ran over and under every inch of his skin. A pain that stabbed and clawed and dug at the very deepest parts of him. A pain that threatened to engulf his entire consciousness.

I have to fight it.

Hundreds of enemy soldiers stood before Xavier, loosing arrows at him and pelting him with fireballs, striking him with lightning, slamming him with rocks, and slicing him with shards of ice, clutching spears and shields with distorted looks of rage on their faces. Rage at the Champion—the human traitor who fought for the elves. The melee fighters were clearly trying to hold themselves back as the ranged fighters did their work. But it wasn't these attacks that were hurting him. Not really. It was what was happening to his body.

Through narrowed eyes and gritted teeth, he read the notification again, trying to understand it through the haze of agony.

Error.
Unable to purge impurities in an F Grade
Denizen.
Attempting to assimilate metal impurities into
muscular structure...

I don't understand. Assimilate metal impurities?

His mind was sluggish. Far more sluggish than it had ever been. But his thoughts turned to... Wolverine from X-Men, of all things. When he'd had adamantium pumped into him in that vat, and his body had healed him, grafting the metal to his bones.

Is that what's happening to me?

There wouldn't have been enough arrowheads embedded beneath his skin for something like that. Would there? Maybe he was just delirious with the pain...

A bright light enveloped him.

Siobhan, summoning me away. She must think I'm in trouble, on my knees like this.

But he didn't want to leave the battlefield. He didn't *need* to.

Your health is at 55%.

His health was still going up. Not down. Despite all of the attacks.

I want to stay. I want to keep fighting.

In the instant the white light enveloped him, he'd felt something *tug* at his body and spirit. The Summon spell. He grunted, then his grunt turned into a roar, his mouth opening wide, every muscle in his body tensing as he dragged himself off his knees and back onto his feet.

Somehow, he *shrugged* off the Summon spell, the tug of it disappearing as the light dissipated. He hadn't even known that was possible—that he could refuse it—but his Magical Resistance must have been high enough for it to work.

All the pain hadn't stopped. It felt like his legs were on fire.

Like the bones inside them were broken. But he needed to *stand*. He wasn't going to take whatever this was on his knees.

You have gained +1 Willpower!
Magical Resistance has reached Rank 5!

What? Willpower? I've never gained that naturally before.
Xavier made it all the way back to his feet, still clutching his Spirit Staff of Might in his right hand, digging it into the ground to help him stand. He straightened up.

He pushed past the pain.

You have gained +1 Willpower!

Really? Again?
A shock ran through his body. It threatened to shake him. To take him back to his knees. But he didn't let it. He stood as even more pain slammed into him.

You have gained +1 Willpower!

This is insane!
Then, as suddenly as the pain had come, it... left.

Success.
Assimilation is complete.
Metal impurities of *Crucible Steel* have been assimilated into muscular structure.
You have gained +10 Toughness!

You have learnt the skill Assimilate Properties!
Assimilate Properties – Rank 1
This is an epic skill that grants you the ability to assimilate foreign properties into your body,

mind, and soul if the perfect conditions are met.
List of Current Assimilated Properties: Crucible Steel (Muscular Structure) – +10 Toughness

The pain gone, Xavier looked down at his body. At his skin. It looked... different. It had the slightest silver tint to it, one that his Spiritual Trifecta spell wasn't the cause of.

I just gained a rank in Magical Resistance, 3 Willpower, 10 Toughness, and an epic skill?

Xavier shook his head in disbelief. He turned his head from side to side, cracking it satisfyingly, then looked out at the enemy soldiers. Their barrage of attacks had ceased, and they were all just staring at him.

Then a series of explosions sounded, mixed with a deep rumbling and high-pitched hissing and the roaring of a jet engine. A dark shadow loomed over the human army.

Their Champion, the three-headed hell beast named the Cerotri Infernum—the same one that had fought for the elves in the previous instance—had arrived behind them.

The trance that had overtaken the human army seemed to disappear. A man bellowed an order. It wasn't Sergeant Bradley—*Did I already kill that man?*—"Clear the way for our Champion! Let the Cerotri Infernum deal with the bastard scum traitor while we move on the enemy!"

Xavier tilted his head forward. "No." Wringing his grip about his staff, holding it tight in both hands, a smile dragged up the side of his lips. "You shall not pass!"

He'd activated Spiritual Trifecta as he'd stood, and still had a few seconds left. He sprang forward, sprinting as fast as he could manage. As he ran toward the clumped-together melee fighters, he flung a Heavy Telekinesis their way.

As the spell struck and dozens of soldiers were flung backward into those behind them, he was assailed with a bunch of kill notifications that he ignored, seeing something far more important.

> **Congratulations, you have reached Level 10!**
> **Your health has been regenerated by 50%!**
> **Your Spirit Energy limit has increased by 100!**
> **You have received +1 Intelligence, +1 Willpower, and +1 Spirit!**
> **You have received +5 free stat points!**
> **All your spells have refreshed and are no longer on cooldown!**
>
> **As you have reached Level 10, you now have the ability to choose your next class. Choosing your class can only happen while you are outside of combat.**
> **You will not receive any further Mastery Points until you have made your choice.**
> **However, you can still upgrade spells, skills and gain attributes while in this state.**
>
> **Title Unlocked!**
> **Minor Butcher: This is an uncommon title. You have slain 50 enemies in a single strike. Whether you have slain small field mice or fearsome dragons, this feat's reward is the same.**
> **You have received +6 to all stats!**
> **Note: As you have a similar title, "Lesser Butcher" has been combined with this title and shares its stats.**

Xavier felt a sudden influx of sheer, bloody-minded utter determination and motivation. He felt like he could achieve *anything* he set his mind to. Like all he would need to do was set a course toward what he wanted, and he would *get* it.

With the level up combined with the title, Willpower had reached over one hundred stat points, breaking another barrier.

Four down, two more to go.

Xavier didn't miss a beat as he kept running toward the enemy. With his spells refreshed, he cast Spiritual Trifecta over himself once more then flung Heavy Telekinesis the other way, taking out another fifty or so enemy soldiers in one fell swoop.

Heavy Telekinesis has taken a step forward on the path!
Heavy Telekinesis is now a Rank 5 spell.
One cannot walk backward on the path.

Spiritual Trifecta has taken a step forward on the path!
Spiritual Trifecta is now a Rank 5 spell.
One cannot walk backward on the path.

Magical Potency has reached Rank 9!

Xavier grinned with near-manic glee.

With so many opponents to attack, it seemed *impossible* for him not to make progress. Perhaps the ranks of his spells and skills were simply catching up to the level of his stats, as he was slaying more enemies than he ever had before.

He didn't know, but he wasn't going to complain. Whatever he was doing was *working*.

Xavier took down another few hundred enemy soldiers. The rank-ups for his spells and skills seemed to dry up, as he mostly used his Heavy Telekinesis spell to deal with the rest.

A part of him lamented at the fact that he wouldn't be gaining any Mastery Points for these kills, but that didn't bother him a great deal. After everything he'd just gained, it felt a little, well, *greedy* to expect even more.

His army—the elven army, this time around—caught up to the massacre, fighting against the humans themselves. Xavier could see Howard, Siobhan, and Justin with them. Howard caught his gaze, a look of awe trapped in his eyes.

Xavier faced the hell beast for the second time. He wanted to slay this thing, then get straight back to the Staging Room so he could discover what options he had for his next class.

He couldn't wait to find out what they would be.

Chapter 52
This Will Bring Me Power

Xavier stared up at the three-headed Cerotri Infernum. Much of the human army lay dead around him. As he'd ordered, some soldiers had been taken prisoner—insurance, to make sure they didn't accidentally clear this floor.

The Cerotri Infernum *looked* like a terrifying beast. Standing at thirty-five feet with those vicious horns jutting from each of its heads. The massive roar that mingled so many monstrous noises all at once.

It was roaring now, back on its hind legs like the first time Xavier had fought it. And for the life of him, Xavier couldn't muster up even a single sliver of fear. He simply stared at the hell beast, tilting his head to the side.

My ears don't sting from its roar anymore. They're not even ringing.

He wrung his grip about his staff. He'd felt a bit guilty about how he'd treated the Cerotri Infernum last time. But this time... he knew what he had to do was necessary.

Xavier raised his staff. He cast Spirit Break, and the hell beast broke. Its weird, rumbling roars turned into wailing moans. It was the first time Xavier had cast Spirit Break since it had reached its second rank.

He could have practised the spell on the human soldiers he'd faced, but he'd had other plans for them.

Previously, when he'd cast Spirit Break, he'd had to focus on which aspect of the spell he wanted: mind, body, or soul. This time, all three of these things happened at once.

What he saw made Xavier take a step back, eyes wide, surprised by his own power.

Reared up as it was, the Cerotri Infernum's hind legs snapped the wrong way and it slumped to the ground. It reminded Xavier of when he'd thrown Giant Mole Rats into the cave walls of the second floor—every bone in the hell beast's body *broke*.

And its mind broke.

And its soul *broke*.

The hell beast was twisted two dozen different ways. Every one of its tree-trunk thick legs. Each of its three necks. Even its horns had broken when the spell had been cast.

And the pain in its eyes was almost unbearable to see, but Xavier did not turn away from it, for he was the one who'd caused it. He swallowed, some of that guilt coming back.

This is necessary. This will bring me power.

Xavier cast Spirit Break ten more times on the moaning Cerotri Infernum. The cooldown had reduced down to thirteen seconds, but it was still a long time to watch the beast writhe in agony.

Spirit Break (All) has taken a step forward on the path!
Spirit Break (All) is now a Rank 3 spell.
One cannot walk backward on the path.

Magical Potency has reached Rank 10!

He was quite sure he gained ranks faster by using his spells on higher-level enemies. And though this spell *broke* an enemy, it never seemed to *kill* it. Perhaps if he let the beast remain here for some time, it would eventually die.

But Xavier wasn't so cruel as to let it remain in such a state.

When the notifications came, he instantly put the poor beast out of its misery, whispering a *thank you* like he had the first time before hitting one of its heads with Heavy Telekinesis, pushing straight down into the ground, even though he knew those two words would be worth nothing.

This beast will be alive once more, once we return. It will live a near infinite number of lives in a near infinite number of instances. It would have killed a trillion times and died a trillion more, and still it has more lives to live. And it will remember none of its lives and none of its deaths and none of the people its killed. It will remain, stuck reliving this instance for longer than I will ever live.

And it will not remember the pain I caused it.

When the beast died, Xavier and the others returned to the Staging Room once more.

The others seemed even quieter around him than they had been the last time he'd killed the hell beast. Xavier wasn't sure how he felt about that. Perhaps they were simply quiet because they now, more than ever, were realising how powerful he was.

They watched me stand there and get pelted by arrows and spells and not take enough damage to need healing. They watched me tear through an army with nothing but my staff, then kill hundreds of soldiers in mere moments with but a few spells.

Do they fear me now?

He didn't want that. He would never hurt any of them, after all.

But he knew having this much power, being capable of what he was, feeling responsible for the people of Earth... it was changing him.

The party sold their items at the System Shop, this time gaining 8,700 Lesser Spirit Coins, which they handed over to Xavier.

After, they arranged their loot boxes in an awkward circle, sitting on them like they were stools. Howard pulled some food out of his Storage Ring. Bacon and eggs atop a plate balanced on his knees—food Xavier had taken from the cafeteria what already felt like an age ago. The others glanced at him.

"What?" the former cop said. "I'm starving."

Siobhan shook her head. "I'm just wondering how you can eat, after..." Her gaze came to rest on Xavier, then slid away from him.

Xavier cleared his throat. They'd all been talking so easily before this. He didn't want to sit around and let things fester. "You don't like what I did to that hell beast, do you?"

Siobhan's forehead creased. Her staff was in her Storage Ring, and she held her hands together in her lap. "You tortured that thing."

Xavier lowered his head, that twinge of guilt coming back in full force, then he looked the redhead in the eye. "You know what's at stake, don't you?"

Siobhan frowned. "Of course I know what's at stake."

Xavier motioned to the door. "There could be armies like that back on Earth already. They could be rounding up our people, turning them into slaves, or..."

"Or slaughtering them in the streets," Howard muttered.

Siobhan winced at that. "You don't have to paint the picture." Her hands clenched in her lap. "We all know what's waiting for us back on Earth."

Xavier continued, despite her protests, "The System that governs this Greater Universe is vicious. Unforgiving. Cold. It doesn't believe in surrender. It believes in power. And all those races that are able to get to Earth? They grew up with that, maybe for countless generations. I didn't *want* to do what I did. But I *need* to get stronger, and it helped me move forward and rank up one of my spells. Could you imagine one of those beasts loose on Earth? How many people do you think would die trying to take that down, people without the advantages we have?"

"The advantages *you* have," Justin said, raising his head. "We wouldn't have been able to take that thing. Maybe with the whole army behind us... and you didn't even break a sweat."

"I think that's what he's trying to say." Howard's food sat on his knees, still uneaten, his fork resting on the side of his plate. "I don't like what he did, but if I were in his shoes, I can't say I wouldn't have done the same. Sometimes the unpleasant is necessary."

Siobhan shut her eyes. She let out a long breath. "I suppose you're right. Just... this was all feeling like a video game. Like an adventure. I know what's at stake. I know Earth is in trouble. I've just been trying not to think about that as best I can." Siobhan opened her eyes, locked gazes with Xavier. "Watching what you did to that hell beast just brought that all into focus. I don't know you very well, Xavier, but I know you're here to protect Earth. And if you're capable of that... then what must others, those who are *against* us, be capable of? What atrocities are occurring *right now*, as we sit around, unable to return to Earth until you clear more of these damned floors?"

"I don't know," Xavier said. "But that's why we must do whatever we can to keep moving forward." He raised his chin. "Speaking of, I've reached Level 10."

Siobhan's eyes lit up, then. Her face had gone white as she'd been speaking of what Xavier had done, and of what might be happening on Earth. Now, the colour returned to her cheeks, and the ghost of a smile was on her lips. "You've reached Level 10? Why didn't you *say* so?" She stood. "What class options do you have? Have you seen them yet?"

Xavier chuckled, raised his hands in defence. "I haven't looked yet. I wanted to... clear the air first. Besides, I still have five free stat points to allocate. Actually, about stats..." He told them about the barrier he'd broken through on attributes once he'd reached 100 in them. How that seemed to take him to a new level of power in each, mentioning that he'd done it for Toughness, Intelligence, Willpower, and Spirit, but still needed to do it for Strength and Speed.

And he told them about the new skill he'd gotten—Assimilate Properties—and what it had done for him.

"Whoa," Siobhan said. As he'd talked, telling them about how the metal from the arrowheads had fused *into* him and given him

+10 Toughness, her eyes had widened, and that smile she'd always seemed to wear had returned in full force. "That's *awesome*! Like Wolverine from X-Men." Her smile turned a little lopsided, her cheeks a little redder. "You're a regular Hugh Jackman."

Xavier rubbed the back of his neck, suddenly feeling a little flushed himself. "Well, I don't know about that..."

Howard had a knowing smirk on his face, an eyebrow raised as he ate his bacon and eggs.

Justin leant forward, resting his elbows on his knees, frowning. "So you haven't looked at the class selection yet?"

"No." Xavier tilted his head to the side. "Why?"

"Well, we've spoken about how what we do before gaining our class *affects* what class we can choose, and the notification said you could still gain rank-ups for your skills and spells, and gain attributes, right?"

Siobhan raised a finger, sitting straighter. Her gaze flicked over to Justin. "I think I know where you're going with this!"

Xavier frowned at the two of them, then thought about what they'd been talking about and had a lightbulb moment of his own. "You think I should get Strength and Speed to 100 points before looking at what classes I can choose from?"

Justin and Siobhan both nodded.

Howard grunted. "Sounds smart."

Xavier thought about that for a moment. He'd been *incredibly* eager to see what classes he would have available. The longer he waited, the more anxious he was to check.

His Strength was at an effective 92, his Speed at 87, and he had five free stat points to use... but all he'd really need to do would be clear the third floor. Even if he didn't get into the Top 100—which was something he certainly couldn't bet on—he would gain at least fifteen stat points to *each* of his attributes.

A smile popped onto his face. He wondered... how often did someone got every one of their stats to 100 before gaining their second class?

Without any titles, assuming someone only gained 8 stats per level, they would need to be over Level 70 to have 600 stats, and that's if they were distributing their stats equally over all six attributes, which is incredibly unlikely.

He remembered what the System notification had said when it tried to expel the metal impurities from his body—that such a thing wasn't possible for an F Grade Denizen, which meant hitting the Toughness upgrade of 100 points was probably *incredibly* rare for someone at his grade, let alone *level*.

Though he still didn't know what level he would need to be to upgrade to E Grade.

That's something I'll find out soon enough.

"All right." He stood up, feeling a sudden burst of excitement at the prospect of what classes he would get after achieving something like this. *There might even be a title for reaching 100 points in all six attributes.* "Let's clear the third floor."

Chapter 53
I'm Going to Tear through This Tower like No One Ever Has Before

FOR THE THIRD TIME, XAVIER AND HIS PARTY STOOD UNDER two suns in a field of purple grass.

This time, however, he planned to clear the floor as fast as humanly possible. Or, Denizenly possible, he supposed.

That's why he'd thrown all five free stat points from his last level-up into Intelligence, further boosting the strength of his Heavy Telekinesis spell, which was already well and truly over-powered.

The second they appeared in the grass, Xavier willed the prompt to appear. After what he'd done the last time they'd come through here, he knew he wouldn't need help from the others, whether in healing or tanking.

I can take that whole army down without breaking a sweat. All I need to do is ensure it happens fast.

And for that, he would need to use every ounce of brute force he had.

Whose call will you answer?

The humans, Xavier willed.

Just like the last two times, Xavier was transported to the front of the human army. He didn't even spare them a glance. Activating Spiritual Trifecta, he turned and ran, sprinting as hard as he could toward the elven army as Howard and the others gave the human army one simple order: stand down.

They wouldn't be needed.

Spiritual Trifecta lasted for twelve seconds with a fourteen-second cooldown, which meant two seconds of downtime between casting.

Once he was in range, arrows and spells came for him. He ignored them. The few that hit him didn't do a lick of damage. Now wasn't the time to work on his Physical and Magical Resistance skills.

Now was the time to wreak havoc.

He cast Spiritual Trifecta three times as he closed the distance, refreshing it for a fourth when he was close enough for his Heavy Telekinesis spell to be in range. Then he cast Heavy Telekinesis, targeting the elven soldiers on the left.

A chorus of cracks sounded in the air, like a dozen bundles of sticks being snapped over a dozen knees.

His cooldown had fallen to a mere one second after all the Intelligence he'd gained, but it still felt like an age. When the spell was ready again, he was even closer. A few more strides and he'd be in skull-crushing range.

Crack!

He cast Heavy Telekinesis to the right.

He ignored every notification that came his way. He would wait until the end to look at all but the kill notifications. He ignored the screams and shouts and agonised moans that rang out from the enemy soldiers ahead of him. And though he couldn't gain any Mastery Points from these kills, he gained more than enough Spirit Energy.

Xavier, now in melee range, barrelled into the front line. He'd killed the elven soldiers on the left and the right with telekinesis so he could reach those in the middle with his staff.

He only managed to kill four in the single second that he had before his spell was ready to be used again, but that was four more than he would have taken down had he just stood there.

The fight continued like this. He took them down so fast he had to sprint toward the next soldiers in the army. The rumbling, jet-engine boom of the Cerotri Infernum's three massive maws roaring in unison came when the entire elven army already lay dead on the ground.

Spiritual Trifecta didn't wear off until the last soldier died, and he only had to wait two seconds for it to refresh.

The Cerotri Infernum reared back, ready to cast whatever spell it was preparing, or to pounce down at him. Xavier didn't know what it would do—he'd never given it a chance to do anything.

Spiritual Trifecta refreshed and was cast once more.

Xavier leapt up.

Heavy Telekinesis!

The hell beast stumbled.

Spirit Break!

The hell beast slammed onto its back. Every limb breaking. Its three necks snapping at awkward angles. Six eyes bulging from its skulls. Strangled whines struggling from its throats.

Xavier ran across its chest until he reached one of its heads. He faced down, and for the third time, he crushed its skull into the ground with Heavy Telekinesis.

The third-floor army of five hundred soldiers had been slain, and their Champion—the Level 40 floor boss—had been defeated.

Xavier leapt off the dead floor boss, stood beside it, and basked in the breeze and the bright, clear day beneath the twin alien suns, letting out a long sigh of relief as he readied himself to read all of the notifications.

He'd cleared the floor even faster than he'd expected to.

Magical Potency has reached Rank 11!

Heavy Telekinesis has taken a step forward on the path!
Heavy Telekinesis is now a Rank 6 spell.
One cannot walk backward on the path.

Not as many as I thought. Though Xavier supposed he'd already gained a lot for both his Magical Potency skill and Heavy Telekinesis from the soldiers on this floor. It only made sense that their progression would eventually slow down.

He didn't gain a single rank in Physical or Magical Resistance —he supposed he hadn't given the enemy enough time to attack him.

How long did I take to clear this floor? Surely I would have made it to the Top 100 with that time...

Xavier read on.

Congratulations! You have cleared the Third Floor of the Tower of Champions.
Party Member Contribution:
Xavier: 501/501 Kills.
Howard: 0/501 Kills.
Justin: 0/501 Kills.
Siobhan: 0/501 Kills.
No shared attributions apply on this floor.

Title Unlocked!
Third-Floor Climber: This title has been upgraded. You have cleared the Third Floor of the Tower of Champions, and shall be rewarded.
You have received +6 to all stats!
Note: The title "Second-Floor Climber" has been stricken from your soul.

Title Unlocked!

Solo Tower Climber 3: This title has been upgraded. You have cleared a floor of the Tower of Champions by yourself. You are either very brave or very stupid for attempting such a feat. Know that whether this feat was achieved through sheer skill or unbridled luck, you shall be rewarded.
You have received +24 to all stats!
Note: The title "Solo Tower Climber 2" has been stricken from your soul.

As he read the second title, every single muscle in his body *tensed* and *bulged*. His heart rate tripled, his breathing turning heavy. He felt like he could bench press the world. Or hold it over his shoulders like Atlas held the Earth.

He looked down at his hands, clenching his fists around his staff, saw the muscles in his forearms hard as rock, the veins like rivers running through a landscape seen from a bird's-eye view. The muscles in his arms bulging beneath his robes. His legs. His shoulders. His torso. Every aspect of him felt *damned strong*, and looked it too.

I guess that title put me over 100 Strength.

After a moment, his breathing steadied, his heartrate slowed back to normal, and he moved onto the next title.

Title Unlocked!
1st Third-Floor Climber: Out of Champions from five competing worlds, your party is the *first* to clear the Third Floor of the Tower of Champions within your instance.
You have received +15 to all stats!
Note: As you have a similar title, "1st Second-Floor Climber" has been combined with this title and shares its stats.

Time seemed to slow right down. Xavier looked at the long, purple grass swaying slowly in the breeze. *Too* slowly. His breathing didn't quicken, nor did his heart rate. In fact, it barely felt like he was breathing at all, and his heart was quiet in his chest.

He looked over the field of corpses toward his party and the human army. His party was jogging over to loot the fallen, and it looked like they were running in slow motion.

My Speed is over 100 now too.

The effect of breaking through that barrier was perhaps the most peaceful of all six of the attributes, as though the universe had finally slowed down, waiting for him to catch up.

The sensation didn't last long, but he knew the shift to his Speed would be substantial—just as every other attribute had been when he'd reached the threshold of 100 points.

The others were right to suggest I do this before selecting my class.

A new title popped up, one he'd wondered if he would get.

Title Unlocked!
All 100: This is a common title that everyone receives when they have reached 100 stat points in all 6 attributes.
You have received +5 to all stats!

Title Unlocked!
First to All 100: You are the first person from your world to reach 100 stat points in all 6 attributes.
You have received +10 to all stats!

Holy crap! Xavier blinked, staring at the two titles. They gave him far more than he'd thought. *I got 15 in all stats just for being the first to do that?*

The System really did favour progenitors.

Part of me was expecting there to be a title for reaching this before gaining my first class, or reaching E Grade... I suppose that would be too greedy?

Xavier shook his head, barely believing just how much stronger he'd become. But there was still one more title to read. The one he'd been hoping to see.

Title Unlocked!
Third Floor Ranked 2 (Completion Time – 1 min 21 sec): Out of all the Champions from all the worlds in the Greater Universe who have completed the Third Floor of the Tower of Champions in every possible instance, you have edged into the Top 100 fastest times at No. 2.
This title is a Temporary Title. If your record is edged out of the Top 100, your title will be lost.
You have received +20 to all stats!
Note: As you have a similar title, "First Floor Ranked 42" has been combined with this title and shares its stats. You may still view the previous title and your standing on the leader-board, if you will it.

Xavier, still struggling to come to terms with how powerful he'd become, stared at the title. He had to read what he was ranked several times before it sunk in.

Third Floor Ranked 2.

He'd cleared the floor in *one minute and twenty-one seconds?* He knew he'd been fast, but *that* fast?

I used Spiritual Trifecta five times, that's a minute and ten seconds. It must have taken a little time for us to be transported to the human army...

In 5 minutes, you and your party will be returned to the Staging Room.

Xavier shook off his awe, looking at the timer. It had already gone down by a minute since he'd been reading all of those titles. Usually a floor only gave them thirty seconds, so he was surprised to get this long.

He began looting the corpses, helping out the others, but all he could think about was what his class choices might be. He hadn't even brought up the selection menu yet, and the anticipation was killing him.

But this had been the right decision. Breaking through the 100-point threshold on all six attributes... he felt like a new man. Like he'd passed some sort of barrier.

And with all those titles he'd just gained...

I'm going to tear through this tower like no one ever has before.

Though, looking at his last title, he knew that mustn't be true. He'd gotten high up the leaderboard. *Very* high. Somehow, out of everyone in the entire Greater Universe who'd ever cleared this floor, he was the second fastest to do it.

And he'd done it in less than a minute and a half.

Who in the hell could have done it faster than that?

The chances of him ever finding out—of ever meeting whoever did it—were incredibly miniscule. Perhaps totally *impossible*. The tower had been around for billions of years, after all.

It made him think of the first Denizen once more. The first... progenitor. If Xavier got these titles for being the first from his world to do these things... what titles had the first in the Greater Universe gained?

Is that who has taken the number one spot? The first progenitor of the Greater Universe?

The very thought sent a shudder up his spine. He knew he was strong, but he couldn't help but remember how many Lesser Spirit Coins a single Grand Spirit Coin was worth.

One hundred thousand... Is that how many times stronger this first progenitor would be compared with me?

Chapter 54
Blazing Your Own Path Is What Creates the Strongest Denizens

Xavier, Howard, Siobhan, and Justin returned to the Staging Room.

Xavier wanted to check his stats. To see exactly how much he'd gained. But more than that, he wanted to check what classes he would get to choose from.

Howard placed a hand on his shoulder. "That was..." The man shook his head. "That was insane." He removed his hand and went over to his loot box, still shaking his head, muttering, "Insane," several more times.

Justin's eyes were a little wide, staring at him. "You defeated an entire army. That Level 40 hell beast. And you did it in less than two minutes! We had to wait longer to get back to the Staging Room! You're a monster, Xavier. An absolute, bloody monster!" He smiled at the end of it, blunting the word "monster," to show he meant it in a *good* way. Though the wideness in his eyes did show a hint of fear.

Justin walked off to his own loot box, and it was just Xavier and Siobhan standing by the door to the tower floors.

Siobhan tucked a strand of hair behind her ear. Her forehead was creased, her head down. She tilted up her chin and looked him in the eye. "I'm sorry I doubted your actions before with the hell beast. The world is... different now. We have to be different. Thank you, for letting us come along with you, up the tower. We wouldn't be able to gain these advantages without you. And, seeing what you did today... you could have just as easily kicked us to the curb and soloed the entire tower yourself. Howard may have been right about you lacking combat experience, but you're a power-house. You can just... trample the enemy without a second thought."

Xavier frowned. He gestured toward the door. "That might be true of the tower, but I don't know how true it will be in the long run." He clenched a fist around his staff. "I know that I could do this on my own, but I don't want to. I fear that by myself, all I would do is focus on the accumulation of power. On reaching the next floor, the next step. I might not slow down to realise I needed more training, or that something could be done in a better way."

He turned to face the door. "If I hadn't stopped to train on this floor, upping the rank of my skills and spells, and getting many of my attributes to the 100-point threshold, there's no way I would have been able to clear the floor in less than a minute and a half." He rubbed the back of his head. "And I would have gone for my next class *before* reaching the threshold for Speed and Strength.

"I *could* do this tower by myself, but having you guys along puts things in perspective. When I return to Earth, it won't just be me against the enemy. There will be millions—billions—of other humans to protect. By helping the three of you level up and gain the first clear title, I'm creating more elites that can help Earth. Not to mention, I'm learning how to keep others safe, a skill I'm sure I'll need... And when we clear the tenth floor and can return, I won't be returning alone. I might be powerful, but I can't be in more than one place at once."

"I was worried you'd realise you didn't need us at all, after that," Siobhan said.

Xavier had considered it. After he'd defeated that hell beast and basked in the breeze, standing beneath the twin alien suns on a battlefield filled with death that he'd been the cause of, he'd considered leaving his party behind.

He'd looked over at Howard, Siobhan, and Justin in the silence that had followed the battle, the timer in the top-right corner of his vision, slowly ticking down to zero. They'd walked around the corpses of the fallen elven soldiers, looting all their weapons and gear, finding any valuables they could, and all Xavier had thought was how much he *didn't* need them.

But that... that was the loner in him talking. The part of him that was used to not taking help from others. They all had value, even if that value wasn't always evident. Howard had helped him decide to farm and train on the third floor. Justin and Siobhan had helped him decide to push his stats to their 100-point threshold before gaining his class.

He might not be able to think of the other ways they could help, but that was half the point.

Besides, he *would* need their help when they returned to Earth. He didn't know how strong the people there would be. He didn't know what danger they were currently in. The titles his party would gain just by being carried by him through the tower alone would make them incredibly strong compared to a normal human Denizen.

He might be able to take down an army by himself, but he didn't know how many armies there would be, and he couldn't exactly teleport from one place to another.

It's better to have them along. Better to help them get stronger. As long as helping them doesn't get me killed. There's no way I would have gotten Rank 2 on the Top 100 list if I hadn't slowed down.

Xavier gestured over to the loot boxes. "Go see what your reward is. I'm going to have a look at my class selection."

Siobhan nodded, turning away from him.

Xavier sat down, cross-legged on the floor a few steps away from the tower door, and willed the prompt to appear. He could have looked at his class selection back on the third floor, but he wanted to do it here, where his mind was the most clear, where he could consult the others on his choice—if he wished to.

When the menu opened up, he frowned, looking at the first few choices.

He hadn't expected them to be so... basic.

Telekinetic Mage – Common Class
Punch Mage – Common Class
Spirit Mage – Uncommon Class

Punch Mage? Really?

Though the class name sounded ridiculous, it also sounded kind of... well, awesome.

For a moment, he imagined himself pummelling enemies with nothing but his fists. Punching through armour. Punching through *swords*. Breaking weapons and skulls alike with nothing but his bare hands.

But the fact that it was a *common* class meant it didn't appeal to him at all. The same could be said for Telekinetic Mage. He wondered what gaining such a class would give him. He'd chosen to specialise in a specific aspect of telekinesis. Would choosing that class let him specialise in *other* aspects?

Spirit Mage was interesting, considering how much he relied on Spiritual Trifecta, and how strong Spirit Break was. But again, it was only an *uncommon* class, and there were more things down the list.

Chain Breaker – Rare Class
Spirit Taker – Rare Class
Death Shaper – Rare Class

Xavier frowned, reading the classes but not really *under-standing* what they meant. He had to admit, the names were pretty badass. But "badass" alone didn't tell him anything.

He tilted his head to the side, staring at the class names. He didn't know what the difference between a common class and an uncommon class was, nor the difference between an uncommon and a rare, but he imagined the rarer the class, the stronger its potential.

Xavier cleared his throat, looking over at the others. "Does the Tower of Champions manual say anything about class selection?"

Siobhan, whose eyes had been glazed over, the loot box open where she knelt on the ground, looked over at him. "It wasn't very specific. It didn't have much more information than what I told you. Apparently in integrated worlds you can buy class manuals, and other information about classes.

"And it said that it can be better to select common classes as it's easier to learn their strengths and weaknesses, as the information is more widely available, but that mastering classes of a higher rarity and blazing your own path is what creates the strongest Denizens in the end... but we haven't come across any of those manuals in the System Shop despite searching for them. Only those Spell Book Primers."

Yet another thing that long-integrated worlds have over us...

"Thanks," Xavier said with a sigh. "I suppose I should have expected we'd be left in the dark." He turned his attention back to the class list, considering what Siobhan had said.

Blazing your own path is what creates the strongest Denizens in the end.

That certainly made sense to him, and he'd already been leaning toward the rarer classes—there were yet more on the list he wanted to look at. He just wished he could be better informed.

Looking at the names of the classes did make him wonder where Spell Books came into play. If, for instance, he chose a Punch Mage, would he still be able to use the Spell Book Primer for a Gravity Mage? Or a Void Mage? *Whatever that is.* Or would learning such spells be a waste? Or, perhaps, not even possible?

One cannot walk backward on the path... There may be spells that are no longer available to me, depending on what class I choose. Yet I have no way of knowing whether that's true or not, do I?

He frowned, willing more information to appear about the classes in front of him. He'd been able to see information about the basic Mage and Warrior classes, after all.

Why shouldn't he be able to see more about these?

Chain Breaker Class (Rare):
A Chain Breaker is a mage that focuses on physical fighting. They can wear heavy armour and use any weapon they wish, and they are able to imbue spells into their weapons and armour to further enhance their power in physical combat.
Attributes per level: +3 Strength, +3 Toughness, +2 Intelligence, +2 Willpower, +13 free stat points.

Xavier's eyes widened, reading the description. *They can imbue spells into their weapons and armour?* That sounded *awesome*, though he had no idea how that might work in practise.

If he imbued Heavy Telekinesis into his staff, what exactly would that do? He could imagine imbuing Spiritual Trifecta into his armour or a weapon...

Xavier shook his head, moving down to the number of attribute points the class offered. He would get ten automatically allocated, and thirteen free stat points. *That's twenty-three! Right now I only get eight per level!* That was almost *three times* as many stat points per level.

Getting to Level 10 really must change the playing field...

He frowned, wondering about something. He brought up the information for one of the earlier classes. The Punch Mage.

Punch Mage Class (Common):
A Punch Mage is a mage that focuses on phys-ical fighting. Where others use weapons, a Punch Mage's fists *are* their weapons. Punch

Mages have a number of spells that increase their physical damage and defences, along with spells that can be imbued into their fists that explode on impact.
Attributes per level: +2 Strength, +2 Toughness, +2 Intelligence, +7 free stat points.

That offers way less attributes! And... fists that explode on impact? Imagining such a thing only made him chuckle.

He supposed it shouldn't come as a surprise that he was being offered classes that were physical fighters after all the skull-bashing he'd been doing with his staff.

Xavier tilted his head to the side. A common class offered thirteen total stat points—five more than his basic Mage class—but ten *less* than a rare class.

All the more reason to choose a higher rarity.

He wondered how many choices most Denizens got when they reached Level 10. Would they even be able to choose anything beyond common or uncommon?

Xavier scrolled down the menu, looking at the final two classes, both of which were a higher rarity. He didn't feel the need to look at the other rare classes available in detail, not now that he was sure he would pick the strongest rarity available.

The two final classes? They were *epic* rarity.

Xavier read the names of the classes:

Bringer of Destruction – Epic Class
Soul Reaper – Epic Class

Well, those sound ominous...

Chapter 55
I Need to Use Any Power at My Disposal

Xavier, still sitting cross-legged by the tower door in the Staging Room, looked at the last two options on the class selection menu. He narrowed his gaze. The names of the two classes sounded rather sinister.

Bringer of Destruction – Epic Class
Soul Reaper – Epic Class

He had an affinity for Spirit—though it was no longer his *strongest* attribute, as he didn't have a skill that enhanced it like Magical Potency enhanced Intelligence—which he supposed was why "soul" was in the title of one of the classes.

Though, as he had that thought, something occurred to him. A skill he'd been neglecting to learn because it would take too long naturally—one hundred hours—and because he didn't want to "waste" a skill point on it.

Meditation.

That sounds awfully spiritual, doesn't it?

Now wasn't the time to think about that. He had two classes to look at.

He looked at the first one.

Bringer of Destruction Class (Epic):
A Bringer of Destruction is a mage that focuses
on magic of the spirit and mind. They are long-
range fighters that destroy everything in their
wake. As a Bringer of Destruction, each oppo-
nent they kill causes the slain Denizen's body
to explode. The size and damage this explosion
causes are a combination of the level of the
slain Denizen, along with the strength of the
Bringer of Destruction's Spirit and Intelligence
attributes.
Bringers of Destruction do not leave anyone
alive in their wake. They scour the land,
leaving only death and desolation from their
passing.
Attributes per level: +10 Intelligence, +10
Spirit, +20 free stat points.

Xavier leant back where he sat, blinking at the text he'd just read.

Bringers of Destruction do not leave anyone alive in their wake... and I get to choose this class based on my actions? He wasn't sure how he felt about that. *Is this because of how quickly I was able to kill that army, and the Minor Butcher title I received?*

Exploding his enemies upon death *would* cause a lot of mass damage—this seemed like it would be an exceptionally strong area-of-effect damage class.

If he'd had that ability while facing the elven army of five hundred soldiers, he might have been able to take them out twice as fast, as each kill could have caused *another* death, which would cause *another* explosion.

Perhaps twice as fast would be an understatement—it would cause a chain-reaction of death.

But... was that really what he wanted to become? A dealer of destruction? Did he really want to scour the land and cause only *death and desolation?*

No. He didn't want that. He wanted to protect Earth, not leave it destroyed. There were so many ways an ability like this could go wrong. So many ways it could backfire on him. *Protection* and *destruction* were two disparate things. What if he were trying to protect someone from an enemy, and that someone was being held with a dagger at their throat?

If I killed the enemy, the person I wished to protect would die from the resultant explosion.

No. This class... this class seemed too volatile. *Too* destructive.

Besides, if he exploded every corpse when he killed, he wouldn't be able to loot them. *Well, that's an awfully selfish yet practical thought...*

But he couldn't help but stare at the number of attributes it offered. The rare class he'd looked at offered 23 total attribute points.

This one offered 40 total attribute points. Even if half of them were in Spirit and Intelligence, he could allocate the rest wherever he wished. That... that would make him incredibly strong, wouldn't it? It almost made him feel like he *had* to make this choice.

The System wants me to do this, doesn't it? To become an instrument of destruction for it?

Xavier bit his lip, and looked at the last class selection.

Soul Reaper Class (Epic):
A Soul Reaper is a versatile mage that focuses on the magic of the spirit. They can be a long-range fighter, a close-range fighter, or a mix of both, and they wield a scythe-staff in battle—a hybrid, melee/magical weapon. They can wear any armour they wish and have the ability to imbue Spirit Energy into their equipment to

strengthen its qualities—though this lasts for a limited time.

Soul Reapers also have the special ability to harvest the souls of those they slay and can call upon those souls in moments of need. This differs from necromantic spells, as the Soul Reaper lacks the ability to communicate with the souls they reap and lacks the ability to reanimate the dead.

Attributes per level: +2 Strength, +2 Toughness, +2 Speed, +3 Intelligence, +3 Willpower, +8 Spirit, +20 free stat points.

Xavier leant back again, expelling a breath. Harvesting souls sounded... sinister, but far less destructive than exploding every single thing he killed.

I should have expected soul harvesting to be a thing, considering the name of the class is literally Soul Reaper.

He didn't fully understand what the implications of the class would be—the Bringer of Destruction's description seemed more straightforward in its illustration of its class's abilities.

Call upon the souls in moments of need...

He had dismissed necromancy for several reasons, but this... Though it sounded plenty sinister, seemed like something else entirely. He didn't exactly *want* to trap souls, but he knew he would need to use any powers he had at his disposal, and he would only use the souls of those he harvested. And he supposed he wouldn't be harvesting *innocent* souls.

If I need to use any power at my disposal, should I choose Bringer of Destruction? The power of that first epic class beckoned him toward it, but the consequences kept him away.

Xavier was intrigued by the part where it said the Soul Reaper could imbue Spirit Energy into their equipment. He always had an abundance of Spirit Energy, and wondered how that would work. Would it strengthen his physical resistance? Magical resistance?

Both? Would it make his weapons deal more damage, or enhance the strength of his magical attacks?

Spiritual Trifecta does all of those things, so I suppose it would make sense that Spirit Energy could boost those things when imbued into equipment. Is the ability some sort of spell? A skill?

The scythe-staff was interesting, too. Though he'd grown attached to his Spirit Staff of Might, he'd long outgrown the weapon. The title of the class, and the staff he'd seen in the System Shop... *Stave of the Otherworldly Void Reaper...* It made him wonder if that weapon was a staff-scythe.

What is an Otherworldly Void Reaper? Is it a class? And if it is, does this class—Soul Reaper—have a path toward reaching that one? Could I one day wield such a weapon?

It was a foolish, fleeting thought, given the price of that staff. It was well and truly out of his reach.

For now.

Xavier snapped his focus back to the two options in front of him. He instantly knew which he would choose. In his mind, it was no choice at all. Though he didn't *like* the sound of harvesting souls, if it brought him power, he would do it.

This class? It looked like the right fit for him. Forty attribute points per level, and those that were automatically allocated were more varied than the last class. The ability to wear any armour he wished... It just felt *right*, calling to him in a way that the first class did not.

His mind returned once more to the staff he'd seen. *Stave of the Otherworldly Void Reaper. This is connected to that somehow, isn't it?*

He pushed the thought away again.

There was a part of him that, admittedly, was curious—*very* curious—about the soul harvesting aspect of the Soul Reaper class. About how those souls could be called upon in "moments of need." What exactly did that entail? How would the souls help him?

He ached to discover what that meant.

Xavier looked over at the others. Howard, Siobhan, and Justin were sitting on their loot boxes, their eyes glazed over. They must have been looking at their own notifications and status screens.

He didn't feel the need to discuss his class selection with them like he thought he might.

This is my choice.

He willed his selection.

Are you sure you wish to choose SOUL REAPER (EPIC) as your class?
Becoming a SOUL REAPER (EPIC) may result in the loss of spells and skills that are incompatible with the class. This is a choice that cannot be unmade.
One cannot walk backward on the path.

Xavier frowned.

I could lose spells, and even skills, by choosing this? Which spells would be incompatible?

He tilted his head to the side. He only had three spells to lose, but he had *six* skills, none of which he wanted to part with. He hadn't even known such a thing was possible. *I suppose it doesn't matter what I lose if it means I can gain even more by choosing this class.*

Yes, Xavier willed, *I'm sure.*

Class selection complete.
Evaluating Class Upgrade of Denizen XAVIER COLLINS from BASIC MAGE to SOUL REAPER (EPIC).
Checking compatibility of spells:
Heavy Telekinesis...
Compatible!
Spiritual Trifecta...
Compatible – Spell Upgrade Available!
Spirit Break...

Compatible – Spell Upgrade Available!

Checking compatibility of skills:
Staff Mastery...
Error – Skill Incompatible – Skill Transfer
Available!
Physical Resistance...
Compatible!
Magical Potency...
Compatible!
Magical Resistance...
Compatible!
Physical Damage...
Compatible!
Assimilate Properties...
Compatible!
Class Upgrade Evaluation Complete.
Commencing Class Upgrade!

Pain gripped Xavier in a hold like never before, then the entire world went black.

Chapter 56
Soul Reaper

"Xavier?" Someone shoved his shoulder. "Xavier, are you all right? Xavier!"

Xavier's eyes snapped open. He looked up. Howard crouched by him, a hand on his shoulder. He yanked his hand away when Xavier opened his eyes, standing and taking a quick step back.

Siobhan and Justin stood behind Howard. Justin's eyes widened, staring into Xavier's. Siobhan's face lit up with a smile.

"Your eyes!" Siobhan said.

Xavier sat up. The pain he'd felt what must have been only a moment ago was gone. He shook his head, feeling a little disorientated. The world looked... different, in a way he couldn't figure out. He blinked over at Siobhan. "What do you mean, my eyes? What's wrong with my eyes?"

"They're silver," Howard said matter-of-factly. "They weren't silver before." He frowned, looked at Siobhan and Justin. "Were they?"

Siobhan shook her head. "They were grass-green. Now they look like the silver of the moon."

"All right," Xavier said. "That's... weird."

"Why did you fall down?" Justin asked.

Howard rubbed at his beard. "I'd like to know the answer to that myself."

Xavier touched a hand to his head. Though the pain was gone, his head felt... tender? No. It felt *full*. Like something had been put inside it that hadn't been there before. He stood up. "I chose my class, and activated the change."

Siobhan's eyebrows shot up to the top of her forehead. "You did? Well, no wonder the System doesn't want you doing that in the middle of combat! You'd likely get killed during the change if it makes you fall unconscious."

Her eyes lit up again, and she was practically jittering with excitement. It was good to see her like this, after she'd been so subdued when he'd used that hell beast to rank up his Spirit Break spell.

"So, what class did you choose?" Siobhan asked. "It must have been a good one, considering how strong you are!"

Xavier smiled, rubbed the back of his neck. He wasn't exactly sure how the others would react to the name of his new class. He still didn't know much about it himself—there were a bunch of notifications waiting for him to look at, ones that had appeared after he'd stood, shaking off the sudden unconsciousness.

"I'll tell you more about it soon. I've still got a lot of things to go through."

Siobhan's face fell a little, though the smile remained. "Well, when you're done, let us know. We were thinking it might be time to head down to the tavern. See if there are any others there. We've got a lot of knowledge between the four of us now. Knowledge that could really help them."

Xavier nodded. Howard had mentioned something about getting rest after the third floor. He supposed visiting the tavern, seeing if there were others from their cohort down there, would be a wise decision.

But honestly, all he wanted to do was keep clearing floors. Especially now he'd gotten his next class.

Soul Reaper.

He waited for the others to head back to the loot boxes, where they started chatting. He tuned them out, sitting cross-legged once more on the floor of the Staging Room by the tower door.

He could barely contain his excitement.

My eyes have turned silver? He looked around at the others again, trying to ascertain what it was that was *different* about them —what it was that he could see now that he couldn't see before. *There's a glow about them. An almost indiscernible glow. Like... an aura, maybe?*

He didn't know what it was, but he looked forward to finding out.

No longer able to contain himself, he opened the notifications that were waiting for him.

Congratulations, XAVIER COLLINS! You have upgraded your class from BASIC MAGE to SOUL REAPER (EPIC).
You have 2 Spell Upgrades and 1 Skill Transfer pending.
You have gained the spell Spirit Infusion.
You have gained the spell Soul Harvest.
You have gained the spell Soul Strike.
You have gained the spell Soul Block.
You have gained the spell Soul Harden.
These spells are locked to your class and cannot be forgotten unless you change to an incompatible class.

Xavier felt floored by the number of spells he'd just learnt. He'd gone from knowing three spells to knowing *eight*? He wondered if that was because he'd chosen an epic class, or if all classes gave that many spells.

He tilted his head to the side, looked at the names of each of them. They certainly seemed to fit a pattern.

All right. Looks like I have a lot to figure out here.

One thing he was very glad for was that he wouldn't need to pick and choose which spells to keep. When he'd gained his first spells, he'd had to "forget" some of them, like Summon and Cast Element. He found it a little bit strange that he didn't have to forget any of these spells, but he was very, very glad for it.

Slowly, he looked at the description of each of the spells that he'd gained.

Spirit Infusion – Rank 1
Spirit Infusion is a rare mage spell that is rarely learnt by human mages and is only available to those with a naturally strong Spirit. Spirit Infusion has two paths: the path of defence, and the path of offence.
The path of defence allows the user to imbue Spirit Energy into their armour and weapons. Armour and weapons infused with defensive Spirit Energy gain a stronger physical and magical resistance and strengthen the durability of whatever material they are infused into.
The path of offence allows the user to imbue Spirit Energy into their armour and weapons. Armour infused with offensive Spirit Energy deals magical damage to those who strike it, and weapons that are infused with offensive Spirit Energy deal more physical and magical damage per strike and per spell.
Unlike other spells, there is no way to generalise with Spirit Infusion. The user must choose which path they wish to follow.
One cannot walk backward on the path.

Xavier frowned. Spirit Infusion sounded pretty great, except for the fact that he couldn't generalise with it like he had with his other Spirit-based spells. He sighed, not sure which he would choose to use as they both had their merits.

I'll decide later, once I've tested out both paths.
Each of the paths sounded great to him right now.
He moved onto the next spell.

Soul Harvest – Rank 1
Soul Harvest is an epic spell specific to the Reaper line of classes. Soul Harvest has only one utility, and one path: it is used to harvest the souls of those a Soul Reaper slays.
One cannot walk backward on the path.

Short and sweet, and exactly what I expected. Xavier wondered if the spell would let him harvest multiple souls at once. Would he need to place his hand on each of the corpses? Or could he do it from afar?

That all sounds rather grim.

He winced at his bad, unintentional pun, then looked at the next spell in line.

Soul Strike – Rank 1
Soul Strike is an epic spell specific to the Reaper line of classes and requires harvested souls to cast. Soul Strike has several different paths, and is a difficult spell to master.
Soul Strike is an offensive spell that uses harvested souls against an enemy. Soul Strike causes soul damage, which is different to magical damage and difficult to protect against.
This spell has three paths: long-range attacks, short-range attacks, or generalising between the two.
The user may use as many harvested souls in a Soul Strike as they wish.
Generalising with Soul Strike weakens the strength of each attack by a third.

One cannot walk backward on the path.

Xavier leant back. Another spell that didn't lend itself well to generalising. *At least it* can *be used to generalise.* That was another decision he would have to leave until later, once he'd had a chance to see what the spell could actually do. *I suppose that means I'll need to harvest some souls.*

The one thing his mind latched onto about the description was the fact that the user could use as many harvested souls in a strike as they wished. It made him wonder if there was a limit to the number of souls that he could keep harvested. For instance, could he have harvested that entire army of souls?

He shuddered, still getting used to this line of thought. *Did I really choose a class that lets me harvest other people's souls? What does that make me? Some kind of devil?*

Xavier pushed that thought away, and ploughed on.

Soul Block – Rank 1
Soul Block is an epic spell specific to the Reaper line of classes and requires harvested souls to cast. Soul Block has several different paths, and is a difficult spell to master.
Soul Block is a defensive spell that uses harvested souls against an enemy. Soul Block can be used to block a single enemy strike.
This spell has three paths: magical defence, physical defence, or generalising between the two.
The user may use as many harvested souls in a Soul Block as they wish.
Generalising with Soul Block weakens the strength of each block by a third.
One cannot walk backward on the path.

Soul Block and Soul Strike looked remarkably similar, like they were sister-spells, designed to work in unison. Though he supposed that would depend upon how many souls one had harvested.

Right now, I can't use a single one of these soul spells, can I?

He looked at the last of the five spells that he'd gained.

Soul Harden – Rank 1
Soul Harden is an epic spell specific to the Reaper line of classes and requires harvested souls to cast. Soul Harden has only one utility, and one path: to protect one's soul.
One cannot walk backward on the path.

Xavier's forehead creased as he read the final spell. He reread the spell three times, trying to glean some hidden information from it. But there was none.

Why would I need to harden my soul, and what does that get me? Xavier wondered. *Protection against soul damage?*

All in all, he didn't know how to feel about the five spells that he'd just gained from attaining the Soul Reaper class, but one thing was certain, something that made him feel a little uneasy, but more than a little excited...

He couldn't wait to harvest his first soul.

Chapter 57
Like Grim Reaper?

XAVIER HADN'T MOVED FROM WHERE HE SAT ON THE FLOOR IN the Staging Room.

There was so much to do. So much to learn.

He opened up his spell list, and selected the Spell Upgrade for Spirit Break, noticing that it was different to an Upgrade Quest.

Spirit Break (All) has been successfully upgraded!
Spirit Break (All) can now be used with a harvested soul.

What?

Xavier leant forward, staring at the text. Not that leaning forward actually made it bigger. He wasn't sitting in front of a computer monitor or reading a book. The text simply moved with him.

Still, he felt like he was on the edge of his seat. He brought up the spell information for Spirit Break.

Spirit Break (All) – Rank 3
Spirit Break (All) combines all three paths of Spirit

*Break. It can break an enemy's body, mind, and
magic.
This power comes at a cost, however. Spirit Break (All)
costs twice as much as the average Rank 3 spell to cast.
Spirit Break (All) can be infused with harvested souls
on casting to increase its effectiveness.
One cannot walk backward on the path.*

Huh. *That didn't really tell me anything new.*
Xavier smiled, however. Increasing the effectiveness of one of
his spells only sounded like a good thing.
He willed the Spell Upgrade for Spiritual Trifecta to appear.

**Spiritual Trifecta (All) has been successfully
upgraded!
Spiritual Trifecta (All) can now be used with a
harvested soul.**

After upgrading the spell, he looked at its updated information.

Spiritual Trifecta – Rank 5
*Spiritual Trifecta combines all three paths of Spiritual
Guidance. When cast, it improves one's physical and
mental strength, physical and mental defence, and
magical strength.
This power comes at a cost, however. Spiritual Trifecta
costs twice as much as the average Rank 5 spell to cast.
Spiritual Trifecta can be infused with harvested souls
on casting to increase its effectiveness.
One cannot walk backward on the path.*

This is exactly the same as the first spell. He'd been hoping for
some sort of new information, but there wasn't any. *I'm just going
to have to test all of these things out in combat on the next floor.*

There was still one more thing he needed to do before he opened his loot box—he needed to see what the Skill Transfer for Staff Mastery was.

He willed the skill list to appear, then selected the Skill Transfer that was available.

Staff Mastery (Rank 2) has been successfully transferred into Scythe-Staff Mastery (Rank 1)!

Xavier nodded to himself. That's about what he'd been expecting. He summoned his Spirit Staff of Might. It felt... different in his hands. Like he'd lost a certain familiarity with it. He grumbled a little about the fact that he'd lost a rank in the skill when it had transferred, but he was glad he'd only gained a single rank in it.

Perhaps it's a good thing I didn't train with it longer. I only would have lost more ranks.

He brought up the skill, wondering what advantages it would give him when wielding a scythe-staff. For a moment, he also wondered why they didn't just call it a scythe. Then he supposed there must have been scythes that were purely physical weapons, meant for warriors, and shrugged the thought away.

Scythe-Staff Mastery – Rank 1
You are a student of the scythe-staff. The scythe-staff is a rare weapon specific to the line of Reaper classes. It is a versatile weapon, one that can be used by melee and ranged fighters alike.
+5% physical damage with scythe-staff weapons.
+5% magical damage with scythe-staff weapons.
+5% Speed when wielding scythe-staff weapons.

+5% Intelligence when wielding scythe-staff weapons.

This skill offers two *attribute boosts?*

Xavier shook his head and smiled. So far, he'd found that whenever one of his skills had ranked up, he'd received an extra percent to whatever boosts that skills had. So, with Staff Mastery at Rank 2 and Scythe-Staff Mastery at Rank 1, he'd only lost 1 percent on physical damage and, and 1 percent to his Speed attribute.

However, he'd *gained* 5 percent on magical damage *and* Intelligence.

That's definitely a win. Is it more powerful because scythe-staves are rare?

Though, currently, as he didn't *have* a scythe-staff, those boosts weren't active.

What caught his attention most from the description was the fact that a scythe-staff was a weapon specific to the Reaper line of classes. *The Stave of the Otherworldly Reaper must actually be a scythe-staff. I can see why they might not have called it that, though. Doesn't really have the same ring to it as stave or scythe...*

Xavier stood up and stretched. He felt like he'd been sitting in that position for hours, though he knew it had probably only taken him a couple of minutes to read through all of that text and consider it all.

The others looked over at him expectantly as he stood. They were all still sitting on their loot boxes, where they'd been chatting quietly.

"So?" Siobhan said. "What class did you get?"

Justin leant forward, curiosity clear on his face. Even normally blank-faced Howard raced an eyebrow, peering over at him.

Xavier let out a breath. *Suppose I've delayed telling them for long enough.* He cleared his throat. "I was able to choose an epic class." He paused. "The class is called Soul Reaper."

Howard grunted, shook his head, sighed. "Soul Reaper? Like grim reaper?"

"That sounds... ominous," Justin said.

"That sounds awesome!" Siobhan said.

The other two snapped their gazes toward her.

Siobhan hesitated. "I mean, I suppose, if this were a video game, it would be awesome. But I guess because it's real life, it's a bit scary?" Her voice went high at the end, like she was asking a question.

Xavier chuckled. "I thought you'd react differently."

Siobhan shrugged. "The world is changing. I have to change with it. Might as well embrace the craziness. That's what I've been trying to do since the start, at least." She didn't mention her reaction to Xavier's torturing of the hell beast, and he wasn't about to mention it either.

"What exactly does a Soul Reaper do?" Howard asked.

Xavier explained to them what he knew about the class. That he could harvest souls and use them in his spells, and about the different spells he'd learnt. He also told them about the fact that he would need to purchase a new weapon, considering his old one was fairly useless now.

"And you should get some armour," Howard said. "You might be able to resist a lot of damage, but those robes of yours clearly can't. You were practically naked after training your resistances on our second time through the third floor."

Siobhan blushed at this, turning away slightly.

Xavier held back a smirk, wondering what he looked like now, beneath all the robes. He clapped his hands together. "All right. Let me see what loot I've gotten. Don't spoil the surprise."

He knelt before his loot box and undid the latch, the familiar notification appearing.

You have gained +1 Skill Point.
You have gained 100,000 Mastery Points.
You have gained 30,000 Lesser Spirit Coins.

You have received 1 Attribute Token (Spirit: 10)!

Xavier raised an eyebrow. His first thought was, *That's it?*

He felt a little disappointed to find that one, he only got a *single* skill point from the loot box, and two, he didn't even get to choose what item he received—that item was chosen for him. And a hundred thousand Mastery Points didn't seem like a great deal after what he'd been able to do on the third floor.

Still, he supposed he shouldn't complain, considering all he'd achieved already. *I'm definitely getting greedy.*

The first thing he did was consume the attribute token. He hadn't been surprised that it was for Spirit. He supposed he couldn't complain about an extra ten points, though it was nothing compared with all the titles he received.

He placed the wooden token into his mouth—it tasted rough on his tongue—and swallowed it with a gulp.

That went down surprisingly easily.

As he'd only received a single skill point, it wasn't a difficult choice what to use it for. He'd been contemplating getting Meditation for a while, and when he realised it might help boost his Spirit attribute—which would be even more valuable to him now, considering the new spells he'd gained—he thought it was a wise plan.

And there was no way he was going to spend a hundred hours in meditation to gain it. *I could clear so many floors in that time.* It would be a clear waste of his most precious resource, the one he couldn't—as far as he knew—buy: time.

You have learnt the skill Meditation!
Meditation – Rank 1
You are a student of the body, mind, and soul.
Meditation lets your body rest, your mind clear, and your soul grow.
+25% health regeneration while meditating.
+25% Spirit Energy recovery while meditating.

+5% Spirit.
+1% Intelligence.

Meditating makes you smarter? Well, not much smarter, but still...

Looking at the Health Regeneration and Spirit Energy recovery bonuses, he could see how this might be a helpful spell for a lot of Denizens. For him, those aspects of the skill were unlikely to come into play. At least, not for a very long time.

I guess I'm going to have to practise meditating now, aren't I? Though he couldn't, for the life of him, figure out *when* a good time for that would be.

Xavier glanced over at the System Shop's terminal, then looked expectantly at the others. Siobhan was the first to notice and chuckled. She took his hand, offering her Lesser Spirit Coins.

The other two came over soon after. They'd gained 9,000 Lesser Spirit Coins from the third floor, and 120,000 from the loot boxes, which meant he now had 214,790 Lesser Spirit Coins sitting in his Storage Ring.

I now have two whole Grand Spirit Coins worth...

That thought dampened his mood, but he didn't let it dampen it for long.

Because it was time to look at the System Shop.

He restrained himself from rubbing his hands together, keen to see what type of scythe-staff he'd be able to afford, and more than a little curious about finally upgrading his flimsy Robes of Intelligence to something more suitable for his new Soul Reaper class.

Xavier walked over to the System Shop's terminal.

Chapter 58
Ghostly Scythe of Darkest Night

XAVIER PLACED HIS HAND ON THE SYSTEM SHOP'S TERMINAL, opening up the menu and feeding in his search parameters.

Scythe-staff, at the maximum I can afford, at the maximum I can wield. He bit his lip, pausing before beginning the search. *This will likely show me what I can only just afford, and whatever the most expensive thing I can get, I know I'll want.*

Xavier paused, considering this for a moment. Armour was important. But... was it important *right now*? He tilted his head to the side. Originally, he'd worried that min-maxing on his attributes would end up getting him dead.

But this was different, wasn't it? He'd already proven he could take a beating, and all it did was literally make him *stronger* by giving him more ranks in his resistance skills.

His Robes of Intelligence might be flimsy, but they always healed right back up when he returned to the Staging Room. If he wanted to clear levels *as fast as possible*, he needed a weapon that would make him *as strong as possible*.

Soon, I might need to focus more on defence, especially in anticipation of returning to Earth. But right now? It's not my priority.

Xavier smiled, easily convincing himself that spending every last one of his Lesser Spirit Coins on the most expensive weapon he could afford was a wise choice.

First, Xavier looked at his Spirit Staff of Might to compare what weapons he came across now, remembering it had cost him 45,000 Lesser Spirit Coins.

Spirit Staff of Might
This staff requires 50 Intelligence, 60 Spirit, and 40 Strength to wield.
+5 Intelligence
+10 Spirit
+5 Speed
+10 Strength
+10% Spirit Energy recovery
+15% magical damage dealt
+15% physical damage dealt

Next, he sold his old staff to the System Shop, a little peeved that the shop only let him sell it back for 30,000 coins.

I lost 15,000 coins just from buying and selling it back?

Then Xavier entered his search parameters and looked at the top five choices within his price range.

Ghostly Scythe of Darkest Night
This staff requires 100 Intelligence, 100 Spirit, and 80 Strength to wield.
+15 Intelligence
+20 Spirit
+10 Speed
+15 Strength
+20% Spirit Energy recovery
+25% magical damage dealt
+25% physical damage dealt
This item costs 200,000 Lesser Spirit Coins

Xavier couldn't help but raise an eyebrow at the name of the weapon. *Ghostly Scythe of Darkest Night.* It sounded so ridiculous it made him chuckle, but he couldn't say he wouldn't mind wielding something with a name like that.

It definitely gave him more stats than his current staff, with the added bonus that his new Scythe-Staff Mastery skill would *actually* work with the weapon.

I'd probably be able to afford decent armour with the money left over, too...

But Xavier didn't stop there. He wanted to see what else there was to offer. The other three scythe-staves he looked at—*Scythe of Reaping, Phantom Stave of Spirit* and one simply named *Reaper Scythe*—all looked remarkably similar and cost about the same as the first had.

Finally, he looked at the fifth and most expensive choice.

Soultaker
This staff requires 150 Intelligence, 150 Spirit, 100 Willpower, and 100 Strength to wield.
+30 Intelligence
+35 Spirit
+15 Speed
+20 Strength
+30% Spirit Energy recovery
+35% magical damage dealt
+35% physical damage dealt
This item costs 240,000 Lesser Spirit Coins

The requirements took him by surprise, but the stats it offered couldn't be denied. Again, it made him wonder how much high-end equipment could offer an incredibly rich Denizen. *Though this weapon would require a high number of stats to even use.*

He itched to take away his search parameters and see what more expensive weapons would offer him—if the attribute requirements would be lower and the attributes offered would be higher, the more expensive the item—but he didn't want to waste time indulging his curiosity on items he couldn't yet afford.

This will be more than enough.

As it was the best weapon he could find, Xavier purchased the Soultaker without hesitation. The scythe-staff appeared in his hand. The moment it did, he felt his attributes rise. His muscles tensed, relaxed. His mind raced, slowed. The world did too. And he felt a warmth, deep inside, that he supposed must be his soul.

I guess there's no threshold when an attribute reaches two hundred points. The weapon had brought his Intelligence over 200, but he didn't notice any difference other than the improvement in stats. *Maybe, if there's another threshold, it's at 500?*

The Soultaker was... well, a beautiful weapon. So far, all (two) of the weapons he'd wielded had been staves. This was a different beast. The blade at the top was larger than he'd expected—as long as his damned arm—yet somehow the weapon was perfectly balanced.

Not to mention considerably heavier than his last weapon.

I guess that's why it requires so much Strength to wield.

It was nine feet long, and he could feel that it was heavier, but he was still able to wield it with incredible ease. He stepped into the middle of the Staging Room, where he had plenty of space, and couldn't help but swipe it this way and that.

The weapon felt *right* in his hands. His strikes smooth and true, but different to how he'd wielded the staff. These strikes utilised the arm-long, vicious looking, sharp-as-anything scythe blade at its top.

A blade that looked like it could decapitate a heavy soldier through their plate armour.

He paused his swipes and examined the shaft of the scythe-staff. The wood was even darker than the wood of his last staff. *Dark as night, much like the grim reaper itself.* There were intricate runes worked into the wood, runes he could barely see—black on black—but ones that he could feel when he ran his hand up it.

Much of the beauty of the weapon was in its simplicity and crafts-manship. In its perfect balance and remarkable weight. In the sharp-ness and strength of its blade—the blade, too, was made of some strange black metal he couldn't identify, though it was perfectly smooth.

Xavier smiled. *I love it.*

Though the others were keen to head to the tavern—not to mention get some rest—Xavier felt more energy than he ever had. He looked over at his party. The three of them were gathered not far off, having been watching as he swung Soultaker.

"I think you guys should go on ahead to the tavern alone." Xavier wasn't even feeling hungry. He just wanted to *train*. He looked over at the door to the tower. "I think I'll check out the fourth floor and farm a few levels on my own. Test out my new spells." He ran a hand along Soultaker. "And test out this beautiful beast."

Howard raised an eyebrow. "You sure you don't want some-thing to eat?"

Xavier nodded. "I'm sure."

Siobhan tucked a strand of hair behind her ear. "You don't want me to come along? In case you need some healing?"

"I think I'll be all right. Don't worry, I won't clear the floor without the three of you."

Siobhan nodded. "All right, then. We'll, uh, be down in the tavern, then I think we'll be able to spare one night's sleep, with the lead we have?"

Xavier nodded. "I think that would be all right." He turned away from the party, too eager to move toward the next floor for idle chitchat, and put a hand on the door.

Congratulations! You have cleared the first three floors of the Tower of Champions! You have reached the first Milestone in the tower. As you have reached the first Milestone, the Tower of Champions will be locked to you for

90 hours. You have 89 hours and 27 minutes remaining.

If you are ahead, you need not worry about losing your lead, as every Champion who reaches this Milestone must pause and reflect for the same amount of time before re-entering the tower.

You may use this time to enter a different party, learn from your fellow Champions in your cohort, or train in the privacy of your Staging Room, preparing your next step on the journey of the Tower of Champions.

Xavier balked at the message. "Are you serious?" He felt a bit of sharp rage threaten to take him over.

"What is it?" Howard asked from the other side of the Staging Room, where the others had been about to leave.

"The Tower of Champions has locked us from entering the floor for almost four days." Xavier stepped back. In his right hand, he gripped Soultaker tightly. Part of him wanted to cleave a hole through the damned door, but he knew he wouldn't be able to.

He'd achieved so much in those past three floors, and now it wouldn't let him move forward? *We've only been here for a day and it's already stopping us!*

Xavier shut his eyes, took a breath.

"That'll slow us down getting back to Earth," Howard said, cursing under his breath. "I was hoping we'd be back there soon. Within the next day or two, at the rate you're burning through the floors."

Xavier let out his breath, opening his eyes, releasing the anger that had clutched at his chest. *It's only a few days,* he told himself, but he was worried about what those few days would mean for the people back on Earth.

"It's all right, Xavier. There's nothing to be done about it.

Come down to the tavern with us. Maybe there'll be others down there," Siobhan said.

Others. Xavier wasn't a fan of other people. Not really. He'd always been a bit of a loner, and the thought of entering the tavern and having to talk to a bunch of other Champions, all displaced from Earth just like the four of them had been... It felt far more difficult than killing five hundred soldiers and a Level 40 hell beast had.

He turned away from the tower door all the same and nodded. Maybe a drink or two down in the tavern would settle his nerves. Maybe... maybe talking with others would put things in perspective.

Then, when he came back, he'd be ready to try out his new class, and plough through the last seven floors as fast as he could before finally returning to Earth.

Chapter 59
True Progenitor

SAMERICALIAN CLEANED THE BAR, DESPITE THE FACT THAT IT was already pristine, subtly observing the patrons in the tavern. Samericalian—or *Sam*, as he liked to go by with people from this planet—was an E Grade Denizen. Not the most gifted Denizen about, but he had some skills, though he wasn't much of a combat fighter.

What he *was*, was good at infiltration. At gathering information. And not being noticed.

Being E Grade also gave him the benefit of having abilities that those of F Grade lacked. One of those abilities was rather valuable when it came to this kind of work—heightened senses. In this case, particularly that of hearing.

He could hear every conversation within the entire tavern. With his level of Intelligence boosting his cognition, he was even able to split his attention and fully follow the thread of several conversations at once.

Though there hadn't been much of anything worth listening to in this place as of yet. He flitted in and out of the different conversations happening, hoping to find what he was looking for.

"...this damned System don't make no sense. There's a goddamned invasion happening. We *chose* to be Champions, yet we're torn away from Earth? And ya know what the worst of it is? The bastard thing took my guns! It's worse than the government, I tell you. Worse than the goddamned government!"

"...if one floor takes a week, seven days, on average to complete, and there are one thousand floors, not including time away from the tower, that's almost twenty years. When I chose this, I didn't think I'd be stuck here for twenty years. How much of my kid's life am I going to miss?"

"...we need to figure out the optimum allocation of stats so that we can distribute them in a logical fashion. We need to gather as much information as we possibly can and factor in every variable before making any decision, maybe survey other members of our cohort, interview them on their experiences in the tower, or else we'll go down the wrong path, and if we go down the wrong path we'll die, and I don't want to die. I thought I could handle this. I feel like all my life I've been *waiting* for something like this to happen so I can prove myself, and now I just feel frozen in fear by *every tiny decision...*"

Sam suppressed a sigh. He'd been placed here for a reason. He knew that. But he felt like he was wasting his time. It was difficult getting a position like this. Being put somewhere where he could watch those from a newly integrated world as they struggle with how their reality has changed.

Trust in the empress.

In the last thousand years, since Samericalian's own world had been integrated long before he was born, the empress was yet to steer them wrong. The woman had been a priestess of the Old Religion—a pre-system fable about a pantheon of gods based on the elements and the celestial bodies in the night sky—and had valued the Spirit attribute above all others.

At least, that's how the story goes.

She was in the Seer line of classes. She won battles before they ever started.

Becoming a cohort's caretaker, like Sam was standing behind that bar, meant knowing something about the people in your instance, meant learning about their ways—that's why he had alcohol from Earth, and knew a thing or two about their culture. And the people of Earth, well, they would look at a chess grand-master and marvel at the fact that he or she had the ability to look fifteen or twenty moves ahead.

The empress of Sam's world? She wouldn't look twenty moves ahead—she would see a million *games* ahead. She was a grand-master of strategy in this sector of the Greater Universe. And even though she was only a C Grade Denizen, it was said she was capable of insights equivalent to that of an *A* Grade.

Because she was a Progenitor. Not just any Progenitor, a *True* Progenitor, one that had taken full advantage of their potential.

And she Saw another Progenitor, one that might soon be on the rise, one from a newly integrated planet by the name of Earth.

Samericalian didn't know much of what she'd seen, only that if he were placed *here*, he would come upon the Progenitor. A part of him thought he already had, but he couldn't be sure.

Progenitors had something most Denizens lacked—an abso-lutely unending well of potential. But that potential, like all poten-tial, could go nowhere.

Take the people in the tavern. It may only be the end of the fourth day since the System integrated their world into the Greater Universe, but it was easy to tell how far some people will go. Today was the day entrance to the first floor of the tower opened for these folks.

All those with true drive would be *in* the tower, not sitting here complaining, *endlessly* talking, warming stools and seats and knocking back pints of beer.

They should be *acting*. Fighting. Practicing. Learning.

Levelling up.

And yet they were here.

And then there was the Progenitor. Sam thought he'd met the man. It would be the first person to walk into his tavern, wouldn't it? That kid he'd talked to. The first one he'd warned about invaders having access to his world.

He was just a kid. Barely looked twenty of their years.

But he was the first to arrive. While the other Champions were still completing their first quests, he was here.

But the potential the kid—the man, he supposed—had could already have been snuffed out. As the caretaker of the cohort, Sam was restricted by what he could say. *Heavily* restricted. He couldn't tell Xavier much, especially not right away, but the more floors he completed, the more those restrictions would be lifted.

He seemed eager enough, when I told him about Progenitors. But he might have been too hasty. He could have jumped straight into the first floor and gotten himself killed trying to clear it too quickly.

There were several ways to take advantage of the Tower of Champions, and a Progenitor just so happened to be in a position to have the *potential* to take advantage of *all* of them.

If they realised what was possible.

He could realise soloing will get him an extra title, that being the first to clear a floor will give him an extra title, and, the least likely, he could realise that reaching the Top 100 could give him an extra title. But if he just figures farming the floors is the better option, like many Denizens who enter the Tower of Champions, then he'll miss out on being first.

That's how True Progenitors were born. They took a lead that wasn't possible for anyone else, and they *never let up*. If Xavier had been lucky enough, determined enough, or *both*, to hit upon this confluence of possible titles, then he might just be who the Seer hoped he *could* be.

Who the empress hoped he could *become*.

A force to be reckoned with. Not just a pawn in the empress's game, but another player. Someone who could help her change the game completely.

Samericalian did the math.

He figured if this Xavier turned out to be the real deal, in two days' time he would stroll into that tavern having completed the first three floors and already be on the Tower of Champions forced rest between Milestones. The first in not just this cohort, or from Earth, but the first of all five worlds competing in this instance of the tower.

Then maybe, just maybe, he could be the one the empress had been waiting for. The Progenitor who wouldn't only become the defender of his planet, but—ultimately—the defender of this entire sector.

But he—as well as the empress—knew the chances of that were slim. This wasn't the first time Sam had stood behind a bar, awaiting to see a *True* Progenitor, only to find himself disappointed. Only to find the Progenitor he'd been observing die, or whittle away their unspent potential, lost before it could be used.

He'd been at this for a hundred years, after all.

Trust in the empress.

He'd been saying that mantra for a long, long time.

The door to the tavern opened. Sam's gaze casually flicked up, still wiping down the same stretch of sparkling-clean bar. A tall man in warrior armour—the *first* warrior armour the system handed Denizens—stepped in. The man had a close-cropped, dark brown beard streaked with grey and a serious look about him. He looked forty or fifty of Earth's pre-integrated years.

Can't be too serious if he's walking in here on day one.

He'd seen the man in here before the first floor opened, chatting seriously with a few others, learning all he could.

A kid walked in after him. This fellow must only just have been old enough to be integrated into the System. Sixteen and fresh-faced, though he looked sharp enough.

Behind them was a redheaded woman wearing a bright smile that felt out of place in a cohort from a newly integrated world. Her blue eyes were just as bright as her smile, and her red hair was down, swaying a little as she walked.

It was the final member of their party that got Sam's full attention.

Xavier. The one he suspected of being the Progenitor. *The first Champion to arrive.* Why was he walking in already? He should be in the tower, trying as hard as he could to clear the first floor as fast as possible!

More unspent potential. Another Progenitor that could have been...

Then Sam saw two things—the man's aura, and the man's eyes. These two details had him stop cleaning the bar. They made his mouth fall open. And suddenly he felt like a complete amateur, unable to remain in character despite having filled this role for a hundred years. Unable to stop himself from gaping at what he was seeing.

Day one, and Xavier had already reached Level 10 and chosen his first class. And whatever that class was, it must be powerful to have changed his eye colour like that.

His eyes have turned silver. A Spirit-based class.

The stronger the aura, the stronger effect it had on the Denizen, going as far to change eye colour and even hair colour later down the line. Though these effects could be veiled and hidden. One could shut down their aura and choose which elements—like eye colour—it changed, once they grew adept enough in Aura Control.

Something a Denizen four days into the System wouldn't know a damned thing about, of course.

None of the others here, none even his party, can see his aura, as they haven't even achieved their first real class, which would grant them Aura Sight.

And the amount of *power* the man was giving off? It could only be possible one way—titles. A hell of a lot of titles.

If Xavier were a True Progenitor, Sam had been expecting him here at the end of the third day of the Tower of Champion's opening, having cleared three floors, attaining his first Milestone.

Now, here he was, on the *first day*. Wired. Fidgety. Hands clenching and unclenching. Jaw working. Teeth grinding. Like a hungry beast pacing back and forth in a cage, raring and waiting to get out.

To *attack*. To *kill*.

That wasn't the demeanour of someone *choosing* to take a break between floors, that was a man who'd hit their first *forced* break and didn't know how to shut off and accept that he had to wait a little longer to keep progressing.

He's cleared the first three floors on day one. This may very well be the one the empress is looking for.

The next True Progenitor. The Denizen that could change the course of the sector.

Assuming he can survive the threats the tower has in store, and the invasion and alteration of his home world, which will be far worse than he could ever imagine.

Chapter 60
Homicidal One

Once Alistair Reed had grown strong enough, he was able to dispense with all subtlety.

It had taken him a full two days to kill all the members of his tutorial. The more of them he'd slain—luring them into dark alleys, taking them out when they were sleeping, or coming upon them when they were alone—the easier it had become.

Not from a moral standpoint. In that way, it had already been easy. Alistair Reed didn't have any moral qualms about killing his own people. He didn't have any moral qualms at all, come to think of it.

Soon, he wasn't bothering to take out loners. Soon, he was taking down whole groups, finding it easier and easier for his daggers to slide through their flesh the stronger he'd become.

He'd managed to get his Dagger Mastery skill to Rank 10, and it drastically improved not only his Speed and the damage his strikes did, but also the amount of piercing damage they had.

To the point where a warrior's flimsy, thin leather armour wasn't enough to stop him from punching a hole straight through it. And a mage's robes? They were nothing to him.

Alistair grew more and more confident, until, at the end, he was striding through the streets taking down people one by one. As a warrior, he didn't possess the same types of spells that mages had, but that didn't mean he didn't have spells.

And one of those spells made it impossible for someone to hit him. At least, for a short period of time.

Phase Shift let him become incorporeal, and he could choose the moment in which he activated it, shifting in and out of the spell's usage to conserve its energy.

It let his *body* become incorporeal. His weapons, on the other hand, remained solid. The spell warned that there were ways to circumvent and cancel it out, but that wasn't something Alistair needed to worry about facing these people.

He'd long ago dealt with any truly competent members of the tutorial before they were ever given a chance to fight back.

When all was done, Alistair had left the section of the city where his tutorial had been set up, leaving 990 corpses behind, searching for the next tutorial worth of people, as he was yet to receive a new quest.

He'd cleaned off all the blood—not a speck of it his own—that he could, but his armour was still caked in the stuff, something he knew he'd have to explain at some point.

But it had all been worth it. In so many ways, it had been worth it. This System coming, integrating Earth into the Greater Universe, it had finally let him take off his mask and show the world who and what he truly was.

An apex predator. One designed for a singular purpose: to kill.

And when he'd completed that first quest, he'd received something he hadn't expected. First, he'd received something called a Storage Ring, which he'd used to strip the corpses of their weapons and armour, figuring he might be able to sell them at some point. Assuming any semblance of society managed to return, of course.

Then he'd received something far more valuable: titles.

Apparently, the titles hadn't activated until he'd finished his first quest. They'd been accumulating, waiting to be activated.

He'd received a title called "Homicidal One." According to the title, he'd been the very first integrated Denizen of Earth to kill another human in cold blood.

The title seemed very specific about it being *in cold blood*, as though there might be other ways humans had been killing each other.

And the title? The title had said it was *upgradeable*. The more of his own people he killed, the stronger the title would become. So he hadn't just received a single title—he'd received a series of them. Each title offered him not only bonus attribute points, but allowed him to deal bonus damage to humans.

Specifically humans.

Like the System *wanted* him to kill his own people. Like it was unlocking his true potential and letting him follow his desires to their ultimate end. Not that Alistair knew what that end was.

He was too busy having fun to think of the bigger picture.

As he strolled through the city of his birth, Alistair Reed began to realise something was off. He didn't yet fully understand what the System had done to Earth when it integrated the world into the Greater Universe, but he was beginning to recognise that things had... *changed*.

Buildings weren't where they were supposed to be. Hell, *streets* weren't where they were supposed to be.

When the integration had happened, as far as he knew the System had plucked everyone from wherever they happened to be and sent them to a little room made out of void-like nothingness, evaluating them, making them choose their moral faction, making them choose their available basic class.

Then the System had thrown them back into the world wherever the hell it felt like throwing them. Those few people that he had spoken to back at the tutorial, and the ones he'd overheard talking, all had said they'd been somewhere else when they'd been teleported away. Whether they'd been uptown or downtown, they hadn't been *here*.

And now, it seemed, no one else was around either.

But that wasn't what Alistair was finding strange.

Fronton, the city he'd lived his entire life in, had its streets built in a grid—much like Manhattan Island. The streets and blocks were uniform, and so were the names of those streets.

Yet things had changed.

When he'd realised this, Alistair had stopped in the middle of Main Street—what *should* have been Main Street—his eyes narrowed, staring at a tall building that shouldn't be there. A building he was sure he'd only seen on TV.

The Empire State Building. A building from a city many miles away.

This confirmed Alistair's suspicions that the System had royally screwed with not only the people and animals of this world, but the world itself.

He kept walking. He could have stolen a car, but it would be tough driving through the streets. Maybe a motorcycle would have worked, as traffic was blocked, everyone having been taken out of their cars at once, but he'd never ridden a motorcycle.

Wouldn't that be a funny way to go in the apocalypse? Crashing a damned motorcycle?

The streets weren't completely deserted. Feral dogs, cats, and rats roamed. Just like Alistair and the city itself, these animals had been altered into something *other* by the System. They appeared as though they had been avoiding the tutorial area, but once he'd left, they began to attack him.

Packs of mutated dogs, grown larger and fiercer than they should be, came out of the woodwork, barking and snarling and barrelling straight for him. His Phase Shift spell helped him remain unharmed, and his daggers carved up the bastard mutts quick smart.

And more Mastery Points flowed into Alistair.

So he made a game of it.

Alistair broke through the side mirror of a car with the butt of one of his daggers and beeped the horn. The keys were still sitting in the ignition. He turned it on and blared the horn in three long bursts.

Then he waited.

Rats drew up from the sewers in droves. Cats, perched on balconies and the sides of rooftops, climbed down fire escapes toward him. Dogs barked and howled, making their presence known, appearing on all sides of the street.

Even pigeons appeared, flying through the sky, mutated and *larger*, their beaks longer and sharper, swooping down toward him.

Alistair threw his head back in a laugh, slashed his daggers against each other to make a satisfying metallic sound, then waited for the mutated animals to come for him.

Three hours later, after doing this at five different intersections, he reached Level 10 and got to select his first class. He chose something called a rare class, as it offered him the most attribute points. And it had a cool name—*Heart Striker*. He could live with that.

Though he made good progress killing animals-turned-beasts, he was beginning to wonder why he hadn't come upon any more humans. Fronton should have had millions of people in it. His tutorial couldn't have been the only one here, could it? There had only been a thousand people.

It didn't make any sense to him that the city would be so deserted.

Then again, what about this new reality *did* make sense, other than him being rewarded for wholesale slaughter?

It made him wonder how the world had been changed. The streets. The buildings. Like this city was a mismatch of six others, and all the puzzle pieces had been jammed together to make something else. Something other. Something altogether alien.

It was bigger than it had been before, too. A *lot* bigger.

He'd gone to the top of one of the tall skyscrapers and looked out. Everything was different. He could see mountains that shouldn't have been there. Could see smoke from fires drifting up into the sky.

Is that where the people are, outside of the city?

It made him wonder how he hadn't noticed this all when he'd first been returned here. It made him wonder, as well, what *else* this System was capable of. If it could take his world and change it in a blink of an eye, it was capable of damn near anything.

Which means the System is essentially God, and God is rewarding me for killing others, for causing chaos. The System itself, changing the world as it has, appears to be an instrument of chaos, just as I am...

A bolt of purple lightning struck the ground a few miles away from where he stood on the rooftop, the breeze playing with his shoulder-length blonde hair. He tilted his head in fascination, narrowing his eyes. Though it was far away, he could clearly make out the appearance of a portal.

And people stepping out of it.

Quest Log Update (New Quest Available)

Alistair smiled, opening his log.

Current Quest: An enemy incursion has appeared in your vicinity. As an instrument of chaos, you have no allegiance to your world. You have two paths: Path 1: Infiltrate and join the enemy. Path 2: Destroy the enemy incursion by any means necessary. One cannot walk backward on the path. Progress: Incomplete Reward:

1. **5 Skill Points**
2. **Bonus Mastery Points.**
3. **Unknown Item**

Alistair smiled, broadly and with far too much teeth.

That's when he realised he'd been wrong about the city being deserted. There *were* others; they were simply difficult to see. They weren't driving cars. They weren't walking down the streets. They were in small clusters. He returned to the street, walked into a sporting goods store, and took binoculars—intended for bird watching, as though *that* were a sport—and headed back to the roof.

With his careful inspection, he spotted signs of a dozen more tutorials around the city, and in the centre of them all, the portal, with enemy soldiers streaming through it. And he was sure there must be more tutorials, in areas blocked by buildings, places he couldn't see.

No, the city wasn't deserted. It was just that each tutorial had been segmented from one another, and the city had been *elongated*, grown, transformed into something far larger than was possible before, so those tutorials could be secluded from one another—like the System didn't want them to coordinate.

Probably the same reason that the internet was down. That phones and radio weren't operating. *The System wants us to play by its rules, not our own.*

For what purpose, Alistair didn't know. But what he did know was that this city, populated as it was, was about to turn into a bloodbath.

And he was the one who would turn on the tap.

Chapter 61
I Can Make Money

Xavier sat beside Siobhan and across from Howard and Justin in one of the tavern's booths.

He couldn't help but notice that Sam, the barkeep in this place, had glanced at him a few more times than he'd glanced at anyone else. A fact which was beginning to make Xavier uncomfortable.

Two days had passed since their ninety-hour forced break from climbing the floors of the Tower of Champions. Forty-nine hours, to be precise. And there were still forty-one left.

Xavier felt more jittery and antsy than he ever remembered feeling. He wanted to *fight*, *gain levels*, but the damned System was making him slow down. He couldn't understand why. He was glad it would in no way slow down his lead and risk losing him the first-clear title, but it *would* slow down his return to Earth.

What is the world going through, without its Champions to protect it?

He hoped that people were banding together. That the government or the military would have some semblance of order and control. He hoped that conventional weapons—the ones the US government had thrown billions and billions of dollars at over the years—would make a difference.

But considering the odds they'd been given by Sam—*a one in ten thousand chance*—of their world surviving... something told him "conventional" weapons and the military weren't going to make much of a difference in all of this.

And, looking down at his skin, he was sure of it.

Tougher than metal. No way a bullet's going to punch through that, unless it's an anti-aircraft round or something...

Guns *might* work at the start, but they wouldn't work once the enemies got higher in level, that was for sure.

Modern weapons weren't really his wheelhouse. He'd always been more interested in fantasy—and medieval—weapons. Maybe that's why he didn't think Earth would be fine just because they had big guns.

"You've got stink-face on again," Siobhan said.

Xavier blinked, looking over at the redheaded mage. "Stink-face?"

Siobhan motioned to her own face, scrunching up her nose, crinkling her forehead. "Like you're walking through a dump or smelling rotten eggs."

"I'm just... thinking about Earth."

"So it's think-face, not stink-face," Justin said.

Xavier sighed. "Suppose it is." He sipped his whiskey. It didn't have the same kick as it used to. In fact, it didn't really have any kick. Probably on account of how much Toughness he had.

But he guessed he liked the taste, at least.

He placed his glass back on the table as a notification popped up over his vision.

Meditation has reached Rank 7!

Xavier smirked.

Howard raised an eyebrow. "Another rank in Meditation? How many is that now?"

"Seven," Xavier said.

Siobhan shook her head. "I can't believe you're meditating

while having a drink with us. No wonder you're so quiet, splitting your mind like that."

"Meditation doesn't split my mind, it focuses it." Though Xavier had initially been frustrated by the System locking them out of the tower—and, honestly, still *was* frustrated at it, as he was sure he would have cleared the tenth floor by now and be back on Earth, probably why the place was on his mind so much—it had given him the opportunity to experiment.

It had given him the one thing he'd been shortest on since getting to this place—the one commodity he still couldn't buy: time.

When he'd decided to learn the skill of Meditation, he'd worried he wouldn't be able to get more ranks in it without the requisite time to focus on it. It didn't seem like something he could rank up in battle, after all, and battle was what he was about. It was one of the reasons he hadn't bothered with the skill earlier—other than the fact that he simply hadn't thought he would need it.

He'd known he wouldn't have the time to simply sit down, shut his eyes against the world, and meditate.

But it turned out that Meditation was quite a versatile skill. Once he'd gotten the skill up to Level 3, he'd been able to meditate while walking. When he'd gotten it to Rank 4, he'd been able to hold a conversation.

And the skill of Meditation—while actively using it—didn't just help him clear his mind and clarify his thoughts, it helped him to *think*. Helped him to *focus*.

What it didn't help him do was fight. He'd walked up to the staging room once he'd reached Rank 5 in the skill. Swinging about his staff-scythe, Soultaker, he'd been more clumsy than ever. Like having Meditation active had somehow cancelled out his Scythe-Staff Mastery skill.

But he was sure that if he ranked the skill up high enough, that could very well change.

Part of him realised he was so good at Meditation from the get-go because of the number of points he had in Spirit. Which was, right now, sitting at an effective 202 since reaching Rank 7 in Meditation.

Another thing he'd found when deep in meditation was that it... it seemed to connect him to something other than himself. Something beyond his frame of reality that he didn't understand.

He wasn't completely sure what it was that the skill was connecting him to—perhaps it was the very System itself—but every now and then he would have insights about the System, and how things worked. Things that he shouldn't have known, things that weren't mentioned anywhere in any notification that he'd received, nor anywhere in that poor excuse for a manual they'd gotten.

It was as though the simple act of meditating was broadening his mind. As though, when he'd begun, his mind had been a small chamber deep in the earth, only large enough to hold himself, and even then he wasn't able to stretch out his arms or even stand higher than a crouch.

His mind had been constricted. Constrained. It had been, well... small.

But as he meditated? Rock was carved and scraped off the walls of the chamber, turning it into a cavernous space. And the more hours he spent this way—the more ranks he gained in the skill —the larger his mind became, broadening and begging to be filled with information.

And, every now and then, as the Meditation skill took a pickaxe to the walls of that chamber, slowly carving chunks off it, making it grow larger and larger, something would be uncovered. Like finding iron ore, gold, or diamonds. Except in this case, what he found was a small insight. An instinct. Or some knowledge he felt like he'd always known but was only now just realising it.

That's why he worried that his thoughts about Earth—about guns not working well against whatever invaders came, about the military being ineffective, about everyone being... unorganised. He worried that these thoughts were more than just fears, that they were insights borne from his practise of Meditation.

You have reached your Spirit Energy limit!
You have 21,200/21,200 Spirit Energy.

Xavier smiled, pushing away his worries.

There wasn't anything he could do for Earth in this moment except keep progressing. Keep learning. Keep pushing forward.

One of the things he'd discovered from these Meditation-related insights was how valuable Spirit Energy actually *was*. He of course knew that Spirit Energy was needed for him to cast spells, and that one could easily get Spirit Energy when killing enemies, eating food, or just generally resting.

And he'd already learnt that one could create Lesser Spirit Coins from Spirit Energy, but when the others had told him about creating Lesser Spirit Coins, they'd said it cost 500 Spirit Energy to create a single Lesser Spirit Coin.

Even Xavier, with 202 Spirit, would only be able to create 42 Lesser Spirit Coins before running out of Spirit Energy with that conversion rate. Considering they'd each gained 30,000 coins from the third floor's loot box... it didn't seem like a good use of their time.

Until Xavier realised the equation they'd given him wasn't from the manual—it had been from their testing. The insight had come to him when he'd been meditating.

All of the currencies the System used were called "Spirit Coins." Lesser Spirit Coins could be created by F Grade Denizens, Minor Spirit Coins by E Grade Denizens, and so on and so forth until A Grade Denizens were creating Grand Spirit Coins.

That, he'd figured out already.

The word "Spirit," however, he should have focused on earlier.

It had come to him all at once when he'd gained his second rank in Meditation. *The higher the Spirit attribute, the more coins one can create per 500 Spirit Energy.*

Until then, Xavier hadn't bothered trying to create Lesser Spirit Coins, and none of the others had done so since Justin had made a few when they'd first learnt about it, back when they'd been huddling in the Safe-Zone cabin on the first floor.

When the insight had come to Xavier, he'd been sitting cross-legged on the floor in his room, too wired to sleep, instead using the time to meditate.

He'd looked down at his hand and focused, imagining what he'd wished.

As he had, he'd felt the Spirit Energy moving around his body, like blood running through veins, except he was able to direct it. Pack it together and make it into something *tangible*.

It had taken him ten minutes of intense concentration, but finally, a Lesser Spirit Coin had appeared.

Not one of them, like he'd expected. Like Justin had done. No, he'd managed to create 38 Lesser Spirit Coins. They'd appeared, hovering in front of him, then fallen in a clump onto the floor of his room.

Xavier had blinked, shaking his head with a small laugh.

He'd looked at his Spirit Energy reserves, seeing he'd only used 500 of them, then quickly did the math, realising what might have happened. At the time, with Meditation being Rank 2, his Spirit attribute had been at an effective 193.

Dividing his Spirit attribute by how many coins he'd created, he'd gotten 5.07. Rounding down, that was 5—which, as he'd found out later, was the exact number of points Justin had in his Spirit attribute when he'd created a single Lesser Spirit Coin from 500 Spirit Energy.

Which brought him to the conclusion: each extra 5 points in Spirit let a Denizen create an extra Lesser Spirit Coin per 500 Spirit Energy. It was an easy enough thing to test. When he'd hit Rank 3 of Meditation, bringing his Spirit attribute to an effective 195, he found he was able to create 39 Lesser Spirit Coins.

I can make *money.*

It still wasn't nearly as much as he'd been able to make clearing floors of the tower, but he knew that not every Denizen had access to the tower. And, he had to imagine, not every Denizen had easy access to the System Shop, or countless beasts to hunt and kill.

He decided to focus on the skill of creating Lesser Spirit Coins. It was something easy he could do to break up the heavy meditation sessions.

Eventually, he got so good that he could create a batch of Lesser Spirit Coins each second, and it took him less than a minute to deplete his entire Spirit Energy reserve.

Then he'd meditate until his reserve was full once more, and start all over again. Though, even with his Spirit as high as it was, it still took him roughly an hour to fully regenerate *all* of his Spirit Energy, as he had so much of it.

Even eating food didn't help him recover it all that quickly, unless he absolutely *gorged* himself, and Meditation proved more effective at quickening his recovery than sleep—not that he'd felt all that tired since clearing the third floor.

Sitting in the tavern, having once again reached his Spirit Energy limit, Xavier looked around the table, cracked his knuckles, then created forty-two batches of 40 Lesser Spirit Coins. One batch per second, forty-one seconds later, and 1,680 coins sat in piles atop the table—though some had surely fallen off onto the ground, rolling to other tables about the tavern.

"God, you're like a damned winning slot machine with that." Howard shook his head. "Making money," he muttered.

Justin's eyes widened and bulged. They always did when Xavier performed this little trick. "How many is that now?"

Xavier ran his hand over the pile, depositing it all into his Storage Ring. "I now have over sixty-four thousand Lesser Spirit Coins."

Justin swore under his breath. "You had less than five thousand when you bought that wicked-looking scythe. That's insane!"

Xavier nodded. Perhaps the forced break from the Tower of Champions hadn't been a *completely* bad thing. As creating more Lesser Spirit Coins?

Well, it wasn't the *only* insight he'd had about Spirit Energy.

Chapter 62
This System Doesn't Like to Play Fair

XAVIER MADE HIS WAY BACK TO HIS ROOM WHILE THE OTHER members of his party headed to the Staging Room.

There was something he needed to do.

When utilising his Meditation skill, he'd found that it didn't much matter if he were holding a conversation with others or not, the rate at which his Spirit Energy and health recovered was the same.

But his insights came less frequently.

Now that he'd used all of his Spirit Energy creating another batch of Lesser Spirit Coins, he wanted to see if he could gain another insight while recovering his Spirit Energy.

He was hoping to learn something about his Soul Reaper class. Something that had nothing to do with his spells, though he was eager to learn more about those. Unfortunately, even though he already had all of the spells for the class, he was only able to use *one* of them. Every spell but Spirit Infusion required souls to cast, and he wasn't in a position to harvest any.

There were souls in the tavern. Other Champions. Weak ones.

Xavier shoved that thought down.

He had been disappointed to find so many of their cohort

drinking in the tavern, drowning their sorrows in alcohol instead of working their way through the first floor of the tower, but at least it had given them the opportunity to spread some knowledge.

Siobhan and Howard had been the ones to do that. When they'd first walked into the tavern, the two of them had gone to every table and talked to each of the Champions at them, explaining all the things that they knew.

Of course, other Champions wouldn't be able to benefit from the same titles that Xavier and his party could. Xavier received the normal title for clearing a floor, a solo title, the first-clear title, and so far, he'd received two Top 100 titles.

Howard, Siobhan, and Justin, though they didn't receive the solo title or any Top 100 titles, received the normal title *and* the first-clear title—without ever having to strike an enemy.

The other Champions? It seemed foolish to recommend that they aim for solo titles, as it would only benefit one of their number, and they would likely not be strong enough to achieve such a feat.

And there was no way they'd ever get into the Top 100. None that Xavier could see, anyhow.

Still, Howard and Siobhan told them everything they knew. Including the fact that they could respawn a floor seemingly as many times as they wished to farm that floor for levels. Though Xavier wished for as many Champions to return to Earth as soon as possible, he didn't think rushing through the levels would be a wise choice for most parties.

In fact, he was sure it would only get them killed.

Unfortunately, that meant their advice skewed toward the other parties in their cohort taking as much time as they possibly could to go through each of their floors.

Howard and Siobhan also spoke about the different skills that were available, and what those skills were capable of once they'd been levelled up.

To Xavier's surprise, not everyone wanted to listen to them. He'd watched from a corner booth in the tavern, listening in from afar to the conversations. It made him wonder if he should *do* something. But what was he going to do? He didn't know how to inspire others. All he really knew how to do was kill a bunch of enemies.

And the people in that tavern weren't enemies. They weren't even idiots. They were just afraid. Paralysed by fear. Maybe even guilt. He supposed, to a degree, he could understand that, but he would have thought the first test of Champions—having to kill another potential Champion—would have weeded out those who would freeze up in these situations.

Many parties *did* listen, however, making their way out of the tavern when their conversation concluded with Howard and Siobhan, a newfound resolve forming in their eyes.

Those, Xavier hoped, had a chance.

One man hung on every word. He was sitting alone, drinking a pint of beer, a serious yet sad expression on his face. He wore the thin armour warriors received when first integrated into the system. His hands were rough and calloused. Fingers thick. He had the broad shoulders of a linebacker, but had a bedraggled look about him. Long hair, tied in a ponytail. A large, bushy beard that went down to his chest.

When Siobhan had asked the man where his party was, he'd told them they were dead. That they'd died on the first floor, faster than he could save them.

That's when Xavier had taken a good look at the others in the place. Not a single one of the groups he saw had more than three members, yet each party would have started with four.

Each party here lost at least one Champion...

Some of those parties linked up, after Howard and Siobhan talked to them about strategy, and headed back up to conquer the first floor, but there were a few stray Champions that looked like they didn't have any fight left in them.

"Happens sometimes," Sam had said when Xavier had gone up to the bar for another drink.

"What's that?" Xavier had been stuck in his own head, thinking on... well, everything.

The barkeep nodded toward some of those stray Champions. "Those from newly integrated worlds. Some catch on fast." He peered at Xavier. "Like you." His gaze flicked away. "Others... they can't handle the new reality. Even if they make it here, and you know what it means to make it here. They shut down the moment the System gives them the opportunity to."

Xavier frowned. "Is there any way to bring them out of it?"

"Let's just say the System won't let them stay away from the tower for too long. Unless someone reaches a Milestone"—the man's gaze trailed back to Xavier for a moment, then peeled away again—"the System won't allow a Champion to stay off a floor for more than twenty-four hours."

"That wasn't in the Tower of Champions manual."

"There're a lot of things not in that manual."

"What does the System do?" Xavier was reminded of what happened to the Navy SEAL. The lightning that had struck the man when he'd refused to fight Xavier. "They don't die, do they?"

"The System gives them one warning. Clear their next floor, all the way through—no stepping back to the Staging Room—or..."

"Or die," Xavier whispered. And they'd probably die on the floor, too, inexperienced as they are. "Why don't you tell them that?"

"I can't." Sam shook his head, gave a weary sigh. "I'm restricted. Told you, when we first met, people from non-integrated worlds... get a bad lot here. There are so many things you learn growing up a part of the Greater Universe that the System with-holds from you."

"Restricted?" Xavier said. He leant forward on the bar, confused. "You... just told me?"

Sam looked him in the eye. "I told you because you've already reached the first Milestone." He poured Xavier another glass, taking the Lesser Spirit Coins he left on the table. "System knows you won't step back now. You've got a taste for it." He raised a finger. "But don't be thinking you've found a loophole. That you can tell the others what I've just told you. Because it won't work. You'll get all tongue-tied and the words will die in your throat." He looked about the tavern. "And anyone listening in? They would soon find they forgot what I said the second I said it."

"This System doesn't like to play fair."

"No. But you know that already, Xavier." Sam pushed the glass of whiskey forward then stepped away, serving a man at the other end of the bar.

Xavier stood there a moment, taking in the man's words. The implications. When he looked back at the Champions in his cohort that had chosen not to keep moving forward, that were still down here, hiding from the first floor of the tower, he wondered what he could do about it.

Part of him didn't want to do a damned thing.

These people made it this far. Survived two trials to get here. Got advice from Howard and Siobhan, telling them everything they knew about the first three floors and what to expect, how to train for it, how to survive. And now they just want to check out? Throw away the opportunity the System has given them to get stronger? To progress? To return to Earth with all the power the tower might grant them and help their world?

He didn't feel pity. Didn't feel understanding. He felt a heaping of disgust, like bile rising up from his throat.

A thought had risen to the forefront of his mind, one that felt dark and alien, but at the same time *true* and *right*. A voice that even now, sitting in his room, falling into meditation, made him shudder recalling it.

These wretched souls aren't worth the bodies they inhabit.

Standing by the bar, staring out at the Champions from his cohort who weren't fighting—thirty-eight of them, he quickly counted—his fingers twitched.

Ached.

With wanting.

A sudden desire to summon Soultaker from his Storage Ring

and live up to the name of his class took hold of him, like the skeletal hands of the grim reaper itself grasping his heart.

For what better use did these poor excuses for Champions have than to be fuel for his spells?

When Xavier had felt that desire. When that thought had popped into his head. He'd taken the glass of whiskey still on the bar and downed it in one go. He'd shoved the thought down. Pushed it away.

And he didn't tell the others in his party what he'd learnt.

By the time a full day had passed—a whole twenty-four hours since the Tower of Champions had opened its first floor to their instance—all the Champions in the tavern except for Xavier and those in his party were gone.

The man Howard and Siobhan had spoken to, with the long hair and beard and the linebacker shoulders, had walked out of the tavern after his conversation with the other two had ended, resolve alight in his eyes.

The man, Alfonso, said he'd tackle the tower floors alone and go after the solo titles, because he didn't want to be responsible for another person's death but his own.

Xavier thought he might have a chance.

The others, he didn't care about at all.

And that's why he sat up here, alone in his room, hoping for some insight about his class, hoping to learn if choosing it had changed him in some way.

Because he *should* have cared about those people, shouldn't he? Should have cared about what they'd gone through? About the fact that they were struggling to push forward?

At the least, he shouldn't have wanted to harvest their souls.

Yet sitting there, what he felt wasn't worry for those people— those people who had no doubt only left the tavern after they'd received a notification saying they would die if they didn't go back and clear their floor—he felt a hunger. A pit somewhere deep inside him. Something dark and unending. Something waiting to be filled. *Needing* to be filled.

No, he didn't feel worried for them.

He felt regret at not having harvested their souls while he'd had the chance.

As he meditated, no insights came, and all Xavier could do was wonder about what he was, and what he might be becoming.

Chapter 63
Er'al'Ealia? Vaegon? Where Do They Come Up with These Names?

MELISSA DONAVAN WATCHED FROM THE TREES.

The elves, she'd found, were difficult to kill. She'd only ever gone after them when they'd been alone. Killing them didn't bring the feelings she'd expected—guilt, heartache, a sense of having done *wrong*.

No, killing them had felt right. Not *good*—but right.

There was a difference, she knew. A difference she understood in her heart. Maybe her soul, if such a thing existed.

These elves were alien invaders, come to take her planet. Worse, come to take her *forest*. It wasn't only the quest that kept her here—the one that told her to survive in the forest with the invaders—it was the fact that these bastards were trying to take her sanctuary.

And so she watched, high up in a tree, peering down at the elven camp. There were at least two hundred of them. After that first elf had stepped out of the portal, she'd almost loosed an arrow at him.

Then more had come, and they hadn't stopped coming for a good while. She'd shrunk back into the wilderness and made herself hidden. Made herself small. Made herself invisible. It was something she'd always been good at.

And in doing so, she'd gained a skill called Stealth, one she'd levelled up relentlessly over the past few days of stalking her prey.

The elves knew they were being hunted. They spoke to each other in a language she didn't understand—a language that the System would not translate for her, but she could *tell* they knew. Their words were melodic and pure. Almost sounded like the bastards were singing instead of speaking.

Tolkien would have, no doubt, felt vindicated. Their language even sounded similar to what she remembered the elves in *The Lord of the Rings* sounding like. Not that she'd spent a great deal of time watching those movies.

That made her mind go on a tangent, something it was prone to do while she spent long hours silent in the trees, observing her enemy, gaining ranks in Stealth the longer she remained unseen.

If elves are real, does that mean we didn't come up with their race on our own? Did we somehow know of their existence? When Tolkien penned his epic, did his creativity tap into some hidden knowledge of the universe? Were the words he inked closer to truth than fiction?

Melissa smiled to herself. *Who bloody knows?*

The elves, not doing much of interest, lost her attention for a moment. Melissa turned her gaze to the rest of the forest. From her vantage point, she could see over the tall canopy of branches. Could see just how far this forest stretched.

In her first days out here, all she'd focused on was survival. Killing animals-turned-beasts, gaining levels, finding water, and cooking food. She'd been in a daze. Maybe even in shock, come to think of it. There were strange things about the forest—beyond the killer bunnies and the elves stepping out through portals.

Then she'd realised there were more animals in the forest than there should have been.

At first, she'd thought she must be in the local nature reserve near the city of Fronton, where she'd grown up. But then she'd encountered a pack of wolves that had almost savaged her to death.

Though she hadn't come out of that encounter unscathed,

she'd certainly discovered the necessity of boosting her Toughness attribute.

Seeing the wolves had snapped something into focus—there were no wolves near Fronton. None in the entire damned state. Which meant she couldn't be near Fronton. She must have been thrown farther afield than she'd thought.

No matter. She didn't have any intention to trek back to civilisation.

But then she'd seen something else. Something she knew certainly *shouldn't be* in her forest. Not in any forest in North America.

A kangaroo.

It was wild. Tall. Had vicious claws that looked like they'd mutated and become strong and sharp enough to punch through steel. And God, it looked like a damned bodybuilder.

But it shouldn't have been *here*.

Which, for a moment, had made her wonder if she'd been teleported to Australia. Only, Australia—she was sure—didn't have wolves, and many of the plants she'd seen were, to her knowledge, native to America.

And that was why Melissa Donavan had taken a moment away from observing the enemy elves—thirteen of which she'd managed to kill when they'd strayed too far from their camp over the last couple of days—to gaze at the rest of the forest.

It's too big. Too varied. The animals here are wrong.

It was still Earth. She was mostly sure of that. But it wasn't *her* Earth. Wasn't the Earth she'd known her entire life. The System had changed it in some fundamental way—in the same way that it had changed her, given her abilities she couldn't have possessed before.

As she stared out at the forest, something caught her ear. Something incongruous, and completely out of place. An engine... a motorcycle engine? She swivelled her head to the left, but the canopy was too dense for her to get a look at it. All she could do was hear it.

Is someone riding a dirt bike out here?

Seemed like a damned foolish thing to do, if she had any say in matters. That was one way to attract just about every hostile animal in the entire forest—and damn near everything was hostile now except the trees themselves, and she could still be wrong about that.

The elves' sharp ears perked, heads turning in the direction of the sound. Weapons appeared in hands. Bows, swords, and staves. Roughly two hundred elves stared off in the direction the noise was coming from.

The revving halted, becoming a low thrum, then a violent noise cut through the sudden quiet.

Pop-pop-pop-pop!

It sounded almost like metal punching through cardboard, but she knew what that was—

Gunfire.

Melissa wasn't much for company. She was happy to do everything herself, if need be. But she supposed someone handy with a gun wouldn't go astray in a situation like this.

She looked down at her own weapon. The bow she'd received when this had all started. Wondered if a gun would be a better choice, even after all the practise she'd had with this thing.

The elves began running. En masse. Toward the noise.

Melissa released a sigh. Whoever that idiot on the motorcycle with the gun was, they were liable to get themselves killed by a whole lot of elves. At least two hundred of them. And that portal was still standing open—it was what they'd built their camp around.

Melissa herself *wasn't* an idiot. She knew that she wouldn't be able to kill this many elves on her own—not all at once, at least—and save whoever that was out there. She'd chosen her moral faction, *fight for yourself*, for a reason, and that reason still held true.

It wasn't that she didn't care about others. She did. She simply wasn't going to put her own life on the line for them. How would her getting herself killed help this situation?

That would just be two people killed by elves in the middle of a massive forest.

No, she knew her actions weren't going to save anyone, but she also wasn't one to let an opportunity slip through her fingers.

Stealth.

Melissa pulled an arrow from her quiver, nocked, pulled back her string, and aimed at the elf farthest back from the pack. A woman that none of the others could see, for she was the last out of the camp. A woman that they wouldn't notice was gone until much later, what with all the excitement.

She loosed the arrow, using Precision Power Shot—a spell she'd ranked up all the way to eight. She'd gotten the cooldown to half a second.

Her aim was perfect. The arrow slammed straight into the back of the elf's head, killing her instantly.

You have defeated a Level 9 Elf!
You have gained 900 Mastery Points.
You have gained 900 Spirit Energy.

Melissa took out three more elves like this before she knew she'd need to get on the ground to pursue.

Stealth.

She slipped down the tree, from branch to branch, quiet as a falling leaf drifting to the ground, and silently set her feet upon the grass.

Then she was off. The noise the elves made bounding through the forest masked the sound of her own rushing feet.

You have defeated a Level 10 Elf!
You have gained 1,500 Mastery Points.
You have gained 1,500 Spirit Energy.

You have defeated a Level 11 Elf!
You have gained 1,650 Mastery Points.
You have gained 1,650 Spirit Energy.

The elves went down easy. Easy as they ever had. Even when they were a higher level than her. Her Stealth skill gave her a double-damage bonus to an opponent unaware of her presence, and she took full advantage of it. Her Precision Power Shot let her hit the target dead-on in the most vulnerable area she could sight.

Killing these bastards was easy as anything.

The sound of the motorcycle's revving grew louder and louder. Closer and closer. After taking out twenty of the elves, Melissa slipped back into obscurity, not wanting to be too close when they encountered whoever had that gun.

I might get hit by a stray bullet.

When she saw the elves slow, she scrambled up a tree, nimble, fast, and quiet, and got a good vantage point. Saw the motorcyclist —the dirt biker—put a foot down and skid to a halt twenty feet from the elves, who had their arrows trained on the man.

The dirt biker swore, shook his head, then dismounted his dirt bike and kicked the stand to keep the thing upright. He had one gun already drawn in his left—looked like a six-shooter revolver— and he drew another into his right once his hand was no longer on the bike's throttle. How he'd managed to clutch through the gears with that gun in his left, Melissa didn't know.

Two bandoleers of bullets were criss-crossed about his chest, and a cigarette jutted out of his mouth. He had a few days' worth of stubble creeping up his neck, across his chin and up his cheeks.

He spoke around the cigarette. "You fellas don't wanna be making any trouble now, do ya? There may be mor'a you than me, but I'll take a good share of you to your graves on my way out." He had his shooters pointed at two different elves, each with arrows pulled back.

Yeah, I don't like your odds, Shooter, Melissa thought. But she was eager to see what those guns could do.

The elves frowned, glanced at each other, and relaxed. To Melissa's surprise, they put their weapons down. The tension didn't escape their shoulders, but their bows were no longer drawn.

One of the elves—looked like the one in charge—stepped forward. His bow disappeared completely, something she'd seen the elves able to do, and he placed the arrow he'd had back in its quiver. He tilted his head to the side, opened his mouth, and began to talk.

In perfect English. More perfect than Shooter, if Melissa were being honest.

"We have claimed this forest in the name of the Kingdom of Er'al'ealia." The elf presented a hand, palm up, to the man. "Relinquish your weapons and your will to the might of our good and ancient King Vaegon, and know that you will live a good life as a slave. Refuse, and you shall instead forfeit your life."

Er'al'ealia? Vaegon? Where do they come up with these names?

Shooter raised a single eyebrow, quite prodigiously, all the way up to his receding hairline. "Slave? There ain't no slaves in 'Merica no more." He pointed one of his revolvers straight at the man's head. "I don't know what in all hell is going on with the world. Got pulled out of my house by some words in my face. Then, when I was thrown back, returned to my home, my damned farm was *gone*. Just had the house and the shed in the middle of a bloody forest. Family was gone too, but they're mostly a nuisance these days anyhow, since the kids learnt to talk and the wife got herself an ed-you-cation and learnt to talk back."

Shooter took a long drag of his cigarette, the ash just about longer than what was left of the cigarette itself. He stepped forward, blew the smoke out of the other side of his mouth straight into the elf's face.

Charmer, this one, Melissa thought, no longer all that worried for the man's life.

"But ya know what I found, in the forest? Some *peace*. Some *quiet*. Not to mention a whole lotta animals that suddenly wanted to kill me." He turned the gun in his left hand, the right still trained on the elf-leader's forehead. "But these still seemed to work on 'em all right. Knew I loaded up on ammo for a good damned reason. The System wanted me to have a sword. HAH. I'd like to see a sword do what *these* can." He tilted his head forward, cigarette still hanging from his mouth. "So why don't you and your white-haired, pointy-eared lot of fancy-looking bastards get the hell out of my forest so I can have me some of that peace and quiet again!"

He looked at the other elves. None of them looked the slightest bit worried.

"Go on, then, *git*! Or I'll blow a hole through the head of your boss-man."

Boss-man, the elf, stepped forward, until the gun touched his forehead. "Your primitive weapons will not work on us. You should have taken the sword that was granted to you by the Holiest Above. You should have adapted, foolish human. I will give you one more chance. Relinquish your will, or forfeit your life."

"Primitive?" Shooter said around his cigarette. "Says bows and arrows over here. Calling a *gun* primitive."

Melissa leant forward on the branch she was perched on.

"Guess there's no talkin' to you bastards."

Shooter pulled the trigger.

The elf's head did not snap back. The elf stayed rigid, standing exactly where he had been.

The gun, however, exploded. Shooter stumbled back. Two of his fingers were missing, blood pouring from the wounds.

The elf touched his forehead. There was a slight red mark where the bullet had contacted his skin, but it healed in a moment, and there was no blood. The elf drew his sword, stepped forward, and pushed the point straight through the man's chest as casually as one might punch a sewing needle through fabric.

The elf tilted his head to the side, peering down at the man who was now spluttering and coughing up blood, the cigarette having fallen from his mouth. "Perhaps you shall have peace and quiet in death."

Melissa's eyes widened, thinking about the implications of what she'd seen and heard.

Guns don't work against the elves.

That man's house was plucked and plopped into a forest, just like kangaroos and wolves were thrown in here together. The world's been all jumbled up, animals have turned into beasts, and invaders stepping through portals have come to kill and enslave us all.

And guns don't work.

The elf's words replayed in her mind.

You should have taken the sword that was granted to you by the Holiest Above. You should have adapted, foolish human.

Part of her had thought the military would be out there, some-where, responding to the threat these weird portals held. Sending in troops. Firing missiles at portals. *Something.*

But the haze that had been over her eyes was lifted. If guns didn't work on much more than weak animals-turned-beasts around here, then could she expect missiles to do much? And what if every member of the military had been scattered, torn from wherever they were, and placed somewhere else?

If there were kangaroos and wolves here, and farmhouses plucked from one place and put in another, could the army bases have been split in half? Would the whole world need to be re-mapped?

Suddenly what had happened to the entire world had been put into stark perspective for Melissa. She was still fighting for herself, fighting for her sanctuary.

But now, she hoped, she wasn't the only one who was willing to adapt. Willing to use the weapons the System handed them.

Otherwise she was rather sure humanity was doomed.

Chapter 64
These Skills Can't Be Bought

As no insight came to Xavier about his burgeoning soul-taking tendencies, when his Spirit Energy was fully restored, he focused on the second thing he'd learnt about the strange energy.

During his meditation the previous day, he'd unlocked an insight about Spirit Energy that had gotten him curious. When he'd first created a Lesser Spirit Coin, he'd felt the energy move through his body like blood moved through veins.

Inherently, he'd known there was something... *important* about that, but he hadn't realised it at the time, too focused on his money-making discovery.

But as time passed, and he meditated longer on the thought-seedling, it had come to him.

Spirit Energy could be controlled.

In a way, he'd already known that. He had a spell that could infuse Spirit Energy into his weapons and armour. Spirit Infusion could turn that energy into either offensive or defensive Spirit Energy.

Using that spell was one of the first things Xavier had done after he'd realised they would be stuck not moving toward the next floor for ninety damned hours.

But the very first time he'd used the spell he'd unlocked its Upgrade Quest. One thing about Spirit Infusion he didn't like was the fact that it *couldn't* be generalised in. He needed to choose a path and stick to it.

It wasn't that Xavier was indecisive. He'd made harder decisions than which path of Spirit Infusion to follow. It was simply that he wanted to test the spell out in both iterations before he chose which way to move forward with it.

His instinct was to move toward offensive Spirit Infusion, because—as far as he could tell—that would be what would help him the most in the Tower of Champions.

More destructive power could only be a good thing if he wanted to clear the floors even faster.

But no, he wouldn't make that decision until he tested the spell. And though he could have technically tested the spell against one of the members of his party, he was worried using even a small amount of offensive Spirit Energy would just kill one of them, considering the discrepancy in their levels of power.

He could have tested defensive Spirit Energy, infusing it into his robes and letting the others strike him, but he didn't think they were strong enough to harm him in the first place.

Besides, he didn't feel comfortable sparring any of them at all, especially not when he *ached* to harvest his first soul. And his second.

And his millionth.

Xavier shut his eyes, quietening that part of him, pushing those thoughts back down into the dark pit inside of him, and moved forward with his practise.

His insight into Spirit Energy.

Thus far, he hadn't made any progress with his insight. It told him Spirit Energy could be controlled... It didn't tell him *how* to control it. But it felt like the information was there, hovering right in front of him, ready to be taken, but completely invisible to his eye.

Xavier fell back into a deep meditation. His health and Spirit Energy were full, so this meditation session was simply to utilise its heightened ability for him to *focus*.

He turned his focus on himself. Onto the Spirit Energy he could feel within him. Whenever he cast a spell, he could feel that energy being torn from him and used. When he cast Spiritual Trifecta, he could feel that energy envelope him in its power. And when he created Lesser Spirit Coins, he felt it flow through him.

But where did it originate?

Xavier sat there for three hours, not moving from his spot. There was a part of him that felt as though what he was doing was useless. His Meditation skill wasn't ranking up, as even though he was using the skill to focus, it only appeared to climb in the ranks when he used it to regain Spirit Energy—he imagined the same thing would be true when he used it to regain health as well.

But simply meditating did nothing for him except increase his chance of gaining an insight, and help him focus more deeply.

Xavier wasn't one for inaction. Especially not since making it here in the tower. He practically radiated with nervous energy.

I should be creating more Lesser Spirit Coins.

He was saving up as many as he could. When he returned to the Staging Room to move to the fourth floor, he would be purchasing armour.

I should be practising with my scythe-staff, Soultaker.

He'd spent a fair few hours in the Staging Room over the past two days practising with the staff already, but he hadn't found that he was gaining much of anything swinging it about by himself, going through the different strikes.

Xavier had of course wanted to rank up his Scythe-Staff Mastery skill to two, thinking it shouldn't be too difficult, but over the hours of practise he'd performed, he still hadn't managed it. He'd wondered if it was because he didn't have an opponent to fight, then he'd worried he was spending too much time figuring that out.

He always worried about wasting time.

That's why, at least a hundred times in those three hours that Xavier sat there, trying to control his Spirit Energy and understand it more, he almost gave up and stopped.

But something kept him rooted to the spot. Maybe it was his stubborn streak. Maybe it was that insight he had. Or some sort of intuition.

Whatever it was, it paid off.

Because he felt *something*. Like a knot of power inside of him. Somewhere in his gut. It was different to the pit—the one that begged to be filled. That begged him to harvest souls.

This knot of power felt like it had always been buried deep within him—perhaps in his own soul, he didn't know—and had simply been awaiting his discovery of it.

He didn't have a name for whatever it was that he had found, but it was the source of his Spirit Energy. What held it. What expanded, whenever he gained a level or added another point into his Spirit attribute.

And after three hours of intense focus, he had finally been able to sense it for the first time. The moment he did, a series of notifications popped into his vision.

You have gained +10 Spirit!

You have discovered your Spirit Core.

Skill Quest Unlocked: Aura-Control
To unlock Aura-Control, successfully contain
the power of your aura with your will 10 times.
Progress: 0/10

Skill Quest Unlocked: Core Strength
To unlock Core Strength, successfully cycle
100,000 points of Spirit Energy through your
core.

Progress: 0/100,000

Skill Quest Unlocked: Cultivate Energy
To unlock Cultivate Energy, successfully draw
10,000 points of Celestial Energy into your
Spirit Core, turning it into Spirit Energy.
Progress: 0/10,000

Xavier's eyes widened, staring at the three different Skill Quests he'd just unlocked.

I gained 10 Spirit? For what? Discovering my Spirit Core?

He'd never heard of such a thing. Siobhan had certainly never mentioned it being written about within the Tower of Champions manual, nor had it been mentioned in any notification he'd ever gotten—he was sure he would have remembered that.

This... this is the insight I had while meditating. This is what it wanted me to discover. My Spirit Core. Like a heart holds and pumps blood, it holds and pumps Spirit Energy.

Though Xavier didn't have any skill points left over, he opened up the skill menu and searched through all of the different headings and subheadings, even running a search for the titles of each of the skills.

He couldn't find any of the three skills he'd just gained Skill Quests for *anywhere* in the skill menu.

These skills can't be bought.

This, he imagined, was another thing that Denizens from other worlds knew about that those from his newly integrated world didn't. At first glance, he didn't understand the implications of any of it, but he knew his Spirit Core was highly important.

He looked at the title of the first skill. *Aura Control.* He frowned. Aura.

When he'd first chosen his epic class, he'd been able to see an aura around those in his party. He'd noticed it immediately, but hadn't known what it *meant*. He'd thought it might have something to do with his Soul Harvest spell—like perhaps it was their very souls that he was seeing.

Stepping into the tavern after having been locked out of the Tower of Champions' next floor, Xavier had noticed he could see other people's auras as well. Every single Champion in the room gave off a faint glow, but the power he felt from them was *lesser* than the power that came from his own party.

As all of them had been lower level, and no doubt lacked titles, that had made sense.

When he'd seen Sam, standing behind the bar, the man had been staring at him, and something had struck Xavier as odd about the man—he didn't have an aura at all. No power emanated from the bartender, yet he was an established Denizen of the System.

Aura Control. Sam was controlling his aura—containing the power of his aura—with his will.

Xavier looked down at himself. He knew *he* emanated an aura, as well. One far stronger than that of the other members of his party. But it wasn't something that they could see.

Sam can see it, though, can't he? If he can control his own, hiding his power from prying eyes, he can definitely see mine. Maybe that's why he's been looking at me differently. And how he knew I'd cleared more floors than the other Champions, reaching the first Milestone.

He saw my power just by looking at me.

Not being able to control his own aura? That could very well make Xavier—and those he was with—a target. If the invaders that wanted to enslave or kill everyone back on Earth saw him, they'd know his strength right away, and know they needed to take him out.

Xavier checked the timer he'd found he could summon, which told him how long he was still locked out of the tower for.

The Tower of Champions will be locked to you for 90 hours. You have 37 hours and 3 minutes remaining.

Xavier released a breath.

A day and a half. A day and a half until I can get back in there.

And now, he knew exactly what he was going to do in that time —other than keep making more Lesser Spirit Coins.

He was going to unlock as many of these three skills as he could.

Chapter 65
Absolutely Impossible

Xavier felt like the universe wanted to open up to him. Like there was so much still left to learn. To discover.

And he didn't know how to access *any* of it.

Ten hours had passed since he'd first discovered his Spirit Core. Gaining those 10 points in Spirit and discovering there were three skills for him to learn had lit a fire underneath him.

But he felt like he was a child trying to understand the heart and the human body's circulatory system by staring at a crude drawing of it. Sure, it got the point in a rudimentary way, but it lacked any deep understanding of what was actually going on.

He could feel his Spirit Core. Knew it was there. He could even feel, when he concentrated hard enough, his Spirit Energy moving around his body. He could see and feel his aura emanating from him, too, but controlling that was like trying to grab smoke with his bare hands.

It just kept slipping through his damned fingers.

Once again, Xavier felt like he was doing nothing more than wasting time. But he'd already gained ten Spirit points by going down this path, and three shiny new Skill Quests, not to mention the knowledge that he had inside himself something called a Spirit Core.

So he persisted. Trying to wheedle out any bit of understanding from the three different Skill Quests.

Aura Control *seemed* straightforward, but again, actually controlling his aura and somehow containing it? That was proving to be absolutely impossible.

And the quest wanted him to do it ten times. *Managing it even once would be a miracle at this point.*

The second Skill Quest, for Core Strength, again sounded reasonable. It wanted him to cycle Spirit Energy through his core. One hundred thousand points of it.

But how exactly did he *do* that?

The way he kept seeing it... it was one thing to understand that you had a heart and it pumped blood through your veins, another thing completely to actively *control* how that blood flowed.

Yes, he had a Spirit Core. Yes, he had Spirit Energy. But what in the world—in the Greater Universe—was he supposed to do to *control* it? Other than cast spells and use Spirit Infusion, he simply didn't see how it was *possible*.

The last of the Skill Quests, Cultivate Energy, was the most maddening of all. The skill wished him to draw ten thousand points of something called Celestial Energy into his Spirit Core.

But Xavier had no clue what Celestial Energy was. It had the feeling of something that might come from the sky, given its name, but that's about as far as he'd gotten with it. He'd tried to sense "energy" around him, wondering if it was just hovering out there in the air somewhere. But if it was, his senses weren't acute enough to feel it.

Xavier looked at the timer again.

The Tower of Champions will be locked to you for 90 hours. You have 26 hours and 42 minutes remaining.

Damnit!

Had he really spent ten hours like this? Not achieving a

damned thing? He sighed and stood up, stretching out his back. Despite the fact that he'd been sitting down, cross-legged on the floor of his room for half a day, he didn't actually feel sore.

A little sluggish, maybe, but he brushed away the cobwebs with a single stretch, then headed down to the tavern.

Maybe I can wheedle some information out of that barkeep, now that I know what questions to ask.

Xavier headed down the spiral staircase that led to the ground floor of the tower. He saw a couple of Champions in the hallway, though it was hard to tell if any of them were from his cohort.

The hallway had thousands of different doors and stretched just about as far as he could see. Every one of those rooms was for another Champion from Earth. But once they got down to the tavern and opened the door, they stepped into a different instance. One only for their cohort.

And there were countless sets of stairs leading down. Just as there were countless sets of stairs leading up, toward the Staging Room—another instance that no doubt had infinite copies of itself, just like the very floors of the Tower of Champions itself.

Xavier had tried heading down a different set of stairs, and stepping through the doors of the tavern, to see if he might end up in a different instance. But of course, that hadn't worked. He'd just ended up in the same place he always did. It was probably the same strange magic that seemed to let him know exactly which room was his own.

Apparently the others—Howard, Siobhan, and Justin—had tried to talk to Champions from outside their cohort in the hall-ways, but they... hadn't been able to. They could see each other, but they couldn't *hear* each other.

The System clearly didn't want them communicating with others outside of their cohort.

Those aren't the people I want to talk to, anyway.

Candles flickered atop tables. A fire roared in the hearth. The tavern was as empty as it had been the first time Xavier had walked into it. He glanced around the place. He had to admit, he loved the atmosphere of the tavern. It had that old, classic, medieval feel that he enjoyed from all the epic fantasies he'd read. Like he was stepping into the Prancing Pony in Middle Earth, or the Waystone Inn in Temerant.

He could imagine taking a seat in one of the booths and pulling out a doorstopper fantasy book like *The Wheel of Time*, nursing a drink as he flipped from one page to the next, or popping out his laptop and getting some good writing done.

My laptop broke when I was fighting the goblins. Even if it hadn't been smashed, the battery would be long dead by now. And even if I did write something... who would read it?

He felt a pang of sadness, a slight mourning for his old life. But he shoved that away. Things were different now. He was different now. The thoughts that had slipped into his mind were remnants of a life he no longer lived.

A life he wasn't sure he'd return to even if he could.

Sam raised an eyebrow when he saw him walk over to the bar. "Still trapped here, I see. What have you got, another day?" The man grabbed a glass and a bottle of whiskey, then gave a questioning tilt of the head.

"Yeah, another day." Xavier sighed at the bottle. "Might as well." He had plenty of Spirit Energy. So instead of using Lesser Spirit Coins from his Storage Ring, he simply created some and deposited the difference.

Sam smiled and shook his head. "You're probably wondering how our economic system works when everyone can just 'make' money."

Xavier had wondered about that. But it wasn't really on his mind right now. Besides, he knew the amount of money he could "make" was nothing compared with those of a higher advancement level.

Grand Spirit Coins are worth so, so much more than these little things...

He sat on a stool and sipped the whiskey. "I have questions."

Sam nodded knowingly. "Must be desperate if you're coming to me. There's only so—"

"So much you can tell me, yes. I know. But..." Xavier took another sip. "I feel like we've been thrown into this mess without... without being given *anything* that will help us get through it," he said, thinking, *except for my titles.* Feeling like he'd wasted so much time as it is, Xavier didn't beat around the bush. "What can you tell me about Spirit Cores?"

That seemed to get Sam's attention. He'd been idly polishing a glass when the words had slipped from Xavier's mouth. He placed the glass down, leant heavily on the bar, and looked into Xavier's eyes. "And how in the Greater Universe do you know about Spirit Cores at Level 10?"

Xavier smiled. Even if he didn't get anything out of Sam, that surprise in the man's voice was worth it. Part of him had been worried that Denizens from established worlds were able to find their Spirit Cores on day one of being integrated.

"I discovered it today. Doing so earned me 10 Spirit points and three Skill Quests." Xavier held his whiskey glass in both hands, looking down at the dark liquid, figuring there was no point in lying to the man. "The first skill is something you clearly already know how to do."

"Aura Control." Sam chuckled. "Was wondering if you'd figure that one out." He looked him up and down. "Though clearly you haven't gotten a handle on it yourself."

Xavier let out a long sigh. "No. I haven't." He stared the man in the eye. *I'm not able to scan him. I can't see his aura, and all Denizens have auras. Level 10s don't usually have access to their Spirit Cores, and he clearly has Aura Control, so clearly has access to his own core.* "What level are you?"

Sam gave a knowing smile. "Not something I can say, I'm afraid."

"Well, what *can* you tell me, then?" Xavier ran a hand through his hair. "Aura Control. Core Strength. Cultivate Energy. I haven't figured out *any* of it."

Sam raised his chin. He gave Xavier a deep, appraising look. One so heavy that it made him shift on his stool. "Well..." He glanced up at the ceiling. The look was somewhat familiar. It reminded Xavier of someone checking if their boss was nearby before doing something they probably shouldn't. "There are a *few* things I can say."

Chapter 66
Candle Flames Don't Produce Smoke

Xavier sat at the edge of his stool, staring at Sam—Samericalian—the barkeep at the bottom of the Tower of Champions, wondering if he would finally get some information about the Spirit Core he'd just discovered inside himself.

The barkeep waved a hand in a circle. "The System prevents me from telling Champions things they haven't already discovered, or other things, like what I told you about being forced to clear a floor." He sighed. "I'm restricted by so much, sometimes it's difficult to know what I can say until I say it."

The man pointed at Xavier's chest. "But as you've already learnt you have a Spirit Core, and the names of those three skills." He shrugged, gave a conspiratorial smile. "Why don't we just see what I can get away with?"

A part of Xavier wanted to ask why the man might even *want* to help him, but he didn't want to make Sam second guess what he was about to do. He remained quiet.

"First, Aura Control." Sam closed his eyes and let out a long breath. Power suddenly rippled off him in waves. A power like nothing that Xavier had ever felt.

The man's aura. Xavier could see it. Feel it. God, if the tavern wasn't a self-contained instance, he'd imagine he would be able to feel it from all the way in his room.

The aura felt so much different to the other auras Xavier had sensed. He could feel his own aura, which was perhaps ten times as strong as the aura of those in his party. The auras of the other Level 4 Champions he'd seen around the tavern? Theirs were incredibly weak.

But this... was like Xavier had waded out into the surf during a thunderstorm. The man's aura was applying a physical pressure on him. One that wanted to push him away. Push him *down*.

And it was even... painful. Physically and mentally.

Xavier didn't move from his seat, however. Even though a small part of him screamed that he should run, he didn't let it take control.

Samericalian was far more powerful than Xavier. Maybe even a higher grade. But he wasn't a threat. He wasn't there to harm Xavier. And Xavier wasn't about to let what he'd felt from that aura appear on his face.

Sam opened one eye, as though he were peeking out at Xavier. A slight smirk appeared on his face as he saw that Xavier hadn't moved. Then, as suddenly as the power had been released, it withdrew until he couldn't feel a speck of aura coming from the man once more.

The barkeep rolled his head from one side to the other with an audible crack. Then he grabbed a glass from underneath the bar and poured himself some whiskey. "Haven't let my aura flow in a while." He sipped the whiskey. Swallowed. Then breathed deeply from his nose. "Felt good."

Xavier tilted his chin up. "You're E Grade, aren't you?"

Sam winked. "I can't answer that."

He took the wink as confirmation. "When can I get to E Grade? How do I get there? What does getting there *mean*?"

"Can't answer that either."

Xavier wanted to slam his fist on the bar. He downed the rest of the whiskey. Slammed the glass on the bar instead, holding back his strength so as not to break it. "Well, go on then, what *can* you say?"

"What you just felt is me letting my aura flow free at"—he wiggled his hand—"about a quarter power."

Xavier blinked. Tried not to let his feelings show. "That was a quarter?"

Sam smiled. "Indeed." He chuckled and waved about the tavern. "You know, if I did that with any of the other Champions from your cohort around, they probably would have fallen unconscious. You didn't even move from your seat. Quite impressive. For a Level 10."

The way he said that—the way he looked at Xavier—he could tell the man had figured a few things out about him.

He would know the only way I'd be strong enough to have cleared three floors that fast is if I had powerful titles.

"I thought the others wouldn't be able to see your aura? My party members can't see mine. Yet they would fall unconscious?"

"They can't yet see the aura, no." Sam frowned. "Not until they gain Aura Sight with their first class. But they *can* sense it, even if they don't realise it. Those of a lower power level than your own, and those who aren't even integrated yet, they'll feel an... urge to listen to you. An urge to follow you. Not a compulsion, mind. Nothing to do with mind control. Just that they'd sense, in a way, that power that emanates from you."

Xavier let that thought swirl around in his mind for a moment. He supposed that made sense. The others had listened to him even after they'd seen his strength. "If your aura could make someone unconscious... what could an A Grade's aura do?"

Sam shook his head, the tiniest flash of fear in his eyes. "Not my business to talk about. Even if I could."

Xavier pulled back, sensing he'd asked a question too far. He brought them back to the topic at hand—the reason he'd come down here in the first place for—though he had to say he was interested in *everything* the man had to say.

He wondered about the implications of having a powerful aura and simply... letting it loose against weaker enemies. Would he one day be powerful enough to kill a low-level beast without even doing *anything*?

It's not low-level beasts I need to worry about killing.

"So, how do you do it?" Xavier asked. "How did you control your aura? I've tried to control mine, but it's like grasping at tendrils of smoke."

Sam inclined his head. "Let's see how much I can say. Maybe if I speak in metaphors..." he muttered. He tapped his fingers on the bar. Then clicked his fingers as though he had an idea. "All right." He raised his left hand. A stick appeared gripped inside it.

Summoned from his Storage Ring?

Sam waved the stick, and suddenly it was alight at one end, a whisp of smoke rising from it, all the way to the tavern's rafters. "You said trying to control your aura was like grasping at smoke."

The man, holding the stick with his left, grasped at the tendrils of smoke above the flame with his right. They flowed over his palm, through his fingers. He closed his fist, but could hold nothing.

"It's an apt comparison." He brought the stick closer to himself. "You can't grasp it. No matter how strong you are, brute strength isn't the thing you need. You need to think differently about it."

The man took a deep, mouth-wide breath, drawing the smoke in. He closed his mouth, held the smoke in like someone taking a pull from a pipe, then released the breath, the smoke wisping out with it.

Sam curled his hand in a fist and put it on his chest. "Think of your Spirit Core as though it were a fire. The power inside it burns, and your aura is like smoke, wafting from you in waves. The stronger the core, the stronger the smoke it can produce. You *can* draw your aura back inside yourself, like breathing in smoke, but it won't be enough. You aren't trying to grasp your aura and pull it into you. Not for the first rank of Aura Control."

Xavier frowned, looked down at the flame. "I can't bring the smoke back, but..." He grasped the flames, closed his fist around them—they weren't strong enough to burn his hardened skin. The flames ceased, the last wisps of smoke fluttering away. "I can stop the fire from burning." He shook his head, looked down at his stomach, put a hand to it. "But I don't want the power in my core to stop burning."

Sam looked as though he were about to speak, but Xavier raised a finger.

Xavier stood from his stool, stepped over to one of the tavern's tables, then whisked a burning candle away from it and placed it on the bar. "Candle flames don't produce smoke." He tilted his head to the side. "Not much, anyway." He ran his fingers through the flame, playing with it. "I remember staring at a candle on my bedside. The power was out, and I was reading a book late at night." He chuckled. "Had a bit of a romantic feel about it, even if it did strain my eyes. When I finished the book, I just stared at the flame for a while, unable to sleep because the ending was so damned good.

"After a while, I noticed no smoke rising from the flame. I suppose I always knew that." He shook his head. "But I didn't know *why*. That thought stuck in my head for a while, until I ended up looking it up." He ran his fingers through the flame again. The heat felt sweet on his skin.

"When a candle is lit, some of the wax melts, turning to liquid. It moves up the wick like water spreads through thin paper. The wax combusts at the tip of the wick, creating more heat, and the oxygen and wax diffuse at the same rate they are consumed."

Even as he spoke, Xavier was surprised he remembered the details of this so clearly. Something he'd looked up on his phone and read only once a few years ago. He supposed he had his stats to thank for that.

"So, when fire burns efficiently, little to no smoke rises from the flame. Candles, unlike a fire in a hearth, were designed with that in mind. Or maybe we just got lucky there." He frowned. "It's about balance. About... efficiently controlling the aura within me?"

Sam's lips twitched at the sides in a smile. "Yes, it's about balance."

Xavier sat on the stool once more and shut his eyes. He felt his Spirit Core within him. That well of energy. Felt the aura around him. The inherent connection between the two. And realised that yes, he had been looking at this all wrong.

He'd been trying to pull his aura back inside of him, but the aura that was around him... was just smoke.

Xavier focused on his core with every ounce of his mental energy, falling into a meditative state. He felt his core more clearly than he ever had. Felt the power roiling within it. Burning. Aching to be free, like he ached to keep progressing in the tower.

He didn't know how long passed with him sitting there, focused on his Spirit Core, on the energies within, but something clicked within his mind when he'd thought of the candle flame, the balance, the smoke.

His Spirit Core was burning fuel at a constant rate. *Spirit Energy. That's the fuel.* Over and over and over. Bit by bit. But his Spirit Energy recovered faster than his core could burn it without casting a spell.

It must always be that way. Even with only 5 points in Spirit, a Denizen would have enough Spirit Energy recovery to constantly be burning Spirit Energy, even if to a minute degree—like 1 point per minute—and that's why the other Champions felt so weak. Their weak Spirit Cores didn't have as much fuel to burn.

And mine is burning like a wildfire...

Xavier took a deep breath, further narrowing his focus.

He could feel it burning now. Feel the Spirit Energy constantly churning through him. Like gas keeping an engine running.

Now, if I just...

Suddenly, his Spirit Energy began to drop. Ten points per second, then one hundred points per second, until it was dropping at a rate of over one thousand points per second.

Available Spirit Energy: 15,438/21,700

His aura flared. Pushing outward in a massive wave, encompassing the entire tavern.

Available Spirit Energy: 10,032/21,700

"Stop!" Sam said. "You'll burn through everything in your core!"

Available Spirit Energy: 5,829/21,700

Xavier tried to clamp down on his core. He'd never felt so *powerful*! But that power, it was leaving him by the second. Draining away from him even as it flared.

The flames are burning the fuel faster than I can recover it. What happens when the fuel is all gone?

Xavier tried to stop it. Focused, hard as he could.

Available Spirit Energy: 432/21,700

But there wasn't anything he could do.

Chapter 67
System-Damned Fool

Xavier snapped his eyes open. He was lying on the floor of the tavern, a stool overturned beside him, a candle tipped over, its wax leaking onto the floor though the flame had blown out.

Sam stood above him, a hand running through his hair, shaking his head. The barkeep sighed. Turned away from Xavier without bothering to help him up, muttering to himself, "System-damned fool children from baby worlds trying to burn through their cores."

Xavier tried to push himself up. He felt... weak. Tired. Like he hadn't slept in a month. Like someone had drained all his blood. His limbs had pins and needles. Raising his arm felt like raising a wet noodle. He tried to make it to his feet, but he just didn't have it in him.

How could he not stand, with how damned strong he'd become?

Available Spirit Energy: 0/21,700

What? Is that why I feel like this? So damned weak?

He thought... thought he'd experienced having no Spirit Energy before. When he'd been facing the goblins. The first time he'd used his spells. It hadn't felt like this. Far from it.

"Why am I weak?" His words came out mumbled, almost like he was drunk. "My Spirit Energy... isn't recovering?"

"Because you're a System-damned fool, that's why." Sam came back around the counter with, of all things, a bar of chocolate. "Eat this."

"How do you even have this?"

"Same way I have whiskey from your planet. Now do as you're told." Sam thrust the chocolate into Xavier's hand.

Xavier struggled just to get the food to his mouth. He couldn't feel it in his hand. After taking a bite, he let out a contented sigh. The weakness inside of him disappeared, like it had never been there to begin with, and he was filled with a sudden warmth. He made it to his feet, not even a little unsteady, and took another bite of the chocolate. "I feel like I've just seen a Dementor," he muttered.

"What?" Sam said, sounding annoyed. The man had made it back around the bar again and was leaning on the counter, a tired look on his face.

"Never mind." Xavier looked at his Spirit Energy. There was a little bit in there now, and... yes, it was recovering on its own, after eating had kickstarted the process. Xavier sat back on the stool, finished eating his chocolate bar. "I still don't understand what happened."

"You burned through your core—*that's* what happened."

"But..." Xavier frowned. "I've used all of my Spirit Energy before. That... never happened."

"You think that number you can see in your vision accurately reflects the *exact* amount of energy in your core at all times? You don't think there might be a minuscule amount that always remains in there to keep the lights on—a percentage of a single point so small it isn't reflected in your stats?"

Xavier sighed. "No. I suppose I never thought of it like that."

"Of course you didn't, because you're—"

"A System-damned fool from a baby world?"

"—someone who doesn't know any better." Sam ran a hand

down his face. "Maybe this was a bad idea." His tone turned serious. His stare becoming blank. "Maybe I'm not supposed to talk to you about these things for a reason."

Xavier stood. "But—"

"But nothing," Sam said. "You're pushing too hard at this. And if you push too hard at something it's liable to break. I thought you were... that you could be..." He shook his head. "If I hadn't been here, if you hadn't done something to get your Spirit Energy back, your core would have reached for the next best thing, and burned through that instead."

"My... my health?"

"Yes, your health. You don't understand how"—he waved a hand—"any of this works. And that isn't your fault, but it is your responsibility." He grabbed the bottle of whiskey. "Now, you're welcome to have another drink, order some food—which would be wise, given your current condition. But otherwise... we shouldn't talk for a good while." He stared hard at Xavier. "What'll it be?"

Xavier put his head down. Part of him felt like he should be angry with the man, but he found no anger within him. Though his core was quickly recovering Spirit Energy, *he* was still recovering from what had just happened too.

From what he'd essentially done to himself.

He inclined his head. "Thank you for what you told me." Xavier walked out of the tavern without glancing back at the man behind the bar. He headed straight for the Staging Room.

It was still a good while until he could go to the next floor of the Tower of Champions, but he figured if he were going to find the other members of his party anywhere, it would be there.

And if the barkeep wasn't going to help him break through and learn this skill, then he'd have to get help from somewhere else.

"So that's what you've been doing locked up in your room for so long," Siobhan said.

Xavier frowned at the woman. "What did you think I'd been doing?"

Siobhan smirked and shook her head.

They were sitting around their loot boxes in the Staging Room. When he'd walked in, he'd found Siobhan practising her elemental spells, Justin sprinting back and forth, touching opposite walls as he went, and Howard lifting the large stone balls on one side of the room.

They've been training almost nonstop. They may not be near as strong as me, but they aren't slowing down. In that moment he'd felt proud of his party, glad they hadn't taken these few days as an excuse to be lazy and slack off.

They'd all gathered around him, and he'd told them about the Spirit Core, the ten points in Spirit he'd gained, and the three Skill Quests.

"Maybe you should heed the man's warning," Siobhan said, her tone turning serious. "He clearly knows what he's talking about."

"But can we trust him?" Justin asked. "He isn't from Earth. He's part of the System."

"We're all part of the System now," Siobhan put in.

"Well, sure, but..." Justin shook his head. "We're also all from Earth, and all want the same thing." He looked Xavier in the eye. "What does Sam want?"

Xavier thought about that for a moment. "If he wanted me dead, he wouldn't have helped me off the floor."

"Maybe. Or maybe Justin's right. Could be the man's giving you just enough rope to hang yourself with," Howard said.

Siobhan sighed. "That's a lovely way to put it."

Howard shrugged. "Nothing lovely about everything that's happening."

"So, what? You're thinking he's telling me just enough that I do something stupid, get myself in danger, and he's not liable for it because I wasn't in his bar when it happened?" Xavier asked.

"Something tells me the System would be mighty disappointed

if a Champion dropped dead in there when he could've prevented it," Howard said.

"The System? The System doesn't care about our lives at all," Xavier said. "I... don't know how much I trust the man." He remembered the barkeep stumbling over a few words, leaving the rest unsaid.

I thought you were... that you could be...

What did he think Xavier could be?

"But he didn't *feel* like he was lying to me with that warning. That he was trying to set me up to do it by myself. He looked... genuinely concerned." Xavier set his jaw. "That doesn't mean he knows what I'm capable of. I'm not going to give up on something just because it could be a little bit dangerous."

"Yeah." Siobhan chuckled. "We've learnt that about you already."

Xavier's mind was running a mile a minute. Once again, he felt like what he was learning was just a drop in the ocean that was the Greater Universe, but he ached to learn *more*.

He'd been doing a lot of thinking about what had happened to him, discovering his Spirit Core. Sam had been surprised to hear that he'd done it at Level 10, which meant it shouldn't be something someone was capable of doing until they were a *much* higher level.

And with the sheer number of stats he'd gotten from titles?

Xavier paused in the middle of their conversation, doing a few quick mental calculations as he fell into Meditation. Assuming someone began with the same number of stats at Level 1 as he did —34—and gained 8 per level until Level 10, then chose a common class and gained 13 per level... not accounting for titles, he had the stats of someone over Level 60.

So, not as high as I'd originally thought, but still damned high.

Now, his Spirit attribute was one of his highest stats, probably higher than most. But let's say someone needed over 190 points in Spirit—which was about how much he had when he'd discovered his Spirit Core—to make the discovery.

Maybe they need 1 80? That sounds like a better number...

He knew this was all just a wild guess, but all he had to go on right now were wild guesses.

If this all tracks, most Denizens probably don't discover their core until somewhere between Levels 50 and 75.

Xavier, still meditating, was struck with an insight. Something that felt *right* and *true*.

Sam's words replayed in his mind: *You don't understand how any of this works. And that isn't your fault, but it is your responsibility.*

Sam was right about that—it was *his* responsibility to understand. To *learn*.

"I think... I think I need to unlock these skills, at least before we clear the tenth floor. Before we're returned to Earth. Because I've got a feeling that's where it will really matter."

He looked over at the door to the Tower of Champions. The one that had been locked to them for far too long. Ached to walk over there. Rip the door open. To get to the next floor.

But he was glad there was still a little time, because that insight he'd gained? It told him something about what learning those skills and mastering the use of his Spirit Core would do.

It told him that it would be his first step on his journey to becoming E Grade.

Chapter 68
The Weight of the World

FOR THE NEXT DAY, BEFORE THE TOWER OF CHAMPIONS opened its floors to them once more, all Xavier did was meditate, create Lesser Spirit Coins, and focus on unlocking Aura Control.

He figured it would be too much to focus on all three Skill Quests at once, and was aiming to unlock one at a time while he grew his understanding of his Spirit Core, auras, and Spirit Energy in general.

In the hours that he practised all of this, he managed to up his Meditation skill all the way to Rank 10. He also created enough Lesser Spirit Coins to bring his total to over ninety-four thousand.

He'd been aiming for one hundred thousand, but as his focus was split, he took that as a win.

Xavier sat in the Staging Room, the others training around him and keeping an eye on him whenever he tried to control his aura. A part of him wondered why he hadn't been meditating here the whole time. He could have blamed it on the fact that the others would be a distraction, lessening his ability to concentrate and develop insights through meditation.

But when he was deep in meditation? It felt like he was the only one in the room.

I hid in my room because I like quiet and privacy and being on my own, he told himself.

But, as the hours passed, he couldn't help but find some comfort in the fact that others were in the room with him. He was glad they were working on their own things and not trying to talk to him the entire time, but their general presence was somehow... soothing.

He shook those thoughts away whenever they sprang up, as they weren't helping him reach his current goals, and pushed forward in what he needed to do.

Six more times, Xavier had tried to contain his aura within his Spirit Core and accidentally burned through his Spirit Energy. The feeling of weakness didn't lessen. If anything, it felt worse.

The first time it had happened, Howard, Siobhan, and Justin had huddled around him. Siobhan tilted his head up, getting him to eat something right away. The other members of his party remained wary after that, constantly glancing at him, making sure he hadn't suddenly collapsed onto the floor.

But on the fourth try, even though he'd accidentally sped up his Spirit Core's burning of his Spirit Energy, he'd actually managed to *stop* it.

The others had been looking at him. Staring at him with worry. And though they couldn't yet see his aura, it was clear that they could, to some degree, *feel* it. His aura wasn't as strong as Samericalian's, but when he flared it, the effects on the others were clearly visible.

Later, they told him that their heads would ache when his aura flared. Not migraine-level headaches, but the stinging, throbbing kind that shook your focus.

It made him wonder what would happen to someone with less Willpower—he imagined Willpower was the mental and magical defence one needed to successfully withstand another's aura, though Spirit could have something to do with it too—like one of the Level 4s that had been in the tavern on the day they'd returned after clearing the third floor.

Would my aura, when flaring, be strong enough to give them a migraine? Make their noses bleed?

Once he'd learnt how to spot the uncontrolled burning of his Spirit Energy, he felt as though he was on the right track. So far, he could speed up the burning, or bring it back to "normal" levels, but he couldn't yet slow it down and bring it into a perfect balance—a balance that would not make his Spirit Core smoke and produce aura.

After the sixth time of causing his Spirit Core to burn through his Spirit Energy faster accidentally, he learnt how to do it *on purpose*. It made him wonder what kind of utility that might have, being able to flare his aura.

The power that swept from Sam back in the tavern when he released his aura... Even if it wasn't strong enough to hurt me, I felt a pressure wanting to push me down. I felt an ounce of the man's power.

He could certainly see how one could use their aura to intimidate others.

Would someone at, say, D Grade be able to kill someone at F Grade with their aura alone?

Unfortunately, though he felt he was gaining some control, flaring his aura wasn't a necessary requirement for finishing Aura Control's Skill Quest.

When only an hour remained before the Tower of Champions let them move to the next floor, Xavier was starting to grow impatient. Or, well, *more* impatient. He was beginning to doubt himself. Though he'd managed to stop his core from burning through, he didn't feel any closer to his *actual* goal.

Skill Quest: Aura Control
To unlock Aura Control, successfully contain the power of your aura with your will 10 times.
Progress: 0/10

Still zero progress.

Xavier sighed, stood and stretched. He wanted to take out Soultaker and kill something. No. Not just kill something. He wanted to *reap*. He wanted to finally harvest his first soul.

Maybe I should just look through the System Shop. Find some armour. Get ready for the next level.

He paced back and forth up the Staging Room. The others glanced over at him. Siobhan was practising her Summon spell, bringing Howard and Justin toward her. She was getting so good she was able to transport them to different places.

At one point, after the second floor, Xavier had asked her why she hadn't used the Summon spell on him to get him out of the hole. She'd said she'd worried it would impact his ability to get a solo title for the floor.

They'd all been trying so hard not to strike out at the rat beasts on that floor. All been holding back so well.

Turned out she'd been right—just like healing another Denizen while in combat got her shared experience even if she didn't attack the enemy, so did summoning an ally in combat to her. The System saw that as cooperation and rewarded the supportive spell in kind.

Fortunately Bulwark, Howard's defensive shield spell, didn't have the same effect. Perhaps because it didn't actively effect someone else, it simply protected what was inside its domain. If it improved the Toughness of those inside it, that would be a different story.

Xavier, in the moment, down in that cave... he wasn't sure if he would have thought of that. If he would have realised the implications. Had he been in Siobhan's shoes, he likely would have just used the Summon spell.

I need to think outside the box on this. I'm still trying to brute-force my aura to be contained. Doing the first thing that comes to mind. That's probably why I keep burning through my core—I'm applying pressure to it, like pushing down on the accelerator in a car.

So far, he'd learnt how to ease off, but he didn't know how to slow down. To put on the brakes.

The Spirit Core needs balance. Which means I need balance. I'm putting pressure on myself. Pressure to clear these floors faster and faster. To gain more and more power. To soar through the ranks until I'm strong enough to save Earth all by myself.

Should I take that pressure off?

Almost by reflex, Xavier fell into meditation, still pacing back and forth across the Staging Room.

I can't take the pressure off. I can't slow down. If I do, I might lose. The world might lose. There's too much at stake and the pressure helps.

But did the amount of pressure he was putting on himself help? Or was it just making him... burn through his energy faster than he needed to? What if there was a better balance to be find here, with these floors?

He was already ahead of the game. Already had a strong lead. He'd ranked *second* on the Top 100 leaderboard for the third floor. Not second in his cohort. Not second in this instance of the Tower of Champions that contained millions of Champions from five different worlds, all of which were from *established* worlds except for theirs.

Second in the entire Greater Universe, where untold trillions of Champions would have gone through the exact levels he had.

And yet, Xavier Collins had ranked *second*.

Perhaps he didn't realise what position he was truly in.

We moved through the second floor too quickly, and for that, I didn't get a spot in the Top 100.

At first, he'd simply thought getting into the Top 100 on the first floor had been luck. And, in a way, of course it was—luck in the titles he'd accrued, luck in not dying when he'd taken on too many Black Pumas at once.

But he'd come a long way from relying on luck.

We trained and farmed levels, spell and skill ranks on the third floor. I found out how to slay the enemy. I upped all my stats past the 100-point threshold. I knew exactly what I needed to do when it came to clearing the floor in the end, and that... that got me to rank second in all the Greater Universe.

I can't just think I'll only get the solo and first-clear titles. The Top 100 is +10 stats all around, and that could very well go up as I move through the floors. Sixty extra stat points per floor... No, I can't let that slip out of my fingers.

Yes, he needed to get back to Earth. But getting the Top 100 spot for each of the next seven floors... it seemed like it could be more than just possible, but *probable,* as long as he played his cards right.

And that would make a difference of 420 stat points.

He would be an absolute monster. And Earth? Earth would be defended, even if it took him an extra few days or weeks to return.

The odds of me getting in the Top 100 for the Tower of Champions floors are millions and millions less than the odds Sam gave for Earth surviving. If I can do that, saving Earth should be easy.

Somehow, this realisation—this slight change of course—relaxed his shoulders. A tension that he'd been carrying since he'd gotten to the tower, since he'd realised the weight of the world rested on *his* shoulders, eased.

It didn't disappear. He still felt pressure to succeed. To save Earth. But now, he knew that if he could do what he needed to in the tower, there's no way he couldn't do what he needed to back on Earth.

One skill, one spell, one level, one rank, one floor at a time. Just focus on that, and I'll get through all this.

Xavier took a long, calming breath. Still pacing back and forth, still deep in meditation, he examined his Spirit Core. In his mind's eye, he saw it as a ball of burning blue fire. Though really, he didn't know what it looked like—all he could do was *feel* it.

Take the pressure off.

He didn't *push* at the core, like he had before when he'd set it to burning through his Spirit Energy. Instead, he... massaged it? He supposed that was the best word he could come up with. Despite the fact that he was a writer, he had difficulty putting the sensation into words.

Like a knot of tension in your shoulders suddenly releases. Or, after a long day of carrying a half-dozen heavy books in your backpack, you take the backpack off and go for a stroll.

No. He couldn't describe the feeling.

All he knew was that it worked.

His Spirit Core still burned, but the flames flickered instead of flared. His core's engine was a low, consistent hum instead of a revving growl.

Wisps of his aura still floated in the air—smoke from before he contained it. He could see the remnants drifting. The energy slowly dissipating into nothing.

Though he imagined the energy had to go *somewhere*.

In three seconds, any remnants of his aura disappeared, no longer visible to him. He glanced over at the others, wondered if, subconsciously, they'd been able to feel the shift in pressure.

He smiled, opening up the Skill Quest.

Skill Quest: Aura Control
To unlock Aura Control, successfully contain
the power of your aura with your will 10 times.
Progress: 1/10

Once he'd figured it out, repeating the process was the easiest thing he'd ever done.

Chapter 69
Your Knowledge Is but a Seed Deep in Damp Earth

AGAIN AND AGAIN, XAVIER CONTROLLED HIS AURA, containing it within his Spirit Core. Until finally, he'd done it ten times in a row. And still with fifteen minutes remaining until the Tower of Champions reopened its door to them.

He couldn't help but pump his fist into the air when the notification popped into his vision.

> **Skill Quest Complete!**
> **You unlocked and learnt the skill Aura Control!**
> **Aura Control – Rank 1**
> **You are a student of the Greater Universe. Your knowledge is but a seed deep in damp earth, but soon it will grow roots and break up through the surface of the ground.**
> **May your knowledge of the Greater Universe blossom.**
> **+5% Aura Strength.**
> **+20% Spirit Energy recovery.**
> **+10% Spirit.**

Xavier blinked, staring at the text before him. The description of the skill was... different to other skill descriptions he'd encountered.

A student of the Greater Universe? May my knowledge of the universe blossom?

The description spoke in metaphor, which he didn't find particularly helpful, but he *did* find it intriguing. *My knowledge will grow... like the insights I get when meditating?*

He shook his head, instead focusing on the material rewards the skill had brought him. He started from the bottom, as those were the ones he understood more readily.

Extra 10 percent Spirit? That brings it up by almost twenty points!

He was surprised the reward was so tangible. Spirit was now well and truly his strongest stat.

Xavier paused, stopping his incessant pacing instantly as a realisation hit him—

After he'd gotten Soultaker, his scythe-staff, he'd tested how it strengthened his stats. He'd felt like there was something different about the weapon than there had been about his last weapon, the Spirit Staff of Might.

While he'd not had much reason to deposit his Spirit Staff of Might into his Storage Ring when he'd had it, basically always keeping the thing in hand since he'd gotten it after clearing the first floor, he'd deposited Soultaker into his Storage Ring many times.

And the stats that he'd gotten from the weapon? They remained for at *least* an hour after the weapon was no longer in his grasp.

He wasn't sure if it was because the weapon was more powerful, if he was more powerful, or even if it had something to do with his class. But he'd made a habit of taking the weapon out once every hour to ensure he got the full benefit of wielding it for his Spirit attribute when meditating and creating Lesser Spirit Coins.

But in the last few hours, he'd been too busy focusing on his Spirit Core and trying to unlock Aura Control.

Without Soultaker in hand, he totalled his stats, including all his percentage bonuses from everything but Scythe-Staff Mastery, as he wasn't holding the weapon.

They equalled 910.

If I take out and hold the Soultaker weapon, it will push me to over 1,000.

He summoned Soultaker from his Storage Ring and held the glorious weapon in both hands, waiting for the title to appear.

His cumulative stats were an effective 1,041...

Yet nothing happened. He sighed, thinking it through. He was 99 percent sure that hitting 1,000 stats would get him another title, but he supposed it didn't count when equipment was what got him there.

Had hitting a 100-point threshold for individual attributes because of equipment-stats count?

He wasn't sure, but he imagined by the time he'd gotten all those titles from completing the third floor, he wouldn't have needed either his Spirit Staff of Might or his Robes of Intelligence for such a feat, so it wouldn't have had any bearing on his choice of class at Level 10.

Xavier deposited the weapon back into his inventory, now benefiting from its increased stats for another hour. Somehow, he had an inherent knowledge that that would only work with a single weapon at a time. He couldn't buy a thousand Soultakers—assuming he could even afford them—and rotate them through his Storage Ring to get a thousand times the benefit.

Which was a shame, really.

Xavier ran through his stats again, taking away any conditional changes—his Robes of Intelligence, the stats he gained from Soultaker, and the stats he gained from holding a staff-scythe weapon.

Without those, his cumulative effective stats were "only" at 904.

Ninety-six more stat points, whether from static percentage gains, levels or titles, and I'll reach 1,000 cumulative effective stat points. I'll reach it on this next floor easily.

Now that little detour was done, and he soon had another title to look forward to, Xavier focused on the other benefits the Aura Control skill gave him. He was surprised by the 20 percent boost to Spirit Energy recovery. Unlike Meditation, it didn't require him to do anything. It was just a flat recovery gain that would always have an effect.

That will make creating Lesser Spirit Coins even easier... and I suppose it will help me in combat.

Then, finally, he looked at the one benefit he felt helped him the least.

+5% Aura Strength.

He supposed it was a good thing that his aura would be stronger when he let it free, or flared it, but though he'd posited a few possible uses for it, he wasn't sure if it would be beneficial to him on a floor-by-floor basis.

Then again... if flaring his aura gave his party members a headache, what might it do to enemy beasts? And now it was a little bit stronger...

It might help me in battle. Even the tiniest bit more edge could help me shave an extra second off clearing a floor, and that might make all the difference in reaching the Top 100.

Another minute ticked by. The fourth floor of the Tower of Champions would soon open up to him and his party. He told the others what had happened when he'd unlocked the skill and about their bonuses, then he'd headed to the System Shop in search of better armour.

He was sick of wearing his Robes of Intelligence and was glad that his Soul Reaper class let him wear any type of armour he wished.

Now, he just had to decide what type of armour that would be.

When he opened the System Shop's terminal, he instantly had second thoughts.

Not wearing heavily protective armour had benefits that wearing armour simply didn't. This was something he'd been debating with himself ever since he'd spent all his coin on Soultaker.

If I'd had armour, my Physical and Magical Resistances wouldn't have been able to level so effectively. If they hadn't levelled so effectively, they wouldn't have pushed me past the 100-point thresholds... and I'd simply be weaker.

He shifted from foot to foot.

Does that rule out something like full plate armour?

Xavier sighed, once again wondering what the right choice would be. *I suppose I could purchase a better set of robes, something that offers me higher stats. It won't help me get the 1,000-point title, but it will help me get stronger.*

More stats would never be a bad thing.

And there was something else we were offered from that first loot box, after clearing the first floor. Enchantments. Is that something that can be applied to our equipment?

Perhaps he should have spent more time contemplating this during his time away from the tower. Then again, if he had, he wouldn't have discovered his Spirit Core.

The Tower of Champions will be locked to you for 90 hours. You have 9 minutes and ten seconds remaining.

Xavier sifted through the different screens, finding that enchantments were like buffs for someone's equipment. They had different ratings, starting at +1 for a single stat, applied to a piece of equipment for a period of time—several minutes to several hours. Then you could purchase an all-stat enchantment at +1, but it cost... *twelve times* as much as the first enchantment.

The most expensive enchantment Xavier could see under his search terms cost 90,000 Lesser Spirit Coins and could enchant armour with +20 Toughness for ten minutes.

That's ridiculously expensive.

Xavier tilted his head to the side. He could see the utility in these enchantments and could imagine that other parties—especially from integrated worlds—would be utilising them heavily.

Especially if they were rich Denizens, backed by strong families.

Seems like a cheat.

He brought this up with Siobhan. The woman perked up. She took her Tower of Champions manual out of her Storage Ring—the first time he'd seen her do that for a little while—and flicked to a page. When she found what she was after, her eyes quickly flicked across the text.

"Only enchantments received from loot boxes can be used within a floor of the Tower of Champions." She nodded, looking up at him. "I remember reading that after the first loot box we looked at. I didn't bother bringing it up because we hadn't seen any more enchantments after that first one."

Xavier wasn't disappointed. In fact, he was *glad*. Established Denizens already had enough advantages. This would've just been one more.

It also meant he didn't need to think about them. At least, not until he was back on Earth.

"Having trouble deciding what armour to get?" Howard asked.

Xavier grunted, explaining his resistance predicament.

Howard nodded along. "Then just go for robes." The man shrugged. "I don't think anything out there can do you serious damage. Not anymore, anyway. Maybe on the later floors, we'll cross that bridge. But a boost to your Spirit or Intelligence? Well, that'll only add to the damage *you* do. It's the obvious choice."

Xavier inclined his head. "Sounds reasonable." Perhaps he'd hang onto his Robes of Intelligence in case training his resistances ripped up his clothes too much again... He didn't fancy standing naked in front of his party, and having something to change into before his new robes healed seemed like a good idea.

Justin shook his head. "So you're going to be wearing flimsy robes because, in the end, it will increase your defence? The logic of that just feels backward."

"What doesn't kill you makes you stronger." Howard scratched at his beard. "Always thought that was a stupid saying. Cause, you know, losing a leg might not kill you but then, hey, one leg isn't exactly going to help you squat more weight. Unless it's a robot leg, I guess... But in the Greater Universe? Maybe it's got more relevance than we realise."

The Tower of Champions will be locked to you for 90 hours. You have 4 minutes 32 seconds remaining.

Xavier turned away from the others, filtering out their conversation as it took a detour about whether the System supported cybernetic enhancements and brought up the different robes available to him.

There were far, far too many. For a moment, the abundance of choices overwhelmed him.

Robes didn't excite him near as much as getting a scythe had, so he flicked through the most expensive ones quickly, discarding anything that offered him more Toughness—and there were a surprising number of those—because he wanted to develop that without equipment enhancing it.

His current robes offered him a whopping +5 Intelligence, which meant they were an incredibly lacking aspect of his equipment.

I wonder how long wielding Soultaker will even make sense.

There were ten different sets of robes, each worth the same amount. Many of the robes had the stat they increased in their name. Intelligence this, Wisdom or Spirit that.

One set of robes caught his attention more than the others from its name alone.

Shrouded Robes
These robes require 100 Intelligence, 100 Spirit, and 100 Willpower to wear.
+20 Intelligence
+20 Spirit

+20 Willpower
+30% Spirit Energy recovery
+30% magical damage resistance
These robes have a self-repair feature fuelled by Spirit
Energy.
This item costs 90,000 Lesser Spirit Coins

While Xavier would have liked it more if the robes didn't
provide him with *any* magical damage resistance at all, he
supposed he could always switch out to his Robes of Intelligence—
which didn't offer any sort of resistances—if he wished to train his
Magical Resistance skill in particular.

The twenty-point bonus to his mental stats *and* Spirit stat?
That... that felt kind of insane to him. It offered fifty-five more stat
points than his previous set of robes.

I've really been missing out.

The Spirit Energy recovery was a great bonus as well, even if
he'd never run out in combat since facing those goblins in his first
real fight.

But the self-repair feature at the end was what made him buy
the robes immediately.

I can heal the robes with Spirit Energy... That's awesome.

No more waiting until the floor was clear to fix his clothes.

Would you like to fast-equip Shrouded Robes?

Yes, Xavier thought, with more excitement than he'd
anticipated.

His Robes of Intelligence were switched out for his Shrouded
Robes in an instant. He took a deep breath, shut his eyes, and felt
the rise in his stats. When he opened his eyes again, Howard, Siobhan, and Justin were all staring at him.

"Whoa. Dark," Justin said, eyes widening. "That's going to
look pretty badass with your scythe."

"You look..." Siobhan smirked. "You look like a Sith lord."

Xavier looked down at himself. He *did* kind of look like a Sith lord. The robes were made of a dark material that was smooth to the touch but didn't look like silk. There was a rope cord at his waist, pulled into a tight knot. The robes had large, billowing sleeves, but as he moved around, somehow the sleeves didn't feel as though they would hinder him in combat. *Weird, System magic, I suppose.*

And the robes had a hood. He flipped the hood on and summoned his staff-scythe, Soultaker.

"He doesn't look like a Sith," Howard said blankly. "He looks like Death."

Xavier smiled. He didn't have a mirror on hand, but he could imagine how he looked.

"God, with that smile, you look bloody terrifying." Howard chuckled nervously. "Suppose you *are* bloody terrifying," he muttered.

"One minute until the next floor," Siobhan said, excitement shining through in her voice, that bright smile she'd worn when they'd all first met alighting her face.

Xavier swung his Soultaker scythe in a pleasing arc. "Time to get moving again," he said, thinking, *and time to start harvesting souls.*

Chapter 70
So Much for This Being a Safe Zone

Xavier was pumped and ready to go. As the countdown timer ticked by the seconds until the Tower of Champions opened their doors to him once more, he looked at his stats and information.

XAVIER COLLINS
Age: 20
Race: Human
Grade: F
Moral Faction: World Defender (Planet Earth)
Class: Soul Reaper (Epic)
Level: 10

Strength: 136 (146)
Speed: 132 (139)
Toughness: 146 (161)
Intelligence: 188 (231)
Willpower: 153 (167)
Spirit: 212 (263)

Mastery Points for this level:
100,000/1,000,000
Available Spirit Energy: 26,500/27,300
Available Skill Points: 0
Free stat points remaining: 0

Titles:
Bloodied Hands, Born on a Battlefield, Settlement Defender, Quester, First Defender of Planet Earth, Survivor, 500 Stats, First to 500 Stats, Minor Butcher, Third-Floor Climber, Solo Tower Climber 3, 1st Third-Floor Climber, All 100, First All 100, Third Floor Ranked 2

Spells List:
Spiritual Trifecta – Rank 5
Heavy Telekinesis – Rank 6
Spirit Break (All) – Rank 3
Spirit Infusion – Rank 1
Soul Harvest – Rank 1
Soul Strike – Rank 1
Soul Block – Rank 1
Soul Harden – Rank 1

Skills List:
Physical Resistance – Rank 6
Magical Potency – Rank 11
Magical Resistance – Rank 5
Physical Damage – Rank 3
Assimilate Properties – Rank 1
Scythe-Staff Mastery – Rank 1
Meditation – Rank 10
Aura Control – Rank 1
Lesser Spirit Coins: 4,070

Xavier was a little taken aback to see how much his Spirit attribute had grown over the past few days. Soultaker. His Shrouded Robes. Reaching Rank 10 in Meditation.

And, of course, unlocking his Spirit Core and learning the Aura Control spell.

It had made an incredible difference. *And all that without actually killing enemies...* That was the part that took him most by surprise—that there were ways to improve so much without levelling up or even gaining titles.

In his first few days at the tower, he'd discovered he could gain attribute points by exercising and training. But back then, he'd only gained a handful of points.

Discovering his Spirit Core? Ranking up his skills? That served him far better.

And I still have two of those skills to unlock.

But Xavier put learning those skills out of his mind as he stepped up to the Tower of Champions' door. Holding Soultaker in his right hand—the shaft so tall its wicked, arm-length black blade hovered high over his head—he grasped the doorhandle, then finally entered the fourth floor.

What greeted him was utter darkness. Black as pitch.

All he could hear was his own breath and the breath of the other members of his party as they appeared around him.

And he could not see a damned thing.

"What's happening?" Justin said, his voice high, frightened, making him sound even younger than he was.

"Keep it together. This floor has a Safe Zone." Howard's voice was strong and sure. "We should be standing right in it."

Xavier turned to where the others' voices came from. They were behind him, and suddenly he realised he could see the light of their aura, even if he could not see *them*. He had not noticed this at first as the light did not spread forth and illuminate anything it touched.

It was an eerie sight. But he supposed a light seen only by those with Aura Sight would not be one that illuminated things. There was a certain logic there that he readily accepted.

Still, it was strange seeing their aura, floating in the air, amid an expanse of black.

"This should help..." Siobhan's voice trailed off. A second later, her aura flared, then bright orange light burst into their vision. At first, harsh in its suddenness, until the warmth of its light flowed around them. A fireball hovered high over her hand, and Xavier was glad she'd gone the generalist elemental route.

"Whoa," Justin said, the fear that had tinged his voice mere moments ago turning to awe at what lay before them.

The flames' light didn't illuminate more than perhaps twenty feet around them, but what he saw took Xavier by surprise. "Good thing we didn't go wandering off into the dark."

As the light didn't reach very far, he wasn't all that sure of what he was seeing. What he could tell was that they were on a platform made from dirt and stone, like something high up a mountain. The wind was strong, billowing and flapping the sleeves of his dark Shrouded Robes.

Xavier stepped over to the edge of the platform and peered down. But it was futile. Nothing but blackness was down there.

"How far do you think it goes?" Siobhan asked.

Xavier dislodged a small rock from the ground and kicked it off the side. He cocked his head and listened for the rock's fall, counting the seconds as they passed, trying to recall what terminal velocity was, though he'd never paid much attention in Physics class.

But the sound never came. He counted a full sixty seconds before he turned to the others. "Very far." If there even was a bottom at all.

Justin looked at the edge of the platform warily. "This can't be all this floor is, can it?" He looked around. "Usually we have to fight beasts. Do you think they're out there... in the dark?"

"We're in the Safe Zone. No harm should come to us here," Siobhan said, though her voice had a hint of shakiness to it.

A notification popped up in their vision.

You are currently in a Safe Zone. Your party has a combined 1 hour they are allowed to spend within this Safe Zone, starting in 5 minutes.

"Only one hour," Xavier muttered. "That's not a long time." The first Safe Zone had given them twenty-four hours. Though he didn't plan to spend any time in the Safe Zone, he wasn't yet seeing a way out of this one.

Howard was staring at the ground with a frown on his face. "Where's the door to the Staging Room?"

Xavier blinked. He hadn't even noticed that it was missing. It should have been the first thing he looked for.

Howard kicked at the ground, took a step, kicked at the ground again. The last exit from a floor had been a trapdoor, but there didn't appear to be anything here.

Xavier's forehead creased. He dipped his head, and an idea came to him. One he wasn't very fond of. "Siobhan?"

"Hmm?" Siobhan looked over at him.

"How well can you control that fireball?"

"Pretty well. I can extend it maybe..." She scrunched up her face. "Fifty feet before I lose control. Though I can throw it farther than that."

Xavier nodded. "Can you send it down around the platform? Let us get a better look at what's around us?" He'd been looking forward to getting back into the Tower of Champions. Aching to find souls to harvest so he could finally test his new spells—and see how his old spells had changed after being upgraded when he chose the Soul Reaper class.

But so far, this floor felt like a disappointment. *Where are all the beasts?* He was feeling nostalgic for the last floor, where he was able to fight an entire army. *That would have been a lot of souls...*

Siobhan walked to the edge of the rounded platform. She

peered over the side with a wary expression. Then, without so much as a wave of her hand, the fireball moved—it must have been responding to her thoughts—and sank down to illuminate whatever was below.

There wasn't much to see, at least not on this side of the platform. Just that they appeared to be standing on a solitary pillar in the middle of a large expanse of darkness. A pillar that seemed to stretch up from a ground that was either miles away or not there at all.

Like a bottomless pit... but it can't really be bottomless, can it?

He supposed it didn't matter. He was sure he could survive a fall from a great height, but there simply wasn't anything to jump down to.

Even if there was, how would he get back?

Not that there's a door to the Staging Room here.

Siobhan walked around the edge of the platform, her fireball drifting as though of its own accord, until it came upon a wooden door embedded in the side of the pillar of stone and dirt they stood upon.

There was the tiniest little ledge jutting out from the bottom of the door that must only have been large enough to let a person stand with their feet out sideways.

"Looks like we found our exit," Xavier muttered.

Siobhan grimaced at the sight of it.

Howard peered down at it with a frown.

Justin's face paled. "That's... that's the exit? But... what if we fall trying to get to it?"

"Then I suppose we die," Howard said.

"So much for this being a Safe Zone." Justin shuddered.

Xavier was getting the distinct impression that the teenager was afraid of heights.

"Don't worry, kid, you'll be all right." Howard slapped him on the shoulder. Justin stumbled forward a few steps—closer to the edge—then swiftly shuffled back to the middle.

Xavier was glad they'd found the way out, but he was still

confused about this floor. "Extend your fireball out. Let's see what else we can see."

Siobhan nodded and did so without complaint.

The fireball hovered away from the platform. Once it got about thirty feet out, it hit a wavy, shimmering wall. The light of the flames couldn't penetrate the wall, only reflecting off it. It made him recall the second floor's Safe Zone, which had been inside a cavern. There'd been a wavy barrier like this one.

Once he'd stepped through the barrier, he'd been instantly attacked by whatever was on the other side. *Maybe it's not so dark through that. But... how are we supposed to pass through?*

The fireball hovered in a great circle around the platform. The wavy wall encompassed it completely, and there was no sign of any other platform—nothing to jump toward.

As the fireball wasn't on their own platform, all Xavier could see of the others was their aura.

"Well, this is strange," Howard muttered.

"Maybe there's light on the other side of the barrier," Siobhan said.

"But... but how do we get through?" Justin asked. "It's too far away."

Xavier judged the distance, thinking about that. *If I did a running jump, with my strength as high as it is, would I be able to get through that wall?*

Even if he did, there was no telling what was on the other side. He would just plummet straight down. Fall and fall until he hit the ground. Or, if there was no ground, he would fall forever.

The fireball flew back toward them, then came to hover above Siobhan's head. She frowned at the edge of the platform then raised her staff. "I might be able to *create* platforms with my earth element."

"Like steppingstones?" Xavier asked.

She nodded. "But... I don't know how well I'd be able to keep them up."

"Do we really think the System is just... making us figure out a way off this rock?" Howard scratched his beard with the top of his shield. "Seems rather cruel."

"When have you known the System to be kind?" Siobhan asked.

Howard grunted. "Suppose you're right."

The five minutes that they were allowed to remain in the Safe Zone before the timer began were almost up.

That's when Xavier spotted something. A large, floating chunk of rock, about half the size of the platform they were already standing on. Except this platform didn't appear to have anything keeping it up. It emerged from the darkness, hovering through the air like Siobhan's fireball had done.

And it was heading straight toward them.

"I guess that's our ride," Xavier said, stepping over to the edge. He tilted his head to the side. He couldn't help but wonder what would have happened if he'd come to this floor alone.

Would he have just stood there, locked in the darkness, unable to see a damned thing? Or would his eyes have adjusted? It didn't appear as though there was any light in this place, so he wasn't sure what his eyes would be adjusting *to*, exactly.

He frowned. *No, I wouldn't be in complete darkness. I could cast my Spiritual Trifecta spell on myself.* He wasn't sure how far that light stretched, but he supposed it would have been better than nothing. Besides, he'd gained enough points in his Spirit Attribute that the spell lasted the same amount of time as its cooldown.

Xavier cast the spell on himself. A brilliant silver light enveloped his body. It was stronger than it had been, with his Spirit attribute at an effective 263. It instantly lit him up with strength of mind, body, and magic. It felt like someone stuck him with epinephrine, and he'd downed five cans of Red Bull. He took a deep breath, flexed his muscles, and grasped Soultaker in both hands.

When the floating platform was still a few feet from reaching the one they stood upon, Xavier leapt over to it. "You guys stay here," he told the others. "Head through the Safe Zone door if I'm not back in forty minutes." Though he didn't want to be without Siobhan's light, he was worried about what might be out there.

This floor wasn't at all what they'd been expecting, and as he wasn't planning on clearing it right away, he could take a moment and check things out.

I don't need to put so much pressure on every single second. I'm already well ahead of all the other Champions.

Howard frowned deeply. Siobhan leant on her staff. Justin looked as though he was trying to hide the relief on his face at having been left behind.

Xavier landed easily onto the platform, glad that it didn't shift under his weight. The moment he stood on it, he felt a mental connection to the platform. He furrowed his brow, focusing his will upon the odd connection, and nudged the platform to float back out of the Safe Zone.

It did so, responding instantly to his will.

The silver light from Spiritual Trifecta spread farther than he'd expected it to. He supposed he tended to use it in the light, not in the darkness, which was probably why he hadn't thought to instantly use it when they'd arrived. It had never held this utility for him before.

Though it didn't extend as far as Siobhan's fireball, and he couldn't move it away from himself like she could make her fireball hover.

It will have to be enough, unless I can think of something else.

Not sure what he should anticipate on the other side, but knowing that each time in the past that he'd stepped out of a Safe Zone he'd immediately been attacked, Xavier used Spirit Infusion on Soultaker.

Spirit Energy flooded into the staff, illuminating it in a silver glow much like the one around himself.

The energy was stored strongest in the blade, making the dark blade look even more vicious and powerful than it already was.

The platform hovered through the wavy, shimmering wall

surrounding the Safe Zone. On the other side, Xavier's eyes widened. Here, the darkness was still all encompassing. But it wasn't just the blackness that Xavier could see.

There were hundreds—maybe *thousands*—of glowing patches of aura.

Though he couldn't see what beasts or Denizens produced these auras, it was clear to him that whatever they were, they were flying, unhindered, through the expanse of darkness.

And ten of them were flying straight toward him.

Chapter 71
Soul Harvest

XAVIER STOOD ON A FLOATING CHUNK OF ROCK IN THE MIDDLE of a great expanse of complete darkness, ten enemies flying toward him at a tremendous speed, closing a large distance—distance enough for him to think and move.

The only thing illuminating the space around him was his Spiritual Trifecta spell. The silver light that enveloped his body reached out only ten or so feet around him, to the edges of the platform he stood upon and no farther.

He was blind to the enemies that came toward him, not knowing what they looked like. All he could see was their auras floating rapidly through the air.

They didn't even make a sound. Not one he could hear. They mustn't be close enough yet.

What would this be like for a Champion without Aura Sight? *I'm glad I've already chosen my class.* He wondered about that for a moment. The others in his party hadn't reached Level 10, but most Champions who got to this floor surely would have farmed a few levels by now, getting their first proper class, wouldn't they?

They would be able to see exactly what Xavier could see. His Aura Sight didn't have anything to do with his discovery of his

Spirit Core—he'd been granted the sight the moment he'd gained his Soul Reaper class.

Still, if someone were out here without the sight... God, that would be terrifying.

He was glad he'd left the others behind in the Safe Zone.

Xavier didn't fear the enemies heading toward him, but he did worry about falling off the platform if they tackled him. He might not take much damage with his Toughness being as strong as it was, but that didn't mean he couldn't get taken out.

He breathed steadily, trying to scan one of the enemies before it reached him.

{Dark Wyvern – Level 14}

Xavier's lips quirked up on one side in a smirk.

Dark Wyvern? Does that mean one day I'll come across dragons?

He had an image of himself riding a dragon mount, reaping souls of those beneath him from astride its back, lording over all those below—

He pushed that thought down with a frown.

Xavier could hear the Dark Wyverns now. Just the flap of their wings at first. Then, as they neared, ear-piercing, screeching roars that might have made him take a step back a few days earlier.

As it was, he stood his ground, relaxed his shoulders, and gripped his Soultaker tightly, anticipating the use of his new spells.

I wish I could see what they looked like.

He imagined massive, black, dragon-like beasts with bat wings and far too many dagger-sharp teeth.

When they were near enough, but still not within the range of his silver light, Xavier cast Heavy Telekinesis on the right half of the ten Dark Wyverns heading toward him. As far as he could see —which wasn't far at all—there was nothing to throw these beasts into. No walls. No Ground. No trees. Nothing but the platform of rock he stood upon, and he didn't fancy the wyverns getting in that close.

Screeches of pain tore through the air. Xavier watched as the auras were ripped to the left, slamming into their brethren with vicious *cracks*. At the same time, all ten auras began to drop.

But they didn't drop for long.

Heavy Telekinesis had done well for him up until now. In any other situation, he'd have falling damage to rely upon. But against flying enemies with no damned ground?

It's like the fourth floor is my Achilles' heel.

Xavier could no doubt take down all the wyverns with Soul-taker alone, but that didn't seem like the most efficient approach. He would have to figure out something *better*.

One of the Dark Wyverns caught flight faster than the others and soared straight at him. Xavier's Heavy Telekinesis spell was already refreshed—down to a one-second cooldown. He could have slammed the wyvern down into the platform.

But, inefficient or not, he wanted to test out his new scythe-staff.

With a wicked grin, Xavier waited until the Dark Wyvern was illuminated by his light. The beast was larger than he'd expected. Its body stretched farther than his light did, but if he had to guess, that dark, leathery body was about as long as a bus. Its wings were batlike and massive, extending far farther than he could see.

Its maw opened wide, a vicious screeching roar tearing from its throat. It looked unharmed from his use of Heavy Telekinesis, perhaps why it had gained its flight faster than the others.

It looked almost exactly as Xavier had imagined. Except ten times more bestial. Two jagged horns curved forward from atop its head, and bone spurs ran down its back.

And its eyes were large pits of absolute darkness.

There wasn't much room for Xavier to move on that floating chunk of stone. He took one step to the side and flashed Soultaker down across the beast's neck, glad for its long reach.

The staff-scythe was infused with Spirit Energy. The black,

arm-length blade sliced through the Dark Wyvern's neck with barely any resistance. The wyvern didn't scream—it didn't have time to scream.

You have defeated a Level 14 Dark Wyvern!
You have gained 1,400 Mastery Points.
You have gained 1,400 Spirit Energy.

Not as many Mastery Points and Spirit Energy as a sapient Denizen at the same level, Xavier thought, a little disappointed. But he supposed that didn't matter—there would be plenty of these beasts to kill with the hundreds, perhaps thousands, of auras he could see floating about in the air.

The instant the Dark Wyvern died—its head cut clean off, falling to roll across the platform with a wet *slap*, dark blood pooling on the dirt and rock as the head came to a stop—Xavier felt a *tug* from deep within him.

A desperate, aching tug.

No, it was *more* than that.

It was a deep yearning. A thirst. A need.

A *hunger*.

The dark pit that had emerged—*or had it always been there, waiting for me to discover it, and I only now feel it?*—when he'd chosen the Soul Reaper class. The dark pit that urged him to *reap*.

The beast's aura was gone, but there was a new glow coming from it. A pure, white glow that Xavier had never seen before, yet he immediately knew what it was.

The beast's soul.

For the first time, Xavier cast Soul Harvest.

Some instinct within him knew he didn't need to be near the body of the Dark Wyvern for the spell to work, though it was an instinct he hadn't had until that moment. Something he hadn't known until the first time he'd actually cast the spell.

He was glad for that knowledge.

The pure, glowing white light poured out of the Dark

Wyvern's massive body, a body that was slowly sliding off the platform, ready to fall down into that great expanse of nothingness, never to be seen again.

But everything felt as though it was happening in slow motion.

The soul streamed toward Xavier. It didn't move like light. It moved like smoke, if smoke were a snake. In swirls and arcs, it made its way toward him.

Then it entered him. Shooting straight through his chest. And the pit inside of him filled with power.

You have harvested 1 soul.
Harvested Souls: 1/10

Xavier smiled.

A wicked, wild, terrifying smile.

Three more Dark Wyverns were almost within range. The body of the first he'd slain fell off the platform, dropping into the dark.

Xavier felt no fear. All he felt was longing. For *more souls*.

Though the fact that he could only harvest ten souls into his reserve worried him, he imagined that would only be temporary.

My reserve's limit will grow, just as my Spirit Energy grew. I will harvest hundreds, thousands, millions, *of souls!*

He aimed his staff-scythe toward one of the Dark Wyverns and cast Soul Strike as a long-range attack.

Then he watched in rapt fascination. Soultaker lit up, power coursing through every inch of it. A bolt of white lightning shot forth from its blade, making sharp, jagged lines through the air as it arced toward the target.

The bolt of white lightning shifted, turning into a white, translucent, glowing wyvern. A wyvern larger and more vicious than the one that he'd just slain.

It tore through the air on wings longer than a semi-truck's trailers.

The apparition glowed so brightly that the nine remaining

wyverns were lit up, revealed in the dark expanse. The soul of the Dark Wyvern Xavier had slain opened its maw and clamped down at the throat of the wyvern Xavier had targeted.

There was no blood. No teeth-to-skin contact. The apparition flew through the Dark Wyvern, its brightness dimming. It slammed into the two wyverns beside the first, dimming farther each time.

But each wyvern it passed through died in an instant, without even a single scratch.

Soul damage.

The apparition disappeared a second later, and all went dark.

Three kill notifications popped up in Xavier's vision, along with a spell Upgrade Quest for Soul Strike. And Xavier could see three pure white souls hovering in the air, about to fall with the bodies they inhabited.

Soul Harvest had no cooldown.

That hunger overtook him once more. Or perhaps it had never left. He gripped his staff-scythe.

And he reaped three more souls.

Chapter 72
Three More Souls

Xavier stood, staring in awe at what he'd just done.

In awe of his first use of Soul Strike.

Though Xavier had certainly killed *more* enemies in a single strike than he had in that moment, that didn't tell him much about the potential of the spell he'd just used.

Soul Strike. It had created an apparition of the soul he'd harvested. That apparition had soared through the enemy wyverns, taking all three down without leaving a single scratch on them.

Xavier's smile grew.

You have harvested 3 souls.
Harvested Souls: 3/10

The dark pit within him filled with three more souls. It did not, in any way, feel sated. No, if anything, the pit had *deepened*. *Widened*, even if the threshold he could keep harvested had not increased. The hunger he'd felt before was nothing like what he felt now. It was as though... as though the hunger had been sleeping, and reaping that first soul had only wakened it.

And all he wanted was *more*.

There were still six Dark Wyverns remaining nearby. He could see their auras soaring toward him, though not near as fast as they had when they'd come his way the first time.

These must be the most injured of the lot.

And there were more heading his way, streaming toward the floating chunk of rock he stood upon—feet shoulder width apart, planted in the dirt, Soultaker grasped tightly in his fists—flying in groups of ten, all their auras in a V formation.

Like flocks of geese.

Xavier turned toward the six wyverns closing in on him. *Soul Strike has area-of-effect damage, and I can infuse as many souls as I want into each strike.* Mere seconds had passed by since he'd used the first Soul Strike, but the spell had already refreshed—he'd only counted a single second for the spell being on cooldown.

That feels overpowered.

Though he wondered how many Dark Wyverns a single soul could take out, he wanted to test all three souls in the spell.

Xavier smiled widely and cast Soul Strike for the second time. Infusing the number of souls he wished into the spell was something purely instinctual. Power coursed through Soultaker once more.

Then three white bolts of lightning streamed through the dark sky, arcing toward the enemies. When the bolts of lightning neared, they came together and created a wyvern apparition even larger than the first.

A single, massive, white-glowing, translucent beast soared straight through the six Dark Wyverns and took every single one of them down. Once again, the soul damage left no visible trace.

The white lightning lit up the area, illuminating the next group of wyverns closing in on him, their dark pits of eyes wide in a fear that brought Xavier joy.

That snagged his attention. *I'm relishing in their fear?* Xavier didn't know how to feel about that, but there wasn't time to think on it.

He refreshed Spiritual Trifecta as it wore off, and harvested the souls of the six enemies he'd just killed, their pure white like streaking toward him in pleasing swirls and arcs.

Like auras, and unlike when he used Soul Strike, the souls he could see did not illuminate the darkness around him.

The souls entered through his chest. He drew in a long breath.

You have harvested 6 souls.
Harvested Souls: 6/10

Xavier released a deep laugh as the pit inside of him filled with souls, the hunger *deepening*.

The limit of ten souls he could store in his reserve galled him, the number offending his eye.

Only then did he realise he hadn't looked at his Upgrade Quest for his Soul Strike spell. He'd been too entranced by the power of it. Too thrilled with the feeling of harvesting souls, and overtaken with the need for *more*.

He quickly brought it up as the next group of ten Dark Wyverns flew toward him, seconds away.

Soul Strike – Rank 1
Upgrade Quest:
As you have now used this spell, you have taken your first step on the path to upgrading it to Rank 2. Available paths:

1. *Soul Strike (Ranged) - Use Soul Strike to attack at range. To upgrade, infuse 100 souls into ranged Soul Strikes. Progress: 4/100*
2. *Soul Strike (Melee) - Infuse a melee attack with Soul Strike. To upgrade, infuse 100 souls into melee Soul Strikes. Progress: 0/100*
3. *Soul Strike (General) - Allows the user to cast Soul Strike in both ranged and melee attacks at the cost*

*of one-third damage. To upgrade, infuse 50 souls
into ranged Soul Strikes and 50 souls into melee
Soul Strikes.*

*This spell is bound to your Soul Reaper class. Gaining
Rank 2 in this spell will not require you to forget
another spell, and this spell cannot be forgotten while
you remain in the Reaper line of classes.
One cannot walk backward on the path.*

Xavier was glad he hadn't accidentally upgraded the spell
without even trying both paths, though he had to say he was
heavily leaning toward the former path—ranged attacks—before
having even used the melee path.

Mostly because of the situation he found himself in.

As he'd been stuck for a few days, unable to enter the next floor
of the Tower of Champions, Xavier had thought long and hard
about whether he should generalise in Soul Strike and Soul Block.
Unlike Spiritual Guidance—the Rank 1 spell that had become
Spiritual Trifecta—and Spirit Break, generalising had a heavy cost.

For Soul Strike, that was one-third damage.

For Soul Block, that was one-third defence.

Seeing Soul Strike in action as a ranged spell, Xavier imagined
the types of battles he would be in in the future. What he saw were
grand armies of invaders, perhaps one-on-one fights against other
World Champions...

Either way, he simply couldn't see himself going with the
melee only path for Soul Strike, and losing a third of the damage
sounded like a high price.

Still, I should test out what it can do.

Xavier aimed his Heavy Telekinesis spell as best he could,
trying to keep one or two of the Dark Wyverns on their path
toward him while throwing the others farther away.

He didn't want to know what ten reaching him all at once
while he was perched on this little floating chunk of rock would do.

Probably have me falling to my death.

But one or two? He could take.

The Dark Wyverns screeched in anger as they were thrown off course. But it wasn't just the screeches he heard. Bones cracked. They'd been heading toward him *fast*, and Xavier pushing them back with Heavy Telekinesis must have been like them slamming into a stone wall.

A stone wall moving toward them at a hundred miles per hours.

It proved far more effective than sending them flying into each other, like the first time he'd cast Heavy Telekinesis on the Dark Wyverns, but it didn't *kill* them.

Though as that hadn't been the plan, it didn't bother him.

What Xavier *had* planned worked. Now, two auras streaked toward him through the dark sky. He widened his stance, bent his knees, and waited.

When the first Dark Wyvern came into view, Xavier's staff-scythe still infused with Spirit Energy, glowing with power, he poured a melee Soul Strike into the weapon.

The shaft and blade *electrified*, white lightning crackling and buzzing up its length. Xavier could feel the power pulsing within Soultaker, ready and eager to be unleashed.

And so Xavier unleashed it.

He stepped aside, out of the wyvern's immediate trajectory but still below its massive wing. Soultaker came down like an executioner's axe. One swift strike. Xavier already knew that he could take down one of these Dark Wyverns with a single hit, so it might be difficult for him to see how much deadlier this attack was.

The moment the blade impacted the Dark Wyvern's black, leathery hide, right at the back of its neck, an explosion of power was released.

This power did not have a physical element to it. It did not explode the platform Xavier stood upon, nor did it destroy the flesh of the Dark Wyvern. Just as in the ranged attack, this was an explosion of soul damage.

The attack was more concentrated than the ranged attack had been. It did not flow *through* the Dark Wyvern as an apparition and then head toward the next. It simply struck and exploded, power rippling and burning through the dead beast.

Though Soultaker still cut through the neck of the Dark Wyvern easily enough.

You have defeated a Level 14 Dark Wyvern!
You have gained 1,400 Mastery Points.
You have gained 1,400 Spirit Energy.

The second Dark Wyvern came at him. Xavier's first instinct was to leap and roll off to the side—but there was nowhere to go.

He cast Heavy Telekinesis on the beast. *Crack* went its bones as the wyvern was sent flying away.

The first eight had found their wings once more, though more than one seemed as though they might be unsteady.

Soul Harvest.

White light poured into him from the Dark Wyvern he'd used the melee Soul Strike on. Xavier drew in a breath as the soul came into him, filling his harvested soul reserve back to three.

As the next few Dark Wyverns came to him, Xavier made a swift decision.

Ranged Soul Strike appears less concentrated than melee Soul Strike, but it causes area-of-effect damage. Melee Soul Strike could probably cause a lot more damage to a single enemy, especially since it wasn't just the power of the Soul Strike damaging a target—it would have the damage of my normal melee strike as well.

The wyvern's decapitated head rolled straight off the platform, its body sliding off on the other side.

Xavier glanced around, rapidly counting the groups of ten auras floating around in the dark expanse.

There are definitely over a thousand of these things here. I need to focus on the challenge in front of me, and this kind of damage will help me win a war against an army better than a single melee strike ever could.

He let out a breath, smiled.

Ranged Soul Strike it is.

It was time to get the spell to Rank 2, and see how truly powerful it was.

Chapter 73
One Dead. Two Dead. Three Dead. Four...

Bolts of white lightning shot forth from Xavier's staff-scythe, zigzagging through the air until they came together in one giant apparition, his largest yet.

Xavier laughed. He'd infused six souls into this strike.

The brilliant, white wyvern soared through the Dark Wyverns heading his way, illuminating them in their moment of death. Instantly, nine kill notifications vied for his attention. He pushed them back, willing them not to appear.

Things were about to get serious here.

Xavier stepped up to the edge of the platform. The floating chunk of rock in the expanse of darkness that was the fourth floor of the Tower of Champions. A darkness teeming with a thousand Dark Wyverns, circling from a distance until they came at him in groups of ten.

Two groups down, only ninety-eight to go.

Not that he would be killing every single one—not his first time here.

Again, he imagined what this floor would be like for another team. He imagined his own party, standing on the chunk of rock. Howard throwing up Bulwark. Siobhan sending elemental strikes through the air. Justin slashing at the enemy as they came close, only to be thrown off the side and have Siobhan summon him back up.

I can see how another group might handle it.

But now that he knew how *he* would tackle this floor—with ranged Soul Strikes—he had to think of the *fastest* way for him to clear it. He could see the auras of the Dark Wyverns. Some looked like they were at least a mile away.

I'll need to test just how long range this spell is.

He also wondered where the floor boss might be. If he looked hard enough, he was sure he'd be able to spot it. Its aura would be stronger than the ones surrounding it. But there was no need to look yet—he had other things that required his attention.

Xavier drew in a deep breath. Pure white light streaked toward him.

You have harvested 9 souls.
Harvested Souls: 9/10

Not enough. His reserve was almost full and it was *not enough*! The pit inside him screamed for more.

And Xavier endeavoured to fill it.

But he noticed something he hadn't the second time he had used this spell—it was still on cooldown. He frowned. The *first* time he'd used the spell, he'd counted the cooldown. It had only been a single second.

Now? It was six seconds.

He quickly realised why. *The cooldown is dependent on the number of souls I use in a strike. The more souls, the higher the cooldown.* He simply hadn't noticed that on his second use, when he'd infused three souls into the strike. He didn't know if that would change in the future, but it was good motivation for him to discover just how many he could take out using a single soul in the spell.

Xavier drew in another deep breath and thought through his situation.

Soul Strike (Ranged) – Use Soul Strike to attack at range. To upgrade, infuse 100 souls into ranged Soul Strikes. Progress: 10/100

Ninety more souls infused in ranged Soul Strikes, and I'll rank the spell up.

It wasn't only his new spells he wished to test and rank up—and he'd only used three of his five new spells so far, he still had to try Soul Block and Soul Harden—he'd also planned to gain a few levels on this floor.

He wondered how long that would take.

Mastery Points for this level: 128,000/1,000,000

I still have over 870,000 Mastery Points to accrue. That would mean killing... 623 of these winged bastards.

Xavier smiled. He wouldn't even have to clear the entire floor to gain his next level.

He didn't wait for the next group of Dark Wyverns to get close. The second his cooldown refreshed, he simply raised Soultaker and cast a one-infused Soul Strike.

The bolt of white lightning arced through the air. The apparition came into being. It tore into the Dark Wyverns, dimming after each one it killed.

One dead. Two dead. Three dead. Four...

Xavier frowned. *A one-infused Soul Strike takes out four Dark Wyverns.* He wondered if that meant he would need a three-infused strike to take out a whole group.

He harvested the souls of the dead.

Only, he couldn't harvest them all. Two of the four souls streaked toward him. He watched the pure white light of the two he couldn't harvest fall down into the darkness. The darkness that seemed to stretch on forever.

As they plummeted, he felt a pang of loss.

I need to keep aware of that.

He hoped reaching Rank 2 in the spell would drastically increase his reserve's threshold. Though he sensed that Spirit and Intelligence helped the damage the attacks dealt, Spirit didn't seem to do anything for the number of souls he could store.

Xavier tilted his chin up. A second had passed. The spell had refreshed.

He sent a two-infused Soul Strike at the remaining six Dark Wyverns. The apparition took them out with ease.

Soul Strike (Ranged) – Use Soul Strike to attack at range. To upgrade, infuse 100 souls into ranged Soul Strikes. Progress: 13/100

This isn't efficient enough.

Xavier dragged in two more souls. His reserve once more at full capacity. He glanced around until he zeroed in on the next group of ten.

Let's speed this up a bit.

Xavier dropped his head down, lips dragging up at the sides in a wicked grin. He gripped Soultaker, and aimed it toward the next group, sending a ten-infused Soul Strike streaking through the darkness toward where their auras flew toward him.

The apparition soared through the Dark Wyverns, causing ten more deaths, and ten more souls for Xavier to harvest.

Yes. This... this will work.

Xavier fell into a rhythm. He waited for his spell's cooldown to end, counting down the seconds, then sent another ten-infused Soul Strike to another group.

He did this eight times.

Once he'd settled on this plan, it took him less than a minute and a half to reach Rank 2 in Soul Strike.

Soul Strike has taken a step forward on the

path, upgrading to the spell: Soul Strike (Ranged).
Soul Strike (Ranged) is a Rank 2 spell.
One cannot walk backward on the path.

Xavier raised his staff-scythe in triumph, unleashing a loud, satisfied laugh into the darkness. He'd already taken out eleven groups of the Dark Wyverns—110 beasts—and it hadn't taken him very long at all.

So far, the range on his Soul Strike hadn't hindered him in the slightest. It seemed to stretch quite a distance, so he didn't know if he could strike the farthest group of Dark Wyverns, which seemed to be a mile away.

How far can *I strike?*

He was *definitely* enjoying his choice of class.

Xavier harvested the souls of the last group he slayed.

You have harvested 10 souls.
Harvested Souls: 10/20

Xavier smiled. A single rank in the spell had doubled his threshold. He tilted his head to the side, sensing a *shift* in the spell, and brought up its description.

Soul Strike (Ranged) – Rank 2
Soul Strike (Ranged) is an epic spell specific to the Reaper line of classes and requires harvested souls to cast.
This is a ranged, offensive spell that uses harvested souls against an enemy. Soul Strike causes soul damage, which is different to magical damage and difficult to protect against.
The user may use as many harvested souls in a Soul Strike as they wish.

*As Soul Strike (Ranged) progresses through the ranks,
its range and area-of-effect damage will only increase.
One cannot walk backward on the path.*

Xavier stared at the second last paragraph. *Its range and area-of-effect damage will only increase.* He had an inkling about that. Something he wished to test.

There's so much for me to test.

He assessed his current situation and objectives. What else did he wish to achieve on this floor?

I want to reach Level 11. I want to further increase my soul reserve's threshold. I want to test the other spells in my arsenal, and test how the spells that had been upgraded to use harvested souls— Spiritual Trifecta and Spirit Break—have changed.

And there was one other thing: Celestial Energy.

He brought up the third of his three Spirit Core Skill Quests.

Skill Quest Unlocked: Cultivate Energy
To unlock Cultivate Energy, successfully draw
10,000 points of Celestial Energy into your
Spirit Core, turning it into Spirit Energy.
Progress: 0/10,000

Xavier sighed. He still had no clue what that *meant.* He looked around, wondering if this so-called Celestial Energy was out there, somewhere, and he simply couldn't see it, or sense it.

All he could see were the auras of the Dark Wyverns, floating through the black.

All right, he told himself. *One step at a time.*

Next step: Reach Level 11.

Then he would test the rest of his spells to his heart's content.

Chapter 74
Every Kill Counts

XAVIER BURNED THROUGH DARK WYVERN AFTER DARK Wyvern, sending Soul Strikes at flocks—

Clutches? Flights? What do you call a group of wyverns?

—of the leathery beasts, taking out ten at a time.

He experimented a little with the strength of Soul Strike, wanting to get a feel for it. Now that it had reached Rank 2, he shot off another one-infused Soul Strike to see how many Level 14 Dark Wyverns he was able to take out.

Xavier smiled. Previously, he'd only been able to take out four wyverns with a one-infused Soul Strike. Now, he could take down *five*.

Which meant he'd only need to infuse *two* souls into a strike to take down a whole clutch.

Yeah, clutch sounds way better than flock or flight.

He did the math, figuring in his cooldown, and the numbers of Dark Wyvern clutches.

The cooldown on Soul Strike is two seconds with two souls. There are a hundred clutches. If I take a clutch out with a single spell, with two seconds apart...

That was less than four minutes.

He frowned. That would mean refreshing Spiritual Trifecta at least seventeen times. *That'll slow me down a second or two, but not by too much.*

Though he didn't yet know how long it would take for him to deal with the fourth floor boss, considering how easily he'd dealt with that three-headed hell beast Cerotri Infernum, he doubted it would take too long.

He tested Soul Strike *without* Spiritual Trifecta active and found a one-infused Soul Strike only killed *three* of the Dark Wyverns without it.

Sometimes I forget how much that spell does for me.

It didn't take long for the notifications to start rolling in.

Soul Strike (Ranged) has taken a step forward on the path!
Soul Strike (Ranged) is now a Rank 3 spell.
One cannot walk backward on the path.

Congratulations, you have reached Level 11!
Your health has been regenerated by 60%!
Your Spirit Energy limit has increased by 200!
You have received +2 Strength, +2 Toughness, +2 Speed, +3 Intelligence, +3 Willpower, and +8 Spirit!
You have received +20 free stat points!
All your spells have refreshed and are no longer on cooldown!

Xavier drew in a deep breath, then released a laugh. "Whoa." He shook his head. He felt like he'd just been granted a title, with how many stats he'd just gained.

And he still had *twenty* to assign.

Apparently, there were perks to choosing an epic class beyond harvesting souls.

I could get used to this.

He also noticed that his health now regenerated by 60 percent instead of 50 percent when gaining a level, and his Spirit Energy's limit increased by 200 instead of 100. Considering how many points he had in his Spirit attribute, he doubted that would make a significant difference, but every point was helpful.

With the plus eight to Spirit, I gain one thousand points to my threshold each level. He paused. *More than that, with Meditation adding 14 percent to Spirit at Rank 10, and Aura Control adding 10 percent at Rank 1.*

Xavier glanced around at the floating auras in the darkness. The remaining clutches of Dark Wyverns he'd yet to take out. He must have taken out over six hundred of them to have reached Level 11, meaning there were only a few hundred left.

He frowned, looking at his stats for a moment and contemplating the twenty free points he'd just received. He raised Soultaker, felt the reserve of ten souls inside of him.

My Spirit attribute empowers almost all I do.

He tilted his head up, making a swift decision, and threw all twenty points into Spirit.

You have added 20 points to Spirit!
Spirit increased from 273 → 298!
You have 0 free stat points remaining.

Twenty-five points for the price of twenty!

Xavier smiled. Shook his head. He shut his eyes—the Dark Wyvern clutches that remained were nowhere near attacking him yet, and he'd hear the flap of their leathery wings and the screeches from their massive maws long before they got close enough to hurt him—and focused on his Spirit Core.

He hadn't been paying enough attention to his aura. When he'd put on his Shrouded Robes, the balance that he'd found within his core had been disrupted, his aura leaking out again—or smoking, as he liked to think of it.

And now, with gaining a level and so many points in Spirit, he had to adjust it once more.

One day, this will become as automatic as breathing is to me now.

It took him several minutes of deep breathing while in meditation to tweak his core until it was in balance again, his aura once more restrained—that was another thing he'd yet to test.

What effect did his aura have against these wyverns?

He chuckled. *So much to do, so little time.*

Aura Control has reached Rank 2!

Xavier blinked, staring at the text that just appeared before him. *What? Already?* He hadn't expected that. He supposed he was still so new to the spell that any small improvement made it shoot up to the next rank. *Maybe adjusting my aura after that much added Spirit wasn't only a small change after all.*

The rank-up of Aura Control pushed his Spirit all the way to 300. The few-point difference only shifted his aura very slightly, taking a few seconds for him to adjust the balance and hide his aura.

He let out a sigh, realising just how often he'd have to change this. Still, he felt *strong*. Gaining that level had felt amazing. He hadn't gained that many stats in a little while.

Fifty-two more, and I'll get that one-thousand-point title.

But by the looks of it, he'd need to kill *double* the number of enemies as he'd had the last time to reach Level 12.

Xavier refreshed Spiritual Trifecta, the spell feeling stronger already, homed in on the next clutch of wyverns, then sent a one-infused Soul Strike at them.

Only moments ago he could kill five with a one-infused Soul Strike. Now, he could kill six.

He smiled, an idea forming within his mind.

I'm definitely going to get onto the Top 100 for this floor.

Xavier took down another thirty clutches of wyverns, standing on the platform, throwing one bolt of pure white lightning after another, brilliant apparitions forming in the dark.

His threshold for soulkeeping—which he'd decided to call the number of souls he could harvest—had gone up to 30 when he'd reached the third rank of Soul Strike, but the Soul Harvest spell itself had yet to rank up.

That made him remember his Spirit Infusion spell. He looked at the Upgrade Quest, which he'd unlocked during the days he'd been stuck, unable to enter this floor.

Spirit Infusion – Rank 1
Upgrade Quest:
As you have now used this spell, you have taken your first step on the path to upgrading it to Rank 2. Available paths:

1. *Spirit Infusion (Defensive) - Infuse defensive Spirit Energy into armour and weapons to gain more physical and magical resistance. To upgrade, take 1,000 hits to equipped armour while it is infused. Progress: 0/1,000*
2. *Spirit Infusion (Offensive) - Infuse offensive Spirit Energy into armour and weapons to deal damage to an enemy who strikes you, and to deal more damage to enemies you strike (whether with spells, in melee or with ranged weapons). To upgrade, strike 1,000 enemies with infused equipment. Progress: 950/1,000*

This spell is bound to your Soul Reaper class. Gaining Rank 2 in in this spell will not require you to forget another spell, and this spell cannot be forgotten while you remain in the Reaper line of classes.
One cannot walk backward on the path.

Xavier frowned. He looked at Soultaker, still infused with

Spirit Energy. *It must be helping the damage I deal with Soul Strike.* He looked at the defensive option once more, then looked out at the auras remaining—only fifty left.

As he'd taken out the last thirty clutches of Dark Wyverns, he'd wondered about his goal of hitting the Top 100.

Wondered if he wasn't aiming *high enough.*

Defence is important... but I think, if I go full offence, I can hit number one.

He tested a one-infused Soul Strike against a clutch of wyverns and found *not* having the spell enhancing his weapon had cost him a kill, bringing him back down to five.

Every kill counts.

He'd told himself he would test the defensive capabilities of Spirit Infusion. But if he were honest with himself, he wasn't worried about his defence anymore.

Xavier had come a long, long way from lying on the ground, fending off Level 2 goblin attacks. Or almost being killed by the Level 11 Black Pumas when he'd aggroed too many of them.

I want to get to number 1. And the only way I do that is by dealing even more damage. By killing even faster.

Xavier raised his chin. He had an instinct for the type of Denizen he wanted to be. For which paths he should take his spells. An instinct he had been struggling to trust. But even if he'd made some questionable decisions getting to where he was, he *had* gotten here.

He must be doing something right.

Xavier felt his determination set. This was the path he would take, and the means were before him.

He struck out, casting four more two-infused Soul Strikes until a single clutch remained.

Magical Potency has reached Rank 12!

Xavier smiled, feeling the slightest shift in his mind, staring at the cluster of remaining enemies. One among that last clutch held the strongest aura of all the Dark Wyverns. He could see the aura in the distance, in the dark. Could feel the strength wafting off the beast, but even though he knew where it was, it was too far away for him to scan.

He couldn't help but wonder what the beast looked like.

I'll be back for you soon.

With his will, he instructed the floating chunk of rock to return to the Safe Zone. He couldn't have been gone from the others for long—certainly not long enough for them to return to the Staging Room.

As the rock floated, he refreshed Spiritual Trifecta—it glowed more brightly than ever, now, and he wondered what he would look like to the others.

Glowing silver, shrouded in dark robes, holding Soultaker, its long blade high above his head.

And thirty harvested souls held within the pit inside him.

Chapter 75
A Quest like That Could Justify Anything

Siobhan paced back and forth, not that there was much space on the pillar of rock that was the Safe Zone.

Justin stood in the dead centre of the platform. His forehead was creased, looking toward the side where the door to the Staging Room was. It was on the side of the pillar of rock that they stood on. When they left, they'd have to lower themselves down, and the kid clearly had a fear of heights.

Howard looked deep in thought, his head down, his arms crossed over his large chest. His eyes were closed too, and if she didn't know any better, she would think he was asleep.

I hate not being able to do anything, Siobhan thought, glancing back over where Xavier had gone, floating alone on the chunk of rock that had taken him away. She looked at the timer for the Safe Zone, keeping it in the corner of her vision. Less than twenty minutes had passed.

Siobhan knew their best course of action was to follow Xavier and support him in any way they could. The man was powerful. With his titles, he *must* be the most powerful human from Earth.

She didn't know exactly *how* powerful he was. He'd told them about the extra titles that he received, but as she couldn't *see* those titles, she didn't understand how wide the gulf between him and everyone else was.

What she did know was that he was her best bet for returning to Earth as quickly as possible. *And when I'm back on Earth, I can find my sister.* Supposedly, those not old enough to be integrated into the System were protected by it, put into Safe Zones like the one they stood in now.

But Siobhan was fairly sure Safe Zones weren't safe. Not *really*. On a floor of the Tower of Champions, *maybe*, but on Earth? When it was being invaded?

One of the first things she'd done when Xavier had left them was turn to Howard and ask if she could test something on him, explaining to him why.

When he'd nodded that she could, she'd set his arm on fire with her fireball. Justin had stared at what they were doing with wide eyes. It wasn't as though they hadn't sparred before, but throwing spells at one another simply wasn't something they had done yet.

Siobhan had been hoping the spell wouldn't harm him. Not that he'd be strong enough to be immune from the flames, like Xavier might be, but that he'd be unharmed because they were in a Safe Zone.

But that hadn't stopped him from getting hurt. Even from friendly fire.

"What the hell did you do that for?" Justin had asked, his mouth hanging open after the words had fallen out.

Siobhan had raised an eyebrow at him. "Weren't you listening?" She used Heal Other on Howard. The burns on his arm disappeared completely.

The fireball hovered over their heads. The three stood in a triangle, facing the middle, their shadows cast behind each of them as the fireball was in the centre between them.

Justin shook his head. "I was... lost in thought."

Howard dropped his arm. "Safe Zones aren't safe."

Justin glanced behind them, staring off into the absolute darkness. "What do you mean, Safe Zones aren't safe?"

"They're safe from the beasts and from any other enemy on this floor, I'm sure. But... I was able to harm Howard."

"O...kay. But we're not going to hurt each other, so what's the problem?"

Howard stared at Justin. His face was a mask. "My children and her sister are in Safe Zones. Those Safe Zones will stop beasts from attacking them, as the wildlife on Earth has apparently been turned into beasts, but will it stop the invaders?"

"I—" Justin's face scrunched up. He shook his head. "I don't know."

"Planets that are integrated like ours are, with interlopers finding them... that barkeep said we have a one in ten thousand chance of our people surviving," Siobhan said slowly. "If that's the case, the Safe Zones probably don't do a damned thing against the invaders. How could they? If we were integrated normally, we'd be locked off from invaders completely, only fighting against the animals that were turned into beasts, levelling up and learning things slowly, rather than having to scramble and defend ourselves from foes that know all about the System."

"Which means my kids might not be safe." That was when Howard dropped his head. Crossed his arms.

And that was when Siobhan had started pacing back and forth on the pillar of rock, wishing she could do *more*, the minutes passing her by as she worried, unable to do a damned thing.

"Xavier's back," Justin said.

Siobhan frowned, glancing over at the direction he'd originally gone, only to see the man standing atop the floating chunk of rock, heading straight toward them.

Her eyes widened involuntarily. The man glowed silver, shrouded in those dark robes of his. Even his weapon glowed. Siobhan knew why. He'd told them about the Spirit Infusion spell.

Still, holding that scythe, draped in black, that dark look on his face, Siobhan couldn't help but feel a shiver of fear run up her spine. While they'd been locked out of the tower floors, hanging out in the tavern or the Staging Room, Xavier had looked... *normal,* in his mage robes.

Now, he looked like something else entirely.

He looks like Death.

Siobhan's rational mind trusted Xavier. She didn't feel as though she had a reason *not* to trust him. She'd seen what he was capable of—the way he'd destroyed that army, the way he'd tortured that hell beast just to gain a few ranks in one of his spells. Not only that, she'd seen the grin on his face as he'd taken down those soldiers. Elves. Humans. It hadn't mattered—he'd enjoyed the thrill.

And that made her worry what else he might be capable of.

He's on a quest to save Earth. A quest like that could justify anything.

The very thought made her shiver, knowing that she was capable of horrible things herself. Flashes of memory assaulted her mind—of the day the System had come. The day she'd been plucked out of her normal life and thrown into *this.*

Thrown onto a plain of grass that looked so perfect it didn't seem real. Pitted against a girl not that many years older than her sister.

She must have only been sixteen. Just old enough to be integrated, like Justin.

The girl had been holding a baseball bat, wearing a baseball uniform. She must have been plucked straight out of a game, as there was dirt on her knees.

The System had made them fight to the death. Siobhan hadn't wanted to.

But she hadn't had a choice. She'd yanked that bat straight out of the girl's hand and collapsed her skull with it.

I didn't have a choice.

She reached up to grasp her pendant. A half-heart, the other half around the neck of her sister. She knew it was cheesy, sentimental, but she'd bought the matching pendants when she'd left home, leaving her sister behind with their parents, it had been a symbol to say she'd come back for her when she could.

But her fingers clutched nothing. The pendant, of course, was gone. Taken by the System, just as she had been.

Siobhan bit her lip, pushing away her memories of the day the System came. Pushing away her worries for her sister—as much as that was even possible—and focused on Xavier as he leapt off his platform and landed neatly on theirs.

There was an air of confidence about Xavier that hadn't been there the first day they'd met, a day that felt years in the past but hadn't even been a week ago. An air of danger. Of power. Something intangible, something that she was sure had nothing to do with his aura, as she knew that he was containing that now.

If we're going to save Earth, we need people like him. People who will be ruthless. People who will do anything to save the world.

Siobhan just worried about what that *anything* might be, and whether they would still be able to hold onto their humanity when their world was finally safe.

She also worried about herself. After what she'd done to that girl... what was *she* capable of, if her life, if the life of her sister, and the lives of all the world, were at stake?

Her fingers grasping at the nothing where her pendant should have been, Siobhan's thoughts went, unbidden, to her sister once more.

I'll find you, Luna. I'll find you, make sure you're safe, and take you away from our parents like I always promised I would. And I will do anything I have to to protect you.

Anything.

"Let's get out of here," Xavier said. Even his voice sounded deeper than it used to, like all the attribute points he'd been getting had had an effect on it. "Then head straight back in." He looked at Siobhan, grinning. "And the three of you will be coming with me. There's something that I want to test."

Before he'd chosen his Soul Reaper class, Siobhan might have found that grin endearing. Now, it sent another little shiver of fear up her spine.

Chapter 76
Did I Just Waste a Soul?

XAVIER KEPT THE FROWN OFF HIS FACE AS HE LOOKED AT THE others. He couldn't help but feel as though they were looking at him differently.

Then again, he supposed he shouldn't be surprised even if they were. He thought about what he'd just done. What he'd just been able to do. Not only had he struck down close to a thousand beasts, he'd done it with ease.

And he'd harvested every single one of their souls.

Yet the pit inside of him still didn't feel full. The pit inside of him felt deeper with every soul he dragged into it. Even now, his soulkeeping threshold at thirty, and thirty souls kept, looking at the others...

He felt *hungry*.

Could Siobhan see that in his grin? Was that why her smile looked wrong?

He shook that worry away. In the grand scheme, what did it matter, what these three thought of him, even if they were becoming his friends?

If they step out of line, I can harvest their souls—

Xavier shook his head.

He didn't need those thoughts. His party had been nothing but good to him. Xavier took a deep, calming breath. His heart was slamming against his chest, invigorated by the power he'd just been able to unleash.

He felt absolutely unstoppable, like that gave him a right... a right to do *anything*. But he knew that wasn't true. Knew that he should feel wary of that impulse.

I'm getting drunk on the power.

It made him wonder what the Greater Universe was like. What kind of people were out there. If this sort of power was going to his head—or trying to go to his head—what did it do to those who didn't share his morals? Who didn't want to use the power for good?

Might makes right was all he could think these people would believe, and in a universe like this, where an individual could one day muster up enough power to destroy entire worlds with a single thought, he was having trouble coming up with an argument against that.

They headed back to the Staging Room, climbing down the platform one by one. Watching Justin shake as he climbed down, Xavier wished he'd had a rope for the kid. Sometimes he forgot just how young sixteen was, and he was only a few years older than that.

They didn't spend much time in the Staging Room. The others had a lot of questions for him, mostly about what had been out there in the dark, considering how long he'd been away.

Xavier told them about the Dark Wyverns. About how he couldn't see the beasts, but he could see their auras.

Then he told them about how easy it had been for him to take them down, to harvest their souls, and the path he'd chosen to take Soul Strike.

"You're aiming to hit the top spot on the leaderboard?" Siobhan asked. Her smile looked genuine, this time. Nothing like the smile she'd given him a few minutes ago back in the fourth floor

Safe Zone. That one, he now realised, had been tinged with fear. "That's amazing!"

"It sounds as though you'd already be fast enough, being able to kill every beast within a few minutes," Howard said.

Xavier lowered his head in a nod. He'd wondered about the same thing. He struggled to imagine how someone else would be able to manage what he could. Then again, he'd completed the last floor in about a minute and a half, and he still hadn't been fast enough to get higher than the second place in the Top 100.

That's still pretty damned high, he told himself, but he still felt disappointed. Felt like he could do *more*.

Besides, he knew that there was always a little something more in store for someone who was *first*.

Though he knew that wasn't *always* the case. He hadn't gained a title for being the first from Earth to choose their non-basic class, nor had he gained a title for discovering his Spirit Core, even though he was sure he was the first. So it clearly didn't work on *everything*.

If he could beat the top record for a floor—maybe for *every* next floor he encountered—he knew in his gut that he'd get a better title.

"It *might* be fast enough, but I don't want to take that risk. I want to gain a few more levels and test out all my other spells. Increase my soul keeping threshold and keep ranking up Soul Strike."

Xavier figured that once Soul Strike reached Rank 10, he should be able to keep 100 harvested souls.

And by then, the gained ranks and the gained points in Spirit from whatever levels he got should be enough for him to take out a clutch in a one-infused Soul Strike.

Then he knew, he could still be even *faster* than that. He remembered the spell's description once he'd ranked it up.

***As Soul Strike (Ranged) progresses through the ranks,
its range and area-of-effect damage will only increase.***

The "area-of-effect damage" part intrigued him. His plan made him smile. If it worked, and he was almost sure it would, he could clear this floor *perfectly*. He could clear it so damned fast that no one in the entire Greater Universe would ever have done it better.

Maybe this power is going to my head.

"But before I do that," Xavier said, "there are other things I need to test. And, when we return to the floor, I want to bring the three of you with me." His forehead creased in thought. He looked at Siobhan. "I think I have a way for you to gain a lot of levels. Fast." He looked at Justin and Howard. "As for the two of you... you're going to help me rank up some skills."

Justin and Howard frowned at each other, clearly not understanding what he had in mind.

Xavier broke off from the three of them. He'd given them a few minutes to focus on sparring or whatever else they might want to do. Right now, he had something else to attend to. Something he hadn't wanted to test while he was in that vast, black expanse.

He headed to the far end of the room. He sat cross-legged, his back against the smooth wall, and fell into a deep meditation within a blink of an eye.

There were many spells he'd yet to test out. Soul Harden was one of them. When he'd first looked at the spell's name, he should have instantly realised *why* his soul needed protecting—to strengthen his soul against soul damage, like the damage he'd caused those Dark Wyverns—yet at the same time, it had seemed like it could be referring to something else. That there was more than soul damage that one had to worry about when it came to protecting their soul.

Because he got a sense that it would be useful for other things, as well. Though he wasn't exactly sure *what* those things were, now that he'd discovered the soulkeeping threshold, he wondered if it might help him to improve that as well.

Either way, he had thirty souls that he could use to test the spell with. Though he should probably save a soul for when they returned to the fourth floor.

Soul Harvest didn't have any cooldown. I wonder if Soul Harden does. The spells were very similar in how their descriptions were structured.

Xavier, eyes closed, cast Soul Harden. He focused on that dark pit inside of him, the one where the souls he harvested resided, and felt one of the souls get wrenched out of that pit.

It was like a bright light in his mind. And the sensation the soul gave off... He had no way of explaining it. It was *like* the power an aura gave off, at least in a small way. But it was also completely different.

Xavier wasn't sure why. He tilted his head to the side, waiting for... something *more* to happen. The spell had been cast. The soul had been consumed. Yet... nothing appeared to have changed within Xavier.

He opened his eyes and looked down at himself, deep lines cutting into his forehead. He didn't feel any different, nor did he look any different. He checked his harvested souls.

Harvested Souls: 29/30

Xavier frowned even more deeply. He had definitely used one of his thirty souls—he hadn't needed to check to know, but it had almost felt necessary, just to confirm that he already knew—yet... nothing had happened?

Part of him had wondered if he would have received more to his Spirit attribute or something. Or gotten some notification mentioning how much stronger his soul had become.

The spell hadn't gone into cooldown, either.

Xavier let out a sigh. *Did I just waste a soul? Is there more to this spell that I simply don't know?*

Sometimes—actually, a *lot* of times—he wished that there could be someone around here that he could turn to. Someone that he could ask these questions of. Someone who would have all the answers.

But... he also enjoyed figuring things out for himself.

Xavier lowered his head, shut his eyes again, and focused once more on the souls within him.

There were twenty-nine left.

How many would he need to consume with Soul Harden for something to happen?

Chapter 77
Plunge to Our Deaths

Sitting in the Staging Room, meditating on his reserve of souls, and casting Soul Harden over and over as he watched them get consumed, Xavier wondered if there was any point to using this spell.

He consumed twenty-nine of the thirty souls he had harvested. And, as far as he could tell, *nothing* had happened.

Though he knew that must have been a deceptive feeling. In his gut, he could feel something changing. It was a small feeling, and he didn't know if he could trust it or not, but he supposed he would have to.

Maybe it's because I can't feel my soul?

He hadn't managed to rank up Soul Harvest, even after harvesting close to a thousand souls, so it came as no surprise that he hadn't ranked up Soul Harden yet.

When Xavier had a single soul remaining in his reserve, he stood and addressed the others. It had barely been a few minutes since he'd come to sit here. The process of consuming those souls with Soul Harden hadn't taken nearly as long as he'd expected it to.

Howard and Justin were sparring, while Siobhan looked deep in thought. She perked up once she saw his approach.

"Xavier! Are we heading back already?" Siobhan asked.

Xavier nodded.

"And we're all coming through with you this time?" Howard asked.

Justin looked warily at the door, sheathing his sword. "What happens if one of us falls off that platform and we plunge to our deaths?"

Xavier nodded over at Siobhan. "She'll summon you back before you fall too far."

Siobhan moved to put her hair in a ponytail, her arms raising above her head. "What if *I* fall off?"

Xavier shook his head. "That's not something I'm going to let happen." Part of him wanted to see what his party could do on this floor without him, but... he honestly didn't know if they could take down a single clutch without his help.

At least, not yet.

He scanned each of them.

{Human – Level 7}
{Human – Level 7}
{Human – Level 7}

The others were only four levels lower than him. That... felt rather strange to him, considering the divide in their strength.

"So... what exactly will you need us for?" Siobhan asked. Her hands dropped to her sides. "I *want* to help. God, I *need* to help. But, ever since you faced that army..."

"It doesn't really feel like you need us." It was Howard who said this. "We were supposed to be your support team, but now... well, you're an army of one. Even more so since you gained that Soul Reaper class." The man frowned. "I had thought you needed more practical battle experience than you'd been getting. That I would be able to train you somehow. But... you don't appear to need me for that. The tower floors are doing that already. And you certainly don't need me to tank for you."

"Or me to heal for you," Siobhan said.

"Or me for anything." Justin hung his head.

Xavier blinked. If he were honest, he couldn't find anything to argue against in what they were saying. He wondered if what he wanted them for was even necessary. Part of him supposed it wasn't, but even if he didn't need them in the same way he'd thought he had before, he *still* needed to make them stronger, didn't he?

"What are you guys trying to say? Do you want to leave the party?"

Siobhan shook her head rapidly. "No, no, no. Just..." She sighed. "Wondering what we can *do*."

Xavier lowered his head in thought. There was no harm dragging them along when there were Safe Zones. Even when there hadn't been. But...

Should I go solo? Kick them to the curb?

Harvest their souls?

The pit inside of him ached. Feeling more empty than ever after he'd used up all but one of his harvested souls.

I don't need them. I don't need them at all.

He shut his eyes, trying to imagine what Earth would be like when he returned. What the Greater Universe would be like. What dangers might lie out there.

His idea of having them as a support system, as people to help him make decisions... The more he fought, the stronger he got, the more insights he received from meditation, the less that seemed necessary, or even desired.

But he kept thinking about Earth.

Yes, technically, Xavier didn't need them. In the *tower*. But the Tower of Champions wasn't everything. The Tower of Champions was simply a path to power.

He was gaining power so he could help the world. Raising these three up would do that too. Besides, as much as he thought he could do everything alone, he didn't *need* to.

And he certainly wasn't about to harvest their souls.

"You can get strong," Xavier said simply. "That's what you can do. When we return to Earth, the three of you will be needed. There are billions of lives at stake. I might be able to clear a floor, but that doesn't mean I can lead an army." He looked at Howard. "That doesn't mean I can heal the sick and injured." He looked at Siobhan. "And that doesn't mean I can be in more than one place at a time." Lastly, he looked at Justin.

Siobhan nodded. "Right." She looked at the door. "We'll be needed. Then."

"And all three of you are needed right now." Xavier walked to the door without further explanation. "Remember I said there was something I wanted to test?"

He heard the shuffle of their feet as they followed.

Moments later, they were standing on the platform atop the pillar of rock in that deep dark of the fourth floor. The others asked a few questions, but Xavier didn't want to answer until he was out there. He liked keeping them in suspense.

Besides, he was interested in seeing what their reactions would be when he cast Soul Strike and they saw the wyvern apparition come to life.

They all stepped onto the platform when it finally floated toward them, and though Xavier enjoyed being alone, he felt a sense of peace at having the others with him. With the pit inside him, that hunger for souls, and the thirst for power that had been driving him to strive ever more within the Tower of Champions... it felt good to have them near, like they balanced his impulses.

And reminded him what he was fighting for.

Each of them had a connection to the world. To Earth. Siobhan, with her little sister. Howard, his wife and kids. Justin, his mum. Having them around made *him* feel more connected to what was at stake.

Perhaps he should have already been connected. His mother was back on Earth, somewhere. A part of him was worried about her. She was his mother, after all. But they'd never been all that close. And they'd always wanted different things from life.

But with the entire world at stake, how could he think of only one person, just because she was related to him?

Perhaps that made him sound callous—maybe he *was* callous.

He wanted to protect *everyone*, not just his mother, and he was beginning to realise he would do just about anything to achieve that goal.

But he didn't want his newfound class and spells to turn him into something he didn't want to be. An emotionless pit that only wanted to devour souls and gain overwhelming power. With the others near, that impulse was somewhat dampened, and his *reasons* for wanting power were more clear.

The platform floated through the wall of the Safe Zone. Xavier gazed out at the thousand different auras he could see. His eyes flicking from one to the other.

Siobhan came to stand beside him. She watched his eyes for a moment, then looked out into that great expanse of darkness. "You can really see things out there?"

Xavier dipped his head. "And you'll be able to see things out there soon too." The first clutch of Dark Wyverns were already flying toward them, but he wasn't worried.

Siobhan frowned, looking out at the darkness without being able to see anything. "You want me to gain levels here, but I don't even know where to..." An idea seemed to occur to her, and the frown disappeared from her face completely. "I'll be healing you and gaining Mastery Points that way, and you'll do all the beast killing."

Xavier smiled, glad he didn't have to spell it out for her.

Howard stepped up, tower shield in front of him, sword drawn. He motioned to Justin. "And you want the two of us to deal you physical damage to build up your Physical Resistance skill, so she has something to heal."

"Yes, I do." Xavier blinked. "How'd you figure that one out?"

Howard smirked. It was good to see something other than a serious expression on the man. "You said you wanted us to help rank up your skills. Seemed like the most logical explanation." He shrugged, looking out into the dark. "From what you explained of this floor, seemed like it would be foolish to try and train your resistances here against the beast themselves. Even if you could withstand their attacks..."

"You'd fall straight to your death," Justin said as he peered over the platform's edge.

Xavier motioned him back toward the middle. "Best you step back." He turned toward the first clutch of Dark Wyverns just as they began to screech and roar. "Let me deal with these enemies first."

He stepped up to the edge, raised Soultaker, then cast Soul Strike, consuming the last soul in his reserve.

Chapter 78
If That's Your Idea of Fun

Xavier watched as a jagged bolt of pure white lightning shot from Soultaker. It streamed through the darkness, heading straight toward the first clutch of Dark Wyverns.

Soultaker was already infused with Spirit Energy. His body, mind, and magic were empowered by Spiritual Trifecta. He knew he'd only been gone from this place for a few minutes, but it felt like far too long.

When the bolt of white lightning neared the beasts, it blossomed into a bright, beautiful apparition of destruction. A wyvern larger than the ones it was about to slay.

Xavier had seen this dozens of times now, yet the sight was still something remarkable to behold.

For the others, it was the first time they'd witnessed his current level of power.

And that was only a one-infused Soul Strike. I can do a thirty-infused Soul Strike now, not that I've tested it.

Five of the Dark Wyverns were instantly killed. Xavier immediately harvested their souls, then sent out another Soul Strike to deal with the remaining beasts.

He turned to the others, not bothering to watch the apparition form. Not bothering to watch the final five wyverns meet their deaths. He'd found he didn't need to be facing a slayed enemy to harvest their soul. He could *feel* them.

When the kill notifications came, he consumed the other five souls.

Soul Harvest has taken a step forward on the path!
Soul Harvest is now a Rank 2 spell.
One cannot walk backward on the path.

Spirit Infusion has taken a step forward on the path, upgrading to the spell: Spirit Infusion (Offensive).
Spirit Infusion (Offensive) is a Rank 2 spell.
One cannot walk backward on the path.

Xavier blinked at the notifications. He'd known Spirit Infusion only needed ten more kills before it ranked up, but he'd expected Soul Harvest to rank up faster than that.

Each spell took 1,000 souls to rank up.

As he wondered what ranking up Soul Harvest might even do, as he could harvest to his heart's content seemingly at any range and without any cooldown, he checked his harvested souls.

Harvested Souls: 9/40

Xavier smiled, delighted to see that his soulkeeping threshold had gone up by 10 when he'd gained a rank in Soul Harvest. *At least I know it does that.*

The more souls he could hold, the more powerful he would become.

He looked at Soultaker, his staff-scythe, and re-infused it with Spirit Energy. *I wonder how much more powerful that will make my spells.*

As he flicked his attention away from the notifications and his staff—which glowed no more brightly than before—he noticed the others gaping at him.

Howard was the first to close his mouth. He scratched his beard with his tower shield, looking out into the darkness. "That... was you using a soul?"

Siobhan had paled, but the colour quickly returned to her cheeks. She stepped toward the edge of the platform. "That was... that was *amazing*! The way it formed into the soul you'd taken. I wonder if that would happen with other beasts. Or... or humans." She tilted her head to the side in thought. "You said you could infuse multiple souls into a strike. What would it look like if the souls were from different beasts?"

"I haven't had a chance to find out," Xavier said. "Though I'm very curious to."

Justin, his mouth still open. "So, souls are just... ammunition to you now?"

Xavier considered. "I hadn't thought of them that way, but yes. I suppose so."

Justin glanced around the darkness. "How many beasts are out there? It's unsettling not being able to see them. But it's almost like I can *feel* their eyes."

Xavier considered Justen's reaction for a moment, wondering if it was their auras he could *actually* feel, even if the kid wasn't conscious of it. "There are almost a thousand beasts out there." He turned to look outward. "Now, I think we should get things started," he said, thinking, *No point wasting any more time.*

As he only needed two souls to take out a whole clutch, and he couldn't hold more than forty, Xavier decided he would consume extra souls with Soul Harden. He still didn't know what benefit he was truly gaining from the spell—especially if he didn't face any other soul-users—but he figured he would find out eventually.

Looking out at all the clutches, he still struggled to believe how powerful he'd become. Though it constantly made him wonder how he would stack up against someone of a higher level. He knew that in the grand scheme—in the Greater Universe—he was just a baby taking his first steps.

He let out a breath. They still had a little while until the next clutch approached. That was something he'd noticed the first time he was here. The clutches of ten wyverns came in intervals—as though the next clutch was waiting for the first to be dealt with.

If it took a party too long to deal with one, then they would be attacked by another at the same time.

He could just imagine what kind of mess that would put a party in.

This tower is going to kill a lot of Champions from Earth. That, or temper them into something stronger. He wished he knew how his fellow Champions were doing. He knew he was a step above them all—maybe several steps. A Progenitor, as Sam called those who gained the "first" titles. *If there was some sort of leaderboard we could see, showing all the Champions from the five instances... see what floor each party had reached, their times...*

He shook those thoughts away. Even if he *could* see where others were, none of that mattered for his own path.

"All right. Howard, Justin, attack me."

"Just, what... stab you in the back?" Justin asked.

Xavier shrugged. "Basically."

"Sounds good to me," Howard said. Xavier raised an eyebrow, looking over his shoulder at the man. Howard had a little smile on his face. "What? It probably won't even hurt you. I might as well enjoy getting a few hits in."

"Well, I guess if that's your idea of fun..." Xavier chuckled.

Justin, who had his sword drawn now, looked down at it. "All my instincts are shouting at me *not* to do this. Sparring is one thing, but you won't even be fighting back."

Howard nudged him with his shoulder. "We might not even be able to do any damage to him. You remember when he took on that army, don't you?"

Justin nodded. "How could I forget?"

Xavier sighed. "Come on, I'm the one who's going to be

attacked here. If anyone should be nervous, it should be me." His Shrouded Robes offered barely any protection at all. In fact, they didn't offer *any* physical protection, only magical. Though they did have a repair feature he was interested in testing out.

And Howard was probably right. This plan might not even work if the two of them were unable to injure him.

Justin rolled his shoulders, gripping his sword. His face shifted. Ever since they'd entered this floor, fear had wafted off the teenager—his fear of heights rearing its head. But it was as though he'd just put on his game-face. An intense look of concentration overtook him. He nodded sharply.

Howard slapped him on the back. "Good man."

Xavier hadn't really bothered to watch these two in action. When they had been gaining a few levels back on the third floor, he'd been too busy fighting the soldiers. And when they sparred in the Staging Room, more than half the time Xavier hadn't even been there. When he *had* been there, he'd been locked in meditation, not paying close attention to what the others were up to.

Xavier faced the front. It was strange, knowing that the two people at your back who were *supposed* to be on your side were about to attack you. He wasn't afraid, but it was an eerie feeling.

He glanced over at Siobhan. She had a look that seemed to be equal parts worry and determination. Her staff was on hand, and she looked ready to heal him at a moment's notice. She nodded sharply at him.

Xavier looked at the oncoming clutch. It was still a little ways away. He wasn't sure if he had to be actively engaged in combat for her to gain Mastery Points from his kills. He waited a moment, heard Howard and Justin step forward, lunging toward his back.

The anticipation proved worse than the attacks themselves. Two red-hot lines cut down his back. Though they were sword strikes, they felt more akin to cat-scratches. Troublesome, a bit painful, but mostly just a minor annoyance. He looked at his health. It had gone down by 4 percent, which surprised him a little bit.

They hit harder than the soldiers back on the last floor. And those soldiers were higher level.

They still wouldn't pose a true threat to him. Not when he could no doubt take them both out with a single spell. But part of him realised it was interesting to find that they could harm each other within a Tower of Champions floor at all. They *were* allies, after all.

A Champion could betray the other members of their party. Kill them during a floor run. Though *why* they'd want to do that, Xavier didn't know.

The damage was quickly healing, but before his health could return to 100 percent, Siobhan had already cast Heal Other on him. He was bathed in light, the pain—such as it was—instantly disappearing.

Xavier sent a two-infused Soul Strike at the clutch slowly heading their way. When the Dark Wyverns died, he didn't need to ask Siobhan to know she'd received Mastery Points.

He'd gained *half* the amount he usually would. For a moment, that rankled him, but he'd known coming in that that would be the case.

"All right. This works." Xavier motioned to Howard and Justin over his shoulder. "Come on. Don't stop at one. Make me *feel* it."

He knew he'd gain levels faster if he wasn't letting Siobhan feed off his Mastery Points by healing him, but he also knew that gaining levels wasn't his *only* goal.

He could farm levels to his heart's content, especially on a floor like this, and gaining a level with his epic class got him a *lot* of extra stat points—stat points that would make it easier for him to get the number 1 slot on these floors—but this seemed like a good way to make sure his skills and spells didn't lag too far behind and that the others got a chance to rank up their skills as well.

He had to imagine that Howard and Justin would be able to gain ranks in Physical Damage by dealing constant damage to him. Siobhan would get ranks in her Heal Other spell as well as gain levels quickly.

And that was half the point of this exercise. He wanted to help powerlevel these people, so they would be more valuable assets when they returned to Earth. But he didn't want to have to *wait* for them.

This way, Siobhan wouldn't have to lift a finger toward the enemy. All she'd need to do was heal him.

Howard and Justin began their attacks once more. This time, they didn't let up at one. They kept striking him, over and over. Xavier watched his health, which was falling faster than he could heal it.

They're doing well. Maybe this will actually work.

A smile kicked up the sides of Xavier's lips as he looked at the remaining ninety-eight clutches. He could only take out ninety-seven of them so as not to accidentally clear the whole floor.

But that should gain Siobhan quite a lot of levels.

All right, let's see how many more ranks I can gain before I hit Level 12.

Chapter 79
Like Fast Travel in a Video Game

IN THE DARKNESS OF THE FOURTH FLOOR, THE ONLY THING visible to the naked eye was the four of them standing on that floating chunk of rock, with Xavier's Spiritual Trifecta spell giving off a silver light, and Siobhan's fireball washing them in flickering orange. Howard and Justin struck Xavier in the back with a constant stream of attacks, slicing through his Shrouded Robes, gouging sharp red lines through his skin that were healed a moment later by Siobhan.

Every few seconds, pure bolts of lightning lit up the darkness that surrounded them, shooting off from the rock and plunging into that blackness before they formed massive white, translucent apparitions that flew through one clutch after another.

They saw the apparitions spark. Saw them pass through the Dark Wyverns and kill them all instantly. Even Xavier was in awe of what he could do, though he'd already done it once before.

Xavier didn't kill the enemies as fast as he could. He wanted more time for his Physical Resistance skill to rank up—wanted to give Howard and Justin more time to strike him.

After a hundred or so strikes to his back, the damage they caused increased.

"Physical Damage ranked up!" Justin said excitedly.

"For me too," Howard bellowed.

A few moments—and a dozen more strikes—after the two had spoken, a notification popped up in Xavier's vision.

Physical Resistance has reached Rank 7!

He smiled, glad his plan was working.

It must have been working for Siobhan, too, as after a while the cooldown on her Heal Other spell reduced. The heals came faster, and worked more effectively.

Xavier destroyed 990 of the Dark Wyverns. During that time, only two more notifications came.

Physical Resistance has reached Rank 8!

Soul Strike (Ranged) has taken a step forward on the path!
Soul Strike (Ranged) is now a Rank 4 spell.
One cannot walk backward on the path.

And, once more, my soulkeeping threshold has increased.

It was at fifty now. With Spirit Infusion at Rank 2 and Soul Strike at Rank 4, he was eager to test how many Dark Wyverns he could take out using a single soul.

And I want to see if I can expand its area-of-effect damage...

He had an idea. One he was eager to try once they refreshed this floor and farmed it for a third time.

Sharing Mastery Points with Siobhan as he was, he'd gotten about halfway to Level 12. If he kept sharing Mastery Points with her, it would take him farming the floor two more times.

Which, honestly, wouldn't take very long.

When only one clutch remained—the clutch holding the beast with the most powerful aura, the one that was no doubt the floor boss—Xavier turned to Siobhan and scanned her.

{Human – Level 10}

Xavier blinked. "Whoa. That was fast."

Siobhan's face lit up with a smile. She was practically beaming up at him. "Right!" She looked down at herself, gripped her staff tightly. "I feel so much more powerful! The System isn't even letting me gain any more Mastery Points now."

Xavier smiled back at her. He couldn't help it. Her enthusiasm brought it out in him. "You'll be able to choose your class when we return to the Staging Room. Do you feel ready?"

Siobhan shook her head. "I can't wait to do that, but I don't think I'm ready yet." Her forehead scrunched in thought. "I won't be able to achieve what you achieved with your stats, hitting the 100-point threshold in each of them—I won't be able to do that in *any*—but there may be something else I can do." She gestured toward him, taking in his Shrouded Robes and his staff-scythe. "Pushing forward a little more clearly paid off for you in your class choice. I know I won't be able to choose an epic class. But, maybe I could get a rare one?"

Xavier dipped his head. "What do you wish to do?" Without gaining new titles, all she could really do was gain more spell and skill ranks before choosing her class. He supposed she could wait until they were on the next floor to choose her class, but he didn't know if another two titles would make much of a difference for her.

Her head down, staring off into the darkness, she seemed to consider this deeply. "I wanted a path that was both offensive *and* defensive, but maybe that's not the best thing for us all." She raised her head, looking at the fireball hanging in the air above them, illuminating them in that burning, flickering light. The light of the flames brought out the red of her hair even more. "The two things that have come most in handy are my Summon and Heal Other spells."

Xavier tilted his head to the side. "Are you really willing to give up an offensive mage path?" That hadn't been what she'd said last time.

Siobhan dipped her head in a nod. "Of course. The path I choose isn't just about me. It's not even just about our party. It's about everyone back on Earth." She stepped to the edge of the rock, scrunching up her eyes, peering into that darkness. "The path I took the Summon spell, it's... not about summoning beasts or anything like that. It's about helping summon allies to where they need to be. And I think... the description seems to imply that it can be used on a grand scale once it's become powerful enough."

Howard frowned. "A grand scale?" he asked, joining the conversation. "What do you mean?"

"I mean, one day, I might be able to teleport an entire crowd out of danger. Or, when I become *truly* powerful, maybe transport an entire army." Siobhan looked at Xavier. "Could you imagine how much that would help back on Earth? The world... the world is *huge*, and we have no idea what's still intact. Getting people from one place to another will be incredibly valuable."

Justin perked up. "And you could get Xavier where he needs to go, like fast travel in a video game!"

Xavier pondered that for a moment. It certainly wouldn't have been something he would have thought to do. *Troop movements.* It was such a logistical thing. His focus was purely on his own power. Hers was on helping others, however she could.

It made complete sense.

Now that she'd brought it up, he didn't realise how he couldn't have thought about it before. And what Justin said about getting him where he needed to go... When they returned to Earth, he might be needed all over the world. And though she likely wouldn't be able to transport him that far *yet*, if she were able to do that in the future, then Siobhan was right. The spell would be invaluable.

Even on a small scale. Crowd control. Getting people out of danger. She could save a lot of lives without even having to resort to healing them, simply by ensuring they weren't there to get injured in the first place.

But it wasn't the small scale that captivated Xavier.

His thoughts went wild, thinking beyond their little blue planet, the third rock from their sun, and about other planets in the Greater Universe. Other worlds. He already knew there was such a thing as portals—he'd seen one with his own eyes—but he wondered if there were *other* ways to get from one world to another.

And if Siobhan might be the key to unlocking that down the line.

We could take the fight to the enemy. Or find allies out there in the Greater Universe.

He was glad he'd decided to level her up. "All right. That makes complete sense. Actually, I love that idea. So, what would you like to do before choosing your class? How can we make you get the best class with this path possible?"

"I want to get my Summon spell, along with Heal Other, up to Rank 10. Maybe... maybe even beyond that. I was able to progress the Summon spell to Rank 5 while we were locked from entering the next tower floor, but I seem to have hit a barrier with it." She frowned. "I think it needs to be used in combat to progress further."

"What rank is Heal Other?" Xavier asked.

"After what we did here? It's Rank 8. So that's almost ready. If we do this one more time, I'm sure it'll reach Rank 10. But... maybe it would be better if Summon was at a higher level when I came to choose my class?"

Justin peered over the edge of the floating platform. "Is this really the best place to practise your Summon spell?"

Siobhan smiled, an idea seeming to occur to her. "Actually, I think it's the *perfect* place." She had a glint in her eye. It looked almost menacing. "And I think I've got an idea for the two of you... How do you feel about flying?"

Chapter 80
What Do You Mean, Flying?

Xavier smirked as he watched Justin step right back from the ledge, then everyone turned their attention onto Siobhan.

Justin was the first one to speak. "What... what do you mean, *flying?*" His eyebrows shot straight to the top of his forehead. "I don't have wings!"

Howard chuckled. "That would be a sight."

Siobhan, still with that somewhat menacing, wicked look in her eyes, turned her gaze back out to the expanse of darkness. She placed the butt of her staff on the rock. A breeze rolled in, kicking up her robes and playing with the few strands of hair that weren't tied up into her ponytail. She motioned, with the hand not holding her staff, out toward the black. "We're going to be on this floor for a few more respawns, right?"

Xavier nodded.

"Well, then I think we should experiment, if Xavier agrees."

"If Xavier agrees?" Justin turned the hilt of his sword around in his hand, over and over. "What about if *we* agree? And, again, what did you mean by 'flying'?"

"I did say I need to use Summon in combat," Siobhan mused. "And Xavier has a telekinesis spell."

Howard laughed, a little manically. "You want him to throw us out into that darkness?"

"She can't want that," Justin said. "You... you don't want that, do you?"

Siobhan grinned. "Actually, that's exactly what I had in mind." She bobbed her head toward Xavier. "He can use Heavy Telekinesis to send you guys out to attack the enemy. Then I can Summon you back after you strike out at them."

"Why don't you send them out with your Summon spell?" Xavier asked. "Aren't you able to do that?"

"The cooldown is about ten seconds. I wouldn't want them in too much danger while they were out there. But I imagine I'll be able to bring that cooldown lower." She shrugged. "Besides, I can't see where the enemy is. And, for this to work, they need to *attack* the enemy, otherwise it wouldn't be considered *in combat*."

Howard furrowed his brow. "Wouldn't it be wiser to... to wait for the enemy to come to us?"

"Yes!" Justin said. "That would be wiser."

Xavier made a "hmm" sound, running a hand over the stubble that had sprouted on his chin since he'd arrived at the tower. "Actually, I think Siobhan's had a great idea. Maybe it will even give the two of you a chance to learn a new skill."

"A new skill?" Justin spluttered. "What skill could we possibly learn by being flung out into the darkness, into enemies we can't see, into a bottomless expanse of *nothing*?"

Xavier shrugged. "I'm not sure, but aren't you keen to find out?"

Howard, brow still furrowed, nodded. "I wouldn't use the word 'keen,' but if this will help Siobhan rank up her Summon spell..."

Justin was still turning the hilt of his sword around in his grip. "Can't we just do this on the next floor? I'm sure there would be somewhere... more *grounded* for this. Besides, you won't even be able to see us out there in the dark!"

"I don't need to be able to see you. As the spell advanced in ranks, I can now actually *feel* your presence," Siobhan said. "Like, I

556

instinctively know where you all are. I think something similar is happening with my Heal Other spell. It's... strengthening my senses, letting me know when one of you is harmed."

"That sounds helpful," Howard said.

Xavier deposited Soultaker into his Storage Ring, then clapped his hands together. "All right, let's head out, then back in." He willed the floating chunk of rock to hover back toward the barrier that led to the Safe Zone, walking to Justin as he did so. He put a hand on the kid's shoulder and squeezed. "Don't worry. I'll make sure you don't get hurt. Maybe you'll get over your fear of heights out there."

Justin nodded, his face paling as he stared into the darkness. "Yeah." He swallowed. "Yeah, maybe." He didn't sound very sure of himself. Then he sighed. "Maybe it'll be... fun."

Xavier smiled. Something told him it would only be fun for him and Siobhan.

Justin shook out his limbs, looking out into the darkness. *I don't like this plan,* he thought. *I don't I don't I don't. It's a stupid plan and Siobhan's stupid for thinking of it and Xavier is stupid for letting her go along with it and I'm stupid for agreeing to it.*

But he was also eager to *do* something. He felt that out of all the members of his party, he was the most useless.

Howard could tank, not that he needed to. But he *could*. He even had that fancy Bulwark spell.

Siobhan could heal and teleport people around.

Xavier was, well, *Xavier*. That dude could do anything.

But me? I can... swing a sword.

The warrior spells he'd gotten to choose from seemed like nothing compared to the mage spells. Perhaps because he'd never really gotten a chance to *use* them. He had something called Power Strike, which made him hit hard—Howard had that one as well—

and the other he'd ranked up was Haste, which let him speed up for a short time.

I can move fast and hit somewhat hard. Whoopie.

He also had his Sword Mastery skill, which was now Rank 4, along with a few other skills like Physical Damage.

Admittedly, fencing and using a traditional, medieval type sword were completely different. Fencing was a very modern sport all about point scoring. Now, he knew he would have been way better off if he'd done something Like HEMA—Historical European Martial Arts.

But who knew the apocalypse would suddenly arrive?

Not me. I sure didn't see all this crap coming.

He stepped over to the edge of the floating chunk of rock, feeling like... well, feeling like an idiot.

I can't see a damned thing out there. How am I supposed to attack what I can't see?

But he knew the answer to that—Siobhan was going to send a fireball along with him, one that would hover by him as he flew, or rather was *shoved*, into the air. And it wasn't as though he was being sent out to deal with an entire clutch.

Now that Xavier had gotten *even stronger*, he could take out seven of those Dark Wyverns using a single soul. The thought of the man using *souls* basically as ammunition sent a shiver up his spine.

It was also really cool. Which, he admitted probably sounded insensitive. But he called 'em as he saw 'em.

Justin turned and watched as Xavier sent a Soul Strike out at the enemy. The apparition sprung to life, soaring through the Dark Wyverns and killing them like they were nothing. The spell didn't even leave a mark. Something he'd noticed the first time Xavier had let them come along. Soul Damage really was something.

At least those wyverns are only Level 14. I mean, I know they're twice my level, but I should be able to take one with all my titles... right?

Not that he had anywhere near as many titles as Xavier. Still, even if he couldn't do much of anything to one of those beasts, Siobhan could summon him back instantly and then heal him.

This is a bad, stupid, dumbass plan.

"You ready?" Xavier asked, a smirk on his face Justin wished he could wipe off.

"Yes. No. Maybe." Justin shook his head. "Fine." He nodded. "I'm ready."

Howard stepped up beside him. "You know, if you like, I could do this first."

Justin shook his head again. "I'm not afraid of doing this," he lied.

Howard clapped him on the shoulder. "All right, then." He stepped back. "Have fun."

Why'd I have to go and say that?

"Don't worry, Justin. I'll bring you back," Siobhan said. She didn't look quite as gleeful as she had when she'd come up with this plan, which to Justin was the opposite of reassuring.

I'm expendable. If I fall to my death Xavier will just find someone else to fill my shoes. Not that he needs to. He shook out his limbs again. *All right. Enough of that self-pity. It's not endearing, so says my mum.*

"Let's do this." Justin held onto his sword for dear life. "Let me at 'em." He took a few steps backward, then ran to the end of the platform and leapt straight into the darkness.

A split second later, a ball of fire appeared to his left, then he was thrust forward by an incredibly strong, invisible force. Suddenly, he was moving at what felt like thirty, forty, fifty miles an hour, soaring through the air.

He let out a less-than-endearing scream.

Siobhan, at least, had been true to her word. The fireball lit up the darkness ahead of him.

Thank god she has some range on that.

He soared through the air, holding his sword up behind him, ready to let it fall down onto the enemy when he came upon it, poised to use his two spells.

The fireball shot ever forward, just ahead of him, keeping apace. And out in that darkness beyond the fire's light, beasts unleashed screeching roars that made fear bubble up in his chest.

Justin held his breath.

Then he saw the first Dark Wyvern. It flew straight at him, its maw open wide, ready to consume him. Justin let out a battle cry. At least, he *hoped* it was a battle cry and not, instead, a most unbecoming high-pitched scream.

Let's go with battle cry.

He activated Haste. As he did, his heart felt as though it were beating twice as fast. Time slowed, and everything came into complete focus.

This is probably nothing compared to how Xavier feels every moment.

He activated Power Strike, slamming his sword down onto the head of the Dark Wyvern before it could clamp its massive teeth about him. The sword, miraculously, cleaved straight through the centre of its head.

Through its skull. Through its *brain.*

Dark blood spurted from the wound, covering Justin.

You have defeated a Level 14 Dark Wyvern!
You have gained 1,400 Mastery Points.
You have gained 1,400 Spirit Energy.

Justin laughed as the notification appeared in his vision. Then, he quickly plunged into the darkness, and the laugh died and was resurrected into a horrified scream.

The other two Dark Wyverns that remained alive in the clutch screeched and roared from either side of him. He heard their wings flap. Could practically feel their ragged, disgusting breath on him as they neared.

Crap, crap, crap!

Then a bright light enveloped him, and instead of falling to his death, he fell two feet to the floating rock where the other members of his party had been watching.

Just as he landed in a crouch, his Haste spell deactivated. He heaved in a long breath and looked up at the others.

"You killed one of them," Xavier said. "How did it feel?"

Always to the point, that one.

Howard stepped closer. "You look really pale."

At least he cares about my wellbeing.

Siobhan had an innocent look on her face. Like *"Sorry this was my idea and I know that must have been scary but at least you're not dead!"* Though maybe Justin was reading a little more into that look than was actually there.

Justin stood, straightening out of his crouch. He looked down at himself, covered in dark blood, his sword held tight in a death grip that was hurting his hand. He blinked, threw back his head, then let out a loud *whoop!* "That was awesome! Oh my God." He shook his head. "My heart is like, trying to explode from my chest." He grinned. "Can I do that again?"

The others glanced at each other. Xavier shrugged. Siobhan grinned. Howard shook his head.

Then Justin went out for a second time.

Then a third.

Then a fourth.

They kept on sending him out, over and over, Siobhan's Summon spell gaining ever more ranks, while Justin's Power Strike and Haste spells ranked up too. Justin even reached Level 8 while he was out there.

Each time he soared through the darkness it felt equal parts terrifying and exciting, but at some point—he wasn't sure how many times he'd done it, he'd long lost count of how many Dark Wyverns he'd killed—a notification sprang up.

You have learnt the skill Aerial Combat!
Aerial Combat – Rank 1
A student of fighting in the sky, you are one

**with the air. You aren't afraid of heights, as
you have mastered the art of falling with style.
+15% Speed while in the air.
+15% physical damage dealt while in the air.
+50% manoeuvrability while in the air.**

Holy crap. Xavier was right. I did gain a skill. Though he had
no idea how useful it would be in *other* situations.

Once again, Justin plunged to his death. But he no longer
feared the fall—he trusted Siobhan to bring him back. As he fell, he
took a deep breath and basked in the feeling of weightlessness,
wondering how the skill he'd gained might affect his future class.

Chapter 81
Growing Impatient

Xavier watched in slight awe at what was the insanity of Justin.

Less than an hour ago, the kid had been terrified of heights. Now, here he was, voluntarily flinging himself off the floating rock's ledge over and over, straight into that pitch darkness, gaining a single kill each time.

The party got into a rhythm once more. It was far slower going than it had been when it had just been Xavier alone killing the Dark Wyvern clutches, but he was glad to see Justin finally lighting up. This was filling him with an energy and confidence he hadn't had before.

And the fact the kid gained a new skill from what he was doing was something rather interesting. *Aerial Combat.* Xavier wasn't sure how it would help him, but he had an inkling that if Justin ranked the skill up high enough, it would *definitely* give him a better choice of class.

I don't know how to guarantee them all gaining a rare class, and I certainly don't see how they'd be able to gain an epic class, but I can at least try to get them there.

As Xavier had watched Justin fling himself off the floating rock with wild abandon, he'd come up with a plan for them all.

I'll get them all to Level 10 before I fully clear this floor. Once they've gained their titles and rewards for this floor, that could be the best time for them to choose their Level 10 class.

They decided not to bother throwing Howard off the rock like they were doing with Justin. The man already had a path in mind —the path of the tank. And doing what Justin was doing wouldn't help him get any closer to that. So, as not to waste an opportunity, Xavier had Howard attacking him as before, with Siobhan healing him whenever necessary, building up Xavier's Physical Resistance skill and Howard's Physical Damage skill once more.

So the Dark Wyvern clutches wouldn't overwhelm Justin when he leapt off the ledge and was pushed by Xavier's Heavy Telekinesis spell, Xavier took out seven of the ten beasts in each clutch, casting Soul Harden whenever he had spare souls.

It wasn't long before the spell ranked up.

Soul Harden has taken a step forward on the path!
Soul Harden is now a Rank 2 spell.
One cannot walk backward on the path.

When the notification appeared, Xavier paused, took a moment to examine himself and see how he felt.

He couldn't decipher any change. As far as he could tell, there was nothing different about himself at all. Though when he checked his soulkeeping threshold, it had once again gone up by ten.

Will this happen whenever I rank up a soul-type spell? It had so far.

Though he didn't yet know what other benefits ranking up the spell would gain him, he figured he might as well continue bringing its rank up. Besides, increasing his soulkeeping threshold was another goal of his in this place. He needed to keep that up if he was going to get it to one hundred before clearing this floor like he planned.

By the time there was only one clutch remaining out there in the darkness, Xavier had ranked up several of his skills and spells.

Magical Potency, which was taking longer and longer to rank up each time, had increased to thirteen.

Physical Resistance had gained two ranks while he resisted Howard's attacks, bringing it to Rank 10.

Soul Strike had ranked up as well, reaching Rank 5, upping his soulkeeping threshold to seventy. His one-infused Soul Strikes killed eight Dark Wyverns now, but he'd fixed that by dispelling the Spirit Energy from his staff-scythe, bringing his kills balanced back to seven. He'd worried it would bring it to six, but was fortunate to find it hadn't.

When he struck the second last clutch, he ranked up Spiritual Trifecta.

The next time we enter this floor, I might be able to take them all out in one go.

Especially since there was still something he'd neglected to test when it came to Spiritual Trifecta—and Spirit Break, for that matter.

He could now infuse harvested souls when casting the spell to improve its effectiveness. *Maybe I should bring my soulkeeping threshold to 110...*

He was also well on his way to reaching Level 12.

Xavier checked his progress.

**Mastery Points for this level:
1,625,100/2,000,000**

I have fewer points left than I gained during this clear of the floor.

He wasn't the only one who had increased the rank of their skills and spells. Justin had apparently increased his Haste and Power Strike spells several times, and his Aerial Combat skill was improving incredibly quickly, already having gotten to Rank 7.

Only three more ranks until ten.

The rate at which the skill improved seemed pretty crazy to Xavier, but he supposed in normal circumstances it would be a difficult skill to rank up. But on this floor, they'd found the perfect storm in which to do it.

Justin was also Level 9 now, which meant he'd definitely reach Level 10 soon.

I wonder what gaining Rank 10 in Aerial Combat would do for his class choice. Maybe he'll be able to fly...

Though that sounded utterly ridiculous, the kid had gone from killing a single Dark Wyvern when he went out there, to being able to kill all three of the ones Xavier left over for him in one go, manoeuvring through the air with extreme ease even as he fell. It was a sight to see.

And, considering the class that Xavier had gotten to choose, which gave him the ability to *reap souls*... flying didn't seem out of the realm of possibility.

Siobhan had gained quite a few ranks in her Summon spell. It was at Rank 9 now, and would soon reach Rank 10. Though they would need it to be at least Rank 12, as Heal Other had gotten to Rank 11 while she'd been healing Xavier's wounds from Howard's attacks, and they wanted the Summon spell to be a higher rank than the Heal Other spell.

We'll have to stop increasing my Physical Resistance, so she no longer needs to heal me.

And Howard himself had gained a few more ranks in Physical Damage, though he said it was taking far longer each time. He had also begun using Power Strike, ranking that spell up several times.

Xavier couldn't help but think about the other skills he'd yet to figure out, like Core Strength and Cultivate Energy.

I'll get to them. Soon. But this doesn't feel like the right floor to figure them out.

When they refreshed the floor, Xavier, feeling a little impatient, stepped to the edge of the floating rock and took out twenty-seven clutches in less than a minute.

His apparitions had grown larger as his spells grew in strength.

Bolts of pure white lightning shot forth from him, crackling through Soultaker then pulsing forth into the darkness one after the other, consuming the clutches with ease, destroying everything in their path.

When the last clutch fell, a notification popped up in his vision, and he grinned at it.

Congratulations, you have reached Level 12!
Your health has been regenerated by 60%!
Your Spirit Energy limit has increased by 200!
You have received +2 Strength, +2 Toughness, +2 Speed, +3 Intelligence, +3 Willpower, and +8 Spirit!
You have received +20 free stat points!
All your spells have refreshed and are no longer on cooldown!

The others stared at him.

"Why'd you go and do that?" Justin asked.

Xavier shrugged. "I was growing impatient." He turned his head from side to side, cracking his neck, feeling the strength of all the stats he'd gained.

Once more—and without any hesitation—Xavier threw all twenty free stat points straight into Spirit, bringing it up to an effective 335. *I wonder how many Lesser Spirit Coins I'll be able to create now.* Perhaps he should have been doing that whenever he had the chance, but right now, his focus was elsewhere.

When Spiritual Trifecta deactivated, he dispelled the Spirit Infusion in his staff, then sent out a one-infused Soul Strike at one of the clutches.

He was surprised to find, with his added points in Spirit, even without those two spells enhancing his magical power, he was able to take out *eight* of the ten Dark Wyverns in a clutch.

Meaning I could definitely take out a whole clutch with a one-infused Soul Strike now, when Spiritual Trifecta and Spirit Infusion are active. That fact made him smile, as he'd been looking forward to when he got that strong.

"All right, Justin." Xavier nodded out at the darkness. "You're up."

Their rhythm continued. As Siobhan's Summon spell gained ever more ranks, she was able to teleport Justin out to the enemies herself, and summon him back with ease, as the cooldown had significantly reduced, and Justin was able to handle being out there for a few seconds.

Now, she could drop him straight onto a Dark Wyvern, then teleport him to fall upon the next.

Once she'd been able to do that, the kills came even faster, until finally, Justin gained Level 10. And, not too long after that, he ranked up Aerial Combat all the way to 10 as well. Siobhan hadn't just reached her required rank in her Summon spell—she'd gone beyond it, reaching Rank 13, which apparently enabled her to use it on more than one person now.

Xavier couldn't help but smile at that.

I've helped them both get to Level 10 and rank up their skills to Rank 10 and beyond. Now, I just need to figure out how to get Howard to do the same.

The way he saw it, Howard had three important things he needed to rank up—his Bulwark spell, his Physical Defence skill, and the Shield Defence skill he'd recently picked up.

Xavier had faced a wyvern or two once the clutches had reached the rock before, and he knew how chaotic it might end up being if he let a whole clutch reach the floating platform with the party there to get knocked off.

As long as I don't let Siobhan fall, she'll be able to summon any one of us back. Besides, I can deal with a clutch in a single second if I need to.

But it was time to find out if they were up to the task, as it was the only way he could see Howard gaining levels on this floor, unless they wanted him to gain Aerial Combat as well—and that just didn't seem like a good path for him.

If it isn't feasible here, then we'll do it on the next floor, but I'm hoping it won't come to that.

Xavier stepped to the edge of the floating rock and dealt with the final few clutches before they refreshed the floor—no point wasting the Mastery Points that were there, free for the taking.

Not to mention the souls he could harvest.

When the remaining clutches were dead, he stepped over to Howard, clapping the man on the shoulder.

"All right, Howard," Xavier said. "Time to see what you can do."

Chapter 82
Hold Your Ground

THEY RE-ENTERED THE FLOOR ONCE MORE, AND THOUGH Xavier was admittedly getting sick of clearing the same floor over and over, he couldn't argue with the results.

At least watching what the others could do never failed to be entertaining.

Darkness spread out before them, only Xavier able to see the auras of the thousand beasts that were out there. He stood at the back of the platform, Siobhan to his right, Justin to his left. The teenager was bouncing on the balls of his feet, like a boxer in the ring before a match, all pent-up energy.

Now that he'd gotten a taste of fighting beasts, it seemed he wanted to experience it even more.

Xavier could understand that.

Siobhan gripped her staff tightly. Her body was somewhere between relaxed and tense. Her eyes were on Howard, as though at any second he might be pushed straight off the platform, and she'd be ready to summon him back. Her posture, slightly hunched forward, chin jutting out, reminded Xavier of a gamer poised at the keyboard and mouse before a competitive match.

Howard stood in the centre of the platform. The big man

looked stiff. His forehead furrowed in a deep frown, his eyes narrowed, trying to pierce through the gloom but unable to.

None of his typical twitches arose. He didn't scratch his beard with his tower shield. Didn't turn around and look at the others. He remained completely alert.

The first clutch was on its way, their auras burning bright in the dark. A moment before they reached the rock, Xavier sent out a Soul Strike, taking out eight of their number, the bright apparition illuminating them all.

The two remaining Dark Wyverns screeched and roared, their maws opened wide. Their leathery, bat-like black wings were hard to make out, blending with the darkness behind them. Howard slid his right leg back, holding his tower shield close. His breath was steady, chest rising and falling.

Xavier stood ready to destroy the beasts should the man get into any true danger.

***

God damned darkness, Howard thought, staring at the Dark Wyverns as they approached, now close enough to be illuminated by Siobhan's fireball.

Howard's jaw was set, teeth gritted. He forced his jaw to relax —if he got hit hard enough while his teeth were gritted like that, he'd be apt to lose or chip a tooth.

I wonder if it would grow back.

Howard liked to keep his feet rooted to the ground, so he was glad the others hadn't insisted he do this the way Justin had. This floor surely hadn't been designed for such a thing.

I can hold this position for as long as I need to. Justin was able to one-hit those things. Surely I'll be able to do the same.

It wasn't just taking out the Dark Wyverns that he needed to do, however. He needed them to strike his protective spell, Bulwark, if he wanted it to rank up.

It's Rank 5 right now, only five more to go.

As he was standing front and centre, the Dark Wyverns came straight for him. He didn't even need a taunt spell to get their aggression.

The Dark Wyverns fell at him in a dive.

Hold your ground.

At the absolute last second, just before the first of the Dark Wyverns snapped its massive teeth at him, Howard activated Bulwark. A transparent shield materialised in front of him. As the skill had grown in ranks, so had his manipulation of the shield.

He could alter the composition of the shield in almost any way he wished. At Rank 5, he could make it cover enough area to protect those behind him, or he could make it encircle himself completely.

Eventually, he would be able to make it encircle his entire party, and even the platform they all stood upon.

One day, I might be able to make it encircle an entire city block. Maybe even an entire city...

The Dark Wyvern slammed straight into it. Howard had no idea how fast the thing had been flying. He knew birds could fly rather quickly. In a dive, they could be faster than a speeding car.

And these beasts were far superior to normal birds.

Blood spluttered out from the beast's face where it slammed into Bulwark. The blood covered the transparent shield, hanging in mid-air.

Howard smirked. God, it felt like that thing hit him hard. Bulwark had been weakened—perhaps by a quarter of its defensive power—but it hadn't broken.

The beast crumpled forward with a great snapping of bones. Like when Xavier slammed an enemy into a wall or the ground with his Heavy Telekinesis spell.

It looked like the thing hit an invisible steel wall. It slumped to the ground, and Howard wasn't pushed back a single inch.

Though, unfortunately, the impact hadn't killed the beast.

That would have been convenient.

The second beast came at him from the left. The damned

things were too large to both come at him directly. Howard expanded Bulwark, making the barrier cover that side of him. Though the larger he made the shield, the more he stretched out its defensive capabilities.

Still, it was enough.

The second beast crumpled just as the first had, hitting Bulwark causing it a fair amount of damage.

Maybe next time I can challenge more than two, until eventually I'm taking down a whole clutch on my own... that will surely get me to Level 10 faster.

He was lagging behind Justin and Siobhan, and was *miles* behind Xavier.

Bulwark took less damage from the second hit. The beast hadn't been going as fast as the first, as it'd had to change direction to hit him from the side.

Howard stood there, waiting patiently for the beasts to stand. His Bulwark spell needed to take vast amounts of hits before it reached its next rank, and unfortunately it had to take those hits in true combat, not sparring.

I'm still not sure how the System discerns the difference.

The first Dark Wyvern struggled to its feet. The beast looked to be in complete agony. Though its wounds *were* healing, they weren't healing fast.

The second Dark Wyvern snapped back up faster, as it had taken less damage. It slammed a wing against Bulwark. The wing glowed as it smashed into the barrier.

Some kind of spell?

A deep slash appeared in the transparent shield. Howard felt it lose another quarter of its energy.

Two more hits like that, and it'll be down completely.

He'd never seen the Dark Wyverns cast spells before. Xavier hadn't given them the chance.

Now that he'd ranked up the spell, Bulwark could technically last indefinitely, assuming it wasn't taking too much damage. Howard could refresh the spell every minute.

That number hadn't changed, no matter how many ranks he'd gained in the spell, or how many stats he'd gotten from levels and titles.

Howard waited for the next attack to come.

The Dark Wyvern slashed out at the shield a second time just as the first Dark Wyvern had gotten to its feet. The first Dark Wyvern didn't slash out like the other had. The beast was shaky on its feet, barely able to stand. It reared back—Howard thought it was going to fall over—then its throat began to glow, and smoke billowed from its mouth.

Oh.

Flames launched from its large maw, pouring into Bulwark.

Bulwark has taken a step forward on the path!
Bulwark is now a Rank 6 spell.
One cannot walk backward on the path.

Though Bulwark had gained a rank, it wouldn't take effect until he refreshed the spell.

The flames destroyed the transparent shield and didn't stop streaming once they had. Howard raised his tower shield, facing it toward the stream of fire. He thrust out his sword, activating Power Strike, and pushed forward.

The flames kept pouring forth. They didn't stop at his tower shield. They covered the surface of the tall metal shield then went *around* it, burning Howard.

Howard set his jaw, resisting the heat, the pain, the blistering of his skin beneath its armour. His injuries would heal. He'd told Siobhan not to heal him unless he was close to death. He needed to learn how to take this punishment.

He stepped forward into his thrust, stabbing the sword straight through the flames and into the Dark Wyvern's open maw. He angled the thrust up, pushing the blade through the soft tissue in the roof of its mouth and right up to its brain.

You have defeated a Level 14 Dark Wyvern!
You have gained 1,400 Mastery Points.
You have gained 1,400 Spirit Energy.

There was no time to celebrate his small victory. A screech came from the left. A line of pain slashed down his back. He couldn't focus on both enemies at once, and he'd paid for that dearly.

Howard planted his feet. They dug into the dirt and rock of the platform. He slid forward, then righted himself, turning around to face the second of the Dark Wyverns—the one least hurt.

It cocked its wing for another of its magical strikes. Howard raised his shield and hid behind it.

The Dark Wyvern struck at his shield five times before his Shield Defence skill ranked up, also to Rank 6. Howard gave the wyvern a dark grin as he turned the shield aside and slammed it in the head with a Power Strike, right as it was rearing up, readying its flame breath spell.

The beast went down.

Howard took a long breath.

"The next ones are on the way," Xavier said. "You want me to deal with some of them?"

"How far away are they?"

"Maybe thirty seconds."

Howard shook his head, still wearing that dark grin. He twirled his sword in his right hand, raised his shield, tilted his head left and right with a satisfying *crack*. His blistered and burnt skin beneath his armour was already healing. He could feel the raw itchiness of it.

And Bulwark would be ready again by then.

"Let me see if I can take all ten."

Xavier stood back and watched in slight awe at what Howard was able to do. He hadn't known what to expect from the man. But again, like Siobhan and Justin, just because he hadn't gotten the same titles as Xavier didn't mean he wasn't benefitting from his party being the first through the Tower of Champions' floors.

The man held his ground to an almost impossible degree. Xavier was sure he would have been knocked off the platform if he'd had to deal with what Howard was dealing with.

When the second clutch of Dark Wyverns came for him, Howard taunted them before they reached him, yelling vile obscenities into the darkness, clearly hoping that would be enough to get them to attack him and not the others.

And somehow, it worked. The man didn't even have a taunt spell.

I wonder if he'll gain one doing this.

As Howard was the only one fighting and the others were all just standing around, the Dark Wyverns circled him, going after only him.

They slammed into his Bulwark spell, which only seemed to be getting stronger and stronger. He hovered it around him with ease, expanding and contracting it at will, slamming Power Strikes left and right, taking the Dark Wyverns strategically, letting them hit his shield for as long as he wished.

He was far more adept at it than Xavier ever thought the man could be.

His spatial awareness, his battle sense, are way more developed than mine. Though I'd easily be able to defeat him in a physical fight, that's only because my attributes make me far faster than him. If we were near in Speed and Strength, it would be a different story. No wonder he wanted to teach me.

Though Howard was able to solo an entire Dark Wyvern clutch, he couldn't do it fast enough. So Xavier kept the next ones from reaching him at bay with Soul Strike.

He also took this opportunity—feeling that if Howard got into trouble, he would need Siobhan before he needed Xavier—to push the limits of Soul Strike's area of effect.

While a small battle raged in front of him, Xavier fell into a deep meditation, focusing on his Soul Strike spell, trying to gain insights into it. At first, his forehead was creased, lined with fierce concentration. As he focused and practised, his forehead began to smooth, and the sides of his lips ticked up.

His Spirit was so high that the insights came more and more easily. He could *feel* the current limitations of the Soul Strike spell, and he knew exactly how to break through those limits.

I know how to clear this floor faster than any Champion before me.

And the second Howard reached Level 10 and his desired ranks before choosing his next class, Xavier would finally clear this floor and blast through the next.

And the next.

And so on, until he returned them to Earth.

Chapter 83
A Speck of Dust

Xavier watched, somewhat impatiently, as Howard was able to solo clutch after clutch on his own. It didn't take the man too long until he was able to take down an entire clutch fast enough to be ready in time to face down the next.

And so it wasn't long before the man reached Level 10. His spell and skill ranks soared straight up to 10 and beyond as well. Like Justin, he gained another skill while fighting. A skill called Immovable.

The skill increased his defence while his feet were planted and also better protected him against getting pushed back or knocked down.

The skill only served to make him an even better tank. The man could simply stand there and take a beating from all ten of the Dark Wyverns—they hit his Bulwark spell, his tower shield, or his armour. It didn't seem to matter which, as he took the hits with apparent ease.

Once the man had reached his goal, Xavier had stepped out and dealt with the remaining wyvern clutches in less than a minute.

Then they refreshed the floor, and Xavier farmed it, clearing all but one of the clutches.

Again.

And again.

Soul Strike ranked up twice more, reaching Rank 7.

Soul Harvest, Soul Harden, *and* Spirit Infusion each ranked up only once, reaching Rank 3.

While farming the floor, Xavier tested his Spirit Break spell infused with a soul, then tested Spiritual Trifecta infused with a soul as well.

He was a little disappointed with the result. Though he couldn't tell for sure, it felt like infusing a soul into Spiritual Trifecta only strengthened the spell a small amount. If he had to guess, which he *did*, he'd assume maybe a 1 percent increase in the spell's power.

Still, the more souls he infused into both Spirit Break and Spiritual Trifecta, the stronger they became.

Definitely a valuable asset, especially when I'll be able to hold thousands of souls.

And he didn't think that was *too* far away, considering he could already hold 110 after ranking up so many of his soul spells.

As he cleared the floors, he focused on his Soul Strike's area-of-effect component, but the insight he'd gained told him he needed more points in Spirit to achieve what he wished.

Still, he was able to *split* the souls he infused into the spell. At first, he could only split the souls once. A two-infused Soul Strike could be sent in two different directions, at two different clutches, creating two separate apparitions.

And with how much stronger he'd become, ranking up Soul Strike, he could take each clutch out with a single soul.

Which meant he could take out *two* clutches with one spell.

As he progressed, he could split the spell into more and more parts. Until finally, when he reached Level 13, he knew he was ready.

Congratulations, you have reached Level 13!
Your health has been regenerated by 60%!

Your Spirit Energy limit has increased by 200!
You have received +2 Strength, +2 Toughness,
+2 Speed, +3 Intelligence, +3 Willpower, and
+8 Spirit!
You have received +20 free stat points!
All your spells have refreshed and are no longer
on cooldown!

Xavier smiled, knowing what was about to come next.

Title Unlocked!
1,000 Stats: This is a common title that
everyone receives when they have reached a
total of 1,000 combined stat points.
You have received +6 to all stats!
Note: As you have a similar title, "500 Stats"
has been combined with this title and shares
its stats.

Title Unlocked!
First to 1,000 Stats: You are the first person
from your world to reach a total of 1,000
combined stat points.
You have received +20 to all stats!
Note: As you have a similar title, "First to 500
Stats" has been combined with this title and
shares its stats.

He laughed, looking at the two titles he'd just gained. Once again, he threw all his free points into his Spirit attribute, bringing it up to a startling 390.

I wonder if there is a threshold at 500 stat points, like there was at 100...

Xavier shook his head. He'd cross that bridge when he came to it. Right now, he had a floor to clear. He instructed the platform to head back to the Safe Zone.

He was ready now. He could *feel* it.

Xavier refreshed the fourth floor of the Tower of Champions.

Leaving the others in the Safe Zone, he leapt onto the floating platform the second it approached through the barrier—he didn't want to lose a single moment—instructing it to float back out of the Safe Zone.

The instant that floating rock passed through the barrier and Xavier could see the one thousand auras, clustered in clutches of ten, he took a deep breath and focused on splitting his attention to one hundred points.

Xavier had 110 souls harvested and stored when he entered the floor, the limit of how much he could hold. He'd used six of those souls, infusing them into Spiritual Trifecta, strengthening his mind, body, and magic. Soultaker was infused with Spirit Infusion, the arm-length blade shining with a silver glow in the darkness, empowering every spell he cast.

He raised the staff-scythe, then cast Soul Strike, infusing 104 souls into the spell—the most he'd ever infused at once.

He split the spell into a hundred parts. Bolts of pure white lightning shot out from his staff, each heading for one of the hundred clutches. For the first time since Xavier had stepped foot on this floor, the pitch darkness that persisted in this place was dispersed.

His lightning lit up *everything*.

The fourth floor of the Tower of Champions was a miles-long domed rock cavern.

But Xavier didn't spend more than a split-second taking in the scenery.

For the ninety-nine normal clutches that didn't contain the floor boss, Xavier sent a single soul toward them.

The final clutch, Xavier sent *five* souls toward. Though he hadn't faced, or even *seen*, the boss for this floor, he was sure this would be enough to take it down.

And if it isn't, I can simply turn back, refresh the floor, and try again.

But he didn't think it would come to that. He *felt* it. He knew this would work. At almost the same time, the pure lightning that Xavier had sent off in a hundred directions blossomed into soul apparitions. A hundred bright, white, translucent wyverns burst into life, all opening their giant maws, all larger than the wyverns they faced.

And for the first time, Xavier was able to see the floor boss. And from what he could see, it wasn't a wyvern at all.

It was drastically larger than the Dark Wyverns. It looked to be the size of a building. A *large*, six-storey building. Like wyverns, it had wings, but its wings dwarfed everything around it. Vicious spikes ran from atop its head all the way across its spine. Its head was massive, its eyes *huge* and as black as its pitch skin.

When it saw the apparition approach, it opened its giant maw and released a plume of flame larger than a fire truck.

It's a dragon. A massive black dragon.

The flames, of course, did nothing to harm the apparition. It couldn't *be* blocked or stopped. At least, not by something as mundane as an elemental spell. Perhaps it could be evaded, but the beast wasn't fast enough—or simply didn't think to avoid it.

All at once, a thousand auras were snuffed out as a hundred apparitions—the final apparition the largest of all—flew through every clutch, destroying every single one of them.

Not a single beast stood a chance.

In place of their auras, Xavier could now see the souls of the beasts. At the sight of so many souls, the pit in his stomach seemed to call out, the hunger he'd been getting better at keeping under control spiking.

Huh. That was even easier than I thought.

A thousand kill notifications appeared in his vision, but he only wished to look at one.

You have defeated a Level 40 Black Dragon!
You have gained 8,000 Mastery Points.

Only Level 40? That's no higher than the last floor boss!

Though, he supposed the last floor boss *could* have had an entire army helping him kill it. This floor was rather different to that one. His party, without him, would likely struggle against something like that.

Still, Xavier felt a burst of pride. Not to mention *power*, as this all went down. Not wanting to waste the souls of the beasts he'd just slain, and hungering for them more than he ever had, he harvested each and every one of them, consuming them to harden his soul as he did, and read the other notifications as they appeared.

Magical Potency has reached Rank 13!

Magical Potency has reached Rank 14!

Spiritual Trifecta has taken a step forward on the path!
Spiritual Trifecta is now a Rank 7 spell.
One cannot walk backward on the path.

Soul Strike (Ranged) has taken a step forward on the path!
Soul Strike (Ranged) is now a Rank 8 spell.
... is now a Rank 9 spell. ...
... is now a Rank 10 spell. ...
One cannot walk backward on the path.

Xavier could do nothing more than stare at the notifications and try to take them all in.

Soul Strike had ranked up *three times*? How was that even possible?

It must have been because I used the spell so differently to before, and maybe because of how many enemies I killed at once— the System saw it as a feat of power?

Was that why Magical Potency had ranked up twice when it had mostly slowed down? And another rank in Spiritual Trifecta...

He shook his head, a little stunned.

Then he read the title that popped up. He had hoped something like this would come.

Title Unlocked!
Greater Butcher: This is a rare title. You have slain 1,000 enemies in a single strike. Whether you have slain small field mice or fearsome dragons, this feat's reward is the same.
You have received +24 to all stats!
Note: As you have a similar title, "Minor Butcher" has been combined with this title and shares its stats.

Twenty-four points to all stats?

He felt like he had skipped a title or two, going straight from "Minor" to "Greater." It made him wonder how many enemies he'd have to kill at once to get "Major" and "Grand"...

As he harvested souls and hardened his own, he gained another rank in both Soul Harvest and Soul Harden, bringing each of them to Rank 4.

My soulkeeping threshold is 161 now!

It was already hard to imagine he'd only been able to hold ten souls when he first got the spell.

But it wasn't these notifications that he was most eager to read.

It was the ones that just started appearing.

Congratulations! You have cleared the Fourth Floor of the Tower of Champions.
Party Member Contribution:
Xavier: 1,000/1,000 Kills.
Howard: 0/1,000 Kills.
Justin: 0/1,000 Kills.
Siobhan: 0/1,000 Kills.
No shared attributions apply on this floor.

Title Unlocked!
Fourth-Floor Climber: This title has been upgraded. You have cleared the Fourth Floor of the Tower of Champions, and shall be rewarded.
You have received +8 to all stats!
Note: The title "Third-Floor Climber" has been stricken from your soul.

Title Unlocked!
Solo Tower Climber 4: This title has been upgraded. You have cleared a floor of the Tower of Champions by yourself. You are either very brave or very stupid for attempting such a feat. Know that whether this feat was achieved through sheer skill or unbridled luck, you shall be rewarded.
You have received +32 to all stats!
Note: The title "Solo Tower Climber 3" has been stricken from your soul.

Title Unlocked!
1ˢᵗ Fourth-Floor Climber: Out of Champions from five competing worlds, your party is the *first* to clear the Fourth Floor of the Tower of Champions within your instance.

You have received +20 to all stats!
Note: As you have a similar title, "1ˢᵗ Third-
Floor Climber" has been combined with this
title and shares its stats.

Title Unlocked!
Fourth Floor Ranked 1 – RECORD HOLDER
(Completion Time – 4 sec): Out of all the
Champions from all the worlds in the Greater
Universe who have completed the Fourth Floor
of the Tower of Champions in every possible
instance, you have completed it in the fastest
time.
This title is a Temporary Title. If your record
is edged out of first place, your title will be
turned into a normal Top 100 title.
If your record is edged out of the Top 100, your
title will be lost.
You have received +40 to all stats!
Note: As you have a similar title, "First Floor
Ranked 42" has been combined with this title
and shares its stats. You may still view the
previous title and your standing on the leader-
board, if you will it.

Xavier was floored.

Four seconds? That floor... it only took me four seconds?

He knew he'd completed it quickly. That had been his plan. What all his training on this floor had been about achieving... but he hadn't thought it was possible to do it *that* quickly.

I ranked first. Out of trillions of Champions over billions of years, I ranked first.

The bonus of forty stats he knew combined the last two Top 100 titles he'd gotten, meaning this one gained him twenty points, where the others gained ten points each.

Accidental Champion

This title is worth double. If I can do this on the next floor, and the next, all the way up to the tenth floor before we return to Earth, including this floor, that will be an extra seventy points for each of my attributes.

Xavier simply marvelled at that fact. At all he'd just achieved. Thinking it all through.

Power begets more power, and so on and so on...

Xavier had gained a lead like never before. If this floor hadn't just been a fluke... he might end up being the most powerful Denizen to ever move through the floors of the Tower of Champions.

He read the last notification.

In 30 seconds, you and your party will be returned to the Staging Room.

As Xavier waited to return to the Staging Room, the countdown timer already ticking, he felt something he couldn't identify. A shiver ran up his spine, and it was almost as though someone—or some*thing*—was watching him.

The feeling only lasted for an instant, but it left a sour taste in his mouth and a pool of fear in his gut.

Whatever that presence had been, all he knew about it was this: it made him look like less than an ant in comparison.

It made him look like a speck of dust.

Chapter 84
Is There Nothing Left Out There for Me, O Great System?

In the centre of the Greater Universe, upon the largest, most densely populated planet in the Traval sector, stood a tower that reached so high into the sky it was above the clouds.

The tower had a thousand floors. The owner of the tower had it made as an homage to the one where he had first gained his strength, and it has stood since before most of the planets in the universe had even been formed.

A monster of a man, with a neatly cropped grey beard and silver hair that draped down over his shoulders, walked to the edge of the tower's rooftop garden. Not many plants were able to grow this high in the sky, where the air was as thin as the celestial energy was scarce. Only those flora hardy enough to survive even the harshest of conditions could thrive up here, just like the man who walked through that garden now.

He did not wear his armour, nor did he wear a weapon. The man was beyond such things. To even draw blood from his skin would take the effort of a thousand of the strongest worlds' greatest armies and elites in the Greater Universe working in unison.

He had not fought a battle in a long time. In a way, he felt as though he'd grown beyond that too. That he had reached the peak, and there was nothing... left.

There were more worlds to conquer—there were always more —but he was satisfied with his dominion. Those thousand strongest worlds, the ones who could perhaps draw blood from his skin if they worked together? They had long been under *his* control.

But sometimes, it was lonely at the top. Sometimes, a challenge was what he craved more than anything else.

He gripped the intricately carved stonework at the side of the rooftop garden. At the four corners of the tower, and every ten yards from corner to corner, statues of beasts stood guard. Great dragons, ferocious griffons, and a dozen other beasts he couldn't care to remember the names of, but knew he'd killed his fair share of in his time.

If the tower were ever attacked—an eventuality that he doubted would ever come to pass—those beasts would come alive and protect it, each equal to the power of a B Grade Denizen. They were an invention he was quite fond of, but one he no longer wasted his time with.

He turned his gaze to the heavens and closed his eyes as though in prayer.

Is there nothing left out there for me, O Great System?

He wasn't expecting a response. The System had *never* given him a direct response. Not once in his vast memory.

The man let out a great sigh. He opened his eyes and turned from the wall.

He felt weary. More weary than he ever had.

Then, unbidden, without his summoning, a notification popped up in his vision. Words floating in front of him. They made his brow furrow in slight confusion, for in the billions of years that he had lived he had never before seen their like.

Your Temporary Title, Fourth Floor Ranked 1 – RECORD HOLDER (Completion Time – 26 sec), has been edged down one spot on the Tower of Champion's Top 100 leaderboard.

The man blinked.

Impossible.

There was further information, about his title turning into a normal Top 100 title for the Tower of Champions, but he dismissed it—a loss of a few measly stat points was no bother to him —bringing up the leaderboard. A leaderboard he had not looked at since he'd conquered the thousandth floor oh so many years ago, defeating every single one of the tower's challenges as the top ranked Denizen.

A ranking he had never once lost for any of the tower's floors.

Until today.

The ladder showed him the names of every single title holder on the Top 100 list for each floor. Seeing the names of the Champions who ranked was only something accessible by someone who both ranked themselves, and had completed the tower's final floor.

The man opened the leaderboard for the fourth floor.

A team must have somehow finally defeated my time. Perhaps a team from my own realm of influence.

In fact, it might even be one of his descendants leading a party into the tower. Someone with the most possible advantages. Though he had no idea just how many direct descendants he would now have out there, he did know about a few promising newcomers in his sect.

Adranial must be sixteen by now, perhaps she's currently in the tower...

The leaderboard opened. He looked at the top name.

Tower of Champions - Fourth Floor Record Holders
1. Completion Time: 4 seconds.
One Denizen listed:

...

Where a name should have been, there were only three dots. The man stared at those dots. He knew what they meant.

This was a Denizen from a newly integrated world. A world that was still under the System's protection. Perhaps that should not have been surprising. Newly integrated worlds were where Progenitors were born.

But this... the man had been expecting a team to have completed the floor, yet he had been mistaken.

It had been a single Denizen.

This... this is something different. *Something new.*

There were Progenitors, those who gained the first titles for their worlds. Then there were *True* Progenitors—those who capitalised upon their position to the best of their abilities, utilising every advantage they had to gain more and more.

Though, technically, *every* Denizen had the potential to do *anything*, it was generally agreed that: a Progenitor had the potential to change a world, and a True Progenitor had the potential to change a sector—an entire galaxy's worth of planets.

But reaching the number one spot?

The man smirked, ran a hand through his beard.

Well, before now, that had only ever happened once. And that man?

He'd changed the entire Greater Universe.

Though the System barred him from seeing the Denizen's name, the man had long discovered ways *around* the System. Small secrets that let him circumvent its control.

He tried not to take too much advantage of these holes, as they tended to be plugged if he used them on too many occasions.

But this was quite the occasion, and he would be remiss if he didn't take a peek.

And so that was how the most powerful Denizen in the entire universe turned his attention upon a mere child who had just completed the fourth floor of the Tower of Champions.

A few moments passed, then the man smiled.

Earth.

The planet was far away. In fact, as far as he could tell, it was the farthest planet in the entire Greater Universe to be integrated into the System, in a small sector that didn't appear to have a Denizen stronger than C Grade.

The man chuckled to himself.

When Adranial breaks from the tower, assuming she survives its trials, I suppose I'll have a job for her.

Xavier couldn't shake the feeling that he was being watched.

As far as he could tell, there was no longer any sort of presence with its attention upon him. No longer any presence looking at him.

But that didn't mean it wasn't there.

What would be strong enough to look at me inside a floor of the Tower of Champions?

Though he didn't know a great deal about the Greater Universe, and what the System allowed its most powerful Denizens to do, he would have thought something like that to be...

Impossible.

Perhaps it was the System itself, turning its attention on him. Something that could consume billions of galaxies and impose its will upon all of them, well, it would certainly make him feel like a speck of dust.

But that didn't seem right. That didn't seem like what had *actually* happened.

But, whoever, or *what*ever, it had been, Xavier supposed there was no point dwelling on it.

If I am being observed by the System, or a super-powerful Denizen somewhere out there in the Greater Universe, it doesn't change what my next step needs to be.

Standing on the floating rock, Xavier patiently waited for the countdown timer to reach zero.

It was time to gain his rewards for completing another floor.

The others had been stunned when they'd been returned to the Staging Room so quickly.

"Four seconds?" Justin said, shaking his head, repeating the words for perhaps the fifth time since he'd heard them. "You completed the floor in *four seconds?*"

"And you got the top spot!" Siobhan looked more excited than ever.

In fact, the entire team looked invigorated. They'd each reached Level 10 on that floor, not to mention ranked up their spells and skills considerably, and all three of them were ready to choose their classes.

But first, Xavier had a loot box to open.

If he were honest, he perhaps wasn't as excited as he should be to look in the loot box. He doubted the Mastery Points he would gain from it would be more than he could get from farming a level —especially a level like the fourth floor. And though he hadn't been able to loot the corpses of the beasts he'd slain there as they'd fallen down into that great pit of nothing surrounding the floating rock, he could always *make* his own Lesser Spirit Coins if he needed them.

Still, perhaps there would be *something* of note inside the loot box.

You have gained +1 Skill Point.
You have gained 100,000 Mastery Points.
You have gained 60,000 Lesser Spirit Coins.
You have received a Sector Travel Key.

Xavier blinked at the text, reading the last thing he'd gotten from the loot box over a second time.

A Sector Travel Key? Is that... is that what I think it is?

The item appeared in his hand. The key looked to be made from well-polished brass. It was large and chunky and looked... old fashioned. He frowned down at it, scanning the key.

{Sector Travel Key}

Well... that was helpful.

Xavier could imagine what it was, though he had no idea how to use it. Clearly, it looked like it was supposed to unlock something. But *sector travel* sounded like something that should let him teleport to another world, or create a portal to one.

This was just... a key.

Perhaps it was time to have another conversation with the barkeep downstairs.

Chapter 85
A New Energy Source

Xavier, still holding the Sector Travel Key in his hand—it felt oddly heavy, given its size, and he got the feeling the key wasn't actually made from brass—looked over at the others.

Howard, Siobhan, and Justin had just opened their own loot boxes. Their eyes had that slightly glazed over look a Denizen got when they were staring at their notifications. None of them looked particularly excited, as though their awards were normal and expected.

"Did you guys get a key?" Xavier asked, though from the look in their eyes he could already tell they hadn't.

Howard frowned, eyes refocusing. "A key?"

Justin shook his head. "No. I didn't get a key." He looked at Siobhan. "Did you?"

Siobhan turned away from her loot box and looked at Xavier. She raised her hand, showing an Attribute Token held between two fingers. "I just got one of these."

Justin rolled his own Attribute Token over his knuckles, tossed it up into the air, then caught it swiftly as it fell back down. Howard raised his own with a shrug.

Siobhan walked up to Xavier. "What kind of key is that?"

Xavier turned it over in his hand, examining it. "It's called a Sector Travel Key."

"Sector Travel Key!" Justin's eyes lit up. "What does that do? It sounds cool."

Xavier smirked. "It does sound cool. It also doesn't *say* anything about what it does, unfortunately."

"I get the feeling it lets you... travel around the sector?" Siobhan mused, sounding a little unsure.

Howard crossed his arms over his chest. "Maybe it's like a passport? Gives you permission to enter certain places?"

"I suppose it could be," Xavier said, sounding dubious. He hoped it wasn't something as mundane as that. A passport wasn't much use if you couldn't get on a plane, after all. And he had no idea how to get to another world.

Do I even want to go to another world?

He internally scoffed at his own thought. *Of course* he wanted to go to another world! Though he knew it wasn't exactly a priority, considering there would be an invasion going on back on Earth, he figured if the System had given him this, it would turn out to be important in the future.

"The question is, why did I get this while you guys got something different?" Xavier didn't mind that the others had gotten an Attribute Token and he hadn't. Though he didn't know how to use the Sector Travel Key, he got the feeling it was far more valuable. It wasn't that he would ever say *no* to more attribute points—it was just that he was confident that he probably had more than just about anyone else at his level would.

"That... doesn't really seem like a question, does it?" Siobhan's forehead creased. "You just ranked *first* on a floor. You made a new record. That... that still absolutely boggles my mind, considering how many *trillions* of Champions would have gone through that same floor in the last few *billions* of years! Honestly, it's kind of insane when you think about it."

Xavier considered that for a moment. "I know that, but the

System has never given us different rewards in the past. Now, it's like it's singling me out."

"The System gives you different titles. Why wouldn't it give you different rewards from loot boxes?" Howard said with a shrug.

Xavier tilted his head to the side, not feeling entirely convinced. It made him think of that presence he'd felt, just after he'd cleared the floor and gotten that title. That presence that had made him feel like nothing more than a speck of dust.

That presence that he'd been sure *wasn't* the System. At least, his instinct had told him it hadn't been.

He lowered his head, deep in thought, turning the key over and over in his hand. *Could this be a gift from that presence I'd felt?* He tilted his head to the side, considering. Could a Denizen really interfere with the rewards a loot box gave?

That doesn't sound like it would be fair... though this key doesn't appear to influence how I'll do on a floor of the tower. If anything, it's technically worse *than an Attribute Token in that regard. At least in the immediate future. So I suppose the System wouldn't be worried about the outcome being influenced if someone were to receive one of these...*

But perhaps he was simply being paranoid. Looking too deeply into this. He didn't *have* any reason to believe that this key hadn't come from the System itself.

Besides, imagining an entity out there that was strong enough to observe him on a floor *and* circumvent the loot box rewards, right under the nose of the System? The very thought made him shudder.

What would it mean, if I've garnered that kind of attention?

Xavier sighed, depositing the Sector Travel Key into his Storage Ring where it would be kept safe. He would definitely visit Sam down at the tavern about this, even if their last conversation hadn't ended too well. Something told him the man would be willing to speak with him again now.

But first, there were other things to attend to. Like Siobhan,

Howard, and Justin choosing their classes. He didn't want to miss out on seeing what they ended up with.

He closed his loot box and sat back on it, crossing one leg over the other. Soultaker was in his Storage Ring, but he imagined he still looked a little sinister, even sitting in this position, with the Shrouded Robes on.

Not to mention his silver eyes.

They're going to be able to see auras soon.

That thought reminded him of his own aura. He'd neglected to adjust it after he'd gained that last level, not to mention all of those titles, and his balance was out of whack. As the others settled down, sitting on their own loot boxes and going through their class selections with that same glazed look in their eyes, Xavier fell into a deep meditation and focused on his aura.

The last time he'd adjusted his aura, it hadn't taken him very long. But this time, he'd gained *quite* a lot of Spirit Energy. It made him worry about when he gained Spirit while being exposed, like when he would be back on Earth.

What if he accidentally revealed his aura, and it gave away his position to the enemy at a crucial moment?

Perhaps as I get stronger with Aura Control, even gaining a vast boost to my Spirit attribute won't throw me off containing my aura.

Once he'd gained the perfect balance, one that didn't have his aura flowing outward from him, the Spirit Energy consumed at the exact rate that he recovered it, a notification popped up in his vision and he smiled.

Aura Control has reached Rank 3!

Though he was glad he'd gained another level in Aura Control so easily, it did make him wonder about the other two Skill Quests.

Celestial Energy... Maybe Sam will tell me about that this time.

"Yes!" Justin exclaimed, pumping a fist into the air. "Hah!"

Xavier raised an eyebrow at the teenager. The kid jumped to

his feet and had a look of glee lighting up his face. "What? Good class?"

"A rare class!" Justin beamed at Xavier. He glanced at the other two. They were still staring at their own class choices. Justin sat back down, smiling broadly. "I'll choose the class now, and tell you when the others have chosen theirs." His eyes shifted focus, then he blinked, stood up from his loot box, and lay on the ground.

"What... Why are you lying on the floor?" Xavier asked.

"Last time you passed out. Figured I'd skip the step of falling." Justin looked at him. "Did it hurt?"

"Yes. Excruciatingly."

"Thanks. I... appreciate your bedside manner." Justin frowned, muttering, "Floor-side manner?"

A moment later, the teenager spasmed, then went still. When he opened his eyes, less than a minute had passed. He let out a breath. "You weren't kidding. That hurt like a mother..." He trailed off, his eyes widening. He must have been looking at his new spells.

Xavier stepped over and helped him to his feet. He checked out the kid's eyes. They hadn't changed colour, but his aura had shifted a little. It wasn't that it was stronger—he wouldn't have gained any attribute points from the class change—but it did seem like... it had more *weight.* "How do you feel?"

Justin shook out his limbs, rolled his head around his neck, then smiled. "I feel great. And these new spells!"

Xavier grinned back at the kid, and they both sat down and waited for the others.

Though Xavier had been hoping that Justin would be able to choose a rare class, he hadn't actually been sure that would be possible. He figured that might be a more difficult feat, requiring more than what the three of them had managed to accomplish.

Then he supposed it must be incredibly rare for Champions to get the first-clear titles that they'd managed to get, and those titles were worth much more than the normal baseline, normal titles for clearing a floor.

And they stack on top of those.

Todd Herzman

Not to mention that Champions in general were probably more powerful as a rule than those who hadn't come through the tower, as they would simply have access to more titles than most.

They probably get uncommon classes as a rule, too... Pushing it to rare couldn't have been that hard.

That made him wonder about his own accomplishment. How much more powerful, exactly, was an epic class compared to a rare class? He remembered reading the descriptions for some of those rare classes. They'd sounded interesting, even kind of powerful, but they hadn't sounded anywhere as strong as the epic classes like Bringer of Destruction and the one he'd chosen, Soul Reaper.

Xavier waited patiently, contemplating what Celestial Energy might be, while he waited for the other two to choose their classes.

At some point, Howard went to lie on the ground. Though it hadn't seemed like he'd been paying attention to what happened to Justin, as his eyes had been glazed over the entire time, he must have been.

Howard grunted, spasmed, shut his eyes, then went still. When he opened his eyes again, he muttered, "Yes. That's the one." His eyes refocused as he made it back to his loot box. Though he wasn't smiling, his shoulders were pulled back, and he was sitting a little straighter than before. Xavier couldn't help but read a bit of pride in the man's posture.

Siobhan was the last one to choose her class. Her face was scrunched up, and she was playing with a strand of hair as she stared at whatever choices she had. Xavier got an image of the woman in her normal—if normal was a thing that existed since the integration or ever would exist again—job as a marketer at an indie games company, sitting in front of her computer, her face all scrunched up like that, one hand on her mouse, the other playing with her hair as she thought through whatever it was that was in front of her.

Eventually, a small smirk slipped onto her lips, and she bobbed her head, making a *hmm* noise. She went through the same procedure as the others. Xavier was there to help her up when she opened her eyes.

When she was back at her seat on her loot box, Xavier rubbed his hands together, finding he was more excited than he'd expected to be, anticipating what kind of classes they'd chosen.

"Did you two manage rare classes like Justin?"

Siobhan and Howard nodded their heads in unison. Howard glanced at the others, then was the first to speak.

"I got the choice of three common classes, two uncommon classes, and one rare class," Howard said.

The others nodded. They must have experienced the same thing.

Interesting. I had more epic classes to choose from than they had rare classes.

"Fortunately, the rare class sounded like exactly what I was after." Howard summoned his tower shield, holding it somewhat reverently. "The class is called Shield Sentinel. And the spells sound... impressive." He tilted his head to the side. "I have gained five new spells. A basic Taunt spell, which says it works to varying degrees depending on an opponent's Willpower and scales with both my Toughness and Willpower attributes.

"A spell called Hold Ground, which I can see working well with my Immovable skill. It decreases the amount of damage I receive when staying in one spot by half." He ran a hand through his beard. "I see that going up in the future.

"I also received a spell called Martyr's Defence. It allows me to intercept a strike or spell meant for another."

"Does it reduce the damage you take from that strike?" Siobhan asked.

Howard shook his head. "No. I take the full damage."

Xavier nodded. That sounded like an incredibly valuable spell. Out of all of them, Siobhan was the most vulnerable. Though she could heal others and teleport them out of danger, she couldn't do any of that for herself. To have Howard able to take damage for her would be quite the asset.

"That's three. What are the other two spells you gained?" Xavier asked.

Howard gave a smile with a bit of an edge. "Backfire. A spell that puts half the damage I receive back onto the enemy. It doesn't reduce the damage I take, but..." He shrugged. "I'm already a tank. And the last one." He ran a hand through his beard thoughtfully. "It's called Toughness Infusion. It gives me the ability to infuse Toughness Energy into my shield and armour."

Xavier sat up straight. "Toughness Energy? What's that?"

Howard shook his head. "I'm not sure. But... when I look at my stats, I now have a new line item. I still have Spirit Energy, but below that... it looks like I have a new energy source."

Chapter 86
Ducklings

"A NEW ENERGY SOURCE?" XAVIER ASKED, HIS CURIOSITY more than piqued, excitement swelling in his chest. "What do you mean, a new energy source?"

The big man shrugged, then scratched at his beard. "It looks like it works off my Toughness attribute." He shook his head. "Which, of course, should be obvious..." He chuckled. "For every point in Toughness, I have 100 points in Toughness Energy."

"Sounds remarkably like Spirit Energy," Siobhan said in a musing tone. "Though I wonder how you'll be able to gather more."

"I thought Spirit Energy was like... like mana in a video game." Justin clenched a fist. "The source of our magical power."

Siobhan tilted her head from side to side. "It's not unusual for there to be different types of energy sources in video games. Something like stamina, to help with running and healing and the like. Though this... this sounds like something else."

"How much information does the Toughness Infusion spell give?" Xavier asked. His thoughts went to Spirit Energy... and then straight to his Spirit Core. The one he'd discovered not long ago, activating several Skill Quests. Xavier frowned, focusing on Howard's aura for a moment. His aura had changed since he'd

603

chosen his class—all their auras had a little. But they hadn't seemed worth examining. At least, not at first.

Xavier narrowed his eyes. Was that...?

Yes. There was a different colour swirling around in the man's aura. Something that hadn't been there before. His aura had taken on a slightly reddish tinge.

Xavier leant backward a little on his loot box, straightening up, thinking about the consequences of this. A different energy source. Something else polluting? Affecting? The man's aura.

Does that mean he has another core? A Toughness Core? Did taking on that new class give him that?

He didn't want to venture his theories to the others. Not yet, anyway. First, he wanted to gather more information.

Howard's eyes glazed over. "The spell doesn't say too much more than I've mentioned. It's defensive in nature... strengthens my armour... reduces damage taken from physical and magical attacks..." The man made an *ahh* sound. "I think I misread it the first time. It's not just *my* armour I can infuse the energy into, I can infuse it into other people's as well!" He smiled, giving a sharp nod. "That will better help me be able to protect you two." He pointedly looked at Justin and Siobhan, clearly not worried about having to protect Xavier. "Though... it looks as if that energy will be trapped when it's in use."

"Trapped?" Justin asked.

"I think it means..." Howard scrunched his eyes almost shut. "I think it means that whatever Toughness Energy I infuse into something won't regenerate until I dispel it."

"Interesting," Siobhan said.

Howard nodded. The smile was still on his face when he turned to Justin. "And what about you? How did your class choice go?"

Justin gave the man a sly smile. That excitement he'd shown moments ago bubbling back to the surface. He looked like he wanted to jump from where he sat, but somehow managed to contain himself.

"I..." Justin almost sounded out of breath. "I can *fly!*"

"What?" Xavier said, leaning forward again, a grin on his face. "Are you serious?" Though Xavier was hoping the kid would be able to develop a spell that would allow him to fly, he honestly didn't think it would be something that would happen this *fast*, that was, assuming it could happen at all.

Developing that Aerial Combat skill of his really paid off.

The others looked almost as excited as Justin did. Siobhan's smile was radiant and bright. And Howard? Well, it was just good to see something other than a sombre, serious expression on that man's face. Since he'd fought on the fourth floor, taking down all of those Dark Wyverns by himself, the man's demeanour seemed to have shifted.

He's still scared for his family back on Earth, but perhaps he's embracing his new role.

Justin, giddy, nodded about four times and finally couldn't contain himself any longer. He stood up from the loot box and stepped over toward a clear space. "The spell doesn't last very long, and I think it will get better over time, but..."

Justin let out a long breath. His hands were beside him, clenched in fists. He seemed to be psyching himself up. He kind of looked like Wolverine about to extend his claws. If Wolverine were a teenager.

Justin threw his head back and let out a fairly good imitation of a bestial roar. Something emerged from his back, about his shoulder blades, punching two holes through his armour—armour that Xavier hoped would be self-repairing, though he wasn't sure if it was.

The *things* extended outward from the teenager's back. They were a dusty, dirty white. And they had feathers.

"Wings!" Siobhan said with a clap of her hands. "You have wings!"

Justin wrenched his neck around, in a way that looked quite painful, and got a look at the wings now protruding from his back. There was a bright, excited look on his face.

Right up until the moment he saw how big they were—or rather, how big they *weren't*.

"What?!" Justin stammered. "These... these look like the wings of... of a baby duck!"

"They're called ducklings," Howard said with a surprisingly straight face. "Not baby ducks. And yes. Your rare class has given you... little duckling wings."

Xavier glanced at Siobhan. The woman had a hand over her mouth and was clearly stifling a laugh. Xavier himself couldn't help it any longer. "The way you threw your head back in a roar!" He laughed, loud and free. "Like, like you were going to turn into a monster!"

Siobhan dropped her hand, joining in. "Then... tiny... little... wings!" she said between gasps of laughter.

Even Howard gave a deep chuckle and a few shakes of the head, looking down at his feet.

Justin crossed his arms at his chest. He looked like he wanted to storm off, leave the Staging Room. And lock himself in his quarters. Instead, he dropped his arms, seemed to force his face to relax, and focused, shutting his eyes and letting out a long breath.

The tiny wings on his back began to flap. Quite fast. Not hummingbird fast—they were still visible—but close.

Then Justin rose from the ground.

"Holy crap." Xavier stood, watching as the kid began to fly upward toward the tall ceiling.

Justin opened his eyes, looking down, saw the floor had left him far behind, and released an uproarious laugh. He pumped a fist into the air—which made him veer off to the right, his whole body tilting—then let out an excited *whoop!*

He lowered to the ground after only about ten seconds in the air. His wings disappeared when he was still three feet from touching back down, and he fell the last little bit.

Justin drew in a deep breath. His cheeks were a little red. "Okay. That was awesome." He glanced at the others. "I'm sure...

sure those wings will grow bigger," he muttered, coming back to sit on his loot box.

Xavier still had a great big grin on his face. They hadn't all laughed like that since... well, they hadn't all laughed like that *at all*. They'd hung out at the tavern. Chatting and having a few drinks, in the time when they were locked out of the next tower floor. But this was... was the closest he'd felt to the others since they'd met.

"So," Xavier said. "What other spells did you get?" He waved a hand, pursed his lips, then said, "Other than the baby duck wings."

"They aren't *baby duck* wings!" Justin burst out.

"Sorry, *duckling* wings," Xavier corrected with a straight face.

The others laughed again, but it didn't take them long to settle down and hear what Justin had to say about his class.

"The class is called Airborne Duellist," Justin said, then went on to tell them about the other spells that he'd gained. The first spell, the one he'd just demonstrated by sprouting wings, was called Winged Flight.

He'd also received Air Strike, which was a physical attack that only worked when he was off the ground. Apparently it used the wind element and allowed him to elongate his physical strikes, turning them into whipping, slashing wind. Xavier had to say he was keen to see that one in action, and not only because it might mean seeing those tiny wings sprout from the kid's back again.

The final spell Justin had received was called Slip Dodge. It was a defensive spell, allowing him to get out of the way of any oncoming strike while it was active. It was a toggled spell, something Xavier hadn't encountered before.

The spell didn't say how long it would last—spells never did in Xavier's experience, that was something you had to find out through experimentation—but it explained that it could be activated and deactivated at will. If it lasted for a whole minute, that minute could be stretched over an hour or a whole day, or even an entire year, if you only used it in sixty one-second bursts.

Xavier was a little surprised Justin had only received a mere three spells, whereas Howard and Xavier himself had received more than that, but as he seemed rather excited about all of them he didn't bother commenting on it.

Though, initially, watching Justin sprout those tiny little wings had been... well, hilarious, Xavier could definitely see the advantage of being able to move through the air, and he knew that the amount of time that Justin would be able to spend flying would only increase as he grew more powerful.

He'll have great mobility, focusing on Speed, and he already has that Haste spell, coupled with flight and Slip Dodge...

Xavier was almost a little jealous. His spells were certainly more powerful, and he didn't want to give up the ability to reap souls, but it did make him wonder what he would look like with wings...

Large, black wings, like that of a raven...

God, he would look even more like the angel of death than he already did. Was that something he *wanted*? The sides of his lips quirked up just thinking about it. *Yes. I do want that.*

Once Justin had finished explaining what the different spells he had did, they turned their attention to Siobhan. It was her class that Xavier had been most excited to hear about. Ever since she'd mentioned what she might be able to do with her Summon spell in the future, he'd been curious where focusing on that would take her class.

He couldn't even begin to imagine what *new* spells she would gain when she already had the spell she needed to accomplish what she wanted—she just needed that spell to grow more powerful, which would happen naturally as she levelled up and the spell grew in ranks.

But what type of rare class would the System have given her now?

Siobhan gave a bright smile, her hands folded in her lap. She looked down, almost a little shyly. "I chose a class called Divine Beacon."

Chapter 87
Divine Beacon

"Divine Beacon?" Xavier's curiosity was piqued. The names of Howard, Justin, and Xavier's own class had felt more descriptive than hers did.

His mind worked, wondering about the name. He supposed the "divine" part could speak of her ability to heal others, whereas the "beacon" part could have something to do with summoning.

But she may have gained other powers seemingly unrelated to those two when she'd chosen her rare class.

Siobhan smiled. "Since I'd gotten that healing spell, I was worried it would make me... a less active member of our party. I always hated playing healers in video games, yet the guys I played with always thought that I"—she rolled her eyes—"as a *girl*, should be the one to play the cleric or monk, as though we can't be fighters too. But..." She dipped her head. "I know that when we return to Earth, there will be so much to do there other than just fight. There will be so many ways for me to help not just this party, but others. And now, I also have ways to help the three of you fight even better."

"What ways are those?" Howard asked.

Justin leant forward on his loot box.

Siobhan's fingers were interlocked in her lap. "Well, first..."

She sighed, her voice turning a bit sad. "I've lost my Cast Element spell." She bit her lip. "The System said I might lose some of my spells if they weren't compatible with the new class, so it didn't come as a surprise. Though it did prove to me that I'm definitely not a combat fighter any longer."

Xavier struggled to imagine what that might be like—to have a purely support class. He assumed she must still be able to cause some damage, even if just by hitting enemies with her staff—he'd certainly proved that that could work—but to not have *any* offensive spells? No, *he* definitely couldn't go down that path.

But he was glad that there were others out there who could.

"I suppose you no longer need it," Howard said in a soft voice.

Siobhan nodded. "Indeed. Fortunately, I have gained more than I've lost." A smile returned to her lips then, her voice no longer melancholy, some of that bright excitement coming back. "One of the spells I received is called Divine Beacon, the same as my class. It says it creates a pillar, something that rises up from the ground, and all those within the pillar receive boosted health regeneration, physical resistance, and magical resistance."

Howard grunted. "If we coupled that with my Bulwark spell as it grows larger, and you were able to summon people into it..."

"Then we could protect a lot of people in the middle of a battle." Siobhan nodded. "And heal a lot of wounded, too."

Xavier could definitely see how useful a spell like that could be, especially in some sort of pitched, defensive battle, like a siege, where a group of fighters were defending a singular place.

That's definitely the type of fighting I can envision when we return to Earth.

"The second spell I got was Banish. It looks like an offshoot of my Summon spell and allows me to teleport an enemy away from us."

Xavier's eyebrows rose. "*That* could be quite an offensive spell. Can you choose where you teleport them?" His gaze flicked to the ceiling. "Like, high in the sky, so they fall to the ground?" He imagined beasts falling down from unimaginable heights, hitting a stone or cement floor at terminal velocity.

"Unless they can fly," Justin said.

Xavier glanced at him.

"What? Then they wouldn't fall."

Siobhan shook her head. "It doesn't appear to allow me to teleport someone to a precise location like my Summon spell. Rather it banishes them away from us to a safe distance. The more it grows in power, the farther I can banish an enemy, and the more enemies I can banish."

"Assuming they aren't resistant," Howard said.

Siobhan nodded. "Yes. Always assuming that. Then there's the third spell." Her smile turned a little sly. "This is where, I think, I could really change the tide of a fight." She looked at Xavier. "It's called Embolden. It allows me to buff a party member, giving them a percentage boost to their attributes."

Xavier blinked. "All their attributes?"

Siobhan nodded. "All of them. There are two paths—one that will allow me to boost an individual, or one that will allow me to spread the attributes between multiple people." She looked at Xavier pointedly once she'd said that. "I haven't decided which way I'll choose to go, yet."

Xavier thought on that for a moment. He could be selfish and push her toward boosting an individual's attributes—namely *his*. But something told him that others would benefit from that boost far more than he would, so he didn't say anything. Though he was glad that the others consulted him about their skills and spells, he ultimately wanted them to make their own decisions on what they should do with them.

"Did you get any more spells?" Xavier asked, as she'd only listed three so far.

"One more," Siobhan said. "This one I'm less sure about." Her forehead creased. "I thought that I'd lost the path of summoning beasts or... lesser deities." Her frown deepened. "So I guess this must be something else? I suppose I'll find out when I use it. The spell is called Divine Guardian. It says that it allows me to summon something called a Construct, which will help defend me from attacks."

"Maybe you haven't lost combat capabilities after all," Xavier said.

"Maybe." She bowed her head. "This is certainly the spell I'm most interested in trying out next."

That made Justin perk up. "When are we heading to the next floor? Because I definitely want to spend some time practising with my new spells before then." He looked over at Howard. "How about a spot of sparring?"

Howard chuckled. "You can see if you can do any damage against me, flying in the air with those little duckling wings of yours."

Justin's expression soured. "And we'll see if you can even land a strike on me, considering how slow you are."

Before their conversation turned into a friendly squabble, Xavier let them know that he wanted to head down to the tavern to visit Sam to see if the man could answer a few of his questions. He told them the questions would only be about the Sector Travel Key, but there were other things he might ask Sam. If the man seemed willing to talk.

Though... he wasn't sure how much he wanted to reveal to the so-called barkeep.

That presence I felt... at the end of the fourth floor...

The more he thought about it, the more he grew sure that it definitely *wasn't* the System that had been looking at him. He hadn't shared that detail with his party. There wasn't anything that he could do about it. The only thing telling them would do was worry them, and they all had enough on their minds as it was.

The fourth floor hadn't taken them very long to clear, so it felt strange heading out of the Staging Room already. Still, he was more curious about this Sector Travel Key than he'd let on, and if he could figure out what it was for sooner rather than later, he was happy to let the others play with their new spells for a little while before heading to the next floor.

In fact, Xavier couldn't help but stop by the door for a moment. He leant back against it, crossing his arms over his chest, and watched as Justin and Howard stood and walked over to the sparring circle.

Justin drew his sword. Howard summoned his tower shield, drawing his own sword from its scabbard. Xavier tilted his head to the side. *Perhaps it's time to outfit them with better weapons and armour.*

Justin began to circle around Howard, sending questing strikes toward him. Howard, true to form, stayed rooted to the spot. One foot never left the ground, only pivoting, his other foot making him turn so he always faced Justin. His tower shield came up, taking a few hits.

Does he already have his new Hold Ground and Backfire spells active?

Justin suddenly burst into action. He leapt up into the air, cocking his sword back, and unleashed Air Strike.

I suppose he doesn't need to fly for it to work.

Howard's tower shield suddenly glowed brown. Xavier narrowed his eyes, peering at the shield.

He's infusing Toughness Energy into the shield.

He watched the two spar for a little while. If he were watching this pre-integration, he doubted that he would be able to follow the movements—they were going so fast. They looked like two veteran fighters that had been at this for years, their skill transcendent, far above that of a normal human.

But Xavier followed their movements easily. And, well, even Justin looked a little slow to him.

Though the two fought hard, it seemed as though they were at an impasse. The two fighters were at the same level, and shared the exact same titles. And their fighting styles were such that neither was able to gain any true advantage against the other. When Justin proved fast enough to get past Howard's shield, Bulwark was summoned to stop his strikes. When that wasn't effective—or when Justin broke through it—the strikes that he was able to land on Howard simply didn't appear strong enough to *do* much of anything.

And Howard? He was certainly tough for his level, but he wasn't near as fast as Justin. Whenever he struck back at the kid, Justin was just too slippery. Xavier wasn't even sure if that was because he was using his Slip Dodge spell or if his Speed was such that he didn't even need it.

After a few minutes of this passed, Xavier couldn't help but chuckle at the two of them. "You don't even appear to be able to hurt each other."

Justin paused his onslaught against Howard, stepping back from the man with a sigh. "I know. It's... well, kind of infuriating."

Howard smiled back. "It is a little frustrating." He stood straight, out of his defensive stance, and rolled his head around his shoulders, eliciting a few cracks. "Also, it appears as though I cannot use the Taunt spell on my allies. Which, I suppose, is fair."

"I can't use Banish on any of you, either," Siobhan said from where she'd been watching on the sidelines. "I just tested. I wonder if that's because we're in the same party, not just allies."

Justin rubbed the back of his neck. "That's probably the reason, right? Maybe the System knows we don't wish any ill will upon each other. But if we were fighting another human... I can't imagine it wouldn't allow us to use some of our spells, especially in self-defence."

Siobhan sighed. "There's still so much we don't know about how this all works, isn't there?" She took a step forward, drew in a deep breath. "Now that your little sparring match has been put on pause, I think it's time for me to see what this Divine Guardian is."

The mage—*or do I call her Divine Beacon now?*—summoned her staff, holding it in both hands. A moment later, a glowing purple light enveloped Siobhan. The glow drained from her, being taken up by the staff.

Then the purple light poured out of the staff and onto the ground, where it coalesced and formed a puddle.

"Your Divine Guardian is a purple... puddle?" Justin said, an eyebrow raised, chuckling slightly. "That's..." He trailed off, eyes widening.

The puddle grew upward until it formed a bulky, seven-foot suit of armour. The suit looked like something you'd see free-standing in a fancy old castle. And like those, this one had no one inside. The helm's visor was up, but it was completely empty. Gripped in the gauntlets of the seemingly empty suit of armour was a great sword.

The Divine Guardian didn't move a muscle. If Xavier didn't know any better, he would have thought it was just a statue.

Justin took a step toward Siobhan, as though to inspect the Divine Guardian. His sword was still gripped in his hand. The Divine Guardian moved swiftly and suddenly, raising his—its?—sword up in a defensive posture and standing in front of Siobhan as though to protect her.

Siobhan grinned, her face lighting up. She clapped a hand on the Divine Guardian's shoulder, having to reach up quite high to do so. "Oh, I think I'm going to like this spell."

Chapter 88
Caretaker

Xavier walked down the spiralling staircase toward the lower floors. He didn't even pause when he reached the floor that contained his chambers. He simply kept on walking, heading to the ground floor, contemplating what he wished to talk to Sam about.

The last time they had spoken, Xavier had burned through his core. If the man hadn't been there, there was a good chance that Xavier would have gotten himself killed doing something as foolish as he had.

System-damned fool.

That's what Sam had called him, and the man had probably been right. But that didn't matter, because his foolishness had paid off—he'd broken through that initial barrier, and now knew how to contain his aura within his Spirit Core, increasing the skill's rank to three.

Only a couple of days had passed since the last time Xavier had stepped foot inside the bar, but he was sure that Sam would notice the change—that his aura was no longer in evidence.

Xavier reached the ground floor. The hallway that headed toward the tavern's door was empty. He summoned the metal key into his hand, turning it over, then tossing it into the air and catching it a few times.

This would be the first thing he asked the man about. But there were other things on his mind: Celestial Energy was one of them, along with the cycling of Spirit Energy through his core.

But the thing that was at the top of his mind was still that presence he'd felt.

Should I trust this man with such a thing?

He would have to explain *why* someone powerful was watching him. Though Xavier might have been a bit of a loner back on Earth—okay, maybe *more* than a bit—he'd never been the secretive type. When people had asked him questions, he'd never felt the need to hide anything about himself. Probably why he'd been so free with the fact he'd gained titles, telling all that to his party when he'd only just met them. Someone else might have felt the need to hide that information.

He already felt bad not disclosing that he'd felt like he'd been watched to them.

But he simply wasn't sure what the right move was. The Greater Universe was more vast than he could even begin to contemplate, and Xavier had never had secrets like the ones he held now. He'd never been in any sort of position of power. He'd been doing a degree in *creative writing,* for god's sake.

Now, he was a Progenitor. More than that, he'd gotten the top spot on the leaderboard. Perhaps only for one floor... but he got the feeling that was a bigger deal than he could even conceive.

Xavier pushed open the door of the bar and was greeted with a waft of warm air. Fires rumbled in the hearths, wood stacked beside them. Candles dotted the tables, their flames dancing.

He couldn't help but smile. There was something about this place that was comforting. Though it was entirely strange to have a medieval-looking tavern inside the Tower of Champions, on the other hand... it felt like exactly what *should* be here.

There were a few people inside the tavern, though not a great deal of them. He couldn't see any of the Champions that had been here when they'd been blocked from visiting the fourth floor. They would either be striving toward conquering the first floor, moving onto the next—or... well, dead.

There were three parties in the place. These Champions looked tougher than the last ones. A tall, broad-shouldered man from the closest table looked Xavier up and down, a frown turning his lips—perhaps because of Xavier's Shrouded Robes—he raised a tankard and nodded at Xavier before turning to the other members of his party.

It wasn't just that they *looked* tougher, Xavier realised. They *felt* tougher, too. Their auras were stronger than that of the last. *Maybe they've actually completed a floor or two.* That would be a good thing to know—that these weren't men and women who'd come to the tavern after having given up, but ones who came down here for the quickest of breaks between floors, to communicate with other parties and share information.

He felt a little less nervous being around people now than he had last time. The gnawing pit inside of him that wanted nothing more than to consume souls was still there. A yawning void that he knew could never be filled... but he seemed more in control of it than he had before.

He only felt a *small* amount of desire to harvest the souls of those he saw, after all. He considered that a win.

Perhaps Soul Harden is doing more for me than I realise, or maybe it's the Willpower I've gained from the last few levels and titles.

Either way, he was glad for it.

Maybe I should speak with those Champions after I talk to Sam.

Though he wanted to blast through the next six floors and get back to Earth as soon as possible—while doing his best to gain more number one leaderboard spots—helping other Champions was important too.

He headed straight for the bar. Sam had noticed him the instant he'd stepped through. The man was casually cleaning a mug, but his eyes were intent, locked on Xavier.

"I guess you figured it out all by yourself," Sam said, looking him up and down. "You can contain your aura now."

"You don't look surprised." Xavier slid onto one of the stools.

Sam poured him a glass of whiskey without having to be asked. "I didn't push you away because you weren't capable." There was a small smirk on the man's lips.

Xavier frowned, passing the man some Lesser Spirit Coins as he took the glass, putting two-and-two together. "You knew I was stubborn. You knew pushing me away would get me working harder."

Sam dipped his head in a nod. "The powerful rarely follow the rules. Rarely heed warnings to slow down on the path. I thought if a few harsh words made you stop trying to gain the Aura Control skill..." The man gave a high, double-shoulder shrug. "Then you weren't who I hoped you were."

Xavier tilted his chin up. "Who, exactly, do you hope I am?"

Sam gave him a significant look. "There are things I can say, and things I can't. It isn't only the System that tells me what those are."

"It's the people you work for."

Sam smiled. "Glad I didn't have to spell that out."

Xavier should probably be frustrated with the man. Feel some indignant rage at being played for a "System-damned fool." Instead, he laughed, then took a sip of whiskey. "I know nothing about the Greater Universe."

"That much is clear."

"But if you're hoping for me to be... *someone*, then you must really be desperate." Xavier waved a hand, trying to encompass not only the tavern, but the entirety of the Tower of Champions. "Looking *here*, working behind that bar, hoping to find... what, help?" He shook his head. "We're all just muddling through, trying to figure out what the hell is going on and how we can survive."

Sam, who had been cleaning the bar after pouring Xavier that glass, stopped what he was doing, standing straight. "The one I work for plays a very long game. Besides, the others here might be doing as you say, but you're well aware that what you've accomplished does not merely amount to *surviving*."

Xavier placed the glass back on the bar. "And what do you know of what I've accomplished?"

"It would be clear to anyone with eyes. You returned on the first day the floors of the Tower of Champions opened, already having cleared three." Sam leant forward on the bar, spoke in a whisper. "You're a True Progenitor."

A True Progenitor?

Xavier knew he was a Progenitor. That much had been clear from the first time he had stepped into this tavern and spoken to Sam. But what did the man mean by *True* Progenitor? What, exactly, was the difference?

"What does that mean?" Xavier asked. He'd leant forward on his stool, eager to listen to the man's next words.

Sam pushed away from the bar. He shut his eyes and let out a great sigh. "I shouldn't have said those words. It is... not wise to tell someone their fate before they are ready for it."

Xavier wanted to argue. To get the man to tell him more. But he supposed he already had an idea of what a True Progenitor might be.

"I need to show you something, Sam." Xavier placed his hand, palm up, on the bar. He summoned the Sector Travel Key he'd acquired from the loot box as his reward for completing the fourth floor. "Can you tell me anything about this?"

Sam's eyes bulged wide, so much so that they looked like they might fall out of his head. Though that reaction only lasted a split second, as the man already looked perfectly composed. "I suppose you already know what it's called."

"A Sector Travel Key."

Sam put out his hand. "Do you mind?"

Xavier hesitated.

Sam smiled. It looked genuine. "I'm not going to steal it, if that's what you're worried about. The System frowns on caretakers stealing from Champions." His eyes flicked up to the ceiling. "And the System isn't something you want to piss off."

Caretakers? Xavier thought. Though he knew the man wasn't simply a barkeep. Never had been. Especially considering how strong he was—he distinctly remembered the power of the man's aura, which had apparently only been at a quarter strength.

Xavier sighed. He placed the key in the man's hand.

Sam turned it over, examining it closely. "Where, exactly, did you get this?"

Xavier decided there was no point lying. "I received it as a reward for clearing the fourth floor." He paused. "Is this not something the System usually rewards in the tower?"

"Oh, the System does sometimes reward Sector Travel Keys."

Xavier's shoulders slumped. That... wasn't what he'd been hoping to hear.

"Except, they don't *usually* get awarded until after a Champion has cleared Level 100. In fact, I've never once heard of someone receiving one before then. At least, not until now."

This made Xavier perk right up. Sam passed the Sector Travel Key straight back to him. Xavier, in his eagerness, was careful not to snatch it out of the man's hand.

"You shouldn't have that," Sam said.

Xavier clutched it close. Though he didn't yet understand what the item did, it was clearly valuable if it wasn't normally a reward until *after* the hundredth floor.

Sam raised his hands. "I'm not going to take it from you. Obviously. I wouldn't have given it back, otherwise." His arms fell by his sides. "What I mean to say is... it doesn't make sense for you to have that item."

"I've gathered that much already. Though you still haven't told me what it *does*."

"Well, first, it can't be used within the Tower of Champions itself. So don't be getting any ideas."

"What ideas could I get?"

"A key like that is exceptionally rare, Xavier. Though the tower *does* reward them on the later floors, it's still incredibly unlikely for a Champion to receive one." He pursed his lips. "A Sector Travel Key, once a year, allows you to open a portal to *anywhere* you wish within the sector."

Xavier's eyes widened. Probably as wide as Sam's had not moments ago. "That sounds... that sounds amazing." He frowned. "What's a sector? And why only once per year?"

Sam shut his eyes, grasped the bridge of his nose with thumb and forefinger, muttering something about System-damned fools from baby worlds not knowing anything about anything.

Then he leant on the bar and told Xavier some truths about the Greater Universe he'd been dying to know.

Chapter 89
The System Is Not Your Friend, Xavier

XAVIER STARED, EXPECTANTLY, AT THE BARKEEP—CARETAKER, or whatever the hell Sam, also known as Samericalian, actually *was* —waiting for him to answer all of his questions. Or, at least some of them.

Sam pulled up a stool on the other side of the bar and slid up onto it. He plopped his elbows onto the bar and let out a sigh. "A sector is..." He waved his hand in a circle. "A very, *very* big area of space. Containing a huge number of interconnected planets."

"Like a galaxy?" Xavier asked with a frown.

Sam pointed at him. *"Exactly* like a galaxy. Though some sectors technically span more than one galaxy, that's very rare— travelling between sectors is..." He shrugged. "Prohibitively expensive, unless you're a part of the zero, point, zero zero zero one percent."

"That's... a fair amount of zeroes."

"Indeed it is."

Xavier looked down at the Sector Travel Key, held in his left hand. "But this lets me travel *within* a sector? Again, while that sounds awesome, how does that help me?" His forehead creased. "Is this how the invaders were able to come to my world? Using keys like this?"

Sam shook his head. "They would have used other means." He stared off toward the other Champions populating the tavern's tables. "The other four worlds participating in this instance of the tower are all from the same sector as your own world."

Xavier pursed his lips together. "While that makes sense... isn't our world integrated differently? Because interlopers travelled there, instigating the System's takeover?" He tilted his head to the side. "Wouldn't the System have integrated our planet long ago if it was already in the same sector?"

"Do you know how large this galaxy is, Xavier?"

Xavier, who'd read a fair number of sci-fi novels in his time, clicked his fingers. "About one hundred thousand light years!"

The barkeep blinked, leaning back a little. He muttered, "light years," then appeared to do some mental calculations. "Yes," he said, somewhat begrudgingly. "About that large." He paused. "But is that something you're able to comprehend?"

Xavier lowered his head, looking into his whiskey glass, thinking about all the things possible in science fiction—wormholes, FTL drives—all the things humans of Earth had imagined that could make interstellar space travel into a "reality." Because otherwise, travelling across the galaxy—even if you *could* get a ship to travel near the speed of light, which would kill a normal human unless they were somehow protected—would simply take far too long. At least, far too long for a normal human's lifespan. Unless relativity was taken into account... though he didn't really know much about that.

Finally, he sighed. "No. I suppose it's not."

"Parts of this galaxy have been integrated into the System for many thousands of years. But the System is still crawling through the stars, integrating one planet after another. We're still... a relatively young sector, when using the metrics of the Greater Universe at large."

Xavier nodded. He supposed he could understand that. It made him wonder about a million things. Like how, exactly, the

System was able to... *do* all that it could, but that was no doubt a question someone such as him could never answer.

Figuring out how all this works will probably only serve to explode my brain. Whether it runs on magic, science, or some twisted amalgamation of the two, it's my new reality now.

"All right, so I'm guessing travelling around the sector is incredibly expensive?" Xavier still couldn't help but remember that portal opening, the goblins coming through. Why spend so much coin on something like that?

"It is, and that key lets you do it for *free*. Which is why it's so damned valuable."

"And the fact it only works once per year doesn't make it any *less* valuable?" Xavier was trying not to show his impatience. The man was actually talking to him, freely giving him information. He didn't want to sound ungrateful—or cause this conversation to end abruptly.

Sam leant more heavily on the bar. "I can understand where you're coming from. Barely any time has passed since your world was integrated, and you've been moving so damned *fast* through the floors. For you, there is a *lot* that will happen in quite a short period of time. Like... the invasion of your world, for instance, and whether or not other forces are able to gain a foothold there, or whether you'll be able to ally with other, stronger forces in the sector who can help protect Earth."

Xavier perked up, sitting straight on his stool. "That... that's something *possible?*"

"Indeed. Not easy, but possible. But certainly not something you'd be able to do at this stage—not without a very high cost..." Sam waved a hand. "What I mean to say is, you're seeing things on a very small timeline because of what you're going through. When in a crisis, a day can feel like a week, a month a year."

Xavier thought on that. He supposed the man was right. He'd been through the COVID pandemic, and that had felt like it had gone on for far more years than it had. What he'd been experiencing lately? It was a crisis on a far, *far* larger scale, and every hour had counted. Though not many days had passed, it felt like this had been going on forever.

"So in the grand scheme, a year really isn't very long," he muttered.

"If you progress through the different Grades, it is not only your power that will grow. Your lifespan will grow as well, far more than you would have ever expected it to." Sam gave a small smile. "Assuming you don't go and get yourself killed, of course."

Xavier's eyes grew wide. He'd expected something like this, even thought of it as a foregone conclusion, but he hadn't thought past each day, each floor. Past returning to Earth, not even knowing what he would find there. "How could I..." Xavier swallowed. "Will I become immortal?"

"Effectively. Assuming you live long enough to reach the higher grades... There could, potentially, be no end to how long you can live. But..." Sam looked down at the bar, his voice turning melancholy. "There are Denizens in the Greater Universe who have stalled their development. Whether they have lived for hundreds of years, thousands, and some—though none in our sector—even for *millions*, many of them hit a wall that stops them from going any further. And if they hit a wall in their development before reaching the very peak, one day, they will die. There are some old monsters out there who ruled entire sectors before their eventual demise."

Xavier took a deep breath. He was... struggling to take all of this in. The scope of it all was a little overwhelming. He'd been having trouble contemplating a *year* passing, and here Sam was talking of centuries, millennia, longer...

Even so, he clutched his Sector Travel Key tight in his hand. He'd be lying if he said he didn't want to see what his sector—his galaxy—had to offer, but he didn't even know what the other worlds a part of his instance of the Tower of Champions were called, let alone anywhere else out there in the black.

"And travelling around the sector will help me?"

Sam bit his lower lip. "It will. There will be opportunities out there that simply aren't available on your world, or even in the tower. There will be items and equipment that cannot be bought in the System Shop. There will be manuals on advancing through to the next grade. And far, far more...

"But none of this will benefit you yet. You're nowhere near ready to leave your little world. It would be far too dangerous for you to venture away from it, especially while you're still in F Grade." He frowned. "There's a reason the System doesn't usually give those out until the later floors. Stepping out into the Greater Universe..." He looked away. "Unless you have friends out there, it's likely to get you killed."

"Friends?" Xavier muttered. "And how, exactly, do I make friends?" He gestured up, trying to point to *the universe*. "I mean, how do I make friends out there?"

Xavier was still reeling from the fact that he might, one day, become immortal. Or at least live for hundreds—if not thousands— of years.

He'd often thought about what life might be like if he were immortal. In a normal human lifespan, there is only so much one person can do. Only so much they can accomplish. Xavier wanted to become a writer. And not just any writer.

He had dreams of mastering the craft. Of toiling at his passion for decades upon decades, until his prose and the characters and worlds he created were as vibrant and real as the ones in his favourite novels, and the stories he told drew people in, immersing them fully, forcing them to keep turning the page.

But to live for centuries? Millennia? How many things would he get to master? How many things would he get to experience?

That was, of course, assuming Denizens got any down time in the Greater Universe, which he found hard to imagine, considering all he'd been doing since Earth had been integrated...

Sam smiled. "There are things I can tell you, and there are things I can't. But... the other worlds that are a part of your instance, there will come a time when you get to interact with them. They may not feel like people you can make alliances with, especially considering—"

The barkeep's mouth kept moving, but no sound came out. After a second, he clutched his neck, as though it were sore. He opened his mouth, working his jaw in a circle.

"Sorry about that. I almost said something I wasn't supposed to." Sam's gaze flicked to the ceiling. "I'm honestly surprised that hasn't happened already. The System is allowing me to tell you far more than it usually would, considering you've only cleared four floors of the tower."

Xavier lowered his head. They would be able to interact with the Champions from other, already integrated worlds? How would they be interacting with them?

Considering all the System had put him and the others through, Xavier got the idea that they wouldn't simply be meeting in a nice, quiet tavern, chatting over a drink.

He looked down at the key again. "If the System doesn't give these out until the later floors, then why do I have one?" Xavier vividly remembered feeling like nothing more than a speck of dust under the gaze of that presence. The one he'd felt after clearing the fourth floor. Like he was an ant and what looked down at him was... a supernova.

Something an ant could never hope to even comprehend.

He'd felt strong. Powerful. He'd just ranked *number one* on the Top 100 leaderboard for a floor.

But... he knew that his feeling of strength was deceptive. He was still but a child. As galling as it felt to be told that it was too dangerous for him to use this key yet, he knew it to be true.

He felt overpowered, and maybe he was. *For his level.* But that didn't mean he was powerful—it only meant he hadn't yet seen what true power was.

"I don't know how you have that key," Sam said. "You... you *shouldn't* have it."

"Could the System be trying to tell me something? Trying to help me?"

Sam laughed. He put his head in his hands, and he laughed. "The System is not your friend, Xavier. Whatever help you might think it gives you..." He shook his head, sighed. "It just wants conflict." He cocked his head to the side. "Why do you think you had to face one of your fellow Champions when you signed up to come to the tower? Because the System was *helping* you?" A bit of venom seeped into the man's voice. Something Xavier hadn't heard from him before, and he had to say he was quite surprised by it.

Xavier supposed the man was right. The System's actions hadn't exactly been benevolent. It forced people to fight. Forced *him* to fight.

He shut his eyes. Now was the time to decide how much he should or shouldn't tell Sam. The man had been helpful—going so far as to almost tell him *too* much—but did that mean Xavier could *trust* him?

"Is it possible that... a Denizen..." Xavier's forehead creased, trying to find the words. "If they were powerful enough... might influence what happens inside the Tower of Champions?"

Sam pushed off the bar and stood straight. "Why would you ask something like that?"

Here goes nothing...

"Because I think I'm being watched." Xavier placed the Sector Travel Key on the bar with a small click. "And I think that's why I got this key."

Chapter 90

Trust

"WATCHED?" SAM ASKED, STARING INTENTLY AT XAVIER. "Why do you think you're being watched?"

Xavier lowered his gaze. Looking down at the key he'd just placed on the bar instead of up at the barkeep. "At the end of the fourth floor, after I received my titles, I felt—" He paused, bit his lip.

Sam raised a hand. "As much as I want you to continue that sentence, Xavier, I think there's something you should know."

Xavier blinked up at the man, waiting for him to elaborate.

Sam seemed to hesitate. Now it was him who looked down, not holding eye contact. He shook his head minutely. "There are things Denizens shouldn't share with one another. Secrets of their class. Secrets of their spells. Things it might even be unwise to share with one's own party."

"Are you saying I shouldn't trust you?" Xavier asked, eyes narrowing. "Because warning me like this makes me trust you more —you didn't have to stop me from speaking."

"I'm not saying you shouldn't trust me. I'm saying you have no *reason* to trust me. It's no secret that I've got my eye on you. Part of what I'm doing here is searching for promise. I've already told you my... employer, plays a long game. But you know nothing about me.

And you know nothing about them. For all you know, my employer could be looking out for threats. Crushing them while they're small."

Xavier downed the rest of his whiskey in one. Placed the glass back on the bar. He didn't believe that's what the man's employer was doing. What Sam was doing. But maybe... maybe that was part of his problem. "You're saying I've been too trusting."

"You've done the right thing in searching for advice, but you must be careful what advice you take." Sam nodded at the key. "Imagine what might have happened if you'd taken that key to someone else. They may have told you of a wonderful place to hunt beasts and gain Mastery Points, only to send you into a trap where they strip you of your wealth and your life, because they want that key in your hand. Because to them, it's worth far more than you are." Not for the first time, he flicked his gaze up to the ceiling. "The Greater Universe is a dangerous place. If you put your trust in others too freely, you'll find you'll never get to enjoy the benefits of an extended lifespan."

Xavier wasn't sure what to say to that.

He *wanted* to talk to Sam about all of this. Wanted to confide in the man. Which, admittedly, was strange. Though he'd never been the secretive sort, he had never sought out these sorts of conversations.

Perhaps it was simply that he had so much bubbling up inside of him. So much to contemplate. So much to *do*.

He wanted to trust this man. And, above all, he wanted to trust his party.

Xavier shifted in his seat, an unsettling thought coming to him. What if there was another reason he wanted to tell this man all of his secrets? As far as he could tell, the variety of different spells and skills the System made available was nearly endless. Could there be some sort of mental manipulation skill, one that made it not only easier to talk with this man but made people less guarded, more free with information when talking to him?

He looked down at his drink. A moment ago he'd been tempted

to get another. Now, that wasn't the case. *Maybe I'm paranoid. Maybe it's just the alcohol, even as a placebo, that loosens tongues.*

Xavier asked the man one more question, "You're saying to trust no one, but how can I thrive if I have no one I can rely on?"

"There are ways to ensure others keep your secrets, or if they divulge them, that they incur a penalty."

"A penalty? What kind of penalty? Like... death?"

Sam inclined his head. "Sometimes. That depends on how severe the terms of the contract are. Some contracts simply prevent one from talking about something entirely." He pointed up at the ceiling, as though gesturing toward the System itself. "I'm a caretaker here, and there's only so much I'm allowed to share with the Champions in this cohort. That's because to be here, I signed a System-bound contract."

Xavier couldn't help but think of non-disclosure agreements, gag orders, and the like. He supposed he should have been more careful. Should have realised there might be measures like this in place. But where, exactly, would he have found such information?

It wasn't as though it was in the manual the System provided for the tower. "All right," Xavier said. "Can we make a contract?"

Sam smirked. "No. At least, not yet. I've told you enough, True Progenitor. Now it's time for you to flounder around in the dark some more."

Xavier snatched his Sector Travel Key from the bar. He couldn't say he was too surprised, or even all that frustrated with the man. Though he hadn't gotten as many answers as he wished— he hadn't even asked about Celestial Energy—he'd found out a few more details about the Greater Universe, and was starting to see Earth's place in it.

And... he was beginning to wonder how exactly they would be able to survive.

Not only would they have to deal with the invaders that could already access their world—invaders capped at whatever level the highest Denizen of Earth had achieved—but in five years their world would be opened up fully to the Greater Universe.

He hadn't contemplated that fact much over the last few days. He'd been far too concerned with what would happen when he returned to Earth. Far too concerned with each hour, each floor, each day, each week.

Thinking in terms of *years* just hadn't been an option.

But now? With the prospect of living for hundreds, thousands, maybe even *millions* of years—something he couldn't even fathom —he knew he would need to think in the long term.

That presence made me feel like nothing. And in the grand scheme, Earth is nothing. If we don't get strong. Don't find allies... how are we going to survive in five years, when our world opens up?

It was yet another thing on his plate he needed to worry about. And part of him wanted to just throw it to the back of his mind and not think about it for... five years. But he knew that would be a mistake. This wasn't like some university assignment he could procrastinate and put off.

Xavier almost walked straight out of the tavern, but he stopped himself, looking out at the three parties in the room.

What could he do to help these people? What would they benefit from the most?

And how much should he even share with them, given what Sam had said?

They're my people. I can't hide everything from them.

Xavier shut his eyes. His instincts told him to just go it alone. To not bother talking to these people at all. But that was the old Xavier. He needed to be different, now. Besides, he didn't have to divulge his secrets to help them.

Xavier walked up to the first table. The one with the broad-shouldered man who'd nodded at him when he'd walked in. Then he looked over to the other two tables.

He cleared his throat. Felt like he was getting up in front of the class to deliver a speech, and suddenly was all nerves.

Then he remembered how powerful he'd become. What he was capable of. What he'd just achieved. He drew in a quiet, calming breath, then spoke.

"I need to speak with all of you."

The broad-shouldered man had already noticed him walking over. Now all three parties—twelve people—were staring at him. There were a few bored expressions. A few raised eyebrows. Some vacant eyes—that made him wonder what they'd all been through.

The broad-shouldered man spoke. "Okay then," he said, his voice deep. "Speak." The word came out as a command. It had that short, clipped, military tone of someone used to giving orders and having them carried out.

Suddenly, Xavier wasn't exactly sure what he should say. Then he figured he might as well get to the point. He didn't have the time to stand around and chat all day. "I want to give you all some advice about clearing the tower."

The broad-shouldered man blinked. "You don't look military, son, and I'm old enough to be your father. What advice could you possibly have for us?"

Xavier raised an eyebrow. He hadn't expected such instant pushback. God, he hated it when people older looked down on those younger, thinking they couldn't possibly know any better than they did.

Arrogant bastard.

Another member of the man's party leant over the table and gave broad-shoulders a shove. "Why not hear what the kid has to say?"

Xavier shut his eyes. *Son. Kid.* He may have been in his early twenties, but that didn't mean he was a damned child. *This is why I don't like talking to people.* He should have gotten Siobhan and Howard to do this like usual. They might have taken Howard more seriously because of his age and profession—*former* profession—as a cop.

Xavier stopped balancing his Spirit Core. He didn't know if any of these guys had reached Level 10, but even if they hadn't, they'd be able to feel it. Even subtly.

He released his full aura and noticed a small shift in the way they all looked at him. He stared down at the man who'd been rude. "How many floors have your party cleared?" he asked in a flat tone.

The man smirked. "Two."

Two?

That actually took Xavier by surprise. Meant that the party might be half-decent, considering the first floor was supposed to take a party from a newly integrated world an average of a whole week.

"Not bad. I've cleared four. Solo. Now do you want to listen to me?"

Broad-shoulders blinked. Gave him another once-over. His expression did not soften. "Four floors? Solo? The four of us have bled to get through two floors, son. You expect me to believe something like that?"

I could kill him in less than a second with nothing but my bare hands... was a thought that Xavier shoved down, knowing it wasn't exactly useful. How did he prove his power to these people without hurting them? He hadn't scanned them, trying to be polite, but he did so now.

That first table were all Level 8. They must have done a lot of farming to get that high just clearing two floors.

Broad-shoulders wore full-plate armour. A warrior. He had a sword at his hip. A big, hand-and-a-half monster. Xavier pulled up the sleeve of his Shrouded Robes. "Cut me."

Broad-shoulders frowned. "What kinda fool are you?"

"A System-damned one. Now, *cut me*. Draw that toothpick you call a sword and cut me. If you can make me bleed, I'll walk straight out of this tavern."

"Maybe he's telling the truth, Dawkins."

"Shut up, Miller. He's just some dumb kid in a costume who thinks he's tough. The world's gone to all hell and the last thing I'm gonna do is take advice from some gamer who thinks he knows what he's doing because he wasted his life in front of a monitor addicted to *World of Warcraft*. I get enough of that crap from my kids."

"Have you even scanned him?" a woman on their table asked. None of the Champions at the other two tables had said a word yet, but they were watching intently. "He's Level 12."

Dawkins grunted. He placed his tankard on the table and stood. "So he farmed a bunch of pumas," the man said, staring into Xavier's eyes but not speaking to him. "Probably hasn't even cleared the first floor yet, just keeps walking in, on his own, killing that one right outside the Safe Zone." He didn't draw his sword. "I don't know why you want me to cut you, son, but I don't need a sword to make you bleed, and I'm not above punching your little punk-ass."

Xavier frowned at the man, struggling to understand why he was so aggressive. Again, he thought he would take a straightforward approach. Social interaction wasn't his strong suit, and he had avoided conflict for basically his entire life. Now, he'd discovered he was good at combat-based conflict, but conversational conflict? That was a different story.

"Why are you wasting time?" Xavier had to tilt his chin up to look the man in the eye. Before the integration, he would have been intimidated by someone like this. That wasn't the case anymore. "Earth is in trouble. Being invaded as we speak. I offer advice and you're too proud to take it. Why?"

If this was the type of thing he would have to deal with when he returned to Earth—people who thought they should be the ones in charge just because they'd been important before the integration and he hadn't... he would need to make some sort of display of power.

It wasn't that he wanted to take *control* of Earth, but if people were to listen to him... they would need to be aware of his strength, wouldn't they?

"Because, what could you possibly have to teach me?"

Xavier took another one of those calming breaths, though it wasn't having the same effect any longer. This felt different to fighting beasts, or fighting on the floors. This felt like it was about to turn into some sort of bar brawl. Old instincts told him to back down, walk away, never talk to this man ever again. Because his old instincts worried this man—and his friends—would beat the hell out of him.

But that isn't something I need to worry about.

"Please don't tell me the only way to open your mind is to open your skull, because I'd rather not make a mess in Sam's tavern." Xavier wasn't actually going to hurt the guy. He'd never really thought violence was the answer to his problems in the past. But the universe... it was a different place now.

"You little sh—" The man cocked back his fist, then swung for Xavier's head.

Xavier didn't move to block it. Didn't raise his arms to protect his head. He could have stepped back or ducked away—it wouldn't have been difficult. With his speed, it would be as easy as avoiding a slowly falling balloon coming at him from thirty feet away.

No, he didn't do any of these things. All he did was smirk.

The fist slammed into his jaw. Xavier, hands casually hanging by his side, was like a stone wall. He didn't budge a hair's breadth.

Dawkins swore, fingers splayed, flapping his hand as though trying to fling away the pain. His knuckles bled. He took a step back. "Damn, is your face made of metal?"

Xavier considered his Assimilate Properties ability and supposed that wasn't too far from the truth.

One of the men from the second table stood. He had shoulder length brown hair and the armour of a warrior. "He might not want to listen to you, but he doesn't speak for us, and we're happy to." He gestured to the other members of his party, which consisted of two mages—a man and a woman—and a female warrior. The man stepped forward, straight past Dawkins, who was still nursing his hand—some of the knuckles might have actually been broken, not just bloody.

The man extended his hand. "My name is Ryan."

Xavier shook. "Xavier."

Maybe he didn't need to bother with people like Dawkins. Maybe people like that could be someone else's problem.

A chair was brought around for him. Xavier sat in front of the second two tables—and couldn't help but see the members of the first listening in—and told them everything he knew about the Tower of Champions.

Well, *almost* everything.

Chapter 91
Never-Ending

Xavier spoke with the Champions down in the tavern for a full hour before he headed back to the Staging Room. He wasn't used to having so many people listening to his every word, but he pushed past any nerves he was feeling rather easily. Especially whenever he looked over at Dawkins. The man was no longer nursing his fist—his broken knuckles would have healed quickly enough—but he was begrudgingly paying attention to all Xavier said.

When he returned to the Staging Room, he found the others were still practising with their new spells. Siobhan's Divine Guardian was battering Howard's shield, while Justin was jumping around, casting Air Strikes left and right.

Xavier was glad they'd thrown themselves into training, and he was starting to see how powerful his party could become in the future. Between them, they had several strong and versatile spells, and he was interested to see how well they could all work together.

But he was more eager to move forward.

The second he stepped into the Staging Room they all paused what they were doing and asked if he'd learnt anything from Sam. Xavier had told them everything the man had said—even the part about how he might not want to trust his party.

Howard nodded sagely. "It makes sense. All those here... they may have chosen to defend our world, but..." He frowned, his face turning serious. "Those who choose to protect, in my experience, are not always up to the job. Sometimes what they're really looking for is authority. I dealt with my fair share of entitled cops. In this instance, perhaps some only chose to be Champions for power. For the opportunities it could bring. It's not as though the System gazed into our hearts when we chose a moral faction."

They had gone a little quiet after that.

Though they each appeared to be quite interested in the Sector Travel Key, they all agreed Xavier shouldn't use it for some time.

Which didn't bother Xavier at all. First, he couldn't even use the key while in the tower. And second, he didn't even know where to *go* yet. And, finally, he couldn't afford to be away for an entire year. Besides, he doubted the tower would even allow for that.

After turning it around in his hand once more, he'd deposited the Sector Travel Key into his Storage Ring and put thoughts of visiting other worlds into the back of his mind.

One day, I'll get that opportunity.

But right now, his mind was on the fate of Earth, and on what lay before them on the next tower floor.

He didn't hesitate. After speaking to the others, he looked at his attributes, spells, and skills.

XAVIER COLLINS
Age: 20
Race: Human
Grade: F
Moral Faction: World Defender (Planet Earth)
Class: Soul Reaper (Epic)
Level: 13

Strength: 205 (219)
Speed: 201 (211)
Toughness: 215 (245)

Intelligence: 266 (338)
Willpower: 231 (252)
Spirit: 365 (460)

Mastery Points for this level:
2,127,700/8,000,000
Available Spirit Energy: 47,000/47,000
Available Skill Points: 1
Free stat points remaining: 0

Titles:
Bloodied Hands, Born on a Battlefield, Settlement Defender, Quester, First Defender of Planet Earth, Survivor, All 100, First All 100, 1,000 Stats, First to 1,000 Stats, Greater Butcher, Fourth-Floor Climber, Solo Tower Climber 4, 1ˢᵗ Fourth-Floor Climber, Fourth Floor Ranked 1 – RECORD HOLDER (Completion Time – 4 sec)
Spells List:
Spiritual Trifecta – Rank 7
Heavy Telekinesis – Rank 6
Spirit Break (All) – Rank 3
Spirit Infusion – Rank 3
Soul Harvest – Rank 4
Soul Strike (Ranged) – Rank 10
Soul Block – Rank 1
Soul Harden – Rank 4

Skills List:
Physical Resistance – Rank 10
Magical Potency – Rank 14
Magical Resistance – Rank 5
Physical Damage – Rank 3
Assimilate Properties – Rank 1

Scythe-Staff Mastery – Rank 1
Meditation – Rank 10
Aura Control – Rank 3
Lesser Spirit Coins: 64,065

Xavier examined his list. There were some skills, like Scythe-Staff Mastery and Assimilate Properties, that he looked forward to ranking up. Though he wasn't sure *how* to rank up Assimilate Properties, and he'd never been good at gaining ranks in Staff Mastery.

I'll figure it out.

He didn't linger too long on his stats. They had changed drastically once more, but he knew that would keep happening for a good while, and it was no longer quite the shock to his system.

Though he had to admit, he *was* eager to see what might happen when he reached 500 points of Spirit. Would there be another threshold for him to pass?

Not wanting to dally, Xavier led his party to the door and entered the fifth floor of the Tower of Champions. He knew he still had a skill he could choose. Knew he still had Lesser Spirit Coins to spend. But he wasn't sure *what* to spend that money on at this point, and he figured it might be better for him to know what this floor had in store before choosing his next skill.

He was happy with his current spells and skills, considering they'd let him clear the last floor in record time. And he didn't want to regret choosing the wrong skill if he found that something important in the skills list would have helped him clear the floor faster.

Xavier was teleported straight into the Safe Zone of the fifth floor. When he materialised in the room—or maybe the room materialised around him—he found it to be made of solid grey stone. A moment later, the others appeared beside him.

He moved to place his hand on one of the walls. It was slightly rough to the touch and cold. The room had four chairs, all angled toward a fireplace. Flames danced in the hearth, logs crackling as they burned.

There were two doors on opposite sides of the Safe Zone.

"This reminds me of the cabin we appeared in on the first floor," Justin said, pacing around, his boots tapping on the stone.

Howard shook his head. "That was more rustic. Made from stacked logs. This place is more like..."

"A room in a castle," Xavier said excitedly. He stepped over to the door and felt a little giddy. Maybe *too* giddy. He'd spent the better part of his life imagining fantasy worlds—whether he was reading about them or writing about them—but he'd never actually *been* in a castle before.

It was something he'd always dreamed of.

The door leading out of the Safe Zone was made from solid oak with what might have been a brass handle. "Perhaps the three of you should remain here while I investigate. Whatever's on the other side of that door could be dangerous."

Xavier summoned Soultaker and held it in his left. He wasn't at all worried about what might be on the other side being able to harm him, so he turned the handle, whipped the door open, and stepped out into what looked to be a large courtyard.

No. This isn't a courtyard, it's a bailey.

Stepping out of the safe room was like turning mute off on the world. A horn was blaring somewhere far away, and there were men and women—soldiers in armour, with capes draped over their shoulders—gathering in the centre of the castle's bailey.

For he had been right. The fifth floor of the Tower of Champions *was* in a castle. Or rather, just outside of one. Turning around, he saw massive keeps rising toward the sky, flanking a large castle with sturdy, double doors up a short flight of stairs.

The Safe Room he'd stepped out of was out of a side door. He looked at the soldiers gathering, gripping his staff-scythe. It wouldn't be the first time they'd worked with an army, and though he was wary, these soldiers might not actually be his enemy.

Though there was something strange about them, he noticed.

For one, they weren't all human. Some of them were, but there were several Denizens of different races. Elves, he'd seen before, their pointy ears, sharp features, and clear complexion familiar.

Others, he'd not seen before. They were all humanoid. But some were... less human than others.

Xavier's eyes widened as he saw what looked like jackal-headed warriors that reminded him nothing more than of the Egyptian god of death, Anubis.

Then there were the lizard men, standing at the back of the line. Faces scaled, large tails idly swishing behind them.

I'll have to get used to that.

There were a few races that didn't look quite as strange. Unless you counted the small horns on their foreheads.

Xavier turned his attention away from the gathering soldiers and to his surroundings. The courtyard—or bailey—looked to be an inner ward, walled off, with a single portcullis leading to the outer bailey.

I wonder if this place has a moat. And a drawbridge.

A bell rang somewhere on the battlements. More soldiers ran out of what looked to be a barracks, heading for the front walls.

A notification popped in front of Xavier's vision as he realised this castle was about to be under siege.

Welcome to the Fifth Floor of the Tower of Champions.
The Fifth Floor of the Tower of Champions is a test of how much you can endure.
Time is frozen on this floor. Outside of this instance, entering this floor will always take a single hour, whether a Champion leaves the floor within one minute or one year.
This castle will soon be under siege from both Denizens and beasts, experiencing increasing waves of difficulty. Unlike other floors, a record on this floor is not based on how quickly

it can be cleared, but rather how many waves
of enemies one survives.
Each wave has a floor boss, or "wave boss,"
and once you have cleared the first five waves—
a feat that takes no less than five hours—this
floor will be considered cleared.
Know this: the castle will fall. You cannot
protect it forever.
The waves are never-ending.

Chapter 92
Champions of the Void

A WIDE SMILE BURST ONTO XAVIER'S FACE AS HE READ THE notification explaining what would happen on the fifth floor of the Tower of Champions.

He was in a castle about to be under siege by countless waves of enemies. Perhaps he should have felt some dread after reading the last line of the notification—

The waves are never-ending.

—but this seemed like the perfect floor for him.

Though he had identified a few issues. First of those issues was the fact that he couldn't play the floor out until the end to see what every wave had to offer. Not only because those waves were apparently infinite, but because after clearing four, he'd need to turn back and head to the Staging Room if he wished to refresh the floor.

Surviving five waves clears the floor.

The second problem was, he didn't know how many waves he would need to defend against to get into the Top 100 of the ladder, let alone grab the number one spot.

A wave-based record, not a time-based one.

Xavier had—wrongly—assumed that the Tower of Champions floors would always be time based, thinking he would need to do each floor as fast as possible.

This changed things.

At least only an hour will pass in here, no matter how long we're on this floor. Though that does mean each refresh—even if we're only in here for a short time—will take an entire hour.

He pushed away those worries and headed back to the Safe Zone to grab the others. Though he didn't want to take the time to have them level up again, he wasn't going to clear the floor on his first time on it. So he might as well let them test out their new classes against the first few waves of enemies.

Xavier opened the door to the Safe Zone and grinned at the others. "I was right. It *is* a castle."

Siobhan smiled back at him. "A castle? Really?"

Xavier stepped aside, holding the door open as she walked through it and into the flagstone-paved bailey.

Her eyes widened as she looked around. She turned and gazed up at the castle. "Whoa! This is just like being back in Ireland. But... I've never seen a castle look so *new*." She chuckled. "Usually they're hundreds of years old." She touched one of the walls. "This stone doesn't look that old."

Howard and Justin stepped out next. Howard's gaze fell straight onto the gathered soldiers. He already had his tower shield summoned. He paused—so did the others—eyes glazing over.

They must not have gotten the notification while they'd been in the Safe Zone.

"Waves?" Howard muttered. "I suppose that means that group of Denizens over there aren't our enemy. Despite how... varied they are."

Siobhan turned around and looked at the soldiers. Justin was already gawking at them.

"Is that... lizardmen? Anubis? Or would it be Anubi...?" Justin took a step back. "And *demons*?"

"I don't think they're demons," Siobhan said. "Though that would be exciting, wouldn't it?"

Xavier couldn't help but chuckle. "Demons would be exciting?"

"Think about the implications! Of all of this! These floors have been around for billions of years. Not only does that tell us that convergent evolution is real." She waved a hand, motioning toward the soldiers, some among them human. "Because, well, *humans*! We've been around for billions of years! Before we evolved on Earth! Isn't that damned fascinating? *Then* we find out elves are real." Her smile widened. "How could *elves* be real? They're supposed to be something we invented. A myth we created. Yet they've been around just as long, and, somehow, we *knew* about them before the integration."

Howard grunted. His forehead creased deeply. "Does your head in, that."

Justin's mouth had fallen open as he stared at the soldiers. "I hadn't even *thought* of that. That's... that's... what does that mean?"

"I don't know!" Siobhan said. "But it's fascinating." She walked forward. Another bell was ringing. The portcullis in the inner bailey was being brought up, the gathered soldiers filing through it.

Xavier was about to follow her out when the double doors to the castle opened. Ten soldiers—knights?—stepped out, flanking a young, stern looking woman with impeccable posture, and an old, stooped, wizened man with a pointed grey beard.

Xavier and his party froze, turning around to look at those walking down the steps. The knights wore golden armour with what looked like a griffon etched into each of their breastplates. Their cloaks were the deep red of blood. Some were human, some elf, and two were demons—or at least, they *looked* demonic.

The woman at the centre, however, was clearly human. And, well, strikingly beautiful. She wore a crown of gold bejewelled with various coloured gemstones, mostly rubies and emeralds. Though as this was another world, Xavier supposed they might be something else.

She wasn't wearing armour or mage robes. Instead, she wore a rich, silver gown that flowed all the way to the ground, though it didn't have any sort of trail. Her hair was a brown so dark it looked almost black, and was pulled up in some intricate bun beneath her crown.

Xavier took a step forward without even meaning to.

The woman looked like a princess and comported herself like a queen. She stopped at the step second to the bottom and raised a hand.

The old man behind her straightened and cleared his throat. "Her Majesty Queen Alastea thanks you for your swift arrival, Champions of the Void."

Champions of the Void?

Xavier had never heard that term before. Looking at the queen, and at the man who was clearly some sort of adviser to her, he had to remind himself that this place wasn't *real*. These people weren't *real*.

They'd been created by the System. Or they were stuck in some sort of time-loop. He didn't know. But they wouldn't remember a single thing that happened once Xavier and his party left. It would all simply... begin again for them.

He stepped forward, standing in front of his party. Queen Alastea turned her gaze onto him. Xavier wasn't exactly sure what to say. "We are honoured to serve, Your Majesty." He gave a small bow and saw a smirk curl the sides of the queen's lips.

"You need not stand on formality with me, Champion. I may be the ruler of this land, but I am not *your* ruler. How can I be, when you are not even of this world?" Queen Alastea stepped down to the bailey. She looked at Xavier, then at the others. "I have garnered the wrath of the Endless Horde." She lowered her head. Sighed. "I do not doubt my fate. I will fight until my last breath, for I know that I cannot be spared." She motioned toward the castle doors. "Half the kingdom has already been evacuated. However, creating portals takes time. It will be some hours until we can create another. Though I know that I and my queendom cannot endure, all I wish is for my people to survive."

"Why can't you leave?" Siobhan asked, a frown on her face.

Queen Alastea raised her chin. "My fate is sealed. I do not wish to speak more on the matter." She raised her right hand. A staff appeared in it.

Summoned from a Storage Ring.

Queen Alastea walked toward the portcullis, her guard trailing behind her. The old adviser, however, stayed behind.

The adviser stared at the three of them with a furrowed brow. "You are Champions of the Void, and you have not heard of the Endless Horde?" He placed a hand on Xavier's shoulder as he passed, releasing a long, weary sigh. "You will learn of them here."

Xavier and his party watched as the queen, her guards, and the tall adviser streamed into the outer bailey, heading toward the battlements at the front walls.

"There felt like there was more... backstory in here than usual." Siobhan pursed her lips. "These people feel so real."

Justin shrugged. "At least... at least we're not here to fight them."

"I guess the portal will open after the fifth wave is cleared. And everyone is supposed to escape through it but the queen," Xavier said. He started heading toward the portcullis. He wanted to get atop the walls. Wanted to see what the enemy looked like. He could hear their horns—horns of war—blaring again in the distance.

"Does that mean all the soldiers will leave after that wave? It will just be us and the queen?" Howard asked.

"Something tells me the waves will get much harder after that," Justin muttered.

Part of Xavier wanted to leave the others behind and run to the battlements to get to them sooner. He couldn't help but be intrigued by what the queen had said. Her fate being sealed. And... what was the Endless Horde? Simply something the System had created for this floor?

Or was it something that existed outside of it as well?

They headed through the gate and into the outer bailey. The wall the battlements stood atop was curved, and Xavier spotted four sets of switchback stairs leading to the top. Gripping Soultaker in both hands, he wondered if he should be out on the ground when the first wave arrived. He hadn't had a chance to rank up his Staff-Scythe Mastery skill, and his Physical Damage skill was lagging behind.

It would also be easier for him to train his resistances, and try out Soul Block, if he were out in the thick of things. Though he supposed it would be wise to see what they were dealing with before stepping out there.

There were ranks and ranks of soldiers gathered in the outer bailey. The space was large enough for several thousand of them, and there were hundreds more on the walls.

That's a lot of defenders. How bad can these waves be if we've got that many soldiers fighting with us in a well-fortified location?

They hurried up the switchback stairs, a bell on the wall still ringing incessantly, and made it up to the battlements. Xavier glanced around until he saw Queen Alastea. The woman had one hand on the parapet, another on her staff. She gazed, wide-eyed, at the enemies gathered below.

Xavier stepped up to the parapet a little ways from the queen and looked over it. "Holy..."

Countless ranks of enemy soldiers, Denizens of all races, shapes, and sizes, wearing dark, spiked armour, were slamming swords, hammers, axes into shields. The bell stopped ringing. The horns stopped blaring. And the sounds of the Endless Horde carried to where Xavier and his party stood.

War drums. Battle cries. Rabid roars, from Denizens *and* beasts. For there were a great many beasts standing alongside the humanoid ranks of Denizens.

"How many are there?" Justin whispered.

The castle was in the middle of a long expanse of flat plains, walled on every side. And the enemy ranks were ringed all around it. And—just as the notification had said—their waves were never-ending.

There were ranks farther than Xavier's eye could see.

"Too many," was all Xavier could find to say in reply.

The first wave began their charge.

Chapter 93
Staff-Scythe Mastery

Xavier, standing on the battlements of Queen Alastea's castle, gazed down at the first wave of enemies charging toward the wall.

There were too many for him to count, but there had to be a few thousand beasts in the wave. None of the ranks of Denizens in the distance had charged forward to fight.

The first wave of beasts were wolf-like creatures the size of horses. They had twin horns jutting out from either side of their heads, curving downward. Xavier could imagine how painful being impaled on one of those things would be.

But, honestly, he couldn't feel any fear looking down at those beasts. They felt like nothing more than the appetiser, and he found that to be confirmed when he scanned them.

{Wolven - Level 10}

They're only Level 10?

Xavier leant over the parapet. Frowned. There *was* a moat around the castle. Even a drawbridge—pulled up—at the main gate. The moat was filled with liquid, but it wasn't water. It was green... and it bubbled.

Some kind of acid?

"You are wondering why they send beasts for the walls, and not siege engines, ropes, ladders, bridges to cross the divide?"

Xavier blinked, looking over at Queen Alastea, surprised that she was addressing him. "It is curious." He motioned toward the first wave. There were archers and mages on the wall among the castle's soldiers, readying their attacks for when the beasts were in range. Though for Xavier, they were already in range. "I don't see how those wolves—Wolven—will be able to get past your defences."

"This is a battle of attrition. For us, and only us. The Endless Horde does not worry about wasting its resources. This first wave will not harm us, this is true, but it will show the enemy how we respond, giving them valuable information for future waves." Queen Alastea sighed. "Though I do warn you. Those beasts? They can leap over our moat, dig their claws into the stone battlements, and climb their way to the top. If we do not respond swiftly and ruthlessly, they will make it atop the wall."

Xavier narrowed his eyes at the beasts. He supposed he shouldn't be surprised by that. He glanced at his fellow party members. None of them were long range fighters. Staying up on the wall wasn't going to do anything for their training.

First, he looked at Howard. "Do you think you can survive being in the middle of that?"

Howard's forehead creased. The big man swallowed. "Maybe. They're only Level 10, but..." He scratched his beard with the top of the tower shield. "There's a damned lot of them."

Justin drew his sword. "I don't want to just stand here. We'll do enough of that when you clear this floor for real."

"It would be easy enough to teleport the two of you out there, then teleport you back," Siobhan said. "This could be a good floor for farming."

Xavier shook his head. "No. We aren't farming this floor. We are seeing what the first few waves are like, then we'll regroup in the Staging Room, and I'll clear it on the next refresh. So you'll have to get as much as you can from these first few waves."

The others glanced at each other, but none of them argued.

"Right, then." Howard sighed. "I best get out there. See what I can do."

Xavier considered the wave. The sheer number of beasts. "I'll join the two of you down there." He looked at Soultaker's arm-length black blade. "I think it's time I got in some more practise with this."

Justin leapt up onto the battlement's parapet, a grin on his face. "You don't need to teleport me down there," he told Siobhan. "I can make my own way." He jumped straight off the wall, spreading his arms wide. When he reached the apex of his jump, wings sprouted from his back, flapping fast as he flew over the moat and landed gently on the ground.

"Those wings," Queen Alastea said. "They're... quite small."

Xavier did his best to hold in a chuckle.

"I understand that Champions of the Void are inclined to do whatever they wish, but please remember why you are here." The woman raised an eyebrow at Xavier. "It would be terrible for your party to lose your lives by taking unnecessary risks."

Xavier dipped his head. "I assure you, Queen Alastea, we know what we are doing," he said, thinking, *for the most part.* For a moment, he paused, wondering how the woman could be so poised, so composed, considering she said she would not survive this siege. Her chin was up, her back straight, her staff held lightly in one hand, its butt resting on the stone floor.

He could not see any fear in her eyes.

She isn't truly real... is she?

He shook away those thoughts and took a few steps back from the wall, then sprinted straight for it, taking a running jump. Though his ranged Soul Strike spell would be able to make short work of this wave, he didn't want to neglect his melee fighting abilities. Besides, it wasn't often that he could test out his newfound Strength and Speed. Not to mention his Toughness.

It would be a good thing for him to get into the thick of things.

A moment before he'd leapt over the parapet, Xavier had activated Spiritual Trifecta, though he did not bother infusing any souls into the spell.

The Wolven were getting close enough to be in range of the archers and mages on the wall now, but they were avoiding attacking the enemies in front of Xavier and Justin.

As Xavier landed, a bright light flashed beside him and Howard appeared.

The big man shrugged. "I'm not really built for jumping and flying."

Xavier slapped him on the shoulder. "We each have to play to our strengths."

Howard gave a small smirk. "Indeed."

Though Xavier lacked any physical attack spells—he'd forgone Soul Strike as a melee spell for the ranged version, which he in no way regretted—his staff-scythe could still cause quite a lot of damage.

He was interested to see how much.

He sped forward, overtaking Justin, and made it to the enemy before the others. The beasts before him became enraged as he neared, as though his very presence infuriated them.

A small part of Xavier, one that still survived from *before*, saw the thousands of enemies and screamed at him to run the other way instead of *directly at them*, but it was an easy thing to ignore.

As much as he knew Howard was a good tank and Justin was extremely mobile and adept at dodging, he wanted to soften the ranks before they reached them, so the two of them couldn't be instantly overwhelmed.

The beasts roared as he neared. Xavier tightened and loosened his grip on Soultaker, infusing offensive Spirit Energy into it, making the weapon glow. He infused his robes with Spirit Energy as well. He hadn't tested that yet. As he'd chosen the offensive route for Spirit Infusion, when enemies struck his armour—or, in this case, his Shrouded Robes—they would take damage.

The Wolven closed in around him. Xavier was still coming at them in a sprint. He swung his staff-scythe in a wicked arc as ten of the beasts leapt straight at him, their lips pulled back in vicious snarls, saliva dripping from their open maws.

The arm-length black blade sliced straight through them. Xavier felt barely any resistance. It felt more like a small gust of wind was working against him than cutting through flesh and bone.

Multiple kill notifications popped up. He only read one of them.

You have defeated a Level 10 Wolven!
You have gained 1,000 Mastery Points.
You have gained 1,000 Spirit Energy.

A thousand Mastery Points seemed barely worth the effort now that he needed a total of eight million to reach the next rank, but he supposed he wasn't bothered about levelling up right now.

Xavier harvested the souls of the dead Wolven and did not relent in his attacks. With his Speed an effective 211, the Wolven seemed to move in slow motion. Even so, there was such an abundance of them that he could never pause the swinging of his staff-scythe.

He *had* used Soultaker in melee before, when taking down some of the Dark Wyvern's from the previous floor, but that hadn't been on this scale. He'd barely gotten a chance to see how the weapon truly performed, and how he performed with it.

Physical Damage has reached Rank 4!

That was fast.

His Physical Damage skill had lagged significantly behind Magical Potency. He knew that was a potential mistake. Though Heavy Telekinesis was a strong spell, and Soul Strike even stronger, he worried about what might happen if he one day encountered an enemy that could withstand soul damage—and if they were able to withstand soul damage, he doubted his telekinesis would be all that effective.

So he couldn't let his melee abilities fall too far behind his magical ones.

Xavier's blade carved through enemy after enemy until his Shrouded Robes were drenched in blood. Somewhere, in his peripheral, he was aware the others were fighting near him. He could see flashes of light in the corner of his vision. Siobhan—safe back on the battlements—healing or teleporting Howard and Justin.

And Xavier simply continued fighting. The Wolven were so damned slow, and his staff-scythe's reach so long, that they never got in close enough to even *attempt* to gore him with those horns or maul him with their razor-sharp teeth.

During that wave, Physical Damage ranked up three more times, reaching Rank 7. And, the longer he fought, the more Soul-taker felt like it was a part of him. As he wasn't struggling to fight, he used this wave as a time to practise with the weapon. He didn't flail around trying to strike as hard and swiftly as he possibly could —instead, he focused on perfecting his technique.

He didn't need perfect technique to deal with Level 10 Wolven. He could swing his staff-scythe around his body with one hand using a fraction of his Strength, and he would still be able to take them out. But he realised that wasn't important. He realised that skills such as Staff-Scythe Mastery—just like Staff Mastery—required a little *more* from a Denizen.

So Xavier measured each strike, turning his body to amplify the force. He paid close attention to his footwork, never crossing his legs as he fought, always keeping a strong stance, even as he swiftly moved around the battlefield.

He felt like an Angel of Death as he destroyed the ranks of Wolven, and he was rewarded for his diligence.

Staff-Scythe Mastery has reached Rank 2!

The longer he fought, the more every action felt *natural*. His body responded instantly to each of his commands. Once he'd gained Rank 2, he could pay a little less attention to his technique and still achieve the same result.

Staff-Scythe Mastery has reached Rank 3!
Staff-Scythe Mastery has reached Rank 4!

Xavier couldn't help but grin as the notifications came. At some point during the fight, without even meaning to, he'd fallen into a deep state of meditation. Something he'd never managed to do while in the middle of a fight. Insights had come. Insights into his Scythe-Staff Mastery skill.

His Scythe-Staff Mastery skill increased several things, balancing between melee and magical benefits. It increased his Speed and Intelligence along with his physical and magical damage. Xavier had killed thousands of enemies with Soul Strike since obtaining the staff-scythe, and apparently those kills contributed to his Staff-Scythe Mastery skills ranking up—except the *melee* side had lagged behind, so he hadn't accrued experience on that side of the skill.

So once he'd truly gotten started, practising his technique and taking down hundreds of Wolven with melee alone, the skill had finally had an opportunity to feel balanced and increase its rank.

Perhaps I should meditate more while fighting. It seemed to be the best way for him to learn more about his class's spells and skills, after all, as it wasn't as though he had any manuals or masters to learn from.

But just as he had that thought, whirling around with Soul-taker, he found no more enemies around him.

The first wave on the fifth floor of the Tower of Champions had been defeated.

Chapter 94
You Know About the Multiverse?

Xavier looked around the battlefield with slight surprise. He'd expected the first wave to take much longer than it had. In fact, he'd been trying to make the wave last a little longer so Howard and Justin would have a chance to practise their new spells in combat.

But only a few minutes passed before all the Wolven were dead around Queen Alastea's castle.

He glanced over at the ranks of enemy soldiers and beasts, expecting them to surge forward. They didn't. They simply stood there. Waiting.

He remembered the notification saying the first five waves would take five hours, and had a suspicion that meant that each wave would take an hour to start moving toward the castle.

Xavier deposited Soultaker back into his Storage Ring, then waved over at Siobhan. A white light enveloped him as the Divine Beacon summoned him back to the wall. Being physically displaced was disorientating. He didn't stumble, but he felt the slightest bit of vertigo as he went from standing on soft ground to standing on stone.

Siobhan had already summoned the others back. Howard and Justin were breathing heavily, both drenched in sweat and blood.

Xavier's breathing was still level, and he hadn't broken a sweat. Though his Shrouded Robes were soaked. There were no tears in them, but Xavier had a sneaking suspicion that if he just...

Ah. That's better.

Xavier's robes dried as he infused Spirit Energy into the robes' self-repair feature. They were no longer drenched in blood. No longer clinging to his skin.

"That..." Justin took a breath. "Was intense."

Howard grunted and gave a curt nod. His tower shield was covered in claw and bite marks. "You certainly burned through them fast," he said to Xavier.

Xavier glanced over his shoulder at the field of battle. "Sorry about that."

Queen Alastea stepped over. Her back was straight, her chin raised, her hands folded neatly in front of her. She must have summoned her staff back into her Storage Ring. Her face was entirely composed but for the slight wideness of her eyes.

"I have rarely seen such strength as yours." Queen Alastea bowed her head slightly, which made her tall adviser frown. "Thank you, Champion of the Void. I am glad that you—and your friends—are the ones that arrived. I knew that my soldiers alone would not be enough to hold back the forces of the Endless Horde long enough to get the portal open."

Before responding, Xavier quickly scanned some of the Denizens along the wall, as he noticed something that he hadn't before. Stepping out of the Safe Zone, he'd been too focused on his surroundings and the fact that there were alien races—for that was what they truly were, as they were people from other worlds—among them to realise their age.

The Denizens all looked rather young. Perhaps not as young as Justin's sixteen years, but quite close. Their levels were low, but more varied than levels on a floor ever were. The humans, elves, lizardmen and Anubis-looking, jackal-headed soldiers ranged between Levels 10 and 15.

Queen Alastea, and her adviser, he was unable to scan.

This place isn't real. If it was, wouldn't the soldiers be older? A higher level? How could they have a kingdom so weak?

The ten soldiers that flanked the queen were the highest level of those he'd scanned, each at Level 20.

"You are welcome, Queen Alastea." Xavier paused before continuing. *She won't remember this.* "Why are your people not of a higher level? How have you survived this long?"

Queen Alastea tilted her head to the side—perhaps the most expressive response he had seen the woman make since he'd met her. "An interesting question, coming from someone at Level 13. Though your level does not appear to reflect your power."

Siobhan was standing to the side, raising an eyebrow at him as though he were speaking out of turn. He supposed he was. But did that really matter?

Queen Alastea turned away. "But if you must know... the bulk of my army..." She motioned toward the ranks of enemies surrounding her castle. "They have already been slain by the Endless Horde, along with my most powerful generals. The enemy has ravaged my queendom, pillaging and burning down town after town until they made their way here. The last bastion. Those you see before you are still new recruits. The civilians, hiding within the castle, are non-combat classes like my adviser."

Non-combat classes. Xavier glanced at Siobhan. *But not support classes? This is definitely more detailed than when those two armies clashed.*

"And you?" Xavier asked. "I am unable to scan you."

"I am a healer, and newly crowned. My mother was the fighter. The protector of our realm." Queen Alastea walked to the parapet. Her head dipped down, the slightest crack in her composure. "She died trying to give us time to escape." Her chin rose. "The second wave will be here at the end of the hour. Your party is welcome to retire. There is an inn nearby, though its keeper is no longer in residence. I shall have my adviser fetch you before the wave is to charge."

Xavier thought of pushing the conversation forward, but the

woman was clearly trying to end it. And even if she wouldn't remember it—even if she wasn't *real*—he wasn't sure what else to ask.

A nearby soldier—one of the lizard men—escorted them to the inn the queen had mentioned. The place was empty. The soles of Xavier's boots got slightly stuck on each step along the sticky floor. There was a large table in the centre of the place. A long bar on one side, with many barrels stacked behind it. A few of the tables had half-eaten food and unfinished drinks still sitting atop them. The clientele must have left in a hurry. At least the candles had all been blown out.

Xavier took a seat at that large centre table and considered what he'd learnt.

The others sat around him. Siobhan spoke first. "These people don't feel as though they were created by the System. They feel..."

"They feel like they're real," Xavier said. "I've been thinking the same thing. But there are things that I..." He sighed. "Things I don't understand." He wished he had someone knowledgeable to turn to. "They should be more powerful than they are. Shouldn't they?"

Howard frowned. "Not necessarily. Perhaps their world is not as warlike as one newly integrated."

"They're being attacked by something called *the Endless Horde*. That sounds fairly warlike to me. Besides, the System promotes conflict. Would it truly let a kingdom survive with low-level Denizens?" He knew he was only Level 13 himself, but that was only because he'd been at this for a very short time.

"The truth is, we have no idea what this world—this *floor*—is like," Siobhan said. "Things on this floor don't add up. These people *feel* real. Whether we're in some locked portion of time from the past, or the System has created these people... well, maybe *they* are real."

Xavier held his head in his hands. "Instances." He sighed. "Pocket worlds. Perhaps they're alternate realities."

"Alternate realities?" Howard asked. "Like... the multiverse?"

"You know about the multiverse?" Xavier raised an eyebrow at the cop. He thought *he* was the nerdy one here.

Howard shrugged. "My kids like Marvel movies."

"Does any of this matter?" Justin said. He ran a hand through his hair, looking a little sheepish when they all turned their gazes on him. "I just mean, figuring out how the Tower of Champions works... It's not really our priority, is it?"

Xavier frowned. "If we're going to be stuck here for as long as we are—for a thousand floors—it seems wise to learn as much as we can about it. This tower, how it all works, where these people and the beasts come from... It could all be common knowledge out there in the Greater Universe. But that doesn't mean we shouldn't try to figure out what's going on if we have the time."

Though he had to admit, Justin had a good point. It didn't *really* matter how these floors were created. He just didn't want to admit that out loud right now. There was something about this floor that made him more curious than usual. Whether it was the castle, the different types of Denizens among the soldiers, or the queen herself.

If this tower has existed for as long as the System, how did the System know to come up with these scenarios? Would humans and elves and all these different beasts even have had time to evolve before the System integrated them?

What Siobhan had said about convergent evolution being real, as there were humans on different planets long before they were on Earth, made him curious too. It made him think there was more going on here. More beyond even the System.

What, like God?

He shook that thought away. Even if there *was* some all-powerful god out there that had created this universe, he was getting way too deep into things.

Siobhan leant her elbows on the table. "This floor could be an opportunity."

"What kind of opportunity?" Xavier asked. "I already told you that I don't want to farm it."

"That's not the kind of opportunity I mean. Remember what the notification said? That any time spent on this floor will equal an hour outside of it?"

"I remember. I still don't know how that's possible, though. Like, is this floor stuck inside some sort of time dilation field?"

"How is any of this possible?" Siobhan said, smiling warmly. "Each wave lasts an hour, but it clearly won't take you an hour to wipe a wave out." She motioned toward the door. "It didn't take you long to take down those waves, and you weren't even trying."

Xavier nodded in understanding. "Which means there will be a lot of downtime between waves."

"And wiping out those waves endears you to the queen. We've already seen that. Whether she's real or not, whether this world is or not, there might be things you could learn from her. Did you try scanning her?" Siobhan asked, continuing when Xavier nodded. "Her level wasn't clear. Something tells me she's the strongest one here."

"She is a healer," Howard said. "When we first arrived, she said she would fight to her last. Even after her people leave." His forehead creased. "Why would she do such a thing?"

"I've wondered about that as well." Xavier folded his hands on the table. "She said she knew her fate. Perhaps the Endless Horde want her, and giving herself up to them will prevent them from going after her people on the world they're fleeing to. I'm not... I'm not sure if there's anything we can do about that, if the waves are never-ending." He looked at Siobhan. "You think she'll know how I can acquire the skills I'm missing?"

Siobhan dipped her head. "In theory. That, and perhaps more."

Xavier's eyes widened as he thought of something. "If... if this place *is* real, there might be a library in the castle!"

"Do you really think you'll have time to *read*?" Justin asked.

Xavier smiled. "Even if I don't." He pointed at the three of them. "You three certainly will, considering you won't be participating in the fighting."

Howard shook his head and gave a chuckle. "I wonder if the System had this in mind when they created this floor."

Siobhan shrugged. "Something tells me the System didn't expect people to have so much time between the waves. Either way... I hope you're right, Xavier." She stood, looking giddy. "If there *is* a library in this place, think of the things we might learn!"

Chapter 95
The Endless Horde

THE NEXT THREE WAVES ON THE FIFTH FLOOR OF THE TOWER of Champions came and went all too fast.

The second wave had been barely more difficult than the first. While the first wave had only contained beasts, the second wave had contained races of humanoid Denizens. Xavier wasn't surprised to see that the Endless Horde contained even more variety amongst its ranks than that of those within Queen Alastea's castle.

Xavier stepped out—or rather leapt clean over the moat from atop the battlements—to fight the different waves. This time, he did it without Spiritual Trifecta and Spirit Infusion active. This second wave of enemies was only one level higher than the last. Xavier wondered how far that pattern would continue. For instance, would the ninetieth wave have Level 100 enemies?

There were several thousand enemies in *each* wave. In the first wave, though Xavier had been limiting his offensive actions, he must have taken out at least fifteen hundred enemies—which was a good step toward his next level.

The wave boss had been taken out by the combined efforts of the queen's forces laying down ranged attacks from the battlements, hence why he hadn't encountered the Wolven Prime.

This time, he'd instructed the queen to command her forces to stand down. She'd looked at him warily. It was clear that though she was new to being queen, she was not used to taking orders from people she deemed below her station. However, as she'd seen what level of power he possessed—and noticed the fact that there was no fear in him—she only protested for a short while, and she did say that if any of his party should die, she would command her forces to attack.

As those terms seemed perfectly reasonable to Xavier—there was no way he was going to let either Howard or Justin die, and Siobhan would be safe back on the wall—he agreed.

That second wave, Xavier had focused hard on his different resistances and that of his Staff-Scythe Mastery skill once more. That's why he hadn't activated Spiritual Trifecta. The spell would cause him to be tougher than he needed for this encounter. And though Spirit Infusion could still use a few more rank-ups, he hadn't used that as he didn't wish to burn through the enemy forces too quickly—with Spirit Infusion in his armour, the enemies would take far too much damage whenever they hit him.

He wanted all that damage to come solely from Soultaker.

Unlike on other floors, his party were not starved for time like they usually might be. He could slow down as much as he wished. While he definitely wanted to probe the queen for more informa- tion as Siobhan had suggested, and find out if there was a library in this place, he knew they would have far more time for that on their second—and final—run-through of this floor.

That's when I'll clear the waves as quickly and efficiently as possible, which will give time for the queen to develop trust in both me and those in my party.

The wave contained even more Wolven, which were easy enough for him to deal with. What he was glad for in this wave was that it had a fair few mages. Human *and* elven mages both filled the ranks of the Endless Horde. The Wolven bounded out ahead of them as the mages came into range, throwing mostly elemental spells.

Xavier could have gone straight for the mages, but his Magical Resistance skill needed the most help. Besides, he wanted to leave *some* enemies for Howard and Justin. Without the army backing them up with ranged attacks, the two of them had to fight far more strategically. Where Xavier simply walked forward, swinging his staff-scythe in perfect arcs and devastating, limb-and-head-separating strikes, Howard and Justin had to rely heavily on their defensive and movement skills, not to mention Siobhan's ability to heal them and get them out of danger whenever necessary.

They'll be improving far more dramatically than I will in this fight.

Xavier took down even more enemies in that wave than he had in the first, purely because the army on the castle's walls hadn't been involved. The wave boss ended up being a human—the first human wave boss that he'd ever faced. Though the warrior hadn't been all that formidable.

A supposed tank class that he'd taken down with four Spirit-infused strikes from Soultaker.

Howard and Justin had also taken out their fair share of enemies during that wave, though not enough for them to gain a level.

The next two waves were similar. They still contained Wolven, but this time there were Denizens on those Wolven's backs. Mounted fighters. Archers and mages alike.

For Howard and Justin, these enemies were more difficult to deal with. Though it did mean that Justin got to utilise his mid-ranged Air Strike spell and his Winged Flight spell. The Airborne Duellist took full advantage of his class's abilities. In battle, it was difficult to think of the teenager as a kid anymore.

Xavier kept pushing. He'd ranked up his resistance spells a fair bit on that first wave, and now he focused on those along with Spirit Infusion, which made the third wave go even faster. His staff-scythe burned through the enemies, slicing them apart with ease. It barely felt like he was cutting through anything at all, as though these enemies possessed zero Toughness. Not even the Denizens' armour helped against the power of his blade.

By the fourth wave, Xavier was getting too close to his next level to hold things in anymore. He felt an impatience growing within his chest to get to the final clear for this floor. Though he knew it would only take an hour on the outside, on the inside it could take *days,* depending on how many waves he was able to clear.

He assaulted the oncoming enemies with everything he had, using his ranged Soul Strike spell with human, elven, and Wolven souls for the first time. White bolts of pure lightning shot forth all around him. Brilliant, terrifying apparitions sprang into being as the enemies around him were slaughtered, the soul damage moving through them with no possible defence. The ghosts of humans, elves, and wolven alike charged through the ranks of those they once fought alongside.

It was quite a sight.

Xavier was gladdened by how easy it was to clear the wave—he did it in a matter of minutes, thousands of bodies lying dead all around him—but he hoped the latter waves, ones beyond ten, or twenty, or thirty, would provide more difficulty for him.

I've no way of knowing how many waves to defeat to take the top spot. Which means I'll simply have to fight until I no longer can.

He couldn't help but feel excited at that prospect.

As the enemies died around him, a notification popped up in his vision.

Congratulations, you have reached Level 14!
Your health has been regenerated by 60%!
Your Spirit Energy limit has increased by 200!
You have received +2 Strength, +2 Toughness,
+2 Speed, +3 Intelligence, +3 Willpower, and
+8 Spirit!
You have received +20 free stat points!

All your spells have refreshed and are no longer on cooldown!

Xavier smiled. He'd gained quite a bit in the last few waves. As for his skills, Physical Damage had gone from Rank 7 all the way to Rank 12. Staff-Scythe Mastery had doubled, going from Rank 4 to Rank 8. It hadn't been the only skill to double either, with Magical Resistance going from Rank 5 to Rank 10. He'd felt the shift in his Willpower, his resolve toughening ever more.

It finally felt as though he was balancing out his skills, though there were still a few heavily lagging behind. Assimilate Properties, which had given him a massive boost the first time he'd received it, one he still benefited from, was a big one he wished he knew how to rank up. Aura Control was also only at Rank 3. But he knew that would change in the future. He hadn't been doing more than simply balancing the burn of his Spiritual Energy within his Spirit Core. Once he delved deeper into those skills, he figured they would advance quickly enough.

As for his spells, Soul Harvest and Soul Harden had gained two more ranks. Considering how many souls he'd harvested, then used to harden his soul, he was surprised he hadn't gained more. But he couldn't complain at the spells both being at Rank 6—it brought his soulkeeping threshold all the way up to 200, after all.

Soul Block was perhaps the one part of his repertoire he'd neglected the most. He'd tried the spell out a few times, but it actively worked against him wishing to rank up his resistances. He knew he was selling the spell short by not using it, but he planned to change that on the first wave of the refresh, knowing that would have the weakest enemies of all the waves, so they wouldn't contribute as much to his resistances anyway.

He'd already decided that he should generalise with the spell. He knew it would mean he would weaken the strength of each block by a third, but he figured that was as good a price as any for such versatility.

Xavier wasn't going to face the fifth wave at all. He knew he would need to take each of the enemies within the wave down to consider the floor cleared, but he was eager to get the real clear of the floor started. The moment he'd gained Level 14, they'd returned to the Safe Zone door. He'd felt a pang of guilt as he'd walked past Queen Alastea without a word, and it felt... it felt as though he was abandoning her and her people.

But he'd pushed past that feeling.

She won't remember this. She's stuck in a time loop, or she's a fabrication by the System. The moment we leave, this whole instance will probably cease to exist.

That's what he hoped for, at least. He didn't want these people to suffer the pain of defeat. He figured these feelings were irrational, but he couldn't help himself. In the past, he'd gotten emotional about characters from TV shows or in novels, or the characters he'd written himself, so it made sense that he would have genuine feelings for people who appeared far more real than characters he would have found in fiction—even if they weren't real at all.

Which he still didn't know yet.

When they returned to the Staging Room, Xavier headed straight for the System Shop's interface. He touched a hand to the crystal atop the pedestal. He hadn't bothered collecting the corpses from those waves. Instead, he'd been *creating* Lesser Spirit Coins— it seemed far more efficient. Especially since he could do over 9,000 by the time his Spirit Energy ran out now.

He'd created 54,144 Lesser Spirit Coins while on that floor, and now had over 100,000 of them in his Storage Ring.

So it didn't bother him at all when he spent the majority of that on 200 Lesser Health Potions. He'd never actually *needed* to use a health potion in the past, but considering the nature of this floor... it seemed prudent.

Xavier also looked through the different skills on offer. He felt as though his skills were well rounded at the moment. His plan had been to spend the skill point after he inspected the fifth floor, but he didn't know what he would benefit from the most. As he looked through the skills list, he heard the others chatting and eating food —which made him wonder just how many days they would need to spend clearing different waves.

The queen had assured him that she had enough food to last months during the siege, though she knew they couldn't be there for months, so food wasn't something that worried her.

One wave per hour... we surely won't be there for that long. One week would be 168 waves.

Xavier stared at one of the skills he'd been putting off getting for ones that had been more useful to him during the floors. But, as he couldn't decide on what else to get, he finally bit the bullet and chose it.

> **You have learnt the skill Identify!**
> **Identify – Rank 1**
> **You are a student of deduction and investiga-tion. Your skills are such that by simply touching an item, you may learn more about it. At this rank, this skill can only be used once every 10 minutes and is limited to touch.**

Xavier blinked. He was fairly surprised by the skill's limita-tions, but he supposed as far as skills went, this one shouldn't be all that difficult to rank up. All he would need to do was use it a lot, right? *It feels almost more like a spell than a skill.*

Xavier summoned his Sector Travel Key to his hand and scanned it normally.

> **{Sector Travel Key}**

Just as before, what appeared wasn't helpful at all. Now, he focused on the key resting on his palm. *Identify.*

> **This item is too advanced for Rank 1 Identify.**
> **Improve the skill before trying again.**

Well, that was disappointing.

Xavier deposited the key back into his Storage Ring and summoned a Lesser Spirit Coin into his hand, using the Identify skill on that instead.

{Lesser Spirit Coin}
Spirit Coins are the main currency in the Greater Universe, and the only currency usable within the System Shop. The Lesser Spirit Coin is worth the least of all the different coins and can be produced with ease by Denizens at F Grade.

Identify cannot be used for another 10 minutes.

Xavier smiled. Though the skill didn't tell him anything he didn't already know, he instantly saw its potential.

This will definitely come in handy. I wonder how many things I'll be able to identify around Queen Alastea's castle?

Though he knew it wouldn't help him identify an enemy very well—not if he had to *touch* that enemy first. He supposed that as the skill progressed, he would be able to use sight alone for the skill.

Once he'd chosen the skill, he still had 20 free stat points to apply.

He thought through his choices, and, instead of throwing all the points into Spirit as usual, he split it between Spirit and Intelligence. Something told him his Soul Strike spell wouldn't pack the same punch against enemies in the fifth floor's later waves. When he spent the points, he now had an effective 374 Intelligence and 483 Spirit.

Xavier smiled. He knew the others had made a fair amount of progress during those waves, each of them gaining another level and reaching Level 11. They'd also ranked up a few of their spells from their new classes. He could see their auras had already been strengthened. Once again, a part of him wished he didn't have to do the floors solo—especially one like this—but he wasn't willing to lose out on the title.

He stood and walked over to where Howard, Justin, and Siobhan sat on their loot boxes, having finished their quick lunch. Xavier looked from them to the door to the Tower of Champions.

He felt good about this next floor. Felt excited for what they might discover from Queen Alastea—even if she didn't end up possessing a library. He didn't know how long they were going to spend on that floor. How many waves he would be able to endure before they had to retreat back to the Safe Zone.

But what he did know was that no matter what, he would be *challenged*. If those waves were never-ending, there would—eventually—be one that was too much for him to handle.

Something about that was absolutely exhilarating.

The pit inside of him—the one he'd managed to quiet soon after gaining his Soul Reaper class—stirred, its hunger mounting. This part of him wasn't only excited about the challenge. No. This part wouldn't stop wondering how many souls he'd be able to harvest.

Thousands and thousands and thousands.

With unrestrained excitement, Xavier smiled at his party and said, "Are you three ready?"

All three gave their assent.

It was time to take on the fifth floor of the Tower of Champions.

Time to face the Endless Horde and see just how long he would be able to endure.

Chapter 96
Balanced on a Knife's Edge

In between the stars at the core of the galaxy, near the supermassive black hole that kept the sector together, the Empress Larona floated in a deep meditation. The vacuum of space had long ago lost its ability to affect her, and there was an appetising silence about the void between the stars that the woman had experienced nowhere else in the Greater Universe.

Though it was completely silent, there were still things to be felt. The Celestial Energy and Void Energy being the main two. They were so densely packed within the vacuum that the first time she'd experienced their presence she'd worried it would overwhelm her.

Now such things were simply the background noise of the universe.

Here, she floated. And thought. And dreamt. And *Saw*. For this was where she came for insights. Here, where everything was quiet but for the future, where she could delve into her mind for almost as long as she wished. Here, where she could not be disturbed by her subjects.

Images swept into her periphery, caught by her consciousness as though it were a net. She peered at each of them in turn, attempting to discern their impact upon her plan.

Her sector, her galaxy, was under threat. She had Seen this a long time ago. It had been one of her first visions. Before she'd even reached the peak of E Grade, the System had bestowed this insight upon her. And for hundreds of years, it had cursed her mind.

Every waking moment, and many of her dreaming ones, this vision had plagued her. Like a parasite, it ate away at all her thoughts until it consumed each one of them. For so long, avoiding this calamity had been her sole purpose. Still was her sole purpose.

The End was coming.

A B Grade Denizen that destroyed everything it came upon in its search for power. She did not know what The End looked like, all she knew was that it would come. For she had Seen it—Seen the aftermath of what it would cause.

Ten billion planets left dead, devoid of their respective energies. Devoid of their respective lives. The End sucked all life into itself. Consumed everything.

She still Saw flashes of that future every day. Saw her own world succumb to that terrible fate. When the integration had come to her world, she had been a priestess of the Old Religion—a religion that had been old even then, and now was all but lost to time, as she was the only surviving practitioner.

Though her faith in any sort of benevolent higher power had abandoned her, she still found herself praying to the old pantheon. To the Mother. The Father. To the Wind and the Sun. To the Earth and the Sea.

And to the Stars. The celestial bodies that she had spent so much of her time staring at, interpreting, identifying, even before she'd become what she was now. Oh, if she had only known what those stars held in store she would have been terrified staring up at them.

That terror struck her as it always did, gripping her heart like icy fingers, as she Saw into the future. For nine hundred years she had known this was coming, and for nine hundred years the vision had remained static.

Death. Destruction. That was all that was in store for her sector when The End came.

And so she made her plans and prayed to dead deities that had never truly lived, following rituals that had been old when she was still young. And she kept looking until she Saw something that she could thread into the futures to change them, for she knew she may never be strong enough to change them on her own.

She had stalled at C Grade half a millennium ago, with no sign of ever being able to push past it. At least, not before The End came.

The future was a difficult thing to predict. One of the most infuriating things about being among the Seer line of classes was that other Denizens tended to think you had it all figured out. It was also one of the biggest advantages. Many a Denizen had called her to fight only to be wary when she arrived.

The thought would enter their mind—*She would not be here unless she knew she would win.* Sometimes, simply placing that thought in someone's head was enough to impact their confidence and lead to their defeat. A self-fulfilling prophecy. A term that always made her chuckle.

But the future wasn't a simple thing to read. It wasn't fixed. It shifted and changed. New threads emerged as old ones were tied or cut forever. It had taken her a long time to figure out how to not only track those changes back to their source, but also be the cause of them herself.

The one thing that had the largest chance of changing the future she Saw was the System itself. For any planet that was not integrated into the Greater Universe was a void of utter darkness that even Empress Larona could not see into.

When a little blue planet had been integrated into the System, thousands of futures she'd thought solid for hundreds of years had been utterly distorted. An occurrence that could only mean one thing—the birth of a True Progenitor.

The future she saw—The End sweeping over the galaxy and destroying everything in its path—had not been one of those solid futures that changed. Floating in the vacuum, she wished to rectify that. To discover if her long game was possible. She could almost See the man now. Each hour that passed in the normal stream of time made him become clearer and clearer.

His fate, however, was yet to be determined. It balanced on a knife's edge.

The Tower of Champions was a difficult realm for a Seer to peer into. The System had blocks in place for eyes such as hers, but she had slowly been unlocking them, one by one, to obtain an unhindered view of the man she hoped would help change the sector's trajectory.

The man who might stave off The End when it finally came for them.

What she found was interesting. Peering through the void she felt the remnants of a presence left behind. Something powerful had been through here. Something powerful which had gazed upon this particular instance of the Tower of Champions. As someone who dealt in futures, she knew such a thing could not be mere coincidence.

Strange.

The power she sensed... it was like nothing she'd ever felt before. Not even as strong as what she felt from The End.

One of the Old Ones?

She followed the path that had been left behind by an entity far more powerful than herself. Someone at B Grade, or possibly even A Grade. She could not tell. At C Grade and a thousand years old, she was the most powerful Denizen in her sector.

But that was because her sector was young, having been around for less than ten thousand years. And in those years, before it had grown strong enough, or found a protector, it had been purged twice before her planet had been birthed into the Greater Universe by the System.

Empress Larona did not know what had caused those purges. Perhaps it had been The End, back then, too. Or one of the Galaxy Eaters she'd heard whispers about. Or someone from her sector had angered one of the Old Ones. When a sector was young, any number of things could cause its demise—its purge or its colonisation. And the strongest Denizens from a new sector often found their way to older sectors, where their paths to power were more assured, and where there were securities against such calamities as purges. Denizens would often spend hundreds of years saving enough to travel away from their sector.

The Seer did not spend her time worrying about the past, or those that had abandoned the sector—those that might have staved off The End alongside her if only they had remained. The only things that concerned her were what was coming to pass in the present, and what would come to pass in the future.

Following the path tread by one more powerful than her, Empress Larona made it into the particular instance of the Tower of Champions that held the one she'd been looking for. The next True Progenitor. When she glimpsed his soul, she almost gasped. Perhaps she would have, had she not been floating in vacuum, unable to breathe.

Millions of threads to the future were connected to the man's heart. More than she'd ever seen on a single Denizen. His power at present was insubstantial, though not for his level and floor on the tower, but the *potential* he possessed.

It was clear to her why he might have been visited by one of the Old Ones.

She could see where those threads led. See where they might end. *The knife's edge.* There was something in his near future calling him toward his death. Something on the next floor—then later, on his return to his little blue planet.

And a thousand more.

She'd never seen someone with a fate in such a state of flux.

Is this why his arrival has not changed the fate of the sector, and the arrival of The End? Because he is destined to die before his time?

Empress Larona followed the threads. One by one, she examined them, using all the considerable powers of her mind, until she came upon the faintest of them all—a line that led to a future she had never seen.

A line so faint, so unsure, so *unlikely* that she feared it may never come to pass.

A line that connected Xavier Collins to The End, that threaded his fate with that of the sector itself.

Accidental Champion continues in Book Two!

Thank you for reading Accidental Champion

WE HOPE YOU ENJOYED IT AS MUCH AS WE ENJOYED BRINGING it to you. We just wanted to take a moment to encourage you to review the book. Follow this link: Accidental Champion to be directed to the book's Amazon product page to leave your review.

Every review helps further the author's reach and, ultimately, helps them continue writing fantastic books for us all to enjoy.

ALSO IN SERIES:

Accidental Champion

Check out the entire series here! (Tap or scan)

Want to discuss our books with other readers and even the authors? Join our Discord server today and be a part of the Aethon community.

Facebook | Instagram | Twitter | Website

You can also join our non-spam mailing list by visiting www.subscribepage.com/AethonReadersGroup and never miss out on future releases. You'll also receive three full books completely Free as our thanks to you.

Looking for more great LitRPG?

Todd Herzman

The world is ending. Only a powerful mage can prevent it. *When he awakens ten years in the past, Kiden Coldsteel dedicates his second chance to becoming a legendary mage to prepare for the terrors to come, when the Acolytes of the Old Gods are destined to shroud the world in darkness forever. Kiden does not have the benefit of years of training as a mage. His martial skills aren't enough alone. He must rely on his method of Law of the Opposites, approaching magic in a way that goes against every establish theory. Until then, he must locate the strongest mage humanity has ever produced and earn his support, or else humanity won't stand a chance...* **Outspan Foster returns with this action packed LitRPG adventure about one man's quest to prevent the coming apocalypse. Can Kiden save everything and everyone he loves?**

Get Return of the Wand Mage Now!

684

Accidental Champion

Accidental Champion

Todd Herzman

**Life at the Magic Deck-Building Academy is
upended when an assassin is reborn in his body.**
*On the cusp of entering the prestigious Lumin Magic
Academy, the young mage Alistair harbors a dark secret: within
him dwells Ghost. A reborn master assassin hellbent on
revenge. Bound together by fate and magic, Alistair and Ghost
embark on a dual journey of vengeance and discovery. As
Alistair navigates the arcane halls of the academy, mastering
battledeck spells and summoning skills, Ghost seeks to unravel
the mysteries of his untimely demise. Their worlds collide and
intertwine, revealing a threat far greater than either could have
imagined...* **Reborn Assassin is the next action-
packed, deck-building LitRPG Series from
Harmon Cooper. It's like My Hero Academia and
Breaking Bad got together to write a progression
fantasy after watching Kill Bill. About the Series:**
*This Isekai magic academy adventure features a three-tiered
LitRPG card system that revolves around summons, wand-
based spells, and abilities. Perfect for fans of All the Skills and
A Summoner Awakens!*

Get Battle Deck Academy Now!

For all our LitRPG books, visit our website.